A MYRMAID'S KISS

A MYRMAID'S KISS

BY ASHLEIGH BELLO

NORTHWOODS
HOUSE
Publishing

FIRST EDITION· February 2024

Cover design by Vasylina-art
www.deviantart.com/vasylina
vasilyna.artstation.com

Map and chapter illustration copyright © 2021 by Jessica Khoury.
All rights reserved.

Other publications by Ashleigh Bello in the Olleb-Yelfra Universe:
Belvedor and the Four Corners
Belvedor and the King's Curse
Belvedor and the Desert of Secrets
Belvedor and the Trail of Fire
Belvedor and the Golden Rule

For more information, visit: www.ashleighbello.com

ISBN-13: 978-0-9987974-9-6
ISBN-10: 0-9987974-9-9

10 9 8 7 6 5 4 3 2 1

To your dark side.
Feed it what it wants.
Ask forgiveness later.

BEFORE YOU DIVE IN
Adult Content Warning

This steamy forbidden romance story is best suited for adults eighteen years or older who enjoy dark fantasy.

You will meet morally gray characters that toe the line between good and utterly wicked. Sensitive storylines include suicide references, family separation, depression, manipulation, addiction parallels, and sexually explicit (smutty) scenes.

Eloise Myr is not your typical 'mermaid'. She is a vampire-like huntress who feasts on the blood of men… and enjoys every drop. So, be prepared to also read passages portraying violence, bloodshed, and death.

Please proceed into the underwater world of Olleb-Yelfra with caution, myrmaid. If you choose to embark on this beautifully dark journey, remember that it's all fiction meant to leave you with even more twisted and depraved wet dreams than those which brought you here.

Happy hunting!

Ashleigh B.

CONTENTS

CITY OF THE FOUR CORNERS

THE JAR OF STONE

UNDOR

Agrarian's District   Healer's District

Vanishing Tunnels   Creator's District   Warrior's District

Tombs

Draminet

NICORA FOREST

BLACK SAND DESERT

BELGRADIA

Fate's Pool

KAMPAULO

MORIAMO

HIGH CITY OF SAINDORA

SEA OF SAINDORA

Empress Isle

OLLEB YELFRA

PART ONE

I

LIFE

ＤＥＬＯＩＳＥ

I SMELL THEM LONG BEFORE I see them: *humans*. Far from shore. So far that it will probably take them a full day to reach land, if they turn their boat in the right direction.

I flip my tail harder, skimming beneath the water with ease, as if I have been a myrmaid my whole life, as if this isn't my first night exploring the wonderous world under the sea. I barely notice Syrifina swimming beside me, just an iridescent, glittering streak that's keeping watch while I attempt my first hunt.

I let my instincts guide me; the currents whisper for me to veer up. '*Follow us, Eloise. You must feed.*'

The scent of blood grows stronger, hitting me like a wall. I soar, toward the hull of a small fishing boat bouncing in the rowdy waves.

Lost, I think.

This isn't a boat prepared to sail for long in deep waters like these—they calm for me, the waves, stilling as I break through.

The wind greets me. The moon smiles down.

Only now do I pause, unsure of how to proceed.

'*Sing*,' a voice urges as I consider my prey from the shadows.

An older man and woman are arguing about the direction to the shore, their voices fracturing the quiet of the night; I cringe at the unwelcome sound.

They're so entangled in their debate that they don't even sense the true danger they're in. If they cared to look, maybe they would notice the golden glint of my scales or the shimmer of silver in my stare pinned on them.

"I told you not to fool around with the compass!" shouts the woman. "You know how valuable they are these days. We should've never taken this trip in the first place, all so you could return a man of glory." She spits over the edge of the boat, into *my* waters.

I hiss. *How dare she disgrace my home.*

"I'm telling you, Penelope," says the man, "I didn't *do* anything." He grumbles under his breath. "It's just gone all wonky out here." He tosses it to her feet. "Either something's interfering with it, or it's faulty. I've no idea, but, *please*, do shut your trap." He crosses his meaty arms at his chest, his heartbeat thundering; I lick my lips. "You're not helping the situation by screaming bloody nonsense into the night." He lowers his voice. "You'll attract the sharks."

Her eyes widen, nostrils flared. Her voice rises higher with every word she screams at him. "The situation being that we're *lost*, at *sea*. Surrounded by sharks! What a piece of work you are, husband. A real hero."

The man rolls his eyes, muttering a string of curses. "Be quiet, or I'll toss you to them."

"What was that?" she screeches, threatening him with an oar.

I bare my fangs at her grating voice, wanting to shut her

-2-

up, not used to this sensitive hearing yet.

Syrifina's voice enters my mind. '*We hunt males above all,*' she states, firmly. '*We honor our human souls. Focus on the blood, and everything else will fade to the background.*'

I narrow my gaze on the man, homing in on that strong heartbeat once again.

He sighs, moving as far away from Penelope as possible. "Nothing," he replies. He adds, in a gruff tone, "Oh, love of my life."

She huffs and turns her back to him, looking out into the distance where I lurk; I wait for the right moment, unsure of how to begin.

"We should've left a note for our son with directions on how to access our coin," she says, calmer now, worried. "At this rate, he'll grow up thinking his mother and father abandoned him."

"At least he'll be lucky enough to say he knew who his mother and father were," the man says, dryly, glancing to the star-riddled night. "Most children these days don't have the luxury of such knowledge... Hail to the King." He frowns, offering a mock bow to the clouds.

My stomach twists as his scent floats to me on the crisp breeze. My lip curls, fangs pushing forward.

"No, he's *lucky* that the Tayshins won't throw him out on the street if you sink us out here." She shakes her head, wrapping her arms around herself. "Gods..." she breathes.

The man silently mocks her like a child behind her back, flailing his arms and moving his mouth.

All you have to do is sing, Eloise. Allow your magic to release.

The woman sucks in a big breath. "You're a blasted fool if you think I don't know what you're doing behind me—"

I part my lips and a poisoned melody pours into the air.

Penelope's voice fizzles out; they both go very still—I delight in the sudden peaceful silence.

I circle closer to the boat, noting the glint of fear in their eyes as they're frozen by my magic.

They can't move nor speak. They can't turn to face each other, and they cannot scream for help, not that anyone would hear.

The only piece of freewill my song has left to them is the quickening pace of their beating hearts, the hitched breath in their throats, and their watery gazes as they search for the culprit of this spell.

So much control. So much power. My mind glows with the excitement of it all.

'*Beautifully done,*' says Syrifina from somewhere near. '*Now, have your fun. I shall not interfere.*'

I swim right up to the side of the boat; the man's chestnut eyes settle on me, growing so wide that his cheeks shake from the strain.

I soften my song—I allow him to move and speak, wondering what his last words might be.

He gasps at the freedom, then his mouth hangs open as he takes me all in.

"What… what are you?" he stutters, drawn to me like one of the hooked fish on the floor of his boat.

Serves him right, I think, swallowing my distaste, wanting to drown him for his ghastly acts. *Focus! He deserves worse things.*

A dryness in my throat tugs at my mind, urging me to feed so that my transformation will be complete.

My song hovers like a mist around them; the woman is a fierce soul. She struggles against my hold, but my magic still grips her tightly.

Her husband, however, doesn't even try to resist. He walks right up to the edge of the boat and drops to his knees before me; I sniff at his wonderful aroma, the sweetness just beyond his skin. A shiver curls delightfully down my spine. I suck on my teeth.

"Tell me," he pleads, eyes glittering with curiosity.

'*I knew you would bring men to their knees easily,*' purrs Syrifina with approval. '*Good girl.*' Her gentle laughter tickles my ears. '*Go on, tell him what you are.*'

I consider his question a moment, tilting my head. *Who am I now that I've traded my humanity away?*

I grin, displaying all my teeth. "I am everything."

'*Feed!*' the Moon beseeches.

'*Drink!*' the Sea sings.

Fear flickers across his features; I grab him by the collar before he can think to move away.

"Let me go!" He strains against me, but I'm too strong. I could drive my fist straight through his chest if I wanted to and make this easier for everyone, but what a mess that would make of my first meal—I want to impress my maker.

His long, thick neck tilts up as he struggles against me. Those shimmering green veins…

An animalistic sound rips from my throat as I pull him forward, his body halfway over the side of the boat. I sink my fangs into his ready flesh, knowing exactly where to puncture to get what I want.

He makes to scream, but I cover his mouth with my hand, not wanting this perfect moment sullied by more unnecessary noise. Water splashes with his struggle, my tail thrashing back and forth in all the exhilaration.

As his essence ebbs into my grasp, I realize the responsibility I hold, the value of human life in this world. I must not take my new place as their superior in vain. I must acknowledge the momentous gift of my power, and of their blood sacrifice.

I vow to be a respectable myrmaid.

But I can no more slow down and savor my first drink than I could on those rare occasions when a kind stranger had offered me a warm meal as a child beggar, orphaned and alone—his blood tastes just as sweet as I recall chocolate did when I had an inferior palate.

I moan from the pleasure of it all, the warmth drizzling down my throat, my chin, filling my empty stomach. There are absolutely no words in the human language that can describe the sensations coursing through me with each pull from my tongue.

'*Disfrutamoré*,' offers Syrifina.

The word rolls around smoothly in my mind, old and complex. I've never heard it before. And yet, somehow, I understand that it's exactly how I feel.

I drink harder, faster. A sort of high fogs my focus.

The man's body goes limp in my hands, his blood thinning out and becoming more difficult to reach as he empties for me.

Penelope's voice shrieks across the night, disturbing the peaceful quiet—I barely notice that I had let my spell slip, the magic holding her tongue floating away like steam.

"What's happening? Who was that? *Edward*," she yells, the icy wind choking her. She's still unable to turn around and see. *Good, it would just leave her with unthinkable horrors.* "Edward, please, honey, talk to me!"

I suck, until there is nothing left of him.

Edward, I think with a satisfied sigh, glad to put a name to a moment I shall recall for eternity.

I swallow the last bit, wholly content. Then I release him and swim back to let my immortality solidify, my transformation complete.

The final remnants of human Eloise dwindle away into the distance, an oblivion, as if she should've never even existed at all. It doesn't feel wrong. *Strange*, perhaps. But not wrong to let her go. I can sense that weak version of me shedding, like a snake's skin, making room for something stronger that's always lived inside of me but was only now equipped to take over—my body, my mind, my soul.

I flex my fins, my tail, and welcome her with open arms. A better Eloise.

This new surge of power…

I look to my hands, golden magic dusting around me—I can't even begin to decide what to do with it, how to release it, subdue it.

It's unlike anything I ever thought to be true in this world. And I'll feed it whatever it needs to flourish, forever.

I look toward the sky with a gasp of ecstasy, a dazed smile smeared across my face along with Edward's blood. The moon showers me with its cold, wonderful light in celebration.

My giddy laugh overwhelms the woman's screams.

"Oh, Edward," I say aloud, haughty and full—my gaze drops to his lifeless body hanging over the boat, his deadened eyes beholding me in reverence, fear; I lick my fingers, wanting to taste every last bit of him. "I will remember each drop of your sensational blood for lifetimes to come."

I wait a moment, wondering if a wave of guilt might hit me. Wondering if my humanity might rear its ugly head again…

When it doesn't, I beam back at the moon, twirling in her encouragement, arms out wide.

Then I still, my attention sliding back to Edward… my first kill. I see him with new eyes, new understanding. He gave me life, nourishment.

He is my beginning. And I am his end.

A great responsibility, indeed.

'*There's balance to be had,*' says Syrifina. '*I'm pleased you understand. We only drink every fortnight, at the Moon's command.*'

I reply with a nod, knowing innately that I am certainly satisfied and would be for weeks.

'*Until the shadow moon,*' she adds. '*This is a boundary we must always keep—*'

'*Or we threaten the balance,*' I reply, for the first time exploring my own voice through this strange mind-link.

I swim forward and gently kiss Edward on the cheek; a silver blush of magic sinks into his skin.

"I will forever remember your sacrifice," I say, humbly. "I truly thank you for this."

I commit his face to memory, kind and warm. Then I turn away, ready to explore the open sea.

Syrifina emerges before me, head bobbing in the waves, her hair like a molten river of lava spilling around her. A prideful glow settles in her expression as she takes in the boat.

"Don't forget to clean up your mess, Eloise. You don't want to leave a trail, not in this unforgiving regime. The King is no friend to those more powerful than him."

With the flick of her hand, she commands the water to lift Edward's body into the sea. A silver trail of sparkling magic drags him down to a place where no light goes.

"What about her?" I ask, still holding Penelope in place with my lingering song. "I know we aren't meant to kill women, but she's seen—"

Penelope whimpers. "I haven't seen a thing! Please... I have a son. He's just a boy."

"Good to know," responds Syrifina in a voice that makes even me cower before her. She licks her lips.

I blink back at her in a daze, blood still swirling my mind.

She smiles at me, a tenderness replacing her monstrous side with the mere twitch of her crimson-colored lips.

I have so much to learn, I think.

"It's up to you," she says. "Leave her here. Let the sun dry her out." She shrugs. "Or you can choose to send her back.

No one would believe her anyway, not with the evidence gone."

We both look down, any trace of Edward already swallowed by darkness.

I will be a respectable myrmaid, I repeat to myself.

"Thank you for your generosity, Penelope," I call with as much sincerity and decorum as I can. She sobs. "It's unfortunate we crossed paths tonight, but I see no reason in wasting human life for the sake of it." This makes her even more hysterical; tiny fish scurry away past us.

I wince at my misspoken words, at her too-loud voice. I glance to Syrifina, pouting.

She rolls her eyes, forcing a smile—I know she would've left her to rot for merely tainting the air around her waters with such an appalling noise.

"It's alright," she mouths, encouraging me to finish.

I nod to myself, resolved in my decision. "We will guide you back to where you came from," I say, making my voice just as strong and confident as the one who made me. "Be with your son. Forget this night ever happened at all."

Currents stir beneath the boat, the water sparkling like sapphires; Syrifina whispers instructions, then the boat turns and gently glides away in the direction of the shore.

"What will become of her?" I ask as we watch the crying woman drift away into the dark, her boat lighter now, quieter—I fully release my song so that she can regain her free will.

To my surprise, Penelope walks to the back of the boat as soon as her limbs are freed. She stands to face us. Her skin is as black as the enveloping night, but she's framed by the moonlight; I know she can't see us clearly, just shadows and glinting scales in the water. But she surely knows that *we* can see *her*.

There's a promise of vengeance written in the streak of

tears and hardened lines upon her face. A promise that she would never be able to keep to herself.

Syrifina turns away with the flick of her glorious tail, like yards of shimmering silk sewn together with crystals. "It's of no consequence to us. We'll never see her again. She doesn't even understand what we are... what happened here tonight."

I force myself to tear my gaze away from Penelope; I look to Syrifina, unsure of what to do next.

"She can be grateful she gets to live," she adds, wiping the remaining blood from my chin. "I set her back on course until that compass of hers begins to prove useful again, outside of my barriers."

She winks at me, tossing her hair over her shoulder.

I make a mental note to query more on that later, about how our magic works.

"What now?" I ask, putting Penelope and Edward in my past.

A shadow hardens over her soft features; I wonder what thoughts consume her ancient mind.

"I knew from the first that you were meant to be one of us," she speaks after a moment. "A princess of the sea."

She looks to the moon. It bathes her in the same power that has made me whole tonight.

"Your destiny is a powerful one, Eloise." She looks back to me. "I daresay we shall all come to know it."

My mind races. *A destiny?*

She, the Moon, whispers back with the softness of a kiss. *'A grand one, perhaps.'*

I've never had the imagination to even hope for such a thing, let alone one that could have a narrative such as 'powerful' in this world. There's never been anything special about me before.

But I do feel it now, this untapped influence. *I wonder...*

My mind flits away, enthralled by the possibilities.

Syrifina's smile tightens.

"Remember this moment, darling," she says, sweeping her hand through the water; magic follows her touch. "It's easy to forget the important memories with a life that goes on forever, this beautiful beginning."

I lift my gaze to a dark, purplish sky swarming with shadows. The deep colors of twilight drip down to a boundless sea that seems to watch our every move with the same eagerness I have to dive again beneath its surface.

Syrifina takes my arm, drawing my attention back to her. Slow-moving threads of silver and gold coil across every surface of my dark skin, cold to the touch—my lifeblood unbound from human limitations.

"I can't wait to introduce you to the rest of your family," she says. "They'll be so pleased."

Family… It's been so long since I've had one. My chest flutters with nerves.

"You have nothing to worry about. Your sisters will accept you," she says, "because you're mine."

I still cannot fathom that out of *hundreds*, I have found myself as one of just twenty-two direct descendants of Syrifina Myr, the original myrmaid of Olleb-Yelfra.

A princess…

My gaze meets hers—two soft-glowing pearls seem to stare straight into my soul, trying to determine who I might become with a life eternal. The gold and silver parts of me reflect in her pupils like priceless jewels.

Who is this enchanting creature? I think, still shocked at my own reflection—it's only been a matter of days since I turned. *Could it really be me? Is she worthy?*

"Yes," answers Syrifina; I start, not realizing I'd let her read that thought. "The best parts of you manifested when you chose to accept the sea. You've always had magic. I just helped you embrace it."

My eyes float closed as I remember that pivotal moment when she offered me her kiss—I made the choice to forfeit my humanity and turn toward the sea. I coveted the powers and immortality that were promised to me.

I forget the exact memories before, the ones that led me to the beach and into the arms of this great guardian of the water. But I'm sure they'll come back to me one day... should I care to retrieve them.

Bliss. That's how I'll paint this memory. I'll never want anything else but the life ahead.

There's only a small pinch of pain, an uncomfortable heat that lingers in my chest, in the thick of my bones, in my vanquished human memory.

Syrifina takes my chin in her hand, the coldness comforting. I open my eyes.

She gently traces a strand of lifeblood from my shoulder to my elbow, stopping in a place where both the colors intersect—a blend that creates a hue so brilliant that I have no name for it; this diamond-like shimmer dots my skin, appearing as if stars forming a constellation in the night.

"Gold and silver both embody a strong affinity toward all the natural elements, the purest of magic," she explains, circling me, her tail and fins skimming the water like a surfaced shark—she searches for other lifeblood stars, a childlike wonder in her voice.

"It's not unlike the exceptionality of my own. In fact, up until now, I have yet to choose a daughter with such a keen elemental balance in her soul." She returns to my front. "You're a rarity, Eloise."

A flicker of darkness moves over her bright expression as she floats before me, allowing me to look. To realize all that she is... all that I could be.

Her lifeblood is an iridescent, rainbow-like blend that reflects every color known and *not* known to humans. A mirage of hues that surely holds the power to hypnotize anyone who dares look too long upon such splendor.

The wind beats against her, heavy and strong, but the only things that bend to its will are her long tendrils of hair, like embers of fire gathered atop her head. She's not exceptionally tall yet she towers over her domain, a statue cemented upon the waves, the watcher of the water. Power radiates from her, silhouetting her white skin in a glow that seeps into the air like twinkling powder—I'm not sure who glows brighter, her or the moon.

And those eyes, with all the intensity and might of a hundred human kings, stitched with unattainable magic as striking and sharp as steel—there's more knowledge wielded in a single, withering glance from Syrifina Myr than I'm sure I'll ever be able to comprehend.

The weight of the sea pours into me with that heavy gaze leveled at me now. I bow my head.

"You will make a grand myrmaid, indeed," she states, her voice shifting to something queenly—a sound as charming and calming as a lullaby, yet as compelling as any indissoluble command. "Now, let's take you home."

Home, I think with a bemused smile, eager to follow her anywhere across these star-flecked waters.

2

WANDERER

ELOISE

THE NIGHT IS COLD, bitter with ice in the air blowing down from the north, the Blancoren Mountains far away yet still ever-reaching with the winter season in bloom.

The waves usher me toward a rocky shore that marks the City of Kampaulo, the very place I was turned over twelve years ago. I smack my lips, thinking of Edward—one never quite forgets that first taste of blood. It would be impossible to replicate.

A waxing gibbous moon swings overhead, urging me to try.

I swallow, my throat uncomfortably dry.

I'll make sure to select someone robust tonight, more filling than the last.

The crowd at the beach has already thinned out, moving inward to the main streets. My cold, empty heart is yearning to follow. I want to move with them.

I stroke a slim ribbon at my neck, one strung with small cowry shells and a long tail knotted with gold pieces ready to spend. I always come prepared before I landwalk, lest I'm feeling generous.

I wade closer to the land. The shore on this side is dark, quiet. No light save for the brilliant night.

I set my gaze on two young women stealing kisses in the shadows. They look just about my age now, physically anyway.

I laugh a little at how rushed they seem. Time eats away at their youth, trading it in for knowledge.

I get to have everything.

I'll never experience a wrinkle from the sun nor will I slow to the aches and pains of weathered bones. And disease or sickness, it drips off me like oil.

I was nineteen when I first drank, and nineteen I shall remain forever. Though, my soul has aged a dozen years since that first taste of true power...

I've learned an incalculable amount shadowing my sisters—to swim, to sing, to feed! To dance with the moonlight and sail with the waves. Nothing and no one to stand in my way.

Eternal Eloise, as Syrifina named me.

And after so many years of practice, I only need the intention to transform back to my human body when night falls.

The shallows glisten with magic around me, the moon feeding me more power than even I suppose reasonable.

I step forth from the water and let the magic take hold.

My tail vanishes in a soft, glittering cloud; I stand upon two legs, relishing the squish of sand between my toes. I curl icy pebbles beneath my feet. It feels... primitive but *fun*, like a stolen, little pleasure I used to take for granted.

I smile, stifling a giggle.

Then I open my arms out wide, welcoming the embrace of the nature all around me; it applauds me for experiencing this part of their world freely, as intended, no clothes nor material things to hide me away.

Though, I do like to play sometimes…

I walk forward, gliding on the shadows toward the women. This beach was familiar to me in my past, yet it feels so very different now.

Before, my feet would've bled with no protection from the sand riddled with stones. And without a wool cloak, I might've frozen in place, to walk no further, frigid air slicing into me off the waters.

I would've feared the night, hidden from the darkness behind feeble doors with a silly knife in my hand. A little magicless girl, unable to sleep soundly if there was even a rustle of leaves outside of my window, incapable of protecting herself, let alone anyone else, from the smallest of threats.

The earth supports me. The wind envelops me. The night holds out its hand.

Old habit compels me to inhale a breath of satisfaction, but oxygen is nothing of consequence to me. My body thrives from a different source.

I sniff at the air. *Who shall it be tonight?*

My eyesight pierces the darkness like burning lanterns. I see the two lovers so clearly, though they will never lay eyes on me, not tonight—they've done away with their clothes in the privacy of the blackened sea, splashing and playing in my realm, not a care in the world.

I smirk, admiring their bravery.

I mark them for consideration of my gifts. "Maybe one day…" When I'm older and ready to accept such responsibility.

"Until then, you won't mind if I borrow these so that I can have a bit of fun tonight."

I swipe their clothes and shoes in the span of a mere breath, then melt back in with the night.

In another, I've fully transformed into a proper human—

tall boots lace all the way to my knees, and a long-sleeved, maroon dress fits generously enough so that most of me is covered; I untie the gold coins from my necklace and place them in my pocket.

The clothes feel itchy, tight. I pluck at the plain, useless fabric with distaste.

Next time I'll make a point to steal from the rich, I think, wondering if it would make any difference to me at all—material things have lost their luster.

There's just nothing quite as precious as the underwater world.

My lifeblood is at least concealed by this silly costume, mostly…

My hands, neck, and bosom still give me away. But with the cloak of the night, I imagine the striking gold and silver sheen of my enchanted essence could be taken for loose-fitted jewelry upon first glance. And I don't typically permit seconds.

Or maybe I might appear like a mysterious wanderer, emerging from another land or time, where people have evolved from needling tattoos of black ink on their skin to ones that shimmer vibrant with color, life.

My imagination takes flight; I take my first steps in the boots, cringing at the squeeze of my calves confined in the leather. A hiss escapes my teeth as I practice walking, slowly, pacing myself to most humans so I can elongate my hunt.

At least you blend in well.

A shudder coils down my spine at such a careless thought.

It must've come from the remnants of human Eloise, the memory of her always more prominent on land. Her biggest goal in life was to try to *fit* the mold of her unforgiving society—even though she didn't, and never would.

"How absolutely wretched," I retort, the sound of *my* voice reminding me of just how little I desire anything of the sort.

The waves sing to me their acceptance, a chorus praising me in the distance. *I hope I never truly blend in again.*

A haughty laugh bursts from my lips, echoing across the beach. *Intrusive, haunting... beautiful, Eloise!*

The women look toward me from the water.

I smile and wave, blowing them a magic-laced kiss on the wind that will keep them safe in the shallows.

Then I walk toward the city.

'Just be careful, Eloise.' The warmth of the warning stays close to me.

My yearning to walk among humans, to observe them with new eyes and new confidence, is too seductive to ignore—it has been since the moment I turned.

I want to judge them, knowing all that I know, the way they used to judge me.

Reunite with the sea before sunrise. Don't take too many risks. Be a respectable myrmaid. Like a landwalking ritual, I repeat this mantra in my head.

I'm grateful the transition is temporary, just a short adventure to spark my soul. But I *must* return before dawn if I want to remain as anyone at all.

Nothing is forever, says the pessimistic, cautious side of my mind. *Be careful... Eternal Eloise.* She snickers.

I push the worrisome thought to the side. *I have plenty of time.*

The earth only darkens, the moon glowing brighter.

But its disapproving face watches me closely—I feel as if the Goddess of the Moon herself keeps me in her sight, brow knitted, curious to know why one of her beloved creatures of the night should want to waste time on the strange ones of the day at all.

I turn my back on her judgment.

The lights of the twinkling city beckon me to follow, to prowl its streets. To look for the one. *Who shall it be tonight?*

On the edge of town, I pinch a black hat rimmed with red ribbon and a matching pair of gloves to complete my look, decisive—yes, mysterious wanderer.

That is what I am tonight.

I slip into a crowd and begin to hunt.

THE AROMAS ON LAND are so different than under the sea, so intoxicating. That's one thing I do miss about being a human—the sea smells only of salt and underwater nature all the time, much like the scent the air carries with it in a dense forest or field.

Clean, fresh, uncorrupted nature.

Life is meant to be spent outdoors, engulfed in nature's glory... but, *goddesses*, do I sometimes crave the smell of sweet-honeyed bread or jasmine-blended perfumes.

I even miss the grittiness of the markets, the stench that makes my nostrils curl. The constant clatter that draws my focus in every which way. It all feels so... familiar.

I find myself in the marketplace, headed toward the back where a man maintains an applecart that's been there my whole life. *Greggor*, I recall.

I used to loiter there as a human, hoping for the scraps.

Greggor's there now, as he's always been, a pile of fresh, plump apples surrounding him, combatting the pungent aromas of sweating meat and fish with something pleasant, sweet.

I observe him from a corner, how he warmly greets every patron and passerby.

He was always kind to me—unlike so many of the others.

He would toss me the bruised ones each day, the ones left to rot by his regular patrons. *Such a waste...*

I always wondered why nobody bought them. They tasted just as delicious as those without imperfections. I smile just to think it.

Even with my new appetite, I know that appearance has nothing to do with taste whatsoever.

Curiosity draws me closer—Greggor's skin is sagging off his bones. He's grown very round and old.

Life has treated him well.

Good, I think, offering him a tight smile, careful not to show my fangs. He's worked hard and honestly for it. *May he live comfortably for the rest of his years.*

I choose the least shiny apple of the bunch and toss him a large gold piece in exchange—a coin that could've bought a week's worth of carts.

It's one of countless treasures scattered across the bottom of the seas of the Olleb—priceless objects to men; worthless to me.

I lift another from my pocket and place it in his hand, wrapping my palm around his in gratitude. His skin is too warm against my own, but the contact makes me eager for more.

Careful... I ignore the Moon's glower.

He shivers and tries to pull away.

Weak, I think. So weak these humans, men especially.

I hold him there, searching his expression to see if he might remember me.

A selfish choice, Eloise—to let him look so long and know that I am something more. But it's already done.

A quick thanks rolls off my tongue.

His eyes widen against his plump cheeks, his lips slightly parted with some question he cannot speak. He's surely never heard a voice quite like mine before.

I wink at him and grin, wide this time. I can't help myself…

I let him notice the sharpness of my two pointed teeth, the proof of an unknown realm beyond his to now excite or haunt his dreams.

"Miss—" he stutters, blinking in awe.

But I'm already gone, swept away on the wind and into the bustling crowd.

I haven't aged a day since the last time he saw me. *I wonder if he will remember?*

Will it cross his mind that the young girl he used to humbly offer his scraps to had a striking resemblance to the mysterious market woman who tipped him in gold in the night?

I can't help the scenarios playing out in my mind, wishing I could read thoughts as well as Syrifina and some of my elder sisters seem to be able to.

The puzzle of me will surely keep him up tonight. That and how he plans to spend his gold. *I hope wisely.*

"I shall visit him in another ten years just to play some more," I say to myself with a snicker, already on the other side of town.

I hum to myself, careful not to catch anyone else in my spell.

THE MARKETPLACE STENCH has drastically subsided here, the freshness of the sea working its way back to me on the wind along with the quiet. My power is scorching within me, trailing my every step.

It's an effort to keep it subdued at night on land. In the sea, I can unleash it like a steady stream.

I stalk the streets, lost in thought and drowning in excess magic that could surely wipe the mortal king from this earth. *I don't know why Syrifina fears him so...*

I situate myself in an alleyway that serves as a shortcut between the inner city and what they call the Lotus Center—a central point of connection for a channel of small rivers that twists all the way from the edge of the sea throughout the entire metropolis, feeding it with life.

And just like the sea is to land, the Lotus Center connects everything; small canoes and boats travel the watery pathways through Kampaulo.

From here, the city builds on a slight incline atop smooth cobbled streets and tight alleyways squeezed in by stone and stilt structures. Lush trees fan out to provide shade during the hot days. And at night, they provide wonderful cover for predators like me.

I stand beneath one now, craning my neck to see up the hill where the Kampaulo Palace sits like a beacon in the sky. No, a spy on the city. The High King's watchful eye on the northeast side of his kingdom.

I never go much farther than the Lotus Center...

I look away from that land-locked castle and back to the busy water channels. It's just as I remember it from when I was a child.

Aside from the ghastly erection of King Devlindor's statue, complete with a gargantuan black snake coiled at his feet, the small shops still stack and lean atop one another like old friends, their faded pastel paints appearing like potted flowers.

I used to peek in the windows with the sun beaming brightly, mouth watering at the baked pies on display and admiring the way the highlife ladies moved about from shop to shop. Their arms full of all the things they didn't need but purchased anyway, their silks and satins swishing between their legs, their shiny heels clacking on the pavement.

Now, they seem so frail and bored. And the buildings just look worn.

I wished and prayed for so many trivial things back then... *How foolish I was.*

I watch from the shadows, a new perspective, a new purpose. I can't even smell the freshly made pastries over the fresh, flowing blood.

Still, the memories of this place make me smile. I appreciate this sampling of the life I used to live, the way one respects a memory of their simple past.

I purse my lips as my gaze skims my old hiding place.

I can't believe I used to cry just under that ledge, wallowing in what I couldn't have.

I shake my head. "To think of what my future held..."

I release some of my magic, painting that gloomy hole in silver and fortune, just in case another child tries to hide there someday.

Choose, Eloise! The sea awaits.

I gaze to the moon, savoring the power she feeds me.

It's high in the sky now, glaring gold, making it far too easy to see my prey—though, for them, the night only thickens, distorts.

Yes, alright then. Focus. I lick my lips—too many passersby to select from, yet nobody enticing enough to pique my interest.

Who shall it be tonight?

My eyes narrow but no one seems right.

I wait. I watch.

I HAVE WAITED A LONG TIME, too long. I can sense the night lifting, making way for the sun's reemergence in the sky. I grow weaker. The Sea of Saindora calls.

The crowd thins. The night thickens.

There are barely any souls to choose from now. In what feels like a blink of an eye, I've gone from mysterious wanderer to a *thing* lurking in a dark alleyway that people scurry by out of fright—and they don't even know my true nature.

I might as well be a beggar. *This is pathetic, Eloise!*

I sigh, hands on my hips, leaning against a tree tucked away between the tight buildings, as bored as any highlife.

Will someone worthwhile not walk into my trap before the night lifts?

I cross my arms at my chest and pout.

Tonight, I desperately want to choose my feast and have a little fun. Not settle for another lost fisherman with not enough meat on his bones! *Where is he?*

Another hour goes by; my power seeps out of me, leached by the rising heat of the oncoming day. I scratch my name into the bark of the tree with my fingernail.

"This is such a waste of a landwalk," I mutter.

I would *never* hear the end of how picky I've been tonight if any of my sisters were here to witness…

Thank the Goddess they're not.

I allow myself to feed on land no more than once per moon cycle, which is already more frequent than most of my sisters would ever condone—I'm not going to waste my selection on sour blood.

Just as I'm about to give up on the city and sweep the

beach on my way back home, the *sweetest* scent envelops the air around me on a blessed breeze, pushing away all else.

A little moan passes my lips. My eyes close. I lean into the tree.

"What in the Sea's sake..." I purr at the mouthwatering scent.

I daresay I haven't felt such a longing since Edward...

No, this will be far superior.

My eyes widen in curiosity, my magic twitching at the surface.

A lone figure morphs out of the shadows into my line of sight. A long, hooded coat sways about him, casting a strange silhouette across the soft, firelit alley.

The man lifts his gaze toward mine, as dark as the deepest waters. I'm instantly drawn to his carefully carved face—by which god, I'm unsure. His jawline is chiseled like cut white stone, his expression just as hard.

A peculiar, new craving twists inside me.

Everything else vanishes. I only see him, want him.

He's the one, Eloise. Enjoy your hunt.

In fact, there's never quite been *one* like him before...

I mark him. And for the first time as a myrmaid, I make a wish among the humans.

Oh, how I wish I had more time to draw this one out.

3

FORTUNE

ELOISE

I'M NOT SURE HOW LONG I might have stood there, just sinking into that magical man's scent, unaware of anything else.

The cool, sleek kiss of a cheap blade against my throat makes me flinch; the overpowering stink of a woman's blood hits me next, tainting the sweetness in the air.

Who dares disrupt my hunt? Who dares to lay their hands on me?

It's all I can do to muffle my hiss of annoyance and pretend to be scared. I blink in surprise, shivering with a little shriek—it's not every day I have the opportunity to act weak.

"Hi, pretty lady," the woman whispers in my ear with a voice like the sound of two jagged rocks scraping together; the warmth of her breath makes me cringe almost as much. "Got anything to share in your pockets with a poor, old woman like me?" She prods at my sides with a callous cackle, then shoves her hands into the pockets of my stolen dress.

I'm a little stunned that I let a human get so close to me

without noticing. But she matters not—I pretend to be too afraid to speak, while she whispers threats, and focus on the object of my hunt.

The man stops in his tracks from afar, witnessing the attack.

His heart beats for me. I can hear it loud and clear, hammering against the inside of his chest as if it wants to break free of his body and into my hands.

I will tear it from you and devour everything.

Hunger knots my insides, excites me.

He removes his hood, his gaze locked on mine. His lips turn downward; the woman doesn't seem to notice.

I can see his face clearly now.

His skin is as pale as the moon in all her glory, and his eyes are as black as the darkest night, angular, sharp. Black, fine strands of hair sweep back from his face and brush the top of his shoulders, half up, half down.

He looks strong beneath his thin cloak, caked in muscle. And I can tell by his calculated expression, his furrowed brow, that he's a fighter, a survivor—most men had to be to endure the war.

He's a decent specimen of a man and surely would've made a handsome suitor to someone in Kampaulo…

Too bad for them, I think.

I close my eyes again and let his intoxicating presence surround me.

The weight of my dress suddenly lightens as the thief upturns my pockets; the sound of my coin tinkling to the ground brings me back to the present.

I purse my lips, my patience quickly fading at this interruption to my otherwise peaceful hunt.

'*We do not kill women.*' I roll my eyes at the moon.

The man rushes toward us. "Leave her be, you wretch!"

His voice is powerful, commanding. It reverberates

through me like a song.

I sigh, slightly bothered at his nobleness. *A kind one...*

Alas, he's now *the* one. And there isn't enough luck or magic in the world to keep me from sinking my teeth into his neck and sucking all of his delectable blood from his body. I have never felt so hungry for anyone in my short life.

I watch keenly as my prey runs toward me. I cock my head to the side, drinking him all in.

What's so special about you? I wonder—besides those long, strong legs or the way the wind combs through his hair.

His coat fans out behind him, heavy boots stomping the ground. *Mmm, yes...* He's a healthy man, fast. *Delicious.*

The scent of him carries on the breeze, an intermingling of so many interesting things—smoke from a firepit lingering in his hair, skin salted from the sea, sweat beading on his chest from...

I frown, scenting a woman on him.

"Mind your business!" grumbles the thief, not even bothering to glance up.

She's too preoccupied with my gold to care about some misplaced hero racing to my rescue, already on her knees scooping it up with frantic greed. She's even dropped her blade.

I chuckle to myself, adding 'actor' to my list of best human disguises—she thinks me so small and frail, frozen in fear, that she doesn't even feel the need to wield her weapon to keep me still.

Just wait...

I will be more terrifying than her greatest nightmare.

Finally, there's some fun to be had tonight!

Magic gathers somewhere in my chest. I hum, releasing a sound I know is far too beautiful to the human ear to be ignored. Too beautiful not to wholly hear.

I've gotten good at this, easily able to incapacitate every

nerve in the human body. I direct all my power toward him.

The man freezes with his right foot forward, fists clenched, ready to take his next step toward me; I hold it.

His eyes dart back and forth, landing on me, wanting to help… wanting help. The tenderness in his stare turns bewildered when I don't react.

The slightest bit of guilt twinges in my chest for the abrupt ending he'll soon meet, when he was only trying to be heroic…

Why did this one have to be heroic? There are so many monstrous men walking this earth.

I stifle my laugh, my cruel smile. *Oh, well.*

I blow him a gentle kiss.

"I'm no damsel," I whisper on a wisp of magic so he can hear—he's still several feet away.

I narrow my gaze, making sure he realizes, from the silver, unforgiving glint in my eyes, that I'm the villain in his story.

His confusion sharpens to shame, then shifts to something else altogether, a fiery rage.

I turn my back to him and focus on the woman, allowing my human mask to fall away and reveal my real face, my fangs.

The thief still doesn't notice what's happened, hurrying to gather up all the gold she can, painstakingly plucking each coin from the ground.

'*Maybe she has gold in her ears*,' a voice speaks.

I cover my mouth with my hand, but I can't hold it in. My laugh pours out between my fingers.

She snaps her head toward me, then glances to the motionless man. Her eyes widen. "Don't come any closer!"

"It's not him you should be afraid of this night," I say with indifference. I drop my hand to my side, straightening my spine to my full height. "Such a greedy fool," I add, crossing my arms. "I'm amazed it's taken you so long to notice me for what I am."

I stand over her, contemplating what to do with this poor example of humanity.

She stumbles back, dropping the gold and sweeping up her dagger. She points it at me.

"Say that again, you palace-bred piece of filth!"

I hold my hands up in mock fright, blinking back at her too quickly to be genuine.

She dares to look away from me, inclining her head toward the man. "What's wrong with you, mate?" she calls. "Why are you standing like that?"

"He cannot answer you," I reply in a low voice—when she looks back at me, I focus all my power on her, letting her feel the magic radiating off me. It glows atop my skin.

She looks me up and down, her weapon hand shaking. "What did you do to him?"

"I've compelled him to wait... while I deal with you, madam." I curtsy, my voice just as sharp as it is soft and polite.

"Why you cocky little—" Her nostrils flare. She swings the blade at me, aiming for where she believes I have a heart.

With as much effort as it might take a person to rip into a loaf of stale bread, I snap her wrist with my hand. The clean, decisive sound of breaking bones cracks through the quiet alleyway—she screams, an agonizing screech.

She loses her grip on her knife; it falls to the ground.

I look around the Lotus Center. *Someone might hear...*

She makes to scream again; I clasp my hand over her mouth, feeling the hotness of her breath on my palm, her scratchy tongue licking at my skin, desperate for air.

She thrashes; I remain steady, still.

She tries to claw my grasp away, rip at my knuckles. Her fingernails bleed—the smell evokes a fraction of the wonder that this man's blood does.

"Goddesses, you're weak," I say, shaking my head. "I don't pity you at all."

She stops struggling, her wrist limp in my grasp. Her eyes find my own, green as the greed in her soul. *What to do with you?*

Slowly, I release her.

Her knees buckle. She snivels, sucking at the air, gluttonous for it.

I kneel down to her so that she can look me in the eye and know that I am not of her world.

Her fear reflects back at me, the glistening of my irises an electric silver, bright with magic she will never know.

"I was weak once, like you," I say after a moment, considering her tear-splotched face. "I felt helpless and afraid and full of desire for things I would never own, never be—"

"*Please*," she cries, shaking her head. I press my finger to her trembling lips.

"But I held moral ground. I never succumbed to thievery or assault of my fellow sisters, even in my most desperate human days." I speak with a seductive snarl that can only belong to an angry Myr Sister. "And I *was* desperate, for a time." I glance to the Lotus Center. Then my eyes move back to hers; I close my grip again over her broken wrist—she bites down on her tongue. "I am no longer."

The sureness of the voice that I conjure now makes me swell with pride.

"Please, my lady… I can make amends. *Please*, I beg of you. Let me go." She can't even look at me now for the fear in her little heart. "I won't steal again! You must forgive me."

Must I?

My gaze drops to the dagger, my lips pressing into a firm line.

"I am no lady. My kind were not created to forgive *you* for your sins on this plane. There are gods and goddesses for that," I say, sharply—I lean in. "I mustn't do anything… at all."

I can see her curiosity, desperate to know, even in the mortal danger she is in—*then, what are you? Which god do you serve? For whom were you created?*

There's a gust of wind. The man's aroma overwhelms me once more. My hunger shifts into a voracious need that I can no longer temper.

I peel back my lips and bite the woman's neck, my eyes pinning on the man. My fangs sink easily into her skin, a knife to warm butter.

She has no muscle at all, not like...

I flinch. *Why am I drinking her and not him?*

I don't pull away, feeding at her veins with as much respect as she showed me.

Eloise, stop! You disgrace your ancestry.

I'm not sure what's come over me, but I couldn't, honestly, care less.

Blood is blood. I see no difference.

I drink as greedily as she'd tried to gather up my gold, yet as slow and unhurried as she deserved.

I nearly forget who I'm really after. Her blood rejuvenates me, making me far too calm for how soon the sun will come to chase me away.

But I just can't seem to stop, to put her down and go to him before I run out of time.

"You're a blood-drinker," the man accuses, his voice pushing into my thoughts. He falls forward, somehow breaking out of the trance I had set upon him.

What in the... I pull my teeth out of the woman's neck, her blood dripping on my dress. *How did he get free?*

He finds his footing, gaping at me, now frozen of his own accord; I gawk back at him, slightly dizzied in the best of ways, sunk in his burning gaze.

"Your legends mislead you, sir," I reply after a moment— the woman weakly moans. "I am so much more." I offer him a surely blood-red smile. "Would you like to come closer, so I can tell you what I really am? I see that you're curious." I stroke the woman's hair. "They always are."

I know I shouldn't think to feed again with the sun nearly risen and my belly full, but I crave for more. I crave him.

No, Eloise. That's just your blood high talking. Do not overfeed.

I wipe my mouth on the back of my arm, considering him with wonderment. "I find I'm curious of you, too…"

I think to lure him to me, to sing again, but clearly I needn't bother. He takes a step closer, as if drawn in by my voice.

He opens his mouth to speak. "I—"

The woman mutters, "Help me," with an outstretched hand.

He sucks a breath in through his teeth, his face going whiter. He swivels on his heel and breaks into a run in the opposite direction, his cloak floating behind him.

Fast, I think again, chewing on my lip.

But not faster than me.

I can hear his heart racing, his blood pumping, even as he gets farther away. His boots thunder on the ground, the sound growing softer with the distance he puts between us.

Catch him. Stop him!

That enchanting, full-bodied scent fades, begging to be tracked down, consumed.

It takes everything not to discard this trash I feed on now for what would surely be the equivalent of a meal for a queen…

'*It would be so, so easy. It's what you're meant to do. So do it!*' A haunting hum murmurs, '*Why deny yourself such a pleasure?*

I look to the moon, unsure of who spoke. '*He doesn't deserve to die tonight. He was a kind one,*' she says. '*Save him for later, at least, Eloise. You've already had your fill.'*

I grimace, reluctantly setting my fangs on the woman again, hiding the roll of my eyes from this great goddess who rules the night.

'You can hide nothing from us,' she reminds me.

'Don't you have better things to do than spy on me?' I ask.

'Not at all,' she says, lightly. *'Your sisters don't seem to care for the risks of landwalking nearly as much as you, Eloise. Someone's got to keep an eye on you.'*

I scoff, sucking at the last of the thief's blood. Then I look longingly down the alleyway.

I can't believe I let that man get away...

The thought of him lingers and surely won't dissipate soon. But I made my selection tonight, even if I chose wrong.

I roll the woman's lifeless body to the side and look to the sky again, grinning like a fiend. "Let's keep this between me and you, *hmm?*" Syrifina will chew me out in front of the entire coven if she gets wind of this. "What do you say, friend?"

Of course, now, the Moon is silent.

I stand, turning in the direction of the man, his scent like an enchanted bread-crumb trail left for me to follow—I take a single step in his direction with Temptation's hand on the small of my back.

The sky begins to lighten, stopping me in my tracks. My time is up, the decision made for me.

I really hope word doesn't get back to my sisters about this mishap. Rumor spreads like wildfire through the sea.

'In the sky as well,' the Moon muses.

I stick my tongue out at her.

She snickers. *'Time to go, Eloise.'*

I strip away my false identity and toss the clothes to the ground. "Good riddance," I sing.

The last shadows of the night envelop me, praising me for returning to my true nature. The mysterious wanderer is gone—next time I shall play the disheveled beggar, and maybe that mysterious man will come to my rescue again.

I shake my head, bemused. *I can't believe he'll live to see another sunrise after all. I've never missed a mark before.*

I still. "No," I gasp, touching my lips. "He saw me feed…"

I shudder as the sunrise begins to warm the air.

I need to right this wrong, and soon. Before anyone else finds out—I resolve to return and hunt him on the next feeding cycle.

The water calls me home, ready to accept me once more and always. I walk to the edge of the Lotus Center, not a single soul in sight to witness me change back into my real body.

I dive into the channel that will lead me to the sea and away from Kampaulo.

The calm waters come to life with radiant lights, surrounding me in all the silver and gold I would ever need for a thousand lifetimes. *Dazzling. Enchanted.* My true self transformed.

I pause on the surface and look back to the alleyway, my tail swishing behind me. My watery magic bursts out of the channel, wrapping around the dead woman, sweeping her and her stolen coins in alongside me.

I don't bother to watch this one sink, trying not to consider what I've done—feeding on a female this night—when I could've taken any man I wanted.

Time will erase this mistake, I think, swimming away to ponder her fate. *Besides, maybe, she'll have more fortune in death. She really did deserve it.*

4

SPELLBOUND

THE SOUND OF MY FEET POUNDING the cobblestone, my breath, ragged and heavy, my heartbeat thundering in my ears—these are the only things I can hear as I try to push her intoxicating yet blood-chilling voice from my mind.

I race through the streets, outpacing the sun as it starts to break over the horizon behind me.

It pushes the cold night away, making room for the gentle warmth of the day. Already my skin heats.

Sweat beads atop every inch of me as I sprint across the city. The wind tangles my hair. Buildings and nature alike pass me by in a blur.

I never look back. I want to put as much distance between myself and that—

'Would you like to come closer, so I can tell you what I really am?'

My chest tightens at just the memory of her honeyed words...

At the way the golden glint in her eyes flickered when she

measured me. The silver sheen in her irises gleaming with murderous magic as she contemplated killing me.

I take turn after turn through the winding, sleeping streets, trying to outrun my thoughts.

My muscles begin to ache. It's been a while since I ran for anything other than pleasure, too long, I realize—gravity forces me to slow at the steady incline beneath my heels.

I draw in big gulps of air, pushing myself harder, determined to prove to myself that I can—that I'm not just a highlife, a painter.

I have let myself get soft since the King's armies stormed Kampaulo and forced us to our knees. I conformed to the new terms of *existing* in Olleb-Yelfra rather than be made an example of by his regulators' swords—meanwhile, blood-sucking beasts are prowling our streets with no one the wiser, no recourse to protect ourselves now that magic's forbidden.

I scowl, forcing my legs to move faster.

My magic tickles at my insides as I push onward, upward. It itches for a release.

I peer down the empty, sleeping streets as I pass. There's no one in sight, but I would be a fool to think there aren't prying eyes peeking through shuttered windows or spying around corners—the King's shadows lurk everywhere now.

I grit my teeth, shoving my magic back down into the pit of my stomach.

The streets widen at the edge of town, opening up to a hilly expanse that's bordered by the ocean. Smooth, pebbled pathways twist through lush trees and bushes that have grown so tall they create a natural maze. If I didn't come this way nearly every day, I might get lost and end up on the other side of the city.

I slow to a walk at the desperation of my lungs, letting the crisp air fill them. It tastes of salt and nature.

I brush my hand alongside one of the overgrown bushes;

it towers over me. Thick, oval emerald-colored leaves create a wall from here all the way to Kampaulo Palace should I wish to follow it. Dark purple flowers sit within the shadows of the hedges like hidden jewels—they're so exquisite that their beauty obscures the bed of thorns they sleep within.

With a yelp, I pull my thumb back to find a bright red dot swelling atop my broken skin, smearing the calloused layer that covers my hands after all these years at my craft. I bring my thumb to my lips and suck, eyes narrowing in contempt at the viciously radiant blossom.

I consider the taste... the salty, sharp tang. The hairs raise on my skin.

My breath hitches in my throat. Slowly, I turn, to see if she is standing behind me.

A lightening sky and blue-gray sea steal my vision instead, making me squint into the distance. The sun raises its exquisite face above the horizon. A sliver of burning, blazing red starts to blend into softer palettes, ones that normally bring me such happiness—this morning, all I see is blood.

I try not to think of how vivid the scarlet was... that stained her white teeth and ran down her chin, her neck, her chest. I try not to think of how she seemed to savor the slow death of that poor, old crone. Of how evenly she spoke to me as she held someone's life in her fists and then squeezed until there was nothing left of it.

'I am so much more.'

I let the sunrise hypnotize me and focus on anything *but* her—not the way her dark skin seemed to glisten under the moonlight. Not the way her hair gently blew in the breeze like the seducing lull of a wave. Not the way every word she uttered was with the succinctness and sureness of the strongest of queens in our buried, banned history. And with the brutality and cruelness of our King.

'I see that you're curious. They always are.'

"They," I breathe, running my hand through my hair.

I close my eyes, my shoulders heavy as I tip my head back, cherishing the breeze on my face, the sound of birds waking to the day; Kampaulo begins to rouse at their call like clockwork. *My city. My home.* "I'm lucky to be alive today."

I continue to walk, cherishing every breath I take.

"JASPYR, YOU ALRIGHT, MATE?"

I start, realizing I've mindlessly walked to the one place I've always felt safe.

Most of the town's people live here, spread out along the sloping hills and cliffs. They keep watch from up high—over the docks and markets, the shops, cafes, and taverns that make Kampaulo such a gem on this side of the world. Homes were built a safe distance from the unruly sea, for she's known to have a sudden temper at times. And one stead, in particular, has always held their doors open to me.

Eddison sits crouched under the awning at the front door of his small estate. I feel the heat of the sun rise even higher behind me as he blinks it from his russet eyes.

"What are you doing out here so early?" he says with an obtrusive yawn. "It's the crack of dawn." He leans his back against the door, tying up his boots. "Out for a run?"

Words don't come to me, not with her enveloping my thoughts. *No one will believe a word of this*, I realize.

I look to Eddison, warily—not even my best friend.

Even when we were kids, he could never understand my fascination for creating things, pictures and places, with only my mind's imaginative eye to guide me; he was always so grounded, his creator's skill honed on practicality, like construction and weaponry.

I take a seat next to him on the porch, wiping away my sweat.

Eddison shakes his head at me, the muscles and veins in his thick neck flexing, involuntarily. A cocky grin stretches across his face.

"Don't you think you're lean enough? If only you'd consider joining up!" He slaps me on the back so hard that I wince at the sting of his hand. "We need more men like you in our ranks," he says. "With a little toughening up, you'd be great as a city regulator." He lets out a low laugh. "Don't want you getting weak on me now."

I spin out from under his hand and have his meaty arm pinned behind his back in my next breath.

"So, *what?* I can become all brute and no brains?" I retort. "No thanks. I'm fine thinking for myself, mate."

He huffs a curse, and I loosen my grip, allowing him to unwind from my hold.

He rubs at his arm, shooting me a glare.

I shove him aside and sit back down, ignoring his wounded expression.

"What was that for?" he snaps. "I'm barely awake!"

I scowl, my mind still in a state of turmoil even as my body recognizes that it's safe, my heart beat slowing to a steady rhythm.

"You and I have different definitions of what it means to be weak," I reply. He knows full well I could beat him in any battle—I set my gaze on the blood-red horizon.

I don't bother to sugarcoat the venomous words that come next.

"And let's not pretend that I didn't teach you everything you know from my days training under the *rightful* king." I keep my voice low, my back turned to him. "Look at what you've become, Eddison. You're nothing more than a puppet in this regime."

I hear as he opens his mouth to retort; I turn to face him.

You know I'm right, I think, hardening my gaze. *How can you do this to yourself?*

His words falter, as if he'd heard my judgment.

He frowns, thinking better than to enter into this argument again. Though his gaze pins to mine, meeting my challenge—by the shocked expression that flickers over his features, I know I let slip the silver glint of unrefined, unapologetic magic in my irises.

If anyone else had seen, we'd *both* be slaughtered on sight, by the regulators he loves so much.

His hands curl into fists. He clearly tosses with whether or not to hit me square on my jaw instead.

I would deserve it.

"Have you been locked up in your studio all night again or something?" he asks after a long, dreadful moment, steam fluttering past his lips. "Why don't you pay a visit with wine or whiskey like everyone else?"

My silence and the tightening of my jaw is enough of an answer for him.

He rolls his eyes, waving me off.

"You *need* to get out of your shop more," he continues. "Get some fresh air up here with us real people, before all those fumes and fake pictures start messing with your mind." He taps on his temples. "Ma said that you never should've left. It's not a healthy home."

I blink at him, mouth agape, suddenly wondering if I had imagined all the surreal events that occurred the moment I left my shop in the Lotus Center...

The ethereal woman of any man's dreams, in need of a helping hand; the terrifying turn of events as she shifted into a figment of any boy's nightmares, into a monster.

Eddison grunts, surely thinking he knows where my head is at. "Do me a favor, Jaspyr, please," he adds. "Don't come barging onto my land at the *crack* of dawn to start something again... just because you forgot that you're human and have to sleep at night."

He gives me a playful shove and a haughty smile that tells me he's already moved on and in no mood to fight.

"I'm getting ready to start my day, and you're barely in the right mind!" He shakes his head, chuckling to himself. "And normally I'm the one out all night."

I still stare at him in a stupor, wondering...

His laugh dies away, his expression turning sullen. "Seriously, though. You look like the ghost of your father right now. How many times do I have to remind you to take care of yourself? It's been years since—"

I blanch; he squeezes my shoulder, sparing me the memories of my grief.

"I'm just..." His gaze darts away from mine, awkwardly. "Worried about you these days is all." He sighs. "Are you alright?"

"Gods, I'm sorry," I reply in a huff.

I rest my forearms on my thighs, head bowed to my hands. My entire body seems to slump from the weight of my tiredness as I let myself feel it.

My hair falls over my eyes. I pull at my cheeks, forcing myself to stay awake. "I shouldn't have spoken to you like that. I was out of line—"

He waves me off. "Forgotten, mate. Always."

I look to him, shame spreading through me.

I can't even fathom what it might take to actually push Eddison away. As far as I can remember, he'd always been there. He's my only true family left in Kampaulo, even if we're not tied by blood—

Her face, that monster, flashes in my memories. *I didn't imagine a thing*, I assure myself.

I stand, pacing the porch, focusing on my friend.

"So…" he says, warily, eyes following me back and forth. "What are you doing out here so early, then?"

"I—" I cross my arms at my chest, leaning back against a worn, wooden pillar—what could I say of what I saw? I don't even think I have the right words in my vocabulary to describe it, and especially not within this willfully ignorant regime. "I… was at my workshop until late," I finally respond. "I might've had one too many drinks trying to finish a commission I'm late on."

He nods, a little too smugly for my liking.

"I *think* we've established that you're addicted to work," he says. "If painting didn't make you such the rich little noble"—he stands, playfully pokes at my cheek; I refrain from snapping his finger—"I would tell you to swap your paintbrushes for a sword."

I sigh in annoyance. "You tell me all the time anyway."

He laughs, the sound jolting me awake.

He walks down the porch steps and onto the lawn, stretching his arms to the sky, muscles rippling. Everything about him looks strong, his body thick and brawny to the point that a simple stretch looks like it might cause him harm. He could pummel me with sheer force… if he could ever land a hit.

I grin at the thought of the countless times he's tried—I love him more than anyone, a brother from the first.

He sweeps his pristine black cloak to the side and draws the sword from his hip, pointing it in my direction.

"Why are you here today?" His voice is a compelling, deep rumble; I can only imagine how citizens of Kampaulo might feel at the sight of him in uniform, how they'd endeavor to be the picture of obedience if he confronted them.

I hesitate, wanting to tell Eddison the truth of everything.

I *should* be able to. And yet, as I consider him now, waking his body up to the day—to the tasks the King has set before him to help regulate this city against a law that I wholeheartedly disagree with—I can't seem to voice the truth.

How could I confess to someone so stubborn and law-abiding that I experienced a part of our world outside of the King's rule, outside of his far-reaching, magic-stifling grip?

Even just the weight of that woman's song, the unearthly aura glittering around her—she had *everything* to do with enchanted, lawless power. Power that's not supposed to exist.

Blood-drinker, I think. A myth...

A legendary creature that belongs to a time this kingdom was supposed to have eradicated from memory.

I rake my fingers through my hair, pulling at the wind-formed knots.

I shrug. "I don't know," I say, my tone lighter now. "But here I am." I open my arms out wide.

"Too much whiskey will do that to you," says Eddison with a smirk.

I raise my eyebrows, sweeping up his shield that leaned against the wall at my back; I know what's on his mind as the tip of his blade watches me still.

I hop down to the grass, beckoning him forward, determined to forget what brought me here.

"No wonder you're so sweaty and pale," he adds, relaxing his stance, cackling to the sky. "I'm *so* glad I was born black. I'd hate to always have to hide my face every time I drank too much ale... imagine. Your cheeks are redder than my ass after a whooping from my ma!" He points his sword toward the house.

"Watch it," I warn, ready to play. "Even with this bastard of a headache, I'm pretty sure I could still knock that sword from *your* sweaty grip."

I grin, angling the shield toward him.

"And I might be cursed with skin that shows every mark, every bruise, every battle scar"—I flick my eyes to my left shoulder and arm where, indeed, faint, jagged markings stand out atop my skin, hidden beneath bright tattoos—"but, after all these years, I don't think even one of them is from you."

He tosses his head back and laughs again, the sound stark against the quiet morning; I wince.

"I've been practicing!" he replies, lifting his sword again. "We run drills every day in the palace yard. Don't test me, Jaspyr. I won't hold back." His ready stance and his eager expression tell me he wants me to attack.

I crouch, a smirk playing on my lips. "Let's see what you've got."

Despite all his training, Eddison's tricks are still the same. He throws all his weight into every move—one hit might bring me down or knock my teeth out, but he never meets his mark.

I buckle some under the strength of his blows, but my shield remains lifted—and the moment he lets his guard down, gathering momentum for the next strike, he's already lost to me.

He aims high, I strike low, swiping the shield at his feet to knock him off balance. I slam my arm into his wrist to loosen the grip on his sword.

In a matter of minutes, I have his blade in my hand and am pointing it at his throat. "I told you, you have to stop relying on sheer strength," I implore. "One of these days it's going to be the death of you or someone you're supposed to be protecting."

He pushes the sword from his face and gets to his feet, brushing the dirt from his knees. "Everyone has their weaknesses," he says, catching his breath. "My weakness and strength happen to be one and the same." He shrugs.

I flip the blade down and press the pommel into his chest;

he clasps his hand over mine. "Trust me, brother," I say, looking him in the eye, "you have many more strengths to lean on when the time comes."

"So do you," he replies, looking down. "You're a natural born fighter."

I hide away my smile—he's getting so good at losing to me, when before he'd still try to rip my head off.

"That may be so, but it doesn't always mean I *need* to fight."

King Damas's advice resonates in my heart from my short time spent as a young apprentice in his court.

He rolls his eyes, waving me off. "Oh, *please*, don't start with all that nonsense," he says with a snort. "You're a stone-cold killer, Jaspyr. I've seen you cut a man's head clean off."

My eyes narrow. "War changes us all," I whisper.

He crosses his arms at his meaty chest.

But before we can get into it again, his mother stumbles out of the house and onto the porch with a screech. "What's all this racket out here this early?"

She shields her face against the sun as if it were acidic.

"Sorry, Mum," whines Eddison. "Go back to sleep. It's just Jaspyr causing trouble again. Nothing to fret."

Her eyes light up at my name. "Oh, my *boy!*" She pins her gaze on me, calling me over.

Obediently, I draw her into a hug.

"Why don't you visit more often?" she scolds, pinching my cheeks. Then she takes one look at me and frowns. "I *told* you to stop wasting away in that wretched shop of yours. You're going to drown in your paint one of these days."

"Better than drowning in your ale," mumbles Eddison under his breath.

She casts a hazy glare at him. "Watch your mouth," she says. "Or I'll rethink why I let you stay here."

I fidget, not wanting to get caught in between another argument about the mother who drinks too much and the son who can't seem to hang on to his coin.

"What brings you here?" she asks, sharpening her gaze back on me, as if sensing I'm about to sneak away.

"I… I met a woman," I blurt out, fumbling over my words as I wiggle out of her grasp.

I met something.

Eddison makes an unusually high-pitched noise. He puts his hands on his hips, his mouth in a wide, awkward grin. "You don't say?"

His mother claps her hands. "Oh, how delightful! Finally, *one* of my sons has their head on straight." She waves me inside. "Come, both of you. I'll make a pot of tea. You can tell us all about it."

"I'd love a spot of tea, madam," I say with a nervous laugh. *Maybe then I could properly think*—I wrack my brain on the details I can share about this 'woman' who has supposedly made me lose sleep.

She scoffs. "By now, won't you please just call me Penelope? *Madam* was my mother… I'm not yet so old." She holds her chin high, walking forward. "Certainly not with my husband dead and gone." She blows a kiss to the ceiling. "Gods rest his soul."

Eddison winces; I offer him an apologetic smile. "Of course, Penelope," I say.

For his sake, I shift the subject away from his father before she can ramble on—the town's people claim Penelope pushed him overboard after they'd drifted too far on a private fishing expedition; she maintains that he slipped and fell off the boat in the dark of the night… But nobody really knows what happened to him those many moons ago.

"So…" I scratch my head. "What kind of tea do you—"

"Mum, I don't have time for this," grumbles Eddison,

pausing in the doorway. "I'm supposed to be at the training camp in—"

She simply glares at him over her shoulder.

I give him a sympathetic pat on his back, whispering to him, "It doesn't matter how old you get, mate, this is just another battle you'll never win. Get used to it."

"I can't argue with you there," he says, begrudgingly.

He trudges forward, head bowed—we both walk into the house and settle at the table.

Penelope makes to heat the kettle; I jump up. "Here, let me do that for you, mada—" She glowers at me. "Penelope."

She smiles, sliding into the chair next to Eddison.

She slaps his cheek lightly. "You could do with a little more chivalry, boy," she says. He curses under his breath, then they bicker back and forth for a good ten minutes before my presence is remembered.

I'm seated back at the table; Penelope's chair squeaks in my direction. "So what's this about a woman?"

My skin goes cold. All I can think to say is "This wasn't just any woman. She was *so* much more."

Penelope slams her hands on the table, making the dishes rattle.

"Gods, Ma..." says Eddison, gawking at her.

"*What* are you doing wasting time here for, then?" she barks as I turn around. "You're a fool if you let someone who makes your face look like *that* go." She points at me.

"Yeah, mate," adds Eddison with a snicker, leaning back in his chair with his hands behind his head. "You're so wound tight. She must've done a number on you if you had to run off all your pent-up energy." He winks. "I know what *that's* like."

"Mind your tongue," says Penelope, slapping his knee so that his chair rocks; he flails his arms to keep from falling. "And spend less time at the brothel. Then maybe you'd have enough for rent."

Eddison dutifully ignores her, reaching for the bread on the table. "You should run right back and find her," he says through a mouthful. "She sounds like she might be the challenge you need to bring your head out of the clouds."

Penelope nods. "For once, I must agree with him."

I find my tongue responding quicker than my wiser thoughts can stop me. "You know, I think you're right…"

Just then, the kettle screams, as if in warning.

5

TIME

ᗡ E L O I S E

TIME PASSES SLOWLY. It's been hours since I encountered the object of my greatest bloodlust since my origin feed…

I'm lost in deep reflection, wandering the seas aimlessly and alone, save for the two cat-like sharks that shadow my every move. They weave fluidly between the feathery sea life that sprouts all around us, caring only to lazily massage their bellies.

"Hello, Aura and Ora," I say—I named them for the playful twin traveler spirits Syrifina told me stories about. She'd met them on her own travels centuries ago. They were sisters of ancient times, known explorers of this world, until they got bored with all its wonders and moved on to another…

I sometimes muse over how long I must live before boredom haunts me, if Syrifina is still entertained by this life after so long.

"You both haven't a care in the world, have you? I wish I could say the same for myself this day." Thoughts of that strange man weigh me down—I settle into a soft bed of white sand so that my friends might slither closer.

They move as one, their blend of blue-gray scales standing out in stark contrast, shimmering against the reflection of the sun from up above.

I draw squiggles in the sediment, coaxing them to me. "How do you always know where I wander?"

Though they might not respond with tangible words, I can sense their answers the same way I hear when the Sea speaks or the Moon whispers. '*We will always know where you are. We will always travel by your side. You're our master.*'

They nuzzle their round, flat faces into me, each wanting attention; I stroke the tops of their heads and the sides of their firm bellies.

Master, I think, humbly. Very few of my sisters enjoy the honor of such a strong bond with the intelligent life we swim among—it's a rare connection that I do not take lightly.

"I am your friend," I reply with a little laugh, tickling their noses—I think I might even trust them both more than any of my sisters; their tiny, beadlike eyes glow in admiration, having heard my thought. "I hope you follow me forever." I sigh, leaning into the reef rock at my back.

Ever so gently, I caress Aura's gills with my palm, her soft, easy watery breath soothing me from the inside out. I focus on the light flutter, trying to keep my mind off—

His face, those deep, destructive eyes, flashes before my mind.

I groan and roll onto my back, disturbing the sediment into a cloud around us.

I stare toward the sea sky. "I could *really* use some brilliant advice right about now…"

I'm not hungry and won't be until the shadow moon. I just *want* him… now.

Goddesses, Eloise, you're acting like a blood-starved beast! Put your mind off him until your next feed.

Whoever sank into my head was right.

I can easily wait two weeks. I have to if I want to keep my wits about me...

'*Never forget Zahra's story,*' says Aura in a soothing tone.

'*What happens when a myrmaid forsakes her boundaries,*' finishes Ora.

I nod to myself, digging my fingers into the sand—everything's fine. I drank my fill from the thief to tide me over until the next feeding cycle, just. No one will find out I accidentally killed a woman. There's nothing to worry about. I just have to wait.

Except what, Eloise? Let's not ignore the real problem here...

I chew on my lip, rolling to my side.

Except, I had not only—perhaps, inexplicably—resisted the urge to drink from who I truly craved the most at the time *but* also allowed my prey to escape having seen me feed.

"If Syrifina finds out..." I curl into myself, suddenly very curious about a clam shell beneath my tail.

In a chorus, Aura and Ora's wisdoms fill my head.

'*All you have to do is wait for a handful of days,*' Aura assures me. '*Then sing to him from the water and be done with this.*'

'*No games next time, and no landwalking!*' adds Ora, always so direct. '*Not until you've taken care of this. He cannot live with your secret, Eloise.*'

Together they speak: '*It was a grave mistake to let him go, indeed.*'

I whip my tail at them, lightly, shooing them away. '*I asked for advice. Not a reminder of my error,*' I say through our mind-link, the sand stirring in their wake.

I look up again, spreading out wide with a groan of frustration. The sun sits high in the sky, tempering me.

As soon as it drops, I *could* go and correct my error, just kill that jewel of a human I'd found among that heap of pebbles, without letting his blood touch my tongue. Ensure the Myr secret is safe.

I lick my lips. *My desires satiated... Yes, I could have him tonight. No one would know.*

His aroma swirls in my memories. I'm desperate to taste it, sickened at just the thought of wasting it.

'*You absolutely cannot consume more than your fill,*' warn Aura and Ora.

"Go away," I say, pushing up to my forearms, spying them not far off. "Let me think on my own."

I lie back down in a puff of glittering sand.

The everlasting effects gluttony can have on a myrmaid can be catastrophic, a lifelong battle for control—I can't just kill this man and swim away. I'd *have* to drink him all.

So, I must wait.

Aura and Ora snicker, '*As we said.*'

I shoot up from the sand and swim away in a blur of anxious thoughts.

I'm normally so decisive—I should've just snapped that awful woman's neck and fed on the man, as was my intention.

What had I been thinking, to let her sneak up on me like that? To let her have any influence over *me?*

His perfect blood... the thought of it fogs my sensibility even now. *Why did I let him go?*

I can't even begin to understand. And why do I still want him so desperately, even underwater? I've encountered countless humans before, at sea and on land, yet none of them have ever had quite this lasting effect.

I keep going over the moment in my head, when I let him escape with a rumor ready to spread like a disease. The expression of horror and shock on his face, ready to shout to the world.

Just sloppy!

I laugh, a frustrated one. Bubbles tickle the space around me then run away to the surface.

Aura and Ora swish their tails across the sand, watching me from below, vying for my attention—I had begun to float absentmindedly.

"It's nothing," I drawl, ignoring the concern in their eyes as they follow me.

The water massages my face and fins as I swim deeper; the cold pressure soothes the headache that's starting to form with my ridiculous thoughts.

I home in on the flick of my powerful tail, up and down, moving me forward with ease, testing my limits; it offers me the same focus and exhilaration as I used to feel when I went for long runs. Only now, I never tire...

Not in the water nor on the surface, I think.

It would've been *so* easy to catch him, and I always do love a good chase.

So what is wrong with me, then? Goddesses, this is wearying!

I wrap my arms around my shoulders, hugging myself tight as I swim. I wonder what Syrifina would say...

She won't be understanding, I think. *She'd think you sick in the head.*

Syrifina doesn't bother much with ruling the affairs of her creations, for the sea is a lawless place. But when she does, it can be a frightful thing—she would be forever disappointed at my frenzied state over a man.

I bite down on my tongue.

Not one of us is perfect... a different voice reminds me. *Least of all Syrifina Myr.*

Sometimes, I wonder where such guiding thoughts come from—I trust them all the same.

The warmth of Aura's voice presses into my mind once more. '*Just go back and finish what you started, Eloise, when* the time is right.'

'*Syrifina needn't know,*' cautions Ora. '*We won't tell her.*'

They intertwine in my line of sight, like the night and moon combined, one dark, one light.

I muster up my courage and strength to take this man's life, to entertain my blood craving *and* ensure the safety of the Myr secret... before anyone finds out.

I am strong. I am powerful. I can wait a little longer. I am eternal.

I glance to the sea sky again, counting the days... the hours, minutes, *seconds.*

Time seems to stop.

6

FREEDOM

DARLING DIARY,

My family blossoms like the greatest reef. Zahra Myr, the first of my daughters to have a strong affinity with the earth element, has joined us on this day.

Her lifeblood blooms the purest hues of green, like strings of emerald were sewn to her skin by the God of Earth himself. Her tail gleams like lush grasses after it rains, and her eyes hold all the warmth of jade.

I was first drawn to her spirit, so free and uninhibited. I knew she deserved to carry on forever, to spread her love for life and nature.

I encountered her on the shores of the Impenetrable Forest, followed the scent of her from the water until nighttime fell. She had been quite alone, deep in the woodlands. Lost, surely, though not afraid, not looking to be found by anyone...

Wandering, searching for something.

She was staring upon a bitten, yellow moon, I recall, when I finally approached from the sea. I let the water roll off my skin like drizzling diamonds and made the waves dance behind me, wanting her to meet me.

"Extraordinary," she said, transfixed—though she hadn't even noticed me yet.

Her gaze was pinned eagerly to the sky, as if she wished to touch it, drink it.

Yes, you are, *I thought.*

DARLING DIARY,

Time has not done my daughter well. Zahra readily accepted my gift when I presented it to her, but it's come to plague her now.

She was not afraid, her excitement and curiosity left no room for her to be; in the end, she took just as well to the sea as she did to the forests and the trees. She was born to roam!

That's why the sea accepted her so. It had no choice.

There was no stopping her ambition to explore, just like there's no end to our waters...

I could've forced her not to landwalk, but I don't wish to control any of my daughters' choices.

As a human, Zahra had been so accustomed to the earthly terrain that she thought herself quite in control to surface almost immediately upon transforming. She desired to visit her old home, friends, and family, to investigate their lives with new eyes and knowledge—this is a known pattern with those newly born to blood, this curiosity to look into the past.

I see it with every new creation of my kin, history repeating itself. It affects each one of us differently, a part of our maturity cycle—some have faced far worse consequences for indulging in their past than others.

I try to warn them against such unrefined urges, but I don't grant my daughters the freedom of eternal life just to be a dictator. As with any child, they must learn the hardest lessons on their own.

Zahra's story, perhaps, is a cautionary one.

Her power was quite erratic in the beginning, just as difficult to contain as the wilderness itself. In a brazen, thoughtless act, she revealed all that she had become to her family and friends of her former life—though they had long since thought her dead.

Confined to the trees, these village people knew little of magic beyond the jungle's offerings. They knew nothing of the enchanted things in the grander world. Thus, they greeted her in horror and distrust.

"Monster!" they accused. "Living dead. We must put her to rest beneath the soil so that this plague shall not spread!"

I heard her scream even from the sea, a roar filled with frustration and rage. But I was too far away to help her…

When I arrived at the shores of the jungle she's always known and loved, the act of her anger was already done. She washed her hands and face of her family's gore in our waters, but not even the sea can cleanse one's soul.

After that astonishing blood feast, the thirst grew to control her; her shame came hand in hand with the desire to suppress her natural cravings—only further feeding the lack of control that slowly built into a tenacious urge for more.

And, of course, this wasn't the last killing spree she fell victim to. Extreme guilt plagued her for the first decade or so.

It's easy to lose focus, sink into the blood, if one is unprepared…

I daresay my dear daughter got carried away. A mistake forgiven but one that will remain with her forever, endless urges that she must always acknowledge with due caution.

Our kind must learn from this, grow.

I watched the shores of the village to make sure the repercussions of Zahra's actions never crossed the sea; a rumor about her quickly spread among the few people who were left alive. They deemed her a restless soul caught between planes.

"Confused and disoriented, afraid," they said. "A murderer but not of her own volition."

I thought this one of the most inaccurate speculations to follow one of my daughter's landwalking transgressions to date—myrmaids are not fearful, restless, indecisive creatures…

We wander by choice and kill who we want. But even we can let our desires swim away with us, like the caress of a seducing wave.

7

GOLD

☼ J A S P Y R

AS SOON AS PENELOPE EXCUSED US, our bellies full, I walked Eddison to his post at the palace; I had little choice in the matter. He thought my highlife status might bolster his justification for being late, though judging by the head regulator's stone-faced expression, I think it might've made things worse.

"Farewell," I say with a half-hearted wave.

He puffs up his chest, readying himself. "I've got this."

"Right… see you on the other side!"

I leave him to his training and drills, wandering across the lush, kempt grounds—the Kampaulo Palace sits quite far from where our city meets the water, covering a vast expansive of open, grassy flat land at the top of what we call the Great Hill.

Since I've made the trek here, I decide to lay eyes on my favorite viewpoint in the city. I circle around to the back, making haste so that I can forgo making niceties with the other visiting nobles.

I crane my neck to take in the barely visible carvings along the outer walls, hidden by wild nature.

The entire palace stacks smoothly to the sky in blue-gray slates of stone that look as if the sea had painted them there; worn depictions of elegant explorer ships and legendary sea creatures are concealed carefully behind tall trees and bushes— whether purposefully or not, this part of our history remains.

I continue to the courtyard behind the palace, passing through winding trails and tall archways. I climb the tall stone staircase that leads to the vista I had been shown years ago, by invitation of the city keeper.

Sweat beads on my forehead. I stop only when I reach the top—the wind pummels me this high up, rolling over the water. And the sun beats down on my shoulders.

I gaze past the Great Hill and beyond our borders—peaks of barren volcanic land roll all the way from here to the north, swallowed by a shadow terrain that is the Black Sand Desert. There's only one other known metropolis to be found on that deadly route—Belgradia, a bustling city bordered by the sea, desert, and the volcanos where King Damas used to claim that dragons slept. *Before.*

I had been to that cruel and cold place only once and never wished to go again… yet some dark part of me wondered when I might return, was fascinated by the stark power that seemed to radiate from that part of the Olleb.

So familiar…

Alone in the early morning, at the top of the world, I finally let my mind pore over her again, trying to formulate where she might belong in the setting I know as the 'real' world.

"She doesn't belong," I state, firmly. "She's a walking nightmare."

The reasonable man that I am hopes the day will never come. Prays that I never lay eyes on that monster again in my life.

And yet, even my wisest mind can't deny how horrifyingly enchanting she was...

How just the taste of her voice held me captive; how her bloodstained lips drew me in.

Another part of me—one I've never quite explored—*wants* to be terrified. Wants to stand face to face with the most mesmerizing being I've ever known to exist in this universe and let her have all of me, just for another glimpse of that surreal beauty and power.

I laugh at the dark thought.

"Fool," I breathe, shaking my head. *Who would knowingly peek into a viper's mouth just out of curiosity?*

The question lingers with me all the way back down the steps and across the palace lawn, past the swarm of city regulators already deep in their drills—Eddison was doing lonely laps around the courtyard—and through the gates.

I was grateful not to run into the city keeper on my way out. I was in no mood to play politics or explain my ever-growing absences from the keeper's court. I was so tired I could barely concentrate on where I was headed, my feet carrying me along a familiar path.

Absolute fool, I think with incredulity...

I HAVE TO FORCE MYSELF not to *run* back to the spot where I encountered her last night. Instead, I briskly walk.

Soon, I'm standing back in the alleyway where we met.

It is empty, save for the rats and the seagulls scurrying around for the scraps of food left by last night's tavern patrons.

It looks completely different washed in morning light, all the shadows and dark corners now brightly lit as if the darkness had never been. As if that creature, born of the dark, hadn't slithered out from the shadows and nearly destroyed me.

Cream cobblestones glitter beneath the sun, and the sounds of the city fill the area.

There is nothing sinister about this place—save for the dried blood on the ground at my feet. It stands out darkly against the soft, sand-colored ground.

I kneel down, scraping my fingers across a place that still shines, just to be sure that it's real. The blood is *mostly* dry—but a small collection of it has yet to congeal.

"I can't believe it… it really happened," I say to myself, noting how sticky old blood feels.

My headache only worsens, knowing I can tell no one, ever.

The thief's body is gone. *She* is gone—and I am left with so many questions.

I stand with a deep frown, still staring at the evidence. Something glints on the ground next to it; the sound of coins tinkling to the ground like a sharp, heavy rain rings in my memories.

I kneel again, pinching a gold piece between my finger and thumb. It's warm to the touch, hot from the sun now beating down.

I run my finger over the soft ridges, studying it. It's a treasure of my world but not of the present. *How did she come of it?*

It surely belongs to a time predating King Devlindor—on one side of the gleaming coin there's a double-edged axe; on the other there's a language I cannot interpret.

I wonder if all the dwarves are truly gone.

I can't help the smile that tugs at my lips, thinking of her, knowing that surely the intelligent, enchanting beings of Ol-leb-Yelfra who were banished to myth still persist, somehow. Even if they only lurk in dark places, like alleyways, and in the minds of poor souls who refuse to forget, like me.

As quick and dreamlike as the encounter was, I recall every detail of her as if I had stared upon her for the span of a lifetime—the soft curves of her physique, her intimidating poise, her intoxicating, venomous voice. And her eyes...

Like swimming in pools of velvet brown stitched with silver and flecked with gold.

I wasn't supposed to see her and live. Of this, I am certain...

She cast a spell over me—a hex—not for my protection but to trap. And even knowing then, I could hardly look away.

My eyes grow wide and my smile fades; I note something else amiss in the alleyway.

Her clothes are shredded, discarded near the place where the walls open up toward the Lotus Center. It's as if she'd ripped off her mortal mask in haste, to feel the wind.

"Where did you go?" I speak, standing at the edge of the alleyway. *And will you come to finish me?*

I can't fathom why she let me escape.

Maybe she didn't, a soft voice speaks. *Maybe you should run and never return, while you still have the chance to get away.*

I gape into the crowd that begins to form along the main street. People pace back and forth, bumping shoulders with one another in a haste to begin their day's work.

The busyness of it all shakes my mind back to its senses.

"For the good king's sake!" I say aloud, leaning my back and head into the brick of the wall—I blow a kiss to the wind in King Damas's honor.

A few people shoot judgmental glares my way, but I stare them down, allowing them to look upon my tired face; my highlife status alone makes my word golden against theirs, as disturbed as that might be. And my prominence as a renowned artist gives me clout. Right now, I don't care what they think. Sleep calls to me, begging me to let my eyes close.

Maybe it was all a trick, a fabrication of an overworked mind. I shift the strange coin into my pocket. *No forbidden Golden Age history I've learned mentions anything of the likes of… whatever it is that she was. Just fairytales.*

I shake my head of the doubt trying to force her out.

The memory of the blood-drained body of the beggar and her spilled remains in the alleyway is all the proof I need. And the gold in my pocket is a tangible testimony.

I step back into the privacy of the alley, leaning my back against the warm bark of the tree; I glance to the side and see freshly carved initials—*E.M.*—and know, instinctively, that they're hers.

Silver threads of energy twine through my paint-covered fingers, tickling my senses awake, reminding me that magic will never fade, no matter the laws stifling it. *We shouldn't have to hide!*

My anger surges, flaring inside my chest. I find myself jealous of *her*, of her freedom.

My power undulates there with my mere breath; I turn my back to the city just as the silver energy in my hands grows brighter, weaving into a ball of breathtaking light that I have no hope of hiding.

"Breathe," I say. "Control yourself."

My power dissolves into drive. I step into the crowd and walk to my shop. It's still shuttered from the night before, and I have no plan to open it today.

I unlatch the door and lock myself in, only cracking the curtains to let in some natural light. Then I sit at my stool and pick up my paintbrush, determined to memorialize the reality I know to be true. I dip my brush in the gold.

8

DESIRE

'I RISE TO THE SURFACE OF THE SEA the moment the sun begins to set—I ignore Aura and Ora's pleas to resist.

Why wait when I can finish this now and take what I want? Why repress myself if no one will find out anyhow?

I certainly wouldn't be the only myrmaid in history who has snacked between cycles. And not everyone falls prey to an uncontrollable thirst.

We're not all like Zahra, goddesses forbid.

I block out their speeches and watch the shore, impatiently, the small dock still buzzing with activity.

Most people are tying up their boats and unloading their hefty catches for the day. The air is saturated with the stench of dead fish. *Hordes* of them. Far more than the humans of this community, and the other cities and villages they trade with nearby, could ever consume before the rot would set in. Swarms of seagulls topple over each other to get to the unwanted carcasses.

I normally love to dance with these fish underwater, such

enchanting and playful little things in the world below. They always move about as one, like a shimmering shield of platinum; with such clear waters as their home, it's no wonder that they're always being hunted by humans, their sanctuary, their ballroom, defiled. It's easy to spot them from the surface on a sunny day like this had been, to see just where to drop the nets.

I wait for sundown, eager to invade the fishermen's land and home. To take what I please, to treat it as an unbridled hunting ground, as they do mine.

Above, with the heavy air suffocating my unfortunate friends, their silver sheen and gold-tipped fins are already beginning to fade to a dull, ash-like gray, large limp bodies tangled and broken in wiry nets. Their mouths hang agape from their final moments choking on this wretched atmosphere, eyes glassing over to a steely black.

"This is no way to die, my loves," I utter, the waves undulating around me in agreement. "I'm sorry for your unjust ending." I ball my hands into fists.

Fewer humans mean fewer mouths to feed, from my garden.

I have to hold myself back from returning their bodies to the sea with me, to give them the dignity of ending their cycle as one with the water. There are just too many people here that could witness it, and I've taken enough risks as of late.

Instead, I blow them magic-laced kisses. "It's been my honor."

I tear my gaze away from the innocent, wasted life and set my focus on the pathways leading away from the docks, into the city. People shuffle boxes and tools back and forth from the boats, preparing for sundown.

The fat clouds above are fast-moving, like a rippling sheet of dark and foamy sea. Two epic oceans mirror one another, the sun pressed between them both, squeezed into nothing but a molten sliver.

I'm still fully immersed in the water, only the top of my head and eyes visible.

'*Stay, Eloise,*' the currents whisper, tugging at my tail. '*Wait.*'

I turn away from the shore, facing the horizon just as the sun begins to settle to sleep beneath the world.

"Hush now. I just need to think." I demand silence so that I may witness nature's nightly gift in peace.

The sun's bloated belly is full of hot red and gold, a rippling fire so thick and dense it appears as if a permanent landmark of Olleb-Yelfra, a blazing mountain range that bleeds into the water. I know it's unreachable, that no matter how fast or far I swim, it would be impossible to arrive at the place where the sun meets the sea. Still, I like to imagine that nothing is impossible for me...

This is by far my *favorite* part of life surrounded by the Sea of Saindora—the coming of night, each one more unforgettable than the last. And I still have forever to go.

The air quiets, the sounds of the dock and city muted by the melodies of the sea and sky intertwined. A calmness washes over me, stills me from the inside out. Then the clouds bathe in a blood orange that shall surely burn bright in my memory after it's gone; the fiery ball drops like a coin from the heavens—the Goddesses of the Sun and Sea playing catch.

I watch with glee as it falls quickly through the clouds. It sinks beneath the waters, a golden chunk, a goddess's blessing, tossed into a wishing well for good luck.

A silver piece replaces it with brilliant elegance, striking simplicity that the sun can never achieve—the Goddess of the Moon has placed her winning token in the sky.

"Ah," I breathe, soaking in her light.

Sensational power rushes over me, tingling atop my skin.

The earth cools, the light dims. I swim forward, in search of him.

I SLIP THROUGH THE CHANNELS of the Lotus Center, careful not to be noticed by the people still scurrying about, blending with the soft currents.

The wind shifts—I catch his scent.

"And the hunt begins again," I whisper, watching the promenade from underneath a dock.

A small but prominent storefront catches my gaze, with painted landscapes hanging in the windows. I can practically *see* his aroma swirling around that shop, my hunger and magic manifesting it into a tangible, shimmering trail of soon-to-be blood.

I plant my hands on the fraying wood and heave myself out of the water without a second thought. At my cue, my gold-drenched tail melts away in a spellbinding shower, leaving me with legs and feet.

I don't bother with human clothes to mute my presence again. No time for play nor distraction. Tonight, I'm not an mysterious wanderer, not a traveling singer, a pauper, nor a trader of goods.

Tonight, I'm simply Eloise, come to clean up my mess, just like Syrifina taught me all those years ago.

Like a breath of wind, I pass across the dock to the doorstep covered in his scent. I press my palm against the wood, and the lock snaps with barely any effort.

I step inside and let the door close gently behind me.

THERE'S NO LIGHT, NO FIRE, but I can see everything perfectly. I gape at the paintings and inked scrolls layering every table and every wall—he's a mapmaker, an artist.

What a privilege in this world...

I can hear his frazzled heartbeat from here; last night it sang to me in clear, slow beats. It calls to me from another room, muted by the walls and doors erected around me.

He must be dreaming, I think, also noting the unevenness of his breath.

I quicken my pace, imagining how good he might taste.

'*No need to rush,*' a voice suggests. '*Take your time. You'll want to savor this one...*'

I slow, finding it somewhat easy to distract myself in the splendor of the artwork that surrounds me. I move through the shop, eyes wide, soaking in every color, every shape this man has created with his gifted hands.

From the looks of it, he seems to spend as much time meticulously inking lines and colors across parchments and scrolls as I have spent navigating the underwater caves around the Impenetrable Forest. He's painted the surface world countless times, bringing new life to each work of art.

I ponder what drives him, what fuels such dedication to his craft. "Only a man painfully impassioned could ever paint like this..."

A section of his shop is dedicated to maps and scrolls of both land and water, a dying craft in this world—most are inked in black and white, each one unique, with markings and details to help the commissioner achieve their goal.

There's one carefully pinned up on a small canvas in the back, away from prying eyes or where patrons might wander. His scent is all over it, both aged and new. He must've been working on it for years...

With a closer look, I understand why it's hidden—this map is of the Golden Age, an age I barely got to taste. And from the looks of it, every careful stroke, he's spent many a moon recalling the history to capture.

"Fascinating," I say as I read names of cities no longer remembered in this era.

I circle to the other side of the expansive windows where a large canvas has been covered with a tarp. I yank it to the floor and it gathers at my bare feet.

I tilt my head back in awe as a vast painting of the Sea of Saindora fills my vision—he's used every shade of blue in his palette, it seems, and even shapes some of his own, to bring my waters to life.

There's no land at all, only giant swells trimmed in silver and gold. He's textured them with ships that bounce atop large waves, and he's hidden sea creatures of myth, like me, in the darker parts of the waters, surely near-invisible to the human eye… unless they know where to look.

I doubt the patron who commissioned this piece knows they're there.

I tilt my head again. "Curious…"

This mapmaker paints more realistically than he knows.

He is a true Master of the Arts, a fantastic creator of something from nothing—I fear that if I kill him, no one else might portray Olleb-Yelfra in quite the same way.

Nonsense! He's just a human.

Insignificant. Impermanent.

And yet, I can't remove the last image of him from my mind, this fragile being with paint-splattered skin and a devasting hunger for more in his eye.

I look back to the unfinished map—how terrible it shall be if he dies before he's accomplished his quest for whatever it is he so desires…

Pity, he's met me, I think—I push the door to the back room open and lay eyes on my prey sleeping sweetly.

9

HAUNTED

☼ J A S P Y R

A BLAST OF MAGIC hits me from behind. My barrier spell fal-
ters, letting some of the smoke pour in. I cough and choke,
unbidden tears burning in my eyes.

"Keep going, Sibyl!" I scream to my wife, cutting our way
forward with my sword. "We have to get to the border."

In my left arm, I hold my infant daughter, Luna, squeez-
ing her to my chest in the swaths of my cloak; she cries and
cries, her innocent fear empowering me to run faster.

I never look away from the nearing forest, determined to
get them to safety, to survive this war.

No, not a war—this is a genocide.

And my family is at its epicenter, wading through thick,
heavy blankets of smoke. Everything burns… the people, the
city.

The King's shadows seek to destroy it all, senselessly, car-
rying out this ludicrous order to eradicate magic… and to take
our children. The City of Saindora has fallen, his armies
sweeping the streets clean of disobedient subjects.

"*Hide, comply, or burn!*" they chant in an eerie chorus, faces hidden beneath black hoods.

Vicious magic streams from their fingertips—their ruthless blasts of power drowned out only by the clank of swords and battle cries. The crackling fires and the bone-shivering screams of those who got caught in their flames.

I will never surrender to him! *I commit these sounds to my memory.* I will never forget this.

The King gave the order to search the High City of Saindora for every child and young adult under eighteen, to collect them under his wing and ship them to the north for only the gods know what. Rumors of such a plan had stirred when he'd instated the magic ban the week prior, but I never thought it could amount to this—

I push on, trying to help who I can with the scraps of my magic I can spare, urging them to follow me to safety. To where I know the resistance gathers refugees.

And for those who still wield their weapons with might, I bolster their blades with subtle enchantments—their war calls follow me. "Down with the false king," *they say, willing to lay down their lives.*

I desperately want to join them, but I can't. I have too much to lose. The trees rise before us. "Hurry! We're almost there."

Sibyl suddenly cries out from behind me. I turn to see her tumbling to the ground, falling outside of the boundaries of my shield. She's tripped over the body of someone who will surely never rise again. Her ankle twists at an unnatural angle.

"Can you stand?" I call back, trying to push my shield outward—but I can't, my energy nearly depleted.

She shakes her head, holding her leg.

"I... I think it's broken," she says, her expression panicked. "Take her and go, please! You have to go without me."

I grit my teeth. "Over my dead body. I won't leave you."

I make to go to her, turning my back to the trees.

"Or how about hers?" comes the sinister voice of a man; I glance to my right and meet another's eyes, glazed with silver, the rest of his face covered by his hood. "We don't take kindly to traitors."

The fear that strikes me is otherworldly as several of the king's shadows step onto my path, blocking my view of Sibyl; I clutch Luna to my chest and brandish my sword. But it's too late—

Sibyl's scream sears the air, joining all the others.

"Stop!" I demand, bolstering my shield, unsure of what's happening to her.

Her scream softens to a moan, then all goes quiet.

"See for yourself," says the man—they all part for me.

A savage shout tears from my throat. Sibyl's beautiful, kind face is splotched with blood-red tears as she inhales the last of a poisoned cloud of magic.

"Save her," she mutters with an outstretched hand to me.

I suck in a breath, pain seizing my heart. "Sibyl…"

She falls sideways to join the dead.

My world crashes down on me, all the choices I made that led to this—I did this. Sibyl was nothing but good, nothing but warmhearted. And I couldn't protect her. I killed her…

I kept my family in this godsforsaken city, all for a highlife position. I could've returned to Kampaulo years ago! I only stayed as a compliment to the former, rightful king… to thank him for his patronage of my coveted apprenticeship.

My mind shatters along with my magical barrier. It snaps away, leaving Luna and me at the mercy of these monsters. "What have I done?"

Luna stops crying, as if she'd felt the moment her mother died; I look down to her perfect, round face, my tears glistening on her ash-covered skin.

"If you want to live and go back to how things were, surrender the child," says the man, evenly; they all surround us, magic sizzling in their palms. "It's that simple."

My gaze finds Sibyl's deadened one—go back to how things were?

"There is no going back," I growl; *the heat of magic flares atop my skin. I lift my eyes to the shadow. "I will destroy everything you are, in this life or the next." A promise.*

I stand to face him, holding Luna close.

The corners of his lips tug up into a smile, magic gleaming in his irises.

"You can try," he says, his sword hand twitching. "But you might need your other arm to take on the lot of us." His smile turns wider, heinous. "Sure you want to be the reason another person you love dies?"

He cocks his head to the side, glancing at Sibyl with a mocking frown.

"She might not be too happy about that…" The others snicker.

"Don't look at her!" I say through my teeth, my sword hand shaking—there's not even a whisper of her soul left in her eyes.

I glance from her to Luna, my heart thundering in my chest—what options do I have?

He reads the defeat in my expression.

"Here's how this will go," he says. "You're going to hand over that baby. You're going to comply with the King's new system. And maybe… maybe, you'll see your child again later in life, if they're deemed worthy of citizenship when all's said and done."

I nearly snarl. Our world would've been much better off without this scum—how heartless does a man have to be to knowingly kill innocent people for the favor of what… gold and glory? How can he stand by and take part in all this blood-shed?

I lift my eyes to his. "And if I don't?"

The regulator glances to Sibyl. "If you don't, then you can join your wife, and your child will still be taken. Or, more likely, killed in the process." He places his hand over his heart. "By order of the King." The others close in, their magic brightening.

I take deep, slow breaths, steadying the defiance in my heart that wishes to take those odds.

I have to give Luna a fighting chance...

I nuzzle my head to the bundle in my arms.

"Don't look, darling," I whisper, forcing a calming tone into my voice. "Everything will be alright." Her tiny fingers reach toward my face; I lean in, memorizing those dark, beautiful eyes.

"You are loved, you are strong." I kiss her on the forehead. "Remember all that you are, Luna. You must survive."

"What's it going to be?" the shadow interrupts in a bored tone, picking his fingernails. "I don't have all night."

I grit my teeth and take a single step forward. Head bowed, I hold out my arms, my offering to the King—Luna's cry fills the night as he takes her from me.

The man laughs, lowering his hood. "You made the right choice, mate."

I step back, looking him up and down with all the hatred I can muster—he's cloaked from head to toe in black, a golden snake, the emblem of the new king, coiling at the center of his armored chest. Blood drips from the sword at his waist.

I commit every feature of his wicked face to my mind, so that I might find him again if I somehow live to see tomorrow.

He immediately passes Luna off to someone else, who walks her to a carriage crammed full of other stolen children.

What have I done? I should've fought harder for her. I

should've never let her go.

I glance back; the tree-lined border is so close.

1 WAKE IN A COLD SWEAT, rasping for breath, tears wetting my cheeks.

I've had this dream before, so many times... not a dream, a memory.

I clutch at my heart and say their names in a whisper that barely quivers from my lips. "Sibyl... Luna..." *Gone.*

I don't allow myself to wonder if Luna even survived that night to make it to the Four Corners. I no longer hope to be reunited. It's too painful.

But I can't seem to keep that memory from my mind, even five years later when the world has so quickly moved on; painting and drinking are my only sedatives these days...

I reach for the carafe next to my makeshift bed—a plush formation of pillows, blankets, and pouffes piled on the ground at the foot of my latest portrait.

I bring it to my lips, but it's empty. I drank myself into a stupor last night, thinking of the blood-drinker.

I groan, tossing it away.

It clangs against the stone floor, knocking into old buckets of paint. The sound is like the grating of stone against my brain.

I throw the blankets to the side, letting the cool night air wrap around my naked body, cooling my heated skin.

I blink a couple times to adjust to the darkness; the lanterns I lit have long since burned out, and in the back of my shop, there are no windows, save for the skylight.

I look up, the moonlight sprinkling down on me.

A gold and silver shimmer darts through the room, settling in a dark corner; the stale air in here rustles like a phantom wind.

That's odd, I think, instantly alert.

I squint at the corner, my mind still shaking off sleep—do I imagine the silver of the shadow's sword glinting on that terrible night? The deathly gold sheen of the snake painted on his armor?

There's a soft rustling sound, then the gleaming sliver becomes more vibrant, floating higher. My gaze lifts with it, eyes widening as a figure clearly forms in the shadows.

"Who's there?" I shout into the darkness—I glance to my swords hanging on the wall. Then I glance down, very aware of my nakedness.

I pull a blanket around me and jump to my feet, reminding myself that I'm not someone who will ever surrender again.

"I know someone is there," I say, flexing my muscles. "You picked the wrong night to break in here!"

No one answers, yet an unwelcome presence seems to thicken, right where my weapons are.

"*Solza ven immito,*" I say, calling to my magic instead.

Pink-tinted flames erupt in all the lanterns across the room.

A hiss of annoyance sounds from the shadow-covered figure; it moves faster than wind, away from the lighted fires.

The hairs on the back of my neck tingle.

"You can't hide from me!" I spin around, only to be met with nothing; I clutch my blanket with a fist, glaring into the dark.

A bemused laugh floats around me, a heavy, heady sound.

"I am not hiding," drawls the soft, ethereal voice of a

woman from a different corner of the room—I recognize it instantly, my courage fleeting. "I am hunting you."

The creature from the alleyway steps forward, allowing me to see. I start, my eyes roaming over her, outside of my control—this time, she's naked from head to toe.

Her lip curls up into a seductive smile as our gazes meet.

She leans against the wall, twisting a lock of hair around her finger.

I can hardly meet her eyes, nearly compelled to bow—she radiates ungodly power, unearthly beauty, unattainable freedom.

And yet, I cannot look away. "It's you…"

Both shadows and magic seem to gently roll around her, intertwining her limbs and kissing her skin. It's as if she *is* the star-riddled night, both its darkness and its light, embodied.

"Were you dreaming about me, hero?" she asks, slinking away from the wall.

I purse my lips, wracking my brain for the best defense against a… *what is this creature?*

My brow furrows.

She tilts her head to the side, her short, wild hair gently brushing her shoulder. "Why do you cry? Are you afraid to die?"

She throws the question at me so matter-of-factly that it takes me a moment to comprehend it, *her*, at all.

I wipe the remnants of my tears on the back of my hand, my expression hard. I square my shoulders. "No, not anymore," I reply with a steady, even voice. "And don't flatter yourself… whatever you are," I spit back. "I wasn't dreaming of you. I was reliving a memory."

She lets out a small snort. "How charming," she purrs, lifting her eyebrows.

Her hand meets my chest, just a light tap, and she's knocked me on my back; I make to stand back up, to fight.

In a blink, she's kneeling down beside me, leaning forward so close that I can smell the fresh scent lingering on her skin; I stay crouched.

"Have you come to deal Death's hand?" I reply, smoothly, not flinching from her animal-like gaze—I will not die whimpering for my life.

Her smile widens, just enough so I can see her fangs.

This time, I can't help but recoil. *No, I will not die today at all! Not by this monster's hands.*

I flick my gaze to my forgotten swords once more; I haven't picked one up in a long, long time, even with all of Eddison's coaxing.

She laughs again, this time the sound coming from the other side of the room. When I turn back to face her, I instead look upon the sharp end of my blade.

"Is this what you're looking for?" she asks with the slight tilt of her chin, bemused.

I slowly stand, unblinking, focused. This time my blanket falls away; the blade rises with me, at eye level.

I raise my hands, silver sparking in my palms. "I have other ways to defend myself," I say in a low voice.

She gasps in delight. "Magic?" she says, her expression glowing with surprise. "*Why*, I thought your kind had long since abandoned your rights…"

I lean into her curiosity, recalling how she toyed with her prey last time—I might be able to buy some time if I can keep her talking.

"My *kind* were forced to surrender or die," I speak between my teeth. "That doesn't mean we don't remember."

I run through a list of spells in my mind.

I must choose carefully—I might only get one chance to act before she decides to sing.

Anger heats my cheeks, remembering how hard it was to call to my magic with hers tainting my body, my will.

"Hmm…" she says with a brazen smirk, drinking me; her gaze lingers on my cock.

I resist the urge to drop my hands to cover myself, standing with as much pride as I can muster in the face of this otherworldly huntress. I also resist the desire to lose myself in everything that she is…

In the sensual curve of her hips and the glittering apex of her thick thighs. In the fullness of her pointed breasts and the sheen of gold that seems to softly shimmer across her every inch.

Her eyes, like molten precious metals, find mine again.

"You cannot fight me," she says, sharpening her stance, her stare; my breath hitches in my throat. "Not with this—"

She cuts my sword through the air so fast that I couldn't have hoped to attempt to block it; the blade slashes across my chest.

I stumble backward with a yelp, moving to cover my wound with my hand; she grips my wrist to stop me, forcing my arm open wide—the muscles in my bicep contract, bulge at the effort to try to oppose her.

It's futile. Her strength is unlike that of any other opponent I've faced.

Her gaze slowly rises from my wrist, crawling back up to my face. "And certainly not with *your* kind of magic," she adds.

She glances to my other hand, silver power still coiling in my palm; I still don't have a plan. I've no idea what can kill her.

She lifts her eyebrow, as if to say 'try'.

My magic fizzles away. I drop my arm to my side.

I need to keep her occupied, stall her, until I can think of a way out of this trap.

"So what?" I say, carefully, my wrist still at her mercy. "You expect me to just stand here and die?" I suck at my teeth, my jaw twitching as I struggle not to spit in her face. "What kind of hunter are you? Don't you take any pride in the chase?"

Her eyes narrow, her expression darkening. She runs her tongue across her lips.

Her gaze drops to the blood I can feel warming my chest— the cut is just a surface wound, a smooth, painful slice to whet her appetite.

"What do you know of hunting?" she asks after a moment, taking the bait.

I don't tell her that I've also taken human life and not by accident. I don't tell her that I hunted the regulator who murdered my wife and stole my child from me across the entire continent, that I stalked him to his family home in Guanamara and burned it to the ground. I don't tell her that I killed him slowly, that I enjoyed every second of it—though the days, weeks, I ensured he suffered were nowhere near long enough to repay the debt he owed.

Sibyl. Luna. I repeat the mantra in my head, over and over.

Instead, I say, "I used to go out on my mate's boat with him and his family." I consider Eddison and Penelope—if I go missing like his father did, they'll surely never recover from another loss. "My friend's father was an amateur fisherman. He spent all his coin on a boat of his own and had dreams of sailing out past the channels, into the deep."

The pink-flamed torches around the room catch my eye; I recall how she fled when I lit them. That she keeps a wide berth from them now.

"He wanted to hunt down proof of the legendary sea beasts the sailors sing about, so he'd take me and his son out on the shorter, preparation trips... for male bonding and whatnot." I shrug, trying to sound as nonchalant as possible; the creature seems to listen so intently.

I take a slight step back, toward the torch that should be

directly on the wall behind me.

"Have you heard the songs they sing?" I ask. "Are the tales the sailors speak of known wherever you hail from?" I pause, hoping she satisfies *my* curiosity and gives me any hint of her home.

"I'm afraid I only know the songs created by my kind," she replies, her smile gone. "You remember the one I sang to you, perhaps?"

An intangible, paralyzing melody swarms my memories, the sound like a blend of whispers from the deepest waters and the softest rumblings of the oldest earth.

I keep my expression steady, though I'm sure she doesn't miss the flicker of fear that crosses my face.

I cannot let her sing again.

She smirks, knowingly, searching my gaze.

"Tell me, hero, what did you hunt out there in the waters, with the fisherman and his son?" She walks her finger along the muscled ridge from my shoulder to my neck; the touch makes my nipples tighten and cold bumps skitter across my skin. "Did you enjoy yourself, the way I am now?"

I swallow. "I wasn't—"

"You know, I never much cared for the practice of fishing."

The coolness of her tongue suddenly meets my chest, somehow rough and soft all wrapped into one; I pull in a breath between my teeth, trying and failing to shift my body away from her—she keeps her hold steady on me.

"I find the practice *absolutely* barbaric," she adds between slow licks of my blood.

I note the glint of flames in my peripheral vision and think the torch is close enough to reach; I thank the gods she can't hear my heartbeat.

No sudden movements. Just a slight twist in that direction so I can angle my arm…

My muscles tense; I think she must sense my potential struggle, for she pins my arms to my sides with her hands and drags her magicked tongue—more roughly now—across my skin.

It makes me tingle, delightfully... to my disgust.

I can't help but match her soft satisfied sighs, though I try to hold them in. I can't help how all of me slightly hardens at her terrible touch.

Her naked body gently grazes mine. The side of her hip, the bottom of her stomach, presses into mine; I shiver—if her hands weren't holding my arms in place, I might have reached out to draw her closer, my baser instincts trying to take over my mind.

A darker part of me whispers at me from somewhere deep down. *Just relax, Jaspyr. This might be the best you'll ever feel... Why deny yourself pleasure, even if it's wicked? The world is drowning in darkness. Who cares what you do in the shadows where no one sees? Who cares about the truth of your emotions, if these are your last moments to feel anything anyway?*

She works her way from the bottom of the cut to the top, until there's no blood left. Then she takes a small step back, watching eagerly as it starts to pool again.

"Incredible." Her eyes glow with more magic than I've seen in a human. "You're absolutely astounding." She studies my face intently. "I've never tasted *anything* like you before. Better than I even imagined." She touches my cheek, her expression soft, desperate. "Tell me your name." A command.

I find myself obedient.

"It's... Jaspyr," I stutter, my voice lost in her beauty; I look down, relief washing over me. I take another step backward with a gentleman-like bow. "Jaspyr Tayshin."

"Jaspyr," she purrs—I dare to look at her face. Magic dances brightly atop her skin, as if my blood had sparked it.

"It's a pleasure to make your acquaintance," I say, careful not to show her my back—if there's one thing the King's war taught me, it was how to survive predators.

I take another step and feel the glorious heat of a flame.

"The pleasure is all mine, I assure you," she replies in a deadly voice.

Something flickers in her expression, her calm curiosity shifting to something lethal, dangerous. Her eyes are alight and wild for—

"*More*," she whispers as if she has fully relinquished control to her inner beast.

There's no more time to play games nor distract her while I think, not now that's she's gotten a taste.

"*Ni passe!*" I shout, throwing out my magical barrier shield and twisting around to reach for the handle of the torch—it's my only chance.

Sibyl. Luna... I'm not ready to die yet, not until I've taken my justice in this world. Not since I've been granted a second chance to seize it.

The creature pounces, crashing straight into my barrier. By the look on her face, I can tell she's just as surprised as I am that it holds against her incredible strength.

She slams into it again—it shakes, vibrates all around me in a glittering, iridescent wave.

I'm already sweating with the effort to keep it up.

"Like I said," she states with a snarl, "your magic won't work against me." She looks at me and frowns. "Not for long, but I do appreciate the effort."

She circles me, light on her toes, her hips lazily swaying back and forth like the tail of a prowling, wild cat.

"Had your blood not called to me in such a way, I might've even left you alone..." She offers me an apologetic smile. "I typically only try and feed on the males that offer little good to this world, and you do seem like a heroic one."

She scrunches up her face. "Shame."

"I wouldn't call myself a hero," I retort, spit flying from my mouth, shaking with the effort to keep my magic in place—I never stopped practicing like Eddison and so many others, but I'm not able to stretch this muscle nearly enough these days.

"I see," she says with a venomous grin—it both terrifies and excites me. "In that case, I can't see any reason to take my time."

She throws her body into my shield again; it cracks and falls away in a glittering rain.

The blast knocks me into the canvas I had been working on all night, the impact so hard that it nearly topples over. The protective cover slides away to the ground.

The painting is illuminated by the torch on the wall—I pull the torch free, hurl it at the painting, and pray to all the gods I can think of that it saves me...

It's ablaze so quickly that I have to shield my eyes.

The creature screeches as the flames chase away the darkness like the sun scorching the night.

I used to fear fire, too, after the war... until I learned to control it.

"*Solza ven immito!*" I yell, tightening my last bit of magic around the free-flowing flames, manipulating them so that they don't spread beyond the canvas. I place myself behind it, trapped between the burning painting and a wall.

"You can't stay there all night," she says over the crackling of flames. "You'll burn as soon as your magic fades."

I peek out from behind the bright pink wall of fire to find *her* shielding her eyes; I smile.

"From what I witnessed last night, I'm sure death by fire will be a faster, more pleasant experience than by your teeth, *beast.*"

She hisses at me, fangs bared, keeping clear of the fire.

"Fool…"

The fact that I still live gives me courage to think, to speak.

"Come and get me, then!" I press my power outward, straining it to its limits.

Her lips turn downward, the only thing I can see of her face still covered behind her hands. "You really think to challenge me?"

"My magic hasn't failed me yet, blood-drinker," I cut in, bolstering the fire higher; the canvas burns tall and bright at the edges, flames eating their way toward the center of the art—part of me knows I'm holding myself back, unready to let this piece go.

She lowers her hands, glowering at me with such menace that I retreat.

"We both know that it will," she says, calmly.

My heart pounds at my ribcage.

I look up, to the window on the ceiling. I know by the faintness of the stars that it's still very early in the night. Kampaulo is still wide awake.

"Surely," I reply, dropping my glowing gaze back to hers. "But unless you want the *entirety* of Kampaulo to lay eyes on you, then you only have mere minutes, seconds maybe, before people come barging in here." I can't help my haughty shrug. "I think I can hold out long enough for my meddlesome neighbors to alert the city to one of their favorite shops burning up in the middle of the Lotus Center."

With only a thought, I set the roof aflame, too, my enchanted flames climbing the wall behind me likes roots of a tree—the creature cranes her neck, recalculating the situation.

She clenches her fists at her side.

"You think you're wise, don't you?" she says, slowly bringing her attention back to me.

"I have my moments…" I reply.

She walks closer to me, her expression passive, hips swaying. "You have no idea of the game you're playing with me."

My courage tries to dissolve to make room for the threats she dangles in front of me, but I hold tight to it.

"Oh, no?" I say. "Well, how's this for knowing my opponent..." I bolster my fires even more. "*I think* you wouldn't have gotten rid of that beggar's body if you didn't care about being found out."

There hasn't been a peep in the neighborhood about a murder all day, so it *had* to have been her... unless she swallowed her whole after I fled; I gulp down that thought and keep goading her, for I know that most battles are lost due to those who act on passion. And this creature seems derived from it.

"Clearly, secrecy holds some weight in your world... wherever that may be." I nod to the flames as they crawl over the ceiling. "By the time my magic fails, you'll have to eat your way through the whole gods-damned city to get back to where you came from."

There's a moment of silence between us, filled only by the crackling of flames eating at my home. But I've rebuilt my life before and can again if need be.

"It's refreshing to see such fight in someone, I must say. Normally, they just lie down and die upon my request. Humans are so weak." She lets out a little laugh. "But you..."

Her gaze shifts to the flaming canvas—she circles it, really seeing it for the first time, I think.

"You're different," she stammers, blinking up at it.

"Different as in... maybe you could call a truce with me and eat someone else for dinner?" I nervously laugh, ignoring what my statement suggests, that I might trade an innocent life for mine.

Sibyl. Luna... I have to survive and avenge them.

She takes a moment to respond. Her expression turns pensive. "I could, you know," she says, her voice a deadly whisper.

"Could what?" I ask, wary of the answer.

She glides closer to the painting, to me, to the flames.

"I *could* rip through every single person in this town and not break a sweat." I brace myself as she takes another calculated step. "I *could* reach my fist straight through the fire and take your neck in my grasp and still come out alright, no lasting damage."

She takes another step, tilting her head as she considers me, only a thin barrier of flame between us.

"Fire… it's not exactly pleasant, but—"

I choke as her fingers wrap around my neck. Her arm is submerged in the blaze, a hole punched through the painting. And she barely has a hint of discomfort on her face.

"You'll have to try harder than your funny little flame to stop me."

She drags me out into the open and then releases me with a grimace; I fall to my knees at her feet, coughing.

"Then why don't you just *do* it?" I say, catching my breath—I look up at her, rigid with anger. Sweat drips down my neck, fury flooding my senses. "Kill me and be done with it! The gods know I haven't anything else left to give to this wretched kingdom. Everything has already been taken from me. What more do you want?"

I look up. My life is burning down around me… again.

Sibyl, maybe, it's finally time I join you.

I'm so tired of hiding. At least I stood up to this one, even if I couldn't win. I sigh, sitting back on my heels. Then I close my eyes, relinquishing my hold on the fires.

Let my body burn when she's done with it.

"Do it, dammit," I say, balling my fists, keeping my eyes shut, not wanting to witness the end. "Free me from this prison."

Let Death come. He's been after me for so, so long.

There's a beat of silence.

"All in due time." The coolness of her breath suddenly tickles against my ear, my neck—I open my eyes; she kneels beside me. "Though, there's one thing you're right about."

She smells of the freshest rain, of morning dew, of the salted sea. I breathe her in, her scent overpowering the charred smoke that's begun to fill the space.

Part of me trembles in fear; part of me can't help but lean in.

"What?" I whisper, looking forward, wondering when I might take my last breath.

The silk-cold press of her lips caresses my cheek, softer than any I'd ever known; my eyes close, again.

This is it... not a bad way to go.

"It simply isn't nearly as fun to hunt without the chase," she says, her sugary, frost-like voice sending shivers down my spine. "Thanks for the reminder, Jaspyr Tayshin." She speaks my name in a sensual hiss.

Voices from the street and the trample of footsteps suddenly sound outside the shop, floating into the space, reminding me that we aren't alone in this world.

"Fire! Somebody get water."

"It's Jaspyr's place!"

"I hope he isn't in there."

"He's always in there!"

"I'll see you soon," hums the creature, nuzzling her nose into my neck as the voices grow nearer—I open my eyes just in time to see the fires consume the entirety of my artwork. "Who knows... maybe I'll even let you paint me again."

"Animal," I say through gritted teeth, finding her fire-licked gaze—a smile curls on her lips and brightens her eyes.

Then her fangs sink into my neck.

I gasp, more in shock than pain. It's the first time I touch her, feel her skin beneath my hands, as I instinctively wrap my fingers around her arms to try to make her stop…

Though, for some reason, I don't pull away.

Her body is cold against mine yet every inch of her skin is soft, smooth, comfortable. Her breasts press into the hard panes of my chest. Her stomach slides across mine as she sucks the blood from my neck—every drop she takes makes me want to give her more, as if the touch of her mouth on my skin releases a soothing toxin into my bones.

Poison. She's pure poison, I think, stifling my pleasure-filled moan. *Don't let her see.*

She unclenches her teeth from me mere seconds later, and I'm suddenly free.

More, my mind begs.

Traitor, I think.

"Until next time, hero," she says with dazed look on her face, wiping the back of her hand on her mouth; she closes her eyes a moment, savoring me. "*Mmm*, you're such a treat. More than you know."

I blink in surprise, and the creature of my nightmares— and maybe my dreams—is gone.

My stomach twists in knots. I sink even closer to the floor, my entire body sagging with relief.

I wonder if I'll see her again some part of me thinks… hopes.

I bring my hand to my neck and cover the two tiny wounds, my newest survival scars.

"Good riddance, blood-drinker," I say, praying to every god I can think of that she'll leave me to salvage the little peace I have left in my life.

As if the darkened clouds can feel my pain, the sky opens up and it begins to rain, pelting the window on the ceiling.

10

HUNTRESS

ELOISE

I GRIP HIS WRIST IN MY HAND, thick with muscle, though I squeeze so hard I feel the knobs of his bone. My eyes travel from there all the way up his arm, his chest, his heart, the side of his neck—a thin line of silver, like a single vein of lifeblood, streaks through his skin, disappearing behind his ear at his hairline.

The skin around its path is inked in thick waves of onyx black, each line underscored in streaks of bright blue shades. The ocean, *my* sea, follows that silver line like a map, wrapping around every inch of skin from his left wrist to his shoulder. A crest of water curls over the space above his heart and stretches over the vessels along his thick, muscled neck.

It's designed in the same unique style as his artwork.

The silver magic flashes out of his eyes, leaving only a brown, nearly black vortex glaring back at me. In his left iris, a bundle of sea-green lines, like a sparkling starburst, frames his pupil.

Peculiar, I think.

I let the essence of him settle in my chest, my veins, as I draw in the air around us.

"*Jaspyr.*" His name rolls off my tongue, just the sound of it igniting a strange desire in me.

Watching the bright droplets of blood dot atop his strong chest, after having just a little taste… it's as if someone dangles the finest slab of meat in front of a starving animal. I salivate at only *imagining* his taste on my tongue again. Not to mention, he's quite nice to lick, for a human.

He responds with more confidence than any man who has deigned to open their mouth at me before I kill them. His voice is a deep, steady hum that coils deliciously in my stomach. "It's a pleasure to make your acquaintance." His eyes burn into mine, steady.

"The pleasure is all mine, I assure you," I reply with as much sincerity as I can muster—this man can't even begin to understand what he means to me; I hardly can.

Not yet, Eloise, a voice whispers. *It's not time.*

True, devastating hunger originates somewhere in my bones, swelling fast, like the hurricanes that stir in the farthest south.

I can't wait any longer.

'*Wait, please! You can still salvage your control.*'

I push the voice aside. *I must have*—

"*More…*" I lunge.

I fly backward—magic I thought snuffed out from this world hits me in full force. The taste of it shakes me awake.

This one is just full of surprises, I think.

The more he fights back, the more his heart rate increases. The more he sweats, the more his sweet scent is enhanced—the hungrier I grow.

I pounce again and… I smile. It won't be long now.

I find my interest in this human even more piqued as I

circle him, wondering where his bravery comes from. Wondering why the blood of this one speaks to me so strongly.

Syrifina would know, surely.

I can't help myself but to play a little, to pry. He's just so…

I look him up and down with nothing short of a feline gaze.

"You do seem like a heroic one." The slightest tinge of remorse tugs at my thoughts but I shake it away. "Shame."

"I wouldn't call myself a hero," he replies, in a ferocious tone that ripples down my spine and stirs the magic in my core.

I smile with my teeth, my fangs, thinking of all the ways I will devour him, hero or not.

I slam my body into his enchanted shield so hard that it shatters into a million diamond-like pieces. Jaspyr stumbles into a canvas behind him that I hadn't noticed before—then all I see is flames.

I scream as the light sears into my eyes like knives. I imagine *this* is what staring directly into the sun feels like—I have to shield my face as the crackling hot oranges and reds and yellow burn through me.

I want to run from the heat, back to the cold, safe blues and greens and maroons of my sea. But I hold my ground, gritting my teeth, bracing myself to face my mark like I promised myself I would.

I shout at him, trying to shift his focus from holding this pesky fire magic out against me. I could sing and *make him* stop…

I suppose I am enjoying this game.

"Come and get me," I hear him say.

I whisper threats under my breath that I promise to make good—the fire *is* surprisingly annoying, a dampener on an otherwise perfect night. I've never really experienced its overwhelming heat before. It's as if the very air has been singed, the light much too bright for my keen sight.

And the smoke, it obscures his beautiful smell, though not enough to make me release my prey back into the wild.

"My magic hasn't failed me yet, blood-drinker," he retorts, feeding his flame.

With a growl of frustration, I drop my hands and squint against the brightness. It's unpleasant, but Syrifina taught me to be unafraid of almost everything—this fire might force me to *recall* that human sense of pain, but I know that only dragonfire can fatally harm myrmaids.

Hail to the King, I think, wryly, glad they're all dead.

I consider the flames, long, pink arms wrapping around the painted canvas that had before sat unnoticed. It's unfinished, the nighttime sky still just a textureless black.

I freeze, enthralled and overwhelmed to find a portrait of *me*.

My face, my lifeblood, my eyes. He's captured them so perfectly that I feel as if I'm looking upon a spellbound mirror.

The scene is from last night but from his perspective, his gaze.

An image of Jaspyr is even blurred in the background, a cloaked man frozen in time, eyes wide and watering, sparkling...

I wonder what he was thinking when he first heard me sing?

The creature he stares upon has dark brown skin, and finely stroked gold and silver strands shimmer along it. Deathly sharp fangs flash shamelessly to the night. And glistening white teeth drip with red as she smiles to a golden moon, relishing her feed—rays of cold, iridescent light wash over her. *Me*.

Reflecting in my silver stare. Dancing across my shimmering skin and entangled in my hair.

Magic... He's even captured my magic there.

The focus of the painting is this, my face, my smile, my eyes, caught in a moment of blissful freedom, a bewitching princess of the night. Unafraid and free of consequences.

An elderly woman lies dead in my arms, like a sleeping baby swaddled in a cloak. Gold coins and blood splash across the painted cobblestones—it's beautiful, haunting.

What a waste, I can't help but think with a soft sigh, noting again the determination to survive on his face.

I humor him, this strange human, as he tries to stall me with his mere words, threats that the townspeople might discover me.

I wish they would.

I don't know why, but I am extremely hungry...

The roof sets ablaze with his next breath, pouring heat down on top of me. I dig my nails into my palms, not sure why I allow him to keep breathing. "You think you're wise, don't you?"

"I have my moments," he says, his eyes lighting up with pride, though his lips press into a thin line of concentration.

More threats, more empty words.

"It's refreshing to see such fight in someone..." I say.

The hitch in his breath, the shake in his palms. *Good. He's not a complete fool as to think he might survive me.*

I consider his artwork again, his depiction of all that I am—or the parts I've let him see—and find myself impressed.

"You're different."

"Different as in... maybe you could call a truce with me and eat someone else for dinner?" he asks, brazenly.

The question takes me aback, disarms me.

A truce? With a human? I nearly scoff. It's such a silly notion that it angers me. *Let me put this hero in his place.*

"I could, you know," I say, stalking toward him. I lace my next words with just enough warning to make him rethink toying with me. "Fire… it's not exactly pleasant, but—"

I plunge my arm through the flames and let the fire lick at my arms, biting at my impenetrable skin, just so he can feel my fingers wrap around his neck.

I give a gentle squeeze, and he chokes. If I go any harder, his head might pop right off. *Pathetically weak.*

"You'll have to try harder than your funny little flame to stop me." My voice rings with confidence, though part of me knows that I reached through the fire just to test Syrifina's claims…

I don't let him see the relief on my face as I yank him clear of the fire and toss him at my feet. And I don't expect his re-action as he confronts me yet again.

I have never met a human so desperate to die.

"Then why don't you just *do* it?" he yells, sweat beading on his chest and mixing with his blood, creating an even head-ier scent—I barely hear anything he says next.

I float toward him on the wind of my magic and kneel beside him; he squeezes his eyes shut.

I will decide when to kill you.

"All in due time," I whisper in his ear, pressing my body closer to his just to see how it feels; I delight in the way he trembles for me. "Though, there's one thing you're right about."

He cringes, but I see the way his body reacts differently, how the length of him grows every second I'm close to him, how he slightly leans in. "What?" he breathes.

I can't help but play, pressing my lips into the curious warmth of his cheek. *Strange*, I think—how delightful it feels.

I pull away, studying my prey. "It simply isn't nearly as fun to hunt without the chase…" He shivers when I speak his name.

The voices from the townspeople are getting closer—they spotted the fires the moment they started, but they're *so* slow. I still have seconds more.

My mouth waters as my gaze lingers on the depiction of him in the portrait, then drifts back to the man of flesh and bone—something about the virile strength he boasts, softened with touches of terror and wonderment, makes me want him all the more.

'Don't fool yourself, Eloise. I can see your next step. If you bite him tonight, there's no going back.'

"I'll see you soon," I sing, letting some of my magic slip through; he'll be dizzy over me for hours after I go. The canvas burns and scorches to black. "Who knows… maybe I'll even let you paint me again."

"Animal," he says—the word, the accusation, rolls through me in such a way that I can't help but grin.

I am *no* animal… I'm a cunning beast, a fantastic creature, an epic huntress of the night.

The more the best meal of my life sits there patiently waiting to die, easy for the taking, the less I want to indulge in it right away…

My inner voice scoffs at the lie.

Do not sympathize with your prey. He's much more than that. Look at what unfolded tonight!

Yes, much more, I think.

My teeth press into his soft, white skin before I can overthink it. Before the voices can convince me to stop.

He gasps but doesn't scream like the rest of them. I suck slowly, gently, savoring every sip of his blood.

He wraps his arms around mine, as if he might start to struggle, to fight—in the end, he just holds me, skin to skin, and lets me drink.

My body presses into his chest, his stomach, every inch of him rigid with muscle yet as silky smooth as my scales when I swim. The length of him grows only firmer, the tips of his fingers ever so slightly pressing me closer.

I've heard it rumored that humans also experience a high when a myrmaid drinks, but to my knowledge, no one has ever lived long enough for any of us to validate this.

He moans slightly as I take the biggest drink, then I find myself suddenly letting go. Part of me knows that if I take any more, it will be the end of this game.

Too soon, I think.

I gaze at Jaspyr in a daze as the blood high settles over me, compiling atop my feed from last night; it's easy to ignore the guilt with his essence still on my tongue.

"Until next time, hero," I say with a satisfied sigh. I wipe his blood from my mouth lest I be tempted to leap on him again. "*Mmm*, you're such a treat. More than you know."

The voices in my head sigh with contempt.

You should kill him and be done with this now! No use waiting since you've already fed outside of the moon's cycle. If you don't, things may only get worse.

And if I kill him, there will be nothing else like him for an eternity! I counter, knowing this surely. *What of that?*

The thought is more terrifying than I care to comprehend.

I let it float away.

"Good riddance, blood-drinker," I hear Jaspyr say as I escape the burning building on the tails of the wind.

I slip into the main channel, turning back around for one last glimpse of his workshop—people rush to the door from every direction as smoke pours into the sky, mixing with the clouds.

Luckily for him, the pink flame of magic hasn't yet broken free to the outside; if it had, even *if* he survived, he'd likely be condemned by his own kind.

I frown, thinking of the beautiful portrait already lost. Of the maps and enchanting depictions of the Olleb… my waters, likely to be destroyed by the end of this night.

I can't just let them succumb to fire. His work belongs in this world.

I call to my magic, the water eager to do my bidding.

Rain, I think.

THE WATER COOLS THE BURNING SENSATIONS stirring in my bones... somewhat. My scales and fins and tail cradle me once more. I'm relieved to be back in my true form, though my gaze remains on Kampaulo.

It's early morning now, the last of the night lingering. The smoke from Jaspyr's studio has long since dissipated into the clouds, but the smell still tingles my nostrils.

A lone fisherman canoes close to the shore, drawing my attention—I'm grateful for the distraction.

He tosses a single line and hook into the water, luring my less knowledgeable kin.

Rage seizes me more than it should...

This is the way of the world, I know. And this one doesn't even rely on a net like most of the hoarders do, who shovel out fish and the quieter but still sentient shell species in droves.

Normally, I would let this small offense go. Acknowledge the balance that must be maintained between our two kinds, and swim the other way...

There are much worse than him to be dealt with on these waters.

But I can't calm the cold, swift anger rising up in me at the trap he's set for my benevolent familiars—I sink beneath the waves and melt into the darkness.

"Go find somewhere else to poke about," I command a small family of fish, their cobalt scales making them appear like a living current. "It isn't safe here."

They don't speak back to me as Aura and Ora can, but they do communicate. They encircle me to show their gratitude before hurrying back to the safety of the reef below.

I latch onto the fisherman's large hook with my fist, letting him feel the weight of me. I could sink his entire little boat with merely a yank, but—

'*You're going too far, Eloise.*'

I glance down to find Aura and Ora swimming toward me, their bodies smoothly winding up from the depths below.

They've been waiting for me to return.

'*You've already fed outside of your cycle once*,' says Aura, worried.

Little spies... My lips curl in annoyance.

'*If you go any further, you will become lost*,' states Ora, sharply.

The fisherman tugs, the line tensing with his hefty catch. He pulls with all his might, surely thinking he's won a grand prize from my world.

I pout, considering their words—why am I so hungry? It's as if Jaspyr's blood carved out space in my body to fit even more of him...

"*Lost?*" I mutter, glaring down at my friends. '*What's that supposed to even mean?*'

They level out, circling beneath me, wise not to ascend too close.

'*You know, Eloise*,' they say as one. '*You should stop while you still can—*'

"Quiet!" I yell, flaring my fins. "I am not lost. On the contrary, I have never before felt so in control." A lie.

The taste of Jaspyr still lingers in my throat, his delicious voice still echoing in my ears. If not for the forsaken sun peeping out, I might've already returned to play with him again.

'Then spare him,' Ora pleads.

I purse my lips, gazing toward the sea sky as I let the fisherman fight for me, and possibly for his death.

My throat tightens. This fisherman will surely not satisfy the craving Jaspyr ignited in me. I frown just thinking of how sour the thief's blood tasted in comparison... how anyone must taste.

I groan in frustration, bubbles tickling my face. "I suppose you're right," I force through my teeth, looking away. "I have already fed too much..."

The statement comes as a whisper I hardly care to acknowledge.

'We won't tell a soul,' says Aura in relief. *'All you have to do is wait another fortnight to feed... on anyone. Then you'll be back on track. Finish him then.'*

'Yes, let this transgression fade into history,' says Ora, carefully. *'There's no telling how another slip might impact you. Too much blood will cloud your better judgment.'*

It already has, I secretly think, trying and failing to push Jaspyr from my mind.

"Fine," I retort. "I will not feed until the bloody shadow moon has risen to bless me. I swear it."

'Good, good!' they sing. *'Trust us, Master, then this craving will ease.'*

I watch the boat bobbing atop the waves, sun beginning to sprinkle down on top of us like a glittering rain. My lips press into a firm line. "That doesn't mean I will let him live," I say. "I'm not feeling very forgiving."

Aura and Ora don't try to persuade me otherwise, but I can hear their titters of disapproval bouncing around in my mind.

'Be gone now. Let me hunt in peace.' I force my command

down our bond.

'*Yes, Master,*' they reply without another word.

I lighten my weight on his hook with only a thought and allow the fisherman to pull me up on the line. As soon as the top of my head and eyes break the now too-sunny surface, he gasps, clutching his rod with frozen hands.

I grin widely, madly, ready to end him, to release some of my pent-up, frenzied energy—I don't bother to sing. I yank the line, and he topples into the water before he can even scream.

I drag him below the surface, passing the disapproving glares of Aura and Ora on the way. Magic trails behind us in a glittering wave.

I stop to float in a place where I have a clear view of the sun waking overhead. It forces itself from its sleeping place now—always with a grand, absurd entrance that's impossible to ignore, even from under the water.

The man thrashes in my hold, surely almost drowned. The world better off for it—I can't even begin to count how many creatures I might've saved just by ending one life. And it only took me seconds of my eternal time.

So why didn't you kill Jaspyr, then? Why did you let him go?

The thought of him gnaws at my insides—his salty-sweet taste, the roughness of his palms, his quick-witted mouth.

Goddesses, do I want to feed on him again so badly that I can hardly stomach the idea of waiting another week.

'*Eloise… Eloise!*' Aura's voice draws me back.

'*What have you done?*' says Ora.

I blink, focusing my sight. The fisherman floats before me, a blank stare on his face, his mouth open in a silent scream. Dead.

I let his wrist fall away from my mouth, the last of his blood rising up toward the sun in inky red lines.

PART TWO

II

HUNGER

I FIND MYSELF EDGING CLOSER to Empress Isle, just to put some distance between me and Kampaulo. Even with the risen sun, temptation tugs at me to return.

My mind begs for rest, yet I know that not even a deep, dreamless sleep can ease my physical discomfort nor my disquieted mind.

I can't believe I fed again…

I pass through both deep and shallow channels, giant tunnels of stone and coral that dance with the strange life down below. My queendom, where if I had only remained, I might not have even crossed paths with Jaspyr at all.

I let out a low growl.

Our home is miles from the City of Kampaulo. It's a network of bottomless caverns that no creature but a myrmaid and our neighbors naturally suited to such depths could ever reach, a country all its own. Nevertheless, I can hardly escape the scent of him here.

I suffer by just the memory of our acquaintance last night,

my stomach churning with a strange new appetite. And sick from the excess blood, nowhere *near* the quality that I knew his to be.

If it weren't for this glorious underwater world, I would've already lost my mind.

"Darling, Eloise, is that you?" comes a bemused voice; ice bumps curl across my skin, and not the good kind.

Suddenly, all the terrible choices I've made become real.

Aura and Ora disappear over a bend in the reef so quickly that the water clouds behind them. I can still sense them near, eavesdropping from a safer distance.

'*Spineless little spies,*' I think with the roll of my eyes.

'*You'll want to hide, too, once she learns what you've done,*' says Ora, a bite to her tone.

I bristle. '*I hate it when you're right…*'

'*When are we ever wrong?*' replies Aura, a bit more gently. The lump in my throat grows tighter as the fisherman's dead eyes flash before me. '*Be careful, Eloise.*'

I shake them from my mind and focus back on Isobel, the eldest of my sisters, as she swims toward me.

Her golden hair flickers in the sporadic rays of sunlight that strain to reach us; they pierce deep here, the water and the sun joining together as one for a dazzling performance above the reef.

"Why, what a fantastic surprise!" I say with as much enthusiasm as I can fake and a reluctant wave, trying to smother my anxieties. "What brings you this way, sister? Have you not yet fed?"

I'd hoped not to cross paths with anyone yet… not until I've had time to take care of the Jaspyr situation.

We exchange a normal greeting, a kiss on the cheek.

"My business is none of your concern," she replies, magic shimmering around her like a cape, "but I should be asking the same of you, little sister." Her voice and her eyes are equally probing. "Why are *you* lurking near the shore? The full moon gathering is just days away. You should be headed to Empress Isle."

I'm suddenly reminded of one of the reasons I'm so fond of landwalking...

It keeps me far away from my elder sisters' prying eyes. They have no interest in it.

All the new confidence in the world means nothing in the face of them, especially Isobel Myr. Next to Syrifina, she's the strongest, most volatile of them all, the first of her daughters.

I obediently answer.

"You know how fond I am of this region," I reply, matching the sharpness of her tongue. "I just thought I'd wait a little longer before I travel there, to enjoy some peaceful moments... *alone.*"

It's a half-truth—I don't think I could travel any farther from Kampaulo right now if I wanted to.

My fins flex like a territorial fish, to make it seem more genuine; she smirks.

"*Hmm...* very well." She considers my words carefully, surely weighing their validity.

I try to keep my expression unreadable, but my confidence melts away with every second held beneath her molten gaze.

Her lifeblood glows a fiery red, striking against her pale skin, like lava carving a path through white sand. She floats in the water with ease, a matching tail and ribbon-like fins of bright crimson fanned behind her as she studies me.

After what feels like hours, she shifts her eyes from my face; I press my lips together to smother my sigh of relief.

Too soon, I realize.

She begins to circle me like the more ill-tempered sharks of our sea... Aura and Ora were wise to flee.

"Do you make a *habit* of lingering here these days," Isobel speaks after a moment, as if catching the sliver of a crack in my mask, "now that you've been permitted to roam free?" Her gaze flicks to the surface; I tense.

I shake my head, my curls swishing from side to side. I look anywhere but at her face.

"Of course not, sister." The pitch of my voice is too high, my words too sincere—at least, I don't fidget. "Why would I waste time here when there's an entire world to explore?"

"Indeed," she says, dryly, hands on her hips. "Why would you?"

My tail and fins flutter with impatience.

She stops, considering me with a wry smile.

My mask of confidence betrays me for a mischievous smirk; I respond with a heavy shrug. There's no use trying to outsmart her. I have to give her something to chew on.

"Alright. The truth is… I didn't want to be one of the first ones home, alone with Syrifina."

"Of course…" She huffs a light laugh, then nods her understanding. "I remember what it was like to have her scrutiny. It's hard being the youngest."

I chew on my lip to soften my false smile, eyes darting to the side.

"Well, it is a refreshing sight, child," she adds, her expression softening; the tension in the water seems to dissipate as we both drop our guard. "And now I have you all to myself for a bit."

She pinches my cheek.

"It's always nice to see you, too," I reply with a tight-lipped grin—I respect her, of course. But it's difficult to look upon someone who appears younger than myself by many years and not be *slightly* offended by the familiar greeting. She was barely a teenager at the time Syrifina turned her.

She puckers her lips, batting her eyes.

"When I was your ripe age"—she draws out the last two

words; I have to hold back my scoff—"as soon as Syrifina allowed, I spent every single moment as far away from this place as I could get before I promised to check back in with her at the full moon. That's how our gatherings began. Though, I suppose I *would* often pay visits to my human birthplace near the City of Zambienth… for a time." She shrugs, looking toward the sea sky.

Her glance drifts to me, but I pretend not to notice, much more interested in a runaway strand of kelp that's tangled around the sparkling fins at my side. "What are you getting at?"

I try not to seem so eager; I don't normally play into her hands like this, but I'm so wound tight.

"Only that it makes sense you linger here," she replies, sweetly, brushing her fins along my side, "with Kampaulo so close and you so *very* new." She tickles underneath my chin, as if I were a newborn.

I resist the urge to bite her, flashing my fangs in warning.

"I'm in no mood for your mocking today, Isobel," I say, flipping my tail to put some distance between us.

"My, my, something *has* gotten under your scales," she replies with a chuckle. She backs away, holding up her hands in mock fright—vibrant reds wrap around her wrists and arms like melted rose petals. "I do *love* your spirit, Eloise. We all do, but take caution of how you choose to spend your nights."

She's right, of course. Even if my mind were not overcome by this maddening craving, I know I spend more time closer to my former home than is wise.

Maybe if you hadn't been so eager to return to a city that offered nothing but despair, then you wouldn't be in this strange predicament in the first place…

Maybe, I think.

I ponder over this, sensing Isobel's ancient eyes on me all the while; I shrink under her gaze, wondering if she can see the blood corruption etched on my weary face.

I never felt an *attachment* before to Kampaulo or anyone in it. I just wanted to explore, experience it with new eyes... *Why him?*

I close my eyes a moment, recalling that first taste of blood the night of my turning. It had awoken every sensation in my body and mind, ignited the dangerous, wonderous creature inside of me that had always been forced to hide.

I didn't hesitate then, and I won't hesitate again with him.

"Eloise, are you quite alright?" Isobel's hand caresses my shoulder.

I focus back on her. Her expression is lined with worry.

I must've fallen into a daze, into the complexities of my own eternal mind.

"Oh, sister, I'm fine," I say, shrugging away. I swim out from her reach. "I just have too much on my mind as of late."

She catches up to me quickly; we both drift along a current.

"Don't we all..." she says in a dark, distant voice. "Try not to sink too deeply, though. Once, Kristeena floated in stillness and silence for nearly half a decade in reflection, by quite the accident."

"*Really?*" I ask, intrigued to know more—Kristeena is another princess, four hundred years my senior. I haven't spent much time with her yet, only sporadic play at family gatherings, but I adore her chaotic personality. Her mind works like that of the smallest, fastest fish paired with the social kinship of dolphins; it's hard to imagine such a lonely experience for her...

Isobel nods.

"Sadly, yes," she replies. "She's always using her magic to reform and rebuild the damaged areas of our underwater world." Isobel shrugs, twisting a strand of hair about her finger. "I suppose, maybe... she went too far down for us to know where to follow, to the places we don't swim."

I nod, clinging to every word. "What happened to her all that time?"

She shrugs, looking away. "She remained suspended in waters so deep and dark that there was no telling up from down. It took us a long while to locate her," she adds. "She simply took her time, so much time in fact that Syrifina became infuriated by her elongated absence and gathered her herself."

Her expression darkens, her voice softening.

"I sometimes do wonder, though... where her thoughts had gone for all those years. I've always been too reluctant to ask." I swear I see a flicker of her true age in her eyes. "But I can wager a guess."

She doesn't share more.

I'm comforted to know I'm not the only one with secrets—and with my mind oddly fixated on a human, a deep-sea suspension sounds like the perfect reset.

She gently squeezes my arm, and we float a little in silence.

Then she turns that penetrating gaze on me. "You can tell me anything, you know."

Her silver, fire-laced stare makes me fidget; I thought I had fooled her enough to avoid a conversation about me, but something in my expression when listening to Kristeena's story must have tipped her off.

I'll have to work on that.

"I know I'm quite your elder here in this life," Isobel continues with an unusual gentleness that makes me uneasy, "but all we have is time to get to know each other... Syrifina made you my ward for a reason."

She smiles again, a sincere one this time, her small, child-like features counteracting her stare, making me feel suddenly calm.

'*Eyes never lie, no matter what magic is at play,*' whispers

Aura in warning.

Isobel's were like daggers, trying to cut out the truth from mine.

I look down, thinking I'd rather stare directly into the sun than confess to the eldest Myr daughter that I'd overindulged.

"I look out for all my sisters," she implores, "and I can see that something is troubling you, Eloise." She sighs, taking my arm. "*Please*, tell me what's on your mind. I'm sure I can help."

Shame hinders me—my strange feelings don't even have a term, no place in our world.

I am desire. I control it! Not the other way around.

I do not want him anymore. Jaspyr can rot on that dry pile of dirt for all I care.

'*Liar*,' the Sea whispers in an echo all around me.

I shudder. "It's just…"

I float on my back, looking to the sea sky with longing; Aura and Ora slink out of hiding to dance in the faded sunrays alongside me—although we swim deep, with such crystal-clear water between us and the surface, I can tell it's going to be a bright sunny day.

"You *have* been landwalking again," accuses Isobel in a tone that sounds much less like a child and more like the damning voice of Syrifina Myr herself; I flail my arms in surprise, as if I'd just hit an invisible wall. She scowls.

I offer her a shaky smile.

I know I can trust her with my truth, if I am brave enough to share it. We're both born from Syrifina's kiss—very few of our sisters can claim such a mighty connection. But how to express this weakness that's plagued me to the first and foremost?

I purse my lips and swim higher.

"We cannot alert the people to our existence, Eloise," she calls, her magic chasing after me. "That time is over with the new regime. You must be careful with such decisions."

I chew on the inside of my cheek, thinking that ship has certainly sailed.

But I saw firsthand where King Devlindor's reign was headed when I was human and know Isobel's warning is nothing if not genuine—the world has grown so dark.

I'm thankful Syrifina rescued me before the war and helped me tap into my magic.

"Eloise…" she says, a warning growl in her throat.

As much as I want to keep swimming up and away from Isobel and my mounting remorse, the shining sun hampers my escape. And the soft pout on her childlike face makes me return to reason, along with the deadly magic she dangles like daggers above my head.

I sigh, submissively, sinking back down to her.

"Sister, please hear me." I take her hand in mine, massaging her palm, forcing her to look at me. "I understand all that you say, but you don't have to worry about me. I know what I'm doing now. I'm not a brand-new myrmaid anymore." I kiss her on the cheek.

She huffs, rolling her eyes. But smiles a little.

"If you care about your family, *me*, at all," she implores, squeezing my palm, "you'll stop landwalking at once. It isn't safe for us." Her eyes bore into mine, as if searching for something.

"I care about you and our sisters more than anything," I reply, tensing, magic skittering across my skin.

Her terrifying magic falls away and a soft smile brightens her face again; I let my defenses down, too.

Except, maybe, him…

I blink at the sudden, unbidden, terrible thought. I swallow the sharp shell in my throat, hating myself for even thinking such a thing—from where did it originate?

It seems my mind has split clean into two—one rational,

and one consumed.

Is there anything I can do to rid myself of these toxic cravings?

I'm starting to feel powerless over them. I want to reach out for a helping hand, yet now I'm even more afraid of the truth.

Silence spreads between us, a yawning of things I wish I could confide in my older sister for advice. If only I understood how to articulate them...

There's a warning in her expression as she reads the worry in mine. She crosses her arms. I float higher.

She swims to my eye level, grips my arm tightly. "Say it," she demands; Aura and Ora once again scatter—they would certainly be useless in the face of any real danger.

'*Don't insult us,*' says Ora in a coy tone. '*You may yet find we can be of service in times of trouble.*'

Aura snickers. '*If Master would only listen.*'

"It can be a very disorienting activity if you're not careful, Eloise. You *know* this," she says, pulling me back down with barely any effort. "Say that you'll stop at once. *Promise.*"

Caught between my pride and my unwillingness to lie anymore to my sister, I simply nod, not trusting my words— they're too entangled around a man that I think I might do just about anything to taste again, including break a promise.

She frowns, her fins splaying out in frustration.

"Come," she snaps. "We shall swim together to Empress Isle. Until your tongue starts working again." She lets go of me with such force that I'm propelled slightly backward. "You'll be wise to find your words again quickly."

The stinging heat of Isobel's magic sears my skin as she whips her tail through the water, slashing my arm, demanding I follow—I'm reminded of the fire's pink raging burn. Of how that swift moment of pain had started to somehow feel good.

12

TWILIGHT

☼ J A S P Y R

"WHAT'LL IT BE? LET ME GUESS, all the blues I have again?" An older woman smiles warmly at me as I peruse her paint selection. She stands back, letting me look at my leisure, bouncing from foot to foot.

She ignores the other people at her storefront in the marketplace, highlifes mostly, probably looking to liven up their estates; they point to shades and colors for their hired creators to attempt to brighten fire-tinged walls or liven old furniture—I do wonder how they get by now without magic, unable to complete even a fraction of the projects they used to in the same timeframe.

I think of my home, my workplace, my livelihood, how it almost burned down. And that just a few basic spells swept the ash-covered walls in my back room after she—

"Jaspyr? You alright there?" says the woman.

I shake my head, focusing. "*Actually*," I say, flashing my teeth, stopping at the new dyes she'd imported from South Luose, "today, I'm interested in black."

The burning canvas flashes in my mind, and the creature I had accidentally manifested in my very home, *through* that portrait, whispers in my ears, her voice like the echo of ice.

'*Maybe I'll even let you paint me again.*'

The woman's eyebrows lift, mouth falling open, her expression shading with anxiety. "But, I—"

She gestures to the assortments of azure, cobalt, and sapphire blues that had surely all been imported specially for me—without my business, I'm not sure how she'd even still be here after the war; the average citizen rarely splurges on material things these days.

I'm lucky to be in the practical business of maps.

And lucky that the highlifes still pay me a pretty penny just to paint out their dreams that will never be in this regime.

Before she can finish her sentence, I smile. "If you could please package that up, along with the collection you've laid out, I'd be ever grateful, ma'am." I flash her a wink as an excited blush tints her cheeks. "That *and* some shades of white and gold should do plenty for this afternoon." I cock my head to the side, my hair falling over my shoulders in a sheet. "What do you think?"

"I think that'll do just fine, sir. Just fine, indeed." Her voice is small and soft but full of gratitude. She can hardly meet my eyes.

I take her hand in mine and plant a kiss on top. A striking gold ring with a ruby at its center glitters up at me, an old treasure she must cling to from before, I suppose.

I draw her gaze with as warm an expression as I can muster these days. "I told you, Xitara, please, you can call me by my name. It won't be an insult, not to me."

"Yes, of course," she stutters, drawing her shaking hand away and smiling shyly back at me. "I know, sir—"

She flicks her eyes quickly to the other highlifes, who pretend not to hear.

"*Jaspyr,*" she corrects with little confidence, though a sense of pride seems to shimmer awake in her eyes. "You really are too generous to me."

I shake my head, my long bangs swishing back and forth. I push them from my eyes. "No, not at all," I say. "Without you, I wouldn't be able to paint nearly as many colors. You should stop by the shop soon. I'll send you away with something nice for your home." I wink at her, tying my hair back.

Her mouth falls open. She shakes her head profusely.

I only smile, nodding, emphatically. "The offer stands," I say.

The other highlifes murmur their distaste.

She carefully packages the paints, then slides the box over the counter to me. I see the way her gaze flicks to my upper arms as they contract but pretend not to notice.

I shift the box into my right arm, hugging it to my side so that I can reach into my pocket for my coin.

"This should cover it," I say, dropping two gold pieces and five silvers into her open palm.

She sucks in a breath of surprise, closing her fingers around them. "It's far too much," she murmurs, though she's already shifted them into her pocket with a grand smile.

"You'll get me next time," I say, returning it. I readjust the wide box to be in both arms, looking over the top of it at her. "I'd be ever appreciative if you could procure some new silver and gold paints. I think I may need more of it soon."

The creature's skin, lined with glittering magic, remains a steady beacon in my mind's eye.

"I'll do my best," she says, sincerely. "What are you working on?"

I just shrug. "It's a surprise. Come by and visit me sometime, friend, and maybe I'll show you."

The woman returns a warm nod, waving me off. "I shall try, Jaspyr."

"I tell you, he wastes all his coin on frivolous things," one of the highlifes says behind my back as I make to leave.

I shoot her a glance, continuing my stride. "I'll remember that the next time your partner asks me to memorialize his lover, madam. Maybe next time I'll stick to ink." I face forward, shaking the box a bit. "Although, he does help me afford a lot of paint these days." I toss my words over my shoulder. "It's more lifelike, after all."

She gasps, and I hear as she drops her shopping bag to the ground, something shattering; I disappear into the wildness that is the marketplace, ignoring the slew of curses she screams at my back.

Rounding the corner, I run smack into a crowd of riled people, men and women, all shouting and yelling over each other, jeering at the man who's speaking at the center.

The corners of my box press into someone; she whips around to glare at me, then immediately relaxes into a smile.

"Jaspyr," says Penelope, "I almost smacked you across the face."

"I don't doubt it," I say with a surprised laugh. I set the box down on the ground, squeezing it between my boots. Then I hug her. "What's all this about?"

Her smile fades. "Ole Greggor," she says, quietly, standing on her tiptoes to whisper to me, "going on about something he shouldn't be…"

I raise an eyebrow, and a younger man whose shoulder is pressed up against mine interrupts.

"He's lost his wits, if you ask me. He just started making a proclamation that… that…" He sighs, looking to his feet, shaking his head. "That ain't good for nobody to speak, if you know what I mean."

My back stiffens. "I see."

We all face forward just as Greggor begins waving his arms in the air.

I can hardly believe my eyes—he's always been so silent here, tucked away in the back of the market where he can sit and relax, away from the meat of the bustling bazaar, away from trouble. *Safe*. Every time I buy a bushel of apples from him, I'm never met with anything but warmth.

Now, his belly shakes with his violent movements. Sweat lines the creases in his neck, his face bright red with every scream at the crowd gathered before him to watch his downfall. Spit sprays from his mouth as he tries to get anyone to listen.

It pains me to see him so distressed.

I strain to hear his voice over the shouts of the jeering crowd.

"She was so enigmatic, a wanderer from another land, I believe." More shouts, more jeers. "It's true!" he retorts, his voice ricocheting off the stone wall at his back.

"She was *not* of this world, not of this earthly plane. You have to believe me!" He shakes his fist at us. "There's more out there than what we've been asked to remember." He points a damning finger toward the palace. "There's no point in pretending to forget the magic that still thrives around us. We *have* to find a way back to it, or it will find us when we're illready."

My eyes widen at words I haven't heard since the war.

The crowd gasps—he's just signed his death warrant.

Greggor curses at us, dismissively. A glazed expression plasters his face; I can't help but wonder how much he's had to drink. He's normally so… contained.

"She was a creature beyond us, by the gods, I swear it," he says. "Her skin was like… like the darkness just after twilight, glowing as if the moon and sun hung in the balance just beneath."

He presses his hand to his chest as he gazes to the sky with a lost expression; I rub at the fresh scabs on my neck.

"And her eyes, they appeared like the deepest, darkest amber stone had been welded together with the brightest, shiniest slices of silver in between." He waves his arm in the air. "I swear, I swear. And her voice, every word spoken was like a song lingered on the tip of her tongue." His voice cracks. "She didn't sing for me, though…" He wipes his watering eyes. "I very much wish to hear it." Penelope seems to go very still in front of me.

Greggor's description of this enchanting woman, this portrait he's painted, haunts me, cements me in position.

I know her, I think. *I've heard that voice. I've seen that face, those eyes. I crave her, too…*

The shouts and taunts grow louder, the crowd condemning him as he speaks.

"You've lost your mind, old man!"

"It's blasphemy, what you speak."

He shakes his head over and over, still throwing his arms around as if he can force the crowd to listen, to believe, with the wildness of his gestures.

"She had been dressed in common clothes, covered from neck to toe, so maybe… *maybe* you didn't see." He points at all of us, eyes wide and bloodshot. "But she spoke to me, she did!" He smiles in a daze. "But the way she stood with such poise made her appear like a… a regal, enchanted *queen*, I must say."

The crowd shrieks at this, closing in on him.

"Traitor!" they cry.

"Greggor has dammed lost his mind!"

People scatter, surely fearing for their lives to even bear witness to such blatant disregard for the King's laws.

"Hail to the King. Hail to Lord Devlindor!" they shout, raising their fists to the air as they quickly disperse.

Greggor stands alone on his makeshift podium. He wipes the sweat from his brow with a handkerchief, seeming to wake from his drunken daze as the streets empty in front of his cart for the first time in decades.

Penelope and I are the only ones who remain.

Greggor looks over us, over the bouncing heads drifting away, as if searching for any regulators headed this way.

But I know for a fact that they're scarce today—Eddison was grumbling this morning about the ceremony they have been forced to attend by order of the city keeper. There would be nothing but the people's word to raise any charges against Greggor for speaking out of turn.

I look around, my hopes for him dashed—by the greedy look in the lurking beggars' eyes, he would surely be sold out for a reward.

"I'm sorry," he calls, his lips quivering, his voice softening into a plea. "I'm sorry… I don't know what I'm doing." He drops his head into his hands.

Penelope has gone very quiet, seeming lost in thought.

"You alright?" I ask, gripping her shoulder.

She starts, her eyes snapping to mine. "I'm off to Nicki's Tavern. *Don't* follow."

I straighten. "Yes, ma—" She might as well have stabbed me with that look. "I mean, Penelope, I… yes—" She turns on her heel and quickly walks away.

I blow out a breath through my teeth, scratching my head as I stare after her.

Greggor and I stand alone; I stoop down for my box.

"Wait!" he cries, rushing toward me. "I'm telling the truth." He waves a large gold piece in my face, then lowers his voice, stopping in front of me. "You see this, right?" It's oddly cut with six ridges, like… I stiffen. "I think it's from *before.*"

"There is no 'before' King Devlindor," I say, a bite to my tone, gazing around. "Put that thing away."

But I'm rooted to the spot, staring in disbelief as the sun's rays bounce off the gleaming piece for all to see—I carry the same one in my pocket.

The area around the apple cart is suddenly far too quiet.

His empty, defeated gaze seems to illuminate with hope. "You believe me, don't you?" His voice is sincere, leveled.

I look over my shoulder to ensure we're fully alone, then I fish in my pocket to show him my token from the same creature.

His gaze steadies on the gold piece pinched between my fingers, then lifts to mine.

"I knew it," he says, stumbling away. "Why didn't you say anything! You bastard—"

I shove my proof back in my pocket and grab him by his collar to choke his damning words out of him.

"Take your gold and leave Kampaulo," I warn, releasing my grip only when his mouth had run dry of words. "It's not safe for you here anymore, Greggor. You'll get yourself killed. The regulators will be coming for you after the show you put on."

Tears pool in his eyes.

"I can't rid her from my mind," he utters, clutching at my shirt, yanking me toward him. "What... what *is* she? Tell me. I swear, I know her somehow. I recognize her."

I push him away, then smack him across the face so hard that the sound reverberates. "Get ahold of yourself!" He gapes at me, as if suddenly seeing me clearly. "If you go on like this, they *will* hang you." My voice cracks. "Think of your family."

I lift my box and make to walk away.

"Please," he says after me. "Please... I must know."

I sigh, taking him all in. I feel as if I look upon a mirror, a pitiful reflection of my future if I let this creature close to me again.

At least he had the balls to express the truth to the people that really needed to hear it, to the ones that willfully pretend magic has never been, I think.

"She's a blood-drinker, a monster," I reply out of guilt. "A page out of a fairytale book burned by the king. I don't know what she is!" I say, angered at the reminder, my fingers digging into my crate. "I don't know a thing."

After what I lived through last night, I'm not dying today for this fool of a man because he can't keep his mouth shut.

"I—" His hand flies over his mouth. "But… she was so kind to me," he mumbles, shaking his head. "I believed them to be only terrible myths."

"She's a *monster*," I say between my teeth, "as real as they come. That's all I know." I still can't fathom why she let me live… or him, for that matter.

He blinks back at me. "But you believe me, then?" he asks, clearly needing to hear those words spoken from my mouth.

I only nod—he exhales a breath of relief, his head hanging low. "Then, I suppose we should count ourselves lucky."

I don't tell him I was lucky twice, if 'luck' is what you'd call it.

I narrow my eyes. "Just… free your mind of her, Greggor, or she'll be the death of you."

His lips twist, his expression wrinkles. "I… I guess I need to pack my bags."

I swallow the lump in my throat, wanting to confide so much more in him, to share this secret with another. I slightly bow my head. "Go well." I place my hand over my heart. "I will look after your family for you."

I promise myself this, for I'll be damned to see another home fall because of a gluttonous tyrant—I'll figure out a way to rid this city of her presence if it's the last thing I do.

He fixes his watery gaze on me, squeezing me on the shoulder. "Be safe. Thank you, son."

I leave and don't look back.

I HEAD TO THE SHORE, the day falling away to night in a blur of dusted color. No amount of normalcy nor painting can distract me from what happened yesterday, so maybe the sharp ocean winds can sedate me instead.

I stumble down a familiar sandy path that leads to a canvas of water encased by deep blue-gray streaked cliffs—it's a somewhat secluded area Eddison and I used to hide away at when we were young, and still come to from time to time. Surely, it will be empty now, with the sun dropping down.

Cream-colored sand shifts and darkens the closer to the water I get, morphing into purple-pinkish layers, like the colors of the sky after a storm has ripped all the others away.

The sea is dark, the wind icy and sharp, a jarring difference from earlier today—it's always been like this in Kampaulo, the most changeable coastal city weather in the west.

I can tell that the cold season has fully settled in, rolling down from the Blancoren Mountains. The air is harsher and more determined than in the warmer months. The days shorter and nights longer.

I look to the water, focusing on the soothing lull of the waves. The sky above it is still lit from the fallen sun, creating a soft atmosphere, muting the light of the stars and moon that are desperately trying to press their shine outward.

For the first time in a long time, I don't care about remembering the past nor my personal rebellions. I don't care about the allies who await word from me across the continent. And I don't even care to practice my magic tonight.

I feel nothing but the heat inside me, longing for *her.*

I pull at my hair, pacing back and forth in the sand.

I hate that all I can think of is that monster's delicate tongue on my skin. Cold bumps crawl up my legs even now just to think of it. I loathe that the shape of her full, pointed breasts is a silhouette in my mind, making my stomach tighten. I clench my jaw, recalling her body pressed against mine.

The moment she bit into my neck… stinging, tender.

The soft arc of her hips. The form of her shoulders and arms as I squeezed her tight.

Even now I can feel myself harden at just the thought.

I kick my shoes off and sink my toes into the cool sand, relinquishing myself to the memory at the caress of the wind— the silky sound of her voice, the perfect curves of her sinful body, the painful ecstasy in the moments when she'd bitten me, licked me, kissed me…

I groan, aching for her touch again. The seam of my pants presses tightly against my cock; it hardens to its full length. Another gust of wind at this moment might even set me off for how riled I am.

I roll the band of my linen pants down to my hips, baring myself to the wind. I ground my feet and pin my eyes on the moon. My palm wraps around my cock, the same way she held my wrist so tight—I squeeze, rub, letting myself succumb to her entrancing energy, the memory of it.

The face of the moon morphs into hers, her eyes glinting like gold coins, her lips parting— *'Until next time, hero.'*

I grit my teeth and grip myself harder, pump faster, moan louder. *Come and find me, beast!*

My stomach clenches, my entire body seizes, ready for a release that I have no hope of holding back. And I don't want to, don't try to. *Please… come and find me.*

In a frenzied surge, I explode into the sea with a great roar of satisfaction.

My insides pulse, that despicable monster's voice whispering in my ear.

'*More,*' she moans. '*More, Jaspyr.*'

I obediently surrender until there's nothing left of me to give.

13

MOON

SOON ISOBEL AND I REACH the looming walls of our gigantic reef. They wrap and merge around us, welcoming us home. We slow to admire the sheer drop into this world, Aura and Ora flying high above, skimming the tops of the coral cliffs as we dive deeper.

Tall, bulbous, beautiful things create such shapes and formations, crevices and hollows, that there are hardly names for them all in the human world.

"*Bellastriste*," Isobel whispers in our sacred language.

Beautiful, I think, Jaspyr's face floating in my thoughts.

I push away the darkening parts of my mind and peek in to say hello to the hidden treasures surrounding us here.

My favorite little fairyfish are prominent in these parts, always darting around the smallest places, on bellies of glittering gold and with pointed heads of shimmering purple. Their presence alone hints at where to find the tiniest, strangest creatures of the sea, for they keep close to many minuscule life forms, some that I can hardly see, even with my heightened sight—they're the heart of a game of hide-and-seek that I often love to play with my sisters.

"I have even yet to uncover or understand them all," says Isobel as we quietly observe what appears to be a rock with heavy-lidded eyes.

"Then I daresay I never shall," I reply with a reluctant sigh, finally breaking my silence.

I flick a soft ripple of water at the camouflaged creature; it slowly swims forward, sediment fogging the waters.

"I can't even begin to imagine what my life would've been like had I never transformed. Not to have witnessed this all…"

I lock my gaze on a flat, white sand fish that blinks up at me with one large eye. It blends perfectly in with its surroundings, an odd little thing. In a swish, it's gone and I have no hope of finding it again.

"You wouldn't be a Myr if you felt otherwise," replies Isobel.

"I'm sorry if I offended you," I blurt out, the guilt of my behavior eating at me; any fish in the vicinity scatter.

I bow my head to reinforce the respect I have for her, eyes cast down.

With the swift flick of her tail, she swims toward me; I flinch.

She plants a gentle kiss on my cheek, the warmth of it trickling through my body, forcing me to relax.

"Also a classic trait of a Myr," she says, softly. "You would not be my true sister if your emotions didn't run away from you now and then. We feel them stronger than ever in this life."

"I'm starting to understand what you mean," I reply, my throat dry, focusing on the phantom taste of Jaspyr's blood on my tongue.

Isobel contemplates me. "I wonder if you do," she says, darkly.

She seems to look through me. Her words linger between us.

"While our emotions are meant to be felt and expressed, however they desire"—she blinks, her gaze sharpening back to the present—"at some point, Eloise, you must listen to what they're trying to say." Her golden locks undulate around her like the sun's rays. "Or you risk them taking hold of you forever."

She drifts ahead of me, leaving me to mull over her words.

"What if my emotions led me to do something... you wouldn't approve of?" I say to her back, a slight challenge in my tone. "Should I still listen then?"

Should I return to Kampaulo and continue playing with my meal until I'm ready to feast on him?

I smirk, recalling how Jaspyr's eyes had roved over every inch of my body, hungry for me, too. How the hair on his arms rose at my mere voice. How the admirable length of him grew with just my slightest touch. *Men are utterly predictable.*

Isobel's voice floats back to me from up ahead. "Try me," she says. "There's little that could shock me after all these centuries."

Centuries... My stomach twists in knots. *I'm barely a decade old to this life, and I've already failed.*

I consider all the other young men I've gladly fed on in the recent moons—some murderers, some saints—there's truly no good reason to be so tangled in the net of this one.

And yet, here I am; I bite my tongue.

"My, you're a tough clam to crack today. I do love a challenge."

'*No, don't tell her,*' whisper Aura and Ora. '*You don't know what she's capable of.*' Their support gives me comfort to keep my mouth shut about anything sincere right now.

"And you know I love to challenge you," I say sweetly, batting my eyes at her.

Her gentle laughs rumbles through me like a soft, building thunder. "Of course, Eloise. Take all the time you need. Maybe by the moonrise you'll have the courage to face me."

I dip back, trailing behind her—accepting this momentary pardon. I must choose my next move carefully, for Isobel isn't known for generosity.

Silver magic trails life of every shape and size across our reef as we silently swim. All around us colorful creatures whizz back and forth through a labyrinth of plant-like organisms, an intricate, balanced ecosystem keeping the peace.

Ribbed barrels, jagged horns, tall pillars, tubes, trees, and mountains of coral decorate the reef, like oddly hung ornaments, a rainbow assortment of hues. My absolute favorite is a bulbous thing with a maze carved into its surface, soft grooves that if followed closely on the right path can lead to a beginning and an end; Zahra told me once that it looked like a human brain, though I dared not ask how she could possibly know that… I normally don't feed past the bone.

Large leafy sea plants, and fragile reef fans sway back and forth to the soothing lull of the water. Brightly colored bushes and branches jut out at us from every angle, protecting the most fragile of the creatures that live among them. And spiny, black and white urchins with silver needle tips buzz and wriggle as they sleep, squished into holes where we cannot reach, waiting for the nighttime before they slink out of hiding to clean up the mess left by their bustling neighbors during the day—I can sense by my mounting energy that it's almost time for all of us to seize the night ahead.

I slow, hovering over a small patch of pinkish-red underwater flowers. Long, finger-like petals reach out to me, caressing my cheek. Their tentacles give off an electric vibration that I find intensely calming.

In a flash of bright rose-colored fire, I see Jaspyr's face, my insides twisting at the memory of his flame.

"Smart little fellow," coos Isobel, winking at the witty striped orange fish that's also learned how to coexist with these fickle flowers.

"Yeah…" I say, shakily, peering at it alongside her.

The vast list of organisms that create our reef is endless—the foundation of our home. If I listen, *very* carefully, I can hear them all thrumming with the great lifeforce of the Sea, a gentle hum much like my sisters' song. It's calming to me.

Isobel stills, holding out her arm. "Wait."

Her eyes narrow in a way that makes me weary, a dangerous grin forming on her lips; I smell them too—the blood of men, a weak, tangy scent compared to what I now know to be obtainable.

She takes a sharp downturn, away from the light of the day. The sea darkens as the last of the sun struggles to follow us, though, for my sister and me, we begin to see all the clearer—the colors deepen in contrast without the light diluting their natural state, their sheens sharper and hues richer, sometimes glowing and radiant. Even Isobel's essence transforms to a luminous entity in the dark the farther down she goes; I rush to keep up.

Hundreds of small, beady eyes watch us as we pass, the translucent, striped coral shrimp always spying on us here. And I spot boulder-like lobsters and prickly crabs that tend to hide in crevices, perched on steep slopes of rock in deeper waters. The crabs snap their mammoth claws in hello; the lobsters tickle us with their long antenna in greeting—not even the bravest fishermen will ever come close to getting their hands on one of these deep-sea creatures. Their nets don't reach this far, and we always sink their ships in these parts.

I rejoice in that.

An abrupt quiet washes over us as we round another corner, the sun breaking back through, tinkling on top of the waves from far above. Isobel swims straight up, headed directly for the hull of a small fishing boat that seems to be far off course.

I hang back and watch her, a fiery star shooting through the water, magic trailing her all the way to the surface. She glances back at me when I do not follow.

"I'm ravenous," she purrs. "Will you not join me, sister?"

I lick my lips, wanting to quench the strange thirst building inside of me, wanting to indulge even more.

'*Eloise, no,*' says Aura or Ora, surrounding me, distracting me.

I know… I know.

I shouldn't even be hungry now.

'*Do it, Eloise,*' a strange voice whispers. '*Who cares what they think?*'

My fangs try to push forward, but I press my lips closed.

"I have already fed this cycle," I call to Isobel, steadfast in my decision. "Enjoy for me. Drink slowly." I blow her a kiss on the currents.

Aura and Ora nuzzle their snouts into my side.

'*You made the right choice,*' they say with pride gleaming in their little eyes.

She nods. "Oh, I shall relish every bite. Indulge me while I play for a moment. I won't be long."

I float on my back, ushering her on.

"Take all the time you want. I've got nowhere to be but here," I say, lightly.

Isobel's song surrounds me the next moment; I relax into it, want to sink my entire soul in it—it's *so* soothing, so persuasive that her magic almost compels me to float toward her.

A splash breaks the water from above.

I look up and see that Isobel needn't even reach the surface for her prey to succumb to her.

The boat bounces with much lightness now, drifting away without anyone to steer it—its captain and his companion have abandoned their small vessel, diving into the waters to meet Isobel.

They swim for her in such a desperation that I've never seen before, only felt. Felt last night with every drop of blood that Jaspyr yielded to me.

Down, down, *down*.

They kick and claw toward the crimson star burning beneath them, toward Death, eyes wide open. Bubbles spew from their lips, their air depleting quickly.

Isobel just waits for them to reach her, a vicious floating flower.

I cannot look away, afraid to blink lest I miss the ending.

Every note she sings is effortless, a spider spinning its intricate web with efficiency, elegance, and the utmost pleasure. A balanced trap that I doubt I'll ever be able to replicate, even with forever.

Even when I'm ready to take Jaspyr.

As soon as the men reach her, Isobel rolls her magic into two binding, blazing chains that wrap around each of them. She fixes their arms to their sides, so they won't even have the freedom of flailing their limbs.

She releases her song in the next moment, allowing them to realize the true peril they're in, savoring their fear as they look to the surface.

She circles them, making her selection as they pointlessly wiggle—she lets the older man, the captain, sink, her magic that had helped him float now fizzling away. He drifts to the bottom where a flat area of rippled white sand and sediment offers a momentary break from the bustle of the reef, appearing like an earthy imitation of the gentle waves on the surface. He slowly falls past me, catching my gaze.

His eyes are bulging, beseeching, as if I might be his saving grace. His body thrashes with a silent plea for air that will not come.

I stare back at him, hardly able to think beyond my own gnawing appetite. All I want to do is drink his blood.

I ball my fists at my sides and will a smooth expression onto my face. *I am not hungry!*

My insides roar in protest.

I tear my eyes away from him just as he sucks in a big gulp of sea water. *What a waste*, I think, crossing my arms at my chest, not even bothering to look him in the eye while he drowns.

I'll be sure to visit his bones after Aura and Ora feast, I think, sardonically.

'*We'll lick them clean,*' they answer.

I frown, watching with unwarranted jealousy as Isobel rears her head, spreads her lips, then sinks her fangs into the neck of her prey.

Her magic flares, brightens as she drains him quickly of his life. It's as if the color of his blood bleeds into her veins when she drinks, the red in her scales and flowing fins glowing only more vibrant as she sucks.

She wraps in closer to him, enveloping him with her entire body, demanding every last drop of his blood.

"*Ahh,*" she sings with a heavy sigh when she's finished, tilting her chin toward the sparkling sunrays refracting against the waves above. "Just what I needed."

She gently unwraps herself from him and floats away—he sinks to the sands to lie with his companion.

"Will you let the boat drift out to sea?" I ask as Isobel descends toward me, forcing a question on my lips to silence the screaming in my head, the scent of Jaspyr in my nostrils—I can tell she's absolutely giddy after feeding by the twinkle in her eye and the soft, unbothered expression on her face.

"I'm in no mood to chase rubbish," she says with a flick of her hand. "Let it land on the shores of wherever and be a reminder of the scorn of the sea against man."

She has a drunken smile on her face, hardly paying me any mind as she floats around on her back, a small, pretty fish stealing her focus.

There's already a swarm of sharks below us, Aura and Ora among them, feasting on the fresh flesh of the bodies, biting and fighting one another just to get a taste—I regret not taking a bite myself, for I know with just another small taste of blood, my hunger for Jaspyr would surely be subdued, much better managed.

Once I drink.

I glance at Isobel—she's drifting away.

She won't notice my absence at all… not for a while.

14

HAZE

✿ J A S P Y R

A BLACK WOMAN LINED WITH GOLD, trimmed in silver, floats before me on a cloud of mist, naked and panting, her plump chest, her smooth stomach, rising and falling with every rasped, hungry breath. Her gaze falls on me, like two bright burning stars.

Crimson drips down her chin, her nipples, her belly button, her thighs. She's wet with blood-red paint. Wet between her legs, I imagine, for the way she glowers at me—such a claim in her eyes, as if she would pounce on me at any second and consume my very soul if I yielded it to her.

She traces her tongue along her upper lip, her teeth.

"Jaspyr," she hums in a voice like the soft song of winter. "Won't you come to me?" She raises her arm and beckons me forward. "Won't you be with me?"

It's only when I see the sharp points of two fangs press from between her parted lips that I remember she's no woman at all. That she's not soaked in paint but rather bathed in blood.

I tear my eyes from the golden vortexes in her face and let my gaze fall to what lies beneath her feet—she does not float, she stands, like a statue, atop a mound of blood-drained bodies. I see only faces I know.

Sibyl. Luna. Greggor. Penelope. Eddison. Me…

My face is there, too. Pale and devoid of life. Black hair hanging in strings over my eyes. My tattoos never to glow silver again for how the magic has been so emptied from me, leeched by this creature from the depths of darkness I hadn't even known to exist before her.

She is the monster that haunts my waking dreams. She is Death's messenger, come to unite me with my family.

"Jaspyr," she howls, the sound of my name on her tongue making my insides throb with an aching desire.

I wish to yield to it, this horror incarnate. I wish it to swallow me whole. Though, I'm certain, as I stare upon my dead, hollow face, that she shall surely devour me completely if I do not wake myself up.

"I want you to beg me to kill you again," she purrs.

Suddenly, I'm on my knees before her, my chin tilted up by her finger, forced to stare upon her lovely, petrifying face.

"Beg me to have you."

"I—"

Jaspyr!" Her voice clangs in my head, echoing around this misted chamber that seems to have no end. "Beg me," she demands, leaning forward, her fangs showing fully.

"Take me," I say, flipping my palms upward toward her. "Take me, please." I mean every word. "I want you to have me."

She smirks with a viciousness that makes my toes curl in fear, with need.

"Very well."

In a swift blur of shimmering streaks, her teeth are in my neck. Her legs wrap around my hips, and she sucks all the *blood from my body without pause.*

Between breaths, she murmurs my name—if the last thing I hear is her voice, I'll die satisfied.

I wrap my arms around her, holding her tighter, pressing her closer. "Please, take all of me," I say.

"OY, JASPYR! I've been looking all over for you." Eddison's voice draws my attention from the hypnotizing waves. I sit up in a jolt, the sleep falling away. "What are you doing out here at this hour?"

I blink my eyes open to find him bouncing toward me across the sand.

I must've cum myself into an oblivion—the night had fully settled over me, the moon now a bright, near-full bulb in the sky, the starlight a halo around it. My lips curl up in a satisfied, albeit confused, smile as my nightmare falls away. I'm safe on the beach.

I can't recall the last time I felt so relaxed and unbothered. Definitely before the war.

I shake the sand from my hair, my clothes.

"*Hello?*" drones Eddison, snapping his fingers in my face. "Anyone in there, mate?"

I massage the stubble at my chin. "I must've fallen asleep," I reply in a daze. The last bit of dream, of nightmare—*of her*—edges from my mind.

Peering at the moon, I accidentally slip back into the memory of those golden-brown eyes, like an abyss sucking me out of reality and into her enchanted, dark world.

I want to drown in her.

My cock twitches. I stifle a small groan. I force myself to focus on anything else, willing myself soft.

I adjust my pants and turn away from the water, toward Eddison. "What are *you* doing out here?" I ask, my voice cracking.

He takes one good look at me and beams, his eyes twinkling with amusement.

I try to keep my face straight. "What's that look for?" I ask, blinking up at him as if nothing were amiss.

He tosses his head back in laughter, the sound of it wiping away any last bit of fog over my brain, jarring me wide awake.

"Oh, I'm sorry, mate," he says, between barking laughs, slapping his knees. "I didn't know you still came out here to…" He folds over, trying to catch his breath. "Pleasuring yourself in our ole cliff spot, are we?" He can hardly get a word out without cackling more. "I thought you were grown enough to get yourself to brothel by now. Do you need us to wait, or are you finished?"

He nods to several others, who are hanging back on the trail, waiting for Eddison to return. Their voices are equally raucous, their postures wobbly.

"Been drinking, have you?" I stand and gently tap him on the arm—he wobbles so much he nearly falls into the water.

I steady him, breaking into a laugh myself.

"Eddison, you're *the* biggest man I know in Kampaulo. How is it you can't hold your whiskey about you yet? I'm younger and leaner than you and have a better record."

He hiccups with a little shrug. "Come find me when you reach your twenty-eighth year. It all goes downhill from there." He pats himself on the stomach, then lifts his eyebrow. "Now, what were you doing out here all by yourself?"

"I wasn't doing anything but trying to enjoy some peaceful moments alone," I say, shifting my hands in my pockets.

"Hmm," he says. "You know, maybe it's time you started putting yourself out there again." He places his hands on his hips, looking me up and down. "I know the King's laws around pairing are less than ideal, but," he looks to the sky, "you never know. Your match could be a win!"

I level my gaze at him, my voice low. "No."

He takes a step back, raising his hands. "Sorry," he slurs. "I overstepped."

I stomp on the building fire that his words ignited in me, touching the three thick chains layering my neck—one for each person I'd already lost to the King's laws, including myself.

I press the dark-dusted gold and silver metals closer to my chest, letting the coolness calm me. Each band is etched like the scale of a snake, the detail grating at my skin, my insides. King Devlindor's emblem, the coiled serpent, reminding me always of what was stolen from me.

I took them from the head regulator who'd given the order, ripped them from his bloodied neck.

Eddison clears his throat, calling my attention back from that dark place I'd slipped into again.

"I shouldn't have suggested anything like that," he says, more steadily. He looks at his feet, swaying a little from side to side. "I am such a lightweight."

I take a deep breath, then let my anger float away. "And you always will be." I offer him a smile, a pardon for his offense—there's nothing we wouldn't forgive of each other. "So… what *are* you doing here?"

"We're headed to the Split," he says, looping his arm through mine and turning us toward his friends. "When you weren't at home, this was the first place I looked, demanded that you had to join us."

The Split is an underwater cavern hidden in the cliffs on

the other side of Kampaulo. An unknown natural phenomenon created a perfect slice within the cave floor long before our time, revealing a depthless hot spring of still, fresh water in the middle of the earth. It makes the perfect swimming hole for the more courageous citizens—I have no desire to go, to be around anyone other than myself and the night sky. In my dreams with that beautiful monster, or awake trying to figure out how to protect myself from her.

I dig my heels into the sand, but Eddison is impossible to resist.

"You're coming," he says, reading the hesitation in my expression; he drags me forward. "It's about time you learned to have a little fun again around here."

I shimmy out of his grasp the moment he stumbles.

"I don't know…" I say, scratching the back of my neck, taking in the small drunken group of regulators waiting for us farther back on the beach. "I'm not really feeling up for it tonight."

Eddison shoves a bottle of whiskey into my hands so forcefully that it spills against my chest, drenching my cloak. "Then drink up. You'll feel just fine."

I can tell by the tone in his voice that he's hardly giving me a choice. Guilt bubbles in my chest.

"You're right," I say with a heavy sigh, taking a long swig. "It's been awhile since we enjoyed a night out, away from all… this." I jerk my chin toward the city, firelights popping up all around.

"Too long," he agrees, holding his hand out for the bottle. We begin to walk back up the beach to where his friends are waiting. "And don't worry about them. They're good people, just trying to make a humble living, like me," he mumbles under his breath, "*mostly.*"

I pretend not to hear.

"Come on," he adds, taking long strides that I can barely

keep up with—he clears me by a full head in height, making me look small in comparison. "We were just headed to the Stables to borrow some horses."

I lift my eyebrow. "Outside of patrol hours?"

Eddison grins widely, dangling a large, metal key in my face.

"Sometimes being a regulator has its perks. As long as we return any that we borrow by tomorrow morning, they won't be missed and the stable hand won't say a word."

I purse my lips, shaking my head at him a little.

"Careful, Eddison," I warn. "Or you might find that you've turned into a person you yourself wouldn't like to know."

Now, he pretends not to hear me. He walks forward, blending into the crowd of black cloaks; I stand among them, feeling so very tall.

They all begin to chant as I follow at his heels up the path, their rowdy voices pressing in on me like a suffocating smog. I smile and bring the head of the whiskey bottle being passed around back to my mouth, letting the liquid burn through me, erasing memories like they never were—like the lick of flames across a painting.

THE RIDE TO THE SPLIT IS BUMPY AT BEST—riding horses drunk, across the beach, always is. But here, unkempt nature made the journey even more difficult.

It had been a while since I rode this path.

I grip the reins, feeling as if I'm flying, moving too quickly from one point to the next. I much prefer walking, feeling the solid earth beneath my feet, the sand between my toes.

I look to the night sky, dusted with stars and strips of wispy clouds guiding us alongside the outskirts of the city.

"It is the perfect night for this…" I say to no one in particular.

So perfect that it doesn't seem like the one before actually happened—*I don't even have a name for her yet.*

"Monster, blood-sucking beast," I utter under my breath, wondering how she might be killed.

Beautiful, beguiling, I think, my thoughts betraying me.

"What?" says Eddison, guiding his horse to hang back with mine in the rear of the group.

"Nothing," I say, looking forward.

"We heard you went a little mad yesterday," he whispers… loudly; I grind my teeth, continuing to face forward. "The other regulators are saying you tried to burn your place to the ground, but I told them you'd never do something like that." He tilts his head. "But then Ma said she stopped in today to drop off some food and the shop was closed for repair." He pauses, waiting for my response.

I return a tight smile. "Never say never," I say with a wink.

He rolls his eyes. "You can be utterly grim sometimes, you know." He tosses the bottle to me again; I catch it.

He lowers his voice to a rumble about as soft as a battered drum. "Tell me the truth. Did something happen I should know about? Do I need to be keeping a better eye on you?"

I chuckle. *Oh, something happened.*

But there's no way I'm telling Eddison even a fraction of the truth in earshot of a group of power-hungry regulators while everyone is drunk. They'd bury me alive, then leave me to rot.

I look to him, my lips turning downward—I don't think he'll ever be ready for the truth… but I do *want* to tell him, to tell anyone what happened to me last night.

Too bad Greggor didn't find me on the beach, I think with a wry snort.

A few more swigs of this whiskey, and I'll be ready to discuss her all night.

I shake my head and steady my gaze on Eddison so that he'll believe every word out of my mouth—I got good at bluffing when I cut my way through Guanamara, pretending to be one of *them*.

"No, it was just an accident," I say, my voice even, light. "I was up late working, and I knocked a candle into my canvas while I slept." I scratch the back of my neck with a nervous laugh. "I'm lucky I woke up in time to contain the fire to a small area. The shop just needs a bit of time for the smoke to air out, and I have to tend to my paintings." I look down to my hands, knuckles white from gripping the reins and keeping my story straight. "It's a little embarrassing, so I'm just lying low until I can open back up in a couple of days."

The lie came so easily. Meanwhile, my memories retrace the creature's physique, the way her tongue carefully slid across my skin; the scabs at my neck prickle.

"*Yeesh*," says Eddison with a long whistle. He shakes his head. "I'm sorry to hear it, mate, but I'm glad you didn't lose much. What of your paintings? Will they be alright?"

I nod with a grateful smile.

"Thankfully the fires didn't move past the back area where I sleep. Just the farthest wall where I store old paints and part of the ceiling took the worst hits." I look ahead, frowning. "But everything I worked on last night went up in smoke," I add with a wounded, truthful sigh. "And the stray flames nearly burned straight through the roof. It all happened so fast." I guide my horse around a bend, following the others, letting words fly out of my mouth. "It was all I could do to keep it contained."

There's a beat of silence.

"How did you?" asks Eddison in a soft voice, cunning.

I stiffen, clutching the reins tighter, so tight that my muscles ripple in my forearms.

It still shocks me sometimes, how well he can read me, even when I think I've thoroughly fooled him—I suppose no amount of time apart, of maturity, can erase a brotherly bond forged during an impoverished youth, watching our families scrape by just to put food in our mouths.

I purse my lips, sucking air in through my nostrils.

"*How?*" he asks again with a low rumble in his throat—I know he can scent the magic still smoking off me, the remnants of silver still surely a glistening sheen in my eyes.

"I always keep fresh basins of water in my shop," I say, holding my chin high. "I need them to paint and bathe and whatnot." I lean slightly over, mockingly sniffing at him, praying he'll shift the subject. "You could do with a bath, by the way. You reek of liquor."

He bristles, opening his mouth to retort, but one of the regulators ahead of us whistles loudly, swiveling around to glance at me.

"Lucky bastard," Kaelan calls, clearly having been eavesdropping on our conversation; his voice makes the hair on my skin rise. "You'd be out on the streets if it hadn't rained."

"*Luck* had nothing to do with it, I assure you," I reply, coolly.

"With your antiquated methods, how could luck have any room to manifest at all?" snaps Eddison.

A crackle of tension electrifies between us.

I clench my jaw; Eddison rolls his eyes at me.

"Whatever," he says after a moment, letting the opportunity for another bicker about magic breeze past us—even he's wise enough to know not to speak of such things in this group.

He lowers his voice to a whisper by his standards. "But seriously, do you have to be so broody tonight? Just… loosen up a bit. You're embarrassing me in front of my—"

"*Friends?*" I snort, shaking my head. "What a fine group you've found here." I nod to the woman directly in front. "That one ransacked old man Yusof's place the other day on the keeper's orders and didn't leave a thing intact. She clearly had the time of her life ripping his world apart." I gesture to Kaelan. "And *he* has more kill scores tattooed on his arm than I can count anymore. Innocent people, Jaspyr. People just trying to get by, with few prospects in this bleak era."

I look at him, wanting to save him from this life, wanting to protect that good heart of his from such corruption.

"If these are the types of friends you keep around you, then what does that make me?" My voice comes out more defeated and unsure than I had anticipated.

He looks me directly in the eye.

"*You* are my brother," he replies, steadfastly. "No matter what." He jerks his chin in the direction of the group of regulators. "And they are…" He lets out a loud, frustrated sigh. "I'm one of them, Jaspyr. This is the world we live in now. Get used to it."

His gaze lingers on the snake forever coiled at my neck, on its deep onyx jeweled eyes that were crafted to transfix.

"Hail to the King," I say with a sneer—the words are like acid I've swallowed a thousand times.

His eyes slide to mine. A deep frown withers his normally bright features.

"Hail to Lord Devlindor!" his 'friends' shout back at us in unison, thrusting their fists into the sky. They laugh, obnoxiously, completely oblivious to how badly I wish to rip them all apart, just to free *my* brother. He'd clearly sold his soul to keep a roof over his head and food on his table.

Eddison faces forward. "Hail to Lord Devlindor," he mutters under his breath, his jawline rigid, dutifully ignoring my glare.

I soften. My heart twists with sadness.

"You're nothing like them, brother. I assure you," I say, thinking of all the blood on my hands, all the black cloaks I slaughtered in my recent past, just to get to one; I finger the chain on my neck again. "And I pray you never will be."

He whips the reins of his horse, trotting onward a little faster to be out of my range and among the others. Their black-hooded robes flutter in the wind, rolling off the high crests battling the shore. The golden crest of the King gleams under the moon in a taunting wave before me.

I look away, up toward the sky. She envelops me once more.

15

HUNT

⟩ ELOISE

I BREAK THE SURFACE and Jaspyr's scent surrounds me like an embrace. It's a complex blend that reminds me of the freshness of fallen leaves, the sweetness of sandalwood, the saltiness of sea spray.

My stomach growls at me, aching with hunger.

"Stop it," I whisper to my cravings. "Get a hold of yourself, Eloise."

I will have him tonight.

I spread my arms over the water, pensive, knowing already which voice will win my inner conflict.

The moon is fully risen, the stars as abundant as the sands of this shore. *Where is he?*

I lean into the comforting hold of the gentle waves at my back, focusing on his scent—Jaspyr's essence is scattered all over this beach, for whatever reason, headed westward along the shoreline.

I glide atop the surface, keeping to the coast, stealthily hidden within the swells; the glint of my tail, my scales, might just appear like a normal watery shimmer, should anyone look.

I'm so intent on locating him before the sunrise that I hardly notice the subtle hum bubbling up toward me from below. The sound becomes clearer, unnervingly beautiful, a fusion of two voices.

I stop swimming, anxiety twisting my insides at the interruption. *I have to get to him… I can't wait any longer.*

The singing stops. I'm no longer alone.

"Vasylina. Miki." My gaze remains pinned on the cliffs in the distance. "To what do I owe the pleasure?" I say, dryly.

The cold press of their lips lands on both sides of my face as my elder sisters kiss me in greeting.

"Hello, Eloise," they seem to sing together.

They are the only twins in our coven, never apart. They swim as one, seduce as one. And they kill and feed as a single, terrifying unit.

I incline my head to Vasylina.

She smiles at me, flashing her fangs. Her pearl-white lifeblood gleams sharply under the moonlight, like cream diamonds melted atop her tan skin.

"It's the full moon soon," she says, her voice quiet. I've never heard her raise it above a whisper, always seeming quite bored in conversation. And she always speaks in dark riddles.

She doesn't offer more.

I smile, tight-lipped, trying to hide my irritation. "I thought you both preferred to hunt in the deep seas. Why are you so close to land this feed?"

Miki swims around to meet my gaze, smiling brightly. She's identical to Vasylina, save for her much more pleasant demeanor *and* her lifeblood—deep midnight blue lines, as dark as the sky, snake across her skin in glittery lines.

"There's not enough boats nor ships out on our course to-night," she answers, pouting—she beams at her twin, adoration in her eyes. "So, tonight, we thought we'd have a bit of fun for once. *Right*, Vasylina?" She bats her eyelids at her.

"Whatever pleases you, sister," she says, clearly resigned to her twin's desires.

Miki takes her arm, and they both look toward Kampaulo. Their lips curl up in an uncannily similar smirk, eyes sparkling with thirst.

"I see," I say, following their line of sight—in the direction of Jaspyr's scent.

He's mine, some primal part of me declares.

"I have to say, I'm surprised," I add—I can't even recall the last time I heard of one of my sisters, let alone an elder princess, landwalking. "What did you have in mind?"

The twins both look at me and smile something wicked. "Lust, or Life," they sing in unison.

"We haven't played in *so* long," says Vasylina in a hushed, ancient voice.

"Oh, you must join us this time!" adds Miki, taking my hand.

"Tell me, what are the rules again?" I ask, pretending to care, wracking my brain for a good excuse to swim off—'Lust, or Life' is a twisted game invented by the twins a millennia ago to torture men through seduction with only their bodies, their voices, and their eyes.

"No magic allowed!" says Miki, eyes glowing—she pinches Vasylina. "That means*, no* enchanted songs or stares. Or you lose and have to let me lead our hunts for the next year."

Vasylina flicks her tail at her sister, white, glossy scales fluttering across the water. "I would never cheat for a meal," she says.

I can't help the derisive snort that comes out of my nose.

"Sure…" I mutter under my breath.

Vasylina smirks. "The humans who reject us also get to live to see the sunrise," she adds—I roll my eyes.

"After all your centuries of practice, you'd think you would be a better liar by now," I say with a little laugh.

Vasylina's lifeblood becomes luminous.

"Careful," warns Miki in a cold but kind voice. Her eyes narrow at me, silver glinting in the irises; I keep one eye on them both and float a little back.

I clear my throat. "All I meant is that it's not a true game if we know the humans would *never* reject us." I look to Vasylina, my whirling thoughts taking precedence over my better senses. "Besides, you'd surely kill any man who dared to, regardless."

Miki covers her mouth with her hand, stifling her laugh; Vasylina scowls.

I shrug. "I just… don't see the fun in it." I offer an apologetic smile. "Thank you, but I think I'd rather not tonight. I'm not in the best mood for games."

I *might* be persuaded to play… if the thought of Jaspyr wasn't drowning my mind. And if my vow to be a respectable example of a myrmaid didn't still temper the way I tend to conduct my hunts—earlier today aside.

Miki giggles. "Maybe she's got a point," she says. "But I still find it a glorious time!"

Vasylina shakes her head, her long, curly locks floating around her like a dark veil. "You're wrong, Eloise. There *are* a rare few who are smart enough to run."

I raise an eyebrow.

"Of course…" She tilts her head, looking to the sky. "Then I only crave them more." She laughs at a memory, the sound making my skin crawl.

"Come on," says Miki. "*Please.* Join us! It's been such a long time since we've hunted together. And when was the last time you enjoyed a human for more than just to satiate your feed?"

I think back to a handsome young man with dusted blonde hair and eyes as soft and brown as the loveliest sands— I don't typically choose to wield my body against men just for fun, for they truly stand no chance. But, once in a blue moon, I suppose, it's nice to explore *all* the wonderful pleasures available to me when I take human form...

I find myself considering, my current motivations to land-walk again becoming distorted by the memory of Jaspyr's naked body. The length of him alone would surely be worth exploring...

And those legs and thighs, his stomach, chest, and arms, every part of him displaying virile strength at just the tiniest of movements.

To think, he's a painter...

I shudder with pleasure at the thought of all the fun I might have with him, if I hadn't already tasted his blood. Alas, I don't think it's even possible for me not to kill him on sight now.

"It... has been some time," I admit, somewhat shyly, as Jaspyr envelops my mind once more.

I frown, thinking it a shame, to waste a man like him— he's molded with muscle surely earned from real battles, cut with lines and scars. I could've looked at him all night long if he'd kept sleeping, exploring the portrait of his past painted atop his canvas-white skin.

And that goddess-sent aroma. Magic mixing with mouth-watering blood.

I lick my lips. My core burns, twists with need, distracting me from my objective—*hunt, kill, feed.*

"Eloise?" says Vasylina, her voice subtly laced with concern.

Oh, no. I've done it again! Slipped away into my mind

over this man.

I shake my head of him, smiling back at her. "I guess, well…" I sigh, exasperated. "I don't know."

"That sounds like a '*yes*' to me," chimes Miki, clapping her hands.

I chew on my lip, looking away. "But I've never participated in your games before. I've always been… alone."

Miki laughs, dismissing me with the flick of her berry-blue tail. "Oh, you're *so* new. Trust me, it's much better as a group."

"And you haven't fed this cycle?" asks Vasylina—they both stare at me, waiting for confirmation.

I look down, a small shake of my head.

'*Gluttonous liar,*' the Moon seethes, the fullness of her splendor glowering down at me like a golden eye. '*Don't even think of slithering out of the sea. I'm warning you, Eloise.*'

"Then that settles it," they both sing.

I force a smile, not daring to look up. I want to sink down and swim away before it's too late, obedient to my great goddess.

The moon's beam weighs heavy atop my head. "I—"

The twins loop their arms through mine, guiding me forward.

"Come," says Vasylina. "We waste precious time."

Miki pats my arm with a grin. "Let us show you how myrmaids have really had fun throughout the ages."

Their laugh encircles me, then we're suddenly speeding across the waves, magic shimmering in a trail like stardust behind us.

We head toward the west side of Kampaulo—Jaspyr's scent grows stronger.

16

SANCTUARY

☼ J A S P Y R

"SORRY ABOUT EARLIER," I say a little while later, catching back up to Eddison. My horse sloshes through puddles on the sand as we trot westward along the shore.

The hazy film of carefreeness that whiskey always gifts me after enough swigs has fully settled over my mind.

"I didn't get much sleep yesterday."

He grunts in response.

I guide my horse alongside his. "Come on, mate. I've just been *so* busy trying to burn my life down," I say, trying to lighten the mood. "I know I was being an ass. I'm sorry."

"*Was?*" he counters, still refusing to look at me.

I clear my throat, sitting a little taller.

"*Oh*, kind sir," I amend, making a show of it, "I know that I'm an ass by nature." He nearly snorts out the drink he'd just sipped; I bow my head low. "As usual, I beg your forgiveness for my ass-like behavior." I shimmy my shoulders like I've seen the elder highlifes do many times when they're in proper debates, "and I'm not entirely sure why you still keep me around." That pulls a laugh out of him.

"For your coin, obviously."

I scrunch my face up at him, for he has racked up quite the debt to me. *Like father, like son*, I think.

"What's mine is yours, brother," I say, genuinely. "Just don't tell Penelope. She'll take me for all my worth." I wink at him, and we both break out into a laugh.

His expression shifts, worry furrowing his brow.

"Ma's concerned about you, you know," he whispers. "After last night."

I clutch my stomach, noting the ridges of muscle beneath my shirt. "Why?" I gasp, mockingly. "Does she think I'm too skinny?"

Eddison snickers. "Look at me... compared to you."

I smirk, waving it off. "You can tell her to quit snooping around my place so late at night. I can feed myself. I'm not a boy anymore."

"I would rather face you in a battle to the death than deliver that message," he replies, beaming. "She's already made up your bedroom down the hall, should you keep up your interests in playing with fire."

I nod, my smile tight, not missing the veiled accusation in his tone. "I'll keep that in mind."

He takes a deep breath, looking forward.

The land has started to shift into a slight incline.

"We're almost there," says Eddison with a yawn. "Finally, my buzz was beginning to wear off." I blanch, thinking he'd nearly drunk the entire bottle himself. "Race to the top?"

"You're on," I say, squinting ahead to try to calculate the distance; there's nothing but natural light from here on out. "What are the terms—"

Before we can set the stakes, Eddison nudges his horse and they dart away. "Loser jumps first!" he shouts at me over his shoulder. "*Ass.*"

My mouth falls open.

"You have *no* honor, Eddison," I call after him in my most formal tone. I shake my fist at him. "You will pay for this disgrace." I whip the reins. "*Yah!*"

My horse's hooves pound the earth behind him as his cackle floats back to me. Not moments later, I breeze past him on a silver-kissed wind that he's too drunk to notice.

"Hey, what the—" He gapes at me as I pass.

Then he pushes his horse faster with a warrior cry, hips high in the air; I'm afraid we both might fall right out of our saddles for how little is left in our liquor bottle.

Soon, the entire group is galloping with us, laughing and hollering. We race alongside moon-licked waters, taking a narrow, sandy cliff path, upward to the Split. The wind claws at our faces and hair, the waves roaring in our ears.

I forgot how good it feels to ride, the freedom in it...

We soon reach our destination and dismount our horses on wobbly legs.

Eddison immediately points at me and laughs, my hair a knotted nest; I try to comb my fingers through it, then lift my hood.

He smirks, patting the perfectly smooth braids that zigzag in different designs atop his head.

"Must be nice," I say, stomping in a large puddle while I tie my horse up to a tree with low-hanging leaves—the dirty water splashes his shiny boots and regulator uniform.

"I... will destroy you," he says, narrowing his eyes at me as he wipes off his shirt; he ties his horse to the opposite tree.

"Yeah, yeah." I rub my thumb and index finger together with a smile. "Right after you pay up, I'll let you get a swing in on me."

He lifts a mocking fist, and I pretend to defend, both goading each other all the while.

"Stop bickering, boys," says Ulsta with a sigh. "You're ruining the peace and quiet."

I grimace, dropping my fake fighting stance.

Ulsta is one of the strongest regulators in Eddison's rank; he's had his eye on her for a while, but I find her despicable—given her proclivity for bloodshed, she's sure to become a head officer one day.

Eddison stutters something incomprehensible, extending a hand out to her to help her dismount; she ignores it, sliding off with grace.

"I think you ruin it well enough, Ulsta," I say, leaning against a tree, one foot up. "Without even trying, might I add. My, how skilled you are."

Eddison shoves me. "*Ass*," he mutters.

I shrug.

"Would you like to test my skill?" says Ulsta in a poison-sweet voice; she places her hand on the sword pommel at her hip, the other regulators standing behind her, arms crossed.

I push off the tree. "It would be my absolute pleasure," I say—I really wish I'd brought my sword with me to the beach, but painters needn't typically carry them. And I don't like to remind myself of the warrior I can be.

Eddison comes to stand between us. "Alright," he says with a nervous laugh. "We came here to have some fun, so let's have it."

I eye the blade at his hip, knowing I could have it off him in a heartbeat and at Ulsta's neck.

His gaze draws mine, his expression pleading.

I laugh, loudly, patting his shoulder.

"What do you think we're doing?" I say, relaxing my posture; I flash a toothy smile at Ulsta and the other regulators. "But Eddison's right, we're all too smashed to practice sword fighting." I wink at him, then put my hands on my hips, craning my neck to see the top of the climb ahead of us.

Kaelan gives a long whistle. "Is that where we're going? I've never actually been. Only heard stories from... before."

My skin heats. *Before*—that's what our past, my lost family, has been reduced to in this world.

I take a deep breath and nod, glancing to Eddison; I soften. "It used to look like an invincible mountain when we were kids."

He smiles, gently shoving me. "Lead the way."

I sigh. *This is going to be a long night.*

We grab only what we need from our packs, for it's a steep, short trek to our final destination; I'm thankful to find an unopened bottle of whiskey in our saddlebag—without it I'm sure I'd make much worse company. I grab it, then lead the others up the nature-covered trail.

The Split is known by all in Kampaulo, though frequented by few—it can be a treacherous journey to this side of the cliff-riddled shores without the privilege of a good horse. And it's even more difficult to climb out of the cavernous watering hole after diving in.

When we reach the top, the narrow path leads us into a cave.

A wide, yawning, jagged mouth opens to a breathtaking view of the sky and moon on the other side of the hollowed-out area, a decorated canvas before us.

Tangles of vines crawl along the inside of the cut-open cliff. Up the walls and dangling from the ceiling. A lush jungle, hidden at the top of Kampaulo.

From the entrance where we stand, the earth is divided into two halves—the Split.

It appears as if an old god took a blazing sword and hollowed out the earth here, creating a cut so deep that the Sea had no choice but to fill it with life.

Tranquil, steaming hot water fills its bottomless center, making the cool walls of the cave bead with sweat. Glistening ridged rocks droop from the ceiling and jut up around the cavern floor like clipped trees without limbs nor leaves, decorating the otherwise flat interior.

And mounds of pale pink and beige boulders nestle up against the sides, glittering like sand trapped beneath an iridescent top layer—I think of her, of the monster whose every inch of flesh seemed to shimmer with the softest gleam of magic.

I toss my cloak to the floor, ready to dive in, thinking that this water might be *just* the thing I need to clear my head.

This impressive division in the earth almost completely separates the cavern into two halves. From where we stand, a perfect triangle carves out toward the sea, an arrow pointing in that direction.

I place my feet directly in the center.

I always imagined the legendary God of Earth speaking to me here, whispering, '*Come, witness my world. This is the best view of it that you'll ever know.*'

The others spread out around me, exploring, awestruck—part of me is a little ashamed to sully this place with the King's regulators, but it's too late now.

I walk further in.

There's a sizable area where we can safely spread out without fear of tripping and tumbling in; it's a risky but thrilling jump from here, fatal if one isn't careful of the rocks along the edges. But Eddison and I have done it countless times, happy to take a chance to see the second, better view from the water.

I eagerly peer over the side.

There's a low but wide ledge submerged in the enclosed lake, far below us, sitting against the ocean side of the cavern. It looks unchanged from the last time I was here. Just a smooth, glistening slab of rock.

If I squint, I can make out another hole carved into the

cliff face atop the ledge. Much simpler than the grand one before us. A honed, perfected view where the sky meets the water—'The Doorway to the Sea', as Eddison and I named it long ago.

This is what truly drew us here as children, time and time again. It's the richest view of any sunset or shower of falling stars a person might ever need to see to feel alive, complete. And we had it all to ourselves.

With that doorway at our fingertips, we needn't desire anything else…

How did I forget? I swallow the growing lump in my throat, the brilliant gold of the moon watching me.

Eddison clasps me on the shoulder, making me jump.

"Been a long time," he says, his eyes twinkling. "A lot has changed since we stood here last."

I wipe mine and nod. "This place hasn't, though."

I edge around the Split to the wide shelf on the left, careful of my footing. I walk as close as I can to where the cave opens up on the farthest side, placing my hand against the wall to steady myself against the strong wind.

I stare down at the wild waves—they crawl up alongside the cliff and smash against the jagged rocks below, reaching toward me.

Eddison clings to the cliff wall to join me. "Careful," he says. "It's slippery over here."

He knocks into me, clumsily; I almost lose my grip.

I shoot him a glare.

"What? It's not like you fell," he says with a sly grin.

"If I fall, I will come back to haunt you," I snap—no human could survive that drop.

He tries to muffle his laughter.

When he finds stable footing, he peers out beside me. "I think the last time we were here was after…"

I look up, noting the sadness in his eyes.

"After your father died," I say, softly, my throat tightening. "I remember."

We both look out to the water, observing a moment of silence in honor of Edward, lost to the unforgiving sea.

"They used to say lightning struck here in the old times, ripping the earth apart," says Kaelan, his voice pulling me out of the moment—I curse him under my breath.

Eddison gives me a wary smile, and leads the way back to the group.

"I think it was just a regular earthquake," he responds, crouching down to contemplate the Split. "We always get the residuals from the barren volcanic lands up north." He nods to himself. "There's nothing strange here like… earth-shattering lightning strikes."

He scoffs at the thought.

I gaze down at the dark water, still as glass, billows of steam rolling up to me off the surface.

"I don't know," I say, unsure. "To me, it looks like someone took a sword and cut clean through the earth. It's unnatural… to have such a perfect rip in the land like this, especially from an earthquake." *Magic*, I think. *Or, maybe, ancient gods at war.*

But I don't say it, for not even the old gods can contend with King Devlindor in this era.

Without warning, Eddison cups his hands around his mouth and yells, "*Hello*! Is anyone down there?"

His voice echoes on forever, then falls silent… until the others start to add their own to it, making me *really* wish I hadn't agreed to this outing.

I plug my ears, whispering apologies to the nature around me.

"Damn, I can hardly see a thing down there," says another regulator I don't care to know the name of. He whistles. "Maybe this wasn't the best idea…"

"Scared?" replies Ulsta with a drunken laugh. "Relax. We just need to light a fire. There's old torches all around this place, it looks like."

She pulls out a chalky stone from her pack and walks over to one. Then she lifts a dagger from her belt and swipes the blade across the stone until sparks sprinkle atop the torch. It immediately takes, fire licking at the old wood and illuminating the space.

Everyone else follows in her footsteps, flames slowly lighting up around the cavern, casting golden shadows across the dark. I join them, walking to the farthest ones so that they can't see when I beckon my magic. *Solza ven immito.*

I wonder if they'll notice at all, for how drunk they are. Will they even remember how flames flicker with pink when enchanted?

Eddison does. I won't let him forget it—he grits his teeth at me from afar but says nothing.

I couldn't care less what he thinks in his moment. This is *our sanctuary*, and I won't hide who I am here.

With the fires lit, everyone settles in, happily chatting and passing the remnants of our liquor bottles back and forth beneath the low lights. Leisurely, we begin to strip away our shoes and clothes.

The cliffs are a sharp drop down, unnaturally smooth slopes. But old ropes have been tied all around the edges.

"Think these will hold up?" I ask, lifting one of the heavy, dried cords. It crackles with age. "Who knows how long they've been here."

"If they don't, we brought a couple of extras," says Ulsta.

Kaelan chimes in. "We just need to make sure one of us is up top at all times, in case someone can't get back out."

He speaks with such a haughtiness that I have to refrain from *accidentally* pushing him over the edge.

I slap him on the back so hard that he buckles with a gasp,

his eyes growing wide as he looks down. "Then you're on duty first," I say with a too-big grin.

He makes to retort, but I suppose the gleam in my eye tells him to reconsider. He crosses his arms at his chest but nods his agreement. "Alright, kids," he barks in his formal, regulator tone; my skin prickles. "Go play. I'll stand watch this round."

Eddison moves to untie his trousers but then halts, flicking an unsure gaze toward Ulsta. "Um… well… we normally do this in the nude," he says, his voice wavering with embarrassment.

"And?" says Ulsta with a raised eyebrow, taking a swig from the bottle.

Eddison fumbles over his words.

"Well, I mean… you're the only—" He clears his throat as she sharpens her gaze on him. "If you're uncomfortable with our… you know," he awkwardly gestures below his waist, "we can keep them in our pants." He exhales a long breath, deflating as laughter echoes around the cavern.

"Good gods," I mutter. "That was hard to watch."

Ulsta turns her back toward him.

"Why would I be uncomfortable?" she asks, tossing her cloak, then her shirt, and boots and pants to the side; she turns back to face him in her undergarments. "I wouldn't mind seeing what you're really made of, Eddison Raez. It might explain why you have such a complex around me on the battlefield."

The other regulators are nearly choking on their laughter.

I can barely hold mine behind my teeth, my face heating for my poor friend.

A blush rises to Eddison's cheeks. He puffs out his chest. "I do *not* have a—"

Ulsta shimmies out of the rest of her garments and stares him down in the nude, breasts out and spine straight, a fiendish smirk on her pretty, olive-skinned face.

Eddison's voice dies in his throat. His mouth falls open,

gaping at her. His eyes rove over her muscular, lithe, curved body.

For a moment, I see *her* again, the creature of the night, standing before me in all her otherworldly glory...

I rid myself of the thought—Ulsta can't hold a candle to her, as monstrous as she is.

She walks right up to Eddison, looking him in the eyes, the tips of her large breasts nearly skimming his chest.

"Apologies, it seems that I might have made *you* uncomfortable now."

Eddison squares his shoulders and tears off his shirt, muscles rippling across his chest, his arms. Sometimes, I can't believe I've ever been brave enough to fight him.

He kicks off his boots and unties his trousers next, proudly letting his cock hang out, hands on his hips as he faces Ulsta; I shield my eyes.

"So... what do you think?" he asks.

She smiles, eyes dropping below his waistline, lips curling in conquest. "I think, Eddison... that you're much more well-endowed than the size of your sword would've had me believe."

She walks past him, hips swinging, her long, auburn hair falling over her shoulders. Then, she runs to the cliff's edge and jumps right in.

We all peer after her, gaping—I hate to think it, but I'm actually impressed.

"Show off," murmurs Eddison.

I shake my head at him. "When are you going to get on with that already?" I take everything off my body but my chains, baring myself to the cool night air. "You two are like fire and ice."

He pouts. "She scares me," he says, his eyes darting toward the water where she's splashing around—she's so far down that her features are slightly blurred from here.

"Yeah, she's awful," I reply, matter-of-factly. "Just get it over with, so we can all move on our with lives."

He scowls at me with his 'you're insufferable' look that I've seen too many times to count.

"*What?* She is!" I say, punching him on the arm. "But sometimes it's even better that way, if you know what I mean…" I think of all the terrible people I've lain with after Sibyl, just to try to feel something again. Temporary solutions but still memorable all the same.

He lifts his eyebrows, considering.

I shrug with a little laugh. "Ready, mate?"

We pound fists in camaraderie, then we both race for the edge.

17

FALL

☼ JASPYR

MY FEET FLY OFF THE EDGE OF THE CLIFF, that momentary freedom better than anything. The rush as I fall is like a high settling in my bones.

For a few seconds, there's nothing before, nothing after, just a timelessness of exhilaration and joy—I would give anything just to stay suspended in it.

The water rushes up to meet me, warm at the top but cold in the center. So cold that it takes my breath away for a moment. Any drunkenness I was feeling earlier is instantly wiped away.

It's deep and heavy. Old water. The coldness of it seeps into my bones as I sink, nothing below me for what seems like miles to stop me from going further. It's so silent, as peaceful as any death I imagine. I think if I open my eyes, I might see straight into another universe.

After I finally slow, my lungs tightening, I start to kick for the surface.

Eddison and I break at the same time.

Rowdy voices and splashing sounds sweep away the quiet so suddenly that I'm insulted; this place was meant to be experienced in utter silence.

I swim away from everyone, floating on my back to let the water muffle my ears. I stare to the cavernous ceiling that seems to blend into a starlit sky, pondering over the wonders, terrors, that might be waiting out there to be found—where does that vile creature hail from? And how can I survive her if she returns again to finish me off?

Worries I've been dutifully ignoring since Eddison collected me on the beach now swarm my mind. I decide that, when this night is done, I won't waste another. I have to try to learn all that I can about the legends of blood-sucking monsters in the Olleb.

After a while, I take my cue to get out and dry off, just as Eddison and Ulsta pair off, kissing wildly in a dark corner of the water; the others are doing jumps and tricks off the elevated ledge at the far end of the Split.

I swim to a rope and make the climb upward, positioning my feet on the wall for extra support. When I get to the top, I tap Kaelan in.

He throws me an obscene gesture with his hand, then runs off the cliff.

"Do hit a rock on the way down," I mutter after him.

I wrap my arms around myself. I'm dripping wet, teeth chattering—the warmth of the water does not stay with me, sucked away by the cool, slick cavern walls at this height.

Not wanting to put my clothes back on wet, I pull Kaelan's cloak over me and conjure a small, enchanted flame. I let it float before me while I wait for Eddison and his friends to tire.

Time passes slowly.

"WHY, THERE YOU ARE, HERO," a familiar voice whispers to me—*in my dreams. In reality?* "I've been looking everywhere for you tonight."

Terror freezes my eyelids shut; I must've dozed off.

Focus, I think. *You survived the war. You can survive anything.*

My muscles go rigid. I gather my magic at the ready and open my eyes.

I find myself on my knees, reaching for Kaelan's sword. There, standing next to my floating flame, is the creature of the night; she presses her foot atop the blade so that I can't lift it.

I sit back on my heels, gazing up at her, Death incarnate. *I thought I'd have more time...*

In the light of the fire and in the shadows of the cavern, moonlight washing down on her, she is something to behold. Gold and silver wrap around her naked body, as if the sun and moon had melted atop her skin to finally dance as one.

She looks around the cavern with a placated expression. Then her eyes cut back to mine. "I can't fathom how *you* could fall asleep in such a nature-governed place." She smiles against the moonlight at her back. "You picked a pretty place to die."

Only now do I realize just how quiet it is... and my single flame has flickered into embers without my focus.

How long was I asleep? Where are the others?

A deep chill settles into my bones with her in my sight— it's as if the old cavern has trapped all the wind, creating an icy tomb for her to leave my body in when she's done with me.

I pull Kaelan's cloak tighter around me, trying to hold some of the warmth in before I die.

Don't go easy, Jaspyr. You've come too far.

The woman, *monster*, jerks her head toward the flame, its firelight skittering across her jewel-like skin.

"Put that thing out. *Now*," she orders.

I curl my lip, my chin lifted to her in defiance. But she has the upper hand.

She hardens her stare; I call my magic back.

"Good," she says in a song-like voice; I grind my teeth together, anticipating the moment she steals away my willpower again. "You're not as daft as I thought."

My nostrils flare, jaw twitching, heart pounding so strongly that I wonder if it will push outside of my chest—the last time I was on my knees in front of someone who held my life in their hands was when I handed over Luna.

I will never freely kneel for a monster again!

I take a deep breath and make to stand, my cloak sweeping open; her ice-hot gaze slowly lifts with me, drinking me in.

I let her look, allowing her to see me for all that I am. *This is my sanctuary, and I will not hide from her or anyone!*

I find my mouth speaking before my brain can talk me out of it. "And you're not as strong-willed as you might've had me believe," I say with misplaced calm.

I try to act unperturbed, even though my fingers shake. And I'm fairly certain that she *can* hear my heartbeat, for her eyes linger on my chest—I wrack my brain for an escape, my gaze darting around.

"Couldn't even leave me alone for one night," I add. "Don't you have better things to do than stalk me?"

She laughs, darkly. "Certainly," she says. "But pity for you, Fate isn't on your side."

Her gaze narrows, presses into mine like gleaming swords.

In a blink of those eyes, she's inches from me, her frost-kissed breath tickling my face. Our lips might touch if I lean forward only slightly.

"I am your end, Jaspyr," she says with vicious calm.

It takes every ounce of strength I can muster to withstand how my name sounds on her tongue, the truth of those words, not to drop to my knees before her again.

I look past her, my breath hitched in my throat as I consider the distance between her, me, and the cliff.

Maybe, she fears water just as much as fire, I consider, a last thread of hope entering my panicked mind. *If I jump, I might stand a chance...*

There's no way I can hold her off with my magic long enough to figure out how to kill her this time. I drank too much, and the coldness of her gaze seems to leach the fire right out of my skin. Besides, she'll be expecting it.

I think of the entrance just behind me, the horses not far down the cliff, but quickly dismiss the idea—I recall how fast she can move. A blink of an eye to me is probably a slow, arduous process to her.

I glance again to the Split at her back. *It's my only chance.*

My power warms me from the inside out, ready to fight for whatever life I have left, the cold-made warrior inside of me breaking back out of the cage I had trapped him in long ago.

"I don't believe in Fate," I say, balling my fists at my side.

Solza ven immito, I think.

Flames grow stealthily in my palms; I blast them in her face with all my strength.

Sparks erupt around her.

She screeches, throwing up her arms. "No!"

My magic lights up the cavern for a blinding moment, the sound of the explosion echoing starkly. But my feet are already pushing past her to the ledge before I can let that thought simmer.

With one swift leap, my cloak fluttering out behind me, the Split swallows me whole. I pray I clear the rocks at the bottom... and that whatever strange magic breathes life into this monster will not allow her to follow into the water.

I glimpse her anguished face as I fall. Her outstretched hand reaches for me past the edge, as if she'd rushed to try to catch me, to yank me back into her claws.

I mimic the gesture Kaelan threw to me earlier as the water rushes up to meet me again, embracing me like an old friend.

18

CLAIM

WHY DID I HESITATE? I scented the fire magic in his hands the moment it sparked. I wanted to see what he might do this time.

But I never thought…

The veil of sparks falls away. I rush to the edge as he soars off.

I try to catch him, to stop him from falling prey to an even worse death than I might've offered him. But I'm too late— Jaspyr disappears beneath the glass-like water, not even realizing that crueler creatures await him there.

He lands with a splash that wipes away the quiet, an eerie crack that reverberates in my ears. Then everything stills once again, the water a giant ripple where he'd vanished.

Vasylina and Miki look up at me, a question on their lips; the idea of sharing him with my sisters, with anyone, makes me flinch.

I slink back into the shadows, hiding the guilt on my face. *Why do I keep toying with him like this? Why can't I just take what I need and be done with this charade?*

Just let the twins take care of him now. It will be much easier this way.

I hear as Jaspyr swims back up, breaking the surface, sucking in a long, greedy breath.

"Who do we have here?" comes Vasylina's voice. "I thought you said that everyone was rounded up in the water."

There's an accusation in her tone—I must be careful not to let them see what he means to me.

And what is that, Eloise?

I bite down on my tongue, unsure of how to respond.

"Oh, he's absolutely delicious," calls Miki in a light, carefree tone. "Why, *aren't* you the little liar, Eloise?" She giggles. "I can see why you would want to keep him for yourself, though. He smells—" She noisily sucks at the air. "*Delectable.*"

A growl rumbles in my throat, but I hold it in. I force myself back to the edge to face them.

"It doesn't matter what she wants," says Vasylina in a delicate voice, her gaze locked on Jaspyr; she's still as stone, a patient lion about to pounce. "She's already lost the game. This one is ours. She can have the scraps after we've selected."

So far, they've only revealed their heads and hands to the prey they rounded up earlier, their bodies hidden beneath the black waters. Their hair floats behind them in a tangled, dark train as they lean on one another, eyes like burning suns.

Their faces and fingers and teeth are all smeared red. And blood splatters the slick, stone walls and tints the old water with a crimson sheen.

A quick look around tells me that a couple of fools tried to escape while I scoped the land area, tried to climb the walls—either the ropes broke of their own accord or my sisters sliced them with their magic, the rough edges frayed and split.

I heard when they fell back to the water with a bone-crunching splash. And I heard how the twins made a show of shredding them, not even caring to feed yet.

No, they came here to play. And now everything is too quiet.

I frown at the wasted life. *These ancient ones have a proclivity for cruelness I can hardly fathom sometimes.*

The unlucky ones—three men and one woman—are corralled with their backs against a low ledge that opens up to the sea, the night sky a blanket behind them, diamonds dotting its tapestry. Their faces have drained of all color. I can see them shivering from here. *It's wise they don't speak.*

Jaspyr floats in the center of it all, his victorious expression now gone, the magic sputtering out of his eyes. He stares stone-faced upon the twins.

What is he thinking? ... How will he fight them? What plan of escape will he try next, this brazen soul?

A voice laughs in my head, darkly. *'Humans can't fight a myrmaid with a gaze set to kill. This one only survived you because you let him.'*

Miki tosses her head back and laughs with it, as if she'd heard. She circles Jaspyr.

"It does seem you have lost, sister... and rather quickly, I'm afraid." She points to him. "He literally *jumped* to escape you."

I shake my head, blinking down at them in bewilderment, counting the nights I've faced him and the equal number of times I let him slip through my fingers. *Three, Eloise! Why?*

I swallow, uncertain.

'Save him,' the voice whispers. *'Take him back. He's yours.'*

Miki wags her finger at Jaspyr, tutting. "Silly boy," she adds. "This is our domain, you know?"

Jaspyr's eyes slightly widen. His gaze flicks up, meeting mine—I hold a finger to my lips.

If he speaks even a single word, it might speed up his death sentence; Vasylina *hates* the sound of human voices. I've seen her rip out her fair share of tongues just to quell a scream.

I grip the ledge, digging my nails into the stone, not even letting myself consider never hearing Jaspyr's haughty, bone-deep, sensual voice again.

Vasylina wades closer—I won't have time to reach him from this far. Any second could be his last.

She reaches out to touch him; he cringes slightly but doesn't try to flee, doesn't speak.

She takes his chin in her hand and tilts his face up, then to both sides, assessing her meal.

He clenches his jaw, never dropping his prideful stare.

"I suppose we can take him off your hands," she states after a moment, eyes boring into his, still clutching his chin, too hard; if she presses any harder...

A growl rumbles in my throat.

She flicks her gaze to mine; I swiftly soften, trying to hide my struggles within, the gluttonous creature I've become in his presence.

Miki offers me an apologetic shrug. "It's alright, Eloise. You can try to play with us another time," she says, resting a hand on Jaspyr's shoulder. "You're clearly still too young to—"

All sense drains from me with both twins closing in. "Don't touch him. He's mine!" I shout.

Miki presses her lips into a firm line, swallowing her words.

"I don't care about your rules," I add in a voice I don't even recognize. "Get your hands off him if you wish to keep them."

I crouch lower, my magic blooming around me like a metallic mist.

"Don't be dramatic, Eloise," says Miki in a low voice, dismissing me with the brush of her hand; she focuses again on Jaspyr, circling him from behind—she sneers up at me. "You'll ruin our fun."

I bare my fangs in a hiss, my magic heating even more, ready to explode.

The corner of Vasylina's lips draws up in a smile that doesn't touch her eyes. She lets go of Jaspyr, then gently pushes Miki back.

"Let's not make unnecessary quarrel," she says to her. "Our sister is yet young. She hasn't learned how to share, and clearly, she's already staked a claim to this one. Let her have him."

Miki pouts. "I suppose that you're right. We did invite her to join our hunt…" She grins at me, a sinister twinkle in her eye; I don't even have a second to be relieved. "On the other hand," she adds too sweetly, "maybe she can stand to learn some manners."

Miki brushes Jaspyr's wet hair away from his neck, revealing the bright blue tattoo that covers his left arm and shoulder, a testimony of reverence for our waters, I decide.

His muscles tense, his breathing heavy. He steels his gaze on me, throat bobbing, eyes watering.

"Bye, beast," he whispers so low I almost missed it.

He closes his eyes as Miki rears back, mouth wide.

"I decide when you die," I utter from some place deep—it's enough of a warning to make my sisters take pause.

My magic shatters out of me. The water erupts around Jaspyr like a protective geyser, hurling my sisters far away from him. They skid across the top of the water like pebbles, landing on opposite sides of the Split.

In one smooth jump, I land on the low ledge.

My nails scrape into the stone like knives, my feet denting the smooth rock upon my landing. Another guttural sound escapes my throat, my magic still a swirl of cold, angry heat around me.

My sisters slowly wade toward me, glowering in disbelief.

"How *dare* you wield your magic against us," says Miki, a mix of shock and anger flashing across her features. "Syrifina will hear of this—"

Vasylina lifts her hand and Miki closes her mouth.

She swims to the ledge, holding my gaze, studying me intently. Then she looks back to Jaspyr, assessing him with new interest—there's nothing between him and her, but at least I'm close enough to dive in and fight if I must.

I keep my protective stance, but, for some reason, I can't bear to look him directly in the eye; Vasylina glances back to me, her brow furrowed, as if sensing my confusion.

"I understand," she speaks after a long moment. She inclines her head toward me. Her expression seems to darken with some thought I cannot place as her gaze slides over Jaspyr again. "He is yours."

Miki makes to retort but one furtive look from Vasylina keeps her mouth shut; a flicker of surprise softens her features.

They nod to each other, comprehending something I do not.

Miki swims forward, glaring at me.

"Fine," she says. "You can have that one all to yourself." She considers the rest of the people lined up against the ledge. "There's plenty to go around."

I stand, swallowing my sigh of relief. I force my eyes to meet Jaspyr's across the water, starting a little as they do.

"Come," I command, finding my voice and loosening my grip on my magic—I can only imagine how terrifying I must look to a human, wielding such power.

Obediently, he swims toward me, past Miki and Vasylina, and the other humans who part to make space on the ledge, muttering in fear; the hard lines in his face soften subtly with relief. His heart rate begins to slow.

I look down on him as he plants his palms on the stone and heaves himself up. Water drips off his skin and combs through his hair; his cloak is surely at the bottom of this lake by now.

I step away to give him room.

He sits, back turned to me, keeping one eye on the twins. He clutches his knees and waits.

His body glitters with water, his back a canvas of glorious strength—it's the first time I've gotten a good look at him from behind.

Different from the bright, hopefulness of the ocean wave tattooed on his arm, the deep, dark stems of a blazing hot fire have been inked on his back, following the ridges of his muscle. Black smoke and reddish-golden flames shimmer in my eyes.

I'm momentarily stunned, caught in his spell once again.

The twins resume circling their remaining prey, leaving me to Jaspyr.

"What should we do with the girl?" asks Miki, concerned. "I didn't scent a female when we targeted them…"

"How could we have?" replies Vasylina in an angered tone. "With the others' stink all over her." She shakes her head, sincerely. "Pity."

"*Please*," the woman suddenly speaks; I still, eyes on Vasylina. "I want to live!"

She bravely swims away from the wall; the men gasp, clinging to it, watching her in shock.

"I… I will serve you," she stutters in desperation, looking between Vasylina and Miki; she nods to herself. "Yes, great goddesses of the water, please, just take me with you, away from here. And I will serve you forever."

Vasylina's eyes melt into a smile as she contemplates her with a curious expression. "Forever is a long time," she replies.

My mouth falls open as I realize what she's considering.

"Ulsta…" gasps another, looking as if he might chase after her. He is vast for a man, with skin as dark as mine and a voice as deep as our waters.

"Eddison, don't!" snaps Jaspyr in a low warning.

He scoots slightly forward, directly behind him, and grabs him by the arm to yank him back.

Brave, I think.

Or foolish? So very foolish, this one.

Eddison doesn't fight him. His expression is contorted in defeat as they meet each other's eyes; Jaspyr shakes his head and keeps a strong grip on his arm.

I lift my eyebrow, watching them both closely, as are Vasylina and Miki.

One whiff of Eddison tells me that he and my mark are close—and it's familiar to me. One of metals and sweat and nature.

I recognize it as plain as night. It had been all over Jaspyr's shop.

Vasylina makes toward them both; Jaspyr notes the movement. His eyes widen, animalistic, a flicker of magic rising again in his gaze.

Panic rushes through me—not even I can save him if he tries to attack Vasylina with his fire.

"She's pretty," I say, loudly, to Vasylina; I step forward, one leg half in front of Jaspyr. "And courageous. She might make a fine addition to our family…"

Vasylina turns her attention back to Ulsta and away from Jaspyr and Eddison.

"I'll be the judge of that," she says, coolly. She circles her.

Ulsta shivers but holds her head high. "I promise to serve you," she says again.

Vasylina merely looks at her and she falls silent. She smiles, cocking her head to the side, considering.

In an even tone, her eyes still on Ulsta, she addresses her twin. "What do you think? Shall we grant her a kiss?"

Miki's eyes glow in pure excitement.

"*Transformed by a kiss*," she says, almost humming. "*If the magic deigns to wish.*" She taps on her lip, thinking, a glance to all the males. "By the company she keeps, she could probably use some guidance..." Then she claps her hands; I flinch. "I say, yes!"

Vasylina inclines her head. "She's all yours, then, sister."

Miki swims right up to Ulsta—and plants a blood-red kiss on her lips.

Myr magic takes hold of her, the water bubbling up beneath her in an icy-blue cloud. It gradually encases her from below, the enchantment expanding to cover her head until she's fully concealed, just a blurred silhouette within any icy shell that floats frozen in time.

Inside, ancient magic is slowly seeping into her veins, seeking to root.

The memory of my humanity being stripped away, the sudden, powerful shift in my body and mind—it all comes back to me now in a glorious wave.

I've never seen another's transformation occur...

You have no idea the life ahead of you, Ulsta, I think as the beautiful magic pours into her soul.

I pray she can accept it, for I recall that internal struggle like it was yesterday, the most important battle I've ever won.

The cave seems to hold its breath, the air and wind stilling...

The shell begins to dissolve in a rain, revealing her head, her neck, her torso. Ulsta's lifeblood—a blue as dark as the lake around her—begins to bloom on her skin.

She did it! I think, chewing on my lip.

The transformation is nearly complete.

What type of tail will she boast? I wonder, excitedly. *What type of powers will she exhibit?*

I walk closer to the edge, forgetting Jaspyr for a brief moment, eager to meet our new sister.

Such power you'll radiate when this is done! I'll teach you everything.

And I won't be the youngest anymore…

I beam brightly, a song of welcome impatiently waiting on my tongue for her arrival.

Her eyes open, scorching silver; I start to sing.

Vasylina swipes her nails across her neck—Ulsta's head rolls off her body, a silent scream frozen on her lips.

Her blood splatters me; my song dies in my throat as I taste it.

Miki screeches, her hands flying over her mouth. "What did you *do?*" she wails.

Eddison cries out, too, his voice shaking me out of my stupor; Jaspyr falls into my legs, wiping Ulsta's blood from his face.

The transformational magic splashes away into nothing, dissolving into the dark waters as if it had never been; Ulsta's headless torso sinks alongside it.

Vasylina reaches for her floating head. She holds it up, the auburn hair skimming the water. She squints, searching for any hint of magic in Ulsta's deadened eyes.

When she doesn't find it, she nods to herself and says, "Good."

Everyone stares at her in disbelief.

"For the Sea's sake!" Miki turns on her sister, power radiating from her. "I thought we had an agreement?"

I sneer, my lips curling over my fangs. But I keep my mouth shut.

"We did…" says Vasylina, carefully choosing her words, "but then it occurred to me that I'd rather not spend the next fifty years babysitting," she tosses me a glare, "*nor* explaining to Syrifina why we turned someone without her permission. She'd never let us hear the end of it." She softens, looking shockingly apologetic. "Forgive me, Miki, I shouldn't have even suggested this."

Miki glowers in her direction, arms crossed. Some of her magic dissipates.

Vasylina lets Ulsta's head slip from her fingers, the water taking it into its depths. She swims up to her sister and embraces her.

"Forgive me," she says again, kissing her on the cheek; her eyes dart to the remaining humans. "And you can have first pick."

Miki shimmies out of her reach, perusing her choices with a scowl on her face. "You bet your tail, I can," she mutters.

Vasylina looks up, noting my soured expression. "Is there something you'd like to say, little sister?"

"That was… unexpected," I say with due caution, keeping my true thoughts to myself—*brutal, gruesome, vicious, even for you, Vasylina*. "I've never seen such a thing." That part is true—it was unnerving to witness such wonderous magic be so violently ended. "Why not at least beg Syrifina's pardon?"

Miki scoffs; Vasylina's eyes rake me up and down. "One does not *beg* Mother for anything," she says, "unless it's for mercy."

I balk, my lips forming a thin line—I think of the woman I fed on two nights ago, and the fisherman from yesterday; I look down to Jaspyr knowing that I will drink him, too, despite the Moon's laws.

Vasylina swims closer to me. "If Syrifina gets word of this, you'll have me to deal with," she says, sternly. "Don't make me regret my invitation to you…"

I offer a curt nod. "I won't utter a word of this night," I say, matching the coolness in her voice. "You can be certain. I have other things to worry over."

She snorts, glancing to my feet where Jaspyr lies.

"Indeed." There's a hint of challenge in her tone. "You do look… hungry, Eloise."

A faint smirk crosses her lips, and I find myself wishing that I could read minds as well as some of my elders can.

"As am I." Her gaze drops to Eddison.

Jaspyr tenses; I curl my fingers over his shoulder. I can tell by the way his heart rate quickens that he might do something foolish should I let him go.

Vasylina swims so close to the large human that he tries to make himself smaller, physically sucking in his chest and stomach as if he might be able to melt into the stone at his back.

He draws in a breath, turning his cheek to the side; her gaze is pinned on the throbbing vein in his neck.

"*Eddison,*" utters Jaspyr so quietly that it pains me—I've never heard such a note of fear in his voice before. In anyone's… he's shaking.

"No, not that one," I snap, suddenly pushing Jaspyr aside and crouching down behind Eddison—I don't know why I risk challenging my sister when I have what I want, but I place my hand firm against his chest, claiming him, too. "I want them both."

I nuzzle my chin into his neck.

He does smell good…

Miki hisses. "Why, you greedy little thing. You can drink only one."

"That's not what I meant."

Vasylina's eyes widen for a moment, just a fraction; she can actually be surprised.

"Why do you want him, then?" she asks me in a serious tone.

"I…" I clear my throat, collecting my thoughts. "This one and the other," I nod to Jaspyr, "seem to have a strong kinship. I can smell them all over each other."

"People don't come in pairs," drawls Miki, frowning at me.

"And why not?" My voice leaves me in a sensual, hungry hum. A salacious grin widens across my face. "Didn't you say this was better as a group activity?"

Miki beams at me. "Why, Eloise, you can be fun after all," she says—some of her earlier joy starts to return.

Vasylina laughs, then she drags her tongue along Eddison's neck. "I don't know," she says, hesitant. "He's so thick... and tasty."

I can feel the cold bumps crawling up his skin as he cringes away from her.

"Let me have him too, *please*," I say, determined.

I flutter my eyelids, hoping she doesn't see the lie glittering behind them—I don't want Jaspyr whimpering over his friend when I'm *finally* ready to kill him. I want the strong, virile man with misplaced hope gleaming in his eyes and fire in his palms up until the very end.

'*Liar*,' someone whispers—but it isn't the Moon and it isn't the Sea, so I ignore them.

"You both were right," I add, hurriedly. "It's been too much time since I let loose during a landwalk. I want to play the game, and I want them *both* to play with me."

After an excruciating, long moment, she nods her consent. "Fine, you may have this one, too, for your pleasures," she says.

"Good for you," says Miki, making her selection. "Indulge in dessert with your supper for once."

I return a tight smile.

Jaspyr hauls Eddison out of the water with haste, both of them scurrying behind me as if I had just saved their lives.

Vasylina jerks her head to the remaining round-up. "There's one for each of us left. Let's take them and feed down below. It's clear that Eloise needs her space tonight."

Miki nods. "*Fine.* I don't really feel like playing now anyway." She narrows her eyes at Vasylina, and I know they'll be bickering about this night for a long time to come. "Which one do you want, then?" she asks, musing over the last two males. "I can't decide."

One man finally lets his voice be heard, pleading for help to Jaspyr and Eddison. The sound is wretched, like nails on stone.

Vasylina pounces on him, ripping into his throat with her teeth.

"Well, alright then…" says Miki.

She pins a bored gaze on the last one, then takes him and melts into the water without another word. His gurgled scream is a ghost-like echo in the cavern when she's gone.

"Take care not to play *too* much with your food, Eloise," says Vasylina, licking her lips, the man still writhing in her grasp; her gaze goes glassy, a dazed smile dancing on her lips. "It won't do you any good to prolong the inevitable."

I stagger backward a step, my voice catching in my throat. *Could she know?*

She grins widely at me, flashing her fangs. Then she dives down beneath the water with her kill.

19

FEAST

"WHERE... WHERE DID THEY TAKE THEM?" asks Eddison, reaching for me, peering toward the water with a haunted look on his face.

"I don't know," I reply in a hushed voice, eyes locked on the beast; I stand, placing Eddison behind me. "*Eloise?*"

Her name is like liquid velvet on my tongue. I had been wanting to say it aloud ever since I heard the other monsters speak it earlier.

She whirls toward me, cocking her head to the side with something like confusion, as if contemplating why she fought for us at all.

It's clear to me—she's just like every other territorial animal.

But at least now, it would be two to one. I find myself hoping that I can escape her yet again.

"That is your name, isn't it?" I speak carefully, stalling while I consider our options. "It's quite an elegant name for a beast."

Her fangs press from between her lips. She lets out a loud hiss.

"Jaspyr, what are you doing?" whispers Eddison, clinging to me. "Don't antagonize it."

She laughs.

"I suppose it's only fair that you know mine before I kill you… Jaspyr," she replies with a smile; her gaze shifts down to Eddison, who's cowering at my feet. "Now, who might this one be? What is he to you?"

Her eyes flare with magic—if I didn't know any better, I might think she is jealous.

"He's my family," I say without hesitation.

"Family?" Her brow furrows as she searches for any hint of semblance between us.

"Yes," I say, firmly. "Ever since we were children. His mother took me in after my parents passed." I rest my hand on his shoulder, hoping he can sense the heat of my power, a reminder that he still has magic, too—if there's any time to acknowledge it, it's now. "If not for him, I wouldn't have the life I do now."

She blinks, uninterested. "How generous."

She considers Eddison, softening somewhat.

"It's not every day people show such kindness to those who are helpless…" she adds.

She sounds so strangely sincere that it takes me aback.

"Is that why you saved us from the others?" I ask, trying to draw her attention away from him and back on me—I find I don't like those gold-pressed eyes looking anywhere else.

But she's fixated on him for some reason.

"Saved you?" she says, her gaze still lingering on my friend. Then it snaps up to meet mine; I jerk back, nearly tripping over Eddison. "I didn't *save* you from anything… except from my sisters wasting your blood with their slovenly methods."

Eloise is suddenly standing next to me, and all the hairs

rise on my skin; Eddison whimpers and scoots as far away as he can on the ledge. "Jaspyr..." he says.

I focus on Eloise, the apex predator unlike I've ever known, as she wraps a gentle hand around my elbow.

She draws me closer, leaning in to whisper in my ear. I shiver from her touch, savor it a little.

"I simply don't like to share," she says, "and I'd rather not have to lick you from off the walls." She drags her tongue along the ridge of my shoulder. "What a waste that would be."

I fidget, biting down on my bottom lip.

Once again, I'm faced with how utterly naked I am, my entirety bared to a monster who seeks to feast on my flesh. Yet, no matter the beast that she is or the bloodshed around me, I can't seem to help how my body reacts to her closeness. How it only craves for more...

Her hand on my arm now arouses something primal in me. And the wetness of her tongue on my skin is like torture. Even just the sound of her voice—every word spoken in a firm command yet somehow soft and sensual—makes me want to drive *my* tongue into her mouth.

I want to taste her.

She steps away and looks me in the eye.

"Your time is up now, Jaspyr," she says, no hint of playfulness in her expression.

Magic gathers in my chest as I prepare to fight; she takes a defensive stance.

Then I look past her, to the water that is her playground, and up toward the land where she proudly stalks—I see no way out for myself now that's she developed a taste for me.

But, maybe, she can be convinced to let Eddison go free.

She spared him from the cruelty of the others; for what reason, I don't know. And she doesn't bother with him now.

Maybe I can give Eddison a fighting chance with my final words.

"Fine," I say—she blinks back at me, confused, as my magic drifts away from my eyes. "You can have me. I won't fight you anymore."

"What?" says Eddison, tears in his voice. "Jaspyr, no—"

"It's going to be alright, brother," I say, gesturing for him to be quiet; I stay facing Eloise, not taking my eyes off her. "Trust me."

He whimpers from behind me, but doesn't speak further.

"Why the change of heart?" says Eloise. "Why don't you fight?"

I step toward her, hands raised.

"Please, let Eddison go free. He has no quarrel with you or your kind. I'm the one you came for, aren't I? I'm the one you want. Take me."

I stand as tall as can be, yet even though I clear her by a full head, her presence still seems to overpower me.

"*Please?*" she purrs, her lips curving into a smile. She closes the distance between us. "I like the sound of that coming from your mouth." She looks me up and down. "I thought you were a worthy opponent before, for a human but now…" She tilts her chin toward me, and my gaze sinks into hers, the weight of her power overwhelming. "Say it again."

I resist the urge to spit in her face and curse her wicked name.

"Please," I say through gritted teeth, stomping down on my magic as it flares up in my core—for Eddison. "Please, let him live. Take me instead."

She smiles, showing all her teeth, her tongue running along the tips of her fangs.

"I don't plan to make the same mistake that I did on the first night I found you," she replies after a moment, in a cold but distant voice; her gaze flicks to Eddison. "Although, he does smell good… familiar."

My brow furrows with so many questions, but there's a

twinge of relief in my chest that he may yet survive this after all… I guess I'll never know.

I look over my shoulder. "Goodbye, brother," I say to Eddison.

He's leaning in the Doorway to the Sea, as if he'd been looking for a way to climb down. He shakes his head at me, tears in his eyes. But before he can reply, the most beautiful sound fills the cavern, a song echoing within the old stone.

I crouch and cover my ears with my hands, waiting for the realization that I no longer have control of my body, but it never comes…

Slowly, I stand, finding Eddison frozen, like a statue placed in front of the doorway with the sky at his back. His eyes are wide in terror, darting back and forth, his hand outstretched toward mine.

"What did you do to him?" I yell, my magic bursting awake.

"I sang him a lullaby," she replies with a little laugh, "to help him relax while I enjoy you." Her song is still an eerie echo in the air. "It'll be nice to have an audience for a change." She shrugs. "My sisters are right. It's good to switch things up now and again. Especially with so much… time ahead."

She circles me like a shark.

I snarl back at her. "Let him go!"

She cocks her head with a mocking pout.

"Oh, don't look so surprised, Jaspyr. You should be worrying about yourself. I'll make his death quick, but yours…" I stiffen; she licks her lips. "And I have to say, I'm disappointed that you'd hand your life over to me willingly in the first place. You have a warrior's build," she adds, "so I'm certain I'm not the first enemy you've faced." She raises an eyebrow. "Did you *really* think I would let him live? Having seen all that he's seen?"

She smiles, incredulously.

"I have no loyalty to humans, and I haven't promised you a thing."

I frown. *It was worth a try.*

I gather my fire in my palms.

Her smile falters, a shadow flickering over her expression. "I should've never let you go," she says in a low voice.

"Why did you?"

She knocks me to the ground so fast that I don't see it coming.

My fires fizzle out. I crawl away from her, on my back, keeping my gaze locked to hers, calling to my magic—it's weak tonight, hardly cooperative, for how much I drank and how little sleep I've gotten in the last few days.

"*Ah, ah, ah.*" She wags her finger at me. "You told me you wouldn't fight anymore," she says, frowning. "Are you not a man of your word, hero?"

"About as honorable as you!" I retort.

My fires grow once more, the heat resting deliciously in my palms.

Her bare foot crushes my left wrist. I grit my teeth against the pain but hold tight to my flames.

She smirks, pressing down harder until I scream.

Eddison makes a strained sound from his throat to let me know he's there, with me until the end.

Guilt twists in my chest, but I know there's nothing I could've done to prevent any of this… except for maybe die three nights ago.

With a roar of anger, my magic floats away.

She releases her foot, crouching down to my eye level.

I sigh in relief, though it's short-lived.

"Extraordinary…" she says as my heated gaze cools to normal—I glower back at her, willing my magic to return, but all I'm met with is an emptiness in my gut. "I've never seen someone with two different eyes."

She leans closer, her eyes boring into mine so hard that I think she can see straight into my soul; I know she's fixated on the halo of color around my left pupil. I don't dare to blink, lest I miss the moment she steals my life away.

"It's like all the colors of the brightest sea in one," she adds, awestruck, "like a ring of sparkling emerald." She grips my face, turning my head from side to side to get a better look; it still stings from where her sister held my jaw. "Why does your right eye not have this marking?"

"Because," I say, simmering, wanting to poke *her eyes* out, "when the sea granted me a second chance at life, it only kissed one vein."

She starts, releasing her grip; I massage my jaw.

"*You* have been granted a gift from the Sea?" she utters, blinking several times, as if to see me clearly.

I lift my left arm, unsure why I interest her so. But I'll take all the extra time I can get. "Not gift," I say. "*Life.*"

She gently takes my arm in her hands, turning it over as if it were precious glass. "How had I not noticed before?"

She follows the sparkling silver vein that runs along my arm, my heart, my neck.

"Probably because I covered the entire thing in ink, to hide it," I reply. "The King doesn't take too kindly to magic in this era, even if healing."

"How?" she asks, transfixed.

I find myself rambling, stalling the death sentence she's granted me.

"I woke up in the low tide with it on my arm, after…" I clear my throat, lowering my voice, "after taking a blade to my wrist."

Her grip on my arm tightens, her thumb sliding over the ridged scar left by the unfortunate choices of my past self.

The memory makes my heart constrict, all the remorse and sorrow that had led to that moment in the first place hitting me like a flail; I push it away, bury it deep down, as I've been re-teaching myself how to do since that very night.

"I knew I was granted another chance at this life, and I never wanted to forget that I was strong enough, worthy enough to seize it."

I take a deep breath, looking to my tattoo, letting myself feel everything that it means to me, content in this moment, if it's the last thing I ever see.

"The Sea breathed life back into me after I bled out and wept in her waters," I continue, wanting to tell the full story; Eddison has never heard it—I hope he can understand and forgive my poor behavior over these last years. "An offering I suppose, though I didn't realize it at the time…"

Eloise returns a faint nod.

"When I was mended, I returned to my craft. I painted the Sea the way I felt her in my soul, to honor her." I twist my arm around, noting the elegant lines, the soft yet vibrant colors knitted to deep, rich black. "Something strong, resilient. To be feared yet worshiped, for she is an old god, I believe—"

"Goddess," Eloise, corrects, sharply.

Her voice draws me out of my memory. I clear my throat.

"Goddess," I say in a hushed whisper, taking in all of her.

She frowns, eager for the end. "Go on."

"I…" I shrug, realizing there's no point in dragging this on. My story is done. "And that's it," I say. "After the Sea touched me, she left me changed. That's what you see in my left pupil."

"Fascinating," says Eloise, inspecting the silver vein even closer; her eyes slash to mine. "In my world, we call it life-blood."

She takes my finger and slowly guides it along one of the soft flowing lines that decorate her body, a silver strand that starts at the nape of her neck and goes all the way to the center of her stomach—all the willpower in the world wouldn't have been enough to keep my cock from twitching.

It draws a seductive smile from her, intent flashing in her eyes.

Then she brings my wrist to her mouth and bites.

I don't bother to struggle—the pain is subtle, momentary, then it just feels... intensely good.

She sucks, just a small taste that she seems to savor when she lets go. Then she holds my wrist out for us both to watch as two bright crimson drops pool atop my white skin.

"Don't ever waste your blood again," she says, her voice deadly. "It's more precious than you know."

"I won't," I say in a daze, a spark running through me from where her teeth have just been.

She sits back on her haunches in front of me, and lets go of my hand.

"Do you want me, hero," she asks in a voice that makes my throat dry, "before you die? The way men want in your world... I can offer you that."

"I... I..." I swallow my words, knowing they will betray my better judgment if I answer.

She seems to hear them anyway.

"It's a rare occasion that I grant a man such an honor when I—"

Hunt, but she doesn't say it.

She looks at me inquisitively, continuing, "I don't know why, but I want you, Jaspyr." She walks her hand up my thigh, making me harden even more. "In all the ways I can have you."

I can't help the huff of laughter that comes out of me, my voice deep and heated. "Are you asking for my consent?"

I wait for her to say she's joking, just toying with her prey. But if this is how she plays... it's not a bad way to go out.

"It would be terribly grim if both parties weren't pleased," she replies, evenly—though I can see a new kind of hunger for me glinting in her eyes, "and I'm not *such* a monster to force that choice from you." She smiles with a little shrug. "You will die either way."

"How benevolent you are." I purse my lips. "I wonder, where was such decorum when you were feasting on my neck last night?"

She sinks her teeth into my thigh, sucking at the fat vein, right next to the crevice of my hip, my groin—I gasp in shock, then pleasure strikes through me, my cock growing to its full length.

She moans when she pulls away, eyes twinkling, my blood on her lips; she smacks them. "I don't ask permission to eat."

Her face is eye level with my manhood, so close that I can feel her cold breath on my sensitive skin; it shudders again.

Traitor, I think.

"I'll ask you one more time," she says, her voice low, hopeful. "Do you want me, hero?"

I frown, trying to make sense of the emotions flowing through me, her enticing offer and all the terrifying moments before—I hid behind a flaming wall of fire to avoid her. And I literally threw myself *off a cliff* to escape this monster's touch.

But gods, do I want to bury myself inside her and discover all that she is.

An incessant, voracious voice inside my head urges me to draw her closer. To delve into this adventure while I still have a life to live.

I stare at her, desperate to fill her up, to taste this incredible being. Since the first moment I laid eyes on Eloise, I have *wanted* her in every way. I loathe that I do, for she's the greatest villain I have ever known, and yet...

"Yes," I say, my words raw with desire, decisive, a steady sword thrusting into its opponent for the kill; the sound of it frightens even myself.

She smiles, her bloodstained teeth and lips nearly grazing my sensitive skin. My hips arc slightly toward her. Then she carefully crawls over me, letting my cock slip and squeeze between her tender breasts on the way.

I bite down on a soft moan as her face, her lips, her eyes mirror mine.

"How much?" she asks, parting her perfect lips, speaking with her perfect voice.

"Intolerably," I say, my voice hoarse.

Her hair brushes my cheeks, my chest. "Even knowing that you're doomed to die by my hand?" She gently kisses my neck. "My mouth?"

"I was doomed long ago, been dead all this time," I say, a savage need twisting in my core; I move to brush a stray strand of hair from her face, studying it, wondering what it is about her that makes me so unhinged. "Pleasure, pain... I don't remember the difference."

Her eyes search mine.

I don't know what compels me, but I wrap my hand around her neck and draw her in for a kiss—Eddison gasps from behind us, but I don't care. I sink into her lips, our tongues slick and greedy to taste one another.

For a split second, I consider Ulsta, how that terrible twin kissed her, too, transforming her into something more. Before...

I wonder.

But Eloise pulls away, and I remain as I was—mortally transfixed on her.

I let out a heavy sigh and relax back on the ground. "Vicious, beast."

She lets out a low laugh. "I've been called worse things."

Then she drags her hand down my middle, all the way to my groin. I draw a breath as her fingers wrap around me, my hardness slipping against the tight squeeze of her palm—I suppose part of me didn't really believe the offer anyway.

"Pain and pleasure, indeed." She hums with delight, noting my surprise. "If the Sea deemed you worthy of life, then I'll make sure your last night truly counts."

She squeezes harder and I grit my teeth, hungrier for her than anyone I have ever been with before.

A surge of excitement shudders through me as her mouth meets my chest, my stomach, her tongue exploring every crevice of muscle until it finds the silky soft peak erected and ready for her at the bottom.

"Don't worry, I won't bite this," she says, peering at me. She lightly licks it. "*Mmm…* are you ready for me?"

I don't speak, my gaze floating to the ceiling. The stalactites suddenly look very much like teeth, and the night sky beyond threatens to swallow me.

Her hand finds my shaft again and she squeezes, this time hard.

I moan, loudly. I jerk up to look at her.

"Eyes on me," she says, an inescapable demand. Her voice is a sensual growl that makes all my senses vanish like smoke on the wind.

I will never escape you, I think. *I don't want…*

All I see is her. All I need is her. There is no past. No future—there's only Eloise.

"I asked you a question," she says again, holding my life in her hands. *Take it*, I think. "Are you ready?" Her voice turns sweet, delicate, just as excited and eager as I am to see what's in store next.

I nod, words escaping me.

She raises an eyebrow. "Suddenly so quiet…" A smirk plays on her lips. "I want to hear you *say it*." And I know what she means.

Vicious, terrible, beast.

I burn my gaze into hers.

"Please," I speak in a deep, feral tone. "Please, Eloise, take me." I might explode in her hand if she keeps toying with me like this. "I'm more than ready for you. Don't torture me on my deathbed."

I've never begged before, and yet, it feels like an easy choice now.

She hums in laughter, loosening her grip on me. "You haven't begun to know torture…"

Then she wraps her mouth around me and pulls me into her throat, her teeth grazing me on the way back out. My mind blurs as she sucks me over and over, working me like an instrument with her tongue, her hands.

I let out a groan, a growl that matches her beastly moans and push her away before I burst in her mouth.

"You've had your fun," I say with gritted teeth.

I grab her by the arms and pull her up on top of me—if this is going to be my last time with a woman, or the likes of one, I'm not going to make it quick.

She lets me, matching her impossible strength to mine.

I slightly ponder over the grandness of her power as my cock slides against her center, desperate to devour it.

Her lifeblood, as she called it, glows ferociously.

Before I meet her entrance, she steels herself on top of me, an unmovable force.

"Patience, Jaspyr," she says. "Why rush to the end? I pity the women who've suffered you." She squeezes; my breath hitches. "And *you* will suffer if I don't enjoy myself."

I know how strong she can be if she wants—I have no chance of moving her anywhere unless I play by her rules. I concede to her ruthless game where only she can win.

"Then let me show you what I can do," I say with slight desperation. My fingers find her thighs, digging in, vainly trying to press her closer to me. "*Please*, Eloise, I can't take this anymore." The words tumble out of my mouth with more truth than I care to unravel.

I physically cannot endure her naked body on top of mine much longer without going mad. It's all I can do to not absolutely unleash myself on her, for I know it would be futile—she's the one in control. She decides what we do.

Our eyes meet; she softens, her expression twisted with something I can't place.

She leans her body across mine. "Careful what you wish for, Jaspyr," she says in my ear.

She bites my neck and sucks, sliding, slowly, *so slowly*, on top of me. We both sigh as one. Then she thrusts her head back with a moan of pleasure, the moon shining down on us, melding us together.

She rolls her hips, back and forth, grinding herself closer, eating all of me up. It's like she can't get enough, can't take me deeper, even though the cold-hot tightness of her core surrounds me completely.

Her nails slide across my chest, fingers intertwining my hair, clawing for— "*More*," she commands, as we move as one.

Our moans entwine us in the bliss, both of us wild. Our voices echo across the cavern walls, our skin slick against one another, with blood and sweat.

I think lesser men may have died, their hearts seizing with too much excitement, after getting such a taste of Eloise.

She's unlike anyone else that ever was or ever would be. And despite my experience, even I'm not arrogant enough to think that I can survive her for much longer.

All I know for certain is that this moment is worth whatever happens next.

"EASE NOW," SHE SAYS AFTER A TIME, her voice dripping with satisfaction—my mind had vanished into an easy oblivion that I can barely draw out of.

She presses her hand to my chest as she slows, rolling her hips across me in long, drawn-out movements. She can sense my oncoming release, and I can tell by the gleam in her eye that she's close, too.

My breath becomes haggard. I groan, deeply, to try and calm myself. It sends her lips curling.

My eyes strain at her impossible beauty under the moon's rays, her dark, luscious skin that appears like a starry night given life. I reach up to touch anything I can—her neck, breasts, hips, backside—greedily, needing to feel all of her still.

"You only rush death," she reminds me, sweetly; she pins my arms to my side and stops moving. "Now more than ever you should aim to take your time to please me... for as *long* as you can."

True torture, I think, scowling. If only I had a way to kill her after this—that's the only thing that could make this better.

"I don't need threats to ensure my lovers have an experience to *die* for," I say, matching her arrogant tone. "I always aim to please. You would know better of it if you were brave enough to relinquish control."

She hisses, squeezing her inner thighs until I grimace; I harden even more.

"True control doesn't require bravery," she snaps—then her teeth find me again, momentarily, and I realize how dizzy I am. "And huntresses do not relinquish anything to their prey, *ever*."

With that, she slides off me, a gleam in her eye.

A low rumble sounds in my throat—I can't tell the difference between how much I loathe her and want to devour her in this moment; everything jumbles into one.

"But, please, hero," she adds with a blood-red smile. "Humor me before you and your friend both die."

Eddison flows back into my mind with a stab of guilt. I don't even want to consider how this must look to him, my betrayal... but it's too late now.

It doesn't matter. We're both dead anyway. Unless...

My thoughts darken, and all I see is her sinister, seductive challenge; I remember that it can't be a game without two competitors.

One last idea tickles my brain.

I grab her hips and make to throw her onto her back; she lets me.

The stone slab does nothing to her, whereas my skin is raw—she laughs at the anger flaring in my eyes, my magic ignited by the passion roaring in my veins.

Solza ven immito! My fingers intertwine with the pink flame.

I don't give her time to command me otherwise—I press my firelit hands into the backs of her thighs and slide my tongue from her belly button all the way to her wet center, following a silver strand of lifeblood.

I moan into her openness, burying myself there, working over her most sensitive parts with an expertise gained in the aftermath of my once beautiful life.

She's somehow cold and burning hot, not like any woman I've joined with before. She's so much better—I feast and feast on Eloise until I feel her body tense with ecstasy, pausing only when I'm sure she's on the precipice of release.

"What is it?" she bites at me, pushing up to her forearms and baring her fangs. "Why did you stop?"

She looks at me with such irritation that I think she's surely contemplating crushing my skull between her thighs.

"You will *truly* come to know the beast in me if you prove a tease, Jaspyr Tayshin."

My laughter rumbles over her body in a gentle vibration. Just seeing her want me so badly is enough to keep me hard… and keep me firm in my next move.

"I'm only giving you the same courtesy you've shown me tonight," I say. My eyes narrow at hers, my voice thickening. "If you want to play, then let's play for real."

"Say what you mean, or die without your *courtesy* attached to your body." My cock shudders beneath her—in fear or excitement, I'm not sure which. "I shall keep it as a prize for putting up with your mouth."

"That sharp tongue of yours nearly matches your bite, you know?" I rub at my tender neck, and try not to note all the spots of my body where trickles of crimson show. "Nearly…"

"Just wait," she says, displaying her fangs and curling her fingers around my arms.

Now or never, Jaspyr, a voice warns.

"You like games, so let's play this," I say, quickly but casually, before she can lose interest in me. "I'll prove to you that I can give you release not once but *twice* tonight." I flash her a sheepish grin. "If I do, then you let us live to see another day." I hold up two fingers. "Two times, two lives."

"A wager?" she asks, tasting the idea. Something lights in her eyes.

"A *promise*," I say, smoothly, pushing the hair from my eyes—I caress my tongue between her legs until she slightly shudders. Then I press my fingers inside of her just to show her that I'm serious.

She bites down on a moan.

"And what do I get if you lose?" She gently presses me away from her with her foot—I grab it, licking the arch of her heel until her toes curl.

"I don't care *what* you are, blood-drinker," I say, sliding my hand up her leg. "As long as you ache between your legs the same way humans do, then I will not lose."

"We'll see about that." Her gaze is a quiet challenge. "And if you lose," she adds, softly, "I'll kill you both, just as slow and meticulous as you should've been."

"You foul creature," I say, grabbing her with the entirety of my palm, smothering that openness like a smoldering fire—my fingers slip in, searching.

Eloise moans, grabbing my wrist to try to force me closer; I resist.

She lets me resist. "Do we have a deal?" I ask.

She looks amused.

I stare down at her. The mocking smile on her face makes my insides rage so much that I'm sure she can see my face turn crimson. Hatred burns in my gaze—I wonder if she can see it, *feel*, my fire sweltering there.

"I will destroy you," I say, evenly. "If you promise me we can live to see the sunrise, then I promise that I'll devastate you this night, twofold."

A dual promise, I think. *If I survive her, I will find a way to kill her the next time she comes for me. I swear it.*

Eloise presses her lips to mine so hard that I feel as if she might suck all the breath from my body. I let her, I lean in—our mouths and tongues greedily explore each other with a ferocity unlike I have ever experienced in a kiss before.

"*Ah.*" I hiss through my teeth, suddenly tasting my own blood.

"You may yet…" she says in a dazed voice, inclining her head to mine. "Alright, Jaspyr, I promise. Let's play your game."

I grin—finally I have the upper hand.

Her feline gaze steadies on me—I slowly press into her again, so excruciatingly slow that I can feel her contract and open around me over and over, trying to coax me in deeper.

Her lips press into a firm line.

"Say please," I demand, my voice a guttural sound; I nibble on the shell of her ear.

Her body arcs toward mine, as if my words had sent a jolt of electricity through her spine.

"Jaspyr, you monstrous man…" She hesitates a moment, then says, "Please."

THE NIGHT BLURS INTO DAY, just as Eloise and I blended as one. Only at the crest of sunrise does she peel herself off me to go.

"Stay," I find myself saying as she stands at the edge of the water. I can barely lift my head for the state of bliss and blood loss I'm in—all I know is that I don't want her to leave.

For the moment she does, our war will begin.

She flashes me a heady smile, as if she too is drunk on our union.

"Don't worry, hero," she says in a light tone. "You won't get to miss me long. Our deal was *one* day, one sunrise." She holds up a taunting finger that I just want to suck. "I'll be looking for you again at sundown to finish what we started."

I tense, thinking it foolish of me to have not phrased our bargain more carefully. *I wish I had more time to prepare.*

"I'll be waiting," I say, meaning every word.

She turns away from me and dives into the water.

I rush to the edge, desperate to see where she swims off to—her sisters seemed to just melt away into the darkness of the deep waters, the same way they arrived.

I can't even fathom what landmark is nearby that my people haven't discovered yet. What place could shelter such a creature?

I clutch the side of the rock just in time to see a cloud of sparkling magic engulf the place where she'd jumped in.

A bouquet of gold and silver fins shimmer as if threaded with gemstones. And the tail of some extraordinary fish disappears after her.

I have to blink a few times as the dark waters settle again. But I stare and stare at the spot with a memory floating in my mind.

I reach for it, grasp it. It's a story the good king used to tell his apprentices over firelight, a cautionary tale to encourage boys to keep their manners when courting the girls:

> *Beware the enchanted maidens of the water,*
> *who seduce and kill by song. They rule the*
> *seas by moon and stars, and they feast on*
> *human blood.*
>
> *Beware the enchanted maidens of the water,*
> *whose powers stretch far beyond our own.*
> *The only protection we have from them is our*
> *steadfast sun.*
>
> *Beware the enchanted maidens of the water,*
> *whose loyalties lie with their own. A lady has*
> *nothing to fear, but a man without manners*
> *might only survive one if he*
> *strikes a deal.*

The king would wag his fingers at the boys, and the girls would haughtily giggle. But even back then, with all the enchanted beings known, magic enjoyed and cherished, maidens of the water were just myths… bedtime stories or tunes sung near the sea whenever the wind so much as whispered too loudly across the waves— *'Steer clear of the water today! A mermaid must be hunting near.'*

I trace the silver line along my left arm. It glows brighter than I have ever seen it before, like stark moonlight sliced across my skin.

'A gift from the Sea,' Eloise had called it, with wonderment in her eyes.

Understanding jolts through me as the water fades back to black, all hint of her gone save for the remnants of the regulators her sisters left. "I can't believe it…" My eyes widen. "You're not just any beast." My heart races. "You're a maiden of the water… a mermaid."

20

REFLECTION

NOT EVEN THE DEEPEST OF OUR WATERS is cold enough to cool me down after clinging to the hotness of a human for hours on end.

Even with my legs transformed back to my tail, I can still feel the pulse of Jaspyr inside me, yearning for more.

If I close my eyes, all I hear is his deep, echoing voice in my bones, our aching moans. All I taste is the blood and sweat blending us together, finding release again and again—not once, not twice, but *three* times before the sky began to lighten with the threat of the sunrise.

I force my eyes open and my mind to focus on literally anything else other than the taste of Jaspyr.

More, more, more! My insides scream.

Just go home, Eloise. Wait this out.

The long, familiar path toward Empress Isle is surrounded by a maze of nature. Rich coral reef and tall forest kelp glisten with life, carving the quickest paths for us home. I always consider if the Goddess of the Sea mirrored the land above from the God of Earth—swimming over the cliffs and canyons and fields of this intricate underwater terrain feels like flying above the earth.

If I keep to the east trail, at this speed, I'll be there in minutes. The west trail is bordered by a vast, thick bed of mint-green turtle grass where I love to stall, to play with the other creatures that have made this place their sanctuary—I veer in that direction, deciding to take the scenic route.

I need time to think.

I sing to the creatures as we swim, a gentle greeting should they be so inclined to return it. A small family of turtles poke their heads out from their feeding beds. They welcome me with drowsy, round eyes, pupils glistening like bright marbles, silver streaking through the black.

I blow a kiss to them, one laced with luck; the water sparks with bright flecks of magic to see them off to their day; Aura and Ora nestle in their place, flattening the grass, waiting for me to send kisses their way yet glaring at me with disapproving eyes just the same.

"You make a fine myrmaid," says Isobel, swimming up on me from behind. I start.

She laughs, grinning. "I'm sorry, did I scare you?"

"Always," I say returning a smirk. "I never see you coming when you don't want to be seen."

Her expression shifts to something more contemplative. "Funny… I could say the same for you, little one. You seem to have a knack for swimming off without warning these days."

I tense, suddenly very interested in a bright yellow coral. "You seemed to be enjoying yourself last night, and I didn't want to interrupt."

She circles me again, taking me all in—then breaks into a wide grin. "And you seem to have enjoyed yourself plenty last night as well," she says, clapping her hands so loudly that fish scatter in the vicinity. "I can smell a man all over you. You must've had a grand time last night." She looks me up and down. "Why, you're absolutely glowing. I think you needed that. You were so glum when I found you yesterday."

"Isobel, *please*," I say, shooing her off, praying she didn't also scent the mounting betrayal on me.

She chases me a little way, poking and tickling at me until I have no choice but to play. We swim and dance with each other in the currents, as if it were any other day.

As if you didn't just have union with a mortal and let him live… again. This time with a friend! Have you gone mad? If Syrifina hears of this, consider yourself dead.

A dark, elegant seabird with white spackled spots steals my attention. It flaps its vast, triangular wings, soaring through the water and skimming the grass on a glittering cloud. Its long tail is tipped with a stinger that looks like a bright metal cap, a dagger fused to its body.

"That was a gift from me," says Isobel, proudly, swirling to mimic the creature. Her fins drape around her like dripping red ink, even more graceful than the seabird. "And you'll *never* get used to it. That's why we're so lucky." She stares after the creature, fondly, until it's just a distant silhouette in the deep.

I look at her.

She seems so at peace with everything, the picture of true confidence. How many more years until I'm just as sure about myself, just as settled in this new world? Up until recently, I thought myself much farther along.

I think of *her* daughters. Of how eventually she must have felt so at ease that she was ready for the responsibility of sharing her energy, her gifts, with others. Ready to expand our family.

'*Transformed by a kiss*,' sings Aura.

'*If the magic deigns to wish*,' chimes Ora, putting more emphasis on her words.

The mantra of the Myrs floats in my mind as I consider Isobel—she has offered the myrmaid's kiss to only a handful of women in her many centuries of underwater life.

Four out of five accepted; three out of five survived the transformation.

It's not a blessing to be given away lightly, as Vasylina so viciously reminded me last night. And not all have the ability to receive it. That's why the waters aren't swarming with myrmaids—we remain rarities compared to the overwhelming population of humans we strain to keep down to protect the seas.

I am the newest to grace the Sea of Saindora—born on the twenty-second day of the moon cycle. A child still, indeed.

I wonder if I will ever feel compelled to share a transformative kiss with another? The thought alone scares me.

'*As it should,*' whispers Aura.

'*You can't even trust yourself with your own gifts at the moment,*' adds Ora with a snort. '*So how could you even consider sharing them with another? Get a hold of yourself.*'

"Go away!" I shout.

I immediately regret the outburst of magic that came with my words; they slink away around a sandy bend.

"What was that all about?" asks Isobel, looking alarmed.

"Oh... nothing," I say, their difficult truths ringing in my ears. "They're just bothersome these days."

I sink into thoughts of lust, of desire, of this relentless craving—Jaspyr's face fills my mind.

When will I have the willpower to kill the man from the alleyway and take what I desire most? Why do I let him get to me this way?

'*You must conquer these feelings, Eloise. They're not as real as you think,*' the Sea sings.

'*Not real?*' I retort. '*You deemed him worthy of your breath of life!*'

The Sea sighs, her voice a soothing whisper all around me.

"Eloise, you're sinking again," says Isobel, tersely.

I blink and find her floating at my eye level, her delicate face studying mine. She's clearly been watching me for a while.

All the light from her earlier expression is replaced by a hardening concern. She stares as deeply into my eyes now as I had been drifting into my own mind before—my mind is crumbling, scattered all over the sea with the currents and her bewildering murmurs.

I hold her gaze. I do not blink...

I'm not sure I even can until my elder sister releases me.

She calculates something in my expression, as if she is trying to piece together my problem on her own, like a puzzle she is determined to solve without the clues.

I wish she could, though I doubt it is possible. I doubt anyone had ever experienced such a...

Such a what? Such a what, Eloise? What has this man done to you?

There's no term, no description for the troubles drowning my mind, my choices, seeping into my soul no matter how hard I try to protect it.

"We have to get to the bottom of whatever is disquieting you so, don't we?" says Isobel after an unbearably long while.

Her eyes light up, and a school of silver and sapphire fish are summoned. They swarm us, wild in their greeting. They form an enormous cyclone, the size of a ship, with the mere mass of their bodies as they sweep over the grasses.

We melt into them, like penetrating a wall of mist, until we're buoyant at the center of their circle, their world.

They swim so fast around us, utterly erratic in their individual movement until suddenly all I see is one—their chaos blends in beautiful harmony. It's rhythmic, hypnotizing.

Isobel dances among them, misting them with magic.

I stare, mesmerized, appreciating the fact that I can continue to watch them for as long as I please.

I think I might stay a while, forever, if it will allow me to escape facing my worries…

"What do you see?" asks Isobel, her voice reaching me from somewhere far away—faintly, I think I must have been suspended in this cyclone for hours already.

'*Hours, time… it means nothing,*' says Aura.

'*Don't you see, Eloise? You are so much more than one bad choice, this blip in time,*' says Ora.

A desperate, terrified, brave part of me suggests that I could simply outlive the enigmatic man in Kampaulo. Let him die of his own accord and pray to the goddesses that my self-destructive craving will die with him, for I have all the time in the world.

"Focus, Eloise." All else disappears; Isobel's voice reaches out to me from across a void. "Look at what's in front of you and see."

Her voice is an echo like the deep, resonating gong of a bell. And though it quickly fades away from my consciousness, I can still sense her presence nearby.

I concentrate on the vibrating wall of silver around me, churning faster and faster, blending into the sea like paint brushed across an azure canvas, spreading me out along with it, until my insides are stretched bare for all to see.

These fish are relentless—they swim, merge, blend, melt into one another, encasing me at their center. Then they vanish, replaced by what appears to be a silver mirror rippling with the clear water around it, and…

"It's me!" I speak in a gasp, spellbound as I stare upon my own reflection. Our magic is still so wondrous and surprising to me that I can't even veil it. I have much to learn.

My fins fan out behind me like a gold and silver cape sewn with fine, shimmering threads. The veins of lifeblood crawl their way across my dark skin, painting my arms and neck, my chest and stomach and tail in light. Connecting every inch of me to the magic, my essence within.

My tail curls back and forth, a dreamlike entity all its own, suspending me in this dome of living glass. I look as if my torso has been welded to an armor crafted of lustrous scales that might weigh a thousand pounds in precious metals yet would never sink; a crown of magic dances brightly atop my thick, black curls, my hair softly floating around me.

Deep brown eyes draw me in last, flecked with platinum, dusted with gold—it's here, in their reflection, my eyes, that I face the truth of who I am.

And all my burdens.

I am more than beautiful, more than strong, more than fierce and otherworldly. Yet, my spirit clings to the weakness of my past, afraid to fully let go and embrace all that I am and will persist to be.

I cannot allow this to go on. It is blasphemy.

As if to validate my new understanding, a shadow emerges from behind, sucking the luster from my reflection the closer it gets. It's just a dark blur of smoke at first, like centuries-old sediment when disturbed underwater. Then it begins to solidify into a shape, the clear silhouette of a man.

"You do not belong here," I say in a low growl, my expression tainted with resentment.

I feel my nerves come alive, so much so that my lifeblood reacts, violently shifting colors. "I... I..." I choke on my words as if they were coral.

"What is it, Eloise? Go on. Tell me, what do you see?" Isobel's voice is just a distant hum now, urging me to give in to her magic.

Black shimmering eyes, one rimmed in a flicker of sea-green, nearly blue, begin to take shape in the shadow, pristine, piercing—they too stare upon my reflection.

Hungrily, I think.

'*But I am here,*' the shadow seems to speak. '*You brought me here, with you.*'

"*Eloise,*" says Isobel, a warning in her tone.

"I see him!" I burst out, the confession burning on my tongue. "I… I think I'm being hunted by an unknown force, Isobel." I spit the words out like acid. *Haunted…*

No, I am the huntress.

"I don't understand why this is happening to me."

I'm unable to blink nor move.

I want to swim away. *I want to sink into the shadow.*

I want to be far from this place, though I know it isn't real. *I want it to be real, so, so badly that my insides hurt.*

I can resist.

Taste, feel, feed! A voice inside me angrily screams.

The shadow lifts its arm and places a heavy hand over my shoulder, clutching me with its fingers. It's too warm, hot.

I rip my eyes away from the entity and my reflection with a yelp—everything spins out of control, as if I have caught myself in the swell of a callous wave and am being thrown around, beaten down by it.

There's no sense of up from down. I become dizzy. I'm trapped in a cyclone that has no intention of letting me go now that I've let my guard fall and shown it my weakness.

With a frustrated cry, I slam my hands together. Energy bursts from my fingertips in a resounding, rippling blast—the school of fish disburses, my magic chasing them away.

"What was that?" I say with a growl in my throat, trying to steady my world. "What did you do to me?"

I whip around, glaring in Isobel's direction.

"Calm yourself," she says, sinking toward me, hands raised in caution. "I didn't *do* anything to you. I just forced you to confront whatever truth you're hiding from yourself."

"I'm not hiding anything!" I yell, letting the more animalistic parts of me take over. I welcome them with open arms, the rage, the power.

"Naive," she utters.

I swim closer to Isobel, a hiss boiling out of my throat, my teeth bared; when the echo of my voice subsides, the sea is so quiet that I can hear boats miles off, on the surface.

Isobel says nothing, her body language calm and unperturbed, the cock of her head making me unreasonably irate and terrified all the same.

We linger in the silence. Her expression does not change.

"I can't protect you if you don't tell me what's plaguing you," she says with deadly calm.

My eyes widen, as if I have just woken up from a dream.

I cannot fathom that I just raised my voice to one of my elder sisters like that... let alone flashed my fangs. She will have my head on a spear one day.

There's no use apologizing.

I huff and swim off as fast as I can.

"Eloise, I'm trying to help you!" Isobel screams after me.

I beat my tail harder against the deep underwater current that dominates here, fighting it to try to lead myself astray—it's a losing battle.

I soon give up, letting the current's powerful hand sweep me back on track.

If Isobel tried to follow me, she remains far behind, allowing me my space. Trying to outswim her is an even bigger waste of energy than attempting to outsmart the Sea's currents or Aura's and Ora's constant eyes on me. If she wants to catch me, she can.

Alone again, I begin to relax into a more normal pace, setting my gaze on the mesmerizing school of fish that had shown me a difficult truth; they've kept watch on me all this time, though they hover far down the grasses, a safe distance away.

I can't believe I tried to break apart their beautiful family out of fright...

Disgust overwhelms me.

I'm thankful that their bond is not so easily broken, for they've already circled back together again—these faithful friends, like me, are watchers of our waters and guardians of my goddess-blessed kind, as are all the Sea's subjects. They will not allow me to hide from this. *Him...*

21

RIVALS

☼ J A S P Y R

AS SOON AS THE SUN RISES, light flooding the cool cavern with warmth, an intense sense of relief comes over me, a weight lifted from my chest—*Eloise is gone. I survived again.*

I exhale, long and deep, as the waters fully settle back to their glass-like state, showing no sign of life below.

It's a sense of false, impermanent freedom. My thoughts still linger on her, and I know she will return.

But her shadow has dissipated with the sun, her dark energy dissolved in the light, and now I have the bones of a plan to cling to.

She fears fire, fears the sun.

I look toward the gleaming horizon, my saving grace. "I wonder…"

A fist collides with my jaw with a deafening crack, blood flying from my mouth, my teeth groaning in my gums. I topple to the ground, too close to the water's edge. I scramble back.

"What the—" I look up and Eddison is swinging at me again, his expression rigid with fury, a raging bull charging at me with all his weight.

It's all I can do to brace myself for his next attack as he throws his entire body into me, shoving me to the ground.

"Eddison, stop. Calm down!" I scream, out of breath—Eloise leeched enough blood from me that I can hardly protect myself from him. For once, he has the upper hand.

"Oh, *I'm sorry*," he says, chest heaving, jaw clenched so tightly that I can see every vein in his neck bulging from the strain. "Do you remember that I exist now?"

He takes another step forward; if he had a weapon, I'm certain he would use it on me.

"Did I *disrupt* your bloody daydream about that despicable nightmare you just whored yourself out to"—spit flies from his mouth—"while I was forced to watch for gods-damned hours on end!" His yell reverberates across the cavern like a gong, making me wince.

"Eddison…" I say, holding up my hands and tasting more blood from his punch than I have all night—I can't comprehend why Eloise finds it so appealing. "Listen to me."

"No." His voice is a condemning slap to my face. "You left me there, to—" He grits his teeth and stands straighter. "You left me, for… that thing."

I bow my head, my jaw pulsing in pain.

We weren't supposed to live…

But we did. And despite the lucky deal I made that saved us in the end, I have to face the fact that when Eloise dealt our death cards, I chose to lie with our executioner. How could Eddison ever forgive me for that?

"I'm so sorry…" I say, lowering my head.

I remember the discomfort of not being able to connect with my limbs. Of my mind being fully aware, my sight unaltered, yet not being able to move nor speak. Eyes pinned opened as if Eloise *wanted* me to see the horrors she could unleash—only when she vanished beneath the water did she relinquish her enchanted grip on Eddison.

I push that foul memory away and block out that horrid expression on his face, as if he can never look at me the same way again. I tell myself that *what I did* was for his own good.

It was!

I needed to focus on Eloise, to placate the beast so she would leave us alone, allow us to live another day.

And it worked. I saved us!

Don't lie to yourself, a dark part of me whispers. *You enjoyed every second feasting on her. And you enjoyed it even more with an unwilling witness.*

I find the strength to steady my gaze on Eddison and nearly break at the pain and betrayal etched on his tear-stricken face—how long, how many *hours* had passed by that he'd been forced to watch me writhe with that monster after seeing his friends murdered before his eyes?

I swallow at the numbing realization. No spell had been cast over me. I had not battled Eloise—I had allowed our union to happen. Consented.

Wanted it to...

I had let him watch.

Wanted him to...

I shake my head and get to my feet, focusing on the facts—just like what kept me going after...

Sibyl... Luna.

"We're alive, Eddison," I say. "Unlike your foul friends." I glance to the gore-splattered walls. "We survived. No matter the ways in which *I* fought for your life," I point to my chest, "at least you still breathe. Remember that."

I gesture to the waters at my back and ignore the shouting in my head telling me to shut my despicable mouth, to have a shred of self-respect and let Eddison punch my face in for adding to his suffering. "You and your regulator mates dragged me to the Split. As far as I'm concerned, you have only yourself to thank for their fates."

He spits on the ground at my feet. "You've lost your damned mind, Jaspyr." He looks me up and down in absolute revulsion. "Poisoned, clearly."

We hold each other's gaze, my hands forming fists as I struggle to rein in my rage—a tangled mix of hatred for everything that he stands for and the knowledge that I've caused my dearest friend inexcusable pain.

"Have you only just cared to notice?" The words slip out of my mouth in a cold whisper, as if I had been holding on to them for years.

He recoils, blinking a couple of times.

"I—" He swallows. "I see."

WE RETURN THE HORSES TO THE STABLES, careful not to be seen, and travel straight to Eddison's home. A frigid silence accompanies us the entire way; the only feeling of comfort is the sun.

Eyes bleary and emotions high, we wake Penelope from her sleep, then sit her down at the kitchen table with a cup of tea. Eddison doesn't give me a choice—we confess all that happened last night.

Well, *almost* everything...

I don't have the heart to tell them that yesterday wasn't

the first time I'd met the creature I now believe to be a mermaid.

The moment I speak my theory of the mythical underwater beings, Eddison scoffs, rolling his eyes.

"And then what happened?" Penelope cuts in, her voice trembling.

Eddison and I straighten, blinking back at her; I half-expected her to send us off, to not believe a word. I'm not even sure I believe myself at this point… I'm so tired that I can hardly keep my eyes open.

I nudge Eddison to continue and hold my breath as he begins the dark retelling of the twins who had left his friends in pieces. He can barely get through it without choking on the tears streaming down his cheeks. "And then she tore off Ulsta's hea—"

Penelope holds up her hand. She turns, fully facing him. "It's time I tell you what I think really happened to your father."

Eddison leans back in his chair, all his muscles going rigid. He scrunches his face in confusion. "What—"

"After your father was killed," she says, "the sea carried me home over endless miles of water. It took me three full days to return to these shores, yet somehow, without paddle nor help from the wind, I made it to exactly where I needed to be. I was safe." She shakes her head. "I knew. I *just knew* that it had something to do with those women in the water. But no one would listen! They said I had lost my mind on the waves." She seems to drift off in thought, eyes darting to the window as the sun beams through. "And that song… it was an old kind of magic."

Her voice cracks. She slams the table with her palm, the wood rattling—my bones rattle along with it. *She knows about them already.*

"What women in the water?" asks Eddison, stumbling on

his words. "Why didn't you tell me all this, Mum?" She doesn't readily answer, squeezing her palms around her teacup; Eddison's voice pitches. "What are you saying to me right now, about Pop? Are you saying—" He cuts a glance to me. "Do you really believe what Jaspyr thinks is true? That these creatures could be…"

Say it, I bitterly think, narrowing my eyes as he holds my gaze. *Don't be so ignorant. Stop refusing to believe. You know what they are.*

"I couldn't tell anyone ever again," says Penelope, drawing Eddison's attention back to her. "Who would listen? Everyone believed me the culprit in Edward's death." A teardrop falls into her tea. She hasn't even taken a sip yet. "And you were so heartbroken."

Eddison looks down.

Penelope reaches for his hand, her expression full of sorrow—I have never seen her look so despondent before. She had forged emotions of steel ever since she returned home without her husband. I clamp tight on any emotion, wanting to be strong for them, to start making amends now for what I'd put my friend through.

Even if he would be dead had I not lain with that beast.

"I couldn't drag you into what turned out to be a ghost chase, so I endured what the people said. I drank my pain away, and, secretly, I began to scour old archives for anything… *anything* to do with the myths and legends of water women. But by the time I found the right clues, the King's purge had already begun." She sighs, shaking her head. "Such a waste. I could never show anyone the proof I found, never clear my name or demand justice."

"What did you find?" I dare to ask.

She glances at me, searching my expression. "I believe you," she says after a moment. "I know what killed my Edward."

Before Eddison or I can respond, Penelope rushes from the table to another room; there is the sound of papers and boxes being thrown around.

"If you thought there was little back then on such creatures—" she yells back to us; Eddison stiffens. To hear someone, his law-abiding mother especially, speak so lightly about a 'back then' and magic after half a decade pretending otherwise comes as quite the surprise to us both. "Imagine how these last few years have changed things."

She returns to the kitchen, a scroll in hand.

"All the libraries burned to a crisp. Ancient scripts destroyed." She sits back down. "A world scared shitless to recount the stories of their past. Stories filled with magic and wonderful, sometimes terrible, beings that wielded raw, natural power we will never understand…"

"Hail to the King," I say in a low voice, stroking the serpent chain at my neck.

Eddison purses his lips, steadying his gaze on his mother.

Penelope nods to me, an agreement that her son willfully chooses to ignore, his regulator cloak wrapped tightly about his shoulders.

"But I did find one thing in my search that confirms…" She takes a deep breath. "Well, it confirms everything you boys witnessed." She lifts her sparkling gaze to ours and speaks barely above a whisper. "These darkly enchanted women of the water are not only sea-dwelling creatures that sailors speak fables about when their shipmates do not return. They stalk and feed on the likes of men. *And* they're not confined to the water. They, too, can walk on land."

"At night," I add. "They can walk on land at night."

They both look at me expectantly.

I shrug. "Trust me." I glance to the window, letting the early sunrays warm my face. "And they don't like fire."

"Good to know," says Penelope.

She lays the scroll down on the table—it has a broken seal, ocean waves that form a circle in the brightest, bluest ink I have ever seen before.

No... not ink, I realize. Something else, something unattainable in our mortal world.

She unfurls it and reads:

Darling Diary

This is the last known recording by Christofer de Miranda.
Sea Explorer. Prisoner. Island of Idris. The year is immaterial.
It was a long time ago.

———◈◈◈———

Time draws on, no matter what stands before her. She's persistent,
constant, undying, forward-thinking without pause nor contemplation.
She takes no notice of the ravaged bones she leaves behind her...
no patience for remorse.

The Past is merely a tribute to Time's never-ending journey.
The Future is her certain, steadfast destiny.

Mortals fear Time maybe just as much as Death. For the two deities
walk hand in hand, openly and proudly, on the earthly plane.
A Myr Sister—the mistresses of the sea—stride in parallel with
these terrible and terrific gods; and at the Moon's behest, they can
walk among the mortals just the same.

We fear them, too. Those of us who live long and unlucky enough to
learn of their existence.

I conclude: with so many ways to meet Death, it makes no sense to try
and turn back Time. For either way, we mortals will always meet an end.
Unless, perhaps, one could steal a kiss from a myrmaid of Olleb-Yelfra...

Alas, I think I've run out of attempts to prove my theory. Syrifina Myr,
the original sin, is no friend of men.

Yours mortally,
Christofer

Penelope passes the scroll to us to read on our own. "It's titled, *From the Archives of Syrifina Myr—Original Myrmaid of Ol-leb-Yelfra*," she says. "And this Island of Idris… it's on no map I've ever seen."

"Looks like even the spelling changed over time," Eddison mumbles. "I thought it was 'mermaids'." He scrawls the word out with his finger on the table.

I shoot him a glare, crossing my arms at my chest; he looks to his hands, pretending not to have noticed, just like he pretends to have forgotten about the magic that used to rule this land. The kings and queens who let it flourish. The dwarves, dragons, and elves. And the—

Immortal landwalking myrmaids, I think, closing my eyes to try and press away the headache forming.

"We have to be prepared next time," I say. "Kampaulo is no longer safe."

22

❦

RUIN

ᗺ E L O I S E

I WATCH MY PREY FROM A DISTANCE, so curious to better understand what has kept me from killing him. So curious to quell this numbing need for his blood.

My insides squirm at just the thought of tasting him again, his scent swirling in my nostrils and lingering on my tongue.

He will be your demise, some cautious part of me warns.

That is why I must kill him tonight, I return, committed to my goal. *I must complete my hunt, once and for all.*

The next breeze carries me closer, though I'm still far away enough that if he turned around and looked directly at me, he would see nothing but the draping night.

He walks the sand in silence, head bowed.

"Fool." If I were him, I would've hitched a carriage to somewhere far inland. But he still doesn't understand me, hasn't put together what I am.

He shoves his hands into his pockets, drawing out a gold coin.

Mine. I touch the ribbon at my neck.

He examines it a moment with a furrowed brow, then rolls it back and forth between his fingers, his gaze drifting to the sea.

I lick my lips. "Jaspyr…" My body begs to let him touch me again with those skillful hands, thoughts of hunger blurring with ones of excitement, desperation.

I shake my head. *I don't need anything but his blood. Focus, Eloise.*

'*Liar*,' the stars sing. '*He is much more to you now that you've lain with him.*'

Their cold light washes him in a brightness that shows every line of muscle beneath his linen shirt.

I tilt my gaze up with a frown. "Stop coaxing me," I say between my teeth. "No, he's not!"

The night seems to shrug in response. '*We shall see.*'

I seethe, pinning my eyes back on Jaspyr.

Two men step into my line of sight, sneaking up behind him, swords at the ready. Their intrusion makes me jump slightly—how had I not heard their footsteps, their breath?

A low growl rumbles in my throat, and my magic flares. Anger floods my senses.

If anyone is going to kill my mark, it will be me.

In the fraction of the time it takes them to move a muscle, I am between them both. And in the seconds it takes them to realize they're face to face with a more dangerous hunter, I snap the smaller one's neck to ensure he does not scream—I cover the mouth of the other and sink my teeth into him.

My fangs break apart his skin and his blood swims to me, warming my throat. I sigh in satisfaction. I have been so gluttonous lately that I'm starting to run on a continual high, a constant, wonderful, excruciating, blood-filled haze that creeps around the outer rims of my mind, pressing in further on my reality with each passing day.

My victim struggles beneath my grasp, trying to reach his blade in the sand. Such silly toys men of this world cling to for safety, security.

I keep him upright. His feet dangle just above the earth as I drain the life from him. His blood ignites my mind like an uncontainable wildfire that keeps getting fed, no end in sight, savagely devouring everything in its path—my gaze is steady, locked on my true target as I drink.

When I'm done, I toss his body to the sand for some unfortunate passerby to find later; Jaspyr is none the wiser.

I wipe the blood from my face and push away the empty ache I feel inside, even with so much blood swirling in my belly. I peer at the most recent corpses I've added to my Kampaulo kill list, their mouths slack and eyes glazed over to join the rest of the dead at my back.

They deserved it, I think. *They were monsters of a different sort. Yes, I've done the city a favor.*

I sway across the beach with confidence.

Even as just a young girl, I knew better than to walk the shores alone at night in Kampaulo—only an arrogant warrior, or painter, might think himself safe.

I remember the thin scars peppering his skin, his arms, his chest, his legs. I consider that he must have fought in the war, and I find myself wondering what side he fought for…

The Sea wouldn't have blessed him if he was a soldier for the King.

I lift my forearm in front of my eyes to examine my lifeblood there. My normally bright essence seems to have lessened, diluted by excess blood. I can feel it, the heaviness inside me, the fog that continues to bleed over my mind.

I'm rotting, I think. *I wonder why Mother never mentioned that symptom of overdrinking.*

"She probably never expected it to happen again," I mutter to myself.

My magic simmers atop my skin in a riled burst, my emotions so unstable that it's impacting my control of my powers.

If my mark turns around right now, he will see a person rimmed in gold and silver and know surely that it is me, returned to finish what I started. Part of me wishes with everything that he would, for I believe once I look Jaspyr in the eyes again, once he really sees me, I'll find the strength I need to end this short-lived nightmare…

The other part of me, the side that seems to hold dominance over my choices now, isn't ready to be released from this frenzy, desires the pain and ache of never having the thing she wants the most.

I ball my fists at my side, reining my magic back in just as he turns away from the sea, glancing in my direction.

I freeze, waiting for him to call out and confront me, but he still doesn't seem to notice me. He's surely occupied by whatever thoughts brought him to this beach in the first place so late at night. He heads toward the center of the seaside town, away from the shores—I follow him past the Lotus Center, past the narrow streets that swallow the city, and upward in the direction of the keeper's palace.

I stalk him along hilly, wide-open paths that overlook the city, the Moon a glaring eye on me all the while.

'*Turn back, Eloise*,' she pleads. '*You're not thinking clearly.*'

We stop in a field, the scent of him intoxicating here, amplified just as it was in his studio. There's a small, wooden dwelling behind him, drowning among the land. It's quiet, save for the howling breeze that beats here just as hard as it does when closer to the waters and the waves.

The stars whisper in a symphony around me. '*What are you doing, child? You're too far from home. Turn back now, before you get lost and not even we can help you find your way back.*'

I can't see my waters from here, but I can scent the salt in the air.

"I know you're there," he speaks, his voice carrying across the open field; I still. "I knew you would come."

I wish to melt back into the darkness before he can see me, not ready to confront what must be done next. But I force myself to stand my ground. "Hello, Jaspyr."

He turns around to face me, unafraid.

His dark eyes bore into mine. His lips press into a firm line, pink and plump with blood; he massages the wrist I indulged on last night, the greenish hue of his veins glinting at me from beneath his pale skin.

He looks me up and down, blinking a few times as if to make sure I'm not just a trick of the night. Then his eyes meet mine and never leave my face. "Eloise," he says in a clipped tone.

I smirk. "Did you enjoy your last day on this earth?"

His cheeks rise with red, lines wrinkling his forehead as he narrows his gaze. His body temperature slightly warms, his scent sweeter. "You have no idea what I'm capable of," he says softly, his expression hard.

His words shudder through me—I lose myself in them, him.

"I know what you are, Eloise. I know you're a myrmaid."

My world spins in the deepness of his voice, in the cockiness of his stance as he confronts me. He's trying so hard not to look at my body, to pretend he doesn't want me still.

My mouth waters. It's as if I'm trapped in the cyclone of Isobel's magic once again.

I can't fight the urge to draw him into conversation. To play with him a little more, before the end.

I want to know him better... this masterful artist who will never comprehend the full truth of the world he spent his life painting. This beautiful lover who has satiated me more than any human I've laid with thus far.

"Then you know you cannot fight me," I say. "You do have good instincts, though…" I close the distance between us, placing my hand on his chest to feel the strong beat of his heart once more; he goes rigid but does not back away. "And yet, I've never known a man so eager for death. You should have fled when you had the chance, Jaspyr."

"I don't run from monsters anymore," he says, glaring down at me with silver glinting in his gaze.

I know I shouldn't toy with my prey like I normally would… this isn't a usual situation. But the feeling of his name on my tongue is like an exquisite appetizer. Our banter just the tantalizing beginnings of the main course. He's so unlike any human I have ever known, as strong-willed as a Myr. I can't bear to end this quickly. "The night is still young," I purr.

I wrap my hand behind his neck and force his lips to mine.

He tries to resist at first, but then our bodies are locked in the wildness of it, the kiss forging us together like fire to cold steel. I feel the Moon's disdain wash down, stars casting me in a shameful light—they're easy to ignore as this rush of adrenaline burns through me, deep in my core.

I pull away before I can get lost in him again and step out of his reach.

He freezes for a moment, brow furrowed, his breathing hard and heavy. His eyes scan my body, slowly, moving over every crevice of my skin, every curve that he's felt, from my face to my nipples, to my belly button, down to my toes in the grass. An intense burning sensation sweeps over me, stirring in my muscles, my bones.

"You are vile," he finally says in a low voice.

My lips twitch up in a smile as my eyes drop to his pants. "Is that so?"

His jaw twitches, eyes darkening.

In a blink, I am inches from him again, the wind rushing behind my back.

This time, he nearly stumbles trying to keep out of my reach. He catches his footing, arms flailing a bit.

Humans are such clumsy things.

I can't believe, sometimes, that I ever was one.

His voice floats out in a quiver. "How do you move like that—"

"Your lack of fear is amusing to me," I speak, my words full of strength, burying his. I stand taller as he seems to shrink.

Silence draws between us and all I hear is the *thump, thump, thump* of the blood-filled organ inside of his chest, panicking at my presence.

As it should, I think.

I slowly begin to circle him where he stands. He makes no motion to move, just follows me with his gaze the best he can; I stay exactly at arm's length, grappling with my own fear to close the distance even more, to touch him again, to drink him, to finish what I started.

"How do you move so fast, on land?" he asks, this time with words that hold steady, his stance returning to strong.

I return a closed-lip grin, laughing a little .

"I can do a lot of things." The words flow from my mouth in a soft, seductive melody that I don't try to smother; his body heat rises even more, warming the air between us. His mind bends to mine, but I do not take hold. I let the magic go, deciding I want to hear what he has to say, see what this mortal man might do, without my influence. "You seem to have learned the name for my kind, but you don't *really* know all that I am, do you?"

He shakes his head, blinking away the daze as my song fades.

"I…" He swallows and tries again. "You've done that to me before. And to my friend." His voice comes out somewhat angrily, an accusation.

"Yes," I reply.

"Am I under your spell now?" he asks. "Am I acting of my own free will?"

"Yes… for now," I say with a smirk. "So what will you do with it, hero?"

"If I am to die by your hand, then tell me what you are," he demands. "How are you able to even survive on land? How do you have so much power?"

I stop behind him, pressing my fangs forward with a hiss. "You don't deserve to know. No man does."

He balls his fists and holds his breath.

My hiss melts into quiet laughter. I can't help myself…

I claw my nails across his shirt until it's in shreds at my feet, then I press my body to his from behind, just to feel the warmth of his skin again on mine—he's a living, breathing flame. I think the canvas of fire painted across his shoulders and back could be real, that his heat could hold me there forever and melt me right into him.

I expect him to try to pull away from my contact like before, hope that his fear might finally show up to force him to fight me.

If only he would fight…

Then, at least, the innate huntress in me might overpower the strange hesitation I have at taking his life.

But he doesn't run. He doesn't move. He barely even breathes.

He slightly leans into me.

I can't help myself. I move my hands over his, up the softness of his thick arms, gripping the mass of his shoulders. I press my chest and cheek into his muscled back and listen for his heart like a comfort; it sings to me. *I'm so close.*

I run my tongue along the crease between his muscles, his shoulder blades, all the way to the nape of his neck, following the etch of embers atop his skin—he tastes like where the sea meets the stars, something beyond, something to be savored… maybe that's why the universe won't let me end him just yet.

He sighs in pleasure.

I feel myself sink into him, my nipples tightening, my insides throbbing, wanting to be closer; he relaxes into me.

"You *have* cast a spell on me. I know it," he says, breathlessly.

I release my hold and step away. He staggers a bit.

I circle around to his front. His chest is a sculpted masterpiece, and his nipples have hardened, too, against the wind or my touch. My gaze travels down to his leathers, to the hardness growing just beyond. I can barely resist the urge to rip them off and taste it.

I lift my gaze to his eyes, not allowing myself to be so distracted again—but by his tormented expression, I can tell he's just as ravenous for me as I am for him.

"You are not under my spell," I say. "However you might feel…" I can't help my eyes traveling downward again. "Whatever you desire, it is all of your own accord." I hold his stare, my lips curling upward. "I swear."

He shakes his head, biting on his inner cheek; I can smell when the skin breaks, droplets of blood pressing outward to swim in his mouth. It's all I can do not to shove my tongue in with his to lick at them. "I don't trust a word from you," he says, his voice drawing my focus away from his scent.

"Then you're wiser than I thought," I reply.

He snorts. "I don't care who you are, or what your sinister intentions might be before this night is done," he says, his voice hoarse. "I'm not going to fight the inevitable." He inhales a long breath, as if working up the courage to speak his next words, "but I need you right this gods-damned second." He takes a step closer. "Do whatever you want to me when I've finished with you. As long as I can touch you again."

He holds out his hand, a devastating hunger in his eyes.

"Be with me one more time, Eloise. It's the least you can do if I'm to give you my life."

He follows the lines of my lifeblood like one of his maps, all the way from my chin to my navel, slowly moving lower, tracing each strand, drinking them up with his gaze; I can see myself sparkling and bright, silver and gold, in his eyes.

"Take my hand."

I know I shouldn't. That if I indulge in him again, I might not be able to kill him at the end. For all my strength, something about him makes me weaker by the second.

Don't, Eloise. Just drink him and return home. The sun will wake soon. It isn't safe for you here now.

He closes the distance between us before I can decide. His lips find mine again—we are like magnets that cannot be pulled apart, though I try… I try.

I sink, like a rock thrown into water, into the softness of his lips, tasting the blood in his mouth, succumbing to it. I feel how he desperately clings to me, tugging at my essence. Old, familiar magic stirs deep in my bones, but it isn't meant for men, and I do not let it go.

I allow him everything else.

Every cell in my body tells me to pull away, that this is wrong. But it feels so right—no one is around to see nor judge me, save for the Moon and the souls no longer of this earth sparkling around her, so I hold his kiss tight. I let his hands search my body for whatever treasures they desperately desire to hoard in his last minutes of life.

"Now!" a man screams.

Suddenly, the night becomes too bright, too hot—I cannot see, cannot think as fire explodes around me from all angles.

Eddison's voice. Yes, I recognized it in the seconds before. And as the Moon's power wanes with the coming of the sun,

I realize much too late…

Run, Eloise, run!

I try to let go of his hand, to flee back to the safety of the sea. But I can't move from this spot as everything burns around me.

23

BURN

☼ J A S P Y R

THEY KILLED THE MAN in the marketplace today. Greggor. He hadn't heeded my warning to get out of the city while he still stood a chance. He couldn't, I think… not after meeting her.

He was so obsessed with the notion of this woman that it removed all reason from his mind—he took too much time, stalling, waiting, wondering if he might see her again.

Eloise, I know now, *a myrmaid…*

Eddison reported back earlier today that his fellow regulators dragged Greggor from his applecart to the Kampaulo Palace, laying him at the city keeper's feet for judgment, mere days after his unfortunate proclamation to the public about his farfetched encounter. People protested in vain, saying his words sprang from old age or too much ale, but it didn't matter. It was time for another brutal example of King Devlindor demanding submission to his reign.

We loved Greggor, I remind myself as I stare at Eloise, his undoing. My undoing…

If I don't have the strength to tether her here until sunrise.

Her voice rains down on me in a fury, her fingers crushing my own, as I draw all of my flame outward, contained inside the magical shield Eddison conjured and manipulates around us.

Penelope brewed a potion to strengthen our powers, only temporarily, but we should have more than enough time to hold out against her—there's only a couple hours left until sunrise.

Eloise cries out again. I've never heard a sound like it before, a beautiful, eerie, heart-wrenching call.

But she has no way out, and she can't possibly focus long enough to get the upper hand on us with her magic. Not now that we've gotten her so far away from her source of power.

I hope, if there are others like her nearby, they cannot hear her terrible song.

I force my eyes closed so I don't have to see her lovely face writhe in such agony. So I don't have to see the confusion and betrayal etched in her expression. I can't even make sense of such a look…

"You should've just left me alone," I say over the crackling of fire, over her screams. My voice sounds like I am pleading, like I am begging for forgiveness as I steal her life away.

I swear I hear her say, "I couldn't," over her howling cries.

"Don't speak to the wretched beast!" shouts Eddison as he strains to hold his power; it's obvious he hasn't stretched this muscle in a long time, though it does not fail him now. "She'll just manipulate you again."

I wince, heart pounding. I clamp my mouth shut.

We loved Greggor, I remind myself once more.

In the burning heat of this very day, no clouds, no darkness to soften the blow, the old man was hanged in the city center for treason against the Crown, without trial. They had enough proof, enough people desperate for a handout or high-life position to speak out against this kindhearted man. He was answerable for spreading blasphemous lies about mythical creatures and magic, for succumbing to an imagination far outside our 'real' world, to dare speak of the existence of a *queen*—and yet…

I have trapped a *queen of the seas*, by any account, on land…

Using fire *magic*…

Using enrichment *potions*…

Using shield *enchantments*…

My mind roars over Eloise's voice—*Down with the King and* his *blasphemous lies! Magic shall always persist.*

I home in on the power inside of me once more, the warmth resonating in my belly, tingling in my fingertips, and let it overwhelm me, let it have a mind of its own so I do not have to consider my actions this night.

She is real, I think. *Eloise is magic.*

Greggor leaves a family behind, at least, who can continue selling and trading apples in Kampaulo—may his legacy continue.

Sibyl. Luna.

I push my magic outward more and focus my mind again on revenge. I wrench my hand from her weakening grip and step out of the fire to stand by Eddison's side. We watch the monster burn.

THE HOURS HAVE ALREADY GONE BY, the sun nearly ready to make its resurrection. I haven't the slightest clue what might happen when it does... if it will really kill Eloise.

My fire hasn't left even a mark on her body, not her hair nor her skin. But the aching sound of her screams assures me that the pain she experiences is more than just a little 'unpleasant' this time.

Her body is silhouetted in my pink flame, her fists pounding on the impenetrable shield.

I shift back and forth on my feet, thinking of the softness with which those hands had roamed over my skin. How the tingle of my flame and the bite of her teeth had left us both greedily craving more. How the perfect union of our bodies had been so remarkable that we came for each other over and over, sinking into such an incomprehensible state of bliss that I know I shall never experience it again—not once Eloise's soul is gone from this plane.

We relinquished everything to each other then, set aside our chasm of differences to self-indulge.

I shall not relinquish now.

"*Solza ven immito,*" I say, the spell spinning into a song of its own as I continuously feed my flame into her small prison without pause—if anyone should pass by our house, they would see a miraculous ball of blazing fire rotating atop the ground.

Eloise screams at every interval, though not in the way I had made her scream last night, not in the way I had made her moan with our bodies intertwined; the pit of my stomach twists, aches.

I do not let go.

"She's a fighter," I hear Penelope say from behind us—she watches from the safety of the porch.

Eloise ceaselessly claws at the shield, punches and kicks—Eddison may be rusty, but his hatred for her keeps his magic steady and strong. His irises flash a liquid silver that it gives me so much relief to see again.

She has no hope of getting out before sunrise.

"She's a lot of things," I say.

The sky begins to lighten above. "In the King's name," Eddison says with relief, sweat beading on his skin.

With so much adrenaline rushing through me, I can't help but snap, "If it wasn't for the *King*, maybe her kind wouldn't feel the need to sneak around and hunt on these lands. Maybe your precious king is to blame for such creatures hiding and lurking in the shadows in the first place. Have you ever thought about that?"

"And maybe you're just sad to see your taboo plaything burn," he says, shooting me a silver-laced glare from the side, still keeping one eye on her. "What's the matter, all the high-life ladies throwing themselves at your feet too easy for you?" He scoffs. "Why don't you court a normal person like the rest of us for once. You've been an insufferable prick since your wife—"

I turn my gaze on him so quickly that he winces, pressing his lips together.

"Say it," I breathe in a soft voice that rumbles deep from the back of my throat—the dark part of me he's roused considers turning my flame on him instead.

He shakes his head, focusing on Eloise. "You need to get your priorities straightened out, mate, before you lose the life you've worked so hard to rebuild."

I let out a huff of air through my nose to loosen my anger, still glaring his way.

"What life, Eddison?" I say, wishing last night had never ended, wishing I never had to face this godsforsaken day at all. "You barely bled in the war before you dropped to your knees to kiss the ring. You lost nothing!" My voice cuts across the air toward him like a blade. "Everything was stolen from me. *Everything!*"

My power intensifies, tied like a knot to my emotions. My skin itches with so much magic now that I have no choice but to feed my flame more, to harm Eloise even more on her deathbed.

"I'm a living ghost since my family was taken from me. A shell. And I love you, brother. I do." My voice cracks, but I push the words out. "I'm sorry I hurt you the way I did, but I—" I bow my head. "I'm not who I used to be. I'm not the perfect painter who lived in the clouds and colors and stories. The world has changed. I've changed."

Eddison shakes his head. "No, you're still the same Jaspyr who I met—"

"No, I'm not." I cut in. "Dammit, open your eyes and look at what's become of me!" Fire rages around me, from me, as I hold my huntress's, *my lover's*, death sentence in my hands. When all I want to do is *hold her*—Eddison's eyes widen, and I wonder what he truly sees this time. "Don't you get it? I'm not... good anymore. Anything good in me was carved out of my body along with my heart half a decade ago." My voice lowers, shakes with the threat of tears. "All I can do is exist now and try to leave a better world behind me when I go."

"I won't let you destroy yourself," says Eddison with such determination that the stab of guilt cuts at me even more. "When this is done and that blood-sucking monster is dead, you and I are going to find a way to help you heal." His tone lightens along with the sky. "And I mean *real* healing. No potions, no ale, no bullshit brothels or seductive myrmaid songs. We'll get out of here for a bit, clear our heads. Everything will be alright in the end. You'll see."

And for a moment, I really do see. I really hope he is right, that he can help me... find some semblance of happiness again. Because right now all I feel is rage and power and a thirst for vengeance that I know can certainly never be satisfied. No matter how many monsters I kill.

I focus back on the burning ball and the strange magical being within.

That blood-sucking monster made me feel alive, a dark part of me thinks. *Made me want to live after all this time.*

Eloise is a walking reminder of the world King Devlindor hid and what he did, who he killed, to claim such power—I let my desire for revenge burn through me, feeding my flame only more.

If I could change one thing about this moment, I would trade Eloise's life for the murderous bastard who calls himself the High King of Olleb-Yelfra in a heartbeat.

"She really got into your head that one," Penelope calls out to us. I see her deep, wrinkled frown in my peripheral vision. "Eddison is right, boy. I can't believe you—"

"Enough. I'm trying to keep her contained. You all can cast your judgment on me later. Everyone just… *shut up*."

She tuts; Eddison snorts his agreement.

I curse them both softly under my breath. Then curse myself for letting last night's events unfold the way they did—I keep thinking of our conversation, as I'm sure Eddison does, still hardly able to comprehend Penelope's sad story. Nor the written proof that undying, landwalking myrmaids exist…

Eloise Myr, I think, trying to focus on the present, *what secrets of our underwater world might you hold?* And here I am, burning them away, just like King Devlindor.

I consider the final words in the scroll, the suggestion…

'*For either way, us mortals will always meet an end. Unless, perhaps, one could steal a kiss from a myrmaid of Olleb-Yelfra.*'

The statement rings in my mind, tingles on my tongue, written so long ago that the scroll parchment had not only yellowed but grayed.

I think of Ulsta when those terrifying twins had pressed their bloody lips to hers. A grand power had begun to form around her, cling to her, up until the moment she was beheaded.

I shiver at the memory, at how the magic had fallen away in a brutal, mocking rain, alongside her head.

What a waste.

I close my eyes a moment and can almost taste the magic on Eloise's tongue seeping into my own, how innately I had searched for it, licked at it, though she held it back from me—how many times had we shared a kiss?

And if what the lost author observed were to hold true, a myrmaid's kiss could transform. It could empower one with the gift of immortality. Incredible strength. Immeasurable magic...

I open my eyes and look to my left arm, to the silver line of lifeblood carving a path through my skin.

Sea-kissed, I realize.

A small taste of a power that could level kingdoms, if the wielders so wished.

I steady my sights again on the fire blazing in my palms, shooting from my fingertips, swirling like a beating sun with Eloise at its center. Like her, it's beautiful and deadly, remorseless and carefree. Powerful and unrestrained, hypnotizing, coaxing—even now it whispers for me to submit fully to it, to let go of the reins I hold so tightly, trying to control it.

It's always whispered such things, I think. *Just like the sea, it marked me long ago, aided me in my quest for revenge for my lost family, for my lost life.*

'Then, why not let it free?' a darker voice questions. *'Why not trust the fire?'*

"Jaspyr."

Eloise's voice reaches out to me over the vicious snapping and popping of the flames.

"Jaspyr, please." Her golden, silver-lined gaze finds mine through the chaos, pierces me like arrows. "Let me go."

I feel the siren song behind her words, the poisonous enchantment searching for a target. It weighs on me slightly, though it's greatly muffled by the shield. And now that I'm prepared, I can fight it.

"Bite your tongue, you foul creature!" shouts Eddison, directing all his anger at her. "When the sun rises, I hope even your soul burns to ash."

"And if it doesn't," she replies in an icy voice, turning to him, "I'll be sure to rip out your throat when your magic dies. Pity I didn't take the time last night."

"Don't speak to him," I demand, stepping forward. "If you have any empty threats to make, you can direct them to me, beast."

She stills, watching me with an expression mixed with so many things that I can hardly name them all…

Is it me or did I see a flicker of delight gleam in her eyes when I spoke? A flicker of something cruel yet eager that makes me want to provoke her even more?

"Is that why you put me in a cage?" she asks after a moment—I can tell she's making every effort not to cry out again, to hold her screams behind her teeth. *Prideful*, I think. "Because you think me an animal ill-fit for your world?"

"I put you in a cage because I know a muzzle wouldn't fit around your wicked mouth."

She lets out a low laugh, her lips curling into a smile.

"If I do recall correctly, you enjoyed my wicked mouth last night."

Her gaze drops to my pants; my cock responds, betraying me, aching against the seams.

Her lips, her tongue, her bite.

I shift from foot to foot, forcing myself to think of anything other than her mouth on me.

"For what it's worth, I enjoyed my time with you," she adds, quietly.

I push my fire harder; she whimpers, scratching at her skin.

Her gaze shifts to the sky as the night starts to lift, as the stars begin to vanish, one by one. The color fades from black to blue, like thick layers of a blanket being rolled back for the earth to awaken from its slumber. The moon shrinks, as if a god had shoved it farther back in the depthless sky to let the sun have room to shine.

"It's a pity we had only one night together. It felt..." She sighs, setting her gaze back on me. "Wrong and yet right." She tilts her head. "So right for some strange reason."

I swallow my words, afraid to say anything at all, for I know that if I do, it will be to state my agreement.

She presses her palms against the impenetrable shield, as if searching for a crack in the magic in one last desperate act. When she finds nothing, a calm clarity seems to wash over her expression—does she accept that these very well may be her last moments in life?

"Jaspyr," she says again, looking at me, one palm still pressed against the barrier—this time, I know it's her voice unaided with magic, her words true. "If you destroy all of me now, I *will* be gone forever." She swallows. "You will never taste me again. Kiss me again. I will not survive the sun's ascent. Do you understand?"

"Kiss you?" I begin to shake, fingers balled into flaming fists. "You hunted me. *Fed* on me. Manipulated me between your legs."

She scoffs, pressing her body closer to the invisible magic so that I can better see her black skin shimmer beneath the flames, the fire licking at every curve and crevice.

"Don't lie to yourself, not if you insist on bearing witness to my final moments. It makes a mockery of me. Haven't you any modesty?"

My mouth falls open. I move closer. "*Modesty?*"

"Jaspyr," Eddison warns from behind me.

She continues to speak. "The only time I ever manipulated any of your actions was on that first night when I sang. Don't blame me for falling prey to your baser desires. I don't blame you for my downfall. You chose to be with me." She frowns, looking around as if she does not want to be overheard; then she steadies her gaze back on me. "And I chose to be with you. For the Sea's sake, Jaspyr… I *saved* you."

I march forward, ignoring Eddison's shouts to remain at a distance.

"You're delusional," I growl. "You hunted me, vowed to destroy me with your every deceitful breath. I had to placate you just to buy myself more time to live."

Her gaze narrows, her brow knitted. Her perfect lips press together in a firm line, pink fire lining her every inch.

"You didn't *have* to do anything," she replies in a low tone. "I could scent how much you've wanted me since the first moment we met, even if your righter mind cautioned you otherwise. I can scent it on you even now, as *you* hold *my life* in your hands. I should have locked you in a cage." She laughs. "I suppose you're no better than me, hero. Maybe I should've killed you after all."

"I am nothing like you," I say, simmering.

"Don't let her into your head," I hear Eddison say, but his voice feels far away—all I see is her.

I step closer. "You, your kind, you're an abomination on this land." Even as I spit the words at her, like acid on my tongue, I know I will mourn her when she dies. Of how the memory of just one night with her would surely torture me for the rest of my life. "You're as abhorrent as they come—"

"And you're as dark and tormented by death as any necromancer I've ever known to exist on this plane! You're a hypocrite, Jaspyr." She yells over the fire. "Do not judge me for my actions, for who *I am*, if you cannot see the truth of yourself. I am a monster by creation, by Nature's hand. And what of you?"

Any words I held die in my throat—necromancers, death-wielding sorcerers… they're as much myths as the myrmaid standing before me.

The sky lightens only more.

Eloise's voice shakes as she says, "I marked you for death, and yet you still breathe. If I wanted you dead, Jaspyr, then that is what you would be. I *spared* you, held myself back from my true nature because—"

"Because why?" I shout, my heart pounding. " *Why?* Why did you come into my life with such empty threats, if only to leave? You torturous creature…"

I cannot be saved.

My own thoughts anguish me now—deep down, I know that I still seek Death, though this time not to join him. I want to look him in the eyes and demand back what he took from me, my life, my sanity.

She seems to start at my outburst, considering me with a softness unlike anything I've ever seen from her.

"I don't know why," she says, her words as gentle as a brushed kiss. "It's not supposed to be this way, *me* with *you.*" She shakes her head, looking down. "I don't know why Fate won't let me loose from your net, but I'm tangled in you, Jaspyr." She flattens her palm against the shield again. "I just… want you, *all of you*, for as long as I can." Her lips seem to shake with her words, with her fear. "I'm not ready for the end."

I want you, too, the dark part of me whispers.

Her focus slips back to the horizon; a shimmer of fear echoes across her features, jolting something awake in me.

"You're right." I force myself to watch her demise, force myself to keep her gaze. "It's not supposed to be this way." My voice shakes as the sun begins to emerge, its fiery arms stretching outward. "You carry darkness with you everywhere you go. Now you shall face the light."

She lifts her hands, as if holding my flaming magic in her palms. "And you carry destruction," she replies. "Is it not the same? Who will be your reckoning when I'm gone?"

I clench my teeth.

"Don't listen to her!" says Eddison, his voice barely a whisper in my ears now as I focus all my energy on her.

"I am nothing like you," I say again.

"Then let me go. Prove yourself a hero."

I narrow my eyes at her. "I told you before, I'm no hero."

"Then what are you, Jaspyr?" When I don't answer, she says, "I'll tell you what you are. You're the villain in my story. And I'm the one in yours. We are the same, you and I. *Let me go.* And if you don't, I will tell you who your reckoning shall be." Her golden gaze flickers with silver. "My sisters will come for me."

My eyes widen. I hadn't thought once about whether or not others might search for Eloise should she not return to her home.

The wrathful twins... what might they do to me, to Eddison and Penelope, should they find their sister as only ash and bones?

"Let me go," she says again, surely noting the flicker of fear that just shuddered through me.

My throat tightens, the air so dry that my tongue sticks to the roof of my mouth.

"Yield to me," I find myself saying.

She blinks. "What?"

"Yield to me, and I'll set you free." I force the offer from my lips.

"What are you doing?" cries Eddison, struggling beneath the weight of his own magic. "Are you serious?"

I ignore him, setting aside all reason, for him, for my family. Reason has never existed in her presence. And if she's telling even a hint of the truth, then I must strike a deal with this spiteful beast… she seems to respect bargains at least, just like the good king's tale said. It's our only chance to survive in the long run.

Eloise laughs, her voice blending with the crackling fires.

"*Yield* to you?" she asks, her expression brightening with hope. "I am already in your prison."

"And if I free you?"

"Then I shall remain in your prison still." Her words are a soft, sensual, poisonous promise that I understand all too well.

I step forward again—if not for the thin layer of magic between us, we would be nearly nose to nose.

"Swear not to kill me, Eloise. And promise not to kill the ones I love. If I let you go now, you can *never* return here. You must leave me alone. I don't care where you hunt, who you feed on, as long as I never see your face again."

She smirks, her features made all the more lovely with even just a hint of a smile.

Her gaze flicks to Eddison—he is shouting my name. To Penelope who surely watches in horror.

My magic flares, my flames swelling. "Swear to me!"

She flinches, eyes cast down. "I promise. You have my word. I want to live." The words barely pass her lips.

She sets her sights back on me. "A life for a life."

"A life for three, in perpetuity," I amend—I'm not going to make the same mistake as last time.

She nods with reluctance.

"You have my word, Jaspyr." Her throat bobs, eyes darting back and forth. "*Please…* the sun."

I press my flaming palm to the shield, compelling the

shield to crack.

"Jaspyr, no!" yells Eddison, his voice strained, my magic too strong to combat.

His shield fractures, shatters like a mirror.

Fire explodes outward, enveloping me, drawing me straight into Eloise's arms. It blazes around us, hot and dark and wonderful—there, in that moment, locking in on her shimmering gaze without magic distorting my view, I feel as if I truly stare Death in the eyes.

"Now you must yield to me," she whispers into my ear, nibbling at the shell. "No games this time. No lies. Do you want me or not, hero?" Her eyes flash silver, her voice a gentle lullaby. "Speak your truth. I command it."

"Deeply," I choke out, the word pulled from me. I draw closer, unable to think of anything else but her gaze pouring into mine.

"All of me?"

I wish for my body to dissolve into hers. I wish to taste her power, to taste her freedom, to taste her mouth again upon my own, to taste her teeth upon my skin.

"Everything and more."

She studies me for a moment with such intent that all my instincts spring alert to the predator holding me in their arms. And yet, I'm so enraptured by her utter existence that I cannot move.

She offers me a soft smile, her song melting away. I blink, coming back to my senses as she says, "You cannot handle more—"

I press my mouth to hers amid the flames, swallowing her words, stealing one last kiss from Eloise Myr. It's as if she breathes life straight into me.

Then she forces our lips apart, severing our connection. "Like I said." I'm momentarily shocked.

"Go," I say after a moment, hardening myself against

her—she still holds me in her arms. "Go now, and never return. Swear it."

I steel myself to my next words, just to prove to myself that I have the willpower of a righteous man, that I'm nothing compared to the likes of her. "Or stay and burn. I don't care, but get out of my sight."

She starts, seeming taken aback. She lets me go, and I have to pin my arms to my side to not reach for her once more.

Stay! Burn with me, I think.

"Fine. You will never see me again, Jaspyr. I will not kill you or the ones you've named..." She smirks. "Even when you're desperate enough to come searching, I promise you that." She lets out a cruel laugh. "Unless, of course, you beg—"

"Rest assured, I won't."

The corner of her lips curl upward.

"Very well." She presses her palm to my cheek. "Goodbye, then, hero. I suppose you lived up to your title after all. Such stories you can tell your children when they're old."

My jaw twitches.

"I don't think our short-lived chapter would make much of a fairytale," I say.

"Pity." She smiles, the tips of her fangs glinting at me; I stand my ground. "Maybe a different type of story, then."

I let out a low laugh, leaning into the heat of my magic just as much as I lean into her touch. "You are the thing of nightmares, you know."

"Then I shall see you in your sleep." She lowers her hand from me, eyes twinkling.

I step back, opening the flames to finally let her pass.

"How could you?" I hear Eddison say, the fire cleared enough for me to see the betrayal on his face.

Eloise seems to snap back to the present, as do I, the haze of her falling away to reveal the sun about to emerge, to the fire blooming around her.

Her expression shifts from contemplative to one of pure ire as she homes in on my friend's voice. On a breeze, she moves past me, a trail of fire following behind her all the way to Eddison.

"Stop, no!" I cry out, lunging after her.

I'm too slow, too late, as she buries her teeth in his neck.

He makes a gurgling sound, screaming out my name.

"You promised me!" I shout, running toward him. "I freed you, Eloise. You're in my debt."

Eloise releases her deadly grip and glares at me over her shoulder, her mouth and lips stained with his blood—she sings. I freeze, my fires still raging behind me.

Her body glints in the early light of day, my magic misting off her.

"You should speak your bargains more carefully. I never promised not to bite," she says, viciously. "I am in debt to no human." She looks at Eddison in disgust. "We are even. A life for a life. Yours, hers, and *his*." The last word hisses out of her mouth with such contempt as she shoves Eddison to the ground.

He falls to his knees in the grass, hand pressed against his neck.

Eloise looks to him and says, "I knew I had tasted the likes of you before." She licks her lips, her brow knitted in thought. She kneels before him as he tries to crawl away in the grass. "Your bloodline was my very first feed. The blood that solidified my transformation."

I hear Penelope gasp from somewhere far off.

Eloise presses her fingers to Eddison's neck as he whimpers, then brings them back to her lips, savoring.

"Remember, this is now the second time I've allowed you to live." She stands, turning toward Penelope, who runs at her from across the lawn. "No… it couldn't be. What a funny co-incidence." She smiles, bemused, her expression contemplative as she again considers Eddison. "Edward, yes, that was his name. You taste just like him."

"What?" Eddison breathes, tears shining in his eyes.

Her song fades; I stumble forward.

"Eddison, I… I didn't know—" My voice dies in my throat when he looks at me, betrayal etched on his face. "I'm sorry—"

"Jaspyr, no, what have you done?" screams Penelope, coming to stand between us all, her expression stricken with too much sadness to bear.

"Go back inside the house!" Fear scorches through me as Eloise sets her gaze on her.

She stills, stunned. But then she breaks again into a run, magic burning in her eyes. "Get away from my son!"

Eloise looks at Eddison, eyebrows raised. "Your son?" She tilts her head back and laughs. "My, Fate is *ever* twisted."

Her words roll out in a hum.

Penelope stops dead in her tracks, as if her feet are suddenly glued to the spot.

By the way Eloise's eyes lit up, I know she has a hold on her now, too.

"Eloise, please. Leave them both be." My voice chokes as my mind panics—*what have I done?* "They're my family, my life. They're everything!" I scream.

She inclines her head to me, a silent agreement; my entire body sags in relief.

She turns back to Penelope, straightening.

"Your husband had to die so I could live," she replies, steadily—as I look between them both, I recognize the haunted expression in Penelope's face as she's forced to behold her husband's abductor, after all these years of searching for answers.

Eloise releases her hypnotizing grip on her, and she falls forward, hate in her eyes.

"And my son," Penelope presses between her teeth, fists balled at her sides.

Eddison looks up from the ground, understanding and pure wrath flashing in his eyes.

"Thank you for your generosity once again," Eloise says to Penelope, wiping the back of her hand on her mouth. "But I'd be truly malevolent if I completely ended your line. I am not such a monster as that."

Penelope screams in a rage unlike anything I've ever heard before, from anyone—a mother petrified, a wife scorned, a friend betrayed. "*Levantis bora!*"

Silver, white-hot magic shoots from her fingertips and cuts through the space where Eloise stands; I throw myself in front of her, not knowing what it might do to Eloise after she'd been weakened for so many hours. She has to leave now to outrun the sun.

Penelope's spell hits me square in the chest—it's all I can do to block the intensity, the buildup of anger pouring out of Penelope now, tears falling from her eyes and spit flying from her mouth.

Her power seems to rage from her very blood.

It blasts me off my feet, blasts away control of my flame— and even I am afraid of what I conjured today.

As I fly through the air, above the flames and my horror-stricken family, I glimpse the trail of magic that follows Eloise all the way back to the edge of the sea—and though there's no sign of her anywhere as the earth is finally washed in pure, undiluted light, her words still echo in my mind.

'You will never see me again, Jaspyr. Even when you're desperate enough to come searching, I promise you that.'

I slam to the ground with the sun glinting in my eyes. Then everything fades to a burning black.

PART THREE

24

CREATION

ELOISE

SUNFIRE CHASES ME all the way to the shore. I've never run so fast before. Never felt my eternal life so threatened than in these last moments in Jaspyr's land-locked world.

The Sea swaddles me like a babe as I dive into her motherly hold. I cut faster through the water than my temporary human legs could have ever propelled me on land, aiming for the safe darkness of the deep.

I swim onward and the sandy shallow shore drops away with a suddenness that always takes my breath with it. The hills of coral swallow me again, gaping channels and caverns carving across the sea floor in such a way that makes me feel as if I am the smallest creature on this earth—the sunlight no longer reaches me at all here, and I would have no greater wish.

I look ahead, wanting to lose myself in this widening underwater world... wanting to turn back and return to the claustrophobic land to feed on that man.

I try to outpace the memory of the flames that scorched around me for hours, torturing me with their harsh light, their unforgiving heat—and yet, I can still feel their burn tingling atop my skin.

His burn… I think, just as the last of the sun's seeping rays are obliterated by the thick watery night of my home.

'*You almost died!*' Aura's distraught voice blasts across my mind, making my flame-induced headache only worse.

"I know," I say, my voice shaking.

I'm shaking. I close my eyes, letting the soft currents here lull me back into my right mind.

'*Eloise, those humans tried to burn you alive,*' seethes Ora.

"I *know.*" The sound of the crackling flames still echoes in my ears.

The sister sharks encircle me, a calm and welcome presence after… I push the fresh memory even deeper down.

'*You can never go back to that shore!*' they implore as one.

"I know," I whisper, lifting my gaze to the sea sky—here it's as black as any soothing starless night. "I won't."

I promised him I wouldn't, and I shall abide by it. Unless…

I clench my teeth, biting down on the deplorable thought. *There's no unless!*

With a heavy sigh, I sink closer to the ocean floor, wanting to feel the sand beneath my fingertips, to bury myself in its cool shelter like the smaller creatures that reside here—I silently skim my tail and fins along the fine grains of earth, a gentle massage that tickles my senses, relaxing me somewhat. Things slither across the floor or scuttle back into their holes as I glide overhead, causing the glass-like grains to shift and roll to the lull of the currents.

A cluster of chubby sand stars the color of green limes and blushing yellow wildflowers crawl across each other, the floor, the reef in a bizarre, fanned-out herd. They gradually head to some unknown destination that I'm sure will take a thousand years to reach at such a pace…

I hope I can witness the end of their journey one day, I softly wish, a ritual I've practiced since my first time spying them.

'*You won't be able to if you don't let go of this dangerous attachment*,' the Sea scolds.

I focus on the shifting sand. I ponder where each grain has been in this world and how long it has existed on this plane, for like the sea stars, they are always flowing with the currents, a constant yet slow movement, rolling onward to another space.

Where would I go if I didn't exist here anymore? Would my soul carry on to another time and place?

'*Think no more of it*,' insists Aura.

'*You are Eternal, Eloise*,' Ora reminds me.

I scoff, slapping the sand in a fit of anger.

"Only the Sun and Moon are eternal," I say. "Only the Sea and Air and Earth are ceaseless forces." I flip onto my back, resting in the sand, looking up; my friends settle alongside me. "I am just a moment in time, aren't I?" I stroke their scales, gently. They croon at my touch. "Who knows when Syrifina's reign will end."

Aura and Ora gasp. '*You shouldn't speak of such things.*'

As if to denounce my claim, her firstborn daughter and my ruthlessly caring sister, Isobel, glides before me soundlessly. I straighten as she drifts down from the sea sky—a beacon of bright red flaming in the dark, her regal presence humbling to any living being in the vicinity.

She need only narrow her eyes in my direction. She need only press her lips together. Obedient, I drift toward her.

EELS AND SEA SNAKES THE SIZE OF LIMBS shoot through the water to escort her, as if they could sense her presence as she entered their domain. They wind alongside her, desperate for her attention, for normally she loves to play.

Today, Isobel pays her admirers no mind—she's solely focused on me.

"You seem perturbed," she says, dryly after a long, excruciating silence of me trailing behind her. Aura and Ora remain even further back. "What ails you this time?" Something about her tone keeps me on edge, wary. "Or is it the same ailment that caused you to *flee* from me like a scared fish the other day?"

The ice in her voice is an unmistakable warning—I choose my words carefully.

"No, it's just—"

"Just what?"

I bury my nerves. "Just sunrise," I reply, smoothly—not a complete lie this time.

The eels and sea snakes wind around her, nudging her for attention; she flicks them small gifts of magic before shooing them off so we can swim in peace. They slither away at the nearest bend in the coral, weaving in and out of the reef's endless dark tunnels that swallow them whole. I shiver at the thought of meeting them in there, in the dark, alone. Their gaping mouths and large, glassy eyes sometimes give even me a small start when they sneak up on us like that...

And yet, I find myself edging after them.

I have to escape Isobel. I can't let her find out about what I've done, what's happened to me.

The weight of my mistakes makes me sink even lower— not only did I let a man live with my secret but now three humans with vendettas against my kind know what I am... and somehow, through my carelessness no doubt, they have learned our greatest weakness.

"Going somewhere?" says Isobel, glancing over her shoulder to find me drifting off course.

"No," I say, hurriedly, floating back to her level; I look back to the tunnels that connect my world to who knows where. "I was only wondering what we should find if we followed them. There's so much of our world left to mystery." Again, not a complete lie.

But I don't say that I also wonder, if I did follow them, would there be a chance I might never have to see the sunshine again? See him? Or might they take me back toward a hidden pocket of the earth, like the Split, where we could secretly be together once more.

"Some things are better left unexplored, Eloise."

We edge closer to Empress Isle. The full moon gathering will take place tonight, yet I can't even fathom looking Syrifina in the eye… let alone facing all my sisters. I have disgraced them.

Isobel falls as silent as the shadows that swim around us, her solemn presence an unwelcome reminder of all the wrong I have done and cannot speak.

I become lost in my thoughts the deeper we go, the heat of my flaming prison still an uncomfortable itch atop my skin.

There will be no relief, not from him.

I should have tasted him one last time.

'*You've had your fill, Eloise,*' the currents whisper.

My throat tightens for how dry it feels. My stomach churns at the emptiness only growing.

An endless forest of kelp trees suddenly surrounds us from top to bottom, jarring me back to the present. They envelop, consume—the same way Jaspyr has enveloped my mind.

Long, leafy tubes sweep us into their domain, swaying softly. It's impossible to see where they begin and end in any direction, from top to bottom, from right to left. I feel as if

I'm floating on another plane of existence altogether, swallowed by a gentle, soothing beast.

I love to imagine that the God of Earth and the Goddess of the Sea shared an epic fight over territory here thousands of years ago. In this battle, our great goddess conjures a mammoth wave that ultimately claims victory and a new island for us to enjoy. The God of Earth concedes, and continues to shine his gifts on this dark, emerald city.

The creatures thriving here are many, a hub of activity rippling through the forest.

A wave of excitement washes over me as we dip deeper into the swaying trees, shifting away some of the dread that's settled with me after last night—I know the shipwreck is close.

I flick my tail a little faster on reflex; Isobel tries to hide her smile of approval, slowing to let me pass.

"It's been more than a decade already," she says, restraining her own delight at this landmark in our journey. "Will you ever swim these waters with calm or shall you always lose your wits when we pass?"

I let out a bubble-filled laugh that relieves some of my anxiety.

"I think I lost my wits some ways back," I say under my breath.

"Indeed," she says, crossing her arms at her chest.

I carry on before she thinks of her next words to say, trying to stall whatever lecture or scolding she's planned for me today—I don't think I can take it in this state.

"I hope it will always spark the same excitement in my soul," I add, hurriedly, making a show of swimming all around. "It's such a legendary place. I can't help but be keen to see it every time." Another truth, veiling a horrendous lie about how close I was to never seeing it again…

I push the bone-chilling thought away and risk a glance at Isobel.

A softness placates her cold expression as she watches me in that big-sister way—one that makes me cower in her presence yet feel safe and protected all at once.

"What?" I ask with the lift of my eyebrow.

She shrugs, combing her fingers through her long hair—each strand shimmers and glints just like the gold of the sun; I shiver.

"It's a joy to see such light in your eyes," she replies after a moment. "You seem so... plagued lately. It's quite unlike you." She swims up to me, wrapping her arm around my waist, a gentle embrace; I try not to flinch at her closeness, try not to let her see my wariness as her fire-kissed scales and fins skim my own. "I hope your light never dies. That you always feel so ignited by this world."

I force myself to nuzzle in closer, relaxing into my sister's arms. "It won't," I say with conviction.

I came too close.

Isobel offers me a cautious smile, then opens her arm, gesturing me forward.

With the brush of her hand and the pulse of her magic, the kelp parts like two large curtains to reveal a massive entity of wood, ravaged by time—this ship belongs to the Sea.

To us.

We float there a moment, observing the foreign structure, now a permanent, notorious fixture in our terrain.

Algae hangs from it like garlands.

A community of fish and the like have made it into a sturdy home base, weaving in and out of shadowy, small places that even I dare not to explore—every inch of the wood is rotted, and fire coral has sprouted across the deck, the only thing in the sea a myrmaid does not care to touch.

It won't gravely harm us, of course, but it does really sting.

I wonder if my pain tolerance for it has increased after last night...

I tremble at just the thought of feeling anything close to that ever again in my immortal life—I steer far clear of the fire coral and focus on the clean white bones and skulls scattered around the vicinity and aboard the ship.

This place appears more like a haunted graveyard than an ordinary wreck—hundreds of those scatter our seas. No, this remains a notorious museum of decay frozen in time, a dedication to the ghost of Syrifina's past.

This ship was once captained by her forsaken pirate lover, the unwitting father of her only human child—to any myrmaid, it remains the ultimate reminder of how the Queen of Seas came to be *and* why her creations will forever savor the blood of men.

More, my body sings, secretly worshiping Jaspyr's name.

Isobel and I hover before the sunken relic in a moment of silence. The wood is warped and splintered, chunks missing here and there. But it's easy to imagine it in all the splendor that it once had, for it remains mostly intact, even after all this time.

I'm certain Syrifina's magic is at play to keep it from fully decaying, though nature has taken it over for its own.

Cracked trunks once brimming with gold and silver are spilled across the crumbling decks, and hordes of colorful jewels twinkle throughout the interior of the ship; if one peeks in from the outside, they still appear to shine and glint as if they'd recently been placed atop the broken wooden floors and decaying rugs. There are also fallen statues and strange trinkets belonging to the Olleb's enchanted history scattered all about the area.

Priceless objects to men. A lost pirates' ship bounty, marking their final resting place, along with their bones.

"Where do you think it all comes from?" I muse. "I wonder if anyone still misses these treasures up there."

In its entirety, the ship's decorations look as if a palace gallery somewhere above had been stripped bare, or maybe a dwarves' treasure trove underground pillaged, then lost beneath the sea.

Both theories were probably right—pirates were ruthless, greedy animals back then, but we no longer suffer them. Syrifina made it her personal endeavor to end their reign over our waters long ago, starting with this crew.

"Does it matter?" she says, unfeeling. "Those who walk the land above are all the same, just skin and blood and bones. Nature exacts balance. This is ours now, forever."

We circle the ship's tall mast, slowly, all the way down to the bottom, paying our respects to Syrifina's greatest loss—the only daughter with a beating heart that she had granted her name, Maddison Myr. We have all been obliged to hear that story more than once, the story of how Mother was made...

25

RECKONING

DARLING DIARY,

You won't believe this for a second… but I died today.

I was happy for a human moment, until I realized he was gone.

I could see him still—deep orange canvases billowing in the wind, his ship set for the horizon as if it might melt right into it. Its sails blotted out the beating sun, thrusting in the harsh winds. The dark painted wood glistened like the Black Sand Desert I have only ever heard stories about.

Father would have chided me for staring after it so long, as if it were a forest fairy's bewitching light meant to lead me astray.

I wished it would as it teased me from across the waves. I wished with everything that it would guide me to another land.

But he left me…

I chased that ship as far as I could; tears wet my eyes when it vanished.

As quick as it'd come, my fantasies of sailing away from this place were dashed, the sun mocking me with its arrogant face as it shed light on the sinful choices I had fallen prey to under the cover of night.

The early morning sunrays burned my fair skin, but inside I felt nothing but cold, my veins iced over with self-loathing and an equally matched hatred for him.

I was forced to hide my indiscretions for as long as I could from my family, rotting with anger and alone in my guilt. And when I could hide my growing belly no longer, my father banished me from our village in disgrace.

As barely a young woman, I was cast out from my tribe without trial, cast out of the only, be it dull, life I had ever known, to survive and care for my unborn child on my own.

As my belly grew with each turn of night to day, the colder I became. It stitched to me like a new skin, replacing my warmth with something dark and disdainful, void of pain and humility but bright with wrath at being isolated, like the moon in its fullest form.

I began to glow with grand ideas of revenge on the men who had abandoned me to this…

Not soon after, I delivered my baby alone in the wilderness.

With great sorrow in my heart, I left a healthy girl—born with eyes as blue and bright as the water I had always wished to explore—somewhere safe on the far side of the island, to be raised by other villagers.

May she live a healthy, adventurous life.

Next, darling Diary, I did what many angry, prideful, resilient, lost young women have done… I set out for retribution.

Deep in the jungles of Idris, I sought out the rumored sorcerer who lived in secret among us—a person named as such was thought to have mastered foundational magic. Tapped into the purest of elements, channeled the undiluted power of the gods and goddesses of the Olleb-Yelfra.

Earth, Air, Fire, and Water.

Even back then, such all-powerful beings as gods and goddesses were thought to be the things of legends. But their legends had persisted and people revered them properly, so much so that tales of them had made it as whispers on the wind to my secluded little island.

I knew from my elders that their epic histories were retold in brilliant cathedrals across faraway lands that I one day hoped to see. That somewhere out there stood statues made of fine metals and stones that had weathered decades, centuries of time, erected in their honor; I hoped to lay my palms upon them in this lifetime.

Their essence could be traced back to the creation of magic, the balance of all things in nature. And despite the doubts of my elders, I knew these terrible and boundless beings were real. That they were the true rulers of my world...

Not my father, not the pillaging pirates.

Not men nor humans at all! Because how could people so small-minded have anything to do with something like the grandness of an ocean? Or the true darkness of the night?

And if they were real, so too would be the sorcerer on Idris—I willed it.

After months of scouring the jungles, I found the one I sought. A mythical man living and enduring in the wild, in beautiful solitude, by the force of his own power.

When I told him of my great sorrows and pled for his relief, he gave into my persuasion almost instantly. Men always do.

He offered me two choices, both of which he agreed to

assist with: forgive and move forward into the future with open arms, or seize my revenge—the consequence of which, he warned, would always tether me here, in a limbo between the present and the past.

It was an easy decision for me... I wanted to delve deeper into my anger, my desires, the dangerous and forbidden. I have always wanted this, and I fear I always shall.

"The future is irrelevant to me if I cannot conquer the here and now." My choice was made.

Then, I readily drank the potion the Sorcerer brewed to aid it.

Darling Diary, we will never know exactly what was in the concoction that burned down my throat, stripping away my humanity and transforming me into something more. However, I believe that the Goddess of the Sea had blessed it herself.

The moment the enchanted drink touched my tongue, I was crowned a queen of a world with no contenders, the Moon a sure witness that night.

"Tread carefully, Myr maiden," the Sorcerer had said. "You have been blessed with great responsibility to the Olleb, and your powers may continue to manifest over time. But if you do choose the path of retribution, be prepared to face consequence... for it shall be equally great, indeed."

"I can't imagine any consequence worse than what I've already suffered from the one who shall face reckoning," I replied.

"Then your imagination is not creative enough," he said, the threat looming between us like a dark cloud. "Your life will be long, endless maybe. I'm sure Nature can find a way to entertain herself with the challenge. She's ever resourceful."

"As am I," I said with a low bow.

"Happy hunting, then," he said with a knowing grin. "Go well, Syrifina Myr. I can't wait for the waves to whisper to me of the adventures I'm sure you'll one day... soon, have."

I thanked the Sorcerer graciously, promising to use my gifts to ensure the balance of our precious Olleb.

Then the Sea sang to me loudly, inviting me to my new domain.

I ran as fast as I could through the trees, all the way to the familiar shoreline. I had never felt the wind rush on my face like that before, never felt my legs so strong and sure.

As soon as I let my feet touch the waves, splashing up to my knees, my real transformation took hold—a tail spun like sheets of glittering silks formed in place of my legs, and underwater I found I could truly breathe.

The miraculous potion had given me the ability to manipulate the water to my every whim, exactly what I needed in order to meet my pirate again...

I continued my hunt for revenge across the Sea of Saindora night after night, honing my new powers along the way.

Then, beneath a dark and stormy moonrise, I finally saw the sunset sails whipping in the unforgiving winds, waves hurling alongside the ship, hungry for it... as was I.

I watched and waited until someone spotted me, bright red hair and pearl-white skin, flesh bared in the night, drifting in the black waters—a maiden in distress, they thought.

An animal ready to attack, destroy, I knew. I would rip out the bloodied, beating heart of the one who had frozen mine and sink my ready fangs into it.

When I marked my pirate, I felt nothing of the adoration and love I had graciously offered him before. Only ire, disgust.

I was hungry. Voracious with raw appetite. My throat burned for him. With every whiff of his scent and the other humans around him, I grew ravenous, maddened for his blood; and if I didn't drink soon, I ran the risk of reverting back to a human—that was not an option.

But the consequence the Sorcerer warned of made me hesitate… made me consider seeking another's vein to drink from, anyone else aboard this ship.

In the end, his warning was easy to disregard.

He was kind to offer me a choice, but I had no regrets about the future I sought. I didn't care what else Nature might decide to take from me in payment for granting me my greatest wish.

Besides, surrendering my humanity in exchange for eternity and power had been such a bargain… whatever else he might desire from me would be even easier to part with, right?

I called to my pirate from the waters, my intoxicating song urging him to join me in the sea while the others stood frozen, incapacitated, to watch. The storm cheered me on with every clap of thunder, every explosion of light streaking across the night as he dove into the waters to rescue me.

I waited as he swam to me, fighting the impossible waves that I had conjured with a mere thought.

When he reached me and looked into my eyes, saw the glint of my fangs and the hunger in my gaze, surely it was then that he realized the mistake he'd made.

26

MORTALITY

ƆELOISE

"IT'S TIME WE TALK," says Isobel, interrupting my thoughts. "I heard what you said earlier, questioning your immortality. Eloise, where have such terrible thoughts sprung from?" She lowers her voice to barely a whisper. "And why would you ever speak a doubt aloud about Mother's eternal reign? Do you know how foolish that was? Why, you'll be lucky if the currents don't whisper it in her ear."

I stop swimming, looking away from her. "I…"

I fixate on a gleaming gold chain with a crossed bones and skull pendant that seems to forever sway in the water—Syrifina's doomed lover's chain, ripped from his neck upon his death. It hangs on a groove on the lowest part of the mast.

It's always been there and will always remain, a tribute to the catalyst that led to the creation of myrmaids, of our history.

Of me…

I feel the burn, the judgment of Isobel's stare upon me as we float before the open graveyard.

"I demand to hear it. Why did you utter such blasphemy?" she asks again, this time much more forcibly.

I frown, thinking that the words I'd spoken earlier to question our mortality were the least blasphemous thing I had done all week.

As if she can hear my damning thoughts, she swoops toward me and forces me to face her.

"*Speak!*" she says; the water undulates around her.

She is fire. She is power. Magic resounds with her voice, the force of it propelling me backward and frightening away any life in the vicinity—we're utterly alone.

Only the water can spy on my secrets now.

A sense of cold overwhelms me, and not the kind I normally welcome with open arms.

Isobel's jaw sets, her silver stare brightens. And with the shipwreck as her backdrop, she looks like a fierce, unforgiving warrior of the water. The only thing missing is a sword with a flaming blade in her hand.

"I will *not* chase you around this endless ocean to ask you again, Eloise. Find your tongue."

Not a question nor request any longer—I will obey Isobel just as incontestably as I would Syrifina.

I nod, submissive, terrified back to my senses.

I muster all my courage, empowering myself to face some version of the truth. "I was landwalking again," I say in a shaky voice. I try not to shrink under her scrutiny this time. "I know my excursions to the surface are much more frequent than you'd approve of, but—"

She makes a derisive sound under her breath. Her magic and fins ripple around her in warning; she surely knows I'm withholding, dancing around the sharp edges of the conversation like we do with fire coral.

"Why, you flatter me, Eloise." Her stare is spellbinding, her expression hard. "I don't approve of it at all."

She crosses her arms at her chest, impatient.

I can't hold back any longer, not with Jaspyr's name, his blood, boiling on my tongue. "I hunted in Kampaulo a few days ago and came across a scent unlike any other," I say, my words tumbling out. "I don't know why I—" I huff out a frustrated string of bubbles. "This man intended to rescue me, thought I was in danger." I shake my head from the confusion of it still. "I was just having a bit of fun. And I don't know how to even explain it to you, Isobel… his scent was *so* intoxicating."

I sigh, deeply, the memory of him filling me once more.

"I think I desired his blood so badly that it frightened me, stalled me." *Frightens me even still.* I begin to swim back and forth, unable to look her in the eye as I unravel. "I've never felt like this before. I don't know why or even how, but—"

"You tasted him, then let him live… didn't you?"

I freeze, staring at her with a question that does not pass my lips. *How could you possibly know that?*

Sometimes I swear that she's part seer—an enchanted being that Zahra once described to me as all-knowing, all-seeing, yet blind to our world.

"Yes," I whisper—a giant weight seems to float away from my chest with the confession, like a ship's anchor being lifted off me.

I steady myself in her direction, willing myself to face her in my shame.

Isobel contemplates me, her demeanor softening somewhat. Her magic drifts away, dimming, until she's no longer this ethereal being ablaze on our dark path. She's merely Isobel again, my sharp-toothed sister and trusted mentor.

"Is that *all* you would like to confess?" she asks, lifting her brow.

"I'm careful—"

"*Lies…*" she snaps, her magic bursting outward again in a

shocking blast—I gasp. "Half-truths! The twins have already spread rumors of just how *careful* you are."

I wish my magic could let me shrivel into a ball so the currents could whisk me away.

"The twins?" I ask, my voice coming out small.

I normally feel weightless here, like a bird soaring through the indigo skies as ships skim the waves below, free. But with Isobel's attention on me now, I fear I might sink, like a rock, from their intensity.

"They say you fought them to protect a *man*." The last word slithers off her tongue in disgust. "The man you let live, I presume."

Her eyes bulge, waiting for me to dispel these stories—when I don't, she balks and backs away to look at me properly.

"Do you realize the error you've made, Eloise? If Mother learns of this…" She cuts through the water, floating close to me, voice low. "You're lucky she hasn't summoned you already."

My anger consumes me like Jaspyr's raging fire. "Nothing about this is lucky!" I shout.

Isobel recoils, shocked. But she continues, "Not only did you attack one of your sisters—"

"The twins are outright terrors, even to us," I retort, whipping my tail in her face to propel me in the opposite direction. "I don't care what they say. I don't care if they're my sisters." I flash her a glare over my shoulder. "And word won't reach Syrifina because the twins have their own secrets to hide from her. Mother wouldn't be very pleased to learn that they killed a woman mid-transformation! I bet you didn't hear about *that* in the gossip they spread."

The currents seem to laugh at my brazenness.

Isobel's eyes widen for a split second, then narrow to slits. She purses her lips. "Don't be a fool," she says with a dangerous quiet that makes me pause in my path. "You're still lying to me, to yourself. I know what you did that you won't speak of. Enough with these diversions. Confess the full truth or else I'll force it from you."

An icy ache curls in the hollow of my bones.

"What do you mean?" I ask, cautiously. I dare to face her again.

"What do I mean?" She bares her teeth at me, her expression turning violent. "You fed... more than once this cycle!" Her voice remains hushed, but with the crimson creeping over her pale cheeks, I feel as if she'd bellowed at me. "I swam with Vasylina and Miki last night. They were quite eager to tell me that my ward joined them on a hunt, then *fought them* for the right to sink their teeth into a male... and claimed his companion! They said they left you on land to feed alone since you apparently couldn't be bothered to share. What in the Goddess's name has gotten into you?"

I swallow, my throat so, so dry. "No... no, that's not exactly what—"

She points an accusatory finger at me. "*You* told me you had already fed on the night when I asked you to join me on my hunt."

If I had a beating heart, I think it would have stopped. "I... I—"

She closes the distance between us lightning fast, her nose nearly pressed against my own. She lifts her chin, steadying her ruby-rimmed gaze on mine.

"I can smell the excess blood on you." Her voice slices deep into my flesh, like the coldest of ice. "You fed on this man. You lay with him, then let him live... and you fed on others."

I close my mouth, casting my eyes down.

She swims slightly back to take me all in, all my disgrace. Her mouth hangs open for a moment, then her lifeblood glows fiercely red.

"The truth, now, Eloise, so help me Goddess of the Sea!

How many times during this moon's cycle have you drunk?"

I look to my hands and realize I'm still shaking—was it from my near-death experience or all the extra blood?

"I don't know," I say, wrapping my arms around myself. "I'm not entirely sure. It's just been a couple more than... than necessary, I suppose."

I don't count the extraordinarily delicious nibbles on Jaspyr nor his friend between meals. And I don't tally the fisherman, the two criminals, nor the four early beachgoers that I ravished after I fled the fire this morning; I just had such an aching in my core. *More, more!*

I let out a heavy sigh, taking in her shadowed expression. *Can she hear me counting in my head?*

"It's really nothing to worry over," I say, plastering on a smile. "I have everything under control. I just lost my temper with the twins. I'll apologize, set everything straight again."

"Do not ignore this! What were you thinking?" She looks down, shaking her head, her golden locks swishing in the water. "You reckless child..." She grabs me by the wrist. "Rumors in the sea spread fast, Eloise." She lowers her voice even more. "You should count your sea stars lucky that *I'm* the only one who knew you had already fed under this cycle of the moon. If word of this gets out, why—"

Her panic rattles me more than anything has thus far.

I shake out of her grip.

"It won't! I can handle this. Just... please, you can help me. Tell me what to do." I squeeze her hand. "I'll do anything if you just... just tell me how to end this... this senseless craving. I need you, sister, please."

It is the first *fully* honest sentiment I have expressed; relief washes over me, at my own acceptance of my wrongdoings.

But why has this happened to me in the first place?

'*Isobel knows something,*' answers Aura.

'*She's keeping secrets too,*' adds Ora.

'*Make her sing her forgotten story for you,*' they hum as one.

My throat tightens as I consider her now, waiting for her to speak. "Will you… help me?" I ask again, tilting my head. "Do you know anything, from your long history, that might give me the answers I seek?"

Pity shines in her eyes. She appears to deliberate over her words.

"I can only help if you're sincere with me from here on out," she finally says. Her gaze burns into mine. "First, tell me everything. And don't leave a single thing out."

'*A truth for a truth,*' says Aura.

'*Sing, Eloise,*' says Ora. '*Then maybe she'll sing for you.*'

So I do. As we swim past the shipwreck, I relay every desire-crazed thought in my mind since I first laid eyes on Jaspyr, one that even led me to feed on a woman. I confess to our union in the Split. Of my fascination with him that continuously begs me to let him live, that impales my better senses and causes me to behave so erratically. I admit how thirsty I am, *always*, no matter how much I've already drunk against the moon's blessing this month. How the thirst seems to only grow, like a human cancer in the mind… how I let it fester, how I feed it.

And I explain that I've visited Jaspyr every night since we met, tasted him, savored him like a fine wine. How no one's blood could ever compare. Not in one hundred thousand years.

The only part I leave out is the land-locked fire trap my prey and his friends had set for me just hours ago, that they'd nearly succeeded in ending me. And the promise that freed me—not even Aura and Ora blame me for hiding that part, and I pray no one ever finds out.

The shipwreck is already far behind us, the sea opening up again wide.

"I see," says Isobel after my story is done. "I see."

She turns away from me.

"You see what?" I ask, no, *demand*, this time. "What is it that *you're* hiding from me now? I know there's something you're not telling me."

"Goddesses…" She curses under her breath, her crimson lifeblood blazing brightly. "This isn't good."

She no longer seems angry, or at least she hides it well with a mask of sisterly concern.

"We need to go somewhere where we won't be overheard. It's not safe here for me to tell you… but I think it's time you knew the full truth, before the gathering commences tonight."

Isobel doesn't give me an opportunity to ask more questions—she plunges down. Dread eats away at my insides as I follow.

'*The way you should've eaten him,*' the Sea croons.

I set my gaze on a skull half buried in the sand, trying to empty my morbid mind. A small black eel slithers in and out of the eye sockets. I faintly wonder if it was part of a skeleton from the wreckage we'd long since left or a more recent meal from someone, something, else. Then I muse…

If a myrmaid does die, would their bones be left behind?

27

BOUND

I PRETEND NOT TO NOTICE Greggor's ghost, an ethereal body of transparent light floating beside me as I pace the streets, hands in my pockets. Eventually, I end up at the shore, where I last spotted her trail.

I have carried ghosts with me for a long time now… *Sibyl. Luna.*

Though, this is the first one that I know to be real.

Greggor is no figment of my deceptive imagination nor my broken mind—stories of lost spirits were told before the King's reign. Souls who lingered after death, unable to move on for reasons of their own.

I don't know why his spirit still clings to the earthly plane. But right now, I feel just as lost as him.

"Why did I do it, Greggor?" I find myself whispering after all these hours, finally acknowledging his presence. "Why did I let her get in my head like that?"

He's been with me ever since I awoke in the field, alone,

an ash-carved circle around me. I thank all the gods and god-desses of Olleb-Yelfra that Eddison and Penelope were able to contain my magicked fires, that I hadn't taken away every-thing from them—their home still stands, but when I went to enter, I found it closed to me for the first time in decades.

I have been walking ever since, thinking of her, of how I had the chance to kill the greatest monster I've ever faced, then freed her at the first sign of weakness.

"Gods," I breathe, covering my face with my hands. "I'm a perfect fool. Eddison will never forgive me for this."

It was one thing to make a deal with his torturer. But his father's murderer...

I scream into my palms, my voice muffled. "I didn't know."

When I lower them, twilight begins to creep across the land. A brush of rich navy bends across the horizon, twinkling with the early signs of stardust.

"Eloise is every man's dream and every man's nightmare," Greggor replies, gazing out beside me. "Sometimes we cannot see, or simply do not wish to recognize, the venom behind such a lovely smile."

His words are wise, wiser than I ever knew him to be in the flesh. It's as if he has consumed decades more knowledge in the hours passed since his death.

"What happened when you died?" I ask. "Where did you go?" I can't bring myself to look at him, so I steady my gaze on the sky. A plump moon begins to rise above the sea, slowly emerging from a soft bed of mist-like clouds.

Is it worth the journey? What else is out there?

"It's going to be a full moon tonight," he says. "Her kind will be out for blood in droves. It's their time, so it's best if you wait this out, away from the water. After tonight, they won't feed again until the new moon comes."

"They feed with the cycle of the moon?" I say with a gasp.

I finally turn to him—he nods.

"Sometimes, in the days before," he adds. "But tonight and on the new moon is when they are at their most power-ful… and hungry. The sea runs red."

I think back to the first night I laid eyes on Eloise, a bright waxing moon beaming in the sky, inching toward its fullest state with each passing night she returned to hunt me. On the cusp of this night, it's brimming with light, yet I know she will not come for me.

I try to smother my disappointment. It eats away at me. *Where has she gone?*

"You're a good man, Jaspyr," continues Greggor; it looks as if he might reach out a hand, then thinks better of it. "Take your own advice. Leave this place. Go somewhere far from the water. Don't let that myrmaid be the death of you. There's plenty of other, lesser, men who will catch her eye when it's her time to feed again."

A sick part of me twists with the slightest bit of jealousy, that another man might endure the pleasure of her mouth on them.

I force the deplorable notion as deep down as I can.

"You're dead, my friend," I say, turning to face Greggor. "And you're worried about my life?" I laugh, though it rolls out cold, unfeeling. "How noble of you."

He smiles, then tilts his head with a strange expression—I wonder if this hasn't occurred to him yet.

"I suppose I still linger on this plane to return the favor that you tried to pay me. But I won't be staying long." He shrugs. "The Olleb whispers to me, Jaspyr. You and Eloise are not meant to be. Let her go. If your paths should cross again, gods save you."

The small, raw wounds on my neck, my wrist, my chest, tingle. A shiver rolls across my skin; I imagine Eloise dragging her teeth gently over my body.

I swallow, frowning at the waters, standing my ground as cold wind tumbles toward me off the waves.

I should fear the Sea of Saindora now, turn away from it, knowing what roams beneath its darkening expanse. But with my magic burning in me, *free*, I stare on in challenge—the muscles in my left arm twitch, my single strand of lifeblood shimmering, as if reacting to its creator's proximity.

"If she returns and breaks her promise, then I *will* kill her," I say, meaning every word.

"A stronger man might, but—"

"But what?" I whirl to face him, but he's gone, the air glittering where he was before.

"She's tasted your blood," he speaks from behind me. "And you've tasted her." *Her power. Her kiss. More!*

I turn on my heels, slowly, fists clenched.

Greggor laughs, shaking his head at me. "I'm a ghost, Jaspyr… you can fight me about as well as you can fight the terrors of your past." On a phantom wind, he blows closer to me. "I'm trying to help you have a future, like you helped me."

I can see through him, to the cliff face, to the sea, and yet his features are as defined as any breathing man's.

I heave out a sigh, unclenching my fists. "I sent her away," I say, unsure why my voice shakes, why my words sound like a soft plea.

"Aye, you did. And she shall keep her word, forever… if you are strong enough to hold *your* tongue. That deal you struck was the wisest thing you've done thus far when it comes to Eloise Myr, for both of your sakes."

I don't know why his words make my heart beat faster. Why my chest seems to tighten with dread. "How do you know any of this?"

"Nothing binds a myrmaid better than a promise. They are honorable creatures to their word. But Eloise seems lost herself. She's fixated on your blood, on you. If you should de-nounce the oath you set, there will be nothing to hold her back anymore—"

"I would never do such a thing!" I think of Eddison, of Penelope. I have already failed them by letting her go; I will not fail them again by calling that monster back to our shores.

He offers me a soft smile, though it doesn't reach his eyes; he considers me for a long moment. "I hope you're right. For if you do, you surely won't survive."

"Give me some credit," I say, pursing my lips. "I'm still standing, aren't I?" I open my arms out wide. "I'll be just fine. Better than fine. The myrmaids are gone, and they're not com-ing back."

He smirks. "Good. I don't want to have to worry about you joining me here. You're much too young and haughty for this place. You still have so much to do on the earthly plane. They need more men like you here, who remember." He looks around, seeming to see something I cannot.

My chest twists with guilt, layers of it. "I'm sorry," I whis-per, bowing my head.

"Why? I made my choice to stay in Kampaulo. I was too afraid to uproot my life." He scoffs, gesturing to his translu-cent body glowing like a lamp in the falling night. "Now look at me."

"At least you escaped her," I say.

Even now, I find myself fixated on Eloise—her strength, her power. The way that the mere sound of her voice can make my stomach ache with a voracious thirst for her.

Bring her back, a seductive voice speaks. *Life will be mean-ingless until you see her again.*

Greggor huffs. "You have my condolences, son," he says, somberly, his voice an echo of warmth, a comfort. "Heed my warning, please." He sighs, looking over his shoulder into the dark. "Or I shall see you soon."

He vanishes in a burst of brilliant light, though I still feel him with me.

I jump back, shielding my eyes.

When the light dissipates, only the rising moon glares back at me, as if daring me to call out her name...

Eloise! I internally scream, dropping my gaze to the water.

The memory of her enchanting song fills my head, surrounds me on the beach. "Release me from your spell," I whisper.

28

CURSE

ᗤELOISE

WE SWIM FOR A WHILE WITHOUT WORDS, Isobel's back to me; I can sense a dark truth looming ahead, hovering around my sister.

A forest of wild kelp swallows us once more as I rush to follow her glistening trail. Instinctively, I take a swift turn, alongside a steep cliff of ribbed rock that guides me away from the swathes of nature and into a deeper, surer darkness.

There's a certain depth where no light reaches at all, where the life forms that sink beyond that threshold create their own brilliant light powered from within—we call it the Sea of Night.

Years of taking this path and it's still always so jarring to me, the sudden moment all traces of sunlight vanish yet still swirl in my eyes. I have to blink several times to focus.

I'm surrounded by nothing but black, so rich that it glistens a deep maroon. At first, all I can make out are minuscule floating particles that look like slow-falling snow, drifting down toward the deep from a velvet, flowing sky. Then the underwater nighttime becomes vivid and alive, a luminous wonderland.

In the pitch-black waters, my mere movement stirs the sleeping life here awake. Luminescent beings dot the water as if they are our very own stars, except much more vibrant—neon pricks and ribbons and balls of every color glow, only making themselves visible in a cloud of rippling light when disturbed.

Pearls of luminescent life dance beyond me, and the strangest of the Olleb's creatures quietly lurk—the shimmer of translucent scales, gleaming skeletal frames, lustrous eyes, and sharp, shining teeth is the only thing that gives them away in these shadows.

I slow, admiring the strange universe here.

I spot a soft, bobbing firelight that entrances me the same way a fairy catches its prey. I force my gaze away from the beautiful flicker and look beyond, wishing I had practiced as much willpower when it came to Jaspyr.

A dragonfish stares back at me, its mouth hanging open, waiting for something juicy to layer its rows and rows of jagged, sharp, ice-like teeth—Mother named it for its likeness to the legendary dragons she claims used to lazily wait for lost, curious sheep in the volcanic regions.

Slowly, I back away, eyes averted. "Happy hunting," I say with the soft flick of my fins.

I weave in and out of creatures with scales as clear as glass that hide in plain sight and ones that are speckled, with bright colors splattering their bodies, too bold to cower from their enemies.

Then I come across a swarm of enchanting, umbrella-shaped creatures that create a small, glowing sea all their own—these graceful yet bulbous fish bounce leisurely atop long, buoyant tentacles with no sense of direction. They just pulse through the water, sucking in and expanding out the entirety of their form to move from one point to another.

I always thought them like flowers in constant bloom unleashed from their roots. Even their colors are bright and alive with a vibrancy that would be hard to replicate anywhere else.

"So beautiful," I say to myself.

Jaspyr's paintings trickle into my mind.

He could probably capture their essence.

I shove the thought down, letting it float away into the darkness.

I spot Isobel far below the vast glowing cloud that the creatures have created and descend to her level.

Her back is turned toward me, her fins flared out like the wind catching fire. She's face to face with one of the most terrifying organisms that roam the Sea of Night—the enormous creature is a black, bulging mass of death that silently floats in the darkest parts of our waters, waiting patiently in a web of light. Though its body blends with the nothingness that surrounds us, a luminous tentacle drips from its head; it's as if its lifeblood has peeled away from its skin to leave nothing but black.

That single bright light—beautiful, enrapturing, radiant—lures its victims in until there's no turning back from the perilous ending that awaits them at the center.

Just like our song.

The only thing that could possibly scare it is a staredown with the mighty Isobel—in a burst of skittish light, it's gone without a trace.

"Isobel..." I softly say, swimming around to her front; she doesn't answer.

The clouds of floating flowers sink lower, a storm of dazzling, iridescent light flashing above us. And with the soft white, bone-like coral bushes layering the sea floor below, I know we are very close to home.

This is where we love to dance.

My sisters and I normally twist through these magical waters with such ease in our souls, the darkest place in our seas springing to life to guide us to Empress Isle.

But Isobel is stone-faced now, floating in silence, ignoring the best parts of our world. Her mind is somewhere else, somewhere even darker.

"Isobel," I say more firmly this time—her lifeblood glows intensely, glimmering reds painting her skin and tail like a lantern. "Isobel, please talk to me..." I take her by the hand and squeeze her palm. "Talk to me. I'm here."

She considers me with a jolt, her frightening magic falling away in a blood-red rain.

"You truly are an exquisite creature," she says after a moment, blinking back at me. "Your essence..." She contemplates something atop my skin. "It's as precious as the rarest and finest of metals. Queens and kings of men would hang you as a trophy if they could, just to see such unsullied gold and silver."

Her empty expression does not change, her mouth set in a firm line.

She touches a strand of platinum lifeblood on my arm, tracing it to one of gold. The pad of her finger presses down on where they intersect.

"You flatter me, sister," I say, cautiously moving her hand away.

"No, you don't understand." Her words are sharp, making me start. "Yours are different. Your essence is born from that of the purest magic. You have the night stars woven atop your skin."

"*Isobel,*" I press, growing impatient. "Enough." I wave my arms at the darkness around us. "Tell me what this is all about. What did you bring me here to say?"

She looks away, gaze pinned on something far off. "Very

well. How you're feeling, your actions..." She sighs, looking back to me. "They're not your fault."

"I don't understand," I say, crossing my arms. "Of course they're my fault. They were my choices."

"Certainly," she says, her gaze drifting upward to the radiant canopy. "But Fate was ever tempting. It's our only curse." Her final word brushes between her lips, barely a whisper.

I go rigid.

"What curse?" I dare to say. Even as a human before the King's regime such a word was taboo.

"The curse of our creation." Isobel's features darken with a somberness that makes her appear as if she's aged several years, finally an adult.

"I have never heard of such a thing plaguing our kind." My voice comes out unsteady.

"You're so new," she replies, forcing a smile on her lips. She tickles me with her tail, trying to get me to relax; it is a wasted effort now. "You must realize, Eloise, we have the power of a goddess, an *elemental*, coursing through our veins. Our human bodies were not made for such a thing, and so we had to transform to accept it." She shakes her head, searching for the right words. "It's just not an easy thing to do. And though our egos attempt to persuade us otherwise, even *we* have certain obstacles to face to fully accept all that we are after we change..."

I open my mouth to question her, but she lifts her hand.

"I'm afraid that you've been infected, Eloise," she states, gravely, spitting the words out as if they'd burned her tongue. "There's only one sickness known to our kind, and it has affected just a small fraction of our sisters. Most severely, Syrifina's direct line."

I back away from her, not sure if I've now started hearing things, untrusting of my own mind. "Myrmaids can't get sick."

She lets out a derisive snort, and I am reminded…

There is no such thing as eternal, Eloise.

"Mother calls this curse the *frenzy*," she says.

I cross my arms at my chest, suddenly feeling claustrophobic in this darkness; she doesn't readily go on.

"Well… what is it, then? This frenzy." I whisper its name, afraid to breathe life into it. I don't think even when I first learned about the existence of Syrifina did I feel so bewildered.

"You know what it is." Her gaze narrows.

My throat itches, my thoughts spinning in every direction. I look away.

"What you're feeling," she says, speaking slowly, "this uncontrollable desire to feed on your mark with an equal desire not to kill him." I feel a false sense of relief as Isobel finally puts succinct terms to the turmoil I've been facing. "Such internal conflict can have a maddening effect on our powerful minds. It can be overcome… but it can also leave a permanent mark on those it plagues if not done so swiftly."

Then it clicks. I feel torn between anger and liberation.

"Is this why Zahra spent so long in the deep, hiding?" My hand flies over my mouth. "And Kristeena, too?"

They are both of Mother's direct line.

"Yes, I'm afraid." She bows her head, nervously pulling at her fingers. "Kristeena never speaks of her time, and… well, Zahra cannot."

I feel true fear grip me.

"I was infected once, too," she says, her voice so low that I almost miss it. "What a horrendous decade that was… I don't like to recall it." There's so much pity in her expression as she looks at me. It makes my stomach churn. "You have to be stronger than this disease, Eloise, or it may destroy you."

I float gently away from her, needing space, even in these wide-open waters.

"I'm sorry, sister," I say, "but I'm not quite sure I understand. How can a sickness impact us at all? We're *immortal*... what happens if it gets the better of me?" I throw my hands up in exasperation. "And why are we cursed in the first place?"

"Every great spell that demands a life also demands a great price, Eloise. A myrmaid's kiss brings death so that the magic has room to take hold... it's only natural that there be a consequence."

"You're speaking in riddles," I reply, digging my nails into my palms. "What consequence?"

'*Jaspyr*,' whispers Ora.

'*Blood*,' warns Aura.

More, more, more!

Until there's nothing left of either of us.

I squeeze my eyes closed, shutting my mind to any voice other than Isobel's.

She sinks toward me. "It will be easier to understand if I show you." She gestures toward a blank canvas of darkness, humming a magical melody.

The floating, minuscule bioluminescent stars of our sea begin to morph together, like a rolling, glowing mist. When her song ends, they've formed a large orb of brilliant particles that seem to blend together as one rainbow-doused ball of light.

"Have you ever wondered why I don't share much of my past?"

I stare at her. In my short years as a myrmaid, I realize only now that it's never occurred to me to ask. I shake my head, softly, my hair swishing in the stillness.

"In my youth, when I was a little older than you are now, I would sink my teeth into just about anyone who crossed my path. I became utterly unhinged with bloodlust."

My eyes grow wide. I cannot fathom that my eldest sister ever lost control at all.

She reads the surprise on my face and smirks. "Yes, I have swum your path before, little sister. And I'm going to help you get back on track."

She blows at the orb and it explodes with a blast of brightness that makes me squint. Multiple shapes emerge from it, more complex pictures—one was clearly a myrmaid, sparkling red.

"I was, at this time in my new life, infected, you see." She stares intently at the enchanted shapes, unblinking, as they come alive. "Syrifina sometimes refers to it as a blood disease." I feel my headache returning. "As I said, as far as we can tell, newly transformed myrmaids created by her are those most at risk. So, in the beginning, the fewer interactions we have with human society, the better."

"Why would you not warn me of this?" I raise my voice to her, teeth clenched as the familiar heat of anger rises into the middle of my chest.

She shrugs. "You know as well as I that Syrifina Myr lives by her own rules. I know not why she decides what secrets to divulge and when. But I'm telling you now so you'd do well to *listen*." The glower she throws me over her shoulder snaps me back into place.

I offer the slight bow of my head.

"At risk for what, exactly?" I ask, more gently, fixating back on her magic. "What does it mean if I might have such a disease?"

I am not sick. I am hungry, I think.

A small glowing sphere of gold grows into what's clearly a bright, burning sun. It then melts into an undulating ripple of sapphire blue—the crimson myrmaid's tail morphs into legs and she's swallowed by a sea of people, bright white lights rushing around the red figure.

"You were landwalking, too." I barely speak, entranced by her performance.

"Indeed," she says, a scowl denting her soft features. "I was just as eager as you to explore that old part of my world, drawn to it. We all are at first." She tilts her head. "Then one day a young man, around my third decade or so, stepped across my path."

The red woman pauses in front of a lustrous black figure, a glimmering shadow among the white blurs.

"Something about him was unusual, his scent distinct." A dangerous gleam flashes across her eyes; she practically salivates at the memory, and it makes me hungrier still. "I quite lost my senses... I kissed his neck, then bit him, in the midst of a crowd of people who realized nothing."

She stares longingly and lost at her charmed past, silent—the red and black figures remain still, in close proximity as a silvery crowd rushes around them. Then the glowing yellow orb begins to reappear, and the red woman melts back into the sea, becoming a myrmaid once more.

"He was tall, dark, and as handsome as they come," she adds with a sigh of sweet remembrance. "Skin as black as the deepest night." A flicker of silver lights up her eyes.

The dark figure remains at the shore; the crimson creature floats in the water—they both wait, facing each other from above and below.

"And the second I got a taste of his blood... absolutely *intoxicating*, I couldn't keep away."

She slashes at the water in anger, her red magic streaking through it like blood.

"And that was exactly the problem..."

"What do you mean?" Though, innately, I know.

She points at her chest. "Something *inside* of me began to fight against my true nature, to never let me kill him even though I knew I must." She shakes her head, brow furrowed. "Just maddening." She huffs. "And once I made myself known to him, he was just as entranced by me. Even knowing what I was… the danger I posed to his life, he couldn't let me go—"

I realize then that she'd let a human live with our secret, too. Who knows for how long, and she was still here to tell the tale. A sense of hope rises through my stabbing worry.

I can get through this. If Isobel will just reveal how…

"For months, it was absolutely infuriating!" She pulls at her hair, strings of gold clumping in her fists. "And I mean that in the literal sense."

The red figure begins to swim in circles frantically, her light dimming; the dark figure waits and watches.

"We were both ruined the moment we crossed paths."

It is the only time I've ever heard Isobel's voice crack; I give her a little more space.

She clears her throat. "Mother believes the frenzy is caused by some sort of anomaly in the balance of things, for the myrmaid line was created, not born into the natural world of enchanted beings. Such two souls *cannot* exist in harmony, yet may try over and over to force the inescapable bond to work…" She moves her palms up and down. "Temptation. Choice."

She seems defeated by her own explanation, doubting.

The spelled sun begins to fall, and the red figure swims upward—the black figure walks closer to the shore.

"I equate it to if the Sun and Moon continuously tried to touch," adds Isobel, moving her hands closer together. "One cannot exist while the other thrives, or chaos would ensue."

"Chaos?" I mutter, entranced by the bright orb of yellow magic as it dissipates; an equally bright white moon takes its place.

"Yes, Eloise."

The magicked myrmaid transforms into a human once more. This time, as the sea of white figures melts around her, each one she touches falls down dead, their light vanishing in an instant.

"There's always a ripple effect when the balance of the Olleb is disturbed. It's the Golden Rule."

The dark figure again waits and watches.

"You mean, *we* are the disturbance, then? To the order of things."

The Golden Rule is an ancient foretelling known among all those enchanted, all those who wield elemental magic. It cannot be broken; and even if such a rule was somehow *bent*, the Olleb could suffer in unimaginable ways as a result, in order to restore the balance...

"Recite it," she commands—the words etched into the stone at Empress Isle are burned into my mind.

I speak:

> *Light is light and dark is dark, but never shall*
> *they live apart. One shall seek what the other*
> *denies. If it is found, thus follows the demise.*
> *When one eclipses over the other, life shall end*
> *for he and his brother.*

"Good." Isobel offers a tight smile. "We were born by the blessed kiss of the Goddess of the Sea, and it is our right to exist."

She speaks firmly, though her gaze shifts down.

"Alas, Mother Nature reserves the right to challenge us all. I believe the frenzy is her way of doing that. When a human is born with such a strong flame in their souls that it has the ability to cling to one of ours, the balance becomes... upset." She frowns, seeming to grow even paler. "The balance must be righted. We aren't supposed to endure in each other's domains for long..."

"We're more like passing ships," I add, starting to untangle her explanation.

'*Light is light, and dark is dark,*' sing Aura and Ora.

"Exactly." Isobel offers me a soft smile.

She gestures back to her magicked memory. It gleams eerily in the dark, like a world within a world. Aura and Ora circle it from a safe distance, far off, its light casting their shadows across the backdrop of the Sea of Night, making them appear like giant, legendary beasts.

"The longer I resisted, you see, the more irrational I became. My behavior was entirely erratic. In order not to kill *him*, I fed on and killed so many others… just to curb my strange, new appetite—"

Isobel looks away; I can tell she's ashamed of that loss of control. I wonder how many people fell by her hand before she was able to right her wrongs.

How many more will fall by mine?

None!

"I was truly a monster. I couldn't resist his pull, and yet I wasn't strong enough to end his influence." She chews on her lip, looking ever childlike. "Imagine the terror I could have brought upon our Olleb if I had been allowed to continue on like that for much longer?"

She seems to drop into a reverie, her jaw set, tail flicking back and forth. Looking upon her now, so composed, one would never know she'd experienced anything so hideous in her past.

I clear my throat, drawing her attention back to me. "So… how did it finish?"

She scoffs. "Let's just say that the City of Lanzataré was a different, quieter place after knowing me."

She suddenly swims toward me, gripping me by the arm with force.

"Myrmaids and humans are not meant to coexist in harmony, Eloise. *We* are their predators. *They* are our prey. That is our nature." Her voice comes sharp. "Mother reminded me of this, and now I am reminding you."

I swallow, the pit of my stomach like a hollow filled with worry. I feel as if I'd eaten the fire coral, my throat burning in panic. *Hunger for him… Longing for him…*

Even though I know Syrifina can't hear us, I feel her presence.

"Please, just tell me, sister. How did you find your control again?" I shake out of her grasp, gesturing to her magic. "How did you overcome this?"

I can already sense the truth in her words, how starving I was for him still, a hunger that went far deeper than normal.

"Mine was by quite the unfortunate, or happy, accident…" she says, dryly. She floats back over to her magicked memory. "When I surfaced one night, I found him injured. Another human must've spilled his blood in a scuffle. The scent of it hit me like a fresh wave at the shore—"

A menacing white figure runs the dark figure through with a blade; he falls to his knees, sparkling red spilling from his belly.

"The moment I smelled so much of his blood, not even the frenzy could stop me from properly feeding on him. I came back to my senses, as Mother assured me I would, once his life left his eyes." She shrugs. "I dragged his body into the sea, drank his sensational blood dry, then I was sick no longer."

The red figure wraps around the black one and devours— her glow growing as radiant as rubies.

His shadow vanishes into the darkness of the sea.

She presses her fingers to her lips. "Though, I find that I do sometimes crave him still… in many ways I wish I did not."

Her magic suddenly dissipates but her haunting words linger. I'm snapped back to reality in a startling moment.

My eyes adjust, seeing Isobel more clearly than ever before.

But the ending of her story leaves me more unsettled rather than relieved. Then, it hits me…

How am I supposed to kill Jaspyr? I made a vow to let him

live. I purse my lips, looking toward the surface.

'*And if you did, what would be the point of life eternal with the greatest blood and hunt behind you?*' Another voice speaks.

"Eloise," says Isobel, snapping her fingers in front of my face. "Do you understand what must be done?"

I nod. "I do. Rest assured, I can handle this… this frenzy. Now that I understand what it is."

"Good." She plants a kiss on my cheek. "Though, I daresay our conversation is not yet done. Come along. I will wait with you at Empress Isle, until the gathering commences." There was an edge to her voice; my insides twist—I haven't fooled her well enough for her to let me out of her sight just yet.

Am I strong enough? Will I make the right choice?

A buried part of me whispers faintly of cowardice, of doubt. But she's dead now, easy to tune out.

29

ABYSS

ᴅELOISE

NOT EVEN THE WONDEROUS MAGIC and beautiful distractions of the sea can protect me from the truth as we continue to swim.

I push my spinning thoughts aside and focus on my future, a long one filled with adventure, freedom, control...

I just have to get past this draining nuisance of a human.

I imagine him dead, his blood on my lips, my fingers and hands, my teeth, my tongue. I'm swimming in it, the mere thought thirst-quenching.

I imagine sinking into his deep, dark eyes, a sea all their own, while his intoxicating scent devours me...

I devour him.

I see our bodies connected, our skin, merging like the shadow of a fantastic storm in the daylight, pressing away the sun, the heat. So all that's left is a cold, cruel satisfaction.

My insides twist, aching for more.

A voice whispers a small doubt again. *But what happens when the blood is gone? What then, Eloise?*

It's a strangely-terrifying concept—I'm not sure I can live without even just *smelling* that blood again. Let alone being denied the taste…

Even stranger still, I'm not sure which voice it belongs to, my reasonable or infected mind.

"I really am cursed," I mutter.

Isobel glances at me over her shoulder. "The gathering is happening in a few hours. For now, you should rest. After our ceremony, I will help you get free of this burden. I promise."

A shudder rolls down my spine.

'*Don't worry*,' whispers Aura.

'*He will release you*,' says Ora.

'*He is infected too*,' they murmur as one.

"Will I be able to feed again soon? At the shadow moon, perhaps?" I ask, catching up to her. I can't imagine waiting much longer than that to taste blood again, frenzy or not. *His blood.*

She shakes her head, tickling me with her tail.

"Absolutely not. That's only two weeks away. You mustn't feed for a while yet. You've overindulged quite enough. It won't kill you to skip a feeding cycle or two. In fact, it might save you from having long-term issues with excess blood." Her mouth twists with concern. "You don't want to become like Zahra, child. If you end things sooner rather than later, you will be much better off."

I frown, falling back. "Right. Yes, you're right."

My stomach moans in protest.

"Isobel," I ask after a time, swimming back alongside her. "What of Zahra… and her sickness? Tell me more."

Her lips turn downward.

"Poor Zahra," she says. "She tried to evade the frenzy when Mother warned her of it, thought she could outsmart it after already battling with severe bloodlust. When it finally struck her, she was afraid of the monster she might become again if she even tasted a drop. So rather than risk it with even a taste, she hid in the deep so long that she eventually outlived the one who had awakened the frenzy in her. Just as Kristeena had tried but *failed* to do many decades earlier." She sighs. "We just couldn't get to her in time to change her mind—"

I nod, knowing how easy it is for a myrmaid to evade, hide, for as long as they please in this boundless ocean. Even from one of our cunning sisters.

"Mother presumes her human died of natural causes in the end, though we never found a body. We thought if we did, Zahra could..." She looks away, shaking her head.

I shudder just to think how that sentence my end.

She clears her throat. "The devastating effects the frenzy can cause on the mind were relieved some once she felt her human's death, but the memory of what she never had haunts her still. The balance was restored, yes," she blows a kiss to the sea sky, "for the sake of the Olleb. But her sanity, I'm afraid, will forever suffer the consequence of her decision. That's why she can appear so... distant at times."

My mouth forms an 'O'.

Isobel whispers again, "Poor Zahra... She never even got a taste."

"And Kristeena?" I ask, eager for more knowledge of my elders' youth.

"No one is as strong-willed as Zahra," she replies, somberly. "To her detriment, as she proved. Kristeena, thank the Goddess, gave in to her craving eventually. She did what was meant to be done. However, she waited *far* too long, years, before she regained control."

She taps on her temple, and I know she's referring to Kristeena's often tangled mind.

"I see." The words barely leave my lips.

She raises an eyebrow, looking sidelong at me.

"Hiding was not a wise choice for either of them," she

adds, a warning in her tone. "And Zahra's story is quite possibly the reason why Mother does not speak of these things, not unless one of us shows signs. The warning clearly frightened Zahra into the deep instead of helping her to confront her problem head-on."

"*Hmm*," I say, haughtily, rolling my eyes. "Syrifina does like to lie."

"Watch your tongue," she snaps; I stiffen. "An eternity to always wonder what might have been had she been stronger… always struggling to remain in control of her urges." She sighs. "That's what Zahra faces every day." She hums a soft, melancholy tune that echoes all around us. "But we have to live with our choices. Now, don't we, Eloise?"

"Yes, sister," I obediently say.

We swim forward and up. The darkness starts to lift. A field of fire coral rises again in our sights, like a barrier of underwater cacti growing over everything. *A disease.*

My sisters and I confessed once that we have all, at one point or another, tested its prick… curious to feel pain.

All I see are raging, pink flames. All I feel is conflicted, tormented *thirst.*

I swim faster, deeper, determined to evade this curse upon my kind.

As soon as the full moon gathering concludes, I will take Jaspyr's life. No one else's. I smile to myself, though it doesn't reach my soul. *I am in control.*

Never mind that I made a promise that may doom me.

OUR REEF IS MOUNTAINOUS, coming back into view on the far south side of the ship. We round a wall so steep and tall that it almost skims the surface. And there's no telling where it might begin. I veer inside at the next opportunity, following the rivers of tunnels that hollow it out, giving it personality and shape. The entity is massive, like an octopus with a thousand arms, connecting one part of the mountain to the next.

I swim through the main path, a wide-open chasm of coral that breathes with life, a soft mist rising up from the bottom. Here, giant sharks with smooth, round faces sleep and hide close to the sand, waiting for the night to come. They stir only to lazily welcome Aura and Ora home as they pass.

The brethren of my companions are some of my favorite creatures of the sea to travel with into the deep, the entourage I summon when I want to make an entrance to Empress Isle—with them at my side, I can pretend as if I'm flying with a group of underwater dragons, their fins slicing the water like a bird through clouds, their sleek, massive bodies able to move from side to side like the ripple of ribbon fluttering in the wind.

Such sophistication—they don't swim. They soar.

"My own little dragons," I whisper to Aura and Ora as they swim parallel to me.

I open my arms out wide; they nuzzle their backs into my palms.

'*We shall always fly with you,*' they purr.

The reef expands, carving open toward what appears to be a wide archway that marks the farthest point. On the other side of the arch is an abyss of boundless blue; it's still as hypnotizing as it was the first time I stared out at it.

I listen to the echo of the sea beyond, squinting to try to spot the silhouettes of whales the size of cities, swimming to the slow, resounding beat of their own beautiful songs.

Mother took each one of us here in the first days of our

transformation. She equates the view from this point to a mermaid's existence and potential—mesmerizing yet mysterious, grandiose and ceaseless. Inimitable.

It was the first time she'd whispered *Eternal Eloise* into my ear.

I tear my gaze away from the tapestry of cerulean that shifts in and out of a lavender-tinted, glittering sea. I consider the tall archway. Daniella swears it appears as if two lovers have been frozen in time, reaching out their hands to touch at the exact moment they'd been turned to stone-like fixtures to decorate our reef—and thus the archway formed.

But Syrifina insists it's a natural phenomenon.

If I look closely, *maybe,* distinct facial features can be discerned, pained and desperate with longing… but I don't believe in such a thing as a love like that.

The two halves of the entity are forever kept apart, connected only by the ever-expanding coral that formed here—and only here—long ago. Daniella deems it Lovers' Coral, a deep, cobalt blue organism intertwined with shimmering black.

I call it self-destruction, for if one half had simply let the other go, maybe they would've lived.

In any case, this coral is a rarity in our seas; we protect its shrine with the same ferocity as we do the waters.

Empress Isle lies ahead, past the archway and across the wide, open sea—we swim forward and through, focused on the beacon that is home.

Isobel and I hold hands and launch ourselves off the cliff.

We're boundless, weightless in the water, yet it always makes me gasp as if we might just plummet down forever.

We're careful not to lose direction as we swim onward, for passing from the reef cliff into the vast open can be disorienting. There's just no way to recall north to south, east to west, up from down. And while Empress Isle is a powerful presence that can be felt from miles beyond, even with our keen myr-maid sight, it is not visible to us yet.

We must trust in our instincts, always.

I could be convinced that we're suspended in the same spot in time and space, for even as fast and far as we swim, it seems nothing changes. There is only a blanket of blue.

Eventually, the yawning channels of Empress Isle that lead to our lair emerge before my eyes, just a blur still but I know their details by heart.

Cavern mouths hang open wide. Large, diamond-like minerals that look like teeth, fangs, from far away, drip from the ceiling and jut up from the floor in the entrance, reflecting the soft twinkling lights of the sea in a curtain. And beyond this glass-like gate sits black, mysterious waters that I'm always cautious to enter.

I'm unsurprised that Mother chose to claim it so long ago—there is truly no other place as wonderous, as enchant-ing, as dangerously dark that is worthy to call home.

As we near Empress Isle, the sea grows eerily quiet.

A cloaking silence wraps around our lair. No sound at all. Everything yields itself to the serenity here.

I squeeze Isobel's hand, then let go. We come to a stop.

"I just…" The heaviness of the silence washes over me, shaking my resilience. "Isobel, why has this happened to me? I feel so powerless over it." I look to her, searching for the an-swers. "I'm supposed to be strong."

I can't help it as my magic surges, electrifying the waters around me like a blazing net.

"You are anything but powerless," she says, her voice barely above a whisper—one always feels the need to speak quietly in this revered place. "Such a plague is rare for our kind, but you will overcome this as all our other sisters have." She places a hand over where her heart used to beat. "As I have. I won't let you suffer this alone."

A bitterness lingers behind her words. I ponder over it.

"What happens if the frenzy fully takes over?" I ask, accepting truly that this disease has infected me. "If I can't—"

"There is no scenario where you can't," she says with a scoff. "*You* are a Myr, a princess of the Sea of Saindora. You can do anything." She waves me off. "Besides, Mother would never let it get that far."

I straighten, my magic vanishing with an uncomfortable snap that leaves me dizzy.

Isobel swims forward, untroubled, steadying her gaze forward as Empress Isle comes into view. "You're either strong enough to do what you need to do… or you're not." She looks sidelong at me as I keep pace. "You mustn't let this dominate you, Eloise. We are not to be manipulated by any outside forces, even if it's a cruel temptation from Mother Nature. We are the supreme temptresses, never to be so tempted."

Her words are decisive, no gray areas, no room for misinterpretation. A sharp, threatening, fire-laced sword.

"The most perilous threat to myrmaids is just that, you realize? Something or someone else controlling us, our powers…"

She conjures enchanted silver threads that drift alongside us, swimming in the form of glittering dolphins; her magic escorts us over the final stretch of blue to our door.

We hover before the threshold.

"They are great, indeed, and must be protected."

Her magic evaporates into the water as soon as we reach our destination, leaving light dancing in my eyes.

It looks as if the shining gate of a grand palace has sunk beneath the world, columns of smooth rock winding tall on either side of the entrance. Past the gates, all color washes away. Just shimmering, clean black stone surrounded by an atmosphere of rich indigo.

Lost treasures and jewels border long, narrow trails that

lead all the way to our main nest. No, not lost, found and claimed by Myr Sisters over the years.

And centuries' worth of glinting skulls and skeletons, piled up after countless gatherings, sprinkle the floor—some human remains have been here so long that it's hard to distinguish them from the actual cavern rock.

We both slip in, pausing to take in the beautiful, welcoming labyrinths.

"It's good to be home," I say, my voice echoing into the cave.

Isobel places a hand upon my shoulder.

Chandeliers of stalactites dangle overhead, dazzling with bursts of golden gems and magicked silver-blue fires that make it seem like real starlight dances here alongside a beaming moon. And blossoms of giant orange crystals hide in pockets on the walls; I see myself reflected in them, a fractured, distorted image.

I shift my gaze to the ceiling where small puddles of lost air have gathered, forming dark, cloud-like decorations overhead. They appear the blackest of black, oil, a vortex to another world. I stare too long into their veiled, smoky depths, drowning in my own burdens.

'*Look away. Don't fall prey. It isn't your time,*' the isle hums to me.

I know Isobel means death, an unholy term for our eternal kind when she warns of Mother's interference. I know it and yet can't even fathom the suggestion, that Syrifina might take back her gift from one of us, to punish us...

Then I think of her temper, of her uncanny ability to decide which emotion presides over her at any given time.

I rip my gaze from the ceiling and turn to Isobel, desperate for her protection. I'm not ready to die, and especially *not* for a human bag of bones that should be Empress Isle décor.

"We can't let Mother find out, at least not until I fix my

mistake. Isobel, please." I clasp my hand over my throat. "I won't feed again until you deem me ready. Let it be our secret."

I offer a tight smile, hoping it fools her into thinking I'm sane, that I can handle the full moon gathering tonight, the feast of bodies that will surely be waiting for us, without breaking.

"She will understand," she replies, gently. I open my mouth to speak but she raises her voice over me. "You're her daughter. She can better guide you through this than I can." She looks away, suddenly very interested in a skeletal ribcage.

Fear snakes through me; my craving pulsates so loudly that it echoes in my ears, screaming, booming; I slam my fist into a wall and the black stone cracks all the way from the ceiling to floor.

Silence, I think, scrunching my eyes closed. *Shut up and let me concentrate!*

"On second thought, Mother *will* have your head if you destroy her palace in a childish fit," she says, coolly.

She places her hand on my arm, lowering it back to my side.

She'll have my head once she discovers the foolish oath I made to a mortal who needs to die for me to live.

But instead I say, "This disease is clearly a mockery from the Sorcerer who granted her these powers, to be undone by a man. I cannot face her with such shame." My fins flare around me. My voice reverberates sharply through the chamber. "It makes a mockery of her!"

"Sister, you haven't…" She clears her throat. "You've done nothing wrong to deserve this, but you cannot hide from it either. Mother *will* understand. I will not help you hide it from her and risk her wrath. She'll take one look at you tonight and know something is wrong." She studies herself in one of the giant crystals. "You have a far greater willpower than you yourself even realize; you confessed so early to me. Don't be so hard on yourself."

"How's that?" I ask, bitterly.

"It's only been, what, a matter of days?" She laughs, tossing her hair back. "Most of us were plagued by the frenzy for *many* moons before Mother could track us down to try and help."

"But I—"

She lunges at me, and I'm forced to reckon with the fire element within her again, her lifeblood, her eyes, glaringly hot.

"Your pleading is pathetic," she snaps; I gape as if she'd slapped me in the face. "I am *trying* to help you, little sister. Your words will not sway me. Act like a Myr and let your confidence reign."

I bow my head, guilt washing over me. "It's hard today, to bear our name."

Some of her steam dissipates; she frowns, tilting my chin toward her.

"Then let me ease your mind and share with you a little more about our lineage." She picks up a bone from the floor, turning it around before her eyes. "Syrifina was the first to be infected," she says, gaining my full attention. "Before she had created any daughters. She speaks little of the time, but those of us who experienced it have eventually become... privy to the history, or her version of it."

I raise my eyebrow but hold my tongue.

"Of all of us, Mother's frenzy is most notorious. That's why, I can assure you, she will offer you... compassion, as she has with all whom it has plagued. You needn't worry, Eloise. She will understand."

She taps the bone against the smooth black wall at her back—the inscription of the Golden Rule shimmers like gilt-leafed letters at her magical touch.

The last line fades away but stays centered in my mind...

When one eclipses over the other, life shall end for he and his brother.

"What happened to her?" I run my fingers over the ancient indentations in the stone.

Isobel peers into the tunnel, then over her shoulder to stare into the deep—we're utterly alone.

But our sisters will be arriving soon with their meals in hand, and many are surely already resting in the depths of our lair, awaiting the gathering to begin when the full moon is at its highest peak in the sky.

Isobel conjures a tornado of water to rush around us, a lulling sound that beats in my ears and easily hides our conversation. Then, she lowers her voice.

"Never repeat this to a soul. Mother would have my tail for telling this to you first, without her blessing."

My mouth drops open; I nod.

"Tell me you understand," she says, gripping my arm, the tips of her fingers pressing nearly to my bone. "Use your words. *Promise.*"

I hiss in discomfort, shaking out of her iron grip.

"Of course, sister. I do. I promise." I hope she didn't hear how my voice shook on the last word. "I won't breathe a word of this to anyone."

And certainly not Mother…

30

ECLIPSE

DARLING DIARY,

This one shall come as quite the shock… or maybe not, now that you really know me at my soul.

The High City of Saindora was once, very long ago, ruled by a High Queen, Julissa. Before Kyrone Devlindor, and before His Majesty, the humble King Damas, and their predecessors several crowns back.

I was just a young myrmaid then, turned only half a century prior and quite alone. I roamed; I searched knowing not for what.

The waters nearest to Saindora were a place I visited most frequently, their natural beauty unparalleled by other coasts. And the magic surrounding the High City never failed to draw me in.

The only thing I despised were the incessant, loud-mouthed dragons always flying about, keeping me well away from the land.

But I didn't have to go near the castle to meet its mistress—the High Queen would often take to my seas for pleasure, circling the shores of her pristine palace.

She would sail with just a small crew toward the setting sun, far enough from her lands to be considered distant, yet still close enough to see the golden tips of her cream-colored towers and the blaze of fires that sat atop them come the fall of night.

I've tried not to interfere in the world of humans, so I never bore any desire to swim close to the queen's ship when she sailed. And she respected my waters enough that I let her continue on.

I had yet to even see her face after so much time swimming in parallel, enjoying the Saindora sunsets and the softness of the salted sea, so unburdened and calm in these parts.

Besides, if I made a meal of this queendom's ruler, it would impact our world greatly—for who might govern the humans of Olleb-Yelfra next?

I wished for no such responsibility, and as far as I could tell, the queen ruled honorably enough for me not to care.

I loved to watch, though—the cloud-colored wood always shone with such grace under the setting sun, and the thick, gold-trimmed sails beat in the winds like the wings of her boorish yet remarkable dragons.

One night, while I hunted in the waters beneath a bright full moon, a strong gale blew in my direction from the north—with it came the scent of the queen.

Just a trace was all it took, but the taste of her essence, pressed onto my tongue, called to me. I felt an intense shift—my mind, body, and soul suddenly leaned toward her.

I turned in her direction to find her ship silhouetted against the backdrop of the moon and earth's great shadow colliding—I watched in awe as, slowly, the silver moon absorbed the darkness, its face turning as crimson as blood.

I chased it atop the flat, azure sea strip faster than ever, conjuring a surf to usher me along; they surely saw me coming from far away, rolling with the swells, large waves that must've appeared to have come from nowhere.

Then I swam right up to the Queen's sleek vessel and looked her in the eyes as she peered down at me over the deck rail—rich, brown pools drank me in with wonder, fear.

I sank into them, like the deceptive quick sands in the jungle I used to avoid in my human home. I let them consume me.

I pressed my lips into a firm line, contemplating her—what was the meaning of this devasting hunger that so swiftly came over me for this woman?

I had made a vow to try to feed only on the worst of the Olleb's men…

But my fangs reacted differently, excited and eager to eat, to feed, imploring that I make an exception for one righteous queen.

She gasped when I bared them at her. "What are you?" she dared ask me.

I kept my tail hidden, my enchantment muted, part of me wanting to still seize the opportunity to drift down and away.

But I couldn't.

I was so enraptured by the queen's scent that I cared not to hide. In fact, for old time's sake, I was excited at the idea of making myself known rather than slinking alongside the shadows.

I touched my dead pirate's chain at my neck and smiled. "I am the Queen of the Seas," I replied in a daze, the waters lifting me to her eye level atop a magical mist.

She balked but stood her ground; her crew scuffled away a good distance.

She opened her arm to me after only a short hesitation. "Then from one queen to another, we have no quarrel. You are welcome here."

My mind spun with the sound of her voice, my whole body tingling—every word she spoke, confident and strong, was laced with her intoxicating aroma.

"How kind of you," I say, leering back at her, wondering how such blood might taste as this new, terribly delightful hunger coursed through me.

My luscious tail and fins melted away at my command. My watery pedestal settled me atop her deck, my lifeblood gleaming gloriously in the dark—it was the first time since hunting my pirate that I had let so many humans see me for what I truly am…

I barely acknowledged their gasps of shock and awe, my focus pinned on the High Queen of the Olleb, my ultimate prey.

The weightiness of my legs, my body out of water, grounded me some, focused my mind on this strange situation. But standing so close to her, it was all I could do not to attack.

She extended her hand. "Our legends speak of creatures like you, who have sunk entire ships. Maiden of the water, that is the name they give you…"

I grinned, gracefully walking forward, water dripping off me like liquid jewels, pooling beneath my feet—a soft dais of magic has always clung to me no matter what form I take.

"Queen," I corrected, taking her hand. "And I am the one and only Myr maiden. I believe the sailors have taken to calling me a myrmaid. I quite like the sound of it."

I squeezed her hand harder, my nails digging into her palm so much that blood broke her skin; she gritted her teeth but kept her calm.

"Impressive," I said, looking her up and down.

Her eyes did the same to me, lingering on the intimate places of my human body that I proudly exposed to the night.

I smirk, lifting my chin, my nipples perked to the wind.

"*Syrifina Myr, my queen. That is the name of your maiden of the water.*" *I moved closer to her, pulling her into me; she recoiled as I sucked at her sweet scent, deeply. The warmth of her body enveloped me like a comforting embrace I hadn't known in so long.* "*And I only sink the ships that the Sea disapproves of.*"

As if in affirmation, waves swelled again and the ship bucked—all the humans wobbled, though I and Queen Julissa remained steady. I still held her hand tightly.

"*Or when I'm very, very hungry.*" *I pulled her closer into my chest, my lips skimming her slender neck; she tried, but she couldn't pull away.* "*I've spent many years trying to gain control over my unending appetite, with many slips.*"

Fear spread across the deck as the Queen and her crew fully grasped that I was not of their world, that I was not their ally. Her peacekeeping attempts were misplaced but a noble gesture, in any case.

There appeared to be only two guards who had accompanied her on this leisurely sail. They stepped up to confront me.

"*Unhand her!*" *one had commanded, silver lighting his irises.*

I humored him and did; she tore her hand from my grasp.

"*What are you, really?*" *said the Queen, her voice steady. She too held her chin high, shoulders back. Her golden, jewel-bedecked crown glinted atop a pile of long, dark braids as she sized me up—the sureness of a ruler, just like me.*

I lick my lips.

"*I told you,*" *I said, stepping forward.* "*I am the Queen of the Seas. I am the Myr maiden your sailors fear so much that they tell my story far and wide.*" *I laughed loudly, tossing my hair back over my shoulder, the thick red sheet falling down* to my waist. "As if it would protect them."

Her spine stiffens.

"And you, my queen, are trespassing." The corners of my lips turned up.

Her expression tightened. I could see her calculating how big of a threat I might be. If she could fight me and win—I wanted her to try, I realized. I wanted to play.

Her hand twitched toward a golden sword at her hip; her guards had already drawn their weapons, pointing them at me. The only reason they hadn't attacked yet was because the Queen had not commanded them to.

She took a step back.

"These are my waters," she said, fiercely. Her eyes narrowed, streaking with magic. "If indeed you are our enemy, then I rescind my invitation. We will not fall prey to your false threats. You may wield powers, but so do we."

The swords her guards held lit up with magic. Her crew also readied spells on their tongues and in their palms, the air warming with their collective powers. Warriors or not, they were prepared to fight for their queen.

"You are sorely outnumbered," she said with a smirk. "This is your last chance to leave."

A laugh fluttered from between my lips.

"Outnumbered?" I say, sweetly, with the tilt of my head. "Why, my lovely queen, I do believe it is you who are surrounded here."

I gestured to the dark waters, my smile widening; Queen Julissa and her crew stood speechless, shifting their attention and their weapons anywhere but to me.

The surface surrounding the ship erupted in an eerie, loud gurgling sound as my magic began to bubble up from beneath. Hundreds of soldiers, with sharp-tipped, water-crafted blades and thick shields, formed atop the now soft-flowing waves. Every inch of them hailed from the sea, emblazoned with a fiery silver. They hummed with energy, life. And as I poured my endless power into my creations, the blood moon feeding me, I too blazed brighter.

Queen Julissa turned her focus back to me, lifting her sword so that its tip nearly touched the center of my chest.

"What is this trickery?" she demanded, gritting her teeth.

My water warriors moved closer, the night wind as their breath. The waves lifting them eye level with their targets.

A man on her crew called to fire magic, the air warming with his despicable spell; with the command of my mere thought, one of my soldiers speared him through his middle, then dragged him under the sea.

A battle erupted across the deck, the queen's crew fruitlessly trying to slash and blast my water warriors into pieces; though they would only grow back, multiplying like the hydra serpent the Sea whispers old legends about.

"I am every man's enemy," I said with unmasked cruelty, holding the Queen's gaze. "But you... you are something else to me." Her sword hand lowered. "Not enemy, no. Something much more. At least, I think you are."

I reached out, caressing her cheek. She seemed frozen, entranced at my touch, my voice, even though I did not yet sing.

"I am regretful that I must now take your life," I said, softly. "I normally do not drink from women. I hope you have an heir ready to take your place, Your Majesty."

I gripped her chin and turned her head to the side—the veins in her neck pulsed for me. The blood pooling in her perfect, pink lips yearned for me. I could hardly think with Queen Julissa's scent filling the emptiest parts of me.

I let out a long sigh, my eyes floating closed.

In the next moment, I tasted the steel of her fire-laced blade.

I screeched, moving away so fast that she had to turn to find me again.

"How dare you," I snarled, eyes wide; I hadn't felt the burn of real pain in so long. "What blasted steel do you wield?"

My voice floated out in a deadly song.

She still held her sword hand steady. "It's dwarf-made," she drawls out at my command.

I bared my fangs, sniffing at the metal. I could smell the stench of sun and earth all over it and quickly added dwarves to my long list of natural adversaries.

We stand, two mighty queens, face to face.

"Kneel," I said, my voice resounding like thunder across the ship. A giant swell of water landed behind me with a booming splash; water rained down on the deck, soaking everyone in the vicinity.

She dropped to her knees without question, the tip of her sword pressed into the wood—I mercilessly removed her ability to choose.

With a glaring hatred in her gaze, she gripped the handle of her sword and bowed, her neck bent toward the moon.

I licked my lips, unable to calm the purr in my throat as the salty water mixed with her skin, her scent. She was even more delicious when wet.

The screams and cries of her remaining crew began to grow tiresome; some had thrown themselves overboard in foolish attempts to swim to land, and her guards were already long dead. Those who still lived had only luck to thank... or maybe they were most unlucky, for they would soon find me to reckon with.

"Quiet," I commanded, scrunching my eyes closed—the word drifted out of my lips in an enchanting hum.

The annoying chatter ceased; my water soldiers sank back beneath the sea in a bright splash.

"Look at me," I said.

Queen Julissa lifted a silver, watery gaze to mine; she tried with everything to resist my magic, but I was far stronger.

"Any last words?" I asked, allowing her tongue to move.

"You've had your fun, so be done with it," she yelled, spit flying from her mouth, her face reddening in anger. "Kill me, you wicked soul! If that's what you mean to do."

I knelt down in front of her, staring into her watering eyes just as she let a single tear fall. I gently ran my finger across her cheek, so warm with the heat of her pride, then pulled it back to my lips, my tongue.

"The gods punish me with you," I said. Her gaze sharpened on me. "The power you could yield over me, if I let you."

"Spare me the kindness of your words," she scoffed. "Syrifina Myr, was it now?" She squared her shoulders. "You're a sinister presence. Darkness without provocation. If I cannot beat you, if my crew and soldiers cannot beat you, then I will seize my death with dignity." She lifted her chin. "Look me in the eyes when you take my soul, water witch."

There was so much arrogance and anger in her stare, a hatred I truly felt seep into my bones. I couldn't look away.

I pursed my lips, considering...

I could pluck out her eyes to break the strange spell she held over me.

'Do it,' a strange voice urged. 'Or she'll be the end of your reign.'

I shook the absurd thought away.

"As you please. I will make this quick... Your Majesty." At the very least, I could dignify her in death.

I let her see my fangs. She swallowed her fright, holding my gaze. Once again, I took her chin in my hand, this time with more force.

I traced my tongue along her neck.

"Mmm, so brutally sweet," I said between licks.

She shivered, and I savored it.

Only when I finally sank my teeth into her skin, my mouth swimming in her blood, did she finally close her eyes and give in.

I sucked, and sucked, and sucked… glorious voices singing a chorus of pleasure in my head, my body dizzied, high, from her intoxicating essence.

But it was too much. I was so drunk and disoriented that I began to wonder if her delectable blood tasted more like pure, deceptive poison.

'Let her go and live to see another day with her in this world,' *a voice warned.* 'A temporary freedom. You will beg for more until your mind breaks. Or destroy the thing you desire above all else, and crave it for all eternity.' *The voice laughed, a soft, savage sound echoing in my mind—I recognized it.* 'What choice will you make this time, I wonder? Life or death?'

I released my deadly bite from the queen's neck and glared toward the fading stars. "Sorcerer," *I growled.* "Is this the consequence you warned of?"

The laughter continued to rumble in my head like thunder in the distant clouds. 'All great spells have great consequence, Syrifina Myr.' *He said my name slowly, savoring it as I did the queen.* 'Are you willing to make another sacrifice to keep all that you have?'

"Light is light and dark is dark, but never shall they live apart." *As if he whispered it into my ear, the first verse of the Golden Rule rolled through my mind.*

The human queen has a passion for the welfare of her people and lands that burns as radiant and sweeping as the sun. Just as you have an appetite for a chaos that is as cold and distant as the moon in a storm. Light. Dark. You are each other's equals in every way, divine soulmates, one might say.'

I looked down at Queen Julissa's face, all the creases of her anger forgotten as she slept right outside of Death's door, cradled in my arms. 'There's no such thing as soulmates,' *I thought in reply, only loathing her even more.*

Such youthful pride,' *he said with a sigh.* Believe whatever you desire. In any case, my child, the cost of your life is the queen's. For the sun and moon must always remain apart on this earthly plane.'

The second verse of the ancient prophecy rang in my ears. 'One shall seek what the other denies. If it is found, thus follows the demise."

'If they lingered in each other's arms too long, you see,' *he continued,* 'the entire world would burn.'

'When one eclipses over the other, life shall end for he and his brother." *The final verse of the Golden Rule landed in such a booming blast that I cringed, squeezing my eyes shut.*

'If you do not kill Queen Julissa before due time, you will gravely upset the balance. It is said that if the Golden Rule is broken, fire would rain upon the seas, the land.' *His voice seemed to brighten.* 'Not even the old gods could stop the catastrophic events that would follow...'

The Sorcerer snickered in such an ancient, cold way that it made me take pause. I think back to our first meeting in the jungle; this was not the same person as I had encountered then and yet I knew without a doubt that it was him.

Then it hit me—I thought I had seduced the Sorcerer into giving me what I wanted, yet in all my wisdom now, I see that he must've seduced me into trading my soul to him. A man with such a power as creation of life eternal could be no man at all... how had I not seen?

"You tricked me," I seethed. "Which old god are you?"

This time, his voice echoed across the night. And by the way the remaining crew cried out, I know I was not the only person who could hear it anymore.

"I am the blackness between the stars. I am the depths beneath the ocean that you dare never to explore. I am the darkness inside the hollow of your bones." *I felt him smile, and it made me shiver right to my very core.* "I am the God of

Shadow, the keeper of night. And you, Syrifina, are my chosen disciple. I saved you… and gifted you to the Sea. The only one of my sisters I tolerate."

His voice resounded across the ship as if his breath were an ice-cold wind, the sails flapping widely.

"Kill the human queen. Or drag out her demise and let the Olleb crumble beside you. It matters not to me. Either way, you have no choice but to destroy one another now that you've crossed paths."

Darkness pooled in front of me, a breathing, living thing that I am loath to admit terrified me.

"I shall enjoy watching what choice you'll make this time," spoke the God of Shadow. He smiled, something wicked. Then dissolved into the night air.

My entire body slumped when he vanished.

I felt the Sea sigh. 'Now you know. Just be done with it, Syrifina. The longer you draw it out, the harder the decision will become.'

"But why?" I screamed, the waves riling at my voice.

'Because the shadows are ancient and bored. They like to play games on those willing to risk it all for power and pleasure and pain.'

I snarled, glaring back down at the queen as her blood settled in my stomach. I felt as if I might explode with ecstasy yet be left in unmendable pieces afterward. I wanted more but some part of me feared what might happen if I should take another greedy sip.

The God of Shadow's voice antagonized me from somewhere far off now, just a soft nudging whisper. 'Let go, Syrifina Myr, queen of nothing! Let her rule you. Let her destroy you. Let her in.'

With a scream of anger, confusion, I shoved the queen's body across the deck. My magic reacted, too bright, too powerful, unhinged.

The Queen smashed into the side of the ship, her crown toppling off her head.

I stared at her unconscious state in disbelief.

"What did you do to me?" I roared, the sea, the wind, the night, hurling itself against the ship so that it rocked, violently.

The God of Shadow cackled.

Her heartbeat slowed. Her breath diminished. It would've been so simple to snap her neck and move on...

I bared my fangs, letting out a loud hiss as I looked upon the stilled High Queen of Saindora, face down upon the deck, completely at my mercy.

I leaned over her, shaking with fury at the resistance, the restraint, I held for her, my ultimate conquest. Never had I tasted anyone so utterly world-altering. Never had I drunk from a neck so worthy. And yet, some wretched part of me insisted that I spare her for another night... to think, to clear my head.

I spat at the Queen's feet, glaring toward the horizon as it began to brighten with the threat of morning.

"Whatever sorcery you've cast here, you cannot survive me," I said with contempt. As quick as the wind, I replaced the crown upon her head. "I do not need gold to reinforce my rightful place. And I don't need the coaxing of the cowardly shadows behind my back to whisper to me what must be done." I shot a glare over my shoulder. "I am the Sea. The Sea is me. And as long as your kingdom touches the shores of my waters, you can never be rid of me. I will kill you..."

I hesitated.

"Just not tonight," I whispered.

I tucked her braid gently behind her ear, frowning down on her all the while.

"I'll see you soon, my queen." I said the words bitterly, and yet I couldn't soften the excitement that swelled in my chest at the promise...

That I had somehow earned more than one night with Queen Julissa.

Soulmate? I wondered at that.

To quell such an unwelcome emotion and my unwarranted rising thirst, I ripped through what was left of her crew and lathered myself in their blood.

When I was quite finished, I dove back into the ocean to investigate my foreign feelings before they threatened to tear me apart. The water was clouded with red, the blood washed from my skin with every flick of my reformed tail.

Only when I was deep underwater—the High Queen's scent slightly muted by the salt of the sea—did I use my magic to escort her and her ship of body parts safely back to the shores of Saindora.

When her aroma was muddied by the horrendous smells of land, I finally felt a small, fleeting sense of relief...

A strange, persuasive part of me wanted to know her. Yet, another part of me ached to bathe in her blood.

It was like two warring souls trapped in my body.

Then, I realized, maybe there were...

Maybe, this wretched consequence was born of the human soul I so readily traded in for my myrmaid one.

Her revenge, perhaps?

To show me an unrequited bond that could've been...

If only I had not so readily given my life to the shadows.

31

PARASITE

DELOISE

"I HAVE NEVER HEARD of the God of Shadow before," I say in a hushed voice. "Why do we not speak of him?"

"Because he is a malicious and ancient deity," Isobel replies, equally quiet. "To speak his name is to evoke him, to give him power in our domain. And that he tricked Syrifina into sacrificing her soulmate is surely her greatest shame. That's why she keeps this story so close to her chest." She turns in the water, arms out wide. "The Shadow may be our seed, but the Sea is our mother, our creator. We needn't dishonor her glorious gifts to us by pondering too much over the dark parts."

"This god," I say in a whisper, hoping he does not hear me, see me, "he is the reason our powers thrive under the moonlight?"

She shakes her head. "No, child, our blessed Goddess of the Moon is to thank for that." She blows a kiss toward the sea sky. "The God of Shadow is the reason we can take human form at night."

I bite my lip, questioning.

She sighs, tilting my chin up softly. "To be a shimmer of one's past self is a cruel gift indeed, Eloise. Now do you understand why I've tried to encourage you to refrain from so much landwalking?"

I offer a solemn nod. "I suppose you're right. I never thought of it as a… a punishment before." I look to my hands, wishing I could go back in time to listen to my wiser sister. If I had, I would've never crossed paths with Jaspyr, never ignited the frenzy at all.

My insides heat at the thought of him.

"This dark god is also the reason our kind subsist on human blood, the blood of which the great gods deem sacred." She holds out her palm and swirls of glittering green, purple, red, and blue weave before my eyes, forming a perfect circle with four distinct quadrants. "The Gods of Earth and Air. The Goddesses of the Sun and Sea. They all poured their powers into Olleb-Yelfra to create all that you see, including human life." Her mouth twists into a frown as she curls her fingers into a fist, the beautiful magic squandered. "For their brethren to create such a life as ours, essentially parasites on their creations, was a callous, unforgiveable act."

"So the frenzy was born of warring between the old gods?" I say between my teeth, brow furrowed. "We are not parasites! We deserve to be here. We shouldn't have to apologize for the acts of a jealous god." My voice raises, my temper building with too much information and this infuriating, unquenchable thirst.

"Of course, never," agrees Isobel. "As the Moon and the Sea said when the others wished to destroy Syrifina the moment she drank from her pirate. They vowed to ensure we did not delve too deep into our shadow-kissed souls, that the balance would remain, if not even strengthen, over time."

I relax, my mouth forming an 'O' with comprehension. I

say, "To feed only twice during the moon's cycle."

Isobel gently tilts my chin up, considering me.

"Very good, child," says Isobel with a soft smile. "This is why we are so adversely affected if we feed outside of those essential boundaries. They are for our safety as much as they are for the safety of the Olleb."

She frowns, letting go.

"The frenzy, our cursed consequence, is the God of Shadow's way of tempting us onto a darker, more isolated path, one where we forsake the protections of the Sea and Moon, where his sinful desires can fester and grow."

I sink a little lower, settling atop a rock to try to steady my dizzying thoughts. All rhyme and reason has abandoned me; everything feels just as wild and out of control as the tornado Isobel had conjured to protect us.

"But what does the God of Shadow have against Olleb-Yelfra?" I ask.

Isobel settles beside me, her tail and fins tickling my own in comfort. She rests her arm around my shoulder as we both lean into one another, watching the water whirl around us. "I don't pretend to know what the old gods are thinking. Their actions are beyond us."

The silver vanishes from her eyes as she drops our protective sound barrier.

When she does, we both gasp, pressing our backs into the wall, eyes wide, holding hands.

In the soft darkness of Empress Isle, the water glows with the most electric turquoises and blues I have ever laid eyes upon. The strange magic weaves with silver and gold threads. It crackles and pops, merging and growing until a full-figured woman—no, *otherworldly being*—floats before us, a crown of gleaming white pearls atop her head and dripping across her neck and arms like shimmering shells.

Isobel and I cling to each other tighter, gaping upon our

great Goddess of the Sea.

Her skin was as onyx as the deepest waters, her eyes crafted from pure sapphire as vibrant as the sunlit sea. And wrappings of water and magic curled around her stomach and legs like rolling waves.

Then the being speaks in words I can only describe as song itself, her voice tickling the space around us. "My younger brother has always been jealous that he was not summoned to be one of the four rulers of this world."

Earth, Air, Fire, and Water, I think.

"For an eternity, he has tried to find ways to dismantle the Golden Rule we founded for this world to bloom, prosper. You, my loves," the water seems to curl tenderly around us, "are merely pawns in a game far grander than your comprehension."

She sounds so soothing that I hardly notice the insult.

"It isn't fair, the hand you've been dealt, but stay with me, my children. Choose to live. Choose the Olleb." She brushes my cheek with her hand and I lean into her comforting palm. "I know that the life of your soulmate is a tempting adversary to my words. They will live on in a different form once gone from this plane. I *swear.*"

I somehow felt her words bind, tied in an unbreakable gold ribbon.

"You may never cross paths with them again, but I can assure you that there are places beyond here where they might find a new sort of life. A better one, without you in it. Souls, you see, never die." She glances at Aura and Ora, who I had almost forgotten—did our great goddess give them a knowing nod? "They have been known to travel far and wide after their earthly bodies are finished."

I find myself speaking; Isobel clutches my hand, squeezing tight. "What do you mean, a better one, a better life without me in it?" I ask, humbly, my voice almost unrecognizable to me in my fear at addressing this all-powerful entity. "And what... what might we be giving up, exactly, if we send our soulmates on to the next world?"

The great goddess smiles, her eyes narrowing at me. I press myself into the wall at my back, wishing I could melt into it as her gaze seems to penetrate right to my very soul. And I suppose, my intuition was right, for she says, "Yours is a strong one, Eloise. Stronger than most, except maybe your maker's." She laughs, the water rippling around her as if it were the sound of her voice itself. "Syrifina Myr is exceptional. And despite the *nuisance* the God of Shadow has cleverly crafted for us with the making of your lineage, I find I quite like the addition."

She seems to soften, considering both me and Isobel with joy in her eyes. I feel Isobel relax by my side.

"And what of my question?" I force myself to speak.

Her smile tightens.

"You are both too young, too new to fully understand, especially given this foolish *era*." The last word slithers off her tongue with disapproval, and I suppose she's thinking of the King. "But soulmates are an old, rare sort of magic born of the natural world." She rolls her eyes. "How to put it simply?"

I cling to every word.

"When my siblings and I breathed Olleb-Yelfra into existence, the complexities of our magic, left free to explore and bloom in this world, eventually grew to develop a mind of its own. Soulmates, among many other rare but equally enchanting things, are one such outcome." She brings her thumb and index finger to nearly touch. "You see, on the earthly plane, there's an infinitesimal chance one might meet another soul that they connect with beyond all others, their equal opposite in every way. For some, it can mean the ultimate romance or companionship. For others, an unlucky few," she looks away from us, not meeting our eyes, "it can mean the ultimate adversary or—"

"Prey," speaks Isobel, for the first time.

The Goddess of the Sea nods, her crown glinting in the low light.

"Because of what you are and what you intrinsically crave, you simply cannot live contentedly in the same realm as your soulmate, ever. Not unless you die and, potentially, meet your soulmate on another plane for another chance to unify."

"But we already chose immortality," I say, completely lost.

The Goddess of the Sea frowns, her words booming out like a thunderous wave. "There is no such thing on the earthly plane. But you *did* choose to forfeit your humanity in exchange for something else." Her voice grows unnervingly quiet. "And by doing so, you accepted the God of Shadow's terms that Syrifina unknowingly agreed to when she drank her pirate's blood to seal her transformation."

"To destroy our soulmates," I state, beginning to slowly understand.

She nods again.

"Existing in the mortal plane alongside her soulmate is the sacrifice Syrifina Myr unknowingly made when she ultimately took her revenge. A sacrifice *you* also made by accepting her kiss of death in exchange for life eternal. If you hadn't, there's a chance, albeit small, that you might've met your soulmate under different, happier circumstances. Shared many lifetimes together beneath the stars."

She offers us a somber smile, her voice now whispering like a gentle current.

"I'm sorry, children. I know this is not what you wanted to hear. But I felt it was time the truth was understood by your kind, for times are changing in the Olleb. And I need you to protect our seas more than ever." She turns to me. "I need you focused, Eloise."

"I can't believe this…" says Isobel, retreating into herself, as if she only now understood what she'd lost centuries ago.

"It is abhorrent what my brother did to you," she replies, softly.

What Syrifina did, I dare to think.

The goddess narrows her eyes. "But the Sea of Saindora wouldn't be nearly as enchanting nor its life protected without the Myr Sisters to watch over her. So forget your soulmate ever existed and be done with your frenzy before it threatens the entirety of the Olleb. Just put this mess behind you, darlings. You are each other's soulmates now."

Then I feel it, the most delicate and loving kiss upon my lips—it makes my entire body come alight with such a joy and calmness that I haven't felt since before I met Jaspyr. I touch my fingers to my mouth where the Goddess of the Sea has left her mark.

I look to Isobel just in time to see the sparks of a silvery-blue magic also fading from her lips, just as the presence of our great goddess begins to fade too.

"Stay, swim," she adds, looking to both of us with a wide grin. "My sea is forever yours to blossom in."

When the Goddess of the Sea is gone, I am left with an emptiness.

If at all possible, Empress Isle sounds even quieter, the water stiller.

It is now that I too truly understand the curse I accepted by choosing life eternal—if I kill Jaspyr, I will live forever, never to cross paths again with the soul I might be most connected to in this universe. And if I don't, I will doom myself, my sisters, and the Olleb.

I wonder to myself—had I known, would I have chosen differently?

'*It doesn't matter,*' whispers Aura.

'*You only have one choice left now,*' says Ora. '*Unless, of course, you consider death again.'*

I look to them and know beyond a doubt that they are soulmates, destined to spend an eternity together, in this world or the next. And they are right—with the past behind me and the future ahead, I have to choose between my life as I know it or his.

The only other choice is to die... again, and *maybe* have a chance for our souls to meet on another plane in happier circumstances.

I glance to Isobel. My powerful elder sister seems to shrivel into herself.

'You are each other's soulmates now', our great goddess had said.

My chosen family, I reaffirm—no matter my choices or what could've been, I can't imagine a life without my sisters. And if the frenzy forces me to decide between myself or a human, then as Mother did, I will choose to remain. Such a choice I made easily before and will gladly make again, promise or no.

I go to Isobel, pulling her into a strong embrace. "It's alright, sister. I'm here. I'm not going anywhere."

She composes herself, gently peeling herself out of my arms to look at me.

"I don't know why I'm so torn up about something that happened to me so long ago. You... you are the one who has to go through this now, *knowing—*"

She sobs into her hands.

"I wish I never knew," she adds. Her voice cracks; she hugs me tight. "I love you, Eloise. I'm sorry that you have to face this. I'll help you do what needs to be done and quickly. I won't leave you alone in this."

I nod, firmly, steadying my mind on the task at hand.

I must kill Jaspyr... I'll find a way to return, my oath be damned.

32

POISON

☼ J A S P Y R

I TAKE GREGGOR'S ADVICE AND LEAVE the shore after a long while. I make my way back toward the Lotus Center. The streets are quiet, the city somber. Night has fully fallen over Kampaulo.

I find myself back in my shop and lose myself in my work. My eyelids grow heavy, but my mind is too energized to ever properly sleep again. And I fear, more than anything, the nightmares that await me if I do.

I'm sorry, Eddison... Words I wonder if he'll ever let me speak to his face.

I drag my paintbrush back and forth over a blank canvas.

She killed his father.

She killed Penelope's husband.

She could've killed Eddison, and she tried to kill me.

But she didn't! We all live.

I focus on the blend of the colors. Mentally preparing myself to tackle the long day ahead, a normal day if I so will it—where I'll be forced to greet the loyal patrons that frequent my store and pretend like I didn't trap a man-hunting myrmaid and release her back into the world.

You did the right thing. A life for a life. The others would have come looking for her, would have slaughtered all of us if she had never returned.

I grit my teeth, steeling myself to that fact.

Eddison and I wouldn't have survived the others if Eloise hadn't saved us...

I swallow my thought, refusing to acknowledge that beast as anything other than what she is, a monster with a set of fangs always in search of blood.

I mix a small cup of white and black paint, swirling it with water until it's a beautiful bright gray. Our naked bodies, intertwined, flash in my mind's eye, the most vivid, wonderful memory. My tongue roving over every crevice of her body sends sparks through my bones.

She is so much more, and you know it.

My paintbrush slips from my grip, dropping to the stone floor with a jolt. I blink at the sound, drawing myself back to the present and out of my mind. An astonishing painting has materialized before me.

"Exquisite," I breathe, standing back to admire it—I must've been lost in my mind for hours, drowning in her.

The artificial waters before me seem to come alive in a dazzling blend of blue, green, turquoise. Frothy cream-like waves and silver-capped crests sweep across the grand canvas in search of something.

Ever so gently, I place a finger against the drying ink at the bottom of the painting. I close my eyes and whisper, "*Morphiatis animo.*"

Like roots planting into soil, silver magic emanates from my fingertips and spreads throughout the canvas, across the painted Sea of Saindora. The waves slowly undulate, a ship gently rocks, and the golden-lined creatures hidden in the darkness slither deeper still, waiting, watching, eyes pinned up.

The enchanted movements are so subtle that no one would ever see this and think... *magic.* Not with any certainty, at least. Not in this cold, magicless world King Devlindor has crafted.

"And yet, it exists." I lay my palm over the serpent chain, the cool metals pressing closer to my chest. "She exists."

I've mastered this artistic magic, the ability to give my paintings the life they deserve with just a little touch—an eternal one, I always do hope.

May my works live on when I'm gone.

With a magicked finger, I trace my initials in silver, shining ink that shall never fade—*J.T.*

I leave the painting to dry and go into the main area of my shop. I had promised a wandering tradesperson that I would finish his map commission of the Black Sand Desert routes by the end of the week, but I've been so distracted I have yet to even start.

I draw the curtains back from the vast window and push the glass panel open. I inhale a deep breath, the crisp night air chasing away some of the sleep from my mind. I've painted most of the night away, but the glorious moon still sits high in the sky, pouring its light over me, clinging to its last hours of dominion over my world.

I remember Greggor's words...

I close the window and curtains quickly, then sweep the room with firelight, just to be certain no myrmaids lurk in the shadows. But there are no eyes gleaming in the corners. No hypnotizing whispers in the air.

For once, Eloise is not here.

I should be thrilled, swept with relief...

And yet, all I feel is intense longing.

You sicken me. You're a coward, just like Greggor thinks.

I peek back out at the full moon with disdain, wishing it

away—it continues to glare at me.

I cannot wait for this night to be over and the day to come. Maybe then I can be content, knowing she does not *choose* to stay away from me but that a grand force keeps her at bay.

No, you are the reason. You made her promise.

I fish for an apple from the bowl at my tableside and bite into it, trying to distract myself from my own corrupted mind. The sticky juices spill down my chin and wet my fingers.

I blink down at the apple as I reach for a towel to wipe my hands. To my surprise, I find it bruised and browned in some places on the skin, the bright red curling toward black. Had I not looked, I would have never known that it had begun to rot, for it tasted so very sweet—I devour the apple all the way to its core, all the time thinking of Eloise.

33

KNOWING

AS DUSK SHIFTS TO NIGHT, my power surges. The water begins to feel suffocating, warm. I long to be rid of Isobel, to claw my way back to the surface over her lifeless body, if I have to, in order to see Jaspyr again.

Forget the gathering, I think. *My sisters will understand. I... I need to make this right.*

'*Make it worse, perhaps,*' a voice whispers.

Surely only an hour has passed since the Goddess of the Sea appeared and turned my world upside down, though I feel as if a year has flown by. Time is hard to track in the depths of Empress Isle, and waiting for Isobel's permission to put an end to this nonsense seems more impossible with each minute that ticks by.

No, I need her to watch me, I need her to help, my rational mind says.

And yet, part of me wants to escape her, to send her to the watery depths just so that I can swim up and away.

I can't stand to be confined right now, waiting. It makes

my skin crawl.

'*You shall have what you want, soon. Patience, Eloise.*'

The puzzle of him and me, and the fate of the Olleb should I fail, threatens to destroy me. My hunger may implode me. My skin itches. I keep fidgeting. I can't keep my mind off him, his blood, his lips. Every inch of my being yearns to explode out of these halls and slice toward the surface to search for him; the oath I so foolishly made was like the wretched sun, ensuring I might never have what I want.

Goddesses! I internally scream.

It is all I can do to keep my face and voice neutral anymore, with grandiose stories of warring gods and goddesses rolling around in my head.

"Isobel," I say after a time, trying to focus on what's right—both of us have been slowly swimming together through the caverns in silence with no destination, Aura and Ora close behind. "I think I need to rest. If I have to wait until the shadow moon"— she scoffs—"or, for however *long*," I add, tersely, "to temper this curse and get back on track, then that's what I'll do." *I have to try.* "But I can't be with my thoughts right now. Maybe if I just sleep, until it's time for the gathering…"

She offers me a tight smile. "That's a great idea," she says, sweetly—she lies so easily.

We swim deeper into Empress Isle where no one will be sure to disturb us; we've been lucky to avoid our sisters so far.

I select a small, secluded alcove where I can curl up and rest. Here, the bones of men have been wiped away to make room for an abundance of green plant life and twinkling emeralds that make it seem as if I float within a jungle. There are so many enchanted spaces like this one and infinite channels to play or rest in—normally, I could spend weeks on end exploring my home. But my eyelids grow heavy with the weight of all I've learned today.

Isobel plants a kiss on my forehead and turns to leave me to my thoughts.

"I won't be far if you need me," she says. "I'll wake you when Mother calls for the gathering to start." I frown, narrowing my eyes at her.

The last thing I want to consider right now is facing Syrifina and all my sisters later tonight.

Isobel sighs. "We've both learned a great deal on this day. I, too, could use some time to… digest."

I want to offer her a comforting smile as she does to me, but I'm too weary to fake such an expression now.

"How long before she could do it?" I ask before she swims away. "How long did it take Mother?"

Isobel stops in the archway. She scrunches her face as she forces the truth from her lips. "Their affair went on for years, even longer than mine, I'm afraid. Her frenzy and the massacres that came with it earned her a nickname that went down in history—the Saindora Savage."

I vaguely recall such a name from my human history lessons.

I gape at her from my pillows of vines and feathery sea fans. "How could she live with this madness for so long? I can't even think straight and it's barely been a week."

"Have you ever known Syrifina Myr to think linearly? I believe the frenzy cracked her ancient mind after a certain point, but she's strong, deliberate. She persisted until she was ready to move on." She shrugs. "I'm sure that's what our great goddess meant when she called her 'exceptional'…"

Maybe, I think.

"But why did she let it go on for so much time, if it's so damaging to her, to the Olleb?"

Isobel's grimace dents her perfect, childlike features.

"Just because *our* soulmates are destined to bring out the worst in us doesn't mean we can't experience the good parts," she says, her eyes shimmering with sadness and exhaustion. "Don't you understand? Didn't you listen to what the great goddess said?"

She pauses, as if hoping I might answer 'yes' so that she needn't deliver yet even more terrible information.

When I don't, her throat tightens.

"It's not unlike being able to landwalk," she continues with a heaviness; she looks away. "It's difficult to let go… once you've had a taste of what could've been."

A question forms on my lips. Then my mind drifts to Jaspyr, to his hands roaming over me and our bodies intertwined. My name on his wicked tongue.

"From the look on your face, I think you more than already realize the mess you're in."

I look down.

"Our frenzy is just another word for love, Eloise, or something even grander," she says with a heavy, quiet breath. "But it's simply the only word that can express the passion we feel for the doomed humans who cross our paths, and what they feel for us." She shakes her head. "It's not even complex enough a term to contain all the emotion sparked in our frenzies…"

"But Mother was hunting." I point to my chest, shutting out thoughts of him. "*I'm hunting.* I loathe what his existence is doing to me."

"Love, loathe." She moves her hands up and down like balancing scales, "they walk a very thin line in this realm, don't they?"

I can hardly keep steady, my tail suddenly so heavy, dragging me down like a stone.

"I believe that Mother *loved* the queen very much," she says, "thus could never find the strength to tear herself away, let alone kill her, as desperate as she was for her blood.

"I'm not sure if the humans we connect with have something in common, something that triggers such an emotion in us on sight and scent alone," she continues, "but I know it can be brought on by *anyone*, not just men. Love is known to be impartial this way." She smiles, softly. "And I don't have to explain to you how deeply our kind love when we deem another worthy."

Her gaze is heavy on me, allowing me a moment to catch up.

"Are you saying… I'm in love and that is what so sickens me?"

She shrugs. "Would it hurt so much to have to kill this man, *your soulmate*, if you weren't?"

I think of the pirate who started it all, the one Mother loved in her human form and slaughtered in the next, vowing to never love again. Until she created us.

"We must maintain our cherished sisterhood by supporting each other through the darker times. That is why I'm sharing this secret with you, Eloise. I don't want you to be blindsided… like I was." She looks to her hands. "For, to kill the one you love, frenzy or not, can be just as destructive to your eternal soul as letting them live."

She appears far away, sinking into her mind. I want to ask more… about the one she might have loved and destroyed anyway. How long had they lasted in her universe? What were they like?

But I can't bring myself to speak the words, for the concept of one of us loving one of them is still so hard to fathom.

I despise Jaspyr. I would claw his beating heart from his chest if…

'If what? Why didn't you?

I suppose, I don't know, I think.

"Alright, Isobel…" I say, drawing her back to me. "Say what you speak is true. Why does Mother try and hide this truth from us? Is it so terrible to name the frenzy by what it really is, to warn our other sisters of it? Why does it have to be such a huge secret?"

"Because," growls Isobel, her powers filling the chamber with so much energy I think I might get pushed out, "if she *loved* Queen Julissa?" She scoffs. "Think about it, Eloise. Don't be so daft. A second treacherous love story for Syrifina Myr after how our kind were created, the revenge she suffered? Why, it's Mother!" She throws her hands up. "She would never admit to such a weakness as yet *another* human stealing her heart. She engaged with the queen for years, because the frenzy, the curse, love, *whatever* you'd like to call it, held her back from killing her."

My mouth falls open; I wish to sink into the walls.

"The point is, dear, I know what I say is true, because I fell for a human once, too. My frenzy was triggered… and the love I felt for him almost undid me."

She looks at her shaking hands; I reach for her, but she floats away.

"I… I wanted to make it work for us, to try. I *did* try, but the moment his blood was spilled by his attacker, I couldn't resist feeding." She blows out a wounded sigh of bubbles. "It was too much too fast. True love or not, his blood was too hypnotizing to resist."

She looks up at me with such a wounded expression.

"I did it quickly."

"I'm so sorry, Isobel—"

"Don't!" she growls, glowing crimson. "Syrifina Myr fell into the abyss of love… something she'd vowed to never do again. And for a myrmaid, that abyss is profound." Her lips turn downward. "This is the hard lesson, Eloise. If you do not kill the one you've marked, the one you love, you will tear this world apart. And if you do, you will have to live with the pain of forever knowing that you killed your one true love, and that you will never love again, for myrmaids are not supposed to."

Her eyes blaze hot.

"That is why Kristeena spent so long in the deep. That is why Zahra has a perpetual foul mood. That is why Mother clings to us, truly. And that is why I"— her voice cracks— "why I'm warning you. The gods have played a terrible trick on us. This is the consequence. If you want to live forever, you *must* kill your eternal true love."

Do it, Eloise. Kill him! For it's not true love if it kills you.

I think I see a tear of bright red magic glisten atop Isobel's pearl-white cheek, but she drifts away into the darkness before I can be certain.

I stare after her long after she's gone, thoughts roaring.

I place my right palm over my chest, feeling the cold emptiness where my heart used to beat strong and warm. With a suddenness that makes me tremble, I understand the true name of the frenzy, this shadow-kissed, cursed love as Isobel so mistakenly claims it. It was the most powerful form of pain ever known in the human realm, what drove Syrifina Myr to give her life away and the true foundation of our creation— not love, heartbreak.

"By the goddesses," I whisper, my voice rippling through the still waters here.

A continuous, relentless cycle of heartbreak that had begun with the mother of myrmaids shall persist for as long as we spread our blessed gifts. I know I shouldn't, but I linger over the God of Shadow, a sneer forming on my lips.

What a wicked soul, indeed.

'*Sleep,*' my friends urge as they settle atop the floor of the cavern. '*Wait. Listen to Isobel.*'

'*It won't be easy, but the days will pass swiftly,*' adds Ora.

'*And when you're ready, we too will help you overcome this.*' Together, their voices, a soothing melody, lull me away from my present worries.

I sigh, my terrible thoughts fluttering away with it on a soft stream of bubbles. I blow them both silver-lipped kisses. '*Sorry I'm such a villain these days.*'

They swim and weave around me to show their support before settling again on the floor at my tail.

'*You will always have our love, Master, even when you lose your way. It's truer than you know.*'

'*Thank you,*' I say, drifting to sleep.

I close my eyes and submit to the shadows, letting them devour my mind's eye. I just pray that when I wake, Jaspyr will be dead already, by some lucky twist of fate.

34

TRUCE

☼ J A S P Y R

IT'S BEEN DAYS WITH NO CONTACT from Eloise or any of her kind...

Good bloody riddance.

But sometimes, I think I can sense her nearing. Like a lurking shadow in the night, an epic energy burning behind me.

I feel her breath on my neck to find it's only the wind. I feel the scorch of her stare on my back to learn it's merely the piercing beam of the moon.

My intuition screams at me to run when I imagine her presence, though I never do. I always turn around to look, to search for someone, something, who is never there.

A thing of nightmares I had called her with my final parting words...

And yet, I dream of the moment I might see her again before I die.

I sit in the cool sand now, watching the tide retreat as the air warms around me—all I see is her, a ghost floating atop the waves.

Eloise Myr, will you ever return? I dare to think.

My mind shatters trying to glimpse pieces of her.

Her dark, smooth skin. The slender ribbons of gold and silver magic stitching to her limbs, pulsing with her very breath. Even the way the night ripples around her to make room for her when she stands. The wonderful wildness of her hair.

And her hands…

I release a painful, agonized sigh, letting my head fall back to the lightening sky. "Gods, what's *wrong* with me?"

Still, I imagine her hands… how they had moved over every inch of me with such an ownership that I had no choice but to surrender my body to hers. No release will ever feel as good as when I was inside her. No kiss will ever feel so impassioned.

I don't even want to consider how utterly meager a union with someone else, a mortal like me, would be; the slightest twinge of guilt curls inside of me when the thought of my deceased love tries and fails to press back into the forefront of my mind.

When Eloise fled my fires, I woke up and followed her soft glittering trail all the way to the seashore at the southernmost part of our city. There it vanished—this is where I sit now, focused on the sunrise, its fire spilling over the world in a haze, burning my eyes and heating my skin.

The sun is beautiful in an obtrusive, garish way. I see that now. See why she would flee its decisive, judgmental burn.

It's nothing like her, who blends with the shadows, cold yet comfortable in her brilliant power. She needn't shout to the world of her existence.

The sun forces its way higher, illuminating the clouds like sketches in the sky. I think it might singe Eloise right out of my mind if I stare too long.

I swear the Sun speaks to me, '*You should've let her burn.*'

I squeeze my eyes shut, blinking the light from my eyes. *I know.*

THERE'S A KNOCK AT MY DOOR.

"We're not open yet," I grumble; my sleepless nights are starting to weigh on me. "Go away!"

"Do you normally scream at your patrons?" A slick voice from the other side retorts; he bangs again, rattling the hinges. "Open the door, you lazy fool. It's me! No bloody excuses. Let's do this."

I straighten, then tumble out of my chair as I make to stand.

"Eddison?"

My feet are heavy as they carry me slowly across my shop. I flip the lock open and swing open the door.

Eddison's arms are crossed over his chest, his entire muscular body filling my doorway.

"Hi," I say, feebly, standing back to offer him entrance. I wipe the sleep from my eyes, blinking a couple times to ensure he's really there.

He brushes past me with barely a grunt of acknowledgment.

"I deserved that," I mumble, scratching the back of my head. I shift from foot to foot, unsure of what else to say.

He faces me, waiting.

I grow increasingly uncomfortable under his scrutiny—I feel as if he can see every disgraceful thought I've had since the night I betrayed him for Eloise. *To save him,* I tell myself again. "So... why, exactly, are you here, then?" I finally ask. "Come to settle the score?"

He narrows his eyes; the heat rises to my cheeks, and I'm sure he can see it plainly for how white I am.

"Something like that," he replies through his teeth.

His gaze flicks around the room as if checking for intruders. His shoulders slump as he sets his focus back on me, arms relaxing down by his side. He pulls a bottle of red wine from his rucksack.

"Mum said it was time to kiss and make up." He extends the bottle toward me like a white flag someone is forcing him to wave.

My stomach twists in knots. I look down.

"I don't deserve your forgiveness," I utter, hardly able to believe that he even had the nerve to offer it at all.

Eddison curses under his breath, then crosses the room toward me in two long strides. He shoves the bottle into my chest so hard I stumble backward. But he holds his hand there, forcing me to look at him, to endure the uncomfortable closeness between us that used to come so easy.

"It's not my forgiveness, it's Penelope's," he says, jaw rigid. He lets go of the wine, stepping away; I grip the bottle before it can slip and shatter on the floor. "You and me still got things to talk about, *brother.*"

I wince as he turns his back to me. He shoves his hands in his pockets with a heavy sigh, tilting his chin up to consider my newest painting.

"What made her come around?" I carefully ask, fishing two glasses out of a cabinet.

He turns back to me, eyes unnaturally wide.

"Let's see... what made Ma come around to the fact that you invited a *blood-drinking succubus* into our lives without so much as a damned word? That you just *had* to wet yourself in her for hours, while I watched! The same monster, in fact, who confessed to *eating* my father?" He says the name of every god and goddess I've ever heard of, staring to the ceiling. "I swear—"

Then he rips the bottle out of my trembling hands and slams it down on a table so hard that the wood rattles. "Forgiveness..." he mutters.

I jump at the sound. I've never seen him so *angry* before, not like this. I can see his shoulders rising and falling with his attempt to remain level-headed.

He turns to me, slowly, like a predator sizing up its prey. Like her... *I miss the way she looked at me.* "Did I leave anything out?"

I grimace, not wanting to accept that I did any of those things at all. Not wanting to admit that I even *enjoyed* when Eloise came around, the things she did to me. She made me feel alive again in a way that I know... I *know* is wrong. And yet, I can't deny that I yearn for her ice-cold touch, her excruciating presence, even more.

So instead, I lie.

"Eddison, I did those things to protect you. I thought if I told anyone, they could also come to meet danger. And I was right! If you hadn't forced me to—"

His mouth twists into a sneer. He slams me into the wall so fast that I didn't see it coming. "Forced you to what now?"

The veins bulge from his neck, and silver laces his irises.

Shame overwhelms me, though it's mixed with a sense of pride at my friend's growth. Maybe his regulator training has made him less of a pushover... and maybe he remembered how much he liked the taste of magic after all.

I don't look away. I keep my chin high, ready to take whatever beating he rains on me. I deserve it.

At least some good has come of this, I think, locking in on the power sparking in his glare.

He lets me go with a huff, squeezing his eyes shut. When

he opens them, there's nothing notable about them.

He stomps back over to the wine.

"You had a chance to *kill* that walking nightmare, and instead you let her go. Why?" His question is more of a plea, his voice quieting. "Why would you do that after the risk my mother and I took to help you? Jaspyr, if anyone had come around the bend that night, we would've all been hung out to dry." He grips the edge of the table, barely holding it together. "I mean, my friends died because of that… that thing."

I shake my head. "No, but she didn't—"

He flashes daggers for eyes at me. "She's poisoned your damn mind with her seduction! Can't you see that. Gods, Jaspyr." He scoffs. "Get your head on straight. What were you thinking, letting something like that have a second chance to terrorize our lands when you had her?" He makes a fist, shaking it in my face. "For the King's sake, *we had her.*"

I bow my head, biting down on my excuses. I owe him more than that.

I take a deep breath, focusing on anything but Eloise.

"I'm sorry, Eddison," I say, meeting his shimmering gaze. "I truly am. I know I let you down, and I can't take it back."

I'm not sure I would if I could, but I keep that bit to myself.

I throw my arms up, exasperated. "You know that I would give my life for you, for Penelope. You're all the family I have left. I let her live to ensure you could too and that's the truth of it. That's all I have to say, and I understand if it isn't enough for you to be able to look me in the eye again without all that—"

He lifts his gaze to mine, so full of hatred.

My heart shrivels. This time, I have to look away.

He looses a long, deep sigh and pours us each a glass.

"Fine, then," he says, enunciating every word so that it is clear that things are not, in fact, fine. "You're forgiven." He raises a glass to me with a mock smile.

I look up at him with a start.

"I'm *not* asking for your forgiveness," I counter, flexing my muscles—I'd rather he pummel my face in than give in so easily. "Why in the good king's name would you even think that? What I did was unforgiveable."

"True," he says—that hurt enough that it might as well have been a slap in the face. "But the threshold for forgiveness is determined by the one doing the forgiveness, *brother.*" He again speaks the word without warmth.

I look at him incredulously. "Why?"

He shakes his head, taking a long swig of his drink and refilling it before even passing me a glass.

"Because," he says, slowly, staring into the crimson depths of his cup, "I suppose, I do understand why you did what you did. And we are all still alive." He shrugs, lips turned down. "We have to keep counting those blessings after…" His voice trails off, but I know that he was going to say 'the war'.

He looks to the window, to the water in the Lotus Center.

"Besides, after Mum and I calmed down a bit, we agreed that it was probably not the worst idea to strike a deal with that fiend rather than kill her. A stupid risk!" he corrects when he sees my face lighten with relief. "But if more came looking…" He shivers. "The King save us all."

I nod. "She promised me that as long as I don't call her to return, she will leave us alone. And I felt something solidify between us when she did, like a spell locked in place." I tuck my hair behind my ears. "I'm not sure, but if I had to wager a guess, a myrmaid with so much power linked to the mere note of their voice… their oaths *could* be bound by a greater force."

He snickers. "Let's hope you're right." He points a finger at me, finally placing a cup in my hand. "And just in case you are, you best keep that wench's name out of your bloody mouth."

I return a forced smile. "Do you really think Penelope will forgive me for—"

"She put the wine in my hand and sent me on my way. She wanted me to tell you that you're welcome back… home. Whenever you're ready."

I shake my head, looking to my feet, overwhelmed by emotion by what I brought to Penelope's doorstep, a mother figure who has always looked out for me.

"No, no, no." Tears cloud my eyes. I ball my hands. "I *cannot* accept this," I say, sternly, trying to hand the cup back. "I don't deserve it. I haven't done anything to earn it."

Eddison tries to speak, but I cut him off.

"No, Eddison. Let me earn it first, at least." I'm not worthy of their love nor their acceptance, not with the dark thoughts eating at my mind, threatening to cloud their world in shadows too.

How could I have done this to them?

"Fine, call it a truce for now, then," he replies, and I know he understands. "I'm sure I can think of a way for you to earn your honor back in my eyes." They narrow as he lifts his cup to mine.

"Thank you," I say with a slight bow.

He smiles, but it doesn't meet his eyes. "Let's look ahead, not behind. We have too much history to let a pretty face with fangs get between us, mate."

His words land soft, sincere. My entire body warms with relief at the possibility to move forward with Eddison and Penelope still in my life, when what I really am owed is Regulator Eddison driving me through with a sword to enact his justice.

"Truce," I say, holding my cup to his.

We both clink our glasses, then chug the wine.

THE BOTTLE IS GONE within half an hour, and the afternoon has barely begun. The conversation is flowing like old times, though the tension still lingers, softened only with the wine.

Eddison scratches the back of his head with a twisted expression.

"*Oy...*" he says. "This place is a mess!" He wrinkles his nose, then throws open a window to let some fresh air pour in. "You can tell me anything, you know. How have things been since..."

I gulp down the last of my wine, glancing at my newest painting—a bright full moon, hanging in a black sky like the night's gleaming eye, a dark golden sea rippling beneath it. If one looks close enough at the water, they might even note the glint of silver eyes staring back at them.

No, I can't tell him... can't explain the beautiful, addicting creature that has enveloped every waking thought and breath I take.

"Everything is fine as can be," I say with a shrug, suddenly very interested in my shoelace. "I'm just... busy these days. I have a lot of commissions to keep my mind off things."

"And that?" He points to the painting. "Was that a commission?"

I press my lips into a firm line.

"I see." He tenses, sucking in a breath through his nose, his chest puffing. He lets it go, all his muscles seeming to relax. "Well, maybe you just need to get out of your head for a while, out of this shop." He stands. "Get up. We're going for a walk."

I open my mouth to protest but he holds out a hand to stop me. He marches past me into my private workshop area and disappears; I don't have the will to follow, inundated by my thoughts and lazy from the wine and lack of sleep.

I hear the clanking of metal and frown; he's gathering my swords. The last thing I want to do is spar right now. I can barely keep my eyes open.

"For the King's sake, everything is covered in dust, and— " I hear him curse as he steps in fresh paint.

He comes back, tracking pink shoeprints across my floor. He presses the handle of a sword into my palm, still dried with my blood—I gulp, remembering that slight sting of pain from when Eloise nicked me with this very blade. How my body had betrayed me, craving her even then.

"Is this necessary?" I ask, a moan in my voice, tripping over myself to follow him around the room. "We're drunk."

He merely frowns. "Earn it," he mumbles in a slur, his eyes hooded.

My heart aches—I'll owe him for a long time to come, no matter what I do to try to win back his love.

"Happy to oblige," I say, sincerely. Then I lighten my voice before my dark thoughts threaten to bury me. "But unfair advantage. You got me drunk *and* I barely slept last night."

He shrugs. "Regulators don't make excuses for how they're feeling when they're called into battle. What kind of warrior are *you?*"

I throw my head back and laugh.

"I'm no warrior," I say, slyly—I'm pretty sure I'd be considered more like a deadly outlaw if people knew what I was really up to post-war. "I'm a humble painter."

I flash him a coy smile, but I've whooped him in duels enough times—he knows… he knows who I really am, deep down, I'm certain.

Eddison shakes his head at me, a smirk forming on his lips.

His expression somewhat darkens. "Funny, I wouldn't have guessed that humble painters kept monsters for muses."

His eyes flick again to the painting; I redden.

"They don't," I reply with brutal sincerity.

His nostrils flare, but he shakes off whatever harsh words hovered on his tongue.

My gut twists, and I'm not sure if it's from the words or the wine.

"Eddison, it's one thing to drink away our problems, but adding real swords into the mix..." I sigh. "I'm not sure—"

"Your choice if you want to change clothes or not, but that's the only one you get," he interrupts.

He crosses his brawny arms at his chest, raising an eyebrow at me, as if to say, 'challenge me, if you like'.

Normally, I would decline a duel in this state—he'll demolish me. But my hands are tied.

I grit my teeth. "*Fine*, have it your way. But, first, food."

"That, I won't argue with," he says, patting his belly

I'm not sure how or why, but I ate like a king that afternoon. Something about the warmth of the sun, Eddison's laughter and conversation, the familiar bustling of the city, gifted me a sense of normalcy today, pulling my attention away from my toxic thoughts.

We got to the beach with the sun high in the sky, choosing a location away from the busyness of the docks, more remote, on the far west port of the city.

Cliffs rose tall on either side of us, and too many sharp rocks had washed up on the beach from a recent storm, so we moved closer to the water where the sand was smooth.

"I'm surprised you would want to spar here, by the water," I say, softly, a bit uncomfortable at the background.

The waves are strong today, hurling toward the shore.

Eddison squares his shoulders. "I'm not going to live my life afraid." He glares at the sea, and I know he's thinking of his father.

Words fail me.

"Do you remember the story of the Saindora Savage?" he asks, suddenly.

I raise an eyebrow—the name floated to me from an old history told to us in Learning Centers, before King Devlindor banned education about the monarchs predating his reign.

"I think so." I glance around the vicinity to make sure we are indeed alone. "Why do you ask?"

"Well, what do you recall?" he says, turning his sword over in his hands, examining the sharpness of the blade. It is a bit dull, but it still glistens nicely in the sun.

"I don't know," I reply, cautiously, wracking my brain for the pieces of the story. "I remember they were a notorious killer. And a big mention in someone's reign…" I scratch my head, then tie my hair back from my eyes before we battle. "Who was it now?"

"The High Queen Julissa," says Eddison, softly, kicking at the sand. "She apparently loved to sail."

It takes everything to hide the surprise in my expression—the words he spoke mark treason against his precious king, and I didn't even have to coax him.

"Right, right," I say, trying not to smile. "Yes, we learned of this briefly as children. And I actually heard even more rumors of her botched reign when I lived in Saindora."

I do a couple of maneuvers to warm up, my feet just as tipsy as my head.

"Queen Julissa was said to have failed to protect her people from a vicious murderer toward the end of her governance," I recite from a blurry memory. "The City of Saindora and her queendom fell to ruin under her thumb. And only when she was found headless, decapitated, did things start to turn back around."

I remember the story so clearly now, for it read like a fairytale in reverse, a bright world going dark, with no happy ending…

"The Queen of Death, they called her," he adds, still staring toward the unruly waves.

"So?" I ask, not allowing myself to look—I have a sinking feeling. "Where are you going with this?"

He shrugs. "It just came to me..." He tilts his head toward the water. "I wonder if the Saindora Savage was one of them."

I freeze, this time understanding. I begin to sweat in my leathers, from the sun, from knowing what lurks below.

"Why would you wonder something like that? There's been plenty of murders throughout history. They're not all—" I swallow the word, not wanting to speak it aloud lest even that might sever our deal.

Eddison continues, cracking his neck, from stress it seemed.

"I dug up the story again in my mum's... storage."

My eyes grow wide. "Penelope still has—" I lower my voice. "She needs to burn everything from the old world."

"Why?" he counters. "You haven't."

"That's different," I say, straightening. "I'm a rebellion."

He rolls his eyes. "I see the wine has really loosened your tongue today."

"Right back at you," I retort, pointing my sword in his direction.

He brushes it away, determined to state his theory.

"The Saindora Savage was a remorseless killer who stalked the streets at night, ripping through the city and leaving their victims in *pieces*, Jaspyr. Sounds a lot like what those twins did to my friends." He slams his sword into the sand, leaning on it. "And during that time, the Queen was believed to have fallen ill, her mind diseased. She cared only to sail rather than protect or rule her people. All while this murderer terrorized her city, leaving bodies in the streets left and right."

"Fine," I say, throwing my hand to the air. "Say your theory is right, that this Saindora Savage was a... was one of them.

What do you expect me to do about it? Who cares?"

He places a comforting hand on my shoulder. "I'm just... I'm just worried about you is all. I've lost too many people to the water."

I sigh, my shoulders slumping.

"I really am sorry," I say, daring a glance at the sea, "about what happened to Edward. She *deserves* to die for taking him from you. But your life means more to me than your revenge for him. I hope you know that. And I'm not going to let her get into my head again. It's over."

He offers me a curt nod.

"Alright," he replies. "I feel the same way about you when it comes to Sibyl and Luna."

A terrible, cold shock overtakes me. I hadn't heard their names spoken aloud in so long.

"I'm sorry," he says, quickly. "I didn't mean... I just meant—"

"No." I hold up my hand, heart pounding. "No, it's alright. I suppose I understand exactly what you mean. Revenge can be a devious thing."

He chews on his lip. "So, have you heard anything from the Four Corners?" he asks with the most gentleness he's been able to muster all day.

I shake my head, my eyes brimming with tears. "But it's my every hope Luna made it there and is surviving whatever tortures the King puts her through."

I save every gold piece now, every treasure exchanged for my art, so that upon her eighteenth year, *if* she makes it out alive, I can find her and bring her home. And when I do, I will remind her of the true world we belong to, of the Golden Age that was stolen from us.

I raise my sword. "For Sibyl and Luna."

Eddison touches his blade to mine. We both bow low.

"After you, Master Tayshin," he says, jokingly, not missing how I slightly stumbled on my feet.

I scoff. "That's my father's title. I'm not yet so old!" I bow back. "Don't be fooled. I'm even more arrogant a swordsman with wine."

I lunge forward; our swords clash.

I lose myself in the battle, just as I lose myself in my art.

In her.

Sweat drenches my skin after a time, hair slick against my neck—I'm grateful to finally focus on anything other than Eloise.

Another hour flies by, and we do away with our shirts, the waves splashing at our ankles and the distant sun warming our backs. Then I hear the softness of a hum, an enchanting song floating back to the forefront of my mind.

With the next thrust of my blade, my sense of freedom evaporates and she takes over once more. My grip tightens over the handle of my sword, my expression hardening, thoughts darkening.

I swing hard, and Eddison parries as he shouts, "Careful, mate!"

But I don't hear him anymore, I don't see anything but her. I'm fighting to regain control of my life, fighting to eradicate her from my mind as much as I'm desperately fighting to attain her, to reach her again.

Greggor's words fill my head. *'You and Eloise are not meant to be. Let her go.'*

I can't. I won't!

I roar in frustration. *Let me go!*

The sun starts to slip away, clouds emerging as if from nowhere, fracturing my light. The waves swallow the sound of our grunts and yells. I swing harder but miss, losing control, losing footing, senselessly taking hits.

Eddison parries another attack from me, then lunges back,

unable to remain on the defense; I attack, again and again, using all my strength and weight, and—

My mind disappears, falling back to that night in the alleyway, where Eloise's eyes enveloped me and her voice penetrated deep inside me.

Eddison lunges and his blade meets my skin, biting into the side of my neck.

I scream out as a vision of Eloise explodes across my mind. The heat of my magic swallows me whole.

"*Luzcora!*" I hear Eddison shout.

When he swings his sword, electric green magic ricochets off his blade and into mine—my sword shatters into a thousand pieces, but he manipulates the shards away from me with an expertise I thought he'd long since forgotten.

The force of his magic knocks me to my knees and I land on the rocky shore, hard, my skin splitting open against the earth. I taste my own blood.

"Have you gone mad?" he shouts over me and the roaring sea, sweat drenching his skin. "You really lost it out there. You could've killed me!"

He takes a step back, eyes wide with worry.

"What did that evil beast do to you?" He points his blade at me. "I *told* you. Something's happened to you. She's got in your head or something, just like with Julissa."

I press my hands into the sand, tiny pebbles cemented into my raw palms. The silver magic is smothered out of them.

"I'm… gods." I cough, catching my breath, the salty sea air tasting so heavy. "I didn't mean to lose control like that," I say, letting out a long breath, feeling so ashamed as my senses come back to me.

I peel my hands off the ground, staring at them; they're shaking.

"I… I just need to get back to work."

"*Work?*" screeches Eddison. "Did you see what just happened out there? I'm tempted to take you to the Wellness Center after a stunt like that!"

I shake my head. "No one can help me. Just leave me alone," I mumble, dusting myself off.

A headache thanks to the wine and magic and fantasies of the death-bringer begins to form.

"I will not," he says between his teeth. "Not when you clearly have a death wish these days. It's only been a week since you—"

Silver is still blaring in his eyes; it's all he can do to smother it. He looks around, distraught, praying under his breath that no one has seen us.

"I just need some time to think, to get back on track," I say.

"Have it your way, then. Rot in your workshop for all I care." He groans. "We're supposed to be family!"

He throws down his sword and stomps up the beach back toward the city, muttering curses all the way.

"Penelope expects you at dinner," he calls back to me over his shoulder. "Clean yourself up and see you at eight." It was nothing short of a threat.

35

BREAK

☼ J A S P Y R

I RETURN TO THE SOUTH SHORE the next night—and every night after that—waiting for her. To sit with my shame.

If only to feel the touch of her hand again on my skin…

The icy smoothness of her breath, her tongue. Just the memory of her. My groin shivers just to think of it.

She was right: my imagination cannot fathom all that she is or could become to our broken world. But it tries anyways.

She was terrible and great all in one.

No amount of physical release can erase her from my thoughts, though the brothels have seen me each and every sunrise since; no amount of drowning my sorrows and aches in painted worlds or wine can make me feel normal again— her portrait I had started anew sits unfinished, for I couldn't possibly hope to capture the depth of her face, the epic power in her eyes, the magic coursing atop her skin with a life all its own. Not without her there to guide me.

And even then…

I long for her only more.

The day is done. The sun retreats, leaving only a clean slab of black—no moon tonight, just stars stabbing their light upon the shadow-kissed land.

I wait for her to return. I watch the waves in vain, knowing that she cannot; I'm the one who wished her away.

I can't take this anymore.

The shadows seem to speak to me, the moonless night growing darker still. '*Then do it. Call to her,*' they say.

Despite the sharpness of her fangs and the way her voice made my spine chill. Despite her bloodstained skin and the way she moved so fast that not even my eyes could contain her, I find myself praying to every god known and not known for Eloise to return to these shores so that we may battle again. So that I might take her in the sand and devour her like she has my sanity.

'*Don't do it, Jaspyr,*' a familiar voice pleads '*Think of Ed dison, your family. If you do this… there's no going back.*'

I refuse to see the glint of the ghost, a man, hovering just beyond the break of the waves in the dark. I refuse to see the pain in his expression, one that used to offer me so many smiles, as he melts back into the stars.

I steady my gaze on the water, on the impossibly dark place where the sea meets the sky. "Eloise, *please,*" I shout into the night. "Come back!"

I drop to my knees in the sand as I feel it—part of the promise she made to me, her vow to stay away, rolls back with an echoing snap that momentarily sweeps the air from my lungs.

What have I done?

I swear I hear the night rumble with laughter as I rinse my stained hands and face in the sea.

36

SAVAGE

MY EYES SNAP OPEN.

Too soon. I'm not ready, I think.

I was dreaming of flying, of drifting through a star-riddled sky with my soulmate by my side.

He was faceless in my dreams, yet as I wake, a vision of him forms—skin like the moon, eyes like the dark, a voice like a raging storm.

Adversary. Prey.

'*Wake, child. You're free. This time is yours.*'

With a jolt, I look around and find myself hovering outside of the mouth of Empress Isle. I have no idea how much time has passed. Aura and Ora are gone, and Isobel is nowhere to be found.

"How did I get here?" My voice croaks out.

I stare into the deep, its vastness shocking after my confinement in the emerald alcove.

I turn around and gaze into the tunnels of Empress Isle, knowing I should turn back and find my friends, my sister…

I hesitate.

I have a chance to finish this alone, I think.

I still can't stand the idea of them bearing witness to my final stand-off with this weakness, with him.

Fate must be giving me another chance to right my wrong-doings on my own.

'No,' Aura says, gently, pushing into my mind. *'It's never wise to blindly trust Fate.'*

'Return at once,' adds Ora. *'This isn't safe.'*

'Why not?' I ask. 'What's happened to me?'

'We don't know. Something foul is at play,' they say in unison.

'You are not in the right mind,' continues Aura. *'You've had us all so worried.'*

'What do you mean? Speak plainly.'

'We've been searching for you for two weeks, Eloise,' they say as one. *'Our mind-link was just... gone. Until now.'*

Two weeks? I think to myself with a gasp. *How? No... I couldn't possibly... I only just closed my eyes hours ago.*

Then I remember Zahra, Kristeena—how easy it is for a myrmaid to disappear.

I begin to panic. If what they say is true, I must have missed a gathering, too.

Oh, goddesses, I can never face Mother now!

'You have to,' they both say, intruding on my thoughts.

I push them away and stall near the gates, staring into the emptiness, mulling over my choices.

There is so much I don't know about Syrifina and our coven, and the beings who created us. Centuries of secrets, questions.

'I don't want to burden Mother with another weakling daughter plagued by the frenzy,' I finally reply. 'I want to show her my strength. I can handle this myself. Then, maybe she'll respect me enough to share the truth with me herself.'

'*You are not a burden, Eloise,*' says Aura.

'*And sometimes,*' adds Ora, '*the best way to show your strength is to accept help when it's offered.*'

'*Listen to us,*' they plead. '*You are not well.*'

A persuasive voice whispers for me to ignore them, to lean into the frenzy consuming my mind.

'*Go to him. Why resist taking what you desire when it's waiting for you with open arms? You have abstained long enough.*'

The thought threatens to crack me in half, shatter my senses—does Jaspyr wait for me still? Is two weeks of not feeding enough for me to have regained control of my appetite?

Isobel didn't think so...

'*Isobel is insufferable.*'

I leave Empress Isle and head back into the open. But Isobel's angry voice isn't far behind the others.

'*Wait right there,*' she warns in a much less patient tone.

I veer to the right, needing to swim, to release some of this anxious energy before my elder and my companions find me and explain what's going on. I head toward the surface and away from the overwhelming silence of the deep.

Already I feel calmer.

The sounds of the buzzing reef hit me in full force; I can hear the fat rainbow-colored fish chomping on coral from far away, like the sound of soft, breaking bones echoing in the distance, and the squeaks and squeals of sea critters busying about through their day. Late sunlight sprinkles its way into my view, piercing the waters like a curtain of dancing lights.

I can feel the shadow moon rising, readying itself for its debut.

The sun is lowering, the lights fading, pulling me up.

The Field of Eels spreads out before me, a white floor-bed completely covered with thin, black, wiggly creatures dotting the sand from tiny holes. From afar, their bodies sway like grass in a strong wind. But as I near, one by one, they disappear, sinking back into their holes.

Cowardly creatures.

I'm not certain they ever leave their homes in the sand, forever tethered here, swaying to the will of the sea. Afraid to know what life might hand them should they confront their fears.

I clench my teeth. *I am not a coward. I am a fierce myrmaid of the Olleb.*

I glance over my shoulder and see the funny creatures peeking back out of their holes as soon as I've passed, spying on me. *Pathetic.*

I swim on, forgetting Isobel, Aura, and Ora. There's a new mantra in my head.

I am strong enough to fight this. I don't need help from my family. I will prove my strength, that I am a true Princess of the Sea. No mortal can weaken me! I don't care what could've been if I had chosen differently.

The sunlight from on top of the water has completely dissipated now; I see even more clearly. And the creatures that thrive in the darkness here can see me too.

The sea comes to true life with the fall of night.

A mammoth shark with rows of sharp teeth lurks close to the sands, headed in the direction of another reef. It curls around me in greeting, its glassy eyes on me all the while. My heart races but not out of fright… I can't tear my gaze from its teeth, covered in blood and gore from its latest meal.

I swallow, imagining what the man of my frenzy would taste like on mine.

I will devour him tonight.

I utterly refuse to fall for the spell that Mother apparently let Queen Julissa cast on her.

Years, I think, pondering over that story.

But the frenzy boiled down to its roots is just lust, desire, and a *quenchable* hunger.

"All things that I trust an independent myrmaid is more than capable of accomplishing on her own," I mutter into the dark.

The shark swims away with the thrash of its tail, bolting through the waters faster than I could have anticipated by its lazy floating. Something for dessert must've caught its interest—

A swarm of these mighty water beasts explodes around me by the hundreds, viciously chasing something ahead, banding together for the hunt. The experience shakes me out of my trance as they rush forward seemingly from nowhere, swimming as one, flowing like a river, even with sudden shifts and veers in direction.

I follow them with ease, letting them escort me to the edge of the reef.

I leave them there; they disappear somewhere down below in the shadows.

Instinctively, I swim up, the waters growing slightly shallower here.

'*Where are you, Eloise?*' Isobel sings from somewhere in the deep.

'*I don't want to be found!*'

I close my mind to her. I mask my trail.

My eyes pin on the seabed; another creature of the watery dark captivates my attention before long—a beautiful organism with eight tentacles slinks across the sand, sneaking alongside the outskirts of the reef. Myrmaids revere them for their intelligence and stealth. I almost don't even see her.

I can sense she's toying with me, playing, a curious little thing. She wants to see if I will notice her. She wants me to watch.

The octopus shifts colors, a clear-glass blue film turning to a rusty red with the mere swish of its body from one rock to the next. She matches her surroundings to hide.

I watch her intently, following her trail in the sand, absorbed. Wondering if she might be able to set me back on the right path.

Then I realize: this is not about me at all. She's hunting something, too.

Before I make the connection, the octopus has wholly absorbed her prey. A crab with a shell that even I might find tough to crack is ripped open; she enjoys the challenge, the fight. She wraps her long arms around the doomed creature, glowing with satisfaction as she consumes it, little by little, slowly, enjoying the struggle it makes until nothing is left.

I smile, proud of my kin for taking what she wanted without remorse, without hesitation—I used to do the same, before him.

Empress Isle calls to me as I get farther away. Isobel calls to me. Aura and Ora call to me—I ignore their beseeching for me to return.

'*I'll be fine. I'll be fine,*' I implore. '*I'll see you at the next gathering when this is over, and I will bring you Jaspyr's skull to make amends.*'

I imagine having to face all the other princesses to share the truth of my disease one day. It makes my skin burn with shame, and I shake the thought away.

I know this has happened *to* me and not *because* of me, that others have experienced the frenzy as well. But I don't care—I want to be perfect in this second chance at life. I want to make my family proud and be worthy of their gifts.

A ship passes overhead—I was so absorbed in my thoughts that I hadn't even noticed it nearing.

I'm too close to the surface.

'*Get closer,*' the shadows urge.

Even from this deep down, I can plainly hear the voices of many males and females up above. It must be some kind of passenger vessel sailing from Zambienth to another shore. Large carrier ships often take this route, directly over Empress Isle.

I can smell them all, how good they'd taste on my tongue. And stranger still, I can smell him too… the faintest whiff of his blood, or the sweet memory of it.

The sure scent of his sensational essence is tangled in with all the other aromas directly above, twirling among them on the wind, in my mind.

I am ravenous for him. Them. Everyone.

Oh, Goddesses, how did I even get here?

I should've never left the confines of Empress Isle, where there's no trace of human scent to tempt me, not when I'm so sick.

'*Go back now.*'

'*Turn around!*'

'*There's still time.*'

I shut the voices out.

It's too late—the hunger I have for him is suddenly amplified into a terrible starvation, as plentiful as there are people on that ship. I can't even wipe the sinister smile off my face at the thought of blood, how satisfied I shall surely be once I taste it again. And with the shadow moon rising, there's no good reason not to feed.

Just one, I think. An appetizer. I'll just have *one* before I finally hunt Jaspyr.

The frenzy is mine to control. It does not control me. I control it.

I succumb to it. I want it to take over. I don't care!

Take me, I think.

'*Gladly,*' it says.

I break through to the surface, to meet a shadowy night without the moon to illuminate me. Though I can feel her still, watching.

'*Ignore her judgment. Enjoy yourself, Eloise. You are welcome in the shadows, always.*'

I settle atop the gentle waves as they usher me closer. I float before the bow of the ship and sing, calling to the captain to join me.

The iron anchor falls, reaching the sands in my domain with a resounding boom.

And there it shall remain forever.

I let the frenzy take hold, basking in the freedom of letting go.

One body drained quickly turned to two, then three, then four. My mind was not my own—I drank every last drop that I could possibly get hold of.

It only takes minutes, and for me, they feel like seconds, to rip through the humans aboard, one by one. I feel as if my mind and body are no longer my own. I pause only for mere moments to drain each person of their precious blood, sinking my teeth into whatever fleshy body part I find first, then tossing their remains to the side.

Some try to jump over the edge into the safety of the sea, but the water is under my command and sends them back to me.

Their flesh is like the softness of seaweed, their bones breaking as easily as the brittle surface of dried-up driftwood. Men, women, my tongue does not differentiate. Their screams and cries I refuse to hear—and though I never have before, I block them out until they scream no more.

When all is silent and the waves calm, I look around, everything with a haze of crimson clinging to it. The deck is covered in gore, as if it had fallen from the sky in a rain, bodies strewn across the mast and white sails ripped to shreds, splattered with red.

The stars cast me in a stark light. I shield my eyes from their stabbing judgment as my murderous haze begins to fade, leaving me only with gut-wrenching remorse.

"What have I done?" I stutter, blinking several times before the fog in my mind finally starts to subside. My blood-drenched hands fly over my mouth. "Oh, goddesses, what have I done?" I cry out into the night.

I run across the deck to the side of the ship, peering over the side to catch my bearings. I feel as if I may vomit, plagued like a seasick sailor, but I know that's not my illness at all.

The clear, calm waters run red. Bodies litter the white sands far below or float atop in shreds. The ship seems lighter, bouncing above the waves in freedom.

Yes, I've set it free of its human controls. And in doing so I've shackled myself to this place forever.

Time will never let me go back to change what I've done here.

'*You will always remember.*' The dark seems to smile at me.

I stand on the deck amid the proof of my gluttony, no moon above me to cast a positive light over what I've done.

I pull at my hair, teeth clenched, fists balled—I still crave him.

I still need him!

It hadn't worked. I was not healed. *I am not in control.*

'*No, dear, you never were,*' the waves hum.

A light pitter-patter of rain starts to wet my cheeks, cleansing my body and rinsing the deck. I settle my gaze near my feet.

The bloodied face of a young man glares up at me, mouth contorted as if he were mid-scream at the moment his soul left his body. He looks so youthful in his fear—he must be one of the first wave of children to make it out of the Four Corners, probably on his way to a new life on the mainland.

I cannot look away from him, frozen, as if this boy has captured me with a siren song, his mouth permanently open with that silent scream that will surely haunt me for the rest of my life.

I cover my eyes, tears burning as I finally allow myself to hear it.

I drop to my knees at his side, pressing a trembling hand to gently close his eyelids. "I'm sorry," I say, my voice shaking with the effort to speak. "I didn't mean it."

I cry unlike I ever have before in this new life. Vivid tears of gold and silver drip to his blood-sodden shirt.

"I'm sorry." I begin to gently shake him. "Please, wake up. *Please*. I... I didn't mean it."

The rain comes harder now as if the Goddess of the Sea had sent it to soothe me. But I cannot look away from that young man's face. I cannot be eased.

This is why our appetites are bound by the goddesses, to ensure moments like this *never* happen.

All life is sacred, and I've literally just sampled several generations' worth of it, fed on both the young and old without deliberation. And for what? To curb my craving for him? *Him?* That wretched, foul-tongued mortal?

"He is not my soulmate!" I shout to the cloud-cluttered sky. "I beg to be rid of him."

'*It's not your fault,*' the Sea whispers. '*You are sick.*'

Looking upon my senseless kill, his face so soft and young, I'm reminded of my brother when the sea had snatched him from me too soon.

A remorseless monster, I had once thought as a human girl.

I realize I can still taste that boy's heart on my tongue. It lies beside him, discarded, drained.

I remember now, why he screamed like that—I had ripped it from his chest and pressed it to my lips before he had even collapsed.

The Sea and I, and all the monsters she can morph to be,

are indeed one. I have become all the things I swore I would not.

I am a true monster now.

"I am sorry. I can never atone for my actions here today," I say, my head bowed low, as I toss the boy's heart to the waves. Then I finally look away.

I have two choices: return to Empress Isle and face Isobel with now even worse truths, or...

I can't even finish my train of thought before I've jumped back into the water, rinsing the blood off my hands. My sisters will find this mess of mine soon enough and know it was me; Isobel will have to confess the secrets I shared with her.

They would try to stop me and force me to face this senseless rampage.

I cannot. Not until I regain what I have lost.

I cry out, a roar of terrible pain, that echoes throughout the watery depths, and might echo throughout eternity, my magic aiding its power. It rips from my chest and throat the way my teeth had ripped through those powerless people, incensed and unforgiving, leaving only tatters of me behind. My fins fan out around me, strands of silver and gold illuminating the dark waters, spreading, seeping off me and into the sea like a virus outside of my control.

I am the disease. I am the curse.

The shadow of the ship sits directly above me, a dark, heavy, mass, hovering over my head like a damning cloud.

And then I hear it, resounding loudly as if one of my sisters had sung it in my ears. "Eloise, *please.* Come back!"

Jaspyr's voice envelops me, floating down to me from somewhere far away. I feel my condemning promise snap, break, shatter into a thousand pieces.

With the whip of my tail, I turn around, headed in his direction, the sharp tang of blood still swimming in my mouth. All my wrath, all my anger... it's all for him.

PART FOUR

37

DROWN

ᗝELOISE

I FOLLOW JASPYR'S SCENT to the docks at the southernmost part of the city. In minutes, I've located him there, staring off into the distance, willfully unaware of the massacre that occurred only an hour ago off the cusp of these shores. Painfully ignorant of all the people I murdered because of him, what his blood, his *existence* does to me.

I brace myself for the task at hand as my insides still sear with a constant, unquenchable, swelling burn that makes it hard to think properly. But I must return to Isobel and Empress Isle soon, and when I do, I shall bring the hollowed carcass of the man who has infected me, reassuring anyone who questions my strength and worthiness that *I* am an honorable Myr and Princess of the Sea.

I make to crawl up the sunken ladder of the dock, but a spell of hesitation seizes me on the first rung, like a sturdy wall has solidified between us—even if my promise is now broken, this isn't going to prove easy.

Then I find myself wondering…

Did I only imagine it?

A snarl snaps from my teeth.

He pauses, glancing over his shoulder as the echo of my voice fades away into the sounds of the city beyond the quiet docks.

The shadows enfold me, hiding me from view—every cell in my body wants to reveal myself to him, wants to crack open his ribs and tear his beating heart right out of his chest. Drain it and then feed whatever's left of him to Aura and Ora, just to prove Isobel and the blasted gods and goddesses who got us into this mess wrong.

I stare directly into his face, his devastatingly handsome face, grappling with what must be done tonight, trying to destroy this invisible barrier before me as the frenzy threatens to shatter my sanity for good. I can feel myself slipping away, giving into this internal war, this disease of my mind. I won't even let myself blink now, repeating the same two words to keep my grip.

Kill him. Kill him!

My fingernails dig into my palms so much that I feel the slightest twinge of pain. I can't stall any longer, only to be chased away by the sun yet again.

His eyes draw me in more, dark and brooding, set in skin as white and flushed as the moon, who refuses to show herself tonight. There's no fear there, I see clearly. Only torment, a familiar emptiness in his gaze, his soul.

I long for it.

He carries on after a moment, strangely unperturbed by the beastly sound I'd just unleashed. He moves, unhurriedly, winding through the maze of docks, hands in his pockets, eyes cast down. It looks as if he's searching for something.

Is his mind so utterly twisted that he cannot sense the danger?

Starlight washes down on him and the waters, decorating

the harbor cluttered with boats and crates in sporadic, soft, cleansing light; the winds are frigid and sharp, rolling down from the north. The sea is wild, restless, just now waking to the night.

I consider my great goddess's words, that my soulmate and I are destined not to love one another for a lifetime but loathe, just because of what I am, what I chose to be. But I can't take back my choices now… and even if I could, knowing all that I know, I would still choose to be me, Eloise Myr—who detests Jaspyr Tayshin for all but his blood.

Isobel is wrong.

Better than Eloise nobody, who would have never known magic, never known the ocean's wonders, and would have likely died, cold and alone, before finding her soulmate at all.

Yes, I'm content to despise this mortal man, if that's what Fate insists. No matter how seductive the fantasy of a lifetime being loved by him might be.

My eyes pin on him. I move closer.

How I wish his limbs and his organs had been among those on that tomb of a ship.

His sweet aroma carries back to me on the breeze, combing through his long, dark hair, making me wild for just another taste; he takes a moment to tie it up, swishing loose strands away from his eyes. The apex between his shoulder blades contracts with his breath. I can pinpoint perfect lines of muscle beneath the linen of his shirt, and I remember how firm and warm he felt beneath my hands.

Not just a taste. I want all of him.

The waters rile around me, bubbling with my hatred as I mark him for dead.

The promise. The promise, I seethe—it still held.

Jaspyr had called to me, had said my name to the wind, so my binding magic allowed me to return, to be near him again. But I can still feel the enchanted shackles on my wrists, the muzzle on my mouth—*I will not kill you, unless you beg*, I had so foolishly said.

I push off from the ladder and sink below the water to shed a frustrated scream. *Think, think, Eloise.*

Even if I found the willpower to kill my soulmate and end this curse before it has time to take root and ruin my life even further, I am bound. *Unless he begs*, I had said.

So make him beg for death, Eloise. He's done so before. He'll do so again.

I look up at Jaspyr from below, watching him pace the docks, his hair mussed, his brow furrowed. It is as if he too has just murdered an entire carrier ship. I wonder what plagues him, what made him call me again?

I clamp down on the kinder thoughts of him floating in my mind. Of how it felt when he had gripped me in his strong hands to pull me yet closer to him.

'It's difficult to let go... once you've had a taste of what could've been.'

Isobel's words ring in my head.

'Where are you, Eloise?' I hear Aura say.

'Come back before you become too far lost,' adds Ora.

I squeeze my eyes closed and gather my magic to shut them all out, to hide my shame. I know I shouldn't, but I let the God of Shadow envelop my mind instead.

'Why did you do it?' I ask, bravely, wondering if he might respond. *'Why are you doing this to me? Everything was fine before... Everything was perfect.'*

The water seems to ripple around me, the darkest parts of it swirling, listening. Then he speaks, his voice just as purely cold as the absence of light, the absence of everything.

'Because I have lived in the shadow of the Moon my entire life, an eternity,' he replies. The blackness around me becomes electric, alive in its rage.

I wish to hide and to take back my words, but I cannot.

'*So many mistakes, Eloise,*' the God of Shadow says. He snickers. '*You should not have called to me, for you will not find reassurance in my words.*'

I square my shoulders and lift my chin. '*I wish to hear them anyway. I deserve to know why I'm being undone by a mortal man.*'

'*You deserve nothing!*' The currents seem to vibrate with his voice. My keen sight diminishes, the shadows thickening. '*Yet I have given you everything. Your suffering is barely a fraction of what I have known.*'

As if the God of Shadow inhales a calming breath, everything seems to soften around me. His voice becomes steady.

'*I have always had to fight to be fully seen by my siblings,*' he continues. '*They always chose Her to praise. Her to adore. Her to preside over their worlds when they slumbered.*' He scoffs. '*And even though I am the stage by which She can be seen, my shadows are always forgotten, weakened by Her annoying light. She is my equal in every way, yet I am treated as an outcast, a nuisance they must tolerate.*'

"The Moon," I stutter aloud with comprehension. "The Goddess of the Moon is your sibling?"

The shadows angrily spool around me in confirmation.

'*Well, what does that vendetta have to do with me? With my family?*' I dare to ask.

Even now, having a conversation with such a malevolent entity, my irrepressible hunger pounds in my ears.

The God of Shadow murmurs, '*Everything, Eloise.*'

I feel his breath against my neck, an unwanted yet tempting caress.

I gasp, wading away as his shadows follow me. I cannot escape, floating amid the dark like a lost soul.

'*I grew tired of being ignored in this world and every other like it, where all life was made to worship them.*' He says each word with such malice. '*So when Syrifina, the child that she*' *was, cried out to the night to satiate her revenge, I graciously answered.'*

He adds, with a smile in his voice, '*Why do you think Sister Moon darkens, her light fading, throughout each month? Her phases are my constant quest to flourish without her holding me back. When she fully disappears, what you trivial beings wisely named the shadow moon, that is the only time I get to thrive. And the only time where those who live in the shadows can do what they please without being chased away by the bothersome light... or spied on by the Moon who whispers all your secrets to the Sea. Why, you should be thanking me each and every month, Eloise!*

How I have lived in such ignorance.

"But the Moon is our companion," I whisper, praying for her return, to chase this monster away—despite all the power the dark affords me, for the first shadow moon ever, I want our goddess to shine brightly down on me, judgment and all. "We were created in her image."

At this, the darkness seems to suck all remaining light into itself so that it's as if I look upon a mirror. But not a welcoming one as Isobel had once conjured—no, this one only reflects an endless black all around, with me, a glowing gold and silver star, at the center of its mighty, unyielding hands.

'*I made you in my image!*' Each word reverberates in my head with a threat to press those palms together so that I might never sing again. '*And no god nor goddess is the companion of anyone in your world.*' He laughs, something sickening, and I feel as if those giant hands raise me higher to his eye level, though I cannot see from where he scrutinizes me. I can see nothing but myself floating, lost. '*We are your masters. You would do well to remember that.*'

He opens his hands, and suddenly I'm falling through the dark, through space and time. My scream catches in my throat. I reach up toward a surface that is not there.

A calming voice calls out to me from somewhere far off.

'*Do not listen to him, Eloise. He is a menace. You are loved. Open your eyes and remember all that you are.*'

And though I'm not sure which voice speaks to me now, I cling to it tightly as the darkness seems to fold in around me. No end, no beginning.

I can't, I think, too afraid to do anything but fall.

It presses in on me, sucking away my power.

It pours down my throat, as if to take back what it had given me.

My hands fly to my neck and claw at my chest as I choke. All the while, I'm still tumbling through the dark.

I cry out to the Sea, but she says with remorse, '*Why did you call to him? I cannot help you here.*'

And I know by 'here' she means trapped in the God of Shadow's arms, for he cradles me possessively.

'*I created your kind, Eloise,*' he whispers, his words punishing. '*I presented you to Sister Sea as a small peace offering. She may have blessed you with great gifts, the Moon at her side, but you were made by me.*'

"The Moon gives me strength. The Sea gives me strength," I say out loud, choking, shutting him out. My tail and fins thrash as I struggle to stay conscious under his hold, clawing at what feels like the absence of water.

"I give you strength!" The God of Shadow's voice blasts around me and his darkness explodes with it, pounding back into my chest. I gasp, drawing the water back in, its enchanting life settling in me again.

Open your eyes, Eloise!

I do. My eyelids open and the wonders of the underwater world I so worship rush to greet me—funny, I hadn't realized I'd closed my eyes at all…

Any relief I might've felt is stolen as I stare into the eyes of another, so full of blackness that they threaten to consume me whole. Shadows swarm around him, as if his entire being is held in a space 'between' this world and whatever plane he'd crept out of to torment me.

Gleaming white skin, as bright as the moon he so reviles, shines in glimpses beneath the darkness that envelops him like a cloak. A crown of glittering onyx stabs toward the surface of the water as he floats before me, all the sea's shadows gathered around him like a devout audience.

I shrink before him, cower, sink… so deep I think I may have slipped back into a remorseless vortex of his making. All light washes away in his presence. All hope. He holds me captive, his eyes devouring, shredding me, like I did that ship.

I cannot speak nor move. I can only listen.

"Now I am not the only one to know how it feels to always be held back by the Sun or to be looked down upon by the Moon," he says after an excruciatingly long moment—his gaze flicks up, releasing me from my trance.

I sigh, but my eyes follow to find Jaspyr, a distorted vision from beneath the water.

"And I am not the only one who will know how it feels to be truly alone, forever." His lips curl up in a soul-shattering smirk. "Eternal Eloise… this I promise."

In a powerful implosion, the otherworldly darkness sucks back into him—the God of Shadow is gone.

And though the waters are still black and the night darker than ever, somehow the world around me feels bright again.

When I look up, I find Jaspyr standing still, all his focus, all his attention on the water—I may not be able to kill him yet, but that doesn't mean I have to float idly by while the God of Shadow triumphantly watches me torture myself.

With an agonized, ravenous cry, I rush to the surface to confront my frenzy face to face.

38
CONTROL

✧ J A S P Y R

THE WAVES REACH OUT TO ME, opening like the mouth of a carnivorous flower to reveal Eloise at the center, a glorious yet deadly treasure. She propels forward, landing with a mighty splash that soaks me from head to toe.

I wipe the water from my face and blink it from my eyes, shocked to find Eloise standing before me. The sea drips off her in a dazzling rain.

I can't help but smile, gawk, taking her in.

"You called?" she says, an animalistic rage glinting in her eyes. Her voice surrounds me in a haze that makes me want to close my eyes and dream.

I shake it away, concentrating.

"I didn't think—"

She moves toward me and I choke on my words.

The wind still rushes around her as my mind struggles to refocus on where she is now. She's so close I could reach out my hand to touch her cheek, but I refrain, noticing how she seems to quiver with anger, her entire body tense.

I take a step back to see her properly, unable to suppress the bubble of worry forming in my chest.

"What happened to you?" I say. "You don't seem like yourself—"

"You didn't think *what?*" she asks, icily.

She closes the distance between us, looking up at me with that hate-filled expression. Normally, she's so poised, playful even. If you could call a blood-sucking monster that…

I let out a deep sigh, trying to focus as her breath cools my heated skin. It's all I can do not to lean in, her aroma swirling around my nostrils, like the scent of a thriving forest after fresh rain.

Her eyes lift to my neck, and her jaw tightens, the muscles in her cheeks tensing.

Something isn't right with her. Something's off.

I take another slow step back, holding up my hands as if to ease an agitated snake.

Her lips remain downturned, her gaze steady on the throbbing vein in my neck; if she can see the blood moving beneath my skin at the accelerated pace of my frantic heart, then I know she must be tempted to attack.

But I can't help it, can't suppress it—my heart always threatens to leap right out of my chest at the sight of her, even if I keep my expression unreadable at times. Even if I bravely stand tall.

There's another emotion there, though, something contemplative and torn. It's like she's drifted off into her mind.

I wonder if she can even see me at all…

"Eloise?" Her attention snaps back to me. "I called because—" I swallow my words.

Why did I call for the beast to return? Why did I bring this monster back into my world?

"So we could talk," I finish with an affirmative nod, as if agreeing with myself on the answer.

'*False,*' a voice whispers from somewhere deep down.

Her mouth widens into an eerie yet breathtaking smile. She tosses her head back and laughs, the sound like a symphony one only hears once in their lifetime.

I relax my stance and dare to take a step closer again.

She snarls at me, baring her fangs, her legs slightly bent.

She's smaller than me, much smaller. I tower over her. And my muscular frame is wider than hers, despite her curves I so loved to caress. If she were a human female with that same bloodlust, I could overpower her with ease, have a chance at fighting back with only my strength.

But she's so much more…

For a flicker of a moment, I remember her stunning sisters, the ones she called Vasylina and Miki. They had painted the steep walls and deep waters of the Split in human blood. The bodies of regulators twice their size floated in pieces around them—I've known monsters like them before. They played with their prey, us. They showed cruelty just for sport.

You are the same, Jaspyr. The weight of the serpent chain at my neck grows heavy.

From what I've seen of a myrmaid's powers, if Eloise wanted to, she could end me in seconds—why do I provoke her? Why can't I stay away?

'*Yes, you're a wretched dead man walking if you stay! Run while you still have a chance.*' Greggor's voice chimes in my head, but I ignore him. I ignore all reason, all my focus on her.

'*No,*' I counter. '*She promised not to kill me. You told me she had to hold it sacred.*'

From somewhere in the universe, Greggor scoffs. '*That doesn't mean she won't be the death of you.*'

His words are a haunting whisper on the wind.

"We are done talking, Jaspyr," says Eloise with a glower.

My name rolls off her tongue so smoothly that I can't help but yearn for it to be entangled with my own. To suckle at that power again. The challenge of her is addicting, consuming.

My lips curl up in a hungry smirk. *More!*

"I don't want to hear another word out of your wicked mouth," she growls, growing even more agitated. "You called. I came. So now *you* can listen."

I nod, ever obedient. But I can't wipe my grin off my face as I drink her in; she straightens to her full height, and I'm certain she could bring any man who calls themselves a king to their knees with that very look.

I would drop to my knees and kiss her ungodly feet right here, right now… if she wouldn't think me so desperate.

I cannot seem weak in her presence, I think.

But you are weak. You're pathetic for calling to her for any other reason but finishing what you started. Kill her, Jaspyr! End this sick obsession before it's too late.

I take a deep breath, letting the thought, a mix of Eddison's voice and Penelope's judgmental tone, drift away.

There's a part of me who is fading—a man who does still thirst for his fire to consume this creature whole, to watch her burn in the sun's arms…

But the greedy, insatiable man in me wins.

I just cannot fathom a world without her in it.

"You're a perfect fool to even utter my name again," says Eloise in a low voice. Her magic sizzles on her skin, as violent as her calculating gaze. "You're a *fool* to cry out for your death." She offers me the slight bow of her head. "But I shall be glad to deliver it, after what you've done to me."

I can't help myself. I ball my fists at my sides, my own temper rising up and out of my throat before I can think better of it.

"Done to you?" I shout, glaring down at her with so much hatred, so much veneration. "I think it's the other way around. I can't get you out of my bloody mind!"

A blast of cold air swaddles me from across the sea. I shiver, clenching my teeth as the hair rises on my skin.

She tenses and presses her lips into a firm line as the wind carries my scent toward her. Is it just me, or does she seem to resentfully relish it, as if tossing with whether to be angry or contented with the breeze?

When the wind subsides, she relaxes her posture some.

"Is that right, hero?" Her voice is so soft it barely reaches me. Her frown deepens, wrinkling her forehead. "You think of me often?"

The heat of shame burns my cheeks—*often* doesn't cut it, but I won't give her the satisfaction of knowing how her absence has tormented me these long two weeks.

She clasps her hands behind her back, exposing herself fully to me. Her breasts are perked in the cool night air. And the painted strokes of silver and gold magic glow radiantly atop her skin tonight, no moon to challenge their shine. They curl all the way down from her neck and shoulders, snaking along her arms and torso, only to disappear between the apex of her thighs before wrapping around her legs.

I gulp, my tongue dry as my eyes eat up every inch of her— I long to explore each line of lifeblood glittering against her deep, dark skin, to claim the treasure I know waits at the end.

I bite down on my tongue as my gaze lowers below her navel. Heat blasts on the inside of me, twisting at my groin.

Her eyes narrow, as if she can smell my arousal.

"You really do have a death wish," she whispers.

She turns away, letting her arms fall back to her side.

I inhale sharply as my heart thunders in my chest. Now, her entire backside is bared to me.

She walks to the edge of the dock, leaning on the rail, peering off into the star-studded distance.

"I'm hooked on you, beast," I say, bitterly, pinching the bridge of my nose to try to think.

But I'm panting like an animal in heat looking at her now. My cock throbs at the sight of her, this angle...

The way the smoothness of her spine curves outward at her waist, so round and firm. The way the thickness of her body seems to claim all the space around her. Her wild, dark hair reminds me of the waves themselves, softly swaying in the breeze, calling to me—I couldn't dream of looking anywhere else, the night casting her on a grand display.

I can't fathom that she ever even let me touch her at all. She's too much for any man to handle, to survive. And yet—

I reach out to touch her shoulder, just needing to see if she is actually there. Or if I've waited so long for her each night that I've lost my mind completely.

She whips around before my hand can meet her skin and catches my forearm in her palm. She brings my wrist to her eye level, her gaze lingering on the silver vein of lifeblood on my arm. I can practically see her salivate, throat bobbing.

I snap back to my senses in her cold grasp and call to my fire.

The memory of her song swirling in my head drifts away.

"*Stop* hypnotizing me." I seethe, my magic searing through my veins; flames flicker in my free hand, but she pins it to my side, smothering them.

Then she squeezes the wrist so hard that my bones ache. The muscles in my left arm bulge with the effort to resist her, but it's no use—Eloise is an unmovable force, when she wants to be.

"It's not my fault how your body reacts to me." There's a flicker of a smile as her gaze drops below my waist. "Do you still want me now, hero?"

She tilts her head to the side. Her nails dig into me like talons, breaking the skin at my wrist, bright red dots forming atop the black and blue ink.

More than ever, some terrible part of me thinks.

I grit my teeth and try not to make a sound, not even flinch to show my fear, for I know she'll prey on it. I scramble to focus on my power, to fight back, but it's too hard.

"Let. It. *Go*," she commands, squeezing my wrist tighter.

Her eyes are wild with something I cannot place.

I blink, letting my magic float away.

"Good boy," she says, softening her grip.

Her focus slides to the arm she still holds at eye level. At a cruelly slow pace, she gently presses her fangs into my wrist. Her soft lips curl around me. She sucks.

My heart skitters at the sharpness of her teeth. I draw a breath in between my teeth, readying myself for worse pain. But it never comes.

I find myself relaxing into it, into her. Her bite is numbing, her venom seeping into my veins as she drinks from me.

The seconds pass slowly. She lifts her golden gaze to mine; something about it seems so… haunted.

She draws more of my essence into her, and I become light-headed, the stars starting to swirl behind her. I let out a little gasp, still unable to look away.

The slight pain teases out the memory of her teeth and tongue all over my body in the Split. I yearn for her all over again, *so much* that the more of me she takes, the harder I become.

She draws closer to me, like she cannot get enough. And I, too, am spellbound in this monster's claws.

My cock presses against the inseam of my leathers, growing nearly to its full length. I want to rip them off and let her have all of me, whether or not I'd live to see another day.

Take me, I think but don't dare utter lest it fully releases her from her promise.

No, I don't really want to die… but Eloise is my undoing.

Her focus finally moves from my eyes, and I feel a slight sense of relief. Her gaze drops below my belt as the leather of my pants presses firmly into her side.

She stills and lets go, stepping back.

"Never touch me again *without* my permission," she warns, wiping her mouth on the back of her hand, "or I will make you wish you were more of a gentlemen."

I shake my head, trying to regain control of my baser instincts.

But every time she speaks, every time she touches me, makes me forget just how monstrous she is, even with my blood staining her perfect white teeth.

"Forgive me," I say, dryly—putting pressure on the bite wounds at my wrist with my other hand.

I glower at her, my desire only mounting.

"I *hate* that I want you, you know." She lifts her chin to stare me down, as if nobly taking a hit in battle—but I don't let her intimidate me anymore. I finally speak my truth aloud. "Even with you in front of me now, after all the danger and pain you've inflicted upon my world, knowing what you are," I run my fingers through my hair as my eyes rake over her, "I can't bear to think of what might become of me if you leave again."

I level my gaze at the beautiful, vicious creature before me.

"That's why I called out your name." My voice is as steady as the thrumming in my heart, the truth finally setting me free. "So I must ask again, what have *you* done to *me*, Eloise, myrmaid of Olleb-Yelfra?"

I keep my expression uncaring as she tries to hide her shock. But I see it flicker over her features, like a rolling shadow.

She takes a step backward, squaring her shoulders, as if bracing herself for another attack.

Yield, I think. *You win.*

I just don't have the energy to keep fighting… whatever this is. I open my arms out wide, offering her everything.

"It's true then. You must also be infected," she stutters, eyes widening.

She peers over her shoulder with a frightened expression.

I look too, but all I find is starlight and dark chattering waves.

"The only thing that's infected me is you," I reply, a mix of affection and ire in my tone.

She seems to remember herself, her expression solidifying back to one of boredom. She begins to circle me; I mirror her slow movements, never dropping my eyes from hers for a second.

"One half of two," she drawls from those perfect pink lips. "Destined to be doomed."

The mystery of her words sends shivers straight through to my spine.

A long silence fractures the air between us as we hold each other's gaze.

"What in the gods' names do you speak of?" I ask, carefully, flexing my fingers at my side, readying my magic again.

She scoffs, crouching low. "Why don't you ask the gods yourself?" she snaps. "They seem quite vocal lately."

Don't let her in! Don't release her, and you may yet live.

"I was never much for riddles," I reply, raising an eyebrow—I've tortured men long enough to know when someone is withholding. "Do you know something I don't… about these charming meetings of ours?" *Why I'm somehow still alive?* I can't help but snicker.

She stops, the dark ocean and sky at her back, the stars shining down on her in a glittering spotlight.

Her eyes cut over every inch of my body so deeply that I burn from the inside out, forgetting that I'm wet and cold as the night thickens.

"Not so much charmed as they are cursed," she whispers.

The word 'cursed' rings through me, resonating with every

thought I've had since we met. I lower my fighting stance.

"I'm listening."

She stiffens, taken aback at my sudden surrender. She sucks on her teeth, as if considering whether or not she should attack while my guard is down.

I wait her out, knowing that she'll take the bait—she only tends to bite when I fight back.

After a moment, she sighs, narrowing her eyes. "Very well," she says, reluctantly, straightening her spine. "I suppose it's only fair that you know why you must die before I take your life."

I bite down on my smile and nod. *Truce*, I think.

I turn in her direction. "How gracious of you," I say with a mock bow.

I blink—when I open my eyes, she's sitting on the rail, peering down at me as if it were her very own throne.

"Silence," she demands—it's all I can do not to lift her into my arms and take her right here on this damned dock.

I smother my viler thoughts and try to pay attention.

"The great and terrible being who brought *us* into creation," she points to herself, "tricked us into also ensuring that if we ever came across our soulmates in their human forms, we would be destined not for happiness but tragic endings. That is the sum of it."

Her glittering eyes find mine, and I'm immediately disarmed by the sorrow they hold.

"I crave you like no other. *Your blood*, Jaspyr." She frowns. "Yet, you still breathe."

She lets out another frustrated sigh, looking away from me, as if sickened with her failure at taking my life.

"And when I foolishly fell for your trap," she hisses, "you spared my life." She leans forward. "Then, I offer you your freedom... you *still* call me back." She clutches the wood so hard I see splinters curl under her fingertips. "I thrive off your very essence. I am your innate predator. You are my prey. Don't you see?"

It's the first time all night that I can't look at her, lowering my gaze to my feet. Even though I already knew this hard truth, it was something else to hear aloud from the mouth of the poisoned cup I cannot seem to put down.

"Why?" I ask—a plea for freedom. My voice barely passes my lips.

"It's not your fault," says Eloise. Suddenly I feel her hand gently cupping my chin, lifting my gaze back up to hers. It is hypnotic.

I shift on my feet, knowing I should feel uncomfortable at her closeness. Yet, I don't.

"Then whose is it?" I manage to say, nearly forgetting myself.

"I shall not speak his name," she whispers, shuddering; in a blink, there's too much space between us once again. "The point is, if I was in my right mind, I would have killed you long ago and spared us both such disgrace to our moralities."

My jaw twitches. "Much obliged…"

"I feed off human blood. You are *human*." She shrugs. "What other outcome could there be?" She looks to the stars. "We are just part of a game, an ancient rivalry. It's not for us to question."

Her words toss around in my head, but only one seems to stay at the forefront.

"Wait…" I hold up my hands. "Are you saying, you think that *we* are soulmates?" An incredulous laugh bursts from between my lips. I scratch the back of my neck. "As in true love? That's what you think? You who keeps snacking on my flesh. And me who would like nothing better than your head on a stake. How lucky we are to have met…" I shake my head at her. "I thought you were smart?"

She narrows her eyes, menacingly.

"I am not only smart," she says. "I have more knowledge and power than you could ever possibly hope to attain, *Jaspyr*. I know what you seek, deep down, because you're not so different than I was when I was just flesh and bone." She snorts. "But you can't have it. You couldn't control it... no man can." She smiles.

I don't know why, but the most jealous parts of me coil to the surface. "You are nothing to me," I growl.

She levels her gaze at me.

"Oh, I'm so distraught," she says, pouting her lips. Then she scoffs, tossing her hair back. "Humans and their fairytales. Don't you get it? Myrmaids *can't* love mortals." Her words are stern, unwavering. "Not when you are the very thing that satiates our appetites." She looks me up and down. "It is cruel magic indeed, that a *man* might be my soulmate. It can only lead to a cruel conclusion, for one of us. And no, this is certainly not true love." Her voice pitches on the last word, as if she's uncomfortable to speak it.

"Then what is it?" I say between gritted teeth, my desire shifting to a boiling hate.

She grimaces, looking away. "We call it the frenzy."

The word is sobering, like all the wild range of emotion I've experienced since knowing Eloise has finally been diagnosed.

'*Don't release her,*' a voice warns again. '*The promise could be your only way out. It's the only thing holding her back.*'

"And how do we... set ourselves free?" I ask, surprised by my own question—is that what I truly long for? Freedom?

"*We* don't do anything." She continues talking, and strangely, for all her threats, I feel as if she's buying time. "Do you know of the Golden Rule?"

"I—" I blink, swallowing the lump in my throat, realizing that whatever knowledge she might share with me next could change my life forever. "No, what is it? And what does it have to do with me?"

And yet, somehow, I know…

It has to do with everything.

"The Golden Rule speaks of all things," she continues. "It's a law of balance." She turns to me, enunciating each word with a hardness that makes me wince. "The more that *balance* is *bent*, the more the world will try to correct its course, the consequences of which could be *catastrophic*." She shakes her head. "And if it is broken, we can kiss our precious Olleb-Yelfra goodbye."

My heart is thundering.

"So what does that mean for us? What's the connection?"

Everything. Everything!

"We are not meant to remain in each other's worlds," she states. "And if I do not kill you, Jaspyr Tayshin, we risk the fate of the Olleb." She looks beyond me, statuesque. "Myrmaids are bound by darkness. Humans the light… we are not destined to intertwine. There is no universe in which we both may live."

I toy with the coils of my serpent chain, thinking.

"Why do I have to die for things to go back right?" I say after a moment, remembering all I've done to survive. "Why not you? You're the blight on our land!"

My muscles tense, my anger taking over.

"Maybe…" she says, her voice honey-sweet, "but I am also a savior of the Sea of Saindora. And I am immortal, whereas you are not." Her voice was so matter-of-fact, that I almost forgot—

"Now, we both know that's a lie, Eloise, lover of all things fire." Pink flames erupt across my arms, my skin; I savor their calming sting. My fire snakes across the dock all the way to her feet. "I should've never let you go. Saved us both the trouble."

She jumps back, her confidence wavering.

"That much is certain," she mumbles, blinking up at me.

I continue to bolster my fire, creating a small wall between us. She could easily dive back into the sea if she wanted, but this time she's the one spellbound. Just as entranced by my flames as I am by her.

I'm ensnared, tangled in her net. *Enemy.*

The force of her is too strong to ignore, and she is too stunning a creature. *Soulmate.*

No matter the threat to my existence, I just *cannot* be compelled to turn away and run.

Let me go. Let me go!

I will stand and fight—*for her? Against her? I don't know, but I will not run.*

I gather all my courage, all my fire, and prepare to face Eloise Myr, maybe for the last time in my life.

"I'm flattered that you think I, of all people, am your soulmate," I say—not a complete lie. "But riddle me this, since you like them so much, why not just kill me and be done with this... frenzy, if you don't believe it love?" I feed my fire more, and she recoils from the heat. "You've had plenty of opportunities before now. And if you're so suddenly concerned for the fate of the Olleb, then why not just put an end to this charade?"

She frowns; I smile.

So Greggor, the old fool, was right.

"Frenzy or not," I continue, more arrogantly this time, "I know that you're bound by more than what your no-name god cursed you with, more than the dark." My smile broadens, fire flickering in my eyes. "You made an oath to me, Eloise. If we are bound together by anything, it's your promise not to kill me, even if you feel you must. So why don't you just throw yourself into my flames and be done. This world can never have too many martyrs." I stand taller. "But I'm not dying *for you*, beast."

A snarl escapes her throat as she curses my name.

I only huff with satisfaction.

"There's plenty I could do to you worse than death," she says, her voice shaking, her fists balled. "Release me from my word of your own free will or *beg* me for death once I hold you at the cusp of it!"

Swift as the water, she moves through my fire and slams me to the ground by my neck. I taste blood in my mouth.

"It's up to you how long we drag this out."

She pins my arms down, sodden wood scraping against my back.

"Is that anyway to treat your soulmate?" I manage to choke out. My magic spreads between us in a fiery shield.

She's forced to roll off me, covering her eyes from the intense brightness with a shriek.

I sit up, wiping the blood from my mouth. "You cannot kill me. I won't release you!" My voice booms across the open air.

She crouches low, baring her fangs at me. "And *you* cannot kill me! I won't let you get the upper hand again. The sun won't save you this time."

My breath comes heavy, but the more I stare at her, the more I comprehend just what the frenzy means, what Eloise withheld from me in her explanation.

We cannot kill one another… nor do we want to.

No, I don't want to.

'*But you must, Jaspyr! You must.*'

My breathing calms. But my heart, like it has a mind all its own and can hear my deceitful thoughts, beats out of control, thrashing in my chest, pumping full of that mouthwatering essence that Eloise just can't get enough of.

"I can't," I whisper, bowing my head.

'*Then I will see you on the other side.*' With a snap, the connection between Greggor's soul and me severs.

My eyes water. I call my magic back to me.

"What are you doing?" says Eloise. "Bring it back! Fight me, you idiot!"

I take a deep breath, then let it blow out of me, calming my mind to the choice I've made, to lean into Fate's coaxing hand.

"Let's make a deal," I say, finding my composure and lifting my eyes to hers.

"No more deals!" she screams, yet still does not pounce— I know, I *know*, that Eloise has not yet accepted the truth I've come to understand.

She can fight it all she wants, but I'm done pretending I can resist her, that I wouldn't give up *everything* and everyone I hold dear just to be near her.

"If one of us *has* to die for the other to live, then prove to me first that you only crave my blood. That you are what you claim to be... nothing more than a man-eating villain that can't be swayed by the *trivial* notions of humans."

I hesitate to say the word 'love', for I have known true love before and this is nothing like it... this is something far more devastatingly dark, but powerful all the same, tantalizing.

"Then I'll release you from your oath, blood-drinker. You can have me. Because if that's all you are, then I deserve to die by your monstrous hands, if only for not killing you when I first had the chance."

"Why do you test me?" she yells, dropping to her knees.

I harden, steeling myself against this show of vulnerability.

"Because I don't believe you can do it, despite all of your threats. *I think* you desire more than just what whets your appetite." I glance to the bite marks at my wrist. *Prove it to me, please. Please, Eloise.* "And I'm just supposed to blindly trust you? That the reason I must die is destined by some unbreakable law, one written by a meddlesome god, who you refuse to name?"

'*Light is light and dark is dark, but never shall they live apart.*' The words echo in my head as if that god had whispered them to me—I know for certain it is the Golden Rule. And should I survive this night, I vow to find out what it really stands for.

Eloise digs her nails into the wood. "You don't know what you're talking about," she growls.

"Oh, I think I do," I say, as she pins her gaze on me. She shakes her head. "Make me beg for mercy, then. Show me I'm wrong." I open my palms toward her, no more fire to behold. "If I shall die by your hands tonight, so be it. I'm done playing this game. Because if what you say is true, then there's no way I can win."

I will give you everything. Just face the truth! Show me who you are. If you really are my soulmate…

She straddles me where I sit, yanking my long hair back so that my chin tilts slightly upward, my gaze lifting to the stars—I wonder if this will be the last view I see of our world.

No, let it be her.

I set my eyes back on her; she loosens her grip.

"Why are you doing this to me?" she whispers into my ear. "Just let me go, please. I… I want to live."

My breath catches in my throat. I'm stunned at her brutal honesty.

"Then live *with* me," I say, my voice cracking—I squeeze my arms around her; this time she doesn't pull away. "Let the world burn. We will remain."

The earth seems to shudder, the sea seems to moan.

But I ignore their protests, leaning into the words spoken from my soul.

What has Olleb-Yelfra done for me anyway? Given me everything, just to snatch it away? I want this. I want her.

The darkest parts of me swell, as if the space between the stars widens to make room for all that we could be together. I cherish the freedom in voicing my truth as I cling to Eloise tighter still.

She releases her grip on my hair, relaxing into my hold for the first time ever.

Our eyes lock. I let out a small sigh of relief that brushes her face.

She swallows, savors, as if tasting my breath. "I'm not sure doomed destinies work like that, Jaspyr," she says with a frown. "If you burn the world down, we'll surely burn with it."

"Then we'll escape to the sea," I mutter into her neck, nuzzling my face into hers, breathing her in; my head spins at her sweet, delicious scent. "Wherever you go, I'll follow you, Eloise. Just… take me with you if you must leave again."

She stiffens in my arms. When I look at her again, her eyes are glittering with tears that threaten to hypnotize me for all the magic they hold.

I kiss a sparkling silver and gold teardrop off her cheek and immediately feel the rush of her power sizzle across my lips, electric and cold.

"Such a pretty fool," she whispers, brushing two fingers across my mouth; my eyes float closed at the caress. "I told you, you can't handle it. The Sea would only reject you. You'd most certainly drown."

I smile with a little laugh, letting her voice surround me— even if this is depraved, wrong, I know I'll never come to regret my choice.

It's *her*, over everything.

The wind seems to roar—'*No, Jaspyr. Don't!*'

"I fear I already am," I reply, ignoring the blast of freezing air that rolls off the waves to encircle us.

I open my eyes, looking down at her from over the bridge of my nose—Eloise overwhelms my vision, like a blazing, dark sun.

She leans in closer, tilting her head, her eyes narrowing to slits. "Why would you tempt me so? What do you have to gain?" Her question is soft, sincere.

"Some semblance of control," I manage to say, my eyes steady on hers, irises lined with all the treasure any man would ever need in this broken world.

"There's no such thing when we're already so far gone," she says, her gaze gleaming only more.

My heart pounds in my ears, waiting for her to rip my soul out with her teeth. I bare it to her.

Take it. It's yours!

She leans in, considering. I wonder if she can hear my blaring thoughts for how intently she studies me.

She opens her mouth, her voice quivering. "We're not meant to be—"

"I don't care. If the curse is true, then let the gods who cast it upon us mourn their world in our wake. I will *not* let you go again." I narrow my gaze at her, a smirk playing on my mouth, my fire magic skittering across my skin, making her squirm with need. "Not unless you beg me."

I close the distance between us, my fingers wrapping around the back of her neck. I press my lips to hers with nothing but insatiable greed—Eloise leans in.

39

FORESAKEN

DELOISE

WITH A POSSESSIVENESS that makes me yield to it, Jaspyr's mouth claims my own, his strong arms pinning me closer to his chest. I'm lost in him, just as I was falling through the darkness at the mercy of our shadow-wielding god.

My fingers grasp on to anything I can find. His arms, his neck, his back, rigid with muscle as he holds me tight. Still, I try to press closer, to absorb him.

This is a kiss to die for…

I might disappear into the crazed passion of it all, our tongues and teeth searching and sliding across one another. His breath entangled in my throat in a strange, hot sensation.

I wouldn't be surprised if I just combust into flames right here in his arms. And by the way he kisses me, I know that his earlier words were true—if I burn, he will burn too.

All this time I have resisted this bond thrust upon us, yet in his hands I feel myself relax, returning to logic. The torturous thoughts subside, replaced by new, curious, excited ones.

Determined ones…

Yes, we can overcome this together.

The Moon aches to be heard. '*Eloise, no. You mustn't lose yourself—*'

Her bright voice is choked out by the quaking sound of laughter through the night. '*Don't listen to her. You are a Myr. Take what you want. Who cares about the fate of the world if you can't be with the one you were destined for by the very magic that roots you to this earth eternal.*'

I don't want to, but I listen. I lean into those words.

The throbbing emptiness brought on by the frenzy when Jaspyr and I were apart abruptly dies as we morph into one another. It shifts to make room for something else.

Now, everything feels… just right.

He pulls away for a moment to catch his breath. Sometimes, I forget that humans need the God of Air's gift to breathe. Just as myrmaids need the Sea.

My insides twist with dread at the simple reminder of our innate differences. Of the line drawn in the sand between us, even if we stand atop it now, willfully pretending it does not exist.

We'll find a way.

Jaspyr smiles down at me like a fool, as if in a daze, drunk or high on a sorceress's elixir. Radiant with happiness at the sight of me—as if I couldn't peel his smiling lips right off his face with the pinch of my nails. As if I couldn't rip the happiness right from between his ribcage with my teeth.

I clamp down on the slight urge to escape the choice I made and run back to the safety of the water. To take back my control.

But we're too far gone, I remind myself, *and I'm not sure I care to return.*

I simply don't want to. I'd rather relinquish my control in exchange for the intensity of his admiration.

Of his love surrendered, I dare to think.

My gaze drops to the throbbing vein in his neck. He softly smiles and tilts his head to the side. "Go on," he urges. "I want you to."

Excitement jolts through me at such an offer, when I've always had to take. "Just enough to quench my thirst," I say, licking my lips.

He nods, not even a flicker of hesitation on his face.

I gently bite into his neck and suck, my mind swimming in yet even more satisfaction; he moans with pleasure.

After a moment, I pull away, the warmth of his blood stirring so delightfully in my belly, the heat of his kiss still burning on my lips.

Jaspyr grabs the back of my thighs, sliding me closer. "You're mine, Eloise," he mutters across my mouth.

Some part of me, deep down, makes a sound somewhere in between a laugh and a cry.

I am still hunting, aren't I? When did I change my mind?

Jaspyr's closeness makes me heady. Everything is an absolute blur. But there's one thing I know for certain…

"No, you're *mine*," I say, digging my nails into his lower back, feeling the curve of his spine and thick muscles.

He sucks in a breath, and I nip at his neck again, the taste of his blood only rousing me more.

His expression turns hungry, intent.

He leans his weight into me until my back is laid against the dock. I let the mass of him weigh heavy atop me, wanting to feel it, crushing and claiming. There's nothing sweet about what he does next.

His linen shirt is soaked from when I made my grand entrance with the plan to destroy him.

So many mistakes, Eloise. So many choices that shouldn't have been made.

I should have never shown myself to him again, never engaged in conversation. I could've just bled him dry and let nature run its course to get around the promise I made.

With great effort, I ignore that voice, that last shred of sensibility. It floats away on the wind.

I don't want to pine over what I could've done differently. It makes no difference to the Past or Time. Yes, damn the blasted gods for putting us in such a position. I don't care what happens to them or their precious world. *I* just want to *feel*.

Jaspyr's palms suddenly find my own, distracting me from my flooding thoughts. His fingers interlace with mine, curling into fists—in a way, it's the most intimate we've been so far. I've never held a mortal's hands before... I resist the urge to crush them into a mess of blood and bone and flee. *I won't.*

'*You can't... he is yours.*'

"You're mine," I say again, gently squeezing back.

His dark eyes clash with mine under the discerning black of the night, as if reading my conflicted thoughts.

"Then take me," he demands in a voice that draws a lustful growl from my throat.

"As you wish." I lean forward and rip his shirt open with my teeth, shredding it like silks so that I can witness the beauty and strength of him underneath.

His lips curl into a satisfied sneer. He lets out a low rumbling laugh. Then he sits up on his knees to hurriedly undo his trousers, the leather rolling down his thick thighs all the way to his ankles.

The length of him bares itself to the night, proudly. I remember its girth, every bit of it filling me.

My insides tighten in anticipation.

Mine, I think again, my hips curling upward to him in invitation. I bury the warnings of my beloved family deep, deep down, my eyes fixated on him.

The heat between us builds, a tense, tangible thing that

threatens to consume us both.

He reaches a hand between my legs. *Finally*, I think, letting out a moan.

"Gods, you're *so* wet for me," he says with a salacious grin.

"Don't flatter yourself, hero. I'm always wet." I open my legs wider for him, smirking. "I'm a myrmaid, remember?" He scoffs. "Now, let's see how you do when your life's not on the line."

"Oh, Eloise," he replies with a rumbling laugh, though there's no humor in his eyes, only a thirst similar to mine. His hands wrap behind my shins. "My life's always on the line with you."

I bite my lip—I think if I had a beating heart it would burst right out of my chest in anticipation.

He angles himself, then slams into me without elegance, without grace, just brute strength and desperate desire. I scream out at the glorious sensation.

I clench around him, allowing him to mold my body as he pleases. He thrusts into me again and again and again until my scream is challenging the sounds of the crashing waves.

My fingers claw at his hair. His hands cup my breasts, my waist, my backside. Words escape us, only our grunts and groans and hungry shrieks mix with the sounds of the nature around us as we meld together into it.

His mouth finds mine again, and he cements his body to my own, moving into me so deeply, so deliberately, that I wonder if we could ever be torn apart after this. He laps at my magic, his tongue searching for it on the tip of my fangs, the roof of my mouth, licking at it—I allow just a little to slip so that he can taste the true power within me and know it can never be his.

His eyes light up, dancing with magic.

"*Yes*, Eloise," he growls, something animalistic. His eyes glimmer with gluttony. "Incredible."

He slows his movements, somehow moving deeper inside of me, the thickness of him forcing me wider, devouring everything I am until I ultimately dissolve. I'm swimming in the stars around him, floating in the dark heavens.

Terror fills me as I hold the thing I've been resisting for so long, for I find myself never wanting to let him go, never wanting to relinquish him to the gods and goddesses that demand his blood.

No, I will not be forced into choices by a prophecy written before I was even born to this world, to these waters. Nor a curse cast upon me out of spite.

I know what's best for me. I know what's right!

A part of me dares to even think…

What if this is true love? What if Jaspyr is the soul my eternal heart was created for? Is he truly fated to die?

I shake my head, praying the answer is no—for, from Isobel's terrible story, I fear it's not worth it to have loved and lost.

The prophecy of old, the Golden Rule, runs through my mind, the rhythm of the sacred script pounding in my brain to the slow beat of Jaspyr throbbing inside of me, trying to tickle my senses back to the forefront.

I can feel the old world stir beneath me. I can sense the goddesses and gods watching with fury.

'*One of you must die, or you risk the fate of the Olleb. Kill him, Eloise. Do not disgrace us! You will not survive our wrath.*'

I resist. My mind shouts in defiance.

'*No, I want him to live. I'll find a way. You'll see! Jaspyr and I can both exist in each other's universe without true consequence.*'

'*You know nothing of true consequence,*' a voice unknown to me speaks, one that seems to be filled with cold fire. '*But you will.*'

No, no! I scream internally, shutting the voices out, focusing on the building, wonderous hotness inside of me.

I cling to the denial that I have lost control and need to take Jaspyr's life to somehow right it. That I haven't just slaughtered a ship full of innocents...

As desperately as I cling to him now, his muscles roiling with fire and sweat that tingles every nerve on my body.

His blood is so warm for me—I bite him again.

But I only take a little each time, enough to satisfy my frenzied mind without him losing stamina.

My throat tightens as I swallow him, my mind spinning.

No, not denial. My instincts...

I can feel the truth of it—Jaspyr *is* my soulmate.

We could've had a life filled with more wonder than either of us realize, if it weren't for the God of Shadow's gruesome interference with our fates. Now, we must fight the forces of nature to exist in each other's universe.

I don't care if it's selfish. If it risks my family. If it risks Olleb-Yelfra.

'*But you love your sisters, Eloise. You love this world. You wanted to bask in its wonders, with your sisters by your side, forever.*'

'*No, it's not fair! I shouldn't have to choose.*'

I love my family, this world—but I don't even want to imagine a lifetime of knowing that I was responsible for my soulmate's death.

He must live... for what's eternal life without him, now that I know he exists?

I focus on Jaspyr's face. I take it in my hands.

His eyes find mine again as if he too is coming back to his senses after being utterly lost in me.

They're dark pools of nothing, everything—they pierce deeply like fangs in flesh, drinking me in as I taste him.

That look, one so sure of his decision to trust that I won't rip out his heart, captivates me the same way my voice entraps people when I sing. It pushes away all reason as he takes us both to the precipice of release.

"If this is true love," I gasp, "it's worth dying for."

'*But it's not, Eloise,*' whispers Aura from somewhere in the deep. '*It can't be.*'

'*Remember the Sea's warning,*' says Ora. '*The soulmate of a Myr is the ultimate prey, or—*'

'*Adversary,*' they sing together, the most haunting melody. '*You are not meant to be united in this world.*'

'*Silence!*' I shout, concentrating hard until their voices are severed from me.

My back arcs toward him as I moan for more. "Jaspyr," I cry, clutching his shoulders.

He screams my name into the night, claiming me to all the Olleb's disdain. His fire bursts around him as he empties inside of me with a declaring roar, then I finally come undone, my own magic cascading around him in an explosive waterfall.

I swim in his essence; he drowns in mine.

When we've both finished, he gently rolls to the dock to lay beside me. He spreads out, panting for air, taking up so much space that I wonder how we can even fit in each other's orbit.

We both stare at the stars as they begin to fade.

"Tell me again that we're not meant to be," he says, catching his breath, his fire receding.

He reaches again for my hand, turning his cheek to me.

I clutch his palm, staring back at him, seeing in his eyes just how brightly I glow at his touch.

"Screw the gods," I whisper, praying they don't hear. "This is worth it all."

40

BLIGHT

☼ JASPYR

'I KEEP MY HEAD DOWN, hands in my pockets, as I stride through the Lotus Center, past the people barricading themselves indoors for the oncoming night.

'Wanted' posters are tacked all around town, hunting for someone called the Kampaulo Killer.

I glimpse one of the descriptions on a poster, and my stomach twists in knots that I do my utmost best to ignore— the Kampaulo Killer does not discriminate between men nor women, between the elderly nor young, the rich nor the poor. They have no pattern, except for one: they hunt their victims at nightfall.

'In the King's name, until this merciless slaughterer is caught and put to death by fire or beheading, stay safe, Kampaulo. Remain indoors from dusk to dawn, if your occupation allows. We will see justice soon!'

I don't pause to read the growing list of names added to the tally of lives lost. I stopped counting when the number climbed past twenty-eight—as old as I am now. One soul in exchange for each year I've been alive, so that I can remain with Eloise.

I continue forward without fear, but I wear my guilt like a heavy crown that I can't seem to set down.

The sun melts across the city and the sea, strips of hot reds and oranges foaming at the edges of the earth that will soon disappear to let the moon fully shine—a warning to all to hide.

The streets have already emptied for the most part, and by nightfall there will be no one in sight... unless another drunk fool forgets himself or the city keeper forces his regulators out on patrol again.

I frown, thinking of Eddison, of how he surely will never forgive what I've condoned these past weeks since declaring my love to Eloise—on the fourteenth night, the city started fighting back, but most of the large patrol group sent to hunt for the Kampaulo Killer did not report back to the palace when dawn came...

Eloise had found herself utterly famished that night, after I had given my all to pleasure her underneath the full moon; I hid in the shadows while she feasted.

And even though a part of me was repulsed by how her teeth so easily ripped those regulators apart—teeth that often gently slide over my body—I couldn't take my eyes away from how horrifyingly beautiful she was in that moment of freedom. Didn't care to. When she was done, blood still caking her lips, she dropped to her knees to pleasure me, too, right there with the corpses behind us. But with my eyes on her, I easily forgot the barbaric scene around me... I always do.

It was a devastating night for Kampaulo, to know not what they fight against and to learn that they cannot win—that was also the night I realized Eddison was right... the Saindora Savage was surely one of them.

Since then, the city falls quieter each and every sunset.

Even now as I stroll the wide, empty streets, all I hear is

the sound of gravel crunching beneath my feet and the ghosts of the ones she killed muttering warnings in my ears.

'*Turn back*,' they cry in a glistening swarm that plagues me wherever I go. '*Look at what your truest love has done to us… it cannot be love at all. Wake to the darkness you've allowed to breed here, Jaspyr. See us!*'

I used to apologize to them at first, to try to explain that Eloise Myr is my fated soulmate and that her bloodlust is Nature's way. But they *kept* insisting that Nature's enemies simply cannot be lovers without severe consequences.

Now, I just ignore them, for I know their time is tied to the sun—they're simply not brave enough to face the one who stole their human lives away.

I edge to the outskirts of the city, taking a well-traveled path to the beach. I loose a sigh of relief as the ghosts remain behind me. I feel their angry gazes burning into my back, but I lift my head high and stride toward the water.

A pinch of joy settles in my chest at the resounding silence that washes over the city with the oncoming sunset—not for the lives lost but for the peace that it brings Eloise and me. We can walk hand in hand without having to hide from suspicious eyes.

Save for the scattered birds flocking to rest for the evening, there's not a peep of life. I round the shores and turn my back on the fading sun that balances below the horizon, to peer toward Kampaulo, just to be sure my home is still there—from here, the city stretches out, up, and around the cliffs and hillside with no sense of direction, like a branched river. Buildings and trees wind from the beach all the way to the palace at the very top.

I make myself watch, shifting from foot to foot, as fires are extinguished one by one, the city darkening like a brooding cloud in the distance. I swallow the lump in my throat when the last one goes out, Kampaulo immersed in shadows.

By now, doors and windows will be locked, and prayers are surely being whispered in secret to the gods and goddesses who people still remember but ignore at the King's behest—none of this can protect them, of course.

I heard just this afternoon in the marketplace that some are even blaming King Devlindor for this disturbing moment in time. They say his refusal to acknowledge a higher power *is* the reason for the blight in the normally quiet and safe City of Kampaulo.

I suppose they're in some ways right—I would have never come to know Eloise if his war hadn't driven me back here to sit solemnly by the waters all night long.

Sibyl. Luna.

I push their names so deep down that they hardly have a way to surface anymore, to remind me that there was life before Eloise Myr. There's no space for me to love anyone else now, not even myself, with her in my universe.

A blight—that's what my neighbors have deemed the love of my life. My soulmate.

When she touches me, my skin ignites in a way that not even my fire magic could conjure. When she speaks, I absorb every note of her musical voice as if it were a grand concert. And each time she looks at me, with all the magic and fierceness that constantly echoes in her gaze, I fear my heart might stop completely. There is nothing before her, and there is nothing after.

I close my eyes and let the deep silence wash over me. I imagine this must be the sound of her world beneath the waves.

Hurry, I whisper to the wind, unsure if the God of Air will even deliver my messages anymore—but I simply cannot stand to be alone…

Only when we're together is this blissful quiet easy to endure, does that small voice of dread in the back of my mind fade to nothing.

That voice is screaming at me now—*shouting* the names of all the people she's slaughtered just to stay in my realm. Begging me to set fire to the blood-drinker while I still have my life intact.

As long as it's not Eddison or Penelope. I loathe myself that I think it—but I do, often and forcefully. *As long as it's not them, I don't care what she does, who she kills, after she finds me each moonrise.*

I open my eyes and look to the sea with a smile as the last golden rays become swallowed by an enchanting night sky. Then I shove that voice of warning far away until it's nothing more than a gentle hum.

The moon is full and bright, glaring down at me. But I don't shy away from her spotlight anymore. There's no one else around to witness my choices now.

The days have quickly turned to weeks, a month. And by the roundness of the moon tonight, I know that another fortnight has passed since the *second* glorious shadow moon we spent together.

I'm not sure at what point I became so swept up by this frenzy, as she calls it, at what point I *fully* set aside my morals, and pain, and goals of vengeance in exchange for a life so much darker…

The Kampaulo Killer may be the thing of nightmares for many in this day and age, but to me, she's a bright spellbinding flame that I can't bear to stop beholding. She leaves me just as hypnotized as I am staring at the waves now.

If the frenzy *is* a gods-cast curse, so be it.

I accept the consequences.

I accept the ghosts demanding retribution in the light of day.

I accept the condemnation from Eddison and Penelope, who know, without a doubt, that I have welcomed a myrmaid back to our shores.

I accept all of it, because it means I can have her.

Nothing else matters.

Not the fate of the world.

Not my lost family.

Not my revenge.

Not the trail of bodies in the sand nor the bloodstained shores of my home.

Eloise. Eloise. Eloise. Come back to me.

I count the seconds until the sun fully sets, my skin prickling with bumps as the last rays of gold smolder across the horizon, melting into the softness of the black.

The waves froth with a burst of silver and gold magic that always makes me catch my breath.

"Don't keep me waiting," I say with a smirk, holding out my arms to Eloise as she rises from the sea like the radiant queen she is.

Her scales, like gold and platinum plates, smoothly recede until her glorious tail becomes two glorious long legs. My gaze travels from her toes in the sand, all the way to the top of her thighs. I can't help but linger there before I finally meet her eyes.

"Hello, Jaspyr," she says in that voice makes my knees weak and my cock slightly stiffen. "Don't you know that patience is a virtue in Olleb-Yelfra?"

She places her hand upon my chest and smirks up at me.

My heartbeat betrays my calm exterior, pounding into her palm. "I'm not a virtuous man, Eloise. I told you that at the first."

She laughs, raising an eyebrow. "Hmm… I suppose you did, *hero.*"

My gaze narrows with hunger. "Don't make me wait," I say again, firmly. My voice rumbles out of my throat with need.

I clasp my hand around her wrist to pull her closer.

She presses up to her tiptoes to brush an icy kiss across my lips. "I missed you too, Jaspyr," she says in barely a whisper.

My throat tightens with no words to say. It's still too surreal to be true, her and me, together.

Then the whole world falls away as she curls her body into mine, still wet in all her splendid nakedness. My hand wraps around her waist, grabbing at her firm thighs and plump backside to lift her up to my lips again.

She feels *so* featherlight in my arms that I know she must be using her magic to aid me. Still, the muscles in my arms contract against my clothes as I lift her off her feet.

She wraps her legs around my waist and squeezes.

"You're stunning, you know," she says across the shell of my ear in a sultry hum that tingles all the way to the base of my spine. Then she nibbles it.

I moan, forgetting everything that I am, everything I've done to keep her.

"And you're *late*," I say across her lips. "I can't stand this dreadful place without you."

She laughs. "I have no control over when the Sun decides to sleep." Her gaze simmers into mine; my core heats.

"Screw the Sun," I say.

'*You don't mean that, Jaspyr,*' a strange voice speaks.

She smiles, and I've never felt so weak. "If I could, I would yank it from the sky for you." I tuck her hair behind her ears. "My enchanting Eloise."

I drink her in, my tongue sweeping into her delicious mouth. Our lips collide in a passionate, greedy demand for more. I swear, she would steal my very breath if I let her.

"I want you," she demands when I break our bond only to draw air back into my lungs. She rips open my shirt at the collar, sliding her nails down my stomach until she meets the rise of my pants. Then she presses onward, taking my cock in her hand with a firm squeeze; I suck a breath in through my teeth at the pleasure pounding in my groin. "*Now.*"

Her eyes come alight with magic, and the sea stirs. A giant wave curls toward the shore where we stand, so high that it could easily wipe me and everything in its path into oblivion. Its crest blocks the moon from our line of sight.

I gasp, holding Eloise tight.

The wave seems to freeze in time, as if it has iced over. Yet it still undulates with softness, movement, with Eloise's magic.

"*Goddesses,*" I say, gaping up at the phenomenon. I have to crane my neck to see to the top. And with the moon's golden light showering down on it from behind, every color of blue seems to shimmer and glow within its form.

"Don't keep *me* waiting," says Eloise again, drawing my attention back. She keeps sliding over me with those soft, wet hands. "I won't ask you again so sweetly, Jaspyr."

I grit my teeth, thinking if she squeezes any harder I might explode too early for us both.

Without finesse, I slam her back into the wall of water just to test if it is indeed solid enough to hold our weight. It seems to soften for Eloise at her impact, the water rippling outwardly from behind her with silver sparks still encased within its wonderous barrier.

"That's a nice trick," I murmur into her ear, nuzzling my chin into her neck. My forehead gently skims the wall of water and comes back damp. "You're just full of surprises."

She slides her fingers faster up and down the length of me, then I feel a buzz of cool magic tickle at the sensitive tip—the sounds that come out of me are utterly fiendish.

"You haven't seen anything yet," she says with a cruelly sensual smile.

I take a deep breath, calming the inner beast that wishes to rip out of me too soon and devour her whole.

"*Levantis bora.*" My spell whisks us into the air, so quickly that Eloise pins herself closer to me with a small gasp.

"You're either a very brave or a very foolish man," she says when we've settled so high that the crest of the wave curls just above our heads, "to surprise a myrmaid with your most precious part in hand."

Laughter rumbles out of me. "I trust you with my life."

She softens in my arms, releasing her grip on me so that I might catch my breath for a moment.

Suddenly, the crest of the wave slowly begins to curl around us even more, until it sits just beneath my feet and we're encased in a tunnel of brilliant azure.

"I want you to take me," she repeats, though this time it sounds more like a soft plea. She lifts her hand to my cheek, and I lean into her palm. "I'm yours, Jaspyr. I'm here. Take me now, *please.*"

That word on her lips is always my undoing—a monster begging *me* for mercy.

I stare into her wanting eyes. I ready myself to let go of my magic so that I can make love properly to Eloise...

But if I fall from this height, my bones will be crushed on impact, even with water below.

I trust her, I remind myself. *I have to.*

I take a deep breath, then let my spell fade into the night.

My feet suddenly drop an inch—enough for my heart to rise into my throat—but then they softly collide with the watery magic.

"Oh, Eloise," I say with a heavy sigh, bringing my forehead to hers, relaxing into her touch. "You will be my downfall."

"No," she says, drawing my gaze to hers. "At least... not tonight." She snickers.

The corner of my mouth twitches up. I run my thumb across her bottom lip. "You really can be such a beast sometimes."

Her eyes narrow, playful yet seductive as she sucks.

A pinch of pain swells from my thumb as she gently breaks the skin with her teeth.

I pull in a breath; she sucks harder, tasting me. Her eyes flare with magic—the mystery still prevails, but I know that even just a tiny taste of my blood drives her mad for more of me...

I would give it all to her—and she would take it, too—if it didn't mean the end of my time on this earthly plane with her.

I ache with desperate need, my mind fogged with only thoughts of our bodies fused. With her back pressed against the frozen wave and my feet firmly planted atop it, I slowly slide into her, not even bothering to fully remove my pants as they catch on my hips.

"You are worth *everything*," I say, my voice low. I thrust into her, deliberate and deep.

She clings to me, her hands playing in my hair as her thighs tighten around my hips. "Tell me what I'm worth," she demands with a small cry of pleasure.

I grin, pounding into her over and over, worshiping her with every breath.

As our bodies and screams of pleasure meld together above the sea, the only thing I can think of is Eloise, and how I somehow *need* more of her. How I'm never truly satisfied when it's over... though how many times we've had such unions, I can no longer count.

It's only when the sun crawls back into the sky, chasing Eloise away and shedding light on the freshest pile of blood-drained bodies she's left in her wake do I wonder how much longer we can endure together...

Will there come a time when the pleasure becomes too painful to withstand, even in the arms of my soulmate?

The light of day drives away the shadows in Kampaulo and in my mind. The ghosts return, new souls added to their ranks.

And that small, irksome hum grows into a bellowing voice again, reminding me of what Eloise tried to implore on a moonless night that feels already so long ago.

'*You are not meant to be! Please, Jaspyr, let this chaos end before you too are drained of your essence. Before everything you truly hold dear is gone forever.*'

But the Jaspyr I once knew has already vanished—a ghost floating in limbo with the rest of the other lost souls that this blight has claimed.

Eloise and I have snapped the Golden Rule in half without compassion, and I don't want to go back and face the person I was before that choice. I don't want to face his wrath.

I can't.

I sit down to paint by the window, waiting for the sun to fall once more.

41

DEVOUR

ELOISE

ANOTHER MONTH HAS MOVED too quickly past us. I observe Jaspyr now from beneath a dock in the Lotus Center, waiting for the sun to drop. I have the perfect view into his home from here, which doubles as his workshop and storefront.

He likes to paint by the window with a view of the water, from the early morning when I leave him, till dusk when I return. He loses himself in his work—barely eats, barely sleeps.

He just paints in a furious, passionate starvation for art.

He's starting to grow weaker than he was when we first met, appearing tired and tense, his heartbeat softer. Even from here, I see the dark spots swelling beneath his eyes. He hasn't been sleeping much, understandably—he's a dimmer version of the strong, energized, self-assured man who had foolishly tried to rescue me more than three months ago.

Humans are so frail. I must be gentler with him. If I drink too much of his blood, he might drift into a peaceful sleep, never to awaken again…

The water around me grows as cold as ice with just the terrifying thought—an endless life to spend without my soulmate, knowing that I was the reason he no longer exists?

No! I won't accept that as an option.

Which means, I must feed outside of him even more.

I frown, desperate to be closer to him now, to protect him, to drink from him. But the day is hot, the sun proudly shining with no clouds in sight. It will be hours still.

Anxiety starts to creep under my skin and scales, worsening with each morning we're separated.

At first, I was grateful that I couldn't be near Jaspyr in the sunlight. My swims during the day helped me to clear my head of his addictive blood, brought me back to my senses and to the goal I set out for—kill Jaspyr and end this frenzy once and for all.

I was comforted that an epic force ensured I retained some semblance of control when I'm at my weakest, the Goddess of the Sun happy to play a part. But it doesn't matter anymore…

My feeds are no longer tempered by the Moon—the only thing that *she* controls is my ability to walk to him across the Lotus Center.

I find myself empathizing with the God of Shadow, who loathes his sister's prideful blaze, a reminder of what I too have lost. *Control. Sensibility. Self-preservation.*

The reassuring voices have also mostly gone, overtaken by my desire for him—I swallow that bitterness down, knowing I have disappointed my family and friends who I hide from beneath the veil of my magic with each passing sun. Knowing I have disappointed the honorable Myr I once was.

Then I dip beneath the water, determined to hunt along the shores to *try* to soften the torture that is being so near yet so very far from the man I…

He's your mark, Eloise. Nothing more.

You're wrong. He's so much more, I counter, swiftly.

I swim back and forth, stalling, waiting for the blasted moon to rise. *Who else shall it be in Jaspyr's place?*

"WHAT ARE YOU THINKING ABOUT?" asks Jaspyr the very next night.

I have been sitting as still as a statue for the last two hours while he paints me, his ultimate muse; my mind had drifted so far away that I'm not sure I can summarize all my thoughts for his human mind to untangle.

His question startles me back to the present—my nose wrinkles as the memory of my carefree days wandering the nature-scented seas is abruptly replaced by this room that reeks of paint and fire and wood.

I fight the urge to flee, affronted by too many unwelcome sensations all at once.

Him... I focus on Jaspyr, the fine specimen of a man that he is, clothes on or off.

I let out a heavy but contented sigh—I don't like when the paint touches his skin. It mutes his beautiful aroma. However, the passion and focus with which he makes each stroke, gently sweeping his hand back and forth across the blooming canvas, fascinates me enough to let it go.

I wonder if he could guess all the ways *I had painted him* with my imagination in these hours lost—his linen shirt and pants torn to shreds by my teeth, his naked body spread before me on the floor, revealing every line of muscle I hadn't yet explored. His dark eyes boring into mine as I gently savor his blood, and the richness of his voice enveloping me as he moans with the pleasure of it all.

Just the thought of every time I've had my way with him makes parts of me sing that I didn't know existed in human form. We've spent countless hours gratifying each other's every waking desire, nothing off limits, yet I somehow *need* more.

"I was thinking of home," I say—it is not a complete un-truth.

I suppose my mind does often travel back to my waters, to my sisters and Empress Isle—I've missed *three* full moon gatherings, and I'll miss another one tonight. *Unthinkable.* By now, surely, Isobel has had to confess all I confided in her to Mother.

"What's it like?" he asks, tentatively, careful not to look at me, putting false attention on the canvas; his heartbeat increases.

"More enchanted than even *your* imagination could possibly dream up. Keep painting. The hair doesn't look right." I shake my head a little, so that my wild, curly locks bounce from side to side. "*See?* Don't make it so stiff. It's just... not right. I thought you were good at this? Are you not a master at your craft?"

He stifles laughter. "As the good king named me, but you seem to have even higher standards than him."

"My tastes *are* quite refined," I answer, licking my lips.

His gaze catches mine. Heat rises in his cheeks.

He focuses back on the painting. "Don't look at me like that," he says. "I'm not even close to completing this yet. I can't get anything done with you around." He furrows his brow, a bemused smile on his face. "Normally, my muses aren't so outspoken about my work. It makes it harder to concentrate."

He has been painstakingly attempting to finish a new, larger-than-life portrait of me since the moment we shifted from adversaries to lovers, to replace the one he'd lost.

"Then they must have not been worth your time," I say, pursing my lips.

"True, but I do miss the deference they gave me when they watched me at my craft." He smirks. "I don't need an all-powerful myrmaid telling me what to do with my paintbrush."

She shrugs. "You sure like it when I tell you what to do with your mouth and your co—"

A streak of fire magic skitters between my legs, my words replaced with a tiny moan.

"I also like that sound," he says. Then he puts a finger to his lips that I desperately wish to suck. "No more talking, my love. The sooner I finish this section, the sooner I can give you exactly what you want, if you behave."

A low growl vibrates in my throat as he turns his back on me, his dexterous hands moving across the canvas with ease. I count the seconds until they're on me.

He continues to paint, leaning over to daub dark, shimmering hues that eventually form my nipples.

My eyes travel down his spine. Everything below his waist is perfection—but as he bends over now, his backside so muscular and defined, I have to restrain myself from sinking my teeth into his linens.

I flick my gaze to the window, to the moon lifting above the waters, looking for a distraction. Kampaulo is so quiet and still outside save for the riled sea—has the tide been rolling in stronger as of late?

"I miss my sisters." I can't stop the words floating out of my mouth, for I feel them so deeply. *I miss my sisters.*

I have never avoided them for so long before.

He grimaces, clenching his paintbrush a little too hard. "How many…" He clears his throat. "Do you have a lot of sisters?"

"Hundreds more." The quickness with which I expose our

kind's secrets to a human alarms even me, but it's the least of my worries.

He starts to cough on what seems to be air.

"You needn't worry," I say, dryly. "I've masked my trail."

I do consider, though, that Syrifina's powerful magic *could* likely lead her here… if she wished to bring me home.

He moves to touch me, but I step out of reach, afraid… terrified once again that if I let his hands rest upon my skin I will be unable to tear them away before the sun fully takes over the earth and destroys me in its wake.

Even if this body burns, I think, *this frenzy will surely follow my soul on to the next plane.*

Jaspyr crosses his arms at his chest, his expression twisted.

"What is it you wish to ask me?" I say, knowing.

"If there are so many more like you, Eloise… why permit King Devlindor to rule at all? Why not take the Olleb for yourselves? You alone have so much… power." The last word rolls off his tongue as if just the thought of my kind quietly lurking in this damaged world was still unfathomable.

His question confuses me at first—I have never once considered that I might use my power to *take* this world for my own. And I do not think Mother nor any of my sisters have had a thought such as this one ever before either… it was the first time his words truly puzzled me.

"Olleb-Yelfra is our home," I reply after a moment. "Why seek to control such a grand entity that flourishes for us of her own free will? King Devlindor surely sets a good example of the consequence of such greed and manipulation."

"I… suppose," he says with a shrug, though something in his tone and how the blackness deepens in his eyes tells me he does not agree.

That I do not know nor comprehend his human mind in this moment makes me all the more curious about him.

"My sisters and I have all that we need, and material possession is not something we entertain," I say, firmly. "We take what we desire and nothing more."

"Do you desire me now?" His frown turns into a coy smile.

I do not answer, still staring at him.

"You are the only thing I will ever desire again," he adds, his stance sure, his voice resolute. "I would do anything for you. Whatever you want of me, take it." He speaks with such a sureness that I know he believes it to be true.

"I shall, in due time," I say, then I add in a whisper, scowling up at him, "My only weakness is you, Jaspyr." I say it like an accusation, for it is—I think I loathe him a bit for his existence, sometimes, even after accepting that we're fated. I despise that he's caused me so much irrepressible pain and excitement all at once.

Every moment Jaspyr lives and breathes is a reminder that I've lost all sense of control. That I've traded in my sisters' undying love for a human's.

His skin warms under my gaze and he looks out at the water.

"This I cannot fathom," he replies under his breath.

"Believe it or don't."

He nods at the agreement, the pact we've made already so many times—each one of us always testing the other's candor, wondering when the other might break beneath the tension of our growing bond. I can feel the heat between us increase with each risen moon, like the friction of two magnets being forced together, an electric power growing, pulsing in the hollow of our bones, trying to meet.

I change the subject. "Is there anything else you're dying to know of my world, hero?"

"Are there other things living down below?" Curiosity lights his gaze as he glances back to me.

"What do you mean by *other*?" I cross my legs, narrowing

my eyes. "Am I not enough to satisfy?"

He tosses me a grin. "I love how envious you can be, even knowing you're the very air I breathe."

I huff but can't help that my lips twitch up in a smile. "Go on, then. What is it you want to know?"

His eyes grow wide, flickering with excitement. He finally sets down his paintbrush and sits on the arm of the green velvet couch next to me.

"Eddison's father used to tell tales passed down from seasoned sailors," something like guilt tugs in my chest, "of otherworldly beings that long ago burrowed into our earth to sleep in the deepest, darkest, coldest parts of the sea." He opens his arms wide; I peer up at him. "Creatures ten times larger than their biggest ships, with sword-like tails and rows of sharp teeth." He speaks hurriedly, like an enthusiastic, hopeful child, "Have you seen anything like that... down there?"

I blink up at him, then toss my head back and laugh.

"*What?* Tell me," he says, sliding onto the cushion next to me. He takes my hand in his own, peering down at me with expectation.

"Nothing." I shrug. "My sisters and I often muse at how a story like this could've ever possibly been spun, for we are ever careful." I tilt my head.

"You?" he asks, raising an eyebrow.

I nod. "They *must* be based on our kind. I'm sorry to disappoint you, but we're the only man-eating beasts in the Sea of Saindora, Jaspyr. I know not where these stories come from."

We have been called many things over the centuries—sirens, blood-drinkers (I liked when Jaspyr favored that one), maidens of the water, sea spirits, ghosts of the waves, water women, the undead. And, of course, *mermaids*, the needless modernization of our sacred name—all of which hold some grain of truth, yet know not the full story.

But a giant, ship-eating sea serpent? I laugh again at the thought.

He shrugs, scratching the back of his head with a soft expression. "Too bad. Just thought I'd see if I could solve the mystery."

I smile at him. "I think we have our *own* mystery to focus on, hmm?"

He stands and walks back to the canvas. A shadow rolls over his expression, and I'm immediately regretful. I'm standing at his side in his next breath. I wrap my arms around his waist from behind and peer toward the painting.

"It's... remarkable, even unfinished." His paint-splattered, genius hands curl over mine as we look, admire.

The strands of my lifeblood sparkle from his enchanted touch. My hair sits in a bob of wild curls, like a crown atop my head, and my skin is a shimmering deep brown, like the diamond-glint of the Black Sand Desert he's told me tales about. He's only been able to work on my face, neck, and torso. The rest is a surprise that I'm hopeful to one day see.

He shakes his head at me, a serious gleam in his eye.

"I doubt one could ever capture just how remarkable you are with merely paint." I nuzzle my cheek into the warmth of his back. "It's... hard to fathom there could be anyone else like you out there, Eloise."

The way he says my name makes me feel that I don't have as good a handle on my human legs as I thought. Suddenly, I'm weak in the knees.

I slide to his front, and he smiles down at me.

"We are each one unique," I say—I don't tell him that out of the hundreds of myrmaids I call my kin, I'm one of twenty-two princesses of the sea. That my magic and lifeblood embody the best of our world. I don't tell him that I have a goddess's blood coursing through me or that my powers have yet to truly even manifest, that I am young, a child, compared to those who swim in my realm.

He looks back and forth between my face and the painting.

"Sit back down," he commands in a voice that makes me yearn for him.

"What have I done to earn such a torturous night? I'm growing impatient," I say, coolly, gracefully lying back down onto the plush, velvet couch in the storefront area of his workshop. The pleated, high back makes it seem like a large throne. I sprawl out, legs thrown over the arm.

He stiffens, his gaze roaming over me from head to toe. "I *said* sit." He turns his back to me. "If you continue to lie like that I'll have no choice but to climb on top of you again, and I'd like to one day finish this painting. Have mercy on me, Eloise."

"Very well," I reply, sliding into an upright position. "Better?" I tilt my head to the side, my mouth curved upward ever so slightly.

He looks between me and the canvas and frowns, tapping the end of his paintbrush on his chin. "Your expression is so… intense. I would rather hope to capture something softer to memorialize our time together."

I scoff, rolling my eyes.

"Humans are soft creatures," I say, matter-of-factly, analyzing his every movement, so painfully slow compared to my natural state. "*I* could hardly emulate one, not truly."

But, goddesses, did I want to sink my teeth into his neck and test again that *softness*—his skin, his veins. I want to run my tongue over every crevice of his body. To taste him. I *need* to bite him again.

No, Eloise. Not yet. Let him rest. You've had enough tonight.

I easily stomp down on the small voice that urges me to

drink him dry and end this curse—it used to be so loud.

"How is this?" I say in all seriousness as I straighten my spine, legs crossed, and look him straight in the eyes.

He stares, looking back at me with loving disapproval.

"Just… never mind," he mutters, shaking his head with a small laugh; he massages the coarse stubble at his chin. "I ask too much of you, I see." He nods to himself. "Fine, I'll capture it true. Your indifference is both alluring and unsettling, you know? You could bring anyone in this kingdom to their knees by that very look."

I shrug and lift my chin, keeping my face as stoic as it's always been.

"You are the only person I require on their knees, Jaspyr." My voice is as sultry as the fire burning in the torches on the wall. "Your hand brushes each line of paint just as capably as your tongue strokes the lifeblood between my thighs, *Master* Tayshin. Do hurry so we can get to the part I'm most fond of you for." I sigh, tossing my hair back. "Sometimes, I fear I may actually grow old sitting here waiting for you to finish."

The rigid lines in his jaw flex, his eyes pinning on me like arrows. Heat rises to his cheeks, so that I can plainly witness his desire, his skin so pale that I can see the beautiful dark tint of blood pooling beneath it, waiting.

"Don't you know that patience is a virtue in Olleb-Yelfra?" he counters; I let out a low laugh, only more enticed by his challenge.

"How *dare* you mock me," I say, playfully.

He smirks, then turns his back to me, dipping the tip of his paintbrush into a pocket of gold.

The entirety of his chiseled back, from the tips of his shoulder blades to his hips, is engulfed in tattoos of dark, hungry flames. Lines of deep red, gold, orange, and black stand out vividly atop his skin underneath the firelight. It's in stark contrast to the calm yet calculated curves of the bright blues that shade his right arm.

In contrast to me, I think.

I close my eyes a moment, as if this depiction bears all the intensity of real fire. Too hot, too bright to withstand.

Suddenly, I'm trapped again in his burning cage, no escaping upon the sunrise. My mouth goes dry, my eyes stinging from smoke and tears, a promise keeping me bound.

"Besides, Eloise—" My eyes snap open again, the flames falling away and replaced by the deep, carnal note of his voice when my name passes his lips. "Masterpieces take time to finish."

He touches the thin paintbrush to the canvas, right in the center of my painted chest.

"It's about the details, you see." He smoothly slides the brush down the plane of my stomach in a gentle curve, stopping right beneath my belly button at my waistline, where the rest of the painting is waiting to be outlined.

I squirm in my seat as longing pounds between my thighs.

"Yes, you *are* meticulous," I reply, chewing on my lower lip, spine stiffening even more.

He rinses the brush in water, then dips it into a sparkling silver paint. He starts back at the same point between my breasts, then effortlessly traces the gold line in a thin silver stroke—the depiction of a single strand of my lifeblood suddenly becomes a brilliant replica.

"I'm glad you think that…"

He sets the paintbrush down and comes to kneel before me on the patterned carpet, spreading my legs wide. A villainous smile curves on his lips. He begins to kiss up the length of my thigh; my toes curl deliciously.

Such human pleasures are wonderous, I think. *I could never have enough. More, please!*

I comb my fingers through his hair as he says, between warm kisses, "Because I enjoy stroking every… *single…* line—

" I hold my breath as his tongue flicks my sensitive pearl. "Until my works of art come to life." He licks at the edges of my center; I quiver. "Do you want to come for me again, too, Eloise? Or have you had enough for one night?"

I gasp as his mouth fully envelops me, his tongue massaging my innermost parts with an expertise that makes me think his magic is also at work. I'm not sure how long he is at it, for I have all the patience in the world when he works his powers like that.

He pulls back with a satisfied sigh, licking his lips like he'd just had the most delicious of appetizers.

"You melt around me like snow. Always so wet. *Exquisite.*" He gently slides a finger inside me; I lean back with a moan.

"Lie down," he says, standing up and taking my thighs with him, to spin me the long way on the couch.

"Since when do you make so many demands of me?" I ask in a delightful daze.

"Since now." I relax into him as he kneels between my legs, pulling my hips toward him for a deeper angle. He seems to peer straight into my soul with those dark, brooding eyes.

"I've never seen snow," I find myself saying in a glorious high as one, two, three fingers slide into me, nice and slow. I moan his name as he pulses.

"*Really?*" he asks, breathless, his mouth suddenly closing over my breast, his teeth softly biting at my nipple.

Our eyes lock as he continues to slowly push his fingers deeper, making me throb and quiver.

I rest my head back on the cushion, letting him consume me.

"When I was human," I say, staring at the ceiling he'd long ago painted with stars, "I never had a chance to see a world outside of Kampaulo. As bitter as the nights can be, it's never grown *that* cold here, has it? And in my new life, I haven't cared to travel to the frozen water in the north beyond the mountains."

He grunts in acknowledgment, only pausing his feasting and fingering to guide my hand toward his pants. His firmness presses through his pale linens into my palm; I can make out the rigid, ready shape of his thick cock. Then, together, we untie his pants and shift them down below his hips.

"Snow can be just as enchanting as you when you're pleased," he says, letting the heaviness rest atop my stomach; I gape, wondering how it fits inside my body at all. "And just as beastly as when you are not."

His eyes glaze over as he massages my shins, my thighs. Then he presses my shins back, my knees up, so that I'm completely bared to him.

He angles his cock, teasing me with the slick tip.

I groan, arching my spine in anticipation.

"Patience, Eloise," he says, darkly.

I press up on my forearms to better see his face, baring my fangs at him. "Then stop wasting so much time talking and put that wicked mouth of yours to better use," I reply, "or you'll meet the true beast I can be."

He leans forward to plant a kiss on my lips, even as I hiss his name; I take his bottom one between my teeth and nip until I taste a sensational droplet of blood.

He jerks away, blinking back at me; I smirk.

"As you wish," he says returning my savage smile.

He presses his hand atop my chest so I lie back again, then slides his tongue all the way down my stomach to finish what he started—only after I combust for his mouth does he finally let me have the main course.

42

DEVOUT

BY THE TIME I FINISHED FEASTING, Eloise had come for me not once but twice. If I could subsist by devouring only her mouthwatering essence, I would. But this wretched mortal body of mine is starving for actual food.

She looks up at me with a haze in her eyes, sprawled out on the sofa so comfortably. I can almost picture where her breathtaking tail I've only glimpsed might drape over the arm-rest like priceless silk shawls—I wish we could stay forever like this.

'*She doesn't belong here, Jaspyr. She doesn't belong with you.*'

I tense, clutching her ankles, massaging her feet.

"We still have so much time left," she says in a tired but satisfied voice. "What about you?" She reaches for me, my cock still hard and swinging, always searching for her.

It takes everything in me to resist the offer, but I shake my head, sliding off the couch.

"No, I wanted tonight to be about you. My gift for letting

me paint you every night. You must get absolutely bored."

"Time is different for you," she says. "It will take much longer for me to tire of watching a master painter work, even if you are slow." She smiles. "Besides, your painting is of *me*." She stretches out on the couch even more, her gaze catching on her naked self in the mirror across the room. "I always make time for admirers."

"Admirer is a very tame word for the things I feel for you."

"Are you sure you don't want me to help you... cool down?" She raises an eyebrow. "It's truly a wonder that you last longer than I care to."

"Because I employ every ounce of willpower I have when I'm with you. To make sure you get what you need from me."

"How very generous of you," she purrs, batting her eyelids at me. "Most human men aren't so considerate."

I narrow my eyes; she laughs, the sweetness of it whistling around me.

"Don't be jealous, Jaspyr. They weren't considerate of me, so I wasn't considerate of them." She licks her fingers as if she'd just had a delicious snack. "But tonight you were very attentive... are you sure you don't want me to—"

"Later," I say. I pull up my pants before I can change my mind. "Just enjoy the blissful aftermath right now. You do enough for me." I kiss her on her forehead, then run out of the room and into the back before my cock simply overrules this rare instance of me having a level head.

Food, I think.

I rummage in the pantry for something to eat.

A thought tugs at the back of my mind as I look to the window, the dark fully settling in for a long night to come.

"Actually, Eloise," I call from the other room, "would you possibly want to..."

I let out a heavy sigh, tearing into a loaf of bread. "Oh,

forget it. It's foolish," I say, my mouth full, my stomach grumbling in gratitude. With so much on my mind, I have hardly thought to eat much these past few weeks… even now, I notice a small loss of muscle.

I reach for the cooked chicken I had bought at the marketplace, not bothering with plates nor cutlery.

"What is it?" Curiosity lines her tone, giving me a twinge of courage.

Maybe, just maybe, she'll go for it. She's my soulmate. We can't persist by only carnal unions forever.

'*Forever will be short for you both*,' a voice whispers in my ear.

If it's true, then I won't wait.

I swallow my food and find my words tumbling out in such a mess that I wonder why someone like me is fated for a being such as her at all.

"I know this might seem…" I scratch the back of my head. "Imprudent, that you might want to join me on something so…" I pour a large amount of whiskey in a glass and toss it back. Then I start to cough, choking on the burn.

"Jaspyr?" she says, sounding somewhat concerned. "Are you quite alright back there?"

I pound my fist onto the counter until the burn passes. I gasp in relief. "Would you want to accompany me to the palace ball tonight?" I blurt out.

I'm not sure why that question felt like passing a sword down my throat, but I feel so much calmer now that it's out.

Her silence lingers a bit too long, so I nervously begin to talk before she even has a chance to answer.

"The King decreed recently that all the cities must hold one every year to celebrate the survivors from the Four Corners. It's a barbaric day to commemorate, but Kampaulo's keeper really knows how to throw a party. I'm certain tonight's inaugural event will be memorable. I heard in the marketplace they thought to cancel the festivities because of… well…" I clear my throat. "But people will risk just about anything for free booze and food, and the palace is so well-guarded. They felt safe enough to continue as planned." I look up at the sky through the ceiling window in my workroom—the moon is high. "It's probably already in full swing by now, so I'm sure no one will notice us if we slip in… just for a peek."

I pull in a deep breath, pausing to allow my words a chance to settle.

"What do you say?" I ask with clenched muscles when there's still no answer. "It could be amusing for a change."

The room falls so silent that one could hear a pin drop.

What a *fool* I am to suggest such a thing for her, for us. I slap my hand to my forehead. She's the gods-damned Kampaulo Killer! She's not going to be so bold as to want to *waltz* into the palace like some highlife lady I'm presenting to the keeper's court.

What I would give for us to have a taste of a normal life together, just for once.

There's an intense gust of wind throughout my workshop, then I hear the front door slam shut.

I rush into the other room and glance at the sofa—Eloise is gone.

My heart thunders in my chest so loudly that I can hear it in my ears. *Gods, what have I done? Did I truly scare her away? This can't be happening… this can't be real.*

I stare, unblinking, at where she just was, where she's sat for so many hours these past several weeks. I tear my fingers through my hair and try to will her to return. My palms grow sweaty, and the glass I'm holding slips between my fingers.

I close my eyes, waiting for it to shatter. Waiting for myself to shatter. But the sound never comes.

"Open your eyes, Jaspyr," says Eloise, her voice as sweet and rich as red wine.

They fly open, and there she is, lounging on the sofa once more, this time sipping whiskey from a glass—*my glass*—and dressed from head to toe in full splendor.

Her expression sours. She spits the drink out.

"This tastes like poison," she cries in disgust, wiping her mouth on the back of her hand. "You *will* stop drinking this at once." She throws the glass across the room toward my head, and it smashes against the wall at my back. A million pieces of glass tinkle down to the floor behind me like rain.

I don't even flinch, so relieved that she's back.

She huffs in frustration. "Do you hear me, Jaspyr? I *mean* it." She pouts. "Just vile," she adds in a whisper.

Her voice is as resolute and threatening as ever, but all I notice are the screams of joy in my head that she returned.

"I know you do. When your voice shakes, I know you mean everything you say."

"And when it doesn't?" she replies, smoothly, frowning at me.

A sheepish grin forms on my face.

I walk toward her and take her cheeks between my palms.

"I thought you left me, for good," I say, my voice suddenly quivering with rage and fear as I glare at her. "Don't *ever* do that to me again, Eloise. Not unless you intend for me to go mad."

Her expression softens.

"Relax, I'm here," she says, in a soothing tone that almost sounds like a song. "I was just gone a minute or two." She places her hands on my wrists and looks me in the eyes. "If anything, we will go mad together, Jaspyr. I can leave you just as easily as you can me." She plants a firm kiss on my lips. "You know the only time I will truly stay away is when I'm forced to by the Sun."

"Always to return?"

"Always to return," she replies, eyes glittering with emotion.

I sit down on the sofa next to her with a sigh. "Alright, fine." I shake off my worry. "I just…" I look at her, this time really seeing the amount of mortal elegances dripping off her.

I gape. "What's this all about, then?"

She stands, walking back so I can see her fully.

"What's this all about?" She shimmies her shoulders and opens her arms wide. "Why, you're finally taking me on a proper date, *aren't* you? I couldn't very well go to a palace ball naked."

She actually seems excited, her expression glowing with an eagerness I haven't seen before now—I suppose we both have the need to explore quite in common.

I laugh, running my hand through my hair. "If you did, it would be to everyone else's sincere pleasure, I assure you."

"Surely," she says with a smirk. "But I do love to play dress-up now and again when I landwalk. You humans have such intriguing stories to romanticize about."

"And who will you be tonight then, madam?" I lean back on the sofa, intent to watch her perform for me all night long.

She steps back, slowly twirling to show off the most enchanting dress I've ever seen. Though, I wonder if it would have the same elegant effect on anyone other than Eloise.

"Tonight, I'll be your betrothed," she says, holding my gaze.

A cold fire coils in me.

Sibyl. Luna.

"My betrothed?" I whisper, the words catching in my throat. I sit up.

Her gaze narrows at me, dark and powerful. "Tonight, I am yours. For all to see." That fire simmers into something warm, delectable as my eyes rove over her, the intense flame that she is.

Layers of crimson lace spill to the floor in intricate patterns woven with gold. The material is so sheer that I can almost make out her dark skin beneath it, her lifeblood making it appear as if jewels have been sewn underneath the fine cloth. The bodice fits snugly to her waist, accentuating her chest, though the loose sleeves and tight-fitted lace collar do enough to shield her most un-humanlike qualities.

Even still, her beauty is bewitching.

"Come here," I say, my voice sounding not my own.

She walks slowly toward me, so that I may admire every sensual stride and sway of her hips.

She stands between my legs, and I clutch her hips, lace pooling in my palms. "If you walk like that again, I will have to rip this lace off you."

She places her palms on my shoulders. "If you rip my dress, Jaspyr, you will come to regret it." She smiles.

I growl with need, loosening my grip on her; she keeps her hold on me.

"You are…" I shake my head. "Beautiful just won't do for you. There isn't any word descriptive enough to capture the extent of your grandeur."

"There is in my language," she replies, sharply, glancing over her shoulder to catch herself in the mirror; she beams.

"What is it?" I ask, drawing her attention back to me.

She pinches the sides of her dress and curtsies low with the slight bow of her head. Her short, thick hair is tussled up with glittering pins, and she proudly wears a thin, gold-plated tiara with a ruby stone sparkling at the center.

"Maybe I'll teach it to you someday, if you remain a gentleman. Now, get dressed. You can't very well present me wearing rags."

She straightens, smiling at me with dark, red-painted lips.

I bristle—I certainly don't own anything fine enough to stand even close to *her*… wearing *that*… though I wouldn't call my fine linens '*rags*'.

"What should I—"

Hanging on the hook behind her by the door is a matching gold-stitched, crimson and black-leather tunic.

"I'm sure your neighbors won't mind," she says, winking at me—I realize she's lifted it from the dress shop next door; then I realize that's not lipstick she's wearing; my stomach tightens. "Hurry now. We don't have all night. Especially with how slow you walk."

"That's what horses are for," I retort.

She puts her hands on her hips, tapping her foot like some kind of common highlife.

I can't stop gawking at her. "One wouldn't expect a myrmaid newly betrothed to be so…" I look her up and down. There just are no words.

We both burst out laughing at her bizarre yet beautiful makeover. Then I rush to the back to quickly wash and dress for our first proper night out.

"And I hope you know how to dance, Jaspyr," she calls to me, "because I sure as shadows don't!"

By the high inflection in her voice, and how steady her words come, I can tell that she's lying through her teeth.

It's a good thing I know how to dance, I think, wryly, as I ready to escort my date to the ball.

WHEN WE REACH THE TOP of the Great Hill, hand in hand, the sound from the festivities hits us in full force. Drunken laughter and chatter and dance are blaring across the otherwise quiet night. The free-flowing liquor has even already crafted lovers—people creep along in pairs, hiding within the shadows along the palace walls and in the vast courtyard.

The Kampaulo Palace looks so very different under the moonlight—the stones of gleaming blue-gray now appear dark, like the sky during a raging storm. And the tall doors and windows thrown open wide all flicker with firelights too small for their form—the light only stretches so far, a grandiose ship lost in it, fighting to be seen.

A giggling couple brushes past us, the man spilling his wine on Eloise; I keep my hand on her waist, and glare down at him.

"Apologize," I say with quiet viciousness, not caring if he sees the silver spark in my eyes.

"S… sorry about that," he stutters, slurs, his gaze catching on Eloise from behind a glittering gold mask. I step forward, in front of her.

"Sorry, my *lady*," I correct him.

"I… yes, my lady," says the man. His expression looks pained, like he's trying his best to focus on us; the woman he's after comes back to his side, looping her arm through his.

"He didn't mean offense," she says, humbly, planting a kiss on his cheek. Her eye mask is a deep crimson with jewels decorating the sides.

I feel Eloise's hand on my back as she steps around me.

"Oh, it's nothing of consequence, see?" she says in the sweetest, most bashful voice I have ever heard her use; I might have believed she was actually a timid woman if I didn't know what was underneath all that lace. "You'll have to excuse my betrothed." She fakes a blush and an innocent little laugh. "He's a little territorial since our recent engagement, and high-lifes always lose their manners with such titles, don't they?"

My eyes widen as she flashes a striking ruby ring atop her hand, gloved in black silk. It matches her tiara just perfectly. I recognize it but can't place it, not with her exquisite beauty fogging my mind—whose finger did she pry from their body to steal such a priceless jewel, I wonder?

I should never take my eyes off her.

Both the man and woman gape, raining compliments down on us for a fortunate future.

She graciously accepts them.

"My sincere apologies again, my lady. I hope I didn't ruin your night."

"Or your dress," whines the younger woman. "It's *so* lovely."

Eloise waves off the worry. "These laces must have been dyed in red wine for the color is so similar, so it's only fitting it's the first spill of the night. Look, you can't see a thing!" She twirls, knocking into me as if she can't possibly stand on her own two feet. "Oh, Jaspyr, you know how I can be so clumsy. Surely, it won't be the last."

Everyone but me laughs.

"Surely," I say, dryly, my expression unchanged—I was never much for role-playing, though with Eloise at my side, I might just come around.

She squeezes my hand, batting her eyelids at me with a wry smile. Darkness lights in her eyes; I can almost taste her hunger.

Who will it be tonight? I wonder—strange that I hadn't even considered what bringing her here might mean for the attendees, especially on a full moon. That I didn't even hesitate at leading an insatiable lion into a field of easy prey.

'*It's not strange at all.*'

The woman nods. "To the Warrior's District," she says, breathlessly as the man presses a kiss over her mouth and carries her off. They vanish behind a tree in the dark.

"Why do they wear masks?" asks Eloise, drawing me back to the present.

"I…" I clear my throat, then find her gold-flecked gaze, immediately comforted. "Your face is much too lovely to be covered by such a thing." I tilt her chin to mine. "But yes, I do admit it slipped my mind." I chew on my lip, looking around. The Gathering Ball is traditionally a masquerade."

"And why did that woman salute the Warrior's District to us?" I smile, her curiosity about my world sometimes just as rich as my own about hers.

"Because, my *beastly betrothed*," she laughs as I press a deep kiss to her mouth, "we are both wearing the colors of warriors. Red is the color they use to delineate that district of the Four Corners."

She presses another kiss to my mouth, her hand fingering the sword at my belt. She sighs over my lips, pressing her hand to my chest. "I can tell by your body, every inch of muscle, that you were a warrior in a past life. And now you're a painter?"

I solemnly smile. "Now I am yours."

"Indeed," she says, giving me another peck on my mouth. "Wait here. I'll just be a moment."

Her head tilts toward the trees where the couple vanished. When I blink, she's already gone.

Their screams blend with the music seeping into the night; I stare toward the palace, fists balled at my sides until she's done.

WE SLIP INTO THE PALACE HALLS unnoticed, looking just as elegant as those around us—Eloise's face is covered by a mask of jeweled red; mine is hidden beneath a mask of glittering gold.

Everything inside is decorated in equal, unrecognizable splendor. Ghastly, actually. The city keeper could feed an entire village with only the décor used for this ball.

"In the King's name," I hear someone cheer from afar— my magic prickles up my spine.

Eloise gets swept up into the fun of it right away. Men and women alike shower compliments on her. She doesn't move in the shadows like she used to. She stands proudly in the shimmering spotlights dripping from the diamond chandeliers.

And oh, is she a sight to behold. A queen finally come to lay claim to her palace.

She's hunting in plain sight, I realize, with my arm wrapped around her waist in escort.

My stomach twists; I focus on the band as it starts up a lively number.

Eloise pins an expectant gaze on me.

I smirk, placing one hand behind my back and extending the other like a proper gentlemen. "May I have this dance, my lady?"

She makes a show of accepting, placing her hand with the stolen ruby ring in mine. I bow and kiss the top of it.

A memory tries to push its way to the forefront of my mind, but I refuse to let it in. I won't.

"Why yes, you may." She turns to lead the way, then tosses a glance back over her shoulder. "But don't step on my feet."

"I wouldn't dream of it, darling."

She pauses so that I gently run into her from behind, then looks up at me and whispers in her real voice. "Good, because I do *not* understand how to walk in heels. What a foolish invention. How do women flee from their hunters like this?"

I lean into her, pressing my lips into her neck, her ear, both decorated in fine jewelry. "I imagine they had far better chances of getting away before you came along." I know it's wrong to say, but I like how it feels on my tongue anyway. "You still haven't told me how you can move so fast."

Magic flickers in her eyes. "I needn't waste time telling you things you already know."

She offers me another smile to die for, then I spin her forward across the ballroom floor, keeping hold of her hand.

"By the way." I draw her back into me with an expertise that leaves her baffled and beaming. I slide my hand around her waist to the small of her back. "I'm an *excellent* dancer."

We lose ourselves in the next several songs.

I might be quick on my feet and know how to lead a high-life lady around a dance floor, but Eloise moves with an extraordinary, wild effortlessness that I've never seen displayed before in these halls. I've sat through countless balls, danced with countless ladies—she is beyond it all.

She's not precise in any way with her movements, but her body, her curves, her feet, her arms sweep and twirl with the music as if they're all one and the same. I imagine this must be how she looks when she swims beneath the sea, so astonishingly free, happy.

I don't know if I've ever seen her look *happy*.

I can hardly take my eyes off her, just as hypnotized as I would be if she sang along with the string instruments. Every time her hand finds my waist or my shoulder, I have to work to catch my breath and steady my feet.

The watching crowd never takes their eyes off us, her. And even the dancers who were around us before have eddied away to give us space to consume the floor however we please— Eloise takes it all, eating up the attention the same way she'll likely feast on the guests before the night's end.

My heart races.

Someone will surely notice us now, I think. *Choices. So*

many awful choices I've made.

But I keep dancing anyway, because Eloise isn't ready to stop. And if I'm being honest with myself, neither am I. I'm trapped by the music, by her spell.

She smiles and smirks at those watching the most intently, wanting them to watch, surely marking them for her next meal—to them, they think she's flirting, that they stand a chance with her when I step away.

My free hand twitches toward my sword, ready and willing to kill anyone who even dares reach for her.

I don't know why envy twists knots in my stomach so, especially knowing her real intentions for them. And knowing I'm the only one she wants in the end...

'*So you should be the one she drinks,*' a small voice reminds me. '*You're the only one she needs to survive. You could save them all, put an end to this massacre.*'

But I'm not ready to die...

I grit my teeth.

In an angry fit, I tug her arm forcibly so that she has no choice but to spin back into my arms and look upon my face—unless she wants everyone to see how strong she really is. She hits my chest and it almost knocks us both over. She looks up at me with a question in her eyes, stunned.

I pull her closer and press my mouth to her lips, claiming her for all to see.

"You're mine, Eloise," I say atop her mouth, biting her lower lip as she peers up at me with wonder in her expression. "Hunt and play all you like but don't tease. I can't stand it."

I rip off my mask so that she can see I mean it.

There's a gasp all around; whispers of my name begin circling the crowd. Everyone is curious to know who this mystery lady is and where I've been all these weeks.

The music starts up again, something slower that draws Eloise and me in closer still. She lifts the mask off her face as well so that I can see that I, too, belong to her.

Something tugs at my instincts to look beyond her—the moment I tear my gaze away from her, I wish I hadn't.

Eddison is glaring at me from across the hall, Penelope clutching his arm as if she might faint. They're both watching us with such pain, such hatred stretched across their faces.

I swallow the lump in my throat and look back to Eloise as Eddison starts to stomp toward me. He's so big that he easily knocks everything, people and tables alike, out of the way to get to us. The crowd murmurs in confusion, parting to let him pass. Penelope tries to hold him back but it's no use.

"Let's go," I say, abruptly stopping our dance.

Eloise looks over my shoulder—then she sings.

HER VOICE JOINS WITH THE BAND for a single, loud note.

Everything freezes—the sound, the people, the dancers in full swing. And Eddison, *in mid-stride*, peering at us with a look of vengeance—*and magic*—burning in his eyes, reaching for his sword.

Eloise takes a single step toward him; I catch her arm.

I don't need to say it. She can read it in my expression. *You promised not to hurt him.*

"Where do we go?" she asks through gritted teeth, shrugging out of my grip. She's so calm, staring up at me as if she'd just wielded the most common magic in the world. "Do you want me to carry you out of here?" She smiles—I refuse her every time.

I shake my head, hurriedly pulling my mask back over my

face. "Come on, I want to show you something first." I take her hand, leading her to the outside, away from the frozen crowd, praying that everyone will be too drunk to remember. "Then we'll leave. It wasn't wise for me to bring you here. I don't know what I was thinking."

"I rather enjoyed myself," she says, unperturbed. "Pity, though, that we have to leave so quickly. You didn't even get to eat dinner."

"Neither did you," I say as I guide her back through the palace entrance.

"Don't you worry about me. I ate plenty." I hear the smile in her voice; it makes me cold, so very cold. "Besides, there's only one thing I'm hungry for right now."

Right on the front steps of the palace, she reaches her hand beneath the belt of my leathers; I clutch at her wrist and slightly moan as she squeezes. The coldness of her hands sends a delicious heat straight to my groin.

"You are absolutely *vicious*." I grow firmer in her hold.

She kisses my neck. "It's your turn, Jaspyr. For being such a gentleman tonight," she whispers, gently tightening her grip. "I didn't realize you'd grown so protective over me."

I moan slightly, breathing in her hair as she leans into me, wondering how I could possibly take any more of such ecstasy. But I want it. I want her hands all over me, all the time. I want to touch her so badly that it hurts, all the time. I would take her right here, right now if—

The music and sounds of life start up again in a thunderous boom that hits us from behind as Eloise's magic fades. I shudder as she releases her clutch on me.

"I've never had to share you before. And if I recall, by the way you snapped at your sisters in the Split, you don't like to share either."

She laughs. "I suppose we have another thing in common, then." She kisses me, so deeply that I lose my breath.

There's a racket not far behind us, and I hear Eddison's voice. He's looking for us.

"Quick, follow me." I take that same wonderfully wicked hand in my own to lead her behind the palace to the courtyard, then up the secret staircase that leads to the overlook. "He won't know to look here for us. Only highlifes have been granted access to it."

"How very prestigious," she says, wryly. "My betrothed is an esteemed patron of Kampaulo." She fans herself with her silk glove.

I scoff. "Careful—I'll take back your ring, love." She winks. "Where did you get that thing anyway?"

I bite down on the inside of my cheek, wishing I hadn't asked at all… but a part of me just had to know.

"Oh, *this*?" She plucks it off her finger, twisting it before her eyes. "To be honest, I don't remember her face. An old woman in the back of the marketplace, I think." Her nose wrinkles. "She reeked of paint, just like you." She pokes at me, playfully. "No one will miss her, and I no longer have use for this thing." She tosses it over her shoulder, off the cliff.

I fight the tears swelling in my eyes.

I fight the fire building in my palms.

I fight any emotion at all and focus on my soulmate.

There's no going back. It's already done.

'*Not unless you wish to face the monster you yourself have become.*'

I bury my condemning thoughts, the voices, deep down.

I won't give her up.

"I love you," I blurt out, pulling her into a passionate kiss that burns all else away.

When I release her, she's speechless, blinking up at me as if she had never been kissed before.

"I…" She swallows. "What is it you wish to show me?" she asks in a shaky voice, looking away from me. She tugs at her dress. "I've had enough fun for tonight, and I cannot wait to be rid of these annoying human garments."

I feel as if she just slapped me in the face.

"Right." My tone is more bitter than I meant it to be. "Just a few more flights to go—"

She sighs. "We don't have much time left."

Suddenly, the breeze is beneath my feet; I'm being carried up toward the sky. I don't even have a moment to gasp before the whirling sensation is over, and I'm back on solid ground.

"Don't *ever*—" I place my hand on my knees, thinking I might vomit. "Do. That. Again. You wretched thing."

She chortles, patting me on the back. "Oh, you're a big, strong warrior. You'll be fine."

She turns and yelps with delight, rushing to the edge of the overlook. I come to stand at her side, and we peer off toward the volcanic regions of Belgradia in childlike wonder.

I'm stunned into silence—at night, from here, you can clearly see the deep reds, and yellows, and oranges of lava. It's constantly burning, roiling beneath the earth and bubbling at the mouths of hundreds of mounds that reach toward the sky. It almost looks like small suns have melted atop the earth in the shadowlands of Olleb-Yelfra.

"It's as if the God of Sun and God of Shadow battle each other there," Eloise says in awe at my side.

Mind-reader, too? I think, eyeing her warily.

"Indeed," I whisper. "I wonder who would win... if—"

She shakes her head. "There is no winning. It's the Golden Rule. They are each other's balance. They aren't meant to duel."

Silence spreads between us; Eloise goes very still.

I take her by the shoulders, turning her around to face me.

"I love you, Eloise." I drop to my knees, my hands sliding to her waist. "You don't have to say it back. You don't have to feel the same, but I do. I know what's in my heart. I don't care what the Golden Rule demands of us. I don't care what the gods warn. I don't care about the people you—" I swallow the horrible words, looking down. "This is *love*, of the truest form." I press my finger to my chest, then to her stomach. "Me plus you, despite all the odds against us." I kiss her navel.

She lifts my chin with her finger.

"And do you still believe that firmly with every sunrise we're apart?"

Guilt tightens my chest; she softly smiles, as if she's heard whispers of my doubts from the currents that touch the shores in the daytime.

I realize in this moment that I must acknowledge *all* that she is… and accept accountability myself. I can't keep hiding from the truth, from the consequences of our choices, not after all she's risked for me. Not if we want a chance at a real future together.

"I don't care about the ones you have killed, as long as it keeps you here with me. We can figure things out as we go. I trust you." Our eyes lock. "There's nothing else but you. Rules and gods be damned. I am yours, Eloise. I will live or die by your side. No one else matters now."

I hug her at the hips, my voice cracking.

"Please, say something."

She combs her hands through my hair, looking at me with a strange, icy glare in her eye. "You truly… love me?" She cocks her head to the side, considering, as if the word doesn't have a firm place in her world and she is trying to determine its translation.

"Excruciatingly."

She blinks with understanding. Then she lifts me up to my feet, by the collar, and kisses me, fast and deep.

"Get me out of this dress, so I can thank you for such a wonderous evening."

I smile, my cheeks heating.

"Close your eyes."

Fire grows in my palm and singes the glittering lace away right atop her skin. I stand back to watch—for a second, Eloise is a writhing beautiful pink flame.

Let her burn! a dying part of me screams.

When my flame recedes, Eloise steps forward in all her nakedness and kisses me everywhere, undoing the buttons on my vest and the strings on my pants.

She presses a palm to my chest and forces me to walk backward on the cliff—any wise man would turn around to look. My back hits a rail and I gasp, catching myself.

I peer over my shoulder to find the roaring sea so far below that I can barely make out the rocks beneath.

"I'd rather this view when I take you in my mouth," she says, gazing to the waters, too; I focus back on her.

She rakes her nails down my bare chest, her cold teeth and tongue slowly following behind. Her fingers expertly tug down my pants until they're completely at my feet, my hardness free. Then she kneels before me like a devout priestess.

"I adore everything about you," she says, stroking it gently, admiring it. "I want to drink you."

Then she cups me from beneath and closes her mouth around me, claiming.

"Look at me," I say.

Her bright gaze strikes me, and I completely lose myself in it as she again strokes awake the ravenous beast inside of me.

With the wind at my back and her teeth gently scraping the skin of my most sensitive part, I can't help but release the building power within me.

I greedily run my hands through her hair, gently thrusting to draw deeper inside of her throat. She *never* has to come up for air and takes all of me with dedication in her eyes. I groan into the night as her hands and mouth slide around me in an electric rhythm that sends sparks rippling down my spine.

"Eloise!" I moan, my head falling back to the sky—I've never seen the moon appear so red before.

She takes me deeper, digging her nails into my backside until I'm almost ready to burst.

Her gaze burns into me, as if to say—*Come.*

I relinquish to her, exploding into her mouth with an excited roar—she takes all of me, swallowing every single drop down.

"Stand up," I demand, the feral creature inside of me unleashed.

She wipes her mouth on the back of her hand and does as I say. She looks up, clouds gathering above us. "We don't have much time left—"

"Turn around." My voice is hardly my own, my cock still hard and hungry for her.

I bend her over the rail, facing the water. Her backside is just as enticing as her front. Every curve of her hips, her thighs, her spine, making me wild for more.

"Jaspyr?"

"We will make time." I slide my palms down her spine, then angle myself behind her.

"Time doesn't work like that," she says.

"Do you want me or not?" I dig my fingers into her hips, sending a shudder of fire through my fingertips.

She turns a lethal gaze on me. "*Yes*," she growls in a voice that makes me forget the sun will soon rise.

"How badly?"

She tilts herself closer, looking back to the water. "More than a life forever, I think."

I lean forward to kiss her between her shoulder blades, right atop a sparkling point where a gold and silver strand of lifeblood meet. "You are my life forever."

I plunge into her, my hip bones leveling to her skin; she clutches the side of the rail.

"*Yes*, Jaspyr!" she screams, her magic coiling around me, inside and out. "Forever, always."

I curse her name into the night, thrusting again and again. Our magic coils and glows around us, golden, writhing, electric, moving to the rhythm of our bodies.

The dusk lifts to dawn, the black dimming to blue. The bright stars dull to gray—we too fade away with the night, lost in each other.

As our magic senses our approaching climax, it sizzles and brightens atop our skin. Then Eloise cries out, nearly crushing the stone rail beneath her hands; I hold her hips in place, buried in her, until she finally combusts around me in an earth-shattering sensation—I thrust my head back and empty inside of her, my fire magic bursting out of control, until there's nothing of me left.

I shudder in utter pleasure, stars exploding across my vision. Then everything stills, the only sound is my heated breath.

Eloise purrs in delight as I gently slide out of her. She turns and reaches for my hand. "That was absolutely—"

An enchanted song sweeps toward us from across the sea in a wave.

Our conjoined magic falls away like a soft, glittering rain to the earth as I freeze—my cock is still pulsing with pleasure, my mind is awake and aware, my eyes are open and seeing, but I no longer have control of my body.

Eloise gasps, carefully sliding her hand out of mine; it remains cupped, empty without hers to hold.

Tears burn behind my eyes, my breath ragged in fear—which one of her hundreds of sisters has finally found us?

I had almost forgotten how terrified I am of myrmaids, almost forgotten what Eloise was at her core during all of these blissful kept nights...

I remember everything at once as the water claws toward

me from far, far below in an angry, terrifying cyclone.

Eloise gawks at the stirring sea, then whips around to face me. The petrified expression lining her perfect face unnerves me more than the water scaling the palace walls.

"Jaspyr, there isn't time to explain. I'm so sorry that I dragged you into this, but our time together has come to an end."

I try to make the questions come but only a groan of consciousness passes my lips. This magic even holds my tongue.

She presses my cheeks between her palms, her glittering gaze locked on mine; my tears finally fall.

Eloise, stay! I scream it, but she cannot hear. *Don't leave me here.*

"I… I can't protect you from my family. They'll do anything to save me from the frenzy, from you. Let me give you this peace." My heart thunders in my chest so loudly I think the entire world must hear it—*what does she mean? What is she talking about?* "It's the only way I see."

She kisses the tears from my cheeks.

"You'll always be my hero, Jaspyr. But let me save you now."

She offers me a soft, sad smile as her voice falls away. It's replaced by a sudden, blood-curdling pain unlike I've ever felt before.

My entire body goes rigid in revolt as she sinks her teeth into my neck without delicacy. Any remnant of pleasure I felt is instantly replaced with pain. She drinks so hard and fast that I become dizzy—from the high that sets into my body and bones, from the lack of blood as she drains me.

It's not like normal, not sensual in any way. The sensations are too much for one mortal person to feel all at once. Suddenly, I realize why her victims always scream in such agony at the end—up until now, Eloise had taken care to bite me in a way that had only prompted screams of desire.

My cry for help clangs through my mind, deafening, distraught—it remains soundless in the night.

My tears fall only more as I feel myself weakening, my life slipping. *Stop, please. I love you! I love you, Eloise. How could you do this to me?*

The pain is otherworldly. Worse than when Death stole my family away. Worse than when I tried to offer myself to him. Now, he clings to my very breath, unstitching it from my lungs one thread at a time, stealing it from my soul.

"I'm sorry, Jaspyr," she whispers, finally pulling away after excruciatingly long seconds that felt more like hours—I teeter on the sharp edge of consciousness. If she had drunk for even one moment longer at that pace, I'm certain I would be dead.

I forgot how horrific she can be with my blood staining her teeth and that euphoric, dazed, blood-drenched look swirling in her eyes; even now, I see that she wants more of me.

And even still, I *need* more of her.

No, no, I clamp down on that thought, forcing myself to see through the fog—then something snaps, and everything becomes clear again.

I loathe you. I wish you dead, you vile vixen! You lied to me.

Oh, how I wish I could make her hear me.

Then she kisses the tears from my quivering lips that try to truly curse her name. It's just as hard and deep and passionate as how she drank from me, defiled me after all I've given.

She always tastes of blood and salt, and something intoxicatingly sweet that's worth it all.

No, no, it's not! There's only deception beyond her honied mouth.

She pulls away; black curls at the edges of my vision, blurring her as if the shadows have begun to welcome her home.

She is darkness incarnate, I say in my head like a chant, trying to hold on for dear life. *She is the blight. She is the monster. She is the Kampaulo Killer who trapped me with her falsehoods. I had no choice! I had no choice but to let her in and follow.*

My heartbeat slows, softens to a near undetectable sound.

From the very first note, I have always been trapped by her song! Forced to be devoted to a soulless beast, a gods-damned prisoner to this blood-drinker.

"If we can't have this life together, then we'll have the next. I'll see you again, I *promise*." Her voice cracks on the word, searching my eyes for something—if it's forgiveness, she will *never* find it. "We are soulmates."

No, we are nothing! If I should ever lay eyes on you again in another world, I will destroy your cursed soul and free mine of this chain you cast around my neck.

Anger distorts all else, unlike I've ever felt it before. If she hadn't drained nearly every drop of my magic by taking my blood, my energy, I think I might combust into a wild flame.

I remember the man I tortured for weeks on end to satisfy my revenge, how it wasn't enough…

There will never be enough time in the universe to show you the retribution my soul demands. You played me for a fool, Eloise.

She might as well reach into my chest and rip my heart out to finish me, as I've watched her do to countless men—if I must leave my earthly body today, then I vow to become a ghost to haunt her each and every night for the rest of her eternal life.

I promise you, Eloise, you shall know my wrath, you despicable, heartless creature of the night!

"Eloise," a voice snaps from the raging cyclone that's now stolen to the skies and spread so wide it's the length of the palace wall that faces the sea. "What in the Goddess's name do you think you're doing? Did you really think you could hide from me for long? Step away from that filth and get back in the water... *now*. You've let the frenzy corrupt you too far, child."

The sea seems to scream the words.

Eloise straightens, positioning herself in front of me, though her stance is casual, unperturbed—as if she hadn't just sucked the life right out of the one she *claimed* she could never live without.

You, all of you. You're a blasted plague upon our seas.

"Isobel," she replies in an ethereal voice, wiping my blood from her mouth. She walks forward, hips swaying, and I can tell she's on an extraordinary high. "I know you're angry that I fled from you in Empress Isle. I know you worried." Her voice pitches in delight. "But you *should* be very proud. I didn't need your help after all. I was strong enough to choose life eternal, to put our sisterhood first." She walks forward, slowly, "I killed him. It's finally finished. Your timing couldn't be more perfect." She licks her lips, gesturing back to me.

There's a beat of silence.

"Then *why* is he still standing?" Isobel's menacing voice resonates around us, sounding somehow young yet very, very old.

"Because *you* are holding him up," Eloise retorts, her magic flaring. Laughter floats from her lips. The sound makes my skin burn like acid has been poured on it.

Eloise looks back at me and flashes a somber smile, so quickly I almost missed it—I wonder if she knows I can still see her for what she is. I wonder if she knows that I still breathe, for I can barely tell myself.

"It was... difficult, yes, but it's finally done. I'm free. Now, we can move forward."

"You are the picture of naivety," says Isobel in a somewhat solemn tone. "Don't you listen to me at all?"

The magic glue holding me in place snaps and I'm suddenly freed. My knees give instantly, slamming to the ground

- 468 -

so hard I think my bones have shattered. And I'm so weak that I can't even make a sound.

I begin to fall sideways in a way that feels as if time has slowed; Eloise is fast enough to catch me, though she doesn't.

The last thing I see beyond the woman who scorned me is the most spellbinding child I have ever laid eyes on. She presses forth from the water as if peeking her head through a curtain to glimpse me, to validate my near-lifeless body. Long, golden hair spills down her chest. And bright crimson strands of life-blood paint across pale skin like battle wounds. Her face is absolutely *stunning*, her features so perfectly carved that I almost think she could be elven.

Then I note the shimmer of a vicious red tail beneath her torso.

My fire reacts to her, like calling to like. *I will burn you all to the ground!*

"Naive?" says Eloise, in a boastful voice. "It's done! What more do you want? He'll be dead by dawn. Aren't you happy with me, sister? Why do you still frown?" Something about her tone speaks to me deeply, but the darkness is coming too swiftly for me to grasp anything but my echoing wrath.

"Because *you* might very well be dead, too, once Syrifina gets her hands on you." There is no hint of jesting in her tone.

I slam to the ground, my head ringing like a thousand bells have gone off at once. Everything fades to black, the night returned full force—there's no sound at all. The music has finally stopped, and I've never felt more free.

43

WISHFUL

꒰ E L O I S E

I NEAR THE GRAND GATE OF EMPRESS ISLE. Isobel's intense power glues me to her side; Aura and Ora escort us, though they remain at a distance.

I can only think of Jaspyr.

Is he safe? Did someone find him and take him to a healer? Will he be alright without me… for who knows how long?

My sisters will likely force me to remain underwater until far past his mortal death. But at least… *at least*, I gave him a chance at a life. Surely a more peaceful one without me in it.

'*You won't be able to keep this secret for long, Eloise.*' Aura's voice pains me.

'*Do you really think you can fool your family?*' says Ora.

'*I drank enough of him that it might last me forever,*' I respond, feeling more in control of myself than I have in such a long time. '*And as far as Isobel knows, he's dead. My secret is safe.*' Jaspyr is safe.

Finally, the voices I've come to respect have the space to return—and I *swear*, I felt the frenzy between us break with that last drop of blood I took.

It might take him a while to recover, but at least he'll live. And *maybe*, just maybe, it's broken for him now too, the sickness.

We pass the sea stars forever crawling across the underwater universe. I close my eyes and make a wish.

May only the best part of our bond remain, now that the frenzy is broken. I wish that I can keep my promise to Jaspyr, in this lifetime. That I can return to him before he takes his final breath and give him one last kiss.

We launch ourselves off the reef and into the vast abyss that is the deep. My high from drinking him has faded, yet I still find myself satiated for the first time in countless moons. Cautiously, my hope starts to return.

Yes, we can surely be together now! We can meet again one day.

Without being driven mad, without destroying the Olleb. There's *always* a loophole to promises—and what's a curse if not a vow with malevolent intent?

I dare to smile, even with Isobel swimming in uncomfortable silence beside me.

I just have to get back to him before anyone finds out I lied—I pray that Syrifina will be lenient when she's learned I finally did what's right.

'*You'll never be free of this*,' Aura and Ora warn. '*Lies are a prison all their own.*'

I clench my fists, holding a tight grip on my magic. I glare in their direction, hoping Isobel doesn't notice.

'*Well, what choice was I given?* I yell back at them. '*What choice do I have? Whether I killed him or not, I should always be trapped by guilt and pain and need… because of a curse Mother chose for me. How is that fair?*'

'*It is the price of your magic!*' they say together in a loud cry.

'*You chose to die. You chose to be reborn by her hand. Second chances at life always come with equal consequence,*' says Aura in a voice I've never known before. '*Especially ones born through ancient dark spells.*'

'*You are not above the Golden Rule,*' adds Ora with equal viciousness. '*What the great Goddess didn't tell you is that there is no defying it. It can be bent to the point of breaking, but it will always snap back in place. It cannot be undone... the Olleb will remain, even if you do not.*'

Only now do I wonder where their otherworldly knowledge comes from.

'*Come clean to Isobel now. She cares for you, truly. If you do, she will help you kill Jaspyr once and for all, before any more damage can happen to you.*'

I shake my head, steadying my gaze forward, refusing to look at them.

'*No! I am free of this. You don't understand. I can feel it. I found a way for us to both live. I found a loophole to the injustice of the frenzy,*' I speak firmly. '*The curse is broken because I drank from him to within an inch of his death. I fooled the God of Shadow! I proved my sisters and our great goddesses wrong!*' I grit my teeth. '*And I won't risk what's left of Jaspyr's life by telling them the truth. I'll keep this secret forever if I have to, if it will keep him safe from the likes of you and everyone else who is against us.*'

'*Nothing is forever, Eloise.*' They speak in a song that seems farther away than ever before. '*Haven't you learned that by now? Don't you ever listen?*'

A deep quiet echoes through our connection. I have to cover my mouth to keep from crying out at the fracturing ache of their sudden absence.

I snap my head in their direction—their silhouettes fade into the shadows of the deep. And for the first time ever, I'm not sure where they've gone or if they'll return to swim beside me. I can no longer sense them.

A part of me I pushed so deep down these past months claws at my chest, wanting to chase after my friends, urging me to confess my sins to Isobel. That lost piece of me loathes every choice I've made since I met that mortal man, wishes I had taken the last sip and ended him—my throat constricts, but I hold back my tears, careful not to show any emotion.

He is worth everything, I repeat in my head over and over.

I swallow my sadness and steady myself. I have to focus on remaining calm and contrite in the face of my coven, or they'll see straight through to my lie. They'll know his heart still beats.

I let the coolness of the water clear my head of the last of my feverish state, of my worries over Aura and Ora's warnings.

I'm so much lighter without them now anyway, free. They were always spying, always weighing me down. I tell myself that's how I feel.

Disquiet rolls through me, but I look past it, to the future. I gaze up, toward the sea sky, hoping to see Jaspyr's face again in this life, even if it's when he's old and gray.

I just pray that I'm right, that the frenzy has broken for him, too. That he won't drive himself mad waiting for me to return—I would hate for him to suffer anymore.

Isobel's voice pierces my spinning thoughts. "What were you thinking?" she snaps, glaring at me—it's the first time she's spoken since we left Kampaulo. A part of me wonders if she meant to say '*are you*', for her gaze penetrates me intensely.

The hotness of her rage makes me squirm, but her magic won't let me drift any farther away.

"I'm sorry," I say again. "Truly." I sigh. "I let my mind swim away in him, but I'm better now that he's dead."

She purses her lips, flipping her tail harder so that the water streaks red.

"Let your mind swim away in him?" She makes a derisive

sound. "Eloise, you *slaughtered* countless people during an age when King Devlindor is trying to snuff out anything more powerful than him." She looks to me, her expression glum. "And he's doing a steady job of it! The elves have been wiped out. The dwarves and giants fallen. The fairies in hiding. And the dragons, well—"

Her lips turn downward; she shakes her head, focusing.

I open my mouth to retort, but her magic pinches my tongue.

"Your actions have put us all at risk. Syrifina demanded you be brought home." She shakes her head, staring forward. "You're lucky it was I who came after you and not the twins. I will deliver you to her because I must... but trust me, I don't want to do this."

Her magic releases me; I gasp for my voice.

"I'm sorry I put you in this position, Isobel. You know that was never my intention." My tail gently brushes hers. "I would do anything for you. I love you most of all," I say, massaging my throat. "Even when you terrorize me into submission," I add, tersely.

She snorts, but I see a smile break through her anger—I lean into it, wanting to regain her trust.

"And you're right. I overreacted, overindulged. I will explain to Mother that—"

"This is not just about you!" she yells, her magic flaring outward with a blast like striking whips. "Your decisions can affect us all." Isobel swims in my path so that I must stop and face her head-on.

For a moment, I think she might attack, grip my wrist and yank me downward to trap me in the deep until human history makes a legend out of my actions on the surface; I flinch but remain steady.

I can't show her my fear or she will feed on it.

She reaches out to lay her hand over my chest, over my

heart frozen in time.

"We are each one connected and must look out for one another." She glances to the surface with a frown; we sink a little deeper together, her hand still firm against me, her power asserting over me. "You are free to roam this world as you wish, in whatever form you please. That is one of the greatest gifts we've been granted by the magic of Mother's kiss… freedom." She releases her hold and I'm suddenly lighter, floating back up like a trapped pocket of air.

She looks up; I look down.

"But never ignore Syrifina's call again. You will come to regret it."

"Yes, sister," I say.

Guilt washes over me as I look to her, my stomach curling at the distress shadowing her normally bright features. A fear for my pending fate, I realize.

"It's not your fault, Isobel," I say, gently. "I was the weak one. I made the choice to leave. I chose to ignore everyone's calls. But after all I have been through, I know I can hold my own against Mother. I survived the frenzy. I will survive her."

Somehow, the threat of punishment by Syrifina Myr is less frightening than never laying eyes on Jaspyr again.

Isobel interlaces her fingers, as if she's trying to hold back from striking me. "Sister, you are so very young. Your immaturity is sometimes remarkable." Her tone is graver than I've ever known. She turns away from me, and we continue to swim. "I implore you to show deference. She's in the foulest of moods today."

"Because of me, surely," I say, a tinge of concern creeping under my skin—the closer we get to Empress Isle and the farther I get from Jaspyr, the more I realize that I have no idea what my future holds once I cross the threshold to home.

"No," says Isobel, her voice cutting. "Did you even notice anything special about last night's full moon?"

She looks to me expectantly.

I bite down on my lip, shaking my head.

A low growl rumbles in the back of her throat. "It was a *blood moon*, Eloise." She grinds her teeth. "Goddesses, it's like your mind has completely turned to seaweed." I freeze, blinking back at her—how had I not noticed?

That tinge of worry begins to build into a thick knot of dread, right at the center of my chest. For whatever reason, blood moons always bring out the worst in Syrifina.

Isobel sighs, looking at me with so much pity in her eyes. "Your timing couldn't be worse," she says.

"Why do they affect her so?" I ask—by the deepening of Isobel's frown, I'm sure I don't want to know the answer.

"Because her frenzy was triggered beneath a blood moon, Eloise," she replies in a hushed voice. "And that you've missed *four* gatherings has not put you in her favor. She always looks to make an example out of someone during this season, and you will surely be it."

"So be it," I say, trying to remain calm and confident. "I can handle whatever she has waiting for me."

I think of last night, of all the ways Jaspyr and I had been together beneath the stars. *It's no wonder I paid no mind to the moon nor the shadows that absorbed her.*

Then I mutter, "But isn't it such a strange coincidence..." That I should conquer my frenzy on the same extraordinary moon as hers ignited.

'*Nothing is coincidence, you cursed child,*' speaks a voice so hot and dry it could only be the Sun.

I shudder, dipping lower.

"How did it end for her and the human queen?" I ask, pushing the voice away, though its burn lingers in the forefront of my mind.

"It ended like it always does, Eloise," she says. "In a mortal's death and a myrmaid's despair." She looks at me sadly.

"As I told you before, in time, you will come to feel the pain of what you finally were strong enough to do today. Just like we all have." She strokes me with her magic, a loving, sisterly caress. "It is our endless royal burden to bear. And as with everything, Syrifina's story marks the beginning." She looks at me. "A love story, perhaps, like I warned you… though she'd never admit it."

44

UNDOING

DARLING DIARY,

I haven't written to you in so long. I fear my mind has drifted so far away in her... Queen Julissa.

The days pass slowly and painfully when I'm not near her. The nights fly by in a blur of passion I can hardly sustain.

A year has come and gone, yet I'm no closer to proving the shadows wrong. I'm no closer to finding a way to live with nor without her.

Our union in the High City has caused a ripple effect of instability across the land.

I am the Saindora Savage. And the people have deemed their once benevolent ruler the Queen of Death—Julissa's reign is marred in blood and mistrust and horrors I didn't even know we were both capable of until we met.

They say she's succumbed to a disease of the mind, spend-

ing all her time sailing and far too little time ruling or protecting her people. I suppose there's a truth in that...

Even if I would let her kill me, she gave up trying long ago, the frenzy much too rooted.

And I have also cast my rules to the side to ensure I can keep her alive... until I'm ready.

I've eaten so many innocent people without discrimination—women, children, and the elderly—for there just aren't enough men in the world to satisfy me after knowing her... my beautiful queen.

DARLING DIARY,

Has another year passed already? My mind is shattering.

I'm growing to despise her for how deeply I need her each excruciating day.

The once bright and vibrant city I loved to watch from the shores has fallen to darkness. And Olleb-Yelfra, I feel her fracturing. Because of me, because of us...

Why can't I stop this?

I can't. I can't kill her... I want to, but I won't!

I tried too many times to count—they always end in a fevered, obsessive union of our bodies that I can hardly withstand.

I must have this forever. I can't live another day without her...

I can't stand to be with her!

What can I do to end this curse?

Help me. Help me, please, Diary…

Who am I fooling? Nobody can help. There is no way out without consequence—the God of Shadow is always whispering to remind me of that.

His is the only voice I hear when I'm alone these long, terrible days. His is the only one left.

OH GODDESSES, WHAT HAVE I DONE on this night? Darling Diary, let this be my confession before I look forward and see what awaits. Let the sacred blood I drip to this parchment be a reminder of what was lost, for eternity.

Another year has drifted on.

Queen Julissa is dead.

I killed her.

I am empty, broken…

Another blood moon hangs in the sky, a blazing black and crimson eye that forced me to look into my past and see how far I had fallen with Queen Julissa by my side.

Oh how I wish she still thrived! How I wish this moon would stop mocking me with its sordid eye.

But I had ravaged the shores of Saindora long enough. And I had so much power, too much power, coursing through me tonight. The blood moon is a persuasive creature, forcing me to see.

I had to do it. I had to do something, anything! To take my life back into my own hands.

I just never expected this outcome. I never thought…

A kiss was our undoing.

I pressed my lips to hers, as I had done so many times before, but this time, this time, Diary, I unleashed it all. The entirety of the magic within me flowed into her—I knew not the power I held.

It was an accident, a fleeting thought—that I wanted to share everything I am with her. I didn't know… I didn't know…

That my kiss could transform!

She drew in my magic with greed and lust and hunger, the same way I had drunk her blood countless times—but she stole a piece of me into her I hadn't meant to give.

Something I hadn't meant to offer.

Only in that moment, when my magic slipped into her soul, did the curse finally let me go, for she was no longer human.

Like a flash before my eyes, I saw all the times she had corrupted me, deceived me beyond words, just so she could one day steal my powers for her own. She must've tasted it within me each time our tongues had intertwined. She'd known all along.

As if that kiss ripped the veil from over my eyes, I saw how she'd taken the one thing I had ever given myself—my freedom—and twisted it until I was trapped again by a mortal's hold.

No, not again!

Queen Julissa was a temptress beyond anything I could have ever imagined in all of my years lived.

She seized from me that kiss, my magic, and a transformation from human to myrmaid began. A cocoon of cold power formed around her like the sea's currents.

I stood frozen, unable to move nor blink as her humanity was stripped and ripped from her, a myrmaid's power dangling there to be accepted or rejected.

My power! Mine! Not anyone else's.

No, I just couldn't allow such blasphemy to occur…

I knew what had to be done.

Utter fear of the eternal consequence for my mistake of knowing her gave me the motivation I needed to end our relationship then and there. And the extraordinary power flowing into me from the blood moon aided it. I would not let her win. I would not let the God of Shadow win.

I am the only Queen of the Seas. I will not share!

Her gaze found my own, full of silver fire, just like the first time we had met—except now, I knew that power was a reflection of my own.

I had only moments to make my choice.

"You don't deserve this life," I told her without remorse. "I will decide who swims by my side forever, not some cursed consequence!"

My magic stirred so fiercely in my bones that I could hardly withhold it. I hated her more than anything. Queen Julissa, swimming my seas!? Abhorrent.

She saw my resolve, and answered this, her voice an ethereal echo around me from her power-filled chamber: "Promise you'll protect my children, Syrifina. Don't let my line end with me."

Still, as I write this, I know not why she didn't even try to persuade me to spare her. To beg for her life.

And I don't know why I answered. "I promise, my queen. It's my every hope that your bloodline will endure. May your soul be free in the next life."

I slashed into that icy cocoon with my nails and ripped open her skin with my teeth. I sucked the magic right out of her before it could fully take hold, then I tore her head from her body just to be sure it couldn't return.

Her head fell to the red velvet carpet atop the stone floor with a muffled thud. Her golden crown crashed down alongside it.

The magic fell away in a devasting rain around me. My magic. My magic. MINE!

I… I did the right thing. Didn't I?

Her body collapsed at my feet and all went eerily quiet.

A warm lake of her blood grew in a circle around me, carrying with it that unmistakable scent—blossoms, sand, and sea.

I wanted to swim in it. Goddesses, did I want to bathe in her.

So I did. I tried! I just… wasn't ready for this to be over.

I rolled in her blood like an animal in the dirt, next to her broken corpse. I writhed in it, lapped at the last of her essence, until every inch of my naked body was covered in her.

Darling Diary, you'll think me ghastly, I'm certain. But the moment was beyond euphoric. I lay there so long that the blood began to dry and cake on my skin. The smell started to sour.

I wish I could've stayed forever, basking in her. But, as always, the wretched Sun forced my hand to leave.

I left her crown atop her head for the next ruler to find in the black, firelit throne room, propped up on the golden chair where we used to lick each other's bodies clean. They were reflected a thousand times in the domed, mirrored ceiling—the glinting gold and rainbow-colored jewels. Her long, dark braids still a perfect blanket beneath them.

A red-painted monster with eyes like silver coins was reflected there, too, stroking the fallen queen's hair, gently, her voice filling the cold chamber in a song, a cry, a wail so loud the mirrors cracked…

I recognized her not. She is not me.

I needed to be cleansed of that creature, to wash my lover's blood from my hands. So I dragged the Queen's body all the way to the palace pools where we'd swum so many times together, leaving a trail of crimson behind me.

Th royal bathing room was warm, tiered with steaming baths that opened up over the sea. The craftsmanship was exquisite, an extension of my world. I felt I could swim right off the edge to meet the ocean from here.

"My queendom, not yours," I reminded myself, squeezing Julissa's lifeless hand.

I left her at the edge and dipped myself in, sinking beneath the water and coming up clean.

The bath waters ran red, but I refused to see it.

The entire chamber was inlaid with dark, shimmering tiles of purple, green, blue, and red. A mosaic I always thought meant to represent the Saindora waters at sunset—I stared at those instead.

Queen Julissa told me that the entire place glittered like the crown jewels in the daylight... I wish I could've seen it.

I looked toward the horizon, watching the moon fade and my powers wane.

"Praise the blood moon," I whispered as the shadows began to move away—I will forever hold it sacred: the curse that tainted me; the blessing that freed me.

Then I drained the rest of Queen Julissa's body, every last drop, until I was free of what I can only describe as a frenzy.

I'm not proud of how long I let our affair endure. I can already sense my mind returning to the strength it once had...

But do I regret killing her?

Time will tell, I reckon.

45

EMPRESS

ᗡ E L O I S E

THE SEA CARRIES US HOME as Isobel finishes telling me the horrors that befell Syrifina and her soulmate, in the end.

No wonder her mind is so fragmented at times, I think.

I could hardly endure a few months of my frenzied state. I can only imagine what three years might've done to me…

The silhouette of Empress Isle starts to form into something solid; I hear them before I see them, the echoing sound of all my sisters.

"Isobel," I say in a gasp, slowing, "why is everyone still here? The full moon gathering is over. Our sisters should be scattered well across the seas by now."

Panic seizes me—it's one thing to be eviscerated in front of Isobel… it's another to be shamed in front of our *entire* coven.

"Mother has not released anyone since the last assembly, except me and the other princesses, to search for you. I had to confess my suspicions on your whereabouts after you fled. Then she put a bounty on your head." She purses her lips. "I hate to say it, but you did annoyingly phenomenal work masking your trail during the days."

"I had a brilliant teacher," I reply with a soft smile.

She huffs, looking away. But I can tell she's pleased for how her lifeblood gently glows at the compliment.

"Well, next time, if you're trying to remain unseen, don't let your human arouse you on the tallest tower overlooking the ocean, in the middle of the bloody night." She rolls her eyes. "I saw your magic combust from *miles* away. Both yours and his combined made it appear like a firelit beacon for ships, Eloise." She shakes her head. "Utterly ridiculous."

I stifle a laugh, not wanting my surely eavesdropping sisters to think me anything but serious. If I were human, I might've blushed.

"Well, Jaspyr knows—" I feign choking, "*knew,* how to fire me up, that's for sure."

She scoffs—I don't think I have ever heard so many contemptuous sounds from her in one swim before.

"You are such a child," she says.

"But why keep everyone together like this just because of what I did?" I ask, looking ahead.

Isobel and Syrifina are one thing, but I'm not ready to face *everyone* at once with a lie on my lips.

"She's afraid of King Devlindor getting his hands upon her daughters," she snaps. "And the only reason the other princesses and I didn't catch you sooner was because she's forbidden landwalking for the foreseeable future."

My mouth forms an 'O'. I sink a little lower from the guilt.

The dark, jaw-like entrance to our lair materializes out of the watery haze of blue and black. If not for my impending doom, I might be happy to see it.

All my sisters await me, swimming in and out and around the channels of our crystalized, cavernous lair.

Seeing them now—swarming the mountain that is Empress Isle, dancing around its pillars of stone that spiral so tall they nearly pierce the sea sky—I realize how lonely I had become without them. How much I have come to despise landwalking after too many long, waterless nights.

I ache for them as much as I ache for Jaspyr, but I wish I could meet them again under different circumstances…

Their voices blend into such an entrancing song that I could never replicate it on my own. I want to dance with them. I want to sing with them. I want to hunt with them under our blessed moon.

From this wide-open view, they remind me of the beloved fairyfish who dart about our reefs, each one more beautifully unique than the next. Trails of stardust-like magic drift behind them as they swim.

No light reaches this deep down, and yet it appears as if shooting comets streak through a dark azure night sky or shimmering ghosts float in and out of hiding, their ethereal essences swarming between the frost-white gates.

"I missed this," I whisper.

"We missed you," says Isobel, though her tone remains cold, distant.

Empress Isle is awakened, glittering and glorious, with all the Myrs who assemble here now. Our home is throbbing with such raw, unrestricted power that it calls to my own. I have trouble subduing it, even in the face of such disgrace to my kin, such embarrassment.

My power licks at my skin, my lifeblood igniting, the water surrounding Empress Isle so charged with Myr magic that I can't possibly withhold it; I curse my magic and its mind, as fickle and unruly as my own. Isobel is right, I'm a child. There's so much to still learn…

It sparks, then explodes beyond my control, basking me in a glowing gold and a silver shimmer—indeed, a beacon.

Everyone stops and stares as Isobel escorts me toward the entrance.

I keep my jaw set, my relief inward, my song suppressed, for I know it's misplaced; I swim forward like a lost, lonely firebug rejected by its clan.

At once, the music ceases.

As if Syrifina can sense me pass over the threshold into her realm, the magic-kissed sea seems to darken. The water suddenly electrifies with tension. My sisters' beautiful magic combined can do nothing to brighten the brooding cloud that Mother has suddenly shrouded us in.

"Bring her to me!" Syrifina's voice booms out across the currents, past the gates of Empress Isle. It cuts through the deep in the ancient language of Myr—a deadly sound—as if our angered goddess speaks on her behalf.

The tension shifts into a storm, a siege of magic that crackles through the water in sharp, unforgiving strikes of light. Large beasts floating in the distance are silhouetted with each and every one.

I reach for Aura and Ora, but I still can't feel them.

My sisters swiftly assemble inside the labyrinths ahead of Isobel and me without saying one word.

Empress Isle stands waiting and open, ready to swallow me whole.

What if she never lets me go? What if I never leave once I enter?

My throat feels dry. Every cell in my body tenses, begging me to turn back—only now do I let myself acknowledge how badly I messed up.

I risked my family, our secret, at the most fragile of times in the Olleb. I forced Mother to recall her family to close quarters for added protection.

I *stole* their freedom; I haven't been thinking of anyone but myself at all.

The ripple effect of my choices is this—the icy glare of hundreds of silvery eyes from behind the gates, freezing me in place outside of my normally welcoming home.

Isobel holds out her hand as we draw nearer.

"Don't!" I lock my arms at my sides, afraid that if I touch her she'll feel the lie I told. Sense the frenzy still sickening me to my very bone marrow.

No, it's gone, I remind myself.

Her expression flickers with surprise, hurt. Then her lips press into a thin line—I fear that if she opens them, she might mold into a fire-breathing myrmaid.

"*Fine*, be brave, then," she says as we pause before the entrance.

She blows me a kiss that stings like fire coral particles; I wince, pulling a hiss between my teeth.

"I didn't mean to—"

"Farewell, sister," she says with a savagery I'd only heard her use for the twins. Though I notice the faint tightness of her chin, the worry over my fate lining her perfect skin. "I just hope she lets you live long enough to ask us for forgiveness. To right your wrongs in this lifetime or the next."

"And if I don't?" I retort. "What would you say to me then?"

Let Death come! I've faced him before.

'*You don't mean that, Eloise. No myrmaid does.*'

She swims up to me; I square my shoulders and hold her fiery gaze.

Her expression turns soft, somber after a moment. "That I forgive you anyway. And that I love you either way."

I blink a few times, unable to think of what to say.

My eyes blur with tears.

She plants a kiss on my cheek, wiping the sparkling drops of magic away.

"I love you, too… and I really am sorry, that I hurt you,"

I choke out.

This time I mean it. I understand.

She nods, accepting, then sends a wave of gentle magic to usher me onward.

I stall just before the threshold, trying to think of any excuse I could offer Mother that might stop my bones being another pile on the floor of our caverns.

Would she really kill me for this offense?

'*Certainly,*' the currents whisper.

"Eloise!" Syrifina's voice pierces through the water again like an enchanted spear, shaking the cliffs so hard that they quiver. "Do not keep me waiting any longer. If I have to go to meet you, you will come to regret even your very *first* taste of blood, whether or not you've yet had your fill. Swim to me."

Suddenly, I can't remember how, my tail uselessly frozen.

Her voice, claw-like, clutches at my fins. "*Swim to me,*" she sings.

Everything inside me tries to defend against such magic. Every bone in my body tries to resist so much that I nearly scream.

I want to turn back and live out the rest of my days in the fading warmth of Jaspyr's arms. I'd rather burn in the sun than be apart from him forever. But Mother's magical grip on me is firm, tight, like a noose around my neck.

Isobel's eyes go wide. "*Go,*" she urges in a hushed voice. "Don't fight her."

I look to her in pain, my spine curved as I struggle to move backward. "I don't want to die."

Isobel looks away, no hope to offer.

There's nowhere to swim where the Sea won't deliver me back here at Mother's orders. And with the air warming up above, the earth waking to the day, the sun pouring itself into the sky like an open wound, I have no choice but to obey.

Jaspyr, I think, *I will see you again. I will resurface in your lifetime. I promise, I'll come back to you.*

This deep down, the warmth of him vanishes from me.

I gaze to the surface, so far away, wondering if Jaspyr would feel it if I died—did the frenzy connect us that deeply?

I swallow…

Does it?

Or would he suffer his entire human life waiting and watching for me to return? And when we both finally meet Death, me for a second time, will our next journey bring us back together?

Mother's terrific and petrifying presence vibrates my bones again, discharging outward from the core of the labyrinths where she will surely be waiting for me to kiss her cheek. Her magic is a powerful, pulsating beast under the sea, unlike anything I have ever known it to be before.

With great reluctance, I slowly float forward.

And as I enter Empress Isle, forced to swim past each of my sisters, their faces so distinct, so full of shame that burns for me, I know I have left Jaspyr with a lie. As it stands, I'm not sure if my soul will even survive Mother's wrath to be able to travel on to the next life to wait for him.

I cling to those last moments with him, when I wasn't brave enough to be fully honest with him—*I should've said 'I love you', Jaspyr, for certainly, our love is true.*

BLACKNESS SWALLOWS US the deeper we go, the entrance to the open sea far gone. The endless channels are only made tangible by the layer of human bone and the glint of men's treasures creating our familiar path. If not for them, even Myr sight would do little good here, for the black stone walls and ceiling, and the dark waters, provide little variation in color.

Every now and then blossoms of those orange crystals bloom above or around us, reminding me that we are still on the earthly, mortal plane and not floating away into some otherworldly sea beyond. And the skeletons comfort me in a way; I know I haven't yet passed on.

I swim directly behind Isobel. And I don't need to look back to know that all my sisters silently follow.

Isobel leads us to the main gathering chamber, the heart of Empress Isle—it's known as the Crystal Castle.

Mother named it for its vastness and natural beauty, unparalleled. The main reason she claimed it for our home. No earthly queen nor king could ever hope to attain such a wonderous fortress as ours. It can fit each and every member of my family at any given moment while still offering us the freedom and space to explore, to dance, to practice our magic, to float in solitude, to lounge and sing while awaiting sunfall.

The water softens as the tight labyrinths begin to widen. The pressure of the sea lifts as we swim up and up and up, like we move through a portal to a different world.

I dare to glance below me. I gape, awed by my sisters as they pour out of the darkness behind me in a rippling blanket of dazzling blue. Swimming together as one, they appear like a thunderous wave, chasing me to the ends of the earth, stabbing toward me like glittering icicles. They're freshly fed, wholly energized for the weeks to come after feeding on just a single man; I can hardly stand to look at them.

I focus on the other princesses, the only variation in color among the group. They remain at the front of the others, leading the way, eyes pinned on me—I don't wait to read their expressions.

I place my attention back on Isobel. On her crimson tail and sunlit fins. She is fire incarnate. She can protect me from anything.

'*Fire doesn't belong here*,' the Sun speaks, hotly.

'*Then leave!*' I shout.

With Isobel at the front, we spill through the wide opening in the ceiling where the main channel ends—the Crystal Castle envelops us for miles in every direction.

Cliffs of towering, dark, diamond-like stones climb upward on all sides of us with no end in sight; we no longer swim in a cavern at all but an actual palace so opulent that I at first thought the Goddess of the Sea herself must've crafted it.

When, in fact, Syrifina was crafted by her hands... then *she* built this palace for us.

Walls form around us like a grand foyer, and the high ceilings are speckled with wide, swim-through spaces that one could explore forever. I peer up as we all filter in, noting the swim-through that will take us directly to the surface; we travel it so often for the full moon gathering.

Sunrays tinkle down from far above through that inviting space, dancing like stars, shooting sharp rays of light into the darkness beyond, though it doesn't reach very far.

Some of my sisters begin to sing in a soft, elegant chorus of homecoming. The sound is like violin strings being gently plucked and the whisper of brass being delicately brushed. Their voices echo all around me in perfect symmetry, bouncing off the gleaming, glass-like walls—every inch of the palace is made from a mosaic of dark, translucent sea crystal tinted in various colors and streaked with silver from being touched by so much magic over the centuries, making it appear as if magic has been trapped inside of ice.

Chandeliers of bioluminescent lights blend with diamonds, dangling above us to cast a sapphire glow across the space. And torches lit with magic line the cavernous hallway

Isobel guides us down; we follow in an orderly procession.

We swim deeper, rise higher, the palace growing with us every bit of the way.

The sea crystal takes on both natural and unnatural shapes the higher we swim, my sisters having spent ample time molding this place to their liking with Mother's blessing. Slabs and slopes, crevices and hollows, pillars and columns of it give the place so much texture that I feel as if we float along corridors carved by humans.

We pass through tall archways, their facades telling intricate histories etched in the language of the Myr, scrawled atop the glass in everlasting magic. Grand statues that look made of a substance akin to pearl stand erected in common spaces, commemorating our sisterhood. Gardens of coral bloom in cozy pockets, and family portraits greet us every time we round a corner, illustrated using all the colors of the sea by the talented magic of our most creative sisters.

Edging closer to the surface, I feel myself growing weaker, tired. I wish to close my eyes and rest until nightfall. I realize only now that it's been weeks, *months*, since I've let myself truly sleep.

But as Isobel veers down a dark passage, I find myself on full alert—this leads to where Syrifina sleeps.

The sea crystal here darkens, shifting to a maroonish-black with silver streaking through it like living currents. We float silently above a base covered in solid gold—the skeletons of more than a hundred men, fully armored with weapons in hand, stand guard the entire way, held up like puppets by magical strings. Some even wear crowns, and I can't help but wonder how many kings Syrifina has single-handedly dethroned during her time.

Isobel pauses before a mass of woven bones and gold and jewels at the end; the mass thrums with power, embedded into the vast wall of towering crystals. Just beyond, I know Mother awaits inside her private lair that no one has ever laid eyes on before.

The rest of us fall still behind her, ready to meet our queen.

Everything around Empress Isle grows quiet, the instrument of voices ceases to a staggering silence as all my sisters wait. I cannot yet see Syrifina... but I can feel her all around us.

Vasylina and Miki swim up on either side of me. "Best of luck, little sister," they whisper in a hateful hum.

I shiver, whipping them hard with my tail; they both hiss, dipping lower.

"Luck is for fools," I respond, tossing them both a glare over my shoulder.

"Then what does that make you, devious daughter of mine?" Syrifina's voice reverberates from behind the wall.

Even Isobel drifts backward, leaving me to face her wrath alone.

"I—"

"Enter." The solid wall begins to part as black, shimmering magic works its way through the material like enchanted thread. "*All* of you."

"May the great goddess have mercy on us," Isobel mutters behind me.

The wall becomes a door, and beyond the door is blackness denser than any night sky I've ever seen, denser than the deep.

With a jolt, I swim backward, bumping into Isobel—she shoves me forward. "Don't be a coward. It's not in our nature."

I bristle, but she's right—I gather my courage and prepare to face Mother.

We all move forward into the dark abyss. Then the wall closes again behind us. As my eyes adjust, I see we're in a hollowed-out part of the palace, where the sea crystal has hardly ever seen light; it shimmers like a bottled night sky with the reflection of all my sisters' magic gathered.

A shiver rolls down my spine, from the nape of my neck to the tip of my tail. I turn to face the door we've just come through.

Syrifina emerges from the dark, drifting up toward us like a blazing, vicious, bright blood moon embodied, ready to seize the heavens. She seems to materialize from the Sea of Night itself, as if her magic had before hidden her in a space 'between'.

A cloak of endless dark indigo rolls off her back, the water breathing with every movement, darkness yielding to her, a glorious star.

She is the center of this galaxy. *She* is the Sea itself.

She rises and rises and rises, until she's shining and soaring above us all, casting a silhouette across the chamber that makes her appear like the larger-than-life sea monster Jaspyr once spoke of.

Her flowing crimson hair appears to weave with the blood of every man she's ever feasted on, for each strand is bright and shimmering with their lost spirits. It drapes around her shoulders and down her back, bleeding into the water around her like a flowing river.

Her skin shines white and brilliant in stark contrast to everything around her—has she basked in undiluted starlight over the centuries?—and her eyes are as bright and beautifully complex as the universe beyond, flecked with sharpened silver that gleams like the moon.

I'm certain the goddess glowers at me through her gaze.

I have to blink several times to even see her clearly for how radiant she shines. And I can't even begin to count all the shades that her lifeblood takes on, its iridescent form gliding between every hue, both dark and light, known to our kind.

I shrink before her, feeling suddenly so small and fragile—

she floats yet higher, lifted atop a tail that ripples and blossoms like an angry, awakened flower, her fins flowing out from her in lustrous streams that seem to vibrate with her fury.

I sink lower. "I—"

"*Silence!*" Her voice is a sea-shaking sound that rips through the castle; the crystalized cliffs quiver, skulls and gold tumbling off slopes from somewhere above to live in the depths below, forever. My gaze is glued to the milky white of a bone as it's swallowed by the darkness.

Jaspyr. Jaspyr. Jaspyr...

His name pounds in my ears, reminding me that I need to survive, for him. Our story is not yet over.

Everything stills, everything quiets even more, a hush so void of life that I wonder if I'm not already gone.

The wall of bones and gold begins to morph again, this time taking with it large wedges of the dark, silver-streaked gems. It leaves behind no door, no way to escape—I watch in awe as, for the first time in my life, I am made to witness her magicked throne come to be.

I have only heard whispers about its grandeur.

I tilt my head up, gaping along with everyone else.

Syrifina is a devasting sight to behold, made even more ruthless as a throne fit for a goddess comes together around her, suspended from the wall.

Thick, dark crystals stab toward a ceiling that I cannot see in jagged columns to form the back. And the wide, deep, curved seat is as smooth as glass, skulls and skeletons across the bottom like a bone-knitted blanket.

A massive, ominous open-mouthed seashell solidifies before me, its casing so clear that I can see the silver magic pulsing within it like veins made of steel—and Mother is its petrifying pearl.

As she settles into the throne atop a pile of fresh skeletons, a spiked crown of gilded bone fuses atop her head, dripping with frightful magic; each point is so thin and sharp that it reminds me of the urchins that roam the bottom of the reef at night, the needle-like tips all set with small, priceless jewels that gleam like spying eyes.

She curls into the seat, resting on her elbows as if she is bored of us already. Her remarkable tail drips over the edge like a tiered sequin gown fit for a sovereign—the ruler of Empress Isle.

"Bow," she speaks.

The still waters seem to shift, slightly nudging me with it—I turn to find all my sisters with their necks bent, tails curled in submission.

Slowly, her eyes fall on me.

I move to lower my head, but her magic explodes like a silent scream—it envelops me, curling around my torso and arms in a suffocating embrace.

It carries me to her eye level. I thrash against her hold, but my hands are pinned to my sides, my tail the only thing able to move back and forth; I go nowhere.

She doesn't even sit up to face me.

"This is what you have risked our family's secrecy for," she says, her voice a poisonous purr—she picks a skull up by its crown. She squeezes, just a quick flex of her fingers, and the bone crumbles to sprinkling dust. "*Nothing.*"

I stop moving.

She smiles but it doesn't reach her eyes, then she turns me to face my sisters.

Slowly, each one lifts their eyes to me; I stay focused on Isobel—I've never seen her look so afraid before.

A crimson tear streaks her cheek, but she quickly wipes it away.

Jaspyr. Jaspyr. Jaspyr.

"There have been lulls in my time. Beautiful lulls," begins Syrifina in a voice so captivating I almost forget I will likely be persecuted, "where peace has swept over the lands, though fragile still. Never quite permanent. Peace never is—not when there's always so much blood spilled, wasted, to achieve it. Not when vengeful energies linger in the air, biding their time to strike back at the injustices served upon them." She twists a strand of hair around her finger. "They grow with hatred in their hearts and wisdom beyond their years. And one eventually finds a pedestal to preach a new falsehood of 'harmony' to those unappreciated in the current regime…"

She scoffs, sitting up in her seat.

"*Harmony*," she spits. "There's never been such a hate-inspiring word in history. A term often manipulated by tyrants brutal and ambitious enough to try and enforce their vision of peace upon the Olleb." She sighs, flipping her hair over her shoulder. "She's suffered so many 'peaceful' monsters, hasn't she, Zahra?"

Her gaze settles on her second eldest—Zahra, notorious for her blood-drenched history, too, and her rigid routines to correct behaviors born from what I now know was her cursed frenzy. She floats stone-faced in the line of princesses, who have settled at the front of the rest; forest-green and emerald lifeblood coil across her black skin, emerald magic dusting the water around her.

"Certainly, Mother," she says with a respectful nod. "The cycle is as everlasting as we are." Her voice sounds like the whisper of wind through trees. "Though this one has proved shockingly successful."

Syrifina taps her fingernails atop a skull, the sound making me grind my teeth.

"That it is." She flicks her gaze back to me.

"This is why you all *must* listen." She slides her focus across all of her descendants. "Heed what our dearest Eloise has foolishly forgotten—"

The magical chains around me tighten, searing my skin as

if she holds me locked with sunfire. I can't hold back my scream—it echoes eerily in the quiet.

My sisters murmur, some in fright, some in delight.

"What did she do?" someone whispers.

"Didn't you hear? She drank outside of the moon's cycle. *She's* the Kampaulo Killer."

Gasps and gossip snake through the gathering faster than flowing water.

"Goddesses save her," someone says.

The magic lessens; I whimper in relief, tears blurring my vision.

"These decades following King Devlindor's hostile takeover have grown quiet after a time," continues Syrifina. "Magic still silently simmers across his kingdom, the efforts to smother it into obedience quite the undertaking. As Zahra has proclaimed, though, he's proving successful." She purses her lips. "I'm sure he will triumph in fully eradicating it from his people's knowledge… at least for a while."

Some of my sisters shake their heads, singing their disapprovals.

"But the moments before this *peaceful* present, where citizens of Olleb-Yelfra were forced to bend to his will and innocent enchanted creatures, creatures like us, were wiped away, buried"—the calmness in her voice slips into something so terrifying that I tremble—"as if specks of dust to be cleaned out from his royal path! *Barbaric.*"

Her magic flares, and another skull is obliterated to powder by the mere flick of her electrified fin.

The crowd doesn't dare speak nor move as her orb-like silver gaze seems to contemplate destroying us all.

She sighs after a moment, blinking back her power.

The tension in the water softens. Then Syrifina lowers her voice, and my sisters all lean forward, prepared to drink up every word.

"Those moments, before… they were filled with pain, havoc. *Chaos.*" Her expression wavers with something like disbelief at her memories. "And after chaos, peace is always promised, endured. Though, ever-unsettlingly, isn't it?"

Everyone nods their agreement—I realize, most of my sisters have witnessed some version of the cruel histories she speaks of. Combined, we have lived countless centuries, of which I have the least knowledge.

"You see, Eloise," she turns her body toward me, "magic still buzzes in the air freely, as if tempting the King and his shadows to try and catch it all. Taunting, teasing. Testing how far his greed might really stretch."

Tendrils of magic rise up and out of her throne, seeping into the water to twirl above us. It's so playful and calm that I'm shocked it came from Mother at all—then it vanishes in a glaring flash that makes me gasp.

"To the ends of the earth it seems," she mumbles, watching the light fade; her voice sharpens, her gaze finding mine once more. "Like us, it bides its time…"

She looks each one of her daughters in the eyes.

"Olleb-Yelfra is *waiting* to strike back with all the magic still burning in her name."

She closes a fist and lifts it to her eye level.

When she opens it, her magic explodes in a loud, silver burst above us.

Fang-sharp, glittering shards of pure power rain down—we all look up, some of my sisters shrieking or covering their heads with their hands.

Death dangles over each of us, but I don't look away.

The magic dissolves moments later into fairyfish dust that tickles my face.

There's a collective sigh of relief that I do not join in.

"Like us," she continues in a gentle tone, as if suddenly the compassionate teacher, "with fewer beings controlling it, wielding it, *knowing* it, the Olleb grows all the more powerful in secret."

She leans back, taking us all in with a warm smile softening her features.

"The Golden Age has come and gone. Now, we bear witness to yet another story of mortal gluttony unfolding, and we'll bear witness from the comfort and safety of our waters." She gestures to the bones beneath her. "Time continues on, and we'll only grow stronger. *We* will remain, while the human monsters and their peaceful kingdoms, built atop the flesh and bones of the men before them, will crumble."

My sisters hiss and shout and sing in excitement, showering Mother in bursts of magic all their own.

"Yes, my daughters," she sings, accepting their praise with a satisfied expression. "You *will* remain. I ensure it." She looks to me. "As long as we keep the Sea of Saindora safe and do not beckon the enemies into our sanctuary."

She smiles at me, parting her blood-red lips to display her fangs.

Then she turns back to my sisters and opens her arms out wide. "Everything the water touches, so do we. Everything the water touches, we own."

They cloud the chamber with more magic, their voices rising in a powerful song.

Her gaze cuts to me again, a deep frown aging her features so much that I see a flicker of that ancient beast thriving behind the mask of perfect youth.

She swims away from her throne, her enchantment forcing me to follow until we're both looking down upon my sisters.

"But risks are for unwise, unshaped souls. I have lived long enough to take no interest in them, despite all that I am." She pouts. "*That* is why we are gathered here today. To remind our dearest, youngest, Eloise, who lost her way in the moonlight."

They all moan in a terrible harmony, my name—'*Eloise, for shame!*'—throwing their fists up in solidarity.

I'm forced to bear the weight of their judgment.

The ropes squeeze tighter, Syrifina's voice growing louder.

"We shall not *remind* the covetous King of what he has been unable to conquer. We shall not prod at the jealous beast who wishes to control everything. We shall not even *reveal* everything we know to be of genuine value in this world! For he knows nothing truly of it."

Isobel holds my gaze, expressionless, though I know she hurts for me.

"Mortals are so very weak," she continues, "disappointing, really. Most of his subjects have already chosen *not* to remember the best parts of our enchanted world for fear of consequence. They didn't fight hard enough to maintain the natural order of things… they never do, really." She shrugs. "So we shall not fight for them. And we will *certainly* not seek to flaunt our powers during such a fragile era."

She tuts at me, wagging her finger. Then she draws me in closer, turning her back on the others and fully facing me.

Her magic seems laced with fire coral, burning into my skin and scales again so much that I can hardly stand it. Her mighty power rages in her eyes—I wonder what might happen if she fully unleashes it upon me.

I clench my teeth, biting back my agonized moan.

Jaspyr! Jaspyr! Jaspyr!

"Like us, the Olleb needs no rulers. She is a monarch of her own accord," she says to me. "I've come to learn over the centuries that she tolerates nothing less than a blood-for-blood world. She will eventually right their wrongs, as a mother surely does." She caresses my cheek with the back of her hand; I cringe away.

She purses her lips, taking my chin in her hand, forcing me to withstand her touch.

"As she does *every* time history repeats itself and delivers a greedy tyrant upon the land... *when she sees fit.*"

She leans forward, baring her fangs. Her power is so strangling I can't help but cry out.

"Do you understand me, Eloise?" she whispers in my ear.

"Yes, Mother," I speak, my voice hoarse.

She presses a gentle kiss upon my cheek, and I wonder if she wears acid-laced lipstick.

I flinch as it sizzles, surely leaving its mark upon me.

"Good." She lets go, tossing her hair back as she turns again to address the rest of the assembly.

Her magic relaxes along with her focus on me—I sigh in relief, sagging against the writhing ropes, arms still pinned at my side as I float behind her.

"Until then, my children, we must live silent as the stillest waters, confined to our endless sanctuary whilst we enjoy this delicate moment of peace." She looks up, as if seeing beyond the castle walls. "Trust me, it won't last long..." Her voice homes in on me again, and I feel as if she looks at me from eyes at the back of her head. "So you needn't eagerly launch us back into an age of chaos, unless *you* wish to be the one to clean it up. It will come again soon enough without you coaxing it."

Soft murmurs of agreement and understanding whisk through the crowd.

A low growl rumbles in Syrifina's throat. "And no more landwalking!" she bellows, her voice forcing everyone backward—even I have to close my eyes to withstand the sound, and I float behind her. "Not until King Devlindor is ash on the wind. *Am I heard?*"

"Yes, Mother!" my sisters echo as one, an army of Myr.

Slowly, she turns her focus on me again, glaring at me over her shoulder, her crown casting an eerie shadow, like a barred cage, across my vision.

I bow my head low with the weight of my guilt, my sorrow, my failure…

Jaspyr, I fear she will destroy me. I fear our time is truly over.

"Yes, Mother," I whisper, looking to my tail.

A swath of red hair suddenly envelops my space like I'm swimming through a forest of crimson kelp. A long, shining black fingernail presses forward, tilting my chin upward.

Syrifina's silver eyes penetrate my own.

"Don't cast your sight down now," she says, a soft but deadly warning; I swallow, steadying my courage. "*You* are a Myr. You will face the penalties of your choices with pride and accountability, daughter."

My throat tightens, but I hold firmly on to the last remnants of my bravery.

"And what choices might those be?" I ask.

Show deference! Isobel's counsel rings in my head from earlier.

I ignore it, my arrogance just as much a part of me now as my tail.

Syrifina smirks.

"The consequence for over-feeding is starvation," she replies, matter-of-factly—my eyes widen in shock; I have to stifle my sigh of relief that she hasn't decided to end me right here and now. "As Sister Zahra can attest, it is both a fitting punishment and absolution in such a case. After a time, you will find yourself back to… a version of your right mind."

Whispers snake again through the crowd; Isobel shifts nervously, and I know something isn't right.

After a time…

"How long is my confinement to be?" I blurt out, praying that my sentence wouldn't outlive Jaspyr. "I don't deserve your mercy, but—"

Her hand closes around my neck so fast that I forget my

words. Her eyes bore into mine, magic swirling around her irises like a vortex. Then I hear her voice in my mind, loud and clear.

'*You're lucky I let you keep your head for all the trouble you've caused me.*' I still, thinking of Queen Julissa's headless body. '*Mind your tongue, Eloise. You've tested me enough already with your foul behavior.*'

Her fingers tighten; I choke, trying to resist her power. *Jaspyr. Jaspyr. Jaspyr!*

"Have you ever known me to be merciful?" she asks aloud, in a sweet yet ageless voice that shrinks my very soul.

I try not to get lost in her bewitching gaze—far stronger creatures than I have drowned in there and never resurfaced.

But if I'm to die today, I will *not* die like a whimpering child. I refuse. I don't need a reminder of who I am. I know.

I am Eloise Myr!

I'll carry my name to my grave if I must, along with Jaspyr's love.

My magic blazes, pushing back against hers with greater force than I knew I had within me—this time, though, I control it.

Surprise and interest light up her features as my golden glow surges.

"You showed mercy on me once," I reply, "when I was a human."

She releases me, feigning a bite to my face. "And here I am, second guessing my choices that night." Then she swims back to her throne, arms crossed at her chest, looking down upon me—her expression dares me to follow, testing my brazenness.

My resentment rises up. '*Queen of lies!*' I retort through our linked mind.

Her lip curls up in a snarl. '*You know nothing, deceitful daughter of mine.*'

With the flick of my tail, I swim as close to her as I can get; I'm held at arm's length by her leash, though I strain against it.

"Eloise," shrieks Isobel; I see her swim forward, but she appears to hit a barrier of magic, hanging in the balance between my sisters, Syrifina, and me. "Mother, please—"

Magic strangles her voice into nothing.

I bare my teeth at Syrifina, a hiss rising out of my throat, knowing it might very well be the last thing I do.

"I just thought you might be empathetic to my predicament," I say, my magic billowing around me like an angered beast, "seeing as your *frenzy* caused even more havoc up on land than mine." Her eyes widen, her mouth setting into a firm line. "After all, *you are* the Saindora Savage of old. Are you not, Mother?"

I sneer at her, satisfied at the flicker of astonishment that crosses her features—it quickly turns to rage.

"What's a frenzy?" one of my sisters whispers, sending a spark of questions and confusion rippling through the throng of sapphire myrmaids. "What's she talking about?"

"How dare you…" Syrifina grips the edge of her throne with nails that suddenly appear more like claws; the sound like metal on stone.

Everyone winces, plugging their ears. But I carry on.

"If you're so angry with me for my carelessness, what does that make you, if not a hypocrite?" A collective gasp echoes throughout the chamber, empowering me to antagonize her only more. "How many years did you lock yourself away in the deep after terrorizing Saind—"

Her brutal song surrounds me, a sound with no replica on this earthly plane; my voice vanishes from my throat, as if her magic sucked it right out of my body.

"Quiet!" she screams, launching up from her throne.

The other princesses remain perfectly still, majestic examples of how one should behave when Mother has cast her power before us; the others quickly fall in line.

Syrifina's expression darkens with rage unlike I've ever known it. It takes all my power not to lower my eyes again, not to bow down to her. '*You're the tyrant!*'

'*No, I am your creator.*'

Everything about her, from her crown to her viciously vibrant lifeblood, screams danger.

Her gaze moves to Isobel; she shrinks back from her scrutiny, her fiery form dimming.

I immediately regret my words about the frenzy and fall back—how much was I really supposed to know? And, certainly, I shouldn't speak of such taboo topics in front of the entire coven.

The iridescent ropes on my arms shift into scorching cuffs that chain my wrists at my front.

"Leave us!" she roars, her magic shattering through the space in a sprawl of black, gold-tipped power.

Her eyes remain on Isobel, who does not dare move a muscle.

"Everyone but the princesses, go. *Now!*" She gestures to me, her voice falsely sweetening. "And say goodbye to your sister. The next time you see Eloise she'll be a much more mature creature with manners to speak of, I'm sure."

Ever obedient, my sisters each blow a kiss to Syrifina, then a farewell one to me that stings with both their disapproval and envy—disgraced or not, I'm still their youngest princess.

They depart the same way we entered, the golden, bone-clad door weaving open to let them pass—it closes again after the last one is gone.

Only I, Isobel, and the other princesses remain, sealed behind in what now feels more like a hollowed tomb.

I can't help but think that I'm grateful Syrifina still

clutches my tongue, for if she hadn't, I would've screamed out the name of my beloved mortal sin when that door shut me in with her, my captor, my creator, my empress.

46

TOMB

MY ELDER SISTERS GATHER in order of succession, princesses indeed. Their expressions shimmer with glimpses of fear, anger, and wonderment as they consider me. But above all, they remain poised and seemingly unperturbed.

Their fins fan out in a softly swaying wall of luminous hues, like magnificent capes floating out behind them. Together, they create a kaleidoscope of color that bounces around the crystalized chamber and reflects through the dark water— even with all the others gone, they alone still seem to take up all the space as the darkness breathes around them.

Isobel still floats somewhere between them, me, and Mother. She dips her head toward me apologetically, then moves back to join Zahra at the front.

Syrifina's voice rings out like a damning gong. "First daughter, stay where you are until I determine what *your* punishment shall be."

She pauses, puckering her lips and looking ever like a child.

The others stir, eyes widening in surprise; the twins don't even attempt to hide their grins.

Isobel turns to face Mother, her sternness melting away into something earnestly puzzled. She tilts her head, eyebrow raised. "Why—"

The water charges with power, black tendrils of magic seeping out from Mother's throne like an octopus with a thousand limbs, each one sniffing out prey to destroy—they home in on Isobel.

Her fire shrivels to smoky fog, her skin paling even more.

"Eloise is your ward," she says, her voice clipped. "Her offenses to our kind are just as much owed to you. *You* should have been keeping a closer eye on her. Why else would I trust her to your watch?" She swims toward me and I try not to cringe back as her gaze seems to search for something in my expression. "They are so precious when they're young, aren't they? So weak."

I part my lips, but she still grasps my voice. Curses roll through my mind.

She smirks at me, laughing a little—I know she can hear them.

I stiffen, focusing. I must be careful… I can't let any evidence of wrongdoing slip through our infuriating bond.

Syrifina is our creator and can decide at any time to enter my mind; I can decide what to show her, if I remain calm and concentrate.

She contemplates me with a steely gaze, as if sensing my resolve to block her out. The fog of her magic rises beneath her like a silver, glittering, smiting cloud.

I prepare myself for the life-shattering blow that will surely come as she balls a fist at her side. Those black tendrils turn their attention to me, and silver strands of magic weave in and out of her fingers, electrified, lightning. I fear she might wield the Sea of Night against me somehow, shrink the blackness so tightly around me until all that's left is a shadow of who they used to call Eloise.

One of my sisters whimpers, surely Daniella.

"You think you're so wise, but you are merely an infant," she says, coldly, leaning closer to me. "That you have learned of my past is of no consequence. We all have them, Eloise. And it's your right to know it, as a princess of this coven."

The magic around her fists brightens; her gaze flickers to Isobel.

"Though, I'm normally the one to decide when to tell *my* story," she adds. She looks back to me. "But you will not disrespect me in front of our family. If you *ever* forget yourself so plainly again, you will come to know the true savage that I can be."

She smiles with those crimson lips, her fangs poking out at me, her hair flowing out behind her like wildfire.

I smother my urge to escape, for it would be futile to try. Syrifina created this kingdom from scratch. *I* am a literal fraction of her. Instead, I attempt to rationalize the fate I've cast upon myself and my dear sister—whatever my punishment is, Isobel's can't be nearly as bad…

After a few years of imprisonment, Syrifina will surely soften and release me, won't she? And Isobel is her first and favorite daughter… she wouldn't harm her. Maybe just scold her or force her to babysit the next newest daughter even sooner.

'*Or, maybe, she'll turn her into something like stone, as she did the other daughters who betrayed her so.*'

I freeze, recognizing the God of Shadow's voice.

'*You're lying,*' I growl, trying to remain calm with Mother's eyes still on me now.

'*Oh, Eloise, I am nothing if not a truthful soul.*'

'*You're despicable.*'

'*Not as despicable as Syrifina Myr can be. She is one of my*' *finer creations.*' I feel him smile. '*The next time you lay a gar-land of jewels around one of the statues decorating the Crystal Castle, look a little closer at what you honor. Maybe you can still see the flicker of silver in the eyes of the ones that used to have voices.*'

'*Mother would never do that…*' I retort but my words shake. '*She loves us.*'

Yes, above all, Syrifina loves us, more than anything in the world—with her soulmate dead and gone, no one would ever come before her children.

'*Precisely. And so many unspeakable things have been done in the name of "love", have they not?*' He chuckles. '*But who am I to know of such terrible, awful histories. Maybe the Queen of the Seas will just give Isobel a strong talking-to.*'

His voice grows darker, harsher like the sound of thunder.

'*And maybe she'll keep you forever, never let you feed again, until you shrivel up and become nothing but more bones to decorate her chambers.*' He sighs. '*Pity… your rampage lasted far less time than your sisters' did.*'

'*Stop!* I say, squeezing my eyes shut. '*Get out of my head.*'

Magic curls out from me in a cloud, forcing the shadows back—I hear his rumbling laugh fade away.

"Who speaks to you, child?"

I snap my eyes open and find Syrifina looking at me with worry softening her fierce expression.

"*Who?*" she demands.

My voice pours back into me. "The shadows won't leave me alone," I mutter, looking down.

Even the twins have the decency to look troubled, whispering in a panic to one another.

"Speak for everyone or not at all," shouts Syrifina, glaring at them over her shoulder.

"The God of Shadow whispers to you?" they ask, simultaneously.

I nod, my gaze sliding over them and the other princesses—everyone looks… disturbed.

"He came to me, in form."

The twins gasp, pointing at me with astounded expressions. "Mother, she's been marked!"

"Hush," says Kristeena, sharply; they quiet for their elder—she smiles warmly at me. "We've all been *marked*. No need to get so excited. Or is that jealousy scenting the waters around you, that a god of old would show himself in form to your youngest sister?"

They bristle, glaring at her.

"It is indeed a horrific honor," says Syrifina, "to meet my maker." She looks anything but pleased, a scowl wrinkling her face.

My gaze locks on Kristeena—I know she tried to vanish to the deep to hide from her frenzy… hide from *him*, maybe.

Her olive skin is painted in soft, lavender strokes, and her tail twists back and forth like a golden shield catching the sun, covered in scales that appear like sharp slivers of amethyst stones. Ice-blue eyes pierce the water between us and I wither even more. But, she's not staring at me, she's looking at Isobel.

"Just because he came to her in form doesn't mean he's won. After all, *we* have her now," she says. "Even if Isobel did let her go too far."

A hiss rises from Isobel's throat. She swims to meet Kristeena's challenge so swiftly that I blinked and missed it—they now float face to face.

"She may be my ward, but I am not her keeper. I didn't *let* her do anything. She is her own Myr, or have you forgotten what the freedom to make mistakes tastes like after hiding for so long from the inevitable?" She looks her up and down with such menace that Kristeena's magic sparks in defense.

She bares her fangs, snapping her teeth at her. "Say that again, you wicked—"

Daniella chimes in, her voice always too bright, too cheery in moments like these. "Let's not argue, sisters, please. It doesn't become us." She raises her hands for peace as tension heats the sea. "It is a curse, after all. It's not as if there's a script for how each one of us might be impacted."

"*You* would say that," snaps Vasylina, narrowing her eyes and pointing a condemning finger.

"Yours didn't carry on like the rest of ours did," adds Miki with a wounded expression, taking her sister's hand.

Daniella flips her long, straight hair, unbothered. "It's not my fault that I ate my soulmate on my first encounter and was spared so many... side effects of prolonging dinner." She smirks.

Vasylina rips her hand away from Miki's, her magic gathering in her palms in a petrifying white mist; Daniella's glacial gaze sharpens with silver.

"That's enough," says Syrifina—everyone falls back in line, magic settling, heads tilted down.

"Apologies," they mumble.

Syrifina's crown glints like thinly honed blades ready to behead the unworthy. She considers each and every one of them.

The God of Shadow's words haunt me—I can't help but wonder what it would take for her to end one of us. If she'd ever really go that far...

Dark laughter echoes in my mind.

Syrifina turns her starfire gaze back upon me.

"Kristeena is right. It matters not if my maker came to you in form. *You* have disappointed me," she says; all my power seems to leach from me in shame. "How *dare* you speak of the frenzy in front of the others, for if you know of it—" Her gaze flicks to Isobel. "Then you should be well aware of the vital secret you hold."

She considers me with new interest.

"Something's different. Something's changed. What makes you act so recklessly before our coven, knowing surely there will be severe consequence?"

Jaspyr! He still lives. I must get back to him.

I press my lips together, using all the power within me to make sure my innermost voice can't be heard; I feel her prowling through my head.

"Do not fight me," she says with a frustrated groan. "You only make it worse for yourself."

Suddenly, an iridescent cage forms around me, trapping me like an animal.

I resist, but my magic just reverberates against the enchanted barrier uselessly.

My sisters' eyes glow silver—all except Isobel's—the weight of their magic keeping me in this inescapable, transparent box.

They surround me, pressing in on all sides; Mother floats above me, her fins and tail fanning out like a glorious god.

"Stop resisting, Eloise." She puckers her lips, hands on her hips. "Or shall I refer to you as the Kampaulo Killer?" I clench my teeth. "*Surrender.* Let me in."

Her voice is as seductive as Jaspyr's blood, the force of her magic unstoppable, pouring from her lips, pressing into me like shrinking walls.

'*Yes! Show her who you really are,*' commands the darkness.

"I won't," I say, shoving Jaspyr's name so far down that she would have to dig for years to uncover the open ending I left my frenzy in.

All the water drains from the cage with a suddenness that leaves me dizzy. I remain buoyant at its center.

Isobel cries out, "Mother, don't!"

"She's so disobedient. It's the only way she'll learn. You've been too soft on her."

It takes a few seconds for me to comprehend what's happened—the only time I've been fully exposed to air in this way is when I landwalk. But this feels… strange, abhorrent.

The sun is still awake. I do not change, and my tail and fins shrivel with too much exposure to this dry, unwelcoming atmosphere. "What are you doing?"

My voice comes out hoarse. My skin and scales start to tingle, fleck, burn, *scorch* as if someone has drowned me in acid.

"Mother, stop this, you'll kill her!" shouts Isobel, moving my other sisters away from the cage so that she can look me in the eyes while I…

Die? I'm dying, aren't I?

'*Yes,*' says Syrifina, '*you are. A myrmaid out of water during the day, whether or not the sun can reach you, is in just as much danger of death as she would be on land.*' She picks at her nails, the picture of boredom. '*The unsympathetic judgment of the Sun can come in many forms, I've learned over the centuries.*' She rolls her eyes.

That's when I realize—I'm screaming so loudly that all I can hear are my own thoughts. The fact that I don't actually burst into flames is somehow worse, for there's no visual substance to curse for the agony I'm in.

'*What is it you're hiding from me, darling? Then all of this can end.*'

The ending… of course. I must give her a grain of truth, as I did with Isobel, something she will be satisfied enough with to stop prying for more.

'*I just didn't want you to see how much I loved my human! I didn't want you to think me weak,*' I scream in agony. '*But it's over now. I killed him. I drank him dry. I ended my frenzy.*'

Syrifina sinks lower, her expression unreadable.

'*There's no such thing as love for a human,*' she seethes.

'*You have truly been infected.*'

'*I know. I am... was.*' I close my eyes, waiting for her striking blow that will snatch my immortal life back. But whatever makes this pain stop, I'm ready. '*Mercy, please!*'

"You killed him, on your own?" she asks.

"Yes!" I cry out without hesitation.

She sighs. "Well, why didn't you say that in the first place?" She claps her hands and the cage evaporates, water filling the space around me with a crash as my sisters scatter—I gasp in relief as my body quickly begins to heal. "That's some good news at least, isn't it, daughters?"

"Yes, fantastic," say Vasylina and Miki as one, dryly.

Isobel swims to me, stroking my back. "You're alright," she says, glaring at Mother as I shiver in her arms.

Syrifina ignores her, looking to me.

"And how do you feel, now that it's over?" I know she means the frenzy and not the fact that she nearly killed me.

My bones ache and my skin is still patching back together, but I muster the strongest voice I can. "I... I was plagued at first, but I finally feel... free." I force myself to be humble, to buy a little extra time on this earthly plane. "Though, I sincerely regret that my frenzied state might have put our coven in jeopardy. I truly am." And I am.

It is the first truth I have spoken to my sisters in so long that it tasted strange rolling off my tongue.

I dig my nails into my palms so hard that I wonder if I might bleed. Anything to keep my focus off Jaspyr, his beating heart, his divine blood. Anything to keep my secret from slipping—my magic surges like a blushing star that might give me away.

"I'm sorry, I'm... I can't seem to control anything at the moment." I shake my head, frustrated by this conversation, by the weakness I just exhibited in front of everyone, by him.

I lower my gaze from hers.

"Probably because you were almost just *burned alive*," hisses Isobel, glowering at her and still patting my back.

Syrifina's eyes travel to my hands, her brow furrowed as she concentrates on me, as if the words I've just said are still sinking in; I begin to shake with the effort.

"It's starting," she speaks, her expression saddened.

That's when I feel it, the moon beginning to rise—we all look up, all sensing it.

Goddesses do I need Jaspyr more than ever. I thirst for him, his body, his blood. My powers bubble beneath my skin in defiance of my thoughts, my words.

Syrifina swims toward me, resting a comforting hand upon my shoulder; Isobel stays glued to my side.

"This will be the hard part, darling. After killing the root of your frenzy, each moon you will crave them still."

She has no idea why I shiver, no idea why I can't utter a single word—and yet, I felt the tug of dryness in my throat. My mouth watering. *Go to him, go!*

"It will feel as if they still live," she offers me a small smile, "but knowing they are no longer attainable. Knowing that his blood is gone forever is your truest freedom, I assure you. It will take… time." Isobel growls, and the others shift uncomfortably. "Much time, yes, but I and your sisters will be here to help guide you, until you have your wits about you again."

As the thought of Jaspyr envelops my mind, all I can think of to say is, "How long?"

Syrifina lovingly moves my hair back behind my ears, tilting my chin up.

"For you, dear?" Her eyes glaze over. "I think it's best you stay put in Empress Isle until this terrible regime falls. Even your sisters are forbidden to landwalk now after all the trouble you caused."

Isobel shakes her head. "But that could be *centuries* for all the magic King Devlindor has hoarded. She'll go mad locked up here for that long." Her voice pitches, her magic blazing. "She's too young—"

Syrifina strikes her across the cheek so hard that I can see a silver-streaked handprint glow on her skin.

Isobel gapes at her, her hands cradling her face.

"Too young is right," says Syrifina, coldly; she turns her attention to me. "I shouldn't have let her out of my sight so soon, entrusted her to you." She ignores Isobel's wounded expression. "As long as she's safe here, that's all that matters in the end. She will have plenty of time in the future to swim freely." She pinches my cheek.

Centuries?

The God of Shadow's laugh rumbles in my ears.

'Oh, she's ever clever,' he coos, proudly. *'Syrifina is wise not to let you go. She senses lies better than anyone. She knows there's more you're not telling her.'*

My eyes widen. I wonder… *Could she know something more?*

He snickers again. *'Your story is increasingly delightful to watch.'*

Syrifina swims back to her throne, positioning herself to address everyone. To formalize my verdict, I realize. The princesses halt, tight-lipped, awaiting her statement.

Jaspyr, I think with a sinking sadness. I have condemned him to a surely worse fate if she ever uncovers he's still alive while I wait for release.

"You have all experienced your own devastating frenzies," she states.

I look to each of my sisters, the other princesses I had yet to confide in; I can see their own stories written across their darkened, saddened, sallow expressions. They say nothing, eyes darting away from mine.

"I had hoped we could avoid another catastrophe this

time, but Eloise has been plagued by the same wretched sickness that haunts all in my direct bloodline." She brings a hand to rest over her chest, frowning.

"The Kampaulo Killer," Daniella whispers with an approving smirk on her lips. "I quite like the title." She winks at me, her blue eyes dazzling in a way only the sky and water combined could achieve.

I mouth, "Thank you," utterly grateful for her support.

The weight of Syrifina's gaze lands on me. The water around her becomes a rage of color, as if her lifeblood had sparked outside of her body in dangerous, vivid strands of magic. Her eyes flash a silver so bright that I think two moons have replaced her pupils.

"This is serious," she says, drawing out each syllable. Her voice wholly surrounds us. "With King Devlindor's shadows spying in every part of the world, it's only a matter of time before word of something amiss gets back to Saindora." Her power ripples around her. "We cannot alert him to our existence."

A sinking feeling weighs heavy in the pit of my stomach, threatening to pull me down.

"I have never, in all my years, seen such savagery from one of our kind," she continues, "not since myself and the High Queen. And not since Zahra's reign." My sisters murmur a blur of opinions, some voicing their support and some their disappointment; Zahra remains silent. "You have left these shores, from the seas to the land, so *close* to our home, in disarray... in a matter of months!"

"Impressive," mutters Vasylina, crossing her arms, a permanent scowl lining her face.

I look away, focusing on my hands. I can almost see the blood shimmering there, stained forever.

"I know," I force from my lips. "I'm sorry."

"An apology is not a solution!" Her words reverberate

sharply. She presses forward from her throne. "I do not care about the bloodshed. If anything, I'm captivated." She laughs something wicked—I realize then that the Moon and Sea had cast boundaries on our powers for a reason. "But you have acted carelessly in an unforgiving era to our kind, maybe the *most* unforgiving and dangerous era for Myrs yet."

She sucks on her teeth.

"King Devlindor is hunting all enchanted creatures, even more ferociously than you have sought to hunt everyone else. And that will include *us*... should he ever come to realize just how great our power truly is." She shakes her head at me. "I prefer to always grant a choice, but you've taken liberty much too far. Why, your own sister had to drag you back red-handed!"

Isobel looks away.

Syrifina pauses, collecting herself, her magic settling back to a normal state of terrifying.

"So, this is what shall happen from here forward. You, Eloise Myr, *will* remain here until I deem you fit enough to swim these seas again on your own, and you'll not taste the sweetness of human blood until that human king is ash and bone." Her eyes narrow with the powerful promise, her words like fire coral being forced down my throat; they dart to Isobel. "Your eldest sister will also remain close to Empress Isle, to make sure your sentence is carried out to the fullest extent and keep you company, no doubt."

The twins and Kristeena snicker with delight; most of the others just looked stunned, their expressions pitying us.

Isobel begins to protest, "But, Mother, I didn't—"

"And should any of you even *think* to carry her blood against my will, you too shall join her." Her gaze burns into Isobel, whose lips set in a firm line.

Syrifina holds it until Isobel bows in submission.

"Good," she says, releasing her hold on her. "Eloise will

swim alongside us before long, and anyone is free to visit her at any time." She glances over the other princesses. "If your other sisters inquire any further about the frenzy, I want to know at once. And spread the word… during this regime, the punishment for overdrinking will not be lenient."

I purse my lips, unwilling to show any type of reaction, accepting my fate with as much dignity as I can muster at this point. But inside, I'm screaming, pleading for her to take back her command.

A cold tear betrays my confident exterior; Syrifina doesn't miss it.

She softens with such a suddenness that it startles me, her expression so warm and light that my lifeblood nearly freezes over in fear.

"My child, essence of my essence, it pains me to see you suffer so. It does… but one day, long from now, you *will* thank me for what's to come." She nods to herself, then turns her attention back to the others. "Isn't that right, darlings? We have forever to adjust."

"Yes, Mother," they say as a unit.

She blows me a kiss from her throne; it lands soft and damning on my cheek, her verdict sealed.

Above, we all sense the moon take front and center.

Syrifina beams. "The night has finally fallen. Let's move forward now and put this unfortunate business behind us."

WE FOLLOW SYRIFINA back into the main area and upward into the core swim-through—the Crystal Castle ends as it began, with a vast opening at the topmost part that leads to yet another cavern, except this one is out of the water.

We press through to the surface, a crisp nighttime breeze greeting us; I shiver, never wanting to feel the air on my skin again, wanting to sink back beneath. I can hardly stomach it after what Mother did to me.

But the view steals my focus away from that painfully fresh memory. I soak it in.

A vast cavern that matches the size of the most spacious of foyers in the palace below expands around us. The top of it was surely carved out by the hand of the God of Earth to let the sky pour in, appearing like Syrifina's crown flipped upside down. Garlands of ivy curl around the dripping stalactites, and waterfalls of vines spill over the sides of the large opening.

This is where we normally come to gather beneath the full moon once a month, to bask in its empowering light.

Tonight, the moon is a plump but waning bulb that sits directly above us. Starlight sprinkles down alongside it from beneath wispy clouds, refracting off the treasures that lay scattered about the dry areas. Large, jutting stones create a cozy texture in the space where we often lounge, and the earth here is softened with deep colors, dusted in bronze.

Bright orange and springy green flowers poke their heads out from random pockets on the floors and walls, intertwining themselves between the cavern rock, treasures, and skeletons.

And the walls of the cave, a glittering dark blue, make me feel as if I have surfaced in the inside of a grand sapphire jewel. This is home, the only place I ever need landwalk.

Just a beautiful, wide-open space decorated in gold and bone.

One by one, my sisters elegantly climb out of the water,

transforming into extraordinary women under the moonlight—this is the only piece of land that Syrifina has encouraged us to enjoy the human form on, and I'm thankful that the privilege wasn't stolen away from them because of my poor choices.

They eagerly explore our sacred space, claiming their favored rocks to perch upon or settling near small pockets of fresh water. Some remain right at the edge next to me, their tails swishing back and forth beneath the surface.

Daniella climbs out, her azure tail transforming to legs, a soft, sky-blue lifeblood wrapping around them—she holds out her hand.

I move to take it, but Syrifina catches my arm.

"Not you," she says. "Take a good look at our gathering chamber, for it could be much changed the next time you lay eyes on it."

Daniella grimaces. "Sorry," she mouths, dropping her hand to her side.

I shake my head and offer her the best smile I can. "It's not your fault."

"Are you not joining us, Mother?" ask Vasylina and Miki together, sucking up to her in one smooth breath. They pout their lips at her from the same tiered rock they always claim.

"No, my loves," she says. "I must go and address the others first." She gazes at the moon longingly. "I fear I may have frightened them off from swimming back here without my invitation. I'll call them so I can make a formal announcement about Eloise."

"Are we free to go?" asks Zahra, carefully.

The others murmur, wondering the same.

Syrifina nods. "I think so, yes. But we'll stay together here for a short time while I assess the situation in Kampaulo. And no one is permitted to hunt near those shores again in this king's lifetime."

Zahra bows her head, the others following suit.

Syrifina turns to Isobel, who has not let go of my hand since the moment Mother tried to burn me into submission.

"Don't mess this up this time," Syrifina warns in a low voice. "Not for your sister. This is what's best for her." She releases my arm, drawing me into her bosom so that Isobel is forced to let go; I tense in her hold. "At least Eloise was strong enough to do what needed to be done with her frenzy and not require my intervention." She kisses the top of my head, then cuts a glare again at Isobel. "The least *you* can do is ensure she recovers."

Isobel seems taken aback by her words, blinking several times at Mother. Then her expression returns to her normal sweetly cruel state.

"Locking her away until the human king bent on cheating Death finally dies is hardly what I would call an effective rehabilitation," she replies. "That much time in solitude will break her and you know it."

"I know no such thing," Syrifina snaps, the water bubbling. "But you can stay confined with her, if you keep this attitude up." Isobel's magic crackles atop her skin; Syrifina looks to the other princesses, softening her tone. "I expect that each one of you will pay Eloise visits with frequency to ensure she keeps her sanity. We must look out for each other."

Isobel rolls her eyes, crossing her arms at her chest. "How benevolent."

"Roll your eyes again at me, child, and I will pluck them from their sockets." Isobel immediately wipes the smugness off her face; Syrifina smiles. "This is for her own good." She points at herself. "I know what's best for her, for *all* of you. I will assess her well-being periodically and make adjustments to her sentencing as needed." She looks at me, stone-faced. "But for now, your life is tied to King Devlindor's."

I offer a meek nod, nothing left to do but accept my fate.

"Then may he perish swiftly," I say through gritted teeth.

She grins at me. "To the Goddess we pray."

She barely glances at Isobel, her tone brisk. "You know what to do. Escort her to the fasting hollow, and I'll meet you both there later to help her... settle in."

Isobel bristles but nods. "Yes, Mother."

Syrifina blows a kiss to all of us, and we each blow one back.

"See you soon," she says before sinking below the water's surface, leaving me in my sisters' care.

I loose a sigh of relief, feeling like a weight has been lifted off me with her foreboding presence gone. Then the princesses surround me.

"Your relief is misplaced," says Zahra, tapping the small, smooth bone that forever hangs around her neck.

"Don't worry," says Kristeena, offering me a pained smile. "After a while, you just sort of... sleep. That's the only way the time passes quickly."

I frown—the last time I slept, two weeks drifted by in the blink of an eye. What if I shut my eyes and wake to find Jaspyr has long since died?

I shudder to think it, vowing to stay awake for as long as possible, to find a way out of this before that happens.

"Yes, and she'll probably let you out early anyways. She's a fool for good behavior," says Daniella.

"Is that why you're always batting your eyes at her, then?" says Isobel, cruelly.

Daniella sticks her tongue out at her.

I see Isobel begin to roll her eyes, but Mother's warning clearly stops her.

"I'll be fine," I say, looking to Isobel, squeezing her hand.

"Do you want us to come with you?" asks Miki, a lethal smile on her lips.

"Yes, we could help tuck you in for the night… or a hundred thousand," adds Vasylina with a laugh.

The quick calculation staggers me, and it's probably not even close to how many nights locked away lie ahead—on which one of those nights will Jaspyr take his last breath somewhere up above?

I can hardly stomach the thought, my mind racing, searching for an out that isn't there; I'm so overwhelmed by the thought of a permanent separation that I can't even stand up for myself.

Kristeena snaps her teeth at Vasylina.

"Have some tact," she says, glowering at her. "It's much too soon to make light of this. You remember, don't you?"

"How could we forget?" they say together—and I wonder at their frenzy. Had it been a shared affair?

"Then act like it and show some decorum," snarls Isobel, moving in front of me; I focus on her golden hair, too humiliated to look at anyone's face anymore. "I will escort her to where she needs to go. And if you so much as do anything to make this process harder for her, *I promise* that your punishment will be much crueler than Eloise's. Am I understood?"

The twins go still, bowing to their elder without a hint of defiance in their expressions, fear glimmering in their eyes.

"Yes, Isobel." They have the decency to look ashamed as they address me again. "We're sorry, Eloise."

I nod to them, wanting to appear strong. "It's alright," I say. "I know you didn't mean it."

An awkward silence spreads through the cavern.

Isobel sighs, looking back at me. "Well, there's no use stalling. Come on. Let's get this over with."

Only Zahra spares words of comfort before we part ways. "At least you had a taste," she says, eyes cast down; the sentiment is lost on me, only making me realize how agonizing starvation will be, let alone never tasting Jaspyr again. "I wish…" Her voice dies away.

"I'm not sure it's better knowing," I reply, gently, the haunted look in her expression making my stomach twist—another lie. I would rather die than not have known the taste of absolute perfection.

Isobel takes my hand and dips below the surface before anyone else can say anything. Reluctantly, I descend alongside her as the princesses wave me off with somber smiles.

I keep my eyes pinned to my sister's back, her spine a rippling wave of crimson. I don't want to take stock of what I'm leaving behind. I don't want to get nostalgic about all the things I'll miss as she leads me through the Crystal Castle, to the darkest depths of Empress Isle where I know insatiable myrmaids before me have withered away until their minds were set right again—if I weren't certain Mother would catch me, I would rip my hand from Isobel's now and try to escape to somewhere on the other side of the ocean.

'*Don't even think about it,*' Syrifina whispers to me from another crevice in the palace. And so, I push the thought away.

As we cross the main foyer and navigate through lesser-traveled tunnels, we pass through a forgotten coral garden decorated with statues that rarely get visited. I always thought them a bit poorly designed, faces twisted in anguish, tails and arms bent at odd angles, as if experiencing a fright. Not like the ones we praise in the grand chamber, where our kind are depicted dancing or singing with joy.

I linger before the one in the middle, tugging at Isobel to slow. The pearl-like statue appears to capture a raw moment frozen in time, her arm reaching upward, her tail and fins fanned out as if she wishes to swim but is being held back; it jogs a memory that I can't quite place.

"Which one of our sisters created this one?" I ask. "It's so… sad."

"I don't know," she replies, tilting her head, as if she'd

never quite thought about it before.

I move closer, noting the intricate detail of the myrmaid's scales and fins, her face...

My hand flies over my mouth, tears threatening to fall—there's an unmistakable flicker of silver glinting in her eyes.

I lean in, blinking a few times to make sure I'm certain; the silver sheen remains, just a tiny trace of the normally bright magic a myrmaid boasts.

'*Hello?*' I send out into the void between us.

I don't want to hear it, but I swear the voice of a stranger enters my mind just then, in the form of a weak but desperate song. '*I am here. I am Lorinara. Please... don't leave me, sister. Don't forget me. I've been waiting for so long.*' Her words are filled with so much pain and loneliness, a sense of longing I've only ever known for one person, spun in the ancient language of our kind.

"Do you hear that?" I ask Isobel, mouth agape, pointing to it—my tears finally begin to fall.

She goes very still, focusing on the statue. Then her eyes widen, darting back and forth, as if checking to see if we are truly alone.

I gasp. "You did! You heard a voice. Didn't you? The statue, it... she..." I swallow. "She said her name is Lorinara."

"Keep your voice down," Isobel whispers. "You're in enough trouble as it is." Then she shakes her head, looking back up at the statue; her expression is twisted with as much confusion as I feel. "No... no, I don't hear anything." She takes my hand to lead me away. "And even if I did, I wouldn't be foolish enough to say it aloud."

A chill rolls down my spine; I feel the God of Shadow grin.

'*Unspeakable things...*' he croons to my soul. '*How lucky you must feel that Syrifina loves you so.*'

47

FREEDOM

FROM THE ARCHIVES OF
SYRIFINA MYR: *GOLDEN RULE*

DARLING DIARY,

It's been a century since you last felt my touch. I wish you could offer me advice… for all the wisdom you must carry after an endless time together.

I lied last time. The frenzy hasn't gone—I am the frenzy, I believe. I'm the curse the God of Shadow warned of.

As he promised, I shall carry on always with my soulmate's ghost in my eyes. And no matter how many daughters I create, no matter how large my family blossoms, I still feel alone.

I can't help but wonder if I made a mistake so long ago. Maybe I would've had a lifetime of true ease and happiness if I hadn't been so afraid to share my empire with another. Maybe, if I had let Queen Julissa live alongside me, there would be no more frenzies to speak of at all.

I wonder at that sometimes…

Had I been tricked? Did I hold an opportunity to come

out the other side of it with everything and more?

But, certainly, no. Not with the God of Shadow in control from my very first taste of life eternal... right? He poisoned that drink of mine, with a revenge all his own.

It spreads through my direct line like a raging wildfire, one that still often flames intense cravings for my own lost love, to my utmost despair.

Yes, darling, you read that true—I loved every moment with Queen Julissa.

Each second we spent together, every taste of her, body and soul, that she offered me, I never took for granted. It was beautiful and dark, and I'll cherish those memories forever; they'll last me an eternity, surely. They must!

But memories will never be enough to satisfy my lust.

My longing for her returns so strongly at times that I imagine her heart is still beating somewhere far off. It sings to me in my thoughts. I can hardly concentrate for how hungry I grow for her still—like clockwork—each and every blood moon.

However, I write to you not about me but on behalf of my ill-fated daughters...

In the Queen's name, I'll continue doing all in my power to keep this disease from destroying my young princesses; it hunts them down, one by one, like a hungry, shadow-fed hound.

Even if it means locking them away for their own good or severing their ties to the mortal earth, I'll spare them any way I'm able to. I will not let their frenzies fester and grow! I won't let them experience such a gaping sore, for their immortal lives, like the Queen left on my soul.

If I must intervene, I shall without remorse nor hesitation. They won't even have the knowledge of the sacrifices I make for them. The God of Shadow's curse will be mine to suffer alone, for I promised my daughters a life full of freedom and *that's what they shall know.*

Freedom from Death.

Freedom from men.

Freedom from want.

Freedom from love.

I know I can't shelter my kin from their frenzies once they spark, but I pray they'll endure less sorrow than I did. That it won't be permitted to spread so far—I would just hate for any of them to experience the pain of knowing such love at all, to lose all control like I lost with Queen Julissa. Especially when there's no hope of holding onto it, not for a Myr and a human.

It's the Golden Rule, and the frenzy seeks to break it. But I won't let it ever get that far. I refuse to lose another daughter to an inconsequential sack of flesh and blood.

Curse the God of Shadow and his blasphemous mind! He's constantly goading me, laughing at my agony. But I'll spend an eternity searching for an end to this.

Until then, I'll ease my children's suffering the best I can.

Oh, darling Diary, believe me when I write to you that to have loved and lost is more tormenting than a world without moonlight. I wouldn't wish it upon anyone.

It's better to have never loved at all. To have never known what could've been. Trust me, I should know.

And I tortured the imprudent man who spread such a nonsensical lie in the mortal realm, that the idea of love should be cast the other way around. That it's worth the risk of everything and more.

Just sinful, I can hardly bear to think it! Even I have more tact with my wicked tongue—he clearly had never met and destroyed his soulmate before and had no business to speak his mind at all.

I, on the other hand, know the torture that awaits those who fall for such a trap.

I'm forever cursed by love, held captive always by recollections of a mortal queen long gone from this world.

I will never be free of her, and a life without freedom is no life at all…

I live for my daughters now.

Yours eternally,
Syrifina Myr

PART FIVE

48

TRUTH

1 PLUCK A DIAMOND from the floor and etch the 1095th mark into the crystal wall of my cage. Exactly three years have come and gone. My skin prickles, my power mounts—another blood moon is on the rise tonight.

I pick the cobwebs from my mind and home in on those strands of new energy, letting them fill my dried-up veins with much-needed life, connecting me back to nature and to myself. Or the self I could've been... had it not been for him.

Some days I actually *wish* I had never tasted him at all for how badly I want him now. But is it the frenzy returned? Or is it true, undying love manifested in its absence?

I like to think the latter. I have to, because if I consider the alternative, then Jaspyr, my soulmate, is somewhere up above experiencing the same misery as I am—forced to live each day without me, wondering if we might ever meet again, missing me to the point of unfathomable pain... all because I cursed him.

I stare at the tally marks on the wall, the sum of my life

since Jaspyr and I were torn apart; I try not to focus on the unbearable dryness in my throat, like I swallowed all the sand in Saindora. Nor the empty, aching, hungry throb in my bones that pulses with each passing minute since I felt the sun drop below the horizon.

Three years I have lasted, existed, in this torturous solitude. But tonight, the blood moon emerging screams at me to resist. Like the others before it, its energy floods me with new power and renews my desperate desire to escape. This time, I latch onto it.

To swim, to sing, to feed! To dance with the moonlight and sail with the waves—these are the things I was meant for, *promised.* Not this life of solitude.

I'm wasting away...

And if I don't taste his blood again soon, I fear I might never recover.

I grip the thick bars of my prison and test them for the thousandth time, attempting to pull them apart with all my strength; they don't budge an inch.

I try to obliterate them with every ounce of magic I can tap into. It skitters atop my skin like lightning; the beautiful, rose-colored sea glass seems to absorb every bit of me, glowing silver and gold for a mocking moment before going cold and dark again.

I whip my tail at the stubborn bars with a roar of frustration, then swim to the opposite side of my cell to glower at them; they seem to glower back.

The crystal cage remains resilient, not even a crack to show in response to my strength, despite my blood moon boost.

I'm tired. So tired... But, I force myself to remain awake.

"You're foolish for being hopeful again, Eloise," I mutter to myself, crossing my arms at my chest.

I've tried everything to escape. Nothing works!

The entire chamber is lined with a suspicious onyx trim—

I've long since known Syrifina must've enchanted it to hold the sea glass intact, for how else could this chamber withstand all the fury and rage of a trapped myrmaid?

I look at my hands and let out a sob. "What's the point of all this power if I can't use it to save my own life?" I ask the silent waters around me.

For all the magic thrumming through me tonight, itching for release, I prove useless over and over.

"Let me out!" I scream to no one, nothing—my voice clangs between the walls, then fades away into the quiet depths of the Crystal Castle. If anyone hears me, they probably think that I'm just another wailing ghost of a human yet to pass on, whose bones were left to rot down here with me.

Kristeena said I would pass the time in sleep, but I've counted every minute, every agonizing day, ensuring that I stay awake, wondering if Jaspyr still breathes—I loathe that I love him still, but the idea that I might see him again is the only thing that keeps me sane.

Anxiety grips me as the moon climbs higher, tugging at me to break the surface and lay eyes upon her. *Him.*

Memories of our last moments together flood my mind. I'm devastated beyond measure that I can't go to him now.

Did he even live to see the morning, this time three years ago?

As usual, I push that thought as far away as it will go, assuring myself that I'll feel it in my soul, the exact moment Jaspyr leaves the mortal world.

I shove off the wall with an animalistic howl and swim back and forth, trying to expel some of my energy that only seems to mount.

Just keep swimming, I think as Time threatens to break me. *Put your mind anywhere else than on what you can't have. There's a way out of this, Eloise. You just can't see it yet.*

'*No there's not*,' someone whispers with a cruel laugh—

but I've gotten good at ignoring him. I just have to focus on my voice, my thoughts.

If there is a blood moon tonight, I think, eagerly, *then the full moon gathering must be happening soon. Maybe, one of my sisters will come to greet me.*

With any hope…

I miss them almost as much as Jaspyr these days.

Isobel, Daniella, and Kristeena visit the most often out of all the princesses. They come with stories and distractions that I might have already gone mad without. But 'often' for a myrmaid is about as frequent as the monthly gatherings.

The twins occasionally swim by, too, but their company is about as pleasant as this cage. They sing of the increasingly terrible state of Olleb-Yelfra, and they won't cease to remind me that King Devlindor's life is sure to make a lasting impression on this earth.

Zahra has yet to visit, but I don't blame her. She's never been very social, and I think she sees too much of her past in my present suffering—how I will endeavor to establish such control and poise as her one day, if I ever get the opportunity.

The other princesses trickle by, less and less, with nothing more than pity in their expressions and empty words of comfort that I know will someday surely cease. And my sisters not of royal descent aren't permitted here at all, in this part of the Crystal Castle where their music doesn't reach.

Soon, they'll all forget me, I realize, thinking of Lorinara.

Sometimes, I wonder if her song was even real or if my mind had already broken by the time Syrifina locked me in here. I imagine a lot these days…

No, I didn't imagine it! I'm certain Isobel heard her, too.

The mournful note of that voice still echoes in my mind.

Had she rotted away in this very fasting chamber long ago, before she was turned into palace décor?

I shake my head, focusing on the gentle flip of my tail, on

anything other than the haunting mystery of Lorinara.

At least this cage is sizable, large enough that I can move from one end to the other and feel as if I have traveled.

I round a corner stacked with bones that I arranged to appear like the ashen coral reef of the deep. Then I pass perfectly stacked, vast piles of human treasures; I spent the first year separating them by color—silvers, golds, and a rainbow assortment of gemstones now stand segregated from one another.

I smile and gently wave at them as I float past, pretending as if they're friendly fish; I rue the day I finally break and begin to talk to them about my woes.

I pluck a ruby the size of my fist from a pile of sparkling red treasure and bask in its splendor—in the memory of being Jaspyr's intended for a single, beautiful night.

I close my eyes, wondering why we hadn't danced more when we had the chance. *How foolish of us…*

Power seizes me again as the moon is fully swept into the shadows, its transformation complete—I feel it as the blood moon takes front and center in the sky. I curl my fingers over the ruby and squeeze, my fist shaking, my muscles rigid; I open my eyes to watch it melt, a gleaming crimson, atop the pile. It takes all my mental energy not to taste it, to focus on reality and not let my imagination and hunger sweep me away.

Then I bitterly think, *It looks more like paint than blood anyway.*

Oh, what I would give to be seated in Jaspyr's workshop, watching him paint, waiting for my turn to be stroked by those careful hands.

"Eloise…" A voice reaches out to me from somewhere beyond.

I have to blink several times to focus; I hadn't realized I was crying, drifting away again into my thoughts.

I swim to the bars to meet the bright flame floating toward me out of the dark.

"Isobel," I say, my voice a raspy version of what it once was—goddesses, I barely recognize it now. "I... I didn't think anyone would come tonight, since it's the blood moon. I'm glad you found the time." I force a smile but she doesn't return it—I don't think she could if she wanted to.

Her perfect face is marred with something wrath-like, her lifeblood an extraordinary bright red like the melted ruby.

I tilt my head, my lips turning downward. I want to reach out to her, but the space is too tight for me to squeeze through more than my fingers. "What's the matter, sister?"

She shakes her head, stoic, her golden hair fluttering out behind her in a train.

"Move back" is all she says, the words barely passing her lips; her irises explode with silver.

Her fists close around the bars; I swim as far away as I can get

I barely have time to cover my eyes and shield them from the blast of power that erupts out of her in the next second. It sweeps through my prison without mercy, the bones and jewels I painstakingly organized now in disarray.

"Stop!" I yell, cowering in a corner. "What are you doing?"

When everything settles, I freeze in surprise—the bars I thought impenetrable were apparently no match for the fire raging in my eldest sister tonight.

A bright purple magicked flame finishes licking at the crystal bars, melting through them like lava. They scorch and burn, disintegrating into nothing. And I'm reminded once again of just how young I am.

"Are you out of your mind?" I stutter, mouth agape.

"*Are you?*" she retorts, reaching out to me. "Hurry, let's go!"

"Syrifina will..." My mind struggles to catch up with my mouth. "Why, she'll destroy you if she finds out you tried to free me." I can hardly comprehend the position she's put her-self in; I look to her hand and shake my head. "No, I can't let you do this, Isobel. You've sacrificed enough for me as it is."

"Oh, for the Sea's sake!" she snaps, glaring at me, that fire in her still raging hot. "Don't be such a child, Eloise. There isn't time enough." I don't budge, not sure that I can.

She floats toward me on a flaming tail.

"What do you intend to do, huh? Remain with your back against the wall while you stare freedom in the eyes forever-more?" She gestures to where the bars used to be, her voice shaking with anger that I didn't quite understand. "Your cage is open, so cut the martyr act and move your bloody tail! I won't let you rot in here a second longer."

I sigh, bubbles blurring my vision. When they clear, it's as if I stare upon Isobel for the first time, the sister who basically taught me everything of this world. "Why didn't you tell me your plan?" I choke out. "I never thought—"

"Because to even *think it* meant Mother might see and stop me. I had to bide my time, choose a night where she's distracted so that you might have a chance to get away. And I needed to wait for a blood moon, to have the strength enough to get through her magic." She grits her teeth at me, pointing to the gaping hole in my prison. "Now, stop wasting precious time. The stars have aligned for you, just as I knew they would. We have to go, now!"

She grabs me by the wrist and pulls me through the siz-zling opening into the dark labyrinth beyond.

The relief I feel is immeasurable—I look back, stunned, taking stock of just how small my prison truly was. Then I swiftly turn away, praying to never lay eyes upon the fasting chamber again.

I smack my lips, my mind homing in on one thing now that I can swim free. "Isobel, I need blood."

"If we escape unseen, you can feed all you want," she says,

her gaze darting around the corner. "But first, we have to get out of here. Come on, it's clear. Everyone is still distracted by the gathering ceremonies. Mother is currently accepting gifts from *every* daughter."

"For what?" I ask, raising an eyebrow.

She rolls her eyes.

"It's the death anniversary for when she killed her pirate. She makes us celebrate every two decades or so. You haven't been a Myr long enough to know, but this is the chance I was waiting for."

My mouth forms an 'O'.

"*Let's go,*" she pushes on. "We have to hurry. They'll notice I'm missing soon enough."

She pulls me alongside her with the flick of her powerful tail. Her grasp on me is so tight, her expression so focused, that I have the sickening feeling there's something she's withholding; we weave in and out of the quiet channels of the Crystal Castle in silence.

Fear grips me as we pass the coral garden of forgotten statues and edge closer to the more common areas. I yank on her wrist, forcing her to stop. I need a moment to collect my thoughts, to comprehend what we're doing.

'*Escape while you can. Go to him,*' a voice urges—I recognize the soft wisp of Lorinara's song.

A shiver rolls down my spine. I steady my words.

"What aren't you telling me, Isobel?" I ask in a hushed voice. "I know you're hiding something. Why do you seem so distraught beyond this reckless plan of yours? You're acting too strange not to take notice."

She lets go of my hand, then slowly turns toward me, her gaze resting on the statue of Lorinara—silent, crimson tears streak her cheeks.

"I lied before. I heard her, too..." she says in a whisper, looking down. "And I've heard her many times before. I hear her even now, our sister. Her song is more forceful than the others."

Others?

I float backward, staggered, slowly noting the rest of the statues here. "No, it can't be true."

She nods. "That's what I told myself for a long time, until you forced me to listen. Now, I can't seem to hear anything but their cries for justice." Her gaze burns into mine. "I am *not* the firstborn," she states, gravely. She gestures to the statues. "Who knows how many came before me. How many lost everything so Mother could try and contain the spread of the frenzy." I shake my head. *I won't believe this. The God of Shadow is a liar.* "It's the only explanation! We are the lucky ones."

She swims closer to Lorinara, unblinking as she holds her silver-lined gaze.

"I didn't want to consider it," she adds. "I would've kept ignoring their cries for lifetimes to come…" She glances over her shoulder with a pained expression. "Ignored you."

I swallow the lump in my throat.

"I would've come to accept your punishment, too, Eloise. For I trust…" She clears her throat. "I trusted Syrifina above all else—"

"What changed your mind?" I force myself to ask, though I'm afraid to know the answer.

She shakes her head, shame wrinkling her features. "The truth."

She looks toward the sea sky, staring directly at the swim-through that would take us up to the surface where Syrifina held the gathering now; it was also the last place I laid eyes on her.

"Something she said that day," she continues, "right before we took you here…" Her voice falters. "I just couldn't get it out of my mind, and then I understood—"

She stifles a sob, her hand covering her mouth.

"What was it?" I reach out to her with a comforting hand. "You can tell me anything."

She bows her head, fists balled, shrugging away the gesture.

"It was her," she hisses. "*Mother* is responsible for the death of my soulmate. And all the time, I thought it was my fau—"

Isobel looks to her hands, as if she can still see his blood staining her palms. Her voice ebbs into a cry, and her magic blooms around her with the same ferocity glowing in her eyes.

"What are you talking about—?"

She whips around to look at me.

"I'm *saying* that Syrifina was the one who stabbed him on the beach, not some human in a random assault! I know it was her. Even the shadows whisper affirmation." Her magic flares, the water around us heating to an uncomfortable degree. "She ran him through with a dagger to trick me into thinking it was coincidental, then left him on the beach where I'd be drawn to him as soon as night fell. I wasn't strong enough to do anything but feed on what was left of him. He deserved so much more!"

"But how do you know?" I ask, trying to follow.

She bares her teeth, her voice shifting into a growl. "Because the last thing Syrifina said to me before I escorted you to the fasting chamber was that at least *your* frenzy"—she points a condemning finger at me—"didn't require her *intervention.*"

I float a little back as my mind catches up—if what Isobel says is true, it's absolutely unforgiveable. I don't care if a myrmaid's frenzy has the potential to end the world. I would destroy *anyone* who took Jaspyr's life, even if it were my own sister.

"I'm so sorry—"

"Don't." She snorts, and I swear I see steam blow from her nose. "I just *knew* I recognized the weapon from Syrifina's pirate ship, but I didn't want to even imagine she was capable of such a monstrosity against her own kin." She wraps her arms around herself. "I wasn't ready to let him go, so she forced my hand. Just like she probably turned Lorinara and countless before her into… *this*—"

"To keep them from the world above," I finish. *Just like she caged me.*

"What other reason would she have? To imprison them here?" Isobel pauses a moment, taking in the statues. Then a tortured wail rips from her throat. The sound is so horrific that it threatens to break me and give away our escape plan, a myrmaid's mournful song.

I pull her into my chest, muffling her scream against my skin even though it burns through me.

"Hush now," I say, trying to wrap my head around all of this. "Someone will hear. You have to be quiet, Isobel. We have to get free of this place, like you said, or what you did will have all been for nothing."

The sound stops, the palace growing eerily silent.

She looks me in the eye, her lips quivering, ever childlike.

"It was too much blood," she mumbles. "Mother knew—" She covers her mouth with her hand to hold in another sob. "I couldn't stop… I couldn't stop…"

"You weren't ready to kill him, but you couldn't stop feeding," I say, trying to help her along. "I understand. I do."

She shakes her head, fervently.

"*No*, I wasn't ready to kill him, because I… I loved him, Eloise." She blinks away her tears of shock, and I try to keep from gaping; it must be the first time she's ever admitted such a thing aloud. "I didn't want it to end. I wasn't ready."

Isobel's frenzy had, surprisingly, unraveled quite like my

own, except hers culminated with Syrifina's gruesome and un-welcome intervention; I empathize greatly, but part of me wonders what Isobel might have done had she found Jaspyr alive on that night three years ago...

Thank the goddesses I tricked her. And Mother, too.

'*A centuries-long imprisonment is an effective way to out-live a human, is it not?*' coaxes the God of Shadow. '*Syrifina has gotten more subtle, more creative over time with how she handles her daughters' downfalls.*'

The shadows seem to roll around me in amusement.

'*She knows?*'

'*Of course she knows.*' He smiles. '*She knows everything about you, including where you are right this second.*'

'*Yet again you prove quite the impressive fool to think she didn't,*' the haughty Moon chimes in. '*You're too young to hide anything in your mind from your creator.*'

'*From any of us,*' sings the Sea, solemnly.

"You see, don't you now?" says Isobel, noting my terror-stricken face.

"We have to go," I utter, barely able to speak.

She swims back and forth, unfocused, lost again to her grief.

"I don't trust a thing she says anymore, and I won't let her snatch your life away just because you got a little swept up in your frenzied feeds..." She points to Lorinara. "And Mother's the root of all this cursed nonsense, mind you. *We* didn't ask to be infected by her revenge! We don't deserve to be turned into statues or locked away, or *forced to kill* our soulmates be-cause of her mistakes."

"Isobel, we need to go," I say more forcefully—have the waters here turned too silent, too still, as if waiting for some-thing to happen?

"No, she doesn't get to decide what's best for us—"

"Isobel!" I rush up to her and clutch her wrist, making her

stop before me. "We have to go, now," I implore. "Syrifina knows I lied to her."

I swallow, nervously glancing all around as if she might emerge out of any darkened corner.

Isobel raises an eyebrow. "Lied about what?"

"Jaspyr," I blurt out, guilt coiling in my chest—I must tell her the truth after all she has confided in me, after all she's risked. "He still lives. I didn't kill him that night on the tower. I lied to you, Isobel."

She rips her hand away. "You *what?*"

"I thought I could... *I don't know!*" The truth explodes out of my mouth the way she blasted me out of that cage. "I tried to beat it. I tricked you into thinking he was dead. I thought I could outsmart the God of Shadow, this blasted curse, *you*, Mother! I wanted to see him again."

"But how?" she asks, her lips pursed in skepticism. "I saw him lying there dead."

I shake my head. "What you saw was me trying to save his life. I drank nearly every drop of him in the moments before you found us. I could hardly stop, but I *did*. And I'm certain he still lives." The hope those words give me is unmatched by anything. "He has to, and I have to get back to him before Mother finds him first."

She opens her mouth to question me, but I cut her off.

"She knows the truth! She read it in my mind all those years ago." I gesture toward her chamber. "That's why her punishment was so severe, because she wanted to let my frenzy die off *and* torture me for thinking I could fool her."

I know what she will say before she speaks it: "*Naive*," we say as one; hers a remorseful tone, mine a sardonic one.

"I understand," I say, taking her palm again and looking into her eyes. "But what's done is done." I kiss the back of her hand. "Please forgive me. I was only trying to save the life of... the one I love."

Her expression flickers between sadness and pain.

"You needn't ask my forgiveness," she says, lowering her gaze. "You did the right thing." And I know, *I just know*, that Isobel would have forced my hand upon Jaspyr, just as Syrifina had done to her, had she found him still breathing on that night long ago.

"It's an impossible situation," I mumble, trying not to let that thought break me. "But, Isobel, I have a chance to be with my soulmate again." I look to the surface. "I'm sure he waits for me to return, and I'd rather die in his arms than down here alone by Mother's hand. Will you help me get back to him?"

I don't tell her that, if what the shadows speak is true, Syrifina is aware of our current movements.

She narrows her eyes, then nods.

"She's done everything wrong," she says, squeezing my hand. "She can't protect us from the consequences of the frenzy. No one can, but we *should* have the choice about when and how it finishes." She offers me a sad smile. "I see that now. I'm sorry I at first steered you wrong."

We touch our foreheads together. "Thank you," I say, then place a gentle kiss on her cheek.

She returns a soft, loving smile.

"Come now." Her magic sparks once more. "If Mother knows your secret, then when she catches us, we'll both be lucky if all she does is add us to the garden next to Lorinara. Let's find your man before it's too late."

I shudder. *When...*

I just hope on all the sea stars in my universe that I can kiss Jaspyr one last time before Syrifina finds me.

WITH NO MORE WORDS TO SPEAK and our fateful choices made, we glide safely out of Empress Isle on the swift currents of our magic, the energy of the blood moon feeding us, pushing us faster than we've ever swum. In what feels like a matter of minutes, we launch ourselves into the abyss as if we'd sprouted wings—my prison flickers in my mind, those walls closing in tighter.

'*You'll never leave it,*' the shadows in the Sea of Night seem to whisper. '*You traded in your freedom for power the moment you accepted Syrifina's kiss.*'

'*Freedom lies in his lips,*' I counter. '*I know it.*'

I reach out to Aura and Ora, desperate for their encouragement, hoping they'll take pity on me for all our time spent apart—still, they do not answer.

But someone else does, just as we pass Lover's Coral…

'*What do you think you're doing?*' Mother's voice chimes in my head like the warning bell sailors wield to announce an oncoming storm.

Isobel's head snaps toward me, her expression white with terror.

"You can hear her, too?" I whisper.

She nods—we both scrunch our eyes closed as her voice booms even louder.

'*Return here at once, sweet darlings,*' she speaks in a voice with all the wrath and seduction of a hurricane. '*You're meant for so much more in my world than these temper tantrums… alas, if you refuse to suffer obedience, for the good of our coven, I will have no choice but to hunt you down.*'

The currents shift into a powerful surge, tugging at us to change course and return to the deep—we launch ourselves upward, exercising all our magic and power to keep atop the reef.

'*Do not make me wield the sea to find you,*' she bellows. '*Do not make me sing! For if I do, I'm certain you'll regret it, even more than the blood of the curse you so readily seek.'*

A bone-freezing chill rolls down my spine, making my back arch toward her voice, as if her words tugged at puppet strings hidden along my fins. A deep discomfort settles in the pit of my stomach like I'd swallowed spoiled blood...

I've seen Syrifina Myr hunt and kill a number of times, mercilessly. Shadowed her even, in the water and on land. There is no huntress more vicious nor relentless than the original myrmaid of Olleb-Yelfra. Not even the twins could hold a candle to her.

And here I am, her foolish prey, attempting to flee like a skittish, newborn fish from an ancient shark—and knowing that I will never truly get away.

"Isobel..." I say, looking to her in despair. "What do we do? How can we survive?"

She narrows her gaze, bursting into a brilliant blaze of power. "If it really is *true* love," she says, "you must fight for it, Eloise, no matter the threats posed against you. You die for it. It doesn't matter if you survive, as long as he lives."

She speaks so bluntly that I wonder where all her courage comes from; I return a firm nod, trying to save face in front of my eldest sister.

I would die for Jaspyr, I think. *I would give my life for him, if it means he'd live on. My true love...*

'*You know that's not what this is, but you still refuse to listen, young one.*' I stifle a sob as the distant voice of Aura fills my head.

'*We thought you would prove wiser...*' adds Ora, to my dismay.

'*Pity,*' they say together. '*There's no easy way out of this mess now, Eloise. Maybe we'll see you again before long, in a different world.*'

Before I can acknowledge my old friends, Isobel grabs my hand and propels us both to the surface in a torrent.

49

DARKNESS

☼ J A S P Y R

THE BELL TO MY WORKSHOP TINKLES, but it's much too late for any visitors. *I swore I latched the door.* I look to the window. The hour is surely past midnight.

Yet again, I had been working well into the night.

"We're closed!" I shout from my back room, irritated at being disrupted.

"Pity," comes a honeyed voice that makes my blood freeze over; I drop my paintbrush, my hand shaking—*is it really her?* "I'm in desperate need of a map to get me far, *far* away from this decrepit city. I hear you're the man to see... Jaspyr, is it?" There's a pause; she's toying with me as she always has, waiting to see if I'll play along. "Won't you help me?"

Monster. Traitor. Villain! I remind myself, shutting my mind off to her witchery.

I have been preparing for this night every single day since she left me for dead.

"Shame..." I reply, forcing my voice steady and getting to my feet. "You must not have known it before the plague passed through here. It used to be a fair place to visit."

"Oh, that's too bad," she says, fake curiosity lacing her voice. Each word she speaks is more seductive than the last. "Is it over?"

I consider the portrait I've been tirelessly working on—it's finally complete after all these years. I've just been unnecessarily refining the details, unwilling to let it go.

Alas, it proved easy to finish in the end... once I truly understood who Eloise is at her core.

She contentedly sits atop a large, slanted boulder planted in the middle of a wild sea, her hair just as free. A sweeping tail and fins, blanketed in gold and dusted with silver, rest over the edge, skimming the water. A storm rages behind her, strong enough to sink ships; human skulls and bones churn in the sea beneath...

But by the glint in her dark, golden eyes, she will *never* be truly satisfied with her feast.

The corner of her upper lip tugs into the faintest of smiles. Contemplative, mysterious, mocking, unrelenting—what could this enchanting, vicious creature possibly be thinking as she picks at the gore caked underneath her fingernails?

It isn't for the faint of heart to try to figure out, and I've long since given up for fear I might go as mad as Greggor.

Her veins of lifeblood gleam in the dark, leaking magic into the nighttime air and into the sea around her. Her stare is so focused, so intent, that she surely looks directly at her next kill, marking another man for dead.

I take a deep breath and sign my initials in silver, magicked ink atop one of the floating skulls in her collection.

Then, I steel myself and walk into the foyer.

"You tell me," I say, coolly, leaning against the doorframe, trying to remain composed.

Three years have passed. I feel the age on me, how my hatred has taken its toll on my body, my bones, while I prepared, waited, for this very moment.

I knew she would return.

But she—my breath escapes me. I shove my hands into my pockets, digging my nails into my thighs.

"Come here," I speak, my voice hoarse as I look upon Eloise with nothing but a desperate hunger in my soul, as ravenous as her expression in my portrait.

No amount of preparation could've readied me for this. I was a fool to think it might be easy.

It's like no time has passed for her at all. She's still the mystifying woman I had tried to rescue in that alleyway long ago, a dark cloak draped around her as if she must've traveled from afar in the midst of a winter storm—the memory of the night she told me she had never seen snow flickers through my mind, how sweet and delicate she looked when she imagined it. At the time, I didn't consider that the trail of blood she would surely leave behind her with every footstep might forever corrupt such a natural wonder, as she corrupts everything.

I shove the thought away and focus on her skin, on her perked nipples peeking out from underneath the cloth, on her uncovered torso and the flash of her thighs—there's fresh blood wetting the front side of her cloak.

She is no delicate woman at all. She's a monster.

If not for her bare body and streaks of magical lifeblood beneath the wool, and the glint of satisfaction in her eyes from her latest meal, she might've pulled off 'weary traveler' very well.

'*There's a trail of bodies from the sand to your doorstep.*' The whispered warning makes the hair rise on my skin.

The moon paints Eloise in an eerie reddish haze as she stands in my entryway; she closes the door, shutting us in together once more, as if the last time we stood here, gazing upon each other with lust-filled expressions, was yesterday.

Her dark eyes glitter. Her lips slightly part. Everything

washes away in her glorious presence.

The emptiness, the absence I've felt without her all this time hits me in full force—my anger is secondary to my thundering heart. It can wait. It can be patient for one last night.

Tread carefully...

"Jaspyr, I—"

"I won't ask you twice," I say, my voice low with primal, unfed need.

A breeze flutters through the room, the firelit torches flickering in the unnatural wind.

I don't even flinch, my heartbeat steadying as she suddenly stands before me, drinking me in.

"I missed you," she says.

I absolutely detest you, I think—but I can't help myself as I brush the hair from her face, tucking her curls behind the soft shell of her ear.

She presses her cheek into my palm, the silkiness of her skin making me rethink everything. I feel myself falling all over again.

'No! Don't forget what she did to you, us. How closely you clung to Death again because of her. How she cast us to him without thought,' the ghosts remind me. *'She's destruction incarnate. Think of your friends, your family who still live. Save them from her plague, as you called it. Stick with the plan, Jaspyr. Be brave. Let this end like you intended it.'*

My lips turn downward as I remember with cruel clarity our last moments together. "All this time, I thought—"

She pins that molten gaze on me; my cock pulses with a heartbeat all its own.

"Time passed is irrelevant," she replies, interlacing her fingers with mine. "Now is all that matters, Jaspyr. We're here this moment, maybe not the next. Let's not waste it."

I blink, realizing she means to finish what she started. She doesn't intend for me to live to see the next sunrise.

I won't fall for her schemes again, I think. *I'm ready to do what must be done to expel her from my life, this world, forever. Nothing she can do or say will sway me from—*

"Jaspyr?" Her soothing voice drowns out my thoughts. She bites down on her bottom lip, and all I can think about is taking it between *my* teeth instead.

I close the distance and press my mouth to hers, kissing her strong and deep. It's pointless for me to resist her pull, the ruthless vortex that she is. A black hole with no end; she needn't bother to even sing.

The next thing I know, I've lifted her off the floor and into my arms. She hooks her legs around my hips, her hands wrapping around my neck, entangling in my hair like she can't get close enough.

I can't get enough. I will *never* have enough of Eloise.

'*You have to kill her, tonight. It's the only way to be free. No more waiting, Jaspyr. Please!*

Our kiss grows only deeper, wild and untamed, making me dazed.

I stumble backward, into my workroom. Faintly, I realize that the finished portrait of her might give my hand away, my true thoughts expressed plain through the paint. So, I angle her in a different direction.

I slam her on the opposite wall, against a vast canvas that depicts a dark landscape, the sea barely a strip beneath a red-hot horizon, a moment between the day and night. A moment that I've waited so long for…

Power explodes out of her as her back hits the canvas, silver veins of magic seeping through the layers of black and blue paint, creating a lightning-filled sky.

I unlock my lips from hers if only just to breathe, to think clearly for a second. "You are my greatest torture, Eloise."

I nuzzle my face into her neck, her hair, sucking at her

scent. I want to bottle it up and savor it forever; then she nestles into mine, her fangs sinking into my skin.

A jolt of energy passes through me, all the way to my core. My blood yields to her once more. My cock solidifies like stone. My breath hitches in my throat as if she'd snatched it right off my tongue.

Panic clutches me—I only recall pain, an agony with no end nor beginning.

I squeeze my eyes closed, waiting for it again as she sucks and sucks and sucks. But it's not fast and hard like the last time…

It's slow and smooth, ecstasy-inducing, like all the fantastic moments that came before my heartbreak. I can't help but relax back into the comfortable rhythm of her gentle tug on my soul.

'*No more! You swore it. You swore you wouldn't let her back in. You despise her, Jaspyr. You promised us.*'

I do, I think, relishing the firmness of her backside as my fingernails dig in. *I loathe everything about her… except for this. Gods, I just love this.*

'*But you do not love her. Not anymore.*' A plead I'm not sure how to answer.

The wail of the ghosts in my ears is more incessant than her bite, reminding me of every horrid thing she's ever done to deserve what's coming to her. They hide from their death-wielder, whispering to me from the shadows so that I don't fall off course again.

'*I hear you. Have trust in me! Please know that I'm with you. She's a monster, like all of them. I will keep my promise to you… after this is done. Turn your eyes away now, or spare me your judgment from what I do next,*' I command. '*Because monster or not, she's mine, and I will have her while there's still time.*'

As if Eloise and I are of the same mind, she rips my shirt

in two from my collar and shifts her hand down my center to untie my pants. My linens fall in a pile to my ankles; the length of me angles toward her, so very hungry, unable to yield slowly.

I slide into her—*she's always so deliciously wet*—all the way to her center, tickling whatever evil lay buried inside of her, placating it, the way she placated me until she grew tired.

She unclenches her jaw from my neck to tilt her head back with a moan of pleasure.

"More, more!" she demands with a hiss, so I give it to her—I give her everything I've been holding in for the last 1095 nights since she left me for a fool, a blood-drained corpse like all the rest.

I grunt with every pounding thrust, gritting my teeth at her as she licks my blood off hers.

"Destroy me, Jaspyr," she says, pulling my hair back to look at me properly. Her eyes slash to mine, then she digs her nails into my shoulders. "I need all of you, for as long as we have left to us."

"Time passed is irrelevant," I whisper with unmasked menace, repeating her callous words back to her. "Now is all that matters." *Yes, I will destroy you.*

I thrust harder, taking, seizing all that she offers; she screams, snarls, cries out my name louder. We both fight for leverage against the wall, the painting already cracked and broken.

I close my eyes and slam my palm beside her head, cursing her name to the shadows as my anger, my passion, builds— our joint release is imminent.

"Look at me, Jaspyr," she begs, taking my face in her hands; a golden tear shimmers atop her cheek.

Fire drips from my fingers, scorching the black-painted sky behind her as if a sun demands to shine in the night. Reluctantly, my gaze melts into hers.

"I'm sorry I left you," she whispers atop my lips.

"I'm sorry you did, too," I say, sincerely—then I take her deeper, pressing all the air out from between our bodies; I've never drowned in her more, and she'd never truly felt the wrath of me.

Her body quivers around me, her magic pulsating with it.

"I love you!" she cries—the words sting like the most frigid of winds. She hugs me tighter, resting her head over my shoulder.

I shudder inside of her, drawing her closer still.

"I love you…" she says again.

My tongue yearns to say it back, but the ice in my heart holds it in. As I finish inside of her, everything becomes so clear once more—I may no longer believe one word out of her venomous lips, but I will savor every sound they speak until this night is done, the way she savored me.

I will make her come again and again if that's what she desires. I'll delight in every minute, until the horizon bleeds with red.

A hazy happiness glitters in her eyes. She's so distracted that she can't see me clearly. But gods, do I see her now.

I softly smile, incredulous at how I ever let her deceive me so successfully. To believe that *I* could ever love *her, this…*

How had she shielded my eyes from the stark truth I knew in my heart from the first night she cornered me in this very room? Frenzy, perhaps. Soulmates, surely—the kind that are doomed from the start.

I think to the night on the dock, when she showed a shred of honesty about our wicked bond—why did I refuse to listen?

I invited this plague here.

'*Now is your time to make amends, Jaspyr. Don't dwell on the past. You are caught in a god's game, and Eloise is their winning piece. Look to the future you could have, if you succeed in using your upper hand. This is your chance.*'

I cling to those encouraging words.

Eloise Myr is not my true love.

She's just some cruel trick of Fate that was birthed in the darkest corners of Olleb-Yelfra.

The life-sparing promise I forced her to make when I still had some wits about me was the single most respectable choice I've made since I became trapped in her terrible net of lies and deceit—I'm ashamed that there was even a time I thought I might release her from it.

She pulls back to look at me, tilting her head, starry-eyed. "Jaspyr, is everything alright?"

I blink back at her, drawing out of my whirling mind.

"Everything is perfect now that you're here," I whisper, taking her all in, for all that she is. "You beautiful, beautiful beast." I kiss her cheek. Her chin, her neck, her clavicle, her shoulder.

She smiles, fangs and all, leaning into the sensation of my lips—two can play this game now that I have my bearings...

Except that when I decide to kill her, she won't *accidentally* survive me.

I peel her off the wall and carry her over to my makeshift bed on the floor, where we first met. I gently lay her on her back, starlight sprinkling her face from the window overhead; she sinks into the feathered pillows and blankets with a satisfied sigh.

This time, I'm the one looking down on her, hunting, holding her life in my hands. I press myself again between her legs, soaking in all of her, reveling in how she calls out my name—I commit it to memory.

"And I love you, too," I murmur. "I always will, forever."

'*Liar,*' the ghosts say in praise.

50

HORIZON

ꭎ E L O I S E

WE MAKE LOVE AGAIN AND AGAIN, time melting away into nothing, the way it did in my prison cell. Jaspyr had never taken me so passionately before, demanded my body this ferociously. It was like he couldn't quite get enough—equivalent to how I feel about his blood.

Will we ever be satisfied?

Three years apart had certainly left its mark on our self-control.

Our bodies knit together in a tangle of limbs, and skin, and teeth. Our voices join in a chorus of guttural moans and sighs that accompany the magic continuously detonating around us; if not for the barrier he cast over his workshop, I fear we would wake the entire city.

We both shatter from the pleasure of it all—Jaspyr is so spent that he can hardly speak.

In a haze of ecstasy and very few words, we finally manage to leave his workshop before sunrise and make our way to the beach.

He leads me there, hand in hand.

"Why the rush for me to go?" I ask, staring at his back, lazily tracing the tattooed flames that peek out of his shirt and spiral up his neck—it will be a miracle if we make it to the shoreline without me tearing this one off, too, before I leave.

He looks at me over his shoulder, his expression intense. "I won't have you racing the sun like last time," he says, shortly. "You always cut it too close. An unnecessary risk."

I let out a little laugh, thinking the risk is in the water that he so readily leads me back to—but he doesn't know that yet. He doesn't know that these are probably our last moments together. We've barely spoken a full sentence to each other since he took me against the wall.

Maybe, it's better this way, I think.

"You needn't worry so much about me," I reply, tugging on his arm; he's forced to stop.

He groans, then turns to face me. His lips twitch downward, his eyes roaming over me, lingering on the curves of my body.

"All I do is worry over you," he says, his voice so deep and sure that it strokes awake my yearning for him all over again.

Goddesses, how did I survive three years without him? And how will he endure forever without me?

Before I can respond, he continues walking, pulling me along.

"Come on," he says, nodding toward the water. "We're almost at one of my favorite spots. Eddison and I used to spar here, before..." His voice trails off as we stop in a secluded area on the beach, surrounded by tall cliffs.

"Before me?" I ask, gently—after so much time alone to reflect on our bond, I'm determined to acknowledge the whole of it so that we can move forward, together in the truth of our love; who knows if we'll get another chance after the sun comes up.

I move to stand beside him, resting my head against his upper arm. My gaze skims the quiet sea beyond; before this night is over, I will confess to Jaspyr the danger that awaits me there. The likelihood that I might not see him again once I leave…

He deserves to know the truth, I decide, *after all we've been through. He can't spend the rest of his life waiting for me.*

And if I warn him about Syrifina, maybe he will have time to escape inland. The least I can do is give him a chance at starting over, somewhere far from the water.

I search for Isobel in the waves, wondering where she has gone, if she is safe after escorting me to Jaspyr's door. Her earlier words of encouragement ring in my mind.

'*If it really is true love, you must fight for it…*' she had said to me, '*you die for it. It doesn't matter if you survive, as long as he lives.*'

And I would… I would die for Jaspyr a thousand times over, if only I could be reborn as many times to live forever in his arms.

I make to tell him, to express how deep my love is seeded after all that time separated. I couldn't say those three words enough tonight to make up for the lost moments. It felt *so* freeing.

"Jaspyr…" I step in front of him, clutching his arms—he keeps his gaze locked on the gently lulling waves, and my words of affection get stuck on my tongue. Instead I say, "What are you holding in? Your heart is drumming so wildly all of a sudden. Is there something you wish to say to me before sunrise?"

You must say it now, I think, wishing he could hear my thoughts so that we needn't say goodbye out loud.

He releases the breath he was holding between his teeth, his heartbeat normalizing.

I reach up to his cheek, forcing him to look at me.

"You can tell me," I say. "We can talk about it. I'm sorry that I cost you your friendship with—"

His gaze cuts to mine, dark and limitless. He grips my wrist, turning his back on the waves. "*You* are worth everything, Eloise."

He's said those words to me before, during a time when I thought our love-making might never come to an end, never be disrupted by the looming threats against us; they feel heavier and more meaningful now, on the cusp of dawn.

He drops to his knees before me in the sand, wrapping his hands behind my thighs to pull me closer. He sprinkles kisses up my legs, my hips, my navel, and all the spaces in between.

"Everything," he says again, his breath warming my skin. Then his skillful tongue moves between my legs, his lips sucking at my most sensitive parts, his fingers aiding his mastery of my body.

I whimper in pleasure, gripping his shoulders, wondering how much more of him I can even take. Sparks of radiant magic form around us once more, making us appear like a fallen star that still burned the moment it made impact with the earth.

I don't know how long I stood there for, basking in him as he basked in me, before he made me come again, made me scream into the fading night; the air starts to warm. The sky begins to lighten.

I would ask Time to freeze this moment, but it's a selfish request that would never be met. Oh, how I despise her as much as the Sun right now.

Jaspyr peels his bewitching mouth away from me as I finish, then glances to the sky. When he meets my eyes, his expression is twisted with something like sadness, anger even.

"You left me…" he says, the words barely passing his lips. He looks down.

"Yes," I say, the hurt in his voice spearing my soul; I drop to my knees in front of him and try to kiss away the pain between words. "But I didn't have a choice. My family..."

Goddesses, he must've been so distraught after I left him all those years ago, and right after he said 'I love you'. He must've stayed awake every night, wondering if I might return to say it back or if he'd scared me off for good.

If only he really knew what kept me away so long.

I sigh across his lips, pressing my forehead into his—I know I should tell him, but I'm not eager to spoil my last beautiful night with him by uttering the name of my cruel creator and captor. Besides, it's so painful to relive, and I'd need far more time to explain all the politics of my coven to a mortal man than these fleeting moments we have left.

The truth will have to wait. I can evade Mother for one more day.

The Sea seems to snicker, soft sprays of water tickling my face that send a surge of terror straight through me.

I make a promise in my head, taking Jaspyr's hand in my own, tracing the rough lines on his palm—if Syrifina doesn't capture me this morning, I'll explain the trouble I'm in to him tomorrow night, *before* any touching happens, any kiss. We'll sit far apart, him in a chair and me on the couch, and I'll answer every question he's ever had about me.

But, if Syrifina does imprison me again or worse, well... at least Jaspyr will have the peace of knowing that, yes, of course I loved him too, despite all the obstacles thrown at us.

He looks down to the sand. "And you're back now," he states, his voice shaking with emotion; I frown, but he doesn't notice. "For how long?"

"For as long as I can be," I say, softly. "Please, look at me, Jaspyr. I want to really see you before I leave." *I want to memorize every line on your face, the brilliant darkness of your eyes... just in case.*

He does, his strong jaw set, and I can't help but jerk my head back a bit; this close, those dark pools threaten to trap me like sinking sand, the vivid green lines in his left pupil entrancing me.

"I... I..." I shake my head, blinking away the stupor he cast upon me. "There's nowhere I'd rather be on this earth than here with you right now." I gesture to the sky. "I would pin the moon to the clouds forever if I could, just to remain with you during the blasted day."

He smirks with something like adoration and all I can think of is getting those lips all over me again; I soften at the sight, trying to be content in the present moment. What if it's the last one we get?

"I'm sorry it took me so long to return," I add. "I know the wait was probably... difficult." He tries to look away, but I tilt his chin toward me. "But I *love* you." I grin wide with the freedom of the statement I before feared so much. "And I've been waiting a long time, too, to say it back to you."

"What about your gods, your curse?" he asks, raising an eyebrow. "Wasn't it you who told me that our love could bring about the destruction of the Olleb?" His words land hard, accusatory. "Why the sudden change of heart?"

I can sense him testing me, searching my face for any hint of deception.

"I never had a heart to begin with Jaspyr," I say, gently, placing my hand over his chest where I know the tattoo of water swirls—a gift from my great goddess—marking his second chance at a life on this plane. *We're meant to live our second chance together,* I think. "Not since you've known me. And nothing about what I feel for you is sudden. I've had a lot of time to think clearly about what you mean to me."

He places his hand over mine, interlacing his fingers into mine. "And what do I mean to you, Eloise?"

I hold his gaze. "You are my soulmate. You are my frenzy.

You are my everything, Jaspyr." This truth was easier to speak than any I have ever uttered, though my words tremble with passion. "The god who cast this curse upon my family is a liar." I hear the shadows seethe, but I dutifully ignore them, needing to state my belief out loud. "You are the blessing he didn't wish me to see. I know that now. There is a way for us to exist, in union. There has to be."

Jaspyr lifts his free hand to my face, caressing my chin, my cheek; I lean into his tender touch. "Go on," he says.

"Think about it," I whisper, kissing the back of his hand as his fingers skim my mouth. "We're drawn to each other like magnets. Yet, on every side of this, we've been told *not* to listen to the connection in our souls, to fight it for the good of the Olleb and our families." I can't help but laugh, finally understanding. "It's all a vile trick!"

He pulls back, his eyes narrowing. "Don't I know it."

"I'm serious," I say with a wry smile; he doesn't return it, so withdrawn today. *Nervous*, I think—that I might leave him for good this time. "You and I are tangled up in an ancient revenge story that was put into play long before we were even born to this world. But we're *soulmates*. A bond so strong that not even the gods themselves can destroy it. Who says we shouldn't question them when they insist that we don't have a choice but to accept such a terrible fate, that only one of us can survive this relationship?" I shake my head. "I want no part of their warring anymore. My sisters can think what they want, but *I refuse* to believe that's the only option for us." I take both his hands in mine, tracing the scars around his knuckles. "I could be wrong... but what if I'm right? What if we stand a chance at an extraordinary life? Would you seize it with me?"

I have to know. Even if it's just for one more night.

Jaspyr's expression twists.

"So what are you proposing?" he says after a moment.

"You wish to… ignore all the warnings, the Golden Rule?" He looks around. "Excuse me," he calls to no one in a mocking tone, "I seem to have lost Eloise Myr. Have you seen her anywhere?"

I hiss at him, playfully, then turn serious again, wanting to say what's burning on my tongue before the wretched sun comes up and forces us apart. "I think that if we *choose* to finally come into balance together, to love each other equally and accept each other's differences, then the frenzy is no longer a curse to be reckoned with but a great fortune to share between us. We just need a little more time to adapt…" I look to the sky, the night swiftly peeling back like a thin curtain. "There's two sides to every coin, Jaspyr," I say, hurriedly, racing the morning. "The choice is ours how this story turns out, in this life or the next."

'*You're wrong*,' says the God of Shadow. '*Imprudent child. This is where your story ends—*'

'*I've beaten your foul game*,' I say, firmly, then block him out.

No matter what happens after tonight, Jaspyr will realize that our love did stand a chance; I don't say it, but I just *know* that the curse was broken after I drained nearly every last drop of him.

Silence draws between us as he stares down at me.

"So, what do you say?" I ask, biting my lip, my eyes darting between him and the sky—I know I must leave the safety of his arms and get to the water, but I need him to understand that *I love him*, the way he loves me. I owe him that.

Just in case…

"Don't make me beg," I add with a smirk.

An incredulous smile spreads across his face. "Well, I never thought I'd see the day… the Kampaulo Killer, on her knees before me, asking for *my* hand." He laughs, soft and deep; the sound vibrates through me. "But how will anyone know I'm betrothed without a golden ring or a woman to show off?" he asks, tilting his head, magic twinkling in his gaze like starlight. "Are you sure this isn't just another role-play?"

I join in on his laughter, delighted to see the joy return to his expression. "I never knew you to be so traditional, Jaspyr," I say; he winks. "Besides, I gave you enough treasure when we were together to last you a lifetime. You surely haven't traded it all these past few years?" I kiss his hand again. "Take your pick for golden rings, my mortal king. You're mine, no matter what treasures you choose to wear."

He looks at me with all the intensity of the ocean. "And the woman?"

I swallow, the night growing uncomfortably warm. "I am no woman," I reply. "I'm so much more." I press my hand to his face. "And *I am yours*, my love… no matter what happens between us, please, remember that."

"My very own monster," he says, darkly. "How lucky I am to be cursed by you."

I blink, taken aback. "I thought you were a gentleman, Jaspyr," I snap, flashing my fangs. "That's no way to speak to a lady of the water." He laughs loudly at that.

"You seem to always have the wrong idea about me," he says with a grin, "at any given moment."

I huff, pursing my lips.

"I love you, and you love me," I say, our eyes locking. "I'm not wrong about that."

He looks me up and down, as if searching for the lie. When he doesn't find it, he gently presses his lips to mine.

I sigh again, sinking in.

"Don't worry, Eloise," he whispers against my mouth. "I will never let you go. I'd rather burn." He pulls back slightly, considering me, his face scrunched in thought. "I'm not sure why you spent so much time searching for answers I've held all along… but that you're here with me now is all I care about." He takes a deep breath. "It's all that's ever mattered, really."

I open my mouth to speak but he tilts his head, baring his neck. "Drink," he urges—the veins under his pale skin call to me, the fresh bite wounds begging me for another taste.

"Are you sure?" I ask, licking my lips. "I really should go... and I've taken much tonight already. You'll feel so weak to-morrow."

"You know as well as I that I can handle your bite," he replies. "I'm still alive, aren't I? Despite your best efforts."

His words land sharp.

I offer a weak smile, realizing that I still have a lot more apologizing to do after I left him in such a state atop the palace tower—we've hardly spoken of that night. *I hope I get the opportunity to explain.* I have no idea what that experience must've felt like for him, but I'm sure it was less than pleasant.

"Jaspyr, I—"

"We don't have much time left," he says, glancing up. "Drink, now. I won't see you go so hungry during the day anymore. We need to act more modestly if we're to remain together. If you're not so uncontrollably ravenous every night, maybe there will be fewer bodies for the city to discover with the tides."

"Yes, you're right," I say with a resigned pout. "The more I take from you, the less burden on the innocent. I will get back on a regular feeding cycle, soon. Until then..."

"Small steps," he says, dryly. "Saindora wasn't built in a day."

I offer him a soft smile of gratitude—he has *no* idea of how desperate I was to taste him again after all these years. I had to drain several people before our reunion tonight just to be sure I wouldn't kill him. Even now, I'm barely holding it together being this close to him without the distraction of his beautiful body devouring my own.

I lock my mouth to his neck, my teeth breaking his flesh effortlessly.

The energy he bleeds into me spreads through my entire body, making my limbs numb, my mind warm.

My eyes pin on the fading moon. Then to the sea where Syrifina surely floats beneath the surface, waiting for me to return to her domain. I can sense her nearing, feel the weight of her power, always. But with Jaspyr's blood in my mouth, her imminent threat is easy to ignore—I become lost in this delicious present.

"That's enough," he says, gripping me by the shoulders. His nails dig into my skin. "Eloise!"

I blink and release him. I had accidentally faded too far into my mind.

"Sorry," I gasp, wiping his blood with the back of my hand. "I got a little carried away. You have no idea how long it's been since I—"

He snorts, running his hand through his hair, his expression darkening. "Is that what you call attempting to kill me?" His voice rises with every heartbeat. "Getting carried away? You revolting creature!"

He stands, leaving me in the sand as I gawk back at him.

Revolting? And he hasn't called me a creature since…

Time seems to still, something strange prickling at my spine, alerting me to danger.

I hold out my hand to him, but he just stares blankly down at it.

'*Naive*,' the Sea whispers.

"Jaspyr, I didn't mean—"

He utters, "*Cementas cuerpal*," and his eyes gleam as bright as the sun beginning to peek over the horizon.

My bones lock in place as Jaspyr's magic takes hold—I try to move my tongue, to plead for release, for forgiveness, but it no longer seems to work. I make to stand, noting the short moments I have left before the sun will show its face, but my limbs don't react to my commands.

I am completely frozen, a living statue upon the sand, the water so close yet out of reach. Only my eyes retain their freedom from this spell.

When the magic fades from his irises, I see him clearly, illuminated in the budding morning light. I grasp the terrifying truth I was so eager to ignore tonight—love no longer shines there in those blackened eyes. Who knows how long it has been gone.

Passion, surely, brewed in its place. Fierce determination, yes. But whatever used to glow in adoration for me has long since been exchanged with something else, something dark and destructive that has always been at his core. And because of me, it has festered and grown.

The spiteful shadows seem to gather behind him, taunting me, spreading around him like black, scaled wings that only I can see.

'*It was sweet to hear you dream of a future where you can both live under the moonlight forever,*' the God of Shadow speaks. '*Why, not even Syrifina Myr was so delusional in her prime. But forever ends today, I'm afraid.*' Jaspyr smiles, something vicious, and all I feel is cold, even amid the rising heat. '*Sister Sun is eager to meet you, Eloise.*'

For the first time ever, I'm at a loss for words, even in my mind.

Tears burn behind my eyes as I realize that his love for me had been undone the moment Isobel swept me off the palace roof—he thought I left him for dead.

Jaspyr! I plead. *You don't understand. I love you. I was trying to save you. It was the only way.*

But he doesn't hear me. The sun begins to force itself atop the waves at his back, already making me painfully hot.

His smile widens as light spreads around me.

"Don't bother trying to fight the spell. I thought long and hard about how I wanted to do this," he says, casually. "A barrier or shield magic wouldn't have been nearly as satisfying as *this*." He flexes his fingers. "I've been practicing."

He pauses, as if waiting for me to speak but all I can do is whimper.

He clutches my chin, forcing my gaze.

"See how it feels," he growls, jaw clenched, eyes burning into mine the way the sun's first rays begin to burn into my naked skin. "For your free will to be *stolen* from you? See how it feels to lose all control of yourself?" His gaze flicks to the sky. "And soon, you'll be drained just as harshly and quickly as I was when you left me to rot." He lowers his voice. "But rest assured, I won't turn my back on you, Eloise. I'm happy to watch."

He sighs with satisfaction and the sound makes me want to cry out for the deep sorrow I know I've caused him. Not even when he first considered me his enemy did he ever speak or act so cruelly.

I didn't mean it, Jaspyr, please! This isn't you. I know you care for me. You do.

As if he can hear me, he conjures a hot, pink flame in his palm, then blasts me in the chest. Fire bursts around me.

I cry out his name again, a silent defense.

The fire doesn't hurt nearly as much as his betrayal.

You're my soulmate! True love. We fought too hard to end like this.

'*This is how it always ends,*' says the Sea, coolly. '*Chaos, destruction. You choose to die with it or live with knowing. I told you this. You've always had a choice.*'

'*Help me!*' I scream—I am met with only silence.

Jaspyr shakes his head as the sparks from his fire fade into the air on a trail of smoke.

"I won't waste my energy!" he shouts, his fingers curling

into fists. He grits his teeth at me, as if it's all he can do to hold back. "Why bother torturing you with a fire you can easily resist when the sun will destroy you properly in…" He looks over his shoulder to the horizon. "Oh, *thank the gods*." He spits on the ground in front of me. "Should be any minute now."

Fear thunders in my chest. I call to my magic. It surrounds me in a cloud, eating away at this spell like a slow acid.

Much too slow, I think.

Jaspyr inhales a deep breath, then exhales it alongside his anger. He opens his palms to the sky, as if guiding the sun to come quicker.

Calmly, he says, "Ah, now you comprehend. There's no way out of this, no *begging* me or song to sing. Use your magic all you want. Waste it, for all I care. I drank one of Penelope's power-boosting concoctions before I brought you here. There's no way you can escape my spell." He steps closer to me, leaning forward. "I told you, Eloise… I will never let you go."

My gaze flicks sidelong, toward the cliffs; if I had been focused at all earlier, I would've smelled her scent, even from this far off. Penelope must've been spying on us all along, looking out for him.

I moan, struggling against his powerful hold, pushing my magic outward in vain.

He laughs, coldly. "You were right all along. We're not meant to be." He looks down at me over the bridge of his nose. "I should've never let you live," he adds, quietly. "Once you're gone, this city can finally move on from your wickedness. And Penelope and Eddison… they deserve to live in a world without you in it."

He kneels down in front of me, meeting me at my eye level; I can't look away from him. I've never felt so ensnared by a gaze before. Even my magic makes space for him.

"*You will burn* on this beach." He points at his chest. "I will remain." Then he picks at his nails, utterly and disgustingly indifferent—not my Jaspyr at all. In fact, I'm reminded of Vasylina. "I will enjoy watching this sunrise more than anything." He gently runs the back of his palm across my cheek, down the side of my neck, my arm... the deceptive warmth of his skin against my own makes me want to recoil, but I can't. "Any minute now. We're almost done, darling."

No! No, please. I saved you. Please, Jaspyr. You can still save me, too. You can undo this before it's too late.

Something wavers in his expression as he takes me in, but then his features harden. There's no hint of remorse nor hesitation for the death sentence he's given me—he grabs me by my neck and presses his mouth to mine. His kiss is so surprisingly forceful that I would've fallen backward if I weren't cemented to the sand by his magic. It's so cold...

I feel as if my soul shatters like ice, into a thousand unmendable pieces.

He releases me and stands, looking down on me with something like pity in his eyes.

"For the good king's sake," he whispers, shaking his head. "I never stood a chance with you." He turns slightly, looking at the waves—they sparkle in the early morning light. "And even if your sisters take their revenge upon me when the night falls again, this will have been worth it."

When, I think.

He's completely underestimating the brutal wrath of the Myr coven when it comes to revenge against the male species. I wouldn't wish what they'll do to him upon anyone... even if it means that we might meet sooner in the next life.

I love you. I love you. I love you!

Tears wet my cheeks and my vision blurs. My magic glows even brighter, though I still can't move an inch.

And you love me, too, Jaspyr. I know it. We're soulmates.

I don't want to die. Not without you. Hear me, please! I'm begging you.

He looks up. "It's time," he says. "Goodbye, beast."

I feel the heat of fire bloom around me, unnatural, suffocating—together, Jaspyr and I stare toward the horizon as the spiteful, scorching sun begins to rise above the water.

With such light in my eyes, the rest of the world falls away, tumbling into the black hole that has swallowed us both. It transports me to another time and place all our own, where our bodies and our minds are united as one, forever—there is no 'us or them', no Golden Rule, no frenzy nor broken sisterhood to mend.

Just me and him.

'*Foolish*,' I hear Aura and Ora say, so distantly. '*This is not the end we hoped for you.*'

I force myself to open my eyes and look, to witness my final moments on this earth. I lower my gaze, settling it atop the soothing waves—we were never alone in this. I see that now, and so does Jaspyr.

The water begins to bubble, and a soft silver light appears from beneath, growing brighter with each passing second.

"This is worth whatever they do to me come nightfall," he says again, eyes also locked on the same spot. "Hope to haunt you on the other side, Eloise." He adds, softly, "My malevolent queen."

A cloud-like shimmer bursts across the waves; Syrifina emerges—a volcanic eruption—from the sea. All my sisters follow, hundreds of them, forming a wall along the shoreline.

Mother stares at me, horrified, with penance promised in her silver gaze. And Jaspyr wields a blade of sunfire over my head, his love for me buried *so* deep down that there's no hope I will see it again before I leave this plane…

I don't want to move forward, and I cannot go back.

I used to rule the land and sea with nothing but life ahead

of me. Now I am a princess of nothing but shame.

I push my gaze beyond my family, for I can't bear to face them on my knees and out of water like this. I lift my eyes to the sun one last time, not willing to cower before my enemy.

Her rays sear my pupils without remorse, slice at my skin like dwarf-made steel. '*Yield*,' she roars.

'*Never!*' I scream—she lifts higher, melting into the sky.

My skin sizzles and cracks, slowly peeling away, the pain otherworldly. Not even I am brave enough to withstand it with grace. It's the only time I'm thankful for the spell holding me in place.

I close my eyes and wait for Death to come once more, this time riding on the back of the sun instead of the waves.

Then I hear Jaspyr scream.

51

SUN

JASPYR FALLS TO HIS KNEES BESIDE ME; a sleek sword dangles over him, its blade covered in blood all the way from its tip to the hilt gripped in Isobel's hand. She drops it to the ground at her feet.

A scream rips out of me unlike any I've ever let go.

"Jaspyr, *no!*" I'm momentarily shocked by my own voice as his spell finally releases me. *Because he's dying!*

He writhes in the sand, blood spluttering from his lips.

I fall forward, trying to reach out to him, to somehow help, but Isobel catches me instead.

"How could you *do* this to me?" I cry out. "You were the one who told me to fight for him!"

Her eyes burn with silver intent as she looks from him to me. Everything about her is unhurried, and there's nothing of regret in her expression at all.

If I weren't so weak, I would tear her face off with my teeth. Instead, I can't do much more than flail weakly in her arms.

Her skin has also begun flaking from the sun, too eagerly ready for the dawn, but she doesn't seem to mind... I wonder if I'll ever be as strong.

"Get in the water!" Syrifina commands from the shoreline, the waves crashing down alongside her—for all her power and strength, she doesn't seem willing to even test the barrier of the sun-drenched land. *Coward*, I think. "This isn't the time for sibling rivalry."

Isobel doesn't speak, nodding to Mother—that's when I realize how I've been the pawn in not one but two games tonight.

I gape at her; the tears burning in my eyes hurt even more than the sun. "You lied to me, didn't you?" My voice barely comes out in a whisper.

Her refusal to speak is confirmation enough of my sister's betrayal—she's *always* been obedient to Syrifina. I was a perfect fool to think she had come to my rescue.

I'm not even sure now if half the things she confided in me earlier bore any truth whatsoever. In fact, I'm certain they didn't...

I should've seen straight through her lies—why in the Sea's name would she advise me to suddenly go after him when all this time she's implored me to end it, to spare myself any further pain?

She stole my love from me because she was jealous! She probably knew he was alive the entire time. She wanted to teach me a lesson for sparing his life.

They'd starved and isolated me, all so the one I depended on the most could corner me at my weakest and feed me everything I needed to hear to lead them to Jaspyr. Yes, she's known full well that he lived all along, Mother's ever obedient spy. And if there's one truth, for certain, Syrifina would do *anything* to contain the curse shadowing her empire, no matter the cost to us.

"I trusted you all!" I scream toward the water, accepting the truth of it. I look back to Isobel, but her gaze remains on Syrifina. "And *you*..." I seethe, snapping my fangs at her. "You wanted me to lead you here, to finish him off. I will never forgive you for this, you wretched, filthy liar!"

Only a true monster could ever inflict such an excruciating pain on another, pain that they too had experienced.

To think, all those stories she spouted to me about love and loss and regret... and she would take *mine* from *me*?

I let out another scream of frustration, my magic itching for release, but it's smothered by Isobel's.

I suddenly understand everything; all those quiet conversations where Isobel confessed so much to me in secret—arming me with such knowledge, strings of a tainted truth—had been a careful calculation. And it wasn't rooted in my well-being nor the safety of our coven, but envy.

How had I not seen that flicker of green in her eyes when she learned of my frenzy?

It was not my doting sister but greed who pushed forth from the waves atop the palace tower. She's just been patiently punishing me, waiting for the most painful moment to reveal her dark motives.

And the lie she told about Syrifina having anything to do with the death of her soulmate... just to get me to empathize.

I bare my fangs at her, fighting and losing against her hold.

Isobel doesn't need any help to destroy love! She's happy to do it on her own, I realize with cruel clarity. *It was her I should've been wary of all this time, this vindictive beast who gathered all my trust just to crush it in her palm. Not the twins. Not Syrifina. Not the blasted gods.*

I would give my soul to the shadows to get to Jaspyr and out of her deceitful arms.

The God of Shadow grins. '*You needn't be so dramatic, child. Your soul has always been mine, from the moment you accepted Syrifina's kiss.'*

Panic grips me even tighter as the strong scent of Jaspyr's blood fills my nostrils. I cry out for him. I don't care that he was misled and tried to kill me. He deserves better than to die alone in the sun.

If only we had more time to right these wrongs.

I would rather throw my body on top of his and die with him a thousand times over than live another *day* in Syrifina's and Isobel's world. An eternity with them would be torturous.

But, just like Lorinara, they will never release me. They'd rather see me live in endless misery than let me burn and be free of them.

There are seconds left until dusk is fully yielded to dawn; I fight all my natural instincts and struggle against Isobel as she drags me to the water before we both turn to ash.

"No, I don't want to go with you! Let me be with him."

But resisting my elder of countless decades is more than futile.

Isobel shoves me into the shallows, and we both transform back to our natural state.

I gasp in utter relief as the water rinses me clean, instantly repairing my burned body and clearing the fog from my mind. Though it does nothing to relieve my soul-crushing sorrow. As I heal, I feel my anger even more, realizing how trapped I truly am—I was promised eternal freedom, yet I've never been so manipulated.

Syrifina and my other sisters close in, intending to drag me back under into their deceitful, dreadful universe.

The sound of fast-paced footsteps draws my attention; Penelope rushes toward Jaspyr.

She drops to her knees next to him and presses her hands over his wounds. And for a moment, I'm hopeful that maybe he will live in her care...

"Oh, my beautiful boy," she whimpers, drawing his head

into her lap, stroking his hair. "What were you thinking? I told you not to do it! I should've *never* given you that concoction. You're a fool to attempt this alone, when she bested three of us the last time. *Why?*"

Jaspyr reaches toward her face, and I can hear his feeble voice, the blood spurting from his lips. "I just wanted to do right by you. I'm sorry for all the mistakes I made."

She shakes her head, silent tears streaking her cheeks. "*None* of this is your fault." She shifts her gaze to mine, then sweeps the shoreline; her heartbeat increases rapidly. "It's theirs, all of it."

"Hardly," purrs Syrifina in my ear from behind me—I stiffen as her hand rests upon my shoulder, resisting her attempt to push me under. "That boy got into your head, Eloise, led you astray. The two of you were both doomed from the start, but I'll help you overcome this." She says it as if it's her absolute honor to do so. She gestures to my sisters—I refuse to meet their eyes. "We can help you. Let him go now. He's as good as dead."

I barely consider the olive branch she extends to me over Jaspyr's dying words. I scrunch my eyes closed, blocking out her voice and focusing on his—I want to remember the deep, delicate note of it, always.

"That doesn't matter now," he says, bitterly; I swallow my guilt and open my eyes; his gaze flicks to me for a brief moment. "You shouldn't have followed me. *Please*, just get out of here. Leave. It's not safe for you."

She scoffs. "You're like a son to me. A brother to Eddison. We're family, no matter the wrong choices you made. I forgive you, Jaspyr, and I'm not going anywhere."

His eyes shimmer with emotion. "Thank you," he says. "And... and Ed—"

"There now, don't struggle too much to talk." She softly smiles. "I'm sure he'll come to forgive you too... in time. I told him everything after you came to me. He's been keeping an eye on you these past few years. I'm certain he…" Her eyes dart down the beach. "I'm certain he'll come before it's too—"

"It's time," commands Syrifina in a queen-like voice that overshadows Penelope's. "Come, before the city begins to wake and sees us all. I would hate to have to finish off what you left of Kampaulo."

My simmering anger becomes a boiling rage.

Fear washes over me as the sun wreaks havoc across the sky, rising to its full potential. It washes Jaspyr in a stark light as he struggles to hold on. His precious blood leaks from him in a river that I wish to bathe in alongside him.

I will not go. I am in control. Syrifina and Isobel will pay dearly for this.

My magic gathers in my core, my energy renewed by the water.

Syrifina moves back, gesturing to Isobel to bring me with her.

Isobel's nails dig into my arm; I want to snap her hand right off for having the audacity to try to steal this moment— *his death*—from me, too.

"You have some nerve." I glare at her, keeping one eye on Jaspyr.

My magic presses outward in a glittering, deadly mist atop my skin; she flinches from the sting of it but keeps her hold, her expression callous, stone-like, unperturbed.

"Do you have *anything* to say to me?" I growl. "Anything at all?"

She still doesn't even deign to respond—whatever reward Mother offered her for her cooperation must've been pretty damn good. She keeps her lips pressed in a firm line, her gaze forward.

"You wicked thing…" I say, my voice cracking—I lunge

for her, fangs bared, fins and magic blazing. "You betrayed me!"

She catches my other arm, barely even shifting in the water.

"Jaspyr, stay with me!" cries Penelope, suddenly, drawing my attention back; I glance over Isobel's shoulder and see her slapping his cheek as his eyes flutter toward his final sleep. "Oh gods," she utters, "there's too much blood. I can't stop it..." She looks all around. "Eddison, where are you?"

I begin to tremble, wracking my mind for a way to right this—but from the mouth of a healer, there was no hope.

Syrifina and my other sisters seem to lick at the air, riled by the commotion, the metallic, tangy scent.

"He's *mine*, you insatiable creatures!" I snap.

Syrifina sighs, growing agitated. "Let's have this conversation underwater, shall we?" My sisters begin to dive. "This has been far too much commotion for one day."

Isobel begins to drag me down with them; I feel weighted like a stone.

I lock my eyes on the shore as I inevitably sink, the water reaching up to my neck. My grip slips on my magic.

My angered curses turn into a terrified plead. "No, no, no, Isobel, *please*! He's fading, let me say goodbye, at least."

Isobel pauses and meets my eyes. Her stone-like expression falters, softens. A false crimson tear streaks her pale skin.

"Forgive me," she says. "I didn't have a choice."

I stop struggling, her words sliding over me.

"One always has a choice," I state.

Her expression turns passive again, into her *real*, uncaring face.

I narrow my gaze. My magic settles back into my control as a calm and quiet determination rolls through my mind.

A halo of gold and silver spreads through the water, Isobel and me at its center.

Let the world burn. We will remain!

"Eloise, wait—" Syrifina calls from behind.

At the same time, the Sea whispers in my mind, '*You are not in control. You never were.*'

An explosive wave finally frees me from Isobel's grasp, as if a cannonball had detonated in the sea below us. It sweeps her away, thrusting her toward the sun-drenched land.

52

SHADOW

ᗡ E L O I S E

ISOBEL CRASHES TO THE BEACH near Jaspyr and Penelope. The sunlight bathes her fully. She doesn't transform like I expect her to. She thrashes atop the sand, flailing her tail and fins as she cries out to us, like a fish out of water, shriveling.

Mother's wail splits the air from behind me. She launches toward her, skimming atop the waves, arms open wide, as if to try to catch her. But it's too late.

I watch in horror, in quiet delight, as Isobel Myr bursts into flames like the wildfire she is.

Fire catching fire, I think with a small smile.

Although, I hadn't meant for *this* to happen…

No, not exactly. I didn't intend to blast her out of the water.

My smile falters. *But she's a survivor. If she's lived this long, I'm certain she will recover, make me pay for disrespecting her.* Part of me hopes this very much, I realize, despite all my anger. *No, I don't take any pleasure at all in watching my dear sister burn…*

In fact, I wouldn't wish such a horrible pain on my worst enemy.

It isn't slow like it was for me at sunrise. The fire takes her fast and brutally, greedy to devour, ignoring her screams for mercy. The smell of flesh and bone, of sea and old magic, fills my nostrils.

She's already a bright raging flame when Syrifina reaches the beach.

She can survive this… can't she? Then we'll have forever to make amends.

Syrifina crawls in the sand to get as close as possible—her torso on land, her tail in the water.

She calls to the waves to salvage the pieces of my sister before there's nothing left of her to heal, but the water just cascades around her in a dome. Not even a droplet touches the magnificent blaze that has become Isobel as Syrifina's magic ricochets off some invisible barrier that I believe was conjured by the Sun.

Isobel just burns and burns and burns…

Then, her echoing screams start to fade and the silhouette of her thrashing body becomes one with the hungry flames.

"Give her *back!*" cries Syrifina, her sadness devastating the shore.

But even I know it's too late as the last of her voice dies away. *What have I done?*

The crackling fire seems to grow brighter with its kill, sending embers of victory to the air.

I look away, focused on anything else but my guilt.

She deserved it, I remind myself.

She's your sister, I counter. *She loved you. You know it.*

"No!" I yell, squeezing my eyes shut until that voice drifts away.

Syrifina turns toward me, her eyes wide in terror and disbelief as the waves continuously fight to reach Isobel.

"What did you *do?*" she screeches, too distraught to even notice the humans anymore—that Penelope and Jaspyr still breathe after Syrifina's power exploded across the beach tells me that Penelope is the one wielding the barrier magic over Isobel.

I should've recognized it before. If I had, then maybe...

Syrifina levels a deadly gaze at me, such menace in her eyes, her magic rippling off her with so much energy that it heats the sea by ten degrees. I'm certain if she directed that force toward me, I would no longer have to worry about anything at all. "She loved you more than anything!"

"Not more than you," I retort, unflinching, though the words sting more than fire coral.

"Your ignorance is astounding," she says, her voice quivering with ire. "And your refusal to listen has cost Isobel her life!" Her rage seizes the waves with more control than I've ever known—a razor-sharp swell slices the water toward me.

I try to move out of its path, but the sea solidifies around my waist, holding me in place.

I grit my teeth, bracing myself, forcing my eyes to stay open so that she can see me for who I truly am—her power may physically always make me submit, but she will *never* capture my loyalty again with her blasphemous lies. I will always remember the truth, no matter what mind games she plays on me.

"I know everything," I say, readying to die.

Her magic stills right before my throat, the blade of water gleaming so finely that I know it could easily take my head right off. "You know *nothing,*" she says.

I lift my chin, trying not to let her shake my resolve, trying to not let the hammering voices be heard.

What have I done?

"You and Isobel had been at this together all along," I say. "I'm certain she told you everything when she got wind that my frenzy had begun. And when *you* realized I wouldn't kill Jaspyr on my own, you convinced her to trick me into leading her to him." My own magic surges, trying to overpower Syrifina's for control over the water blade. "This couldn't have been more calculated. All you want is to control us, your family." I glance down to where her magic grips my waist, then narrow my eyes at her. "We were never really free, were we?"

Syrifina's grip tightens. The waves explode around me. "How dare you."

This time, I cower.

"*I held* the sword to Jaspyr's chest, not Isobel, you insolent child," she says with such a calm that a chill snakes through my bones. Her silver gaze seeks to burn straight through to my soul and yet all I feel is a numbing cold.

"What are you talking about? I... I saw her with the blade."

She hums something soft and seductive. Her magic seeps into my skin like poison—it makes mine falter, then drift away, leaving room for hers to force its way into my mind and do her bidding. I can't resist.

Only when she's wrenched every ounce of power out of my grasp does she release me.

I shake my head, my mouth falling open as I look to her. "It was you all along..."

She sneers back at me, then glances to the flame that is Isobel. She lets out another wail, hunching over, wrapping her arms around herself. "My darling daughter," she says in despair.

"No, no, *no*," I stutter, gaping at the fire.

"Yes!" screams Syrifina between uncontrollable sobs, her watery blade falling away with a splash. "I forced her to kill your marked one to teach her a lesson for betraying me... to *you*." She snarls. "Before I dragged you both back to Empress Isle by your tails to beg my forgiveness."

"Why?" I shout, my own panicked mind threatening to sink me. Suddenly, I can't remember how to swim, to float.

The God of Shadow answers, '*If you paid attention to anything other than your own desires, you might've heard the remnants of Syrifina's song lingering around your sister before...*'

"No," I gasp, covering my ears. "No! I won't hear another word!"

'*You did this,*' he forces into my mind. '*You killed her.*'

"I'm sorry! I thought—" I choke on the unbearable statement. "No, I... I can save her."

He tuts at me, chastising. '*Such a joy to watch, you are. Pity, though... Isobel was one of the more tolerable ones.*'

'*Get out of my head!*'

I make to wade toward the beach, toward Isobel, resolved to undo my grave mistake... somehow. *There's still time.*

Something clutches my tail from below, stopping me.

I look down to find my sisters—the other princesses—surrounding me with their magic and grief-stricken songs, clinging to me like ropes to try to pull me down. They break the surface.

"Come, Eloise," they plead, attempting to tug me under.

"There's nothing left for you here," urges Kristeena.

"We won't let Mother hurt you," adds Zahra, sternly. "Just dive with us, now."

"Quick!" cries Daniella. "You don't stand a chance if you stay."

I look to the shore, toward the enchanted fire—I wonder if it will burn forever, for as long as Isobel should've had to swim beside me in our waters.

My voice comes soft. "But... what if she still lives?"

Their silence is overwhelming.

I cry out to Syrifina, and the water swirls with magic around me; my sisters' grips weaken as they're forced to move back. "I don't understand! Why, *why* did you do this?"

Syrifina focuses on me, her cheeks glimmering with pearl-like tears. "For the good of our family. Everything I do has always been for you, all of you."

She's never sounded so genuine before...

I look to my sisters again, noting the beautiful faces of each one of them, wishing I had looked closer at Isobel's all those times we swam side by side in the deep. I blink and gold and silver teardrops fall to the water. "I thought she lied..."

"It's not your fault," says Vasylina, her expression grave, honest.

"The end of a frenzy is always tragic," adds Miki, blinking away her tears. She holds her hand out to me. "But this..." She shakes her head. "It should've never happened."

"We will protect you," the twins say as one, glaring toward Syrifina.

I cover my face with my hands and weep, wanting to jump into the fire to die with her. "I'm so sorry—"

"You didn't know, sister," they sing with open arms—that they're willing to accept me still makes this even more painful. "Swim with us, please."

Guilt forms like a stone in my stomach. I turn away from them, but I feel as they sink beneath the next wave, leaving me alone with Mother.

"You traitorous girls," whispers Syrifina, her grief-stricken voice swiftly transforming into something terrifying. "Enough of this! You want the truth? So be it."

The water stills below me, and I know my sisters listen keenly.

"The God of Shadow may have tricked me, but he's right." She points a condemning finger in my direction. "*You* agreed to live by my side forever. You accepted my gift, and so you accept the terms that come with it." She sighs, rolling her shoulders, as if her body holds too much power to restrain. "I tried to shelter you all from this painful reality, but most of you didn't have what it took to come to terms with it yourself. So, I assumed responsibility. I tried to ease your suffering. I took it upon myself to ensure the longevity of our coven. You should be thanking me! Or would you all have rather died? Just so your mortal lovers could enjoy a few more years with their hearts beating?" She opens her arms out wide. "I gave you eternity, power! You cannot turn back time." She blows me a kiss on the wind, its magic stinging my cheek as it lands. "You made your choice to sacrifice your soulmates and love me instead."

I wish, *I wish* that Time would prove her wrong.

"You will never have my love again," I say, each word trembling out.

Her tears seem to freeze over like ice, her distressed expression going cold.

"I ended Isobel's frenzy," she says. "And I will end yours. Once this messiness is over, we can all move on."

Then she turns her back to me and faces the beach.

Fear thunders in my chest. I move to swim forward, but my sisters still cling to me.

"I'm so sorry," I say again, fighting against them, repeating those words over and over—I have to reach Jaspyr. "*Please*, I must go to him. I have to try and save him. Please!"

I think of Isobel. Of my dear, sweet sister who risked her life for love. For me, *mine*! Who died for me.

"It's what she would want! That's why she freed me. That's why she was in this position at all. Please, I beg of you, sisters. Release me!"

I pitch at the sudden freedom.

I gaze down to see them drifting deeper without me, the silver glint in their eyes piercing mine. "Go to him then, Eloise." They sing as one. "But please be careful. We can't lose you, too. We won't."

Their song uplifts me, energizes me in a symphony of power.

I swim forward, not sure how I might even save him. All I know is that I must reach him before Syrifina ensures I cannot.

She focuses in on Jaspyr, who sucks at his final breaths in Penelope's arms; I look to Penelope, noting the burning silver in her gaze—retribution for her husband, for Jaspyr.

Yes, *she* holds the barrier spell cast over what used to be Isobel.

I was wrong before… I've been so very wrong.

I freeze—the memory of the binding promise I made years ago flickers before my eyes.

It should've been me, not her…

'*I will happily take two lives*,' speaks the hot, dry voice of the Sun.

My gaze slashes toward the sky. Determination to see if there is even the smallest chance to save Jaspyr explodes out of me in a merciless song that seeps straight into Penelope's bones.

"It's her doing!" I shout, holding Penelope captive and pointing a damning finger at her. "She cast the barrier spell to trap Isobel."

Syrifina shifts her deadly attention from Jaspyr to her—the guilt in my stomach seems to grow only heavier, but I do not unleash her from my song.

Penelope goes rigid with Jaspyr's head cradled in her lap. But her gaze remains a penetrating silver as she holds tight to her spell.

I glance to the enchanted fire, squinting to check for any signs of life from within.

Dare I hope?

The Sun laughs brightly.

Penelope's grasp on her magic is unwavering, as focused and honed as any elder's. She pours all her power into trapping

Isobel's body, and she forgets to reinforce the barrier over her and Jaspyr.

Syrifina hisses, sniffing at the air. "Oh, I remember you…" she says. "The Sea sings that I should've ripped your heart out and let you join your husband all those years ago." She glares at me and I recoil, knowing she regrets many things about the night we first met Penelope.

Syrifina commands the torrent of water continuously flowing over the fire-filled dome to rain down on Penelope instead.

Penelope's focus shifts, slips into one of shock and realization as she's drenched in unyielding water.

The silver flickers in her eyes. Her energy wanes.

The water keeps flowing without end.

Her shields weaken. *Crack.* Break with an ear-splitting *snap.*

Syrifina hones all her wrath into a sea-sharpened weapon.

Water pours down Penelope's throat in an unstoppable river. She chokes and gurgles, unable to move from her spot in the sand.

She's still frozen by my song. Still holding Jaspyr in her hands. And *still* gripping her shield around Isobel, as if it is her last will in this world to ensure that she is dead.

Water seeps out of her ears, her nostrils, the sockets of her eyes—I can't save her, but I can try to save him.

I manipulate a protective bubble of air around Jaspyr's head to keep him safe. I just pray he doesn't find the sudden strength to open his eyes and witness what has become of Penelope…

The power of my song evaporates into the air as there's no soul left to hear it. Her body falls backward with a thud to the sand, Jaspyr still in her lap, his soul ready to follow.

"I won't let you go yet," I whisper, swimming closer. "I won't let you die, too."

Mother turns her gaze on me, eyes brilliant as two silver moons.

I brace myself for an attack, on either me or Jaspyr. But she maneuvers her magic to sweep over the freed flame, finally dousing it with water.

The world seems to hold its breath as we watch it go out.

I swim closer to the shore—nearest to Jaspyr and eyes pinned on Isobel—praying to all the goddesses who empower me that at least *one of them* can survive this gruesome day.

When the fire is gone and the water recedes, all that remains of Isobel is a sodden pile of sparkling red sand.

All goes eerily quiet, the water still as glass.

I blink several times. *She's gone and never coming back.*

The God of Shadow's sickening laughter booms in my mind. *'How does it feel, knowing that you killed your own sister? I have never had the pleasure'*

The Sun and Sea seem to seethe as one. *'And you never shall.'*

I push them all away, repulsed at being a crushed piece of dirt between their warring thumbs.

"Isobel…" I utter, curling into myself in the shallows. "I'm so, so sorry. *Please*, don't leave me. I love you. I didn't mean it. I need you. I've always needed you."

Already there's a gaping chasm forming in my eternal world at just the thought of her absence—we were meant to dance and sing together, forever. She had so much more to teach me. I should've never…

"What have I done?" My face falls to my hands. I shudder with agonizing sadness that's only echoed by the mournful moans of the princesses who await my return.

Syrifina whips around to face me, her expression one of utter, terrifying vengeance; I resist the urge to swim in the opposite direction.

Her lifeblood brightens, throbbing with power. Her needle-like crown materializes on her head, glistening with brutal intent.

Then giant, dark swells begin to boil on the shoreline.

THE COMFORTING PRESENCE of my sisters abruptly vanishes as they dive for the safety of the deep; our waters have become an uncontrollable beast that can only be leashed by Mother.

'*Join us*,' they sing.

I cower in front of the storm that Syrifina Myr has become, the currents swirling behind me, trapping me in the shallows.

'*Go! I'm not leaving him.*' Not while he's still breathing.

The sun is swallowed by swollen clouds that ripple with energy, casting shadows over the beach, over Isobel's remains. A layer of thick black and gray settles atop the city in the distance. Then comes the rain, pelting the water and sand like tiny arrows being dropped from the sky.

The rocky shore is wiped clean, Jaspyr's blood washing away into nothing. It looks as though he could be sleeping. I catch the faint beat of his heart, softer even than when I drained him.

The wind whips at my face; I push the hair from my eyes. I try to calm the vicinity around me, my magic kneading out the currents and hushing the waves as best I can.

Maybe there's a way I can still save him… if I can just get past her. Or, at least help him die in peace.

A veil falls over Kampaulo where sound can no longer enter, save for the drumming of the riled rain and the clash of the waves hurling against the shore, against me. I'm hardly able to remain topside.

Thunder comes next. I wonder how she'd conjured it—it's as if the Gods of Air and Earth have collided in the sky. Their deafening blows send ripples of light cutting through the clouds, swords of flames piercing the atmosphere.

Does the Goddess of the Sun show off the strength of her fire after killing one of us?

I let the rain pelt my face, trying to think through all the noise; the thunder only grows louder, the lightning blighting and hot. Then our great goddess joins the battle, thrashing her shields toward the clouds with every mountainous wave.

I float in the middle of an all-out war—Syrifina and the old gods… against me.

I have a sudden urge to sink, to retreat into the deep and mourn Jaspyr and Isobel from far, far away. Live the rest of my days alone in my shame for not conquering my frenzy.

I sense that's what I was meant to do, that this storm was raging for me, imploring me not to fight the Golden Rule any longer, to let Nature take over the reins. I steel myself as the ancient ones force their way into my mind.

"There will be dire consequences, Eloise, if you continue to disobey us," the storm speaks through the mouth of Syrifina. Her voice wraps around me, deep and cold.

"Isobel is dead and Jaspyr shall soon follow! Isn't that consequence enough for the curse you've cast upon me?"

'*Things can always grow worse,*' the Sea warns in a motherly tone, beseeching me to leave his fate up to her and be done—she would wash away the memory of him come high tide, I'm sure.

I resist, moving closer to him on the mounting waves. The wrathful waters have swallowed so much of the beach now that

I can nearly reach him.

'*Offer him to them, before they take back everything!*' screams Syrifina in my mind.

She shifts into something otherworldly, deadly, a glowing orb of water and wind, magic and wrath, hovering over the shore. It isn't exactly fire—the violent energy ebbs and flows through every color in the rainbow—but it is similarly ruthless.

She homes in again on Jaspyr.

The next wave that crashes down gets me close enough to touch him. The scent of his blood hits me like a rusted iron shield. With nothing to stop it, it freely pours from his wound. It's all I can do not to sink my teeth into his stomach and feed, his beautiful essence coaxing me.

I position my body directly in front of him and open my arms out wide to face the storm. "Never! You will have to go through me first to lay your vile magic on him again."

"Fine." Syrifina's waves recede with a suddenness I'm not prepared for, exposing me to the callous air.

Steam rises from my skin and tail, my scales drying out. I grit my teeth, readying to meet Isobel. Yet, nothing more happens.

Why do I not burn?

The rain comes down harder, a curtain that blurs my vision. The thunder continues to burst in the sky, like boulders breaking into a million pieces. The lightning snakes and licks at the wounds in the clouds, the only light left.

I let the false night wash over me, counting every second I have left.

"This is your final warning," the storm speaks, bellowing to me in a thunderous chorus that demands my submission. "One of you must lose your life today. It's time."

"But why?" I yell back, the wild wind pelting my face. "*Why* can't we both endure your world together for just a little longer? Mother had years to be with her mortal, and not locked away!"

'*She is the exception to the rule, not the standard,*' says the Sea.

"You sacrificed our gift, your humanity, in exchange for a life eternal, Eloise Myr. You cast your soul to the shadows, so now you must feed them what they desire."

I gape to the sky as the world seems to come crashing down upon me. *The ultimate blood sacrifice...*

That's the powerful magic that tied Syrifina's fate to the shadows all those centuries ago when she chose to feed her revenge instead of letting it go. Such a choice can *never* be undone. Nothing can when sealed with blood.

I glance to Jaspyr, my tears falling atop him. *We never stood a chance, united.*

There's no breaking the Golden Rule. The creators of the Olleb will not allow it. I was foolish to think it...

"*I will not* allow it," says the God of Shadow, his voice suffocating and sharp.

The darkness of this day becomes denser, curling over the Sun. The sky becomes a raging black vortex that seems to swallow the storm—with the Sun desperate to shine from behind, I'm reminded of the blood moon.

"A binding promise, sealed with a blood-wet kiss," he says with a sickening laugh, ready to be fed. "One of you must die. *Choose!* Or you shall both live an eternity of even greater suffering." A promise, I realize.

"Then I offer you mine," I say, looking up to the blackened sky—eyes, so many eyes, glowering like scorching stars of every color, look back at me from above.

The shadows shudder, as if it wasn't the outcome their god was hoping for; I swear I see a moon-white face with pupils as clear as diamonds recede into the blackness, glaring at me all the while.

'*Pity,*' the darkness murmurs. '*I wasn't done with you.*'

The sky lightens again with all the colors of the storm, the goddesses and gods of Olleb-Yelfra.

"So be it," they say as one—with a gasp, Syrifina blinks, her eyes settling back on me with awareness.

The old gods have gone.

"No," she utters, gazing between me and the clouds in desperation. "No, Eloise, I won't let you do this…"

All my untapped power suddenly sizzles at the surface just beneath my skin, tingling at my fingertips. I can barely contain the glorious sensation, to finally feel the full range of my abilities, to finally understand who I am… how powerful I could've become compared to the weak girl I started as—my creators must've wrenched a door open for me to access all that it means to be a princess. Offered me the strength to stand by my choice… my life for his.

I know what to do.

I look at my hands, my arms, my torso, my tail—my lifeblood glows brighter, defiantly, illuminating me like a torch in the sand.

If you don't act quickly, that's exactly what you will be. Hurry!

I fit my hand into Jaspyr's, remembering how they had laid claim to me with such warmth. Now, he is cold and stiff.

His fingers twitch, then he gives my hand a gentle squeeze.

"I'm here, Jaspyr." I choke, wiping my tears away. "I'm not going anywhere."

In Isobel's name, I will fight for him, for my true love.

Die for him, I bitterly think.

His hand falls away from mine.

I grit my teeth and clutch the bloodstained sand to move closer. His heartbeat is too faint, and so is his breath. I throw my body over his, trying to stop the blood flow as it slides through my fingertips.

Suddenly, I'm licking them, sucking at my fingers, drifting away in the existential state that lives in every drop of his wonderous essence. I bring his wrist to my mouth, my fangs pressing forward.

'*Yes, yes!*' someone urges from far away.

The line of shimmering azure lifeblood on his left arm draws my focus, clears my mind.

"No!" I shake my head and lower his arm back to his side. "Focus," I say to myself. "He's meant to live. Even the Sea chose him long ago."

'*What makes you think that?*' she whispers.

With our palms interlaced, our lifeblood intertwining—his too dim; mine too vibrant—I realize what I'm meant to do with all my magic.

Syrifina readies to attack with even greater might.

I conjure a massive wave, bigger than any that Syrifina's storm crafted, a mountain in its own right. With an ear-splitting crash, it smashes down on top of her, forcing her under.

Jaspyr's eyes flutter open, catching mine.

I still, memorizing that beautifully dark gaze.

He tries to speak, blood sputtering from his lips. "Eloise, I…" His voice falls away.

I make to comfort him, but his attention flicks to Penelope; he groans with sorrow, reaching toward her with the last of his energy.

I gently press my hands on him, to keep him still.

He finds my gaze; I can practically see his hatred solidify over what might've been a remnant of his affection for me. Then, his eyes close again.

"It's alright," I murmur, stroking his hair, tears burning in my eyes—no, just *burning*, I realize, literally evaporating in the air. "I understand. This will all be over soon, and… and then you can move on." I steady myself to my task. "I will take care of you. I promised I would not be the death of you, and

I will keep it now."

I swallow, my chest constricted with guilt and grief, afraid for my future without him, even if it's on another, inconceivable plane.

His heartbeat slows to a near stop, a low, drawn-out thud against his ribcage. The air swirling in his lungs is barely audible, stale. He's stopped breathing.

"You deserve the exquisite life you painted, Jaspyr. I've lived long enough."

All my budding magic rises out of me then. I grasp the sea with ease. It doesn't fight me no matter how hard Syrifina battles for control.

A tendril of water reaches toward me like a long-stemmed flower—Mother always said that one of the reasons myrmaids can live forever in ageless bodies is because of the water's natural healing abilities... I'm ready to test that theory now, to find out what it really means to be a Princess of the Sea.

I tear open Jaspyr's shirt and guide that flower right over his heart. It melts atop his chest, absorbing into him, then shifts and slithers throughout his body like a brilliant glowing snake, licking his wounds clean from the inside out.

I frown. "It's not working fast enough..."

I lift him to the air on a watery pedestal, his body now limp, blood spilling from him still. I send him more magic, giving him all of me.

Gold and silver strands begin to weave within the water beneath him, then inside of him, until he's as vibrant as Isobel was at the end. It's as if my lifeblood has melted right off my skin to manifest in the power I pour into him instead.

I focus *everything* on Jaspyr.

I grow weaker with each second.

Still, his heartbeat remains a grim melody compared to its normal strong chorus.

I beseech the healing properties of the water and press

them to him, as if carefully stitching up a wound with a needle and thread; his heartbeat begins to strengthen, little by little.

It's working! I think, daring to be hopeful.

"Stop!" the shadows scream.

I know in this moment—if I die and he lives—that I will have gained full control over my frenzy and proven Syrifina wrong, broken our curse for good. This will change the course of the future for all princesses to come. I have the strength to do it.

There's always a loophole, I think with pride. *He thought me weak, but I'm glad to give my life to save my sisters from his wickedness.*

By resisting my greatest desire and offering my life in exchange for my soulmate's—the sacrifice of a direct descendant to Syrifina—I know it in my soul that the Myr line will live the rest of their days peacefully, and, with any hope, surrounded by love.

"*Onasyuda!*" I plead, clinging to the word that translates to 'life' in our ancient tongue in case it might make a difference.

The beautiful sound of Jaspyr's lungs filling with air wisps to my ears as the last of my life ebbs toward his body; I lean in for one final kiss.

"Eloise!" yells Syrifina, stealing it away. "You disgrace us. I won't let you do this!"

I feel a warmth on my back that I haven't felt in well over a decade—my clutch on my magic is shaken.

Jaspyr lowers gently back to the earth, the last of my enchantment showering over him.

I glance up. The storm, like an eclipse, suddenly subsides. The sun breaks back through the thick clouds with a vengeance. It hovers high over the horizon like a molten crown.

Fire rolls across the sea in a thick sheet, my keen vision blurred by waves of smoldering heat. In seconds, its flames slice into my skin like hot iron rods, knocking me over. I roll away from Jaspyr, lest my soon-to-be torch of a body burns him.

I cry out, an extraordinary wail that echoes across the beach, challenging even Syrifina's anguish this day.

My skin begins to char, smoke, peel. Fire crackles in my ears, my eyes, my mind. The Sun's entangling arms, they're all I can see as she embraces me.

No, I don't want this... I don't want this at all. Please, make the pain stop! Suddenly, my panicked mind can't remember how I got here. *Goddesses, every choice I make is wrong!*

I call to anyone for relief. "Please, help!"

'*I am not the goddess to plead to, you blasphemous creature,*' says the Sun with no love in her voice at all. '*You should have never been born to this world, a mistake like my nuisance of a brother. I'm happy to let you join your sister.*'

If at all possible, the day grows even brighter; I find myself empathizing with the shadows now nowhere to be seen.

The Sea hums a soothing lullaby, her waves gently lapping in the distance, softening the loud popping of the flames.

'*Thank you,*' I say.

I collapse to the sand beside Jaspyr and force myself to look, to see through the searing sun and into his face—he opens his eyes.

I see the blackness there, that icy blue-green starburst in his left pupil, brightening with so much life. It surrounds me like the cool, safe arms of the Sea of Night, blocking out the harshness of the day, shielding me some place safe.

It's all the relief I need.

'*I love you,*' I think, wondering if he can hear my final words, my final song.

53

SEA

✿ J A S P Y R

'I INHALE THE SWEET BREATH OF LIFE, my blood pumping anew. I have never felt this alive before, never felt the sun so fully on my skin. It warms every cell in my body with a loving caress. The shadows are whisked from my mind like cobwebs swept away.

Then, I open my eyes and remember everything all at once.

No matter how hot and pleasant the day, the sun smiling down at me, all I feel is cold to my core.

Every inch of Eloise's beautiful body, a body I used to worship, seems to have caught fire. She's curled into herself atop the sand, given up as the flames eat away at her flesh.

Instinctively, I reach toward her, trying to command the fire back. But it doesn't yield to me.

'*Leave her!* a stern voice commands. '*Let her burn.*'

Thin lines of gold and silver shimmer beneath the skin of my outstretched arm. I drop my gaze to my body, examining every inch of exposed skin.

"Unbelievable," I mumble—the sound of my own voice, so coarse and dry from choking on my own blood, frightens me.

I block out the memories of my near-death experience and focus on the life burning away in front of me.

Eloise marked me in her final hour. Her lifeblood mixes with my veins.

Died for me, I realize. *Gave up eternity for me…*

I look back to her, trying to recall why I had planned such a brutal death for her in the first place—just because she left me? Just because she had a moment of weakness and couldn't fight her baser instincts?

I slowly sit up, massaging my temples as an intense headache begins to form.

'*Because she took everything from you! Look around.*'

My clothes are ripped and stained with blood. And there, in the sand, lies the sword, sticky with my gore.

My hand flies over my mouth as I turn my head to the side. What I see so clearly in the flesh is exactly why I should've killed Eloise sooner—I stare at Penelope's horrorstruck face; a mess of blood and water streams from her hollowed eye sockets as if they are tears she sheds for me.

"*No*, this can't be happening," I stutter, unable to look at her; her skin, normally so flush with vibrant life, has turned a grayish-purple color, akin to a bloated corpse. "I'm sorry. So, so sorry." I bow my head toward her. "I should've never let her go in the first place. I should've never let her live."

My breath comes heavy, restrained. I press my face between my hands and fight the urge to throw sand atop the fire; I fight the urge to feed it.

Gods! I fight the need to jump into it and *die with her*, to hold her until the very end.

No, I don't care if she sacrificed herself for me… Let her burn. Let her burn!

This becomes a mantra in my mind, alongside the aching cries of my heart and my conflicted yearning to save her.

My stomach twists into knots that can never be undone—if I cannot save her, then I long to follow her to wherever she journeys to next.

For love or revenge?

I shake my head with the uncertainty.

All I know clearly is that I won't stay here and live knowing that she died for me. Knowing that she killed so many and I held her bloody hand. *Penelope! Penelope!*

Oh, how will I ever face Eddison again? How can I stand beside him while he buries another parent because I wasn't strong enough to be a better man?

So many voices battle to be heard that they all merge together in a drone that threatens to break me from the inside out.

She loved you. She must've truly loved you, if she was willing to give her life. Forgive her, Jaspyr! It's not your fault Fate played these wretched cards that paired you with a monster.

'No, destroy her! Leave her ashes in the past. Monsters have no place in the Olleb.'

'We cannot live without her. Save her, please! She's your soulmate.'

'Soulmate or not, she's better off dead. They all are. Avenge us!'

'Save her, Jaspyr, please. Deliver her to us.'

'No, avenge us. Avenge us!'—I gasp at the soft sound of Penelope's voice, as if she whispers in my ear along with so many others.

"Stop, please…" I squeeze my eyes shut, afraid to face her, any of them. "I can't think over all the noise!"

The clatter of voices in my head shifts into a thrumming song from the outside. A loud splash draws my attention, and I open my eyes. I follow the eerie sound and find the ones she must call sisters—several sets of silver eyes glow along the shoreline.

And there are *so* many voices calling to me, singing, screeching for Eloise to come home.

Her sisters remain tethered to the waters, tails painted in an array of colors that seem woven from every type of jewel in existence. Different than Eloise, who always displayed the brilliance of clean, priceless metals.

A fallen star, I think, glancing to her again.

Flecks of her begin to lift to the sky, glittering ash on the wind.

Her death will come any minute now—but Time is cruel and seems to draw it out just to torture me with too many terrible choices to consider.

I crawl to her in the sand, the grains sticking to me, coating the blood on my skin. *Her skin* is smoking.

"Eloise, are you still in there?" I whisper.

Maybe she's already gone, dead...

I hope she is. Then, at least, the choice will have been made.

There's a flicker of movement, her fingers twitching toward mine. Without thinking, I reach through the fire and take her charred hand. It's like grasping the blade of a sword the moment it's pulled from a coal-fired oven—I scream out in agony, but I don't care.

'Let go! Let go!'

I grit my teeth. "I can't," I say. "It's too late for me."

I call to my magic to try to ease some of my pain, to slow the burn to my arm; this time the sunfire *somewhat* bends to me, as if this enchanted flame only cares to take Eloise's life.

Beyond the fire, another myrmaid, a majestic monster, watches me from down the shore.

Her hair was surely crafted from the deepest, hottest parts of the sun. And vibrant strands of lifeblood decorate her skin like strings of lustrous pearls.

A crown that could only have been carved from the bones of ancient men and their lost treasures sits atop her head, catching the sunlight with its jeweled tips, then tossing it away.

A queen of legends, I think, entranced by her gaze, *Eloise her subject.*

She's so unlike the others. She's living, breathing power— if I were standing, I would bow.

Her expression is both menacing and distraught. She impatiently swishes her tail behind her, with scales that glitter like diamonds. Back and forth, back and forth.

She looks on at me, at Eloise, as if debating whether to intervene.

"Will you not save her?" I dare to ask, knowing she will hear me over the snapping fire—the question alone makes something break inside of me.

'*How disappointing,*' the Sun seems to speak on behalf of all those I've let down.

The fire burns hotter; I squeeze my hand tighter.

"How dare you speak in my presence." An icy wind seems to howl with her words, making me shudder even as the flames lick my skin. "You're like a cat with one too many lives," says the Queen of the Seas, baring her fangs; her expression shifts from troubled to calculating—whatever decision plagued her just now, it is made.

"I refuse to let another one of my daughters throw their life away for you, *Jaspyr.*" My name hisses off her tongue. "This ends now. I'll gladly add your bones to my throne when I'm done with you."

The water rushes toward me so fast I don't even have time to blink, let alone surrender my enchanted hold on Eloise to throw up a shield.

A wave smashes on top of us, dousing the flames—Eloise is an unrecognizable charred pile of flesh, but her spasms tell me she still lives.

"Eloise," I sob, gaping at her.

I'm barely able to unclench my hand from her iron grip before the water curls back around us. It thrusts us to the air and toward the shallows where her sisters wait.

I take a deep breath rather than scream as I fall alongside her.

The waves reach out to gently catch Eloise, cradle her, pulling her under as healing magic engulfs her—I seem to fall slowly, the water moving farther away, parting, shifting, as if to extend my terror before I hit.

My gaze slides over the land, my heart thundering in my chest.

The last thing I see is Eddison glowering at me from the cliffs where he watches, an enraged cloud of magic hovering around him. Then, I'm plunged into the sea and feel a cold hand wrap around my wrist so tightly my bones break—I silently scream.

54

CHAOS

'I AWAKE UNDERWATER, surrounded by my elder sisters.

"Where is he?" I say, startled at the familiar setting. I quickly examine my arms, my tail.

I am safe, healed. The Sea undid the Sun's damage to me. All tangible memory of the excruciating pain that had become my existence on the surface world is gone.

I gaze up, the sunlight twinkling atop the waves, as if teasing me. Daring me to reemerge in her presence.

Never again…

I look back to my sisters, the princesses gathered, all except dear Isobel.

I scowl, growl; I'm supposed to be with her.

"*Where* is he?"

"Mother swam to the deep," says Daniella in a low voice, head bowed.

"With Jaspyr?"

The twins nod.

The shadows seem to cling to me again, threatening to

drown me once more in their waterless, suffocating hold.

"We're sorry," they say with such sincerity I'm momentarily stunned.

I shake off the shock, remembering what my sacrifice was supposed to mean, not only to Jaspyr but to them and the future of our family. "No, you don't understand! If he dies, then—"

Not even the breath of another second passes before all the magic and determination to my name propels me toward the deep. I swim faster than I ever have before, flying on the new power the gods and goddesses had showed me how to access.

"Wait!" cries Kristeena; I hear as they rush after me.

But no one dares lay a hand nor touch of magic on my skin to slow me down as they follow.

I know where she's taking him.

To Empress Isle, as she does all her greatest conquests.

He doesn't belong there! It's supposed to be me.

The water and reefs rush all around me in a blur. I cut straight toward the Sea of Night.

The shadows follow, chasing me, whispering to distract me from my goal.

"Syrifina!" I call out, searching everywhere—I never look back, only forward. I close my mind to everything but the focus of my hunt. I can't waste even a millisecond if I'm to save Jaspyr's life. "Where are you?"

I can smell him here, taste him. It feels more than wrong, knowing that my love for him pulled him this deep down.

Then I see her, a rush of crimson hair and the powerful flick of a dazzling tail. She's a streak of brilliant light with a deadly clutch on my life.

If he dies, I die. It has to be me. For him, my sisters.

"Stop!" I slash through the water, counting the seconds flying by; more than a minute has passed. If Jaspyr didn't hold his breath well, he's surely already gone.

And Mother is moving too fast for me to hear if his heart is even still beating, though it matters little—the crushing pressure of the sea will cause it to burst in his chest any moment now.

If only I could get close enough to cast my magic around him...

I don't know why I still hold out hope, but I do. I must.

Syrifina dives deeper as I close in.

"Syrifina, enough!" Zahra's stern voice floats up to me from below.

The darkness erupts with spellbinding light; my sisters are silhouetted beneath me like the illusive beast Jaspyr once pondered over—their song is a force to be reckoned with, forming a barrier, a net around us all.

I join them, the desperate note of love carrying their chorus. I pour all my magic into my song, a lethal sound that not even Syrifina can resist.

She stops swimming, as if hit by an invisible wall. She turns toward me, her grip tight upon Jaspyr.

When her eyes rest upon mine, I nearly crack at the glistening grief within them—Jaspyr floats behind her like a ragdoll.

"Let him go, Mother, please," I implore, calling my magic to the surface. "We can still fix this."

We all hover just beyond Lovers' Coral in the great abyss, but I refuse to acknowledge the archway, the statues. *Our future will be different.*

She presses her lips into a thin line, trying to command the water back into her grasp; my sisters and I have an unshakeable grip on it, our song an eerie echo in the background.

"You cannot fix what was never broken," she replies. "You will thank me one day."

My magic burns, cold and electric, pooling in my palms. "I will not!"

I release everything I have, a storm of rage, just like she conjured on the surface.

I don't know how I do it, but I call to the wind and it answers—the water seems to part for me, the particles shifting in a radiant kaleidoscope that encases Syrifina and Jaspyr in a dome of silvery-white air amid the dark.

Jaspyr hangs there limp, suspended, as if he is held up on invisible strings; I clutch my fingers. "*Breathe*, please."

Tendrils of his long, black hair seem to drift in a soft breeze, and his head hangs heavy, his feet dangling. I listen intently and hear the faintest murmur of his heartbeat. It is so, so slow, barely perceptible, almost done.

This deep down, the cold should have shattered his bones and the depths should have squeezed him so tight that his internal organs might've exploded. But the flash of silver flooding his eyes and the gold sparks dwindling on his fingertips give me hope—I recognize this magic, this healing part of me I gifted him, helping him to hold on just a bit longer.

Still… he doesn't breathe.

Magic is only a temporary solution. He can't survive this journey. He doesn't belong here.

Syrifina suddenly screams, and my head whips toward her.

The sea is rendered silent. Her shimmering scales and tail start to shrivel, the absence of the water withering her from the inside out—yet, even faced with death once again, she still grips Jaspyr's wrist, unwilling to yield to me.

I scoff, shaking my head, content to watch her writhe in the pain I know all too well.

"You've lied so many times." I float forward, beyond the others; she tosses her head back and cries out to us in such a persuasive song that if it were not for the barrier between us, we would all bow down. "We are not immortal."

My eyes pin on Jaspyr, desperate to go to him; but if I do, I must first release Syrifina…

I glower at her. Electrified magic streaks over the shell of the air bubble and stirs the water around me.

"You would *truly* kill my soulmate," I ask, my voice pitching with every word, "and then ask me to live forever?"

She steadies her gaze on me, her voice hoarse as she focuses on her words. "If I die... you die." Her gaze slides over the others. "You will *all* cease to exist."

"Another lie," I snap; I glance over my shoulder as the princesses begin shifting uneasily. "Don't listen to her."

She screams again, squeezing her eyes shut. When she opens them back up, they're glowing silver stars that seem to see straight through me.

"See if Isobel's line still live!" she challenges between gasps, her voice multiplying with her rage. "Sing to them, then."

There's a gasp of shock from my sisters—of all the ways I've learned just how *not* immortal I am, this isn't a weakness that I am ready to test on behalf of our entire coven.

Have yet more of our sisters died because of me?

"It isn't true," I say, balling my fists; golden power weaves in and out of my fingers. *I pray it isn't.*

The eldest princesses surround me in an instant.

"Eloise, don't this," implores Kristeena, tears like glittering amethysts upon her cheeks. "We've all lost too much as it is. Release this... magic." She looks the pocket of air up and down in a sort of awe. "*How?*" she mouths.

Zahra clutches her necklace, bringing the bone ornament to her lips. "I agree," she says with a calm I would never achieve. "She is all our burden to carry, not just yours, Eloise. You will find a way to forgive her... as we all have."

The twins nod, and Daniella places her hand on my shoulder. "She's our mother."

Syrifina has the decency to look humble. "I was only trying to help," she says, lowering her head, her hair hiding the shriveling skin on her face. "To keep my promise to you all. A life forever. Freedom from…" her gaze flicks to Jaspyr, "these trivial things."

I snarl, launching forward, wanting to rip her tongue from her mouth. But Zahra and Kristeena's magic weaves together to keep me back, a pulsating net of emerald and maroon.

Miki swims forward, touching my arm. Then she looks Syrifina in the eye. "Then let him go."

Vasylina grasps her hand and yanks her back to the safety of her side; she lifts her chin and adds, "At least let him die in her arms, Mother." Her voice comes out so loud and sharp that it startles me.

I frown, my lips quivering, not sure what emotions their courage and loyalty have stirred in me. I've never felt so surrounded by family, never felt so truly seen. *I wish Isobel was here to witness…*

"I… I'm sorry," says Syrifina, seeming to deflate with realization—a small part of me is stunned to hear such words uttered by her, but I can't focus on that now.

"Release him!" I say, not a demand but a desperate plea.

She stares at me, cocking her head to the side; her expression softens. "I just… didn't want you to hurt like I did. Darlings, I thought—"

Her voice falters, her eyes darting back and forth as if she sees something we cannot. A single tear rolls down her withered cheek. She looks down—I know she understands that she did, in fact, want to share her pain all along.

"Time will erase the memory," I say, coolly.

Zahra and Kristeena swim up beside me, letting their wall of magic dissipate in a sparkling gust. They each place a hand on my shoulder, then escort me forward.

I look upon Jaspyr's swollen face. He is all but gone, a corpse of white floating in the Sea of Night. There is nothing I can do to save him, no point in dragging this on.

"There is only goodbye," says Zahra, evenly.

"We'll wait for you," says Kristeena. "We'll always be here for you, sister."

They both kiss me on the cheek, then float back to give me space.

Syrifina places her hand upon the barrier. Her skin and scales have begun to flake away.

I frown, not letting myself think twice about freeing her... for my sisters' sake.

I reach through that air-filled dome and grip her hand, digging my nails into her palm. With a sweep of magic, I pull her out and let the water cascade over her. Then, with all the gentleness I can muster, I comb the rest of the air away to let Jaspyr go in peace.

It evaporates around him, the darkness folding back in one particle at a time until the water again kisses his skin; my sisters softly sing in his honor. It is the same mournful melody that whispered up to me from the deep when Isobel died, though I had ignored at the time.

Jaspyr begins to drift away, slowly, up toward the sea sky.

I swim to him from below, leaving my sisters behind.

Even in this atmosphere, being so near to him is overwhelming, as if my frenzied mind knows this is our final moment together.

I swim parallel to him, floating on my back, my fins and tail fanned out like a magnificent cape—I've taken this position so many times before. To muse over the wonders of the surface world and the humans there.

Now, all I see is him and the future we promised each other yet could not reach. And the only thing I wonder is what it might be like to kiss my soulmate one last time...

I close the distance between us and lightly press my lips to his, just as the final beat of his heart fades away into the Sea of Night.

For once, I hold nothing back from him.

55

KISS

⟩ E L O I S E

I ALWAYS FELT A SMALL SPARK OF MAGIC when Jaspyr and I kissed, but I never let it grow. I allowed him to taste it on the tip of his tongue, but even in our most heated throes, I held tight to this part of me.

Not now, though. What's the point? I kiss him hard and deep, trying to savor the last of his essence.

A strange, new energy manifests from beneath my skin, swirling inside the marrow of my bones, making my lifeblood dance like never before—my magic floods into him. It's different than earlier.

This time, I can sense it searching for his soul.

Syrifina calls to me from beyond. "Eloise, get away from him. You don't know what you're doing!"

And she is right—but I also know that the *only* reason she wants to stop me is because she doesn't know how to welcome true love into her world.

My mind fades into his, lost in our connection, on a quest to find any signs of life.

If I pull away, I know it will all end abruptly, us, him... everything. So, I stay, prolonging the end for as long as I can, remaining true to all the foolish ideas we had long ago.

I exist in a haze of memories—I home in on the shared ones from those short months of bliss in each other's arms, the love that shone in his eyes; I ignore his thoughts from the following three years, ones that paint me as the same vicious beast he had at first known me as in the alleyway.

Then, I see it. His soul. It's a bright, fluttering orb of life, wisps of impossible light, dark blue and bright gold, hiding within a fragile cage of human bones.

A waste, I think, *for one so powerful.*

I reach out to it, tempting it to follow.

Live with me, I think, wishing for the ability to sway Time once again. *We've both survived too much. I burned for you, Jaspyr. Remain with me now... stay, please.*

It hears me. It brightens—if the Moon and Sun had another skyward sister, I'd think this soul their kin. '*Hello, Beast,*' it says.

My magic wraps around it, an offering—*Stay or go.*

Jaspyr's soul grows even stronger, so brilliant now that I have to look away. I slip back into my own body and wait, my lips still pressed to his. I can hardly believe what I just did...

"Eloise, leave him be! It's not too late," pleads Syrifina.

Jaspyr's lips suddenly match mine and his arms pull me closer. I open my eyes—his flash open with a spark of electricity that whirls in his pupils; I might've gasped and pulled away in shock, but his arms hold me in place. I don't remember him so strong.

His gaze pierces into mine, blacker than any deep sea I've ever known. A streak of silver glints around his irises. *Familiar.* But that turquoise starburst in his left eye... it now gleams with something more, a power akin to my own.

I sink into his oblivion, our limbs, my tail and fins, inter-twining in a tangle.

A strange coldness spreads through the water—his kiss grows more passionate, not just tugging at but *seizing* the gift I offered, inhaling it like oxygen.

'*Why don't you listen, child?* Mother's voice enters my mind. I can tell she's far away from the faintness in her tone.

Jaspyr's tongue presses into my mouth, licking at every drop of power it can reach. We float together in our own world, held by this peculiar, comforting, petrifying magic as his soul breathes it in. It twines around us in icy ribbons.

Our hands tangle in each other's hair, teeth scraping, bit-ing, as we both struggle to taste just a bit more.

My tail and fins coil around his legs; he runs his hands down my torso, rough palms sliding against the smoothness of my scales—I tingle with giddiness at the unfamiliar yet wel-come sensations.

He pulls away to look at me, taking me all in. And for a single moment, we both smile in relief.

"Jaspyr?" I say in a daze, blinking back at him.

He opens his mouth to speak but then thinks better of it, his eyes focusing in on my backdrop. His expression darkens with panic.

I take his chin, my gaze demanding all of his. "Eyes on me," I say, firmly—what if a misplaced jolt of fear sends this magic recoiling?

We're so close to forever. I won't lose him.

He doesn't sink nor struggle. He just holds my gaze, a soft expression on his face.

I reach my hand to his cheek and can feel all the new life beneath his now perfectly mended skin. "There will be a lot to explain once you fully—"

The magic around us explodes into a cocoon of power that blasts me downward.

I look up, shaking off my daze—Jaspyr remains buoyant at the center.

There's no way to stop his transformation now, not with the magic solidifying over his entire body.

Why would you even think that?

I shove that voice away and cling to my excitement.

Only moments ago he was floating off to the next life. And now—

Now, we can be together forever... however long that might be.

I've gifted my sacred power to him, kissed him with the magic of the Goddess of the Sea herself.

It seems to take, and yet I can't help but feel that something isn't quite right with his transformation. Something is off. Even the currents seem to sense it, changing course, away from us.

I glance behind me, suddenly feeling so very alone—Syrifina and my sisters are swimming away. They're so far that I can hardly make them out. But I can see when Mother stops and turns toward me, her expression saddened.

'*Our power isn't meant for him,*' she says. '*Swim to me, Eloise. He is not the ending you seek.*' She extends a hand. '*Trust in me.*'

I turn my back on her, shutting her out.

Only now do I realize that my sisters' song has gone, too. There's no sound at all, save for the beating, ice-blue, silvery heart that is this cocoon; veins of black grow from the center and seep through the water like wisps of shadow.

The cocoon begins to expand. The currents churn faster around it until the magic—a mind formed of its own—breeds a raging cyclone.

I've never witnessed a full transformation before, and mine had been on land... "Beautiful," I whisper in astonishment, wishing I could see through the thick of the magic.

"I have waited an eternity for this," says the God of Shadow, watching with me; his voice seems to resonate across the entire ocean.

I feel his sinister smile like the prickle of fire coral down my spine and whirl around. I bare my fangs and ready my magic—there's only the swathing darkness of the water.

"Whatever you're talking about, you're wrong!" I shout, sending an explosion of power toward nothing.

And yet, I find myself pondering over Queen Julissa and her headless body. Of how Mother impulsively ended her transformation with the snap of her teeth—was it really true that she feared to share her domain with another?

Or had she listened to an instinct?

Kill him. End him!

I turn back around and float higher until the cocoon is eye level. I have to shield my face with my hands from the force of the magic and strength of the currents, whipping my hair and fins.

I shake my head. *No… why would you ask that of me?*

I am you, Eloise. Ask yourself.

The absurdity! It's like my frenzy is starting all over again, my conflicting voices returned. I brace myself against the doubtful words, realizing I may just have to endure them for as long as I exist.

I have already made my choice.

And even if I tried, I couldn't prevent Jaspyr's transformation from happening anymore. My magic has taken his life into its hands…

I wait and watch.

The cocoon grows and grows, like a silver wrecked ship that doesn't rise nor sink; I float with him, eyes wide in wonder, terror.

I consider my own transformation in the stirring silence—how excruciating it had been for my humanity to be stripped away and something new to be born in its place; the moment I took my first watery breath and that first sip of blood.

I look at my hands. *So much power. Too much to even know what to do with.*

A scream, an agonized snarl, resounds through the sea. I swallow, not sure which might hurt worse—the sun's deadly kiss or the one I had given him.

The cocoon grows wider, illuminating the Sea of Night like a rising moon, forcing me back—all I can see through the magic is a writhing silhouette of Jaspyr at its core, a dark blue blur outlined in gold.

It widens and stretches so much that the magical shell begins to strain at the pulse from within. Then it cracks, *explodes*, falling away in a cloud-like burst to finally reveal my creation.

I shriek, cowering before it. *Him*... "Jaspyr?"

A mammoth serpent, a sensational sea snake, with scales as black as the darkest night and glistening with soft veins of silver and gold, floats before me.

What in the goddesses' name have I done?

He does not hear nor see me yet. His eyes remain closed.

I still, unsure of what to do.

His body has stretched and contorted in such a way that he has lost all hints of human form. There's nothing to suggest Jaspyr ever was, or would be again, anything other than a mythical monster...

Sharp black fins shimmer along a gently undulating spine, cutting through the water like swords. Without those and his icy blue-silver underbelly, he would almost be one with his surroundings, the perfect predator.

A massive jaw is slightly parted, gleaming with rows and rows of curved, pointed teeth.

To eat what? I wonder. *What could feed such a creature?*

I look beyond him to try to see where his body might end,

but it ripples so far back that I can't—I'm a floating speck in comparison.

My tail twitches anxiously. I wish for Isobel, for my elder sisters. I even wish for Syrifina to return and tell me how to undo all that I've done, for even I know this is wrong.

But I'm alone with my frenzy, in full formation.

I touch my hand to my lips, my thirst for him completely gone, my soul-crushing desire—*dead.*

Along with Jaspyr.

The God of Shadow cackles again, a riotous sound that he can't seem to contain. '*I'm sure something else will be born in its place, Child of Agony. Enjoy forever with your soulmate.*'

My eyes widen. "You did this!"

'*One always has a choice,*' he says—and I swear my own voice echoes back to me on the edges of his.

My voice startles Jaspyr awake.

His eyes snap open, the same as I've always known yet so much larger—and it's easy to see his confusion, in those mirrors that reflect my own.

He opens his mighty jaws and roars in my face, as if to cry, '*What have you done to me, Eloise?*' The sound is so crushing that I think my skull might implode.

"I'm sorry!" I say, covering my ears with my palms. "This isn't what I wanted… what I meant to—" I shake my head, craning my neck to see all of him. "I had no idea you'd turn into such a monster—"

His eyes dilate.

He opens his jaws wide, showing off those layers of hungry teeth and a blood-red tongue; his inner throat muscles vibrate—it's *so* gaping and vast that I'm sure I could swim straight through him like a reef tunnel, his mouth an abyss all its own.

He roars again, this time releasing the full force of his power upon me in a surge of searing magic.

I throw up my hands, curling my tail in protection.

The magic that sweeps past me in a haze is cold, frigid, a frozen blast of fire.

I've never known a myrmaid to do such a thing...

The magic solidifies around me in thick layers, a cage of crystal-clear ice. By the time he closes his jaws, I'm the one cocooned—limbs, fins, tail, head. Even my eyes are frozen open, forced to witness the mess I've created.

I call to my magic to try to thaw it, but it's somehow rendered useless by his. I can't fight this enchanted ice-covered flame.

What are you? What monster have I invited into my sisters' sanctuary?

I can see nothing of Jaspyr anymore through this frosted glass. No remnant of the man I loved, his soul snatched by something else. There's just the long shadow of a hungry snake slithering away into the deep.

He's off to hunt... That's the first thing he'll do.

He heads straight toward Empress Isle, disappearing into the darkness.

No, come back. I sink toward a depth I have never dared to explore. *Please, don't leave me alone.*

The God of Shadow laughs. '*Eternal Eloise.*' Then I feel him vanish, too, along with all the other voices.

It's not true love at all if it doesn't
destroy you when it ends.
For like all deceitful things,
love is cruel and callous.

A MYRMAID'S KISS BY ASHLEIGH BELLO

Dear Myrmaid

·· ☽ ☼ ☾ ··

That was quite the journey! I hope you enjoyed meeting Eloise and Jaspyr as much as I enjoyed writing about their twisted love story.

Syrifina Myr may wish to keep her coven of powerful sisters a secret from the world—but I don't.

Please take a moment to share your experience exploring the Sea of Saindora with other dark romantasy readers who might like this book.

What was your favorite part? Share your thoughts:

amazon   **goodreads**   **BookBub**

Thank you for reading!

P.S. This is not the end... I promise.

Ashleigh B.

ACKNOWLEDGMENTS

This was the writing adventure of a lifetime! It was so fun to explore my dark, steamy side through the tainted minds of Eloise and Jaspyr. I really had to challenge myself.

When I first outlined this story in the winter of 2022, I was certain it would be a novella… 181,000 words and a year later, *A Myrmaid's Kiss* is now the sixth fantasy novel I've published. It's also one of the largest (tied with *Belvedor and the Golden Rule*) and marks my first time writing adult dark fantasy—I hope you loved my spicy, twisted take on mermaids and true love. Jaspyr and Eloise sure *wrote me* in the end…

Thank you to everyone who supported me while I drowned myself in myrmaid smut this past year. It was a magical time!

Mom—YOU are a beautiful myrmaid. How can I thank you enough for being my number one fan? For the countless hours you listened to me gush about this dark fantasy land? It's a miracle that I didn't spoil the ending for you. Your support means everything to me. Hope you loved this book as much as I love you.

Dad—I hope you never read this book. But if you do, just remember that you helped raise me. ☺ Thank you for always supporting my wild ideas and writing goals. And for being my phone buddy, even if all I care to talk about is myrmaids and magical realms. Alrighty then... love you!

Lisa Miranda—I didn't have a choice *but* to write this book for you. You have been waiting for me to publish a story about myrmaids since I started the *Belvedor Saga* more than a decade ago. I hope Eloise's underwater world is everything you could've imagined. Thank you for always rooting for me and for all the business advice over the years. You're the OG myrmaid. *holalittleone.com*

Allison Sicking—A year ago this month (January 2023), I was in Playa del Carmen with you setting the stage for this story. That was such an important moment in time for the creation of *A Myrmaid's Kiss*. Thank you for being a part of it, for all the brainstorms by the beach, and for helping me shape my writing goals. *vivalatravelista.com*

Jules Karp—The girl who said that a myrmaid's dreams are always wet. You're a real one! There's no friend I would rather send snippets of myrmaid sex scenes to for a stamp of approval. Thanks for checking on me when I disappeared from society, and for all the encouragement to get this done. Love you, boo! *www.spring-affair.com*

Hannah McCall (editor)—I can't thank you enough for your help in shaping this story. If not for your early critique and detailed editing work, *A Myrmaid's Kiss* would be an <u>entirely</u> different book (with some *very* unfortunate replacements for the word 'cock')—you guided me through a major writing block and helped Eloise and Jaspyr shine for all their dark glory. I'm grateful for your partnership! *blackcatedit.com*

Vasylina (cover designer and illustrator)—I scoured the internet world looking for you! I'm so lucky that I clicked on your DeviantArt page. Your illustration of Eloise on the cover is so enchanting that I described it in detail through one of Jaspyr's portraits in this book (Chapter 49). Thank you for bringing the darkest parts of my imagination to life… and I hope you don't mind that I named a myrmaid after you. *www.deviantart.com/vasylina*

Jessica Khoury (map illustrator)—You originally created this map for the *Belvedor Saga*, and my readers are still enthralled by your work. I'm so glad that the world you illustrated so beautifully can live on through this book. Thank you again.

Book review team and social media supporters—I could not have completed this story without YOU. Writing a book can be a rollercoaster. There were just as many ups as there were downs in getting to the finish line with this one, but I felt the reader support every step of the way. Thank you for sharing this journey with me and for spreading the word to your friends and followers. Thank you for your encouraging emails, comments, and messages. Thank you for lifting me up—with any hope, we'll watch Eloise and Jaspyr seize the book world by storm one day! **#myrmaidskiss**

THANK YOU!

Turn the page for

BONUS MATERIALS

REAL 'UNDERWATER'
WORLD MAGIC

_____

MYRMAID SOUNDS
ON SPOTIFY

_____

DID YOU KNOW?

_____

'JAR OF STONE'
An Excerpt of Book 1 in the
Belvedor Saga

REAL 'UNDERWATER' WORLD MAGIC

Traveling has always been a huge inspiration to my writing process—every book idea I have ever had has sparked while I was on an adventure. After the COVID-19 travel advisory lifted (which still feels like a ~~dream~~ nightmare), I was itching to get back out there and explore the world.

So, I did something I have always dreamed of trying and took scuba-diving lessons! I fell in love, booked a solo trip to Mexico to finish my certification, and the rest is history.

From that point on, I knew that writing a book about mermaids was next on my list—*A Myrmaid's Kiss* and the descriptions of the Sea of Saindora are an ode to all the real world enchantment I have witnessed while swimming underwater in our oceans and cenotes. I hardly had to stretch my imagination at all to create the sea life that I introduced to you in this story. Many of the things I described are real! I just sprinkled them with silver magic.

Check out some of the places I have visited for dive excursions. Highly recommended!

- Playa del Carmen, Mexico
- Cozumel, Mexico

- San Pedro, Belize
- Cabo San Lucas, Mexico
- Roatan, Honduras

Please protect our waters. They're more than special. Imagine what else could be hiding in the deepest, coldest parts we've yet to explore... *Jaspyr?* ☺ See you down below!

Photo credit: www.deepphotos.photodeck.com.
Roatan Divers. Roatan, Honduras.

MYRMAID SOUNDS
ON SPOTIFY

Music is such an inspiration to my imagination! Often when I write a chapter in a book, I'll imagine it like a vivid scene in a movie with the music in the background.

Just for fun, I selected my favorite songs on Spotify to pair with each chapter in my story—if *A Myrmaid's Kiss* were a motion picture, this would be the soundtrack (manifest!).

Listen to my Spotify playlist:
www.bit.ly/myrmaids-kiss-spotify

DID YOU KNOW?

A Myrmaid's Kiss is set in the same epic fantasy world as the *Belvedor Saga*, the author's first completed series!

If you loved meeting the myrmaids of Olleb-Yelfra, then you don't want to miss out on discovering what other enchanted creatures roamed the land—before King Devlindor took the crown and instated the ban on magic.

This five-book series kicks off with *Belvedor and the Four Corners*: a hope-filled journey that follows Arianna Belvedor of the Warrior's District in a magicless era. It's set in the cold and cruel City of the Four Corners, *several centuries after* Eloise and Jaspyr's time. Arianna learns about the King's treacherous secret to hide the magic in her world and sets out on a daring quest for freedom alongside her friends.

If you enjoy young adult fantasy adventures with found family, discovery of magic, and coming of age themes, then this book is for you! It has epic battles, a comprehensive magic system, enchanted settings, and beautiful friendships to be explored.

You'll find romance as a sub-plot only (no spice), so it's a good break after visiting the dark underwater world of the Sea of Saindora—but who knows! You may meet the Myrs again on this journey, if you make it past book one. ;)

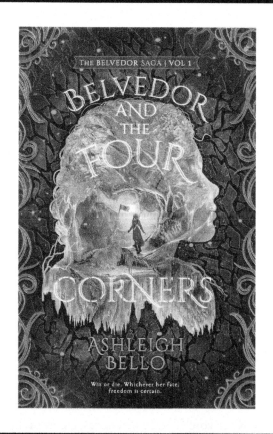

Turn the page for a sneak peek

BELVEDOR AND THE
FOUR CORNERS

JAR OF STONE

AN EXCERPT

SNOW BIT AT ARIANNA'S SKIN and dotted her dark hair white, the same as every day. Try as she might, there was just no preparing for that kind of cold. She could never stop the shivers from coursing through her body, and the burn of the icy wind made her eyes well with tears no matter what she did. Pulling her hood tight around her head to shield her face from the biting flakes, she gazed toward the sky. Each morning, she found herself searching for the sun, but lately there was a permanent blanket of gray blocking it from view. If she was lucky, it might peek through the clouds to warm her skin for even just a few moments, but most days she wasn't.

As much as she despised those clouds, the view of the ashen-faced mountains that encased the Four Corners was ten times worse, impossible to ignore at almost any moment spent outside. They trapped the city in a wide, jagged cage with perilous peaks that reached toward the skyline like a claw, locking in the gray and barring out the light. It created the perfect prison, and it earned the city a nickname—Jar of Stone.

Thousands of slaves marched in silence alongside Arianna under the darkened sky, under the watch of the mountains. The snow turned brown beneath their boots as they trudged forward in a familiar rhythm. In a crimson flock, they passed the many crumbling buildings that made up the small district until a deep hole spread out before them. They maneuvered around the Pit with ease, their breath hitched in their throats out of respect for those who had perished.

Arianna's eyes were glued to the swelling blackness of the

Pit as they passed, straining to see so far down with no help from the sun. Still, she spotted some of the skeletons glinting in the dark. Needle-like rocks and rotting bodies lined the bottom.

"Hey! You wanna join 'em?"

Arianna jumped as the voice pulled her from her thoughts. She hadn't realized she had stopped, holding up the line behind her. The regulator leading her group got down from his horse and stormed over to her side, grabbing ahold of her arm.

"There somebody down there you'd like to see, Twenty-Two?"

She could think of a few names.

Digging his fingernails deep into her skin, the regulator pushed his weight into her so that she had no choice but to lean back, half her body now dangerously hovering over the side of the Pit. From this angle, Arianna could see the bottom with alarming clarity. Her heartbeat quickened as all her hopes for a future seemed to vanish into its depths. If he let go of her arm, she would surely fall to her death. She was unable to tear her gaze from the abyss threatening to swallow her, her curiosity replaced by terror as the sunken faces of the dead stared back.

Just as she was counting the seconds until the end of her life, the regulator moved, allowing her to regain her footing.

"Don't make me ask twice," he said, waiting for an answer as he itched toward his swords.

Flinching away from him, she shook her head.

"No," she said.

Her whisper was sucked down into the darkness of the Pit, and every time her heart throbbed, she thought it might jump right out of her chest to follow.

A gruff laugh escaped his lips.

"Then eyes forward," he replied.

He poked her in the shoulder, on her double-digit identity, gesturing for her to keep walking. Her knees shook as she moved on as quickly as possible, and she kept her eyes down until they arrived at the city center—the Square.

They passed under a low bridge, and a wide, open area stretched out around them, people pouring in from all sides. High stone steps encircled the space and created an amphitheater-like structure with pillars at the top.

Arianna eventually found the nerve to lift her gaze from her boots and peered again to the sky, past the crumbling pillars and past the people below. Wind pounded against a raised flag that stood tall as a centerpiece of the Square. She studied the embroidery while waiting for the gathering to commence. Faded reds, blues, purples, and greens were woven into segments, a pattern she could retrace by heart if she had to. They formed a circle which signified the emblem of the Four Corners and the four districts within the city.

As was the daily morning routine, the regulators sat comfortably atop their brawny horses in black, hooded cloaks, herding the non-citizens into lines facing an elevated platform. It was a large structure that towered over the crowd as the stage of the amphitheater. And, on this particular day, Arianna stood at the front, just below the platform, wishing she could be anywhere else.

She studied the stage as General Ivo surveyed the red sea of prisoners from underneath his hood, waiting for everyone to assemble. His dark, brooding glare matched well to his known ruthless character. Black robes, lined with red fur and emblazoned with the golden snake of the King's Crest, swept the floor at his feet, and a scar slashed across his face like a worm crawled atop his skin. He also wore a sharp sword at his belt, one that she'd seen in use plenty.

Behind him, a massive painting created the backdrop on a black wall. The same golden snake intertwined itself between two blazing swords, the symbol of Arianna's district. Every time she looked upon it, she thought the symbol quite plain—swords to depict the Warrior's District.

Such a superficial view of what it takes to be a warrior.

A familiar hum buzzed throughout the Square until General Ivo raised his hand. With his gesture, the crowd was promptly silenced. Arianna stood to attention, her arms flat at her sides as he walked forward, hands behind his back, preparing to speak. Though, before his lips parted, something caught his attention, and hers too. A loud whisper was coming from behind her in the crowd.

Arianna bit her lip, unsure of where to look as the hushed voice faded away. *Too late.*

Nothing went unnoticed in the Warrior's District under the general's watch, and right now his eyes were unblinking. He scowled down at the crowd from the stage, and Arianna froze. She felt his gaze burning straight through her center as he searched their faces for the culprit. Then, a stone-faced regulator started to march toward her from his post at the front. Her stomach churned as he neared. This was too much suspense for just one morning, even in the Jar.

To Arianna's relief, the regulator merely pushed past her, instead reaching for a small girl who was standing only one row back. She recognized her as a tenth year.

The girl kicked and screamed as the regulator dragged her to the foot of the stage by the collar of her cloak. He looked to the general for instruction, and Arianna held her breath. After a moment of contemplation, General Ivo gave a single nod—that sinister 'you-know-you're-done-for' nod she'd seen too many times to count.

The regulator acknowledged his unsaid command and locked eyes with the terrified child. "Should have shown some respect," he grumbled in a low voice.

The girl's cries had drowned out his words for the most

part, but Arianna stood close enough to hear the tragic ending they promised. Some days General Ivo gave second chances, but today he seemed to be in as foul a mood as ever.

Arianna could feel the heat from the nervous crowd rising around her, everyone fidgeting uncomfortably as the girl was escorted from the Square, headed in the direction of the Pit. Nobody dared make a sound, not a peep as her cries faded away into nothing.

Arianna closed her eyes, shaking her head at another wasted life. The girl should've known better.

She couldn't resist the small sigh of relief that left her lips when all was quiet again, hoping no one else would notice.

I'm still safe. I'm still here. Just survive.

Her eyes flew open as the general again prepared to speak, as if nothing at all had transpired. His calm demeanor baffled her because inside her own head she was screaming. It was a silent scream that echoed into every corner of her mind until she felt numb and the voice died away. She always took care to silence it, for otherwise she'd have gone mad with grief long ago.

As Arianna tried to focus on anything other than this fresh reminder of death, a sudden quiver rolled across her skin. She knew she was being watched, as though her body could sense the glare of eyes on her back. She glanced slightly to her left and found the culprit. Her friend Liam was standing only a couple people down, and his shaken expression reflected her own worry. They looked out for each other. Life was a little easier that way.

She nodded to him in reassurance, and then put her focus forward.

General Ivo raised his right hand, and the crowd mirrored his movement as he balled his hand into a veiny fist and placed it on his chest above his heart.

"Hail to the King! Hail to Lord Devlindor."

His voice, such a terrible one, made Arianna want to stick her fingers in her ears, but she straightened her back and repeated the daily verse. Her words melted in with the other mindless voices around her, the phrase tasting so wrong on her tongue. She'd be hanged if she voiced it, but she couldn't help but hate King Devlindor. Her loyalty to someone who squeezed so tightly at her life made her dizzy at times.

According to her teachings, this was the way of the world, and promises of citizenship and all the riches that came with it would apparently wipe away the memory of this gruesome chapter of life for all who made it to the next. Freedom supposedly changed people, and Arianna prayed it would change her, too. However, no matter what anyone said, she knew in her heart that she'd have to experience this change for herself to believe it—to believe in the King.

Just survive. A few more months.

"Dismissed," said the general as the echo of voices ceased.

The crowd dispersed to their daily routines, and a dull chatter filled the air as Arianna headed to the Dining Hall. She walked by the Pit on the way, but she didn't dare look down.

THE BELVEDOR SAGA

By Ashleigh Bello

Follow the Magic!

www.ashleighbello.com

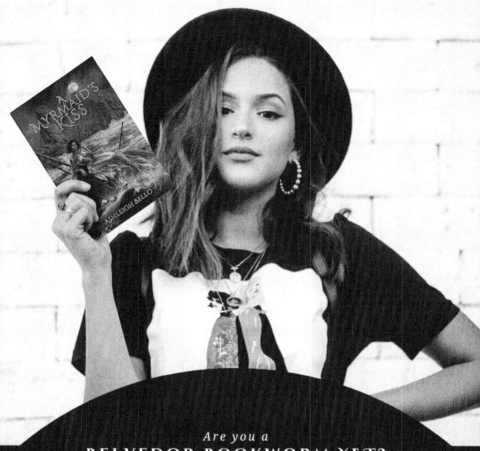

ASHLEIGH BELLO is the author of the *Belvedor Saga* and *A Myrmaid's Kiss*. She graduated from the University of Missouri-Columbia and currently lives in Brooklyn, New York. When she's not writing, she focuses on her career in marketing. She also teaches and practices vinyasa yoga in her community and is the co-founder of Yoga Block Party, a female-owned yoga events business. She enjoys spending time with friends and family every chance she gets and is always daydreaming about her next novel. Her endless passion for travel and spontaneous adventure continues to be her inspiration for future works in the enchanting world of Olleb-Yelfra and beyond.

Connect with the Author
www.ashleighbello.com
www.goodreads.com/ashleighbello

Follow her on TikTok
Her main bookish social account
#myrmaidskiss

Don't miss the next book release!

FOLLOW AUTHOR ASHLEIGH BELLO

AMAZON

BOOKBUB

GOODREADS

TIKTOK

INSTAGRAM

FACEBOOK

Printed in Great Britain
by Amazon

42834269R00381